THE ZODIAC DECEPTION

FORGE BOOKS BY GARY KRISS

The Zodiac Deception

The Houdini Killer (forthcoming)

THE ZODIAC DECEPTION

GARY KRISS

A TOM DOHERTY ASSOCIATES BOOK

NEW YORK

THE ZODIAC DECEPTION

Edited by James Frenkel

A Forge Book
Published by Tom Doherty Associates, LLC
175 Fifth Avenue
New York, NY 10010

www.tor-forge.com

Forge® is a registered trademark of Tom Doherty Associates, LLC.

The Library of Congress Cataloging-in-Publication Data is available upon request.

ISBN 978-0-7653-2759-8 (hardcover)
ISBN 978-1-4299-4963-7 (e-book)

Forge books may be purchased for educational, business, or promotional use. For information on bulk purchases, please contact Macmillan Corporate and Premium Sales Department at 1-800-221-7945, extension 5442, or write specialmarkets@macmillan.com.

First Edition: May 2014

Printed in the United States of America

0 9 8 7 6 5 4 3 2 1

For Pat
*My wonderful, talented, beautiful wife, the love of my life
and the best person I've ever met. You are, and will always
be, the alpha and omega of my life.*

ACKNOWLEDGMENTS

There are so many people to thank that some will inevitably be overlooked, and I apologize for this in advance.

One person who can't be overlooked is James Frenkel, my editor and my friend. Jim's the kind of editor they're not supposed to be making anymore. He brings his entire self to the development of a novel, and of a novelist. This book took a while, but Jim never stopped believing in or fighting for it or me. I owe him more than I can express.

Even before Jim, someone else went out on a limb for *The Zodiac Deception*—June Clark, my agent. June's faith in the book never flagged and, together with Peter Rubie, the CEO of FinePrint Literary Management, she gave it her all. She still does and I love her for it.

An author couldn't want for a better publishing group than Macmillan and, specifically, Tom Doherty Associates, headed by Tom Doherty himself. They are a textbook example that old-fashioned publishing, done right, can quiet all the naysayers. Tom didn't hesitate to take a gamble on me, and while I *wouldn't* play poker with him, as an author I would follow him anywhere.

Speaking of Macmillan would be woefully incomplete without speaking of Kristin Sevick, a highly gifted editor who took this book and me under her warm wing during the final phases of publication. She's a gem in every sense of the word.

The Zodiac Deception involved a tremendous amount of research. Besides the classic older works and personal accounts, current scholarship on World War II, the Third Reich, and espionage is plentiful and of extremely high quality. I've tried to incorporate this breadth of knowledge in *The Zodiac Deception*. Any mistakes, however, are my own.

In conducting my research, I've had the privilege of being associated with two of the world's greatest academic institutions. Through appointment,

Williams College opened up its arms and its wealth of resources to me, and I'm proud that it remains my academic base, anchoring me to my "home away from home," the beautiful Berkshire Mountains. I'm particularly indebted to President Adam Falk, College Librarian David Pilachowski, Professor and Former Dean William G. Wagner, and Professor Peter Just for allowing me to become an "Eph" and to live the Williams experience on an ongoing basis.

Closer to my actual home, Yale Divinity School has been and continues to be extremely accommodating, making me feel like one of its own. Among the riches that it and the entire university has afforded me is the expertise of its renowned faculty. I want to especially thank John Collins, Holmes Professor of Old Testament Criticism and Interpretation, Adela Yarbro Collins, Buckingham Professor of New Testament Criticism and Interpretation, Harry Attridge, Sterling Professor of Divinity and former dean of the school, and Dale Peterson, Associate Dean of Student Affairs, for their personal help and for their friendship.

In addition, public libraries and bookstores have nourished me as they have so many others. I can't express how important these are and how much we need to support them.

The British had their "Magic Gang" that created deceptions during World War II, and I was fortunate enough to have my own magic gang that created deceptions for this book. Many of my fellow members on The Magic Café were kind enough to brainstorm with me. When it came to the specifics of crafting the more involved illusions, I relied on the creative and technical skills of David Becerra and Matthew Olsen, and I greatly appreciate their contributions.

Bob Cassidy, the Dean of Mentalists and arguably the most respected member of the profession, was kind enough to sign on as an advisor, as was Anthony Jacquin, the legendary British hypnotist. Bill Palmer, a renaissance man with an encyclopedic knowledge of magic history, always answered my questions, no matter how foolish. Damon Reinbold, friend to some of the greats in mentalism and magic, became my friend as well, regaling me with little-known information and valuable insights. Rick Roth, who many, myself included, consider the best when it comes to devising bizarre effects, kept me on the right track, while Rich Hennessey, one of the finest craftsmen of magic accessories, lent me his counsel and provided me with some magnificent pieces unique to the book. The late John Wells shared his vast knowledge of hoodoo and of its use as a premise for magic effects. Those who wonder if some of the seemingly "far-out" techniques I describe in the book—the ones requiring a transformation, if not a suspension, of disbelief—really work, they do and I have my good friend Bill Montana to thank for demonstrating this. An underground legend, Bill graciously agreed to let me use some of his groundbreaking work.

In writing *The Zodiac Deception*, I drew on a lot more astrology than I included. Some very generous people made this possible by providing both guidance and copies of their highly effective astrology software. I'm extremely grateful to Madalyn Hillis-Dineen of Astrolabe, David and Fei Cochrane of Cosmic Patterns, Alphee and Carol Lavoie of Air Software, and Ernst Wilhelm of Kala Occult Publishers. When it comes to anything that's astrology related, few would disagree that the greatest resource, and the one I tapped often, is Hank Friedman of Soulhealing, who always had time to point me in the right direction.

My membership in three terrific organizations—the International Thriller Writers, the Mystery Writers of America, and the Romance Writers of America—is very important to me. I cherish my involvement, my fellow members and all the benefits I've received.

To the crew at the Tunnel Café, my "office" in Williamstown, Massachusetts, and to the great gang at Ross' Bread, my "office" in Ridgefield, Connecticut, continued thanks for everything.

Being a writer can often prove a challenge to relationships. But I've been blessed with some extraordinary people who kept on giving of themselves no matter what. Thank you so very much Dick and Alice Rapasky, Mert Rymph, so very missed. And Jackie Rymph, Bob and Gretchen Naylor, Stanley and Barbara Solomon, Larry and Bernadette Gotch, Jahn and Leah Marmon, Marcy Reed, Sue Swanson, Bill Ryan, Marty Rogowsky, Mike Amodio, Anne Skinner, Sam Humes, Harry Montgomery, Don Washburn, and the one-and-only Herman Geist, my personal hero of the Greatest Generation.

I also want to acknowledge my furry family, who also helped keep me sane.

I can't close without honoring the memory of my parents, Charles and Anne Kriss, who taught me to love reading and writing before I could even walk, and of my uncle, Peter Colman, who raised me like his own and taught me by his own example that the human spirit can transcend even the horrors of the concentration camps. And in remembrance of the millions who weren't as fortunate and of those known and not named who risked all for others. You are this book.

PREFACE

In January 1933, Adolf Hitler, head of the rapidly growing and often violent National Socialist or Nazi Party, was named Chancellor of Germany. Hitler's political enemies engineered his appointment, arguing that once he was in government they could control him.

They were wrong.

Within three months Hitler forced a new election that swept his party into power, and almost immediately it passed legislation allowing him to govern without Parliament. Hitler, a failed artist, was now the absolute ruler of Germany. An enormously effective orator, Hitler used every opportunity to proclaim the superiority of the German "Aryan race." He also promised to restore Germany, humiliated and severely sanctioned after starting and losing the First World War, to a position of greatness.

Instead he destroyed it.

By 1939, the Nazi Party had imposed dictatorial control over every aspect of German society: schools, press, churches, courts and the arts. Even family life was regulated, with the Party deciding who could marry and the number of children they were expected to have. Paranoia was rampant. Neighbor spied on neighbor, reporting questionable individuals to the Gestapo, the dreaded secret police—a sure death sentence. Under the direction of Heinrich Himmler—a former fertilizer salesman who became Hitler's right-hand man—the Nazis worked relentlessly to rid Germany, and ultimately Europe, of entire groups, foremost the Jews, through mass murder.

Some 12 million men, women and children were systematically and horribly murdered in German concentration camps. Of these, more than 6 million were Jews, the rest "enemies of the state," gypsies and other "undesirables" and those deemed mentally or physically unfit and, therefore, of no value to society. While a few Germans of conscience stepped forward and risked their own lives to shelter or help Hitler's targeted victims escape to other countries, most either condoned the atrocities or were too intimidated to get involved.

By the end of 1941, the German military, viewed by many as unstoppable, had seized Austria, Czechoslovakia, Poland, Denmark, Norway, Holland, Belgium, Luxembourg and France and had attacked Russia. It was all part of Hitler's 1933 master plan, to create a new and glorious German Reich that would last a thousand years.

It lasted twelve.

During those twelve years of iron-fisted repression, Hitler plunged the world into a lingering war of devastation unrivaled in the history of humankind. More than 60 million lives were lost. Not that Hitler was totally unopposed. Some Germans joined various secret resistance movements. Their motives often differed, but their aim was the same: replace the Nazi government. Early on these groups sought to avoid war. After 1941 they sought to end it. At first they thought that they could act without violence. Later they realized violence was the only course of action.

They had to kill Hitler.

The resisters included soldiers, students, conservatives, communists, intellectuals, socialites, celebrities, everyday citizens, high-ranking Nazi Party members, clergy and even Jews still in Germany leading underground lives.

Often the resisters maintained loose alliances with like groups in countries under German rule. Occasionally they were aided by forces beyond Germany, notably the United States and Great Britain, both of which formulated their own plans to remove Hitler and topple his government. So, too, did their military ally Joseph Stalin, the Russian ruler who matched—or surpassed—Hitler in tyranny and in the taking of innocent lives. After the war the German resisters were widely regarded by their fellow Germans as traitors.

Today they are honored as heroes.

Some may see what follows as a chronicle of failure. After all, there was no assassination nor was there a governmental overthrow. Hitler remained *der Führer*—the Supreme Leader—of Germany until April 30, 1945, when, in a bunker beneath Berlin, he shot himself in the head. A week later, on May 7, the war in Europe, which he had started, was over.

But this isn't a story about success or failure. This is a story about how even the smallest good can eventually overcome the greatest evil. The story is based on a number of facts. If it isn't true, then perhaps it should be.

THE ZODIAC
DECEPTION

1

Berlin, Germany: December 1933
Your Stars Today: Now is the time to act on your bold visions of the future, but only if you have the determination and leadership strengths needed to do what must be done.

The door was unlocked. He knew it would be. He entered the old half-timbered house, pausing for a moment to savor the lingering aroma of fattened carp poached in a pungent vinegar sauce.

There was no need to flick on the foyer light. The stairway leading to the second-floor bedrooms was right in front of him. He headed up, carefully treading toe-to-heel so his shoes wouldn't make a noise as they struck the wooden steps. The door to the children's room was directly across from the landing. With a thin-gloved hand he turned the knob, which was still sticky from some jelly dessert, pushed it and went in. The moonlight, which had bathed everything in bluish white, made it bright enough for him to see all he needed.

The eight-year-old was asleep in the first bed, next to his most prized possession, a toy helmet, adorned with an Iron Cross decal on one side and a swastika on the other. For now the boy was a pretend soldier, but in two years he would join the Hitler Youth, receive his first military training and pledge his life to Adolf Hitler. How quickly time passes, he thought as he leaned over, lifted an unused pillow and, in a single motion, pressed it firmly over the boy's face. It only took a moment.

There was no resistance.

As he backed away from the bed, his foot caught on a lamp wire. He managed to grab the shade before the lamp went tumbling, but the slight commotion was enough to awaken Liesl, the six-year-old.

"Shhh," he said before she could speak. "It's all right." He knelt beside his favorite and brushed a wisp of fine blondish-brown hair from her eyes.

"I thought you were *Krist Kindl* come with the presents," she said.

"Not yet, Liesl." He pressed his lips against her forehead as he had done so many times before. "Are you disappointed?"

"No." She reached up and put her hand on his neck. "I love you."

"And I love you, too, little one."

"Did you bring it?"

"Of course. Don't I always?"

"Where is it?" she asked.

"Here." He tapped his left coat pocket, which responded with a crinkling sound.

"Can I see it?"

"It's all tightly wrapped. But it'll be there in the morning. I promise. Now go back to sleep."

"Wait! Where's Teddy?"

He scanned the bed. "Oh, poor Teddy's trapped!" He put his hand over his mouth in mock horror before dislodging a stuffed Steiff bear, which had gotten jammed between the mattress and the footboard. "But look. . . ." He ran his hand over the bear, fluffing its matted blond mohair fur as best he could. "I've saved him." He placed the bear in her waiting arms. "Off to sleep, Liesl. You and Teddy."

"Will you stay awhile?" she asked, cradling the bear.

"Only if you shut your eyes." He waited. "That's a good girl." He reached into his right coat pocket and drew out a Walther PPK pistol, small and not too loud.

"Are you still there?" she asked.

"Yes, but if you open your eyes, I won't be."

"Then I'll keep them shut."

"Very good." He lifted the pistol and held it close to her temple, making sure the tip of the barrel didn't touch her skin. He would have preferred to use the pillow again, but she was awake and might struggle, and he didn't want to cause her any pain. "Very, very good," he said, and squeezed the trigger.

Anticipating what would come next, he headed to the hallway.

"What's happened?" The woman burst out of her bedroom not even bothering to put on her robe. "What's happened? What was that noise?"

The first shot hit her shoulder and spun her around. She grabbed hold of a picture on the wall, a Dürer pencil study for his *Christ as the Man of Sorrows* that had been a wedding gift from her parents.

The second shot hit the back of her head. She crumpled to the floor, taking the Dürer with her. The impact of the fall drove her elbow through the picture. Pity. It was a regrettable accident, but still he was dismayed over destroying such a thing of beauty.

He walked over to where she was lying, not quite dead, trying to say something but managing only a gurgle. It didn't matter. He could read her question in her dilated eyes, and he answered by firing two more bullets, one into her heart, the other into her skull. Satisfied, he went back to the children's room and shot the last bullet into the middle of the dead boy's forehead.

Only a few housekeeping matters remained. He removed an ash-wood crucifix that hung on the wall between the children's beds and carefully pried off the crucifix corpus—the figure of Jesus on the cross—which he placed in his shirt pocket. Then he broke off the crossbar, lifted the boy's nightshirt and, with a single forceful swing, plunged the piece into the exposed left side, just beneath the ribs. Using the cross stand, he repeated the process with the girl.

Returning to the hallway, he knelt and ripped off the dead woman's sleeping gown, leaving her naked. From the side pocket of his suit jacket he took two communion wafers, which he moistened with the tip of his tongue until their centers were slightly sticky, then placed them on her nipples, applying just enough pressure so they adhered. Next, using the overlapping feet of the crucifix corpus as a pen and her blood as ink, he drew a faint line from each of her breasts to a spot at the base of her sternum. Finally he positioned the crucifix corpus on her body so the head with its crown of thorns was just below where the lines converged. When he finished, he stood and with her torn gown blotted away the little stray blood still on his hands. Looking down at his handiwork, he smiled approvingly.

Now everything was perfect.

He walked down the stairs, and turned into the study where two other men were waiting.

"Just making sure," one of them said.

"There was no need," he snapped. "I did what I had to do. Now get out of here, both of you, and do what *you* have to do."

"Who are you to give orders?" the other man said.

"Do you want to debate, or do you want to finish?"

After some grumbling, the other two men headed for the foyer, and he accompanied them, opening the door to make sure they left. He watched them trudge down the walk, then closed the door and went back to the study to refocus. Music always helped, so he flicked the switch on the nearby lowboy radio console and pushed in one of the eight small ivory tuning buttons jutting out from the face of the mahogany cabinet. A fast flow of words streamed from the radio's arched speaker grill urging "all true Germans" not to buy from Jews. He immediately recognized the impassioned, high-pitched voice. Even at this late hour, a radio station was trying to curry favor with the new Nazi government by running State Propaganda Minister Joseph Goebbels' wire-recorded message.

He pressed another button and got another speech. No, wait. . . . Not a speech, but a sermon, and from the snippets he caught—"tonight God has given us a new Prince of Peace in Adolf Hitler" and "God speaks in blood"—he knew who was giving it: Joachim Hossenfelder, leader of the Berlin branch of the rapidly growing German Christian Church movement, which was nothing more than an arm of the Nazi Party.

"Let us never forget that the German Christians are the storm troopers of Jesus Christ." When he heard Hossenfelder bellow his signature line, he switched off the radio in frustration and turned to the tabletop gramophone. The needle was already on a disk. He gave the handle a few cranks and sound began to flow. He recognized the piece immediately, the immolation scene from Wagner's opera *Die Walküre,* one of his favorites and, by chance, a fitting selection.

He lifted a half-full crystal decanter of cognac from a silver tray to the left of the gramophone, poured some into a snifter, then settled into a chair where a book had been left open, straddling the wooden arm. He picked it up, looked at the ornate gold title stamped into the green cloth cover— *New German Poetry*—and flipped the volume over to see what she had been reading before going off to bed. Something by Georg Heym—"The Demons of the City"—written, the notes said, in 1910. He scanned the first lines:

> *Through the city night they roam,*
> *Darkness cowering under their feet*
> *Their chins adorned with sailors' beards*
> *Of soot and smoke-blacked clouds.*

Closing his eyes, he inhaled deeply, recalling the smell of the curling smoke that rose from the great square near the Berlin opera house on a May evening this year. There he watched as thousands of chanting university students heaved tons of books the Reich leaders considered incompatible with Nazi ideology onto a massive bonfire. Despite raucous cheering from the throng of spectators, he was close enough to hear the crackle as fingers of flame thumbed through the pages, notating them in ash. *Heinrich Heine, Thomas Mann, Sigmund Freud, Karl Marx*—degenerates all being cleansed by fire from Germany's soul. He turned back to the poem.

The city's shoulders crack.
They straddle the ridge of a ruptured roof,
Amid the flares of freed flames,
Howling at the heavens.

Leaning forward, he tossed the book onto a pyre of logs in the fireplace and watched as bright orange flames reduced the book to a small pile of charcoal and ash. Then he reached for the phone and placed a call.

Wagner's seductive "Slumber Music" filled the room. Wotan, the much-feared Father of the Gods, had placed his favorite daughter, Brünhilde, leader of the Valkyries, into a deep sleep and surrounded her with a magic wall of fire. Only the kiss of a hero who braves the fire can awaken her. Siegfried was that hero then, and Hitler that hero now, braving the fire and awakening Germany from the nightmare created by Jews and communists. He listened to the magnificent "Slumber Music" with its promise of rebirth and unbounded greatness, thinking of the wondrous destiny that lay ahead for Germany.

And for him.

The voice at the other end of the telephone brought him back to the present. At first he spoke softly, but soon he grew more agitated. "I don't care what night it is. Tell him that I'm on the phone and tell him now!"

While he waited, he noticed some blood that he had missed was trickling down the back of his left hand. Putting the receiver down, he took a neatly pressed handkerchief from his breast pocket, dabbed it in the cognac and began to rub. The blood was still fresh and came off easily, revealing a small tattoo just above his wrist.

"Are you there?"

He heard the faint voice on the phone and quickly picked up the headset. "*Reichsführer?* . . . Good. *Krist Kindl* has left you a present. . . . No, no problems. Have the police come in twenty minutes. Everyone will be gone. . . . Yes, thank you, *Reichsführer,* and a most blessed Christmas Eve to you as well."

Drawing himself up, he started for the foyer but stopped abruptly. With everything, he had almost forgotten, and that would have been unforgivable.

The tree, a seven-foot balsam, was in the corner of the study, wedged between two windows, the needles of its outspread branches tickling the glass panes. As usual, it wasn't overly decorated, which only enhanced its beauty. Laced with two electrified strands of tulip-shaped handblown and -painted glass bulbs, its green was mottled with a small and tasteful collection of colorful ornaments, some new, others dating back to the last century.

From his right coat pocket he removed a small, crinkly bundle and carefully tore away the tissue wrapping to reveal a five-inch Dresden Angel in white holding a palm leaf on which the name "Liesl" had been carefully lettered. Having already decided on the proper spot, he draped the gold hanger over the end of a branch, positioning the ornament so it was prominent.

As he stepped back and looked at the ornament dangling there, he felt a sense of satisfaction over the wonderful and unique Christmas surprise he had given Liesl, his "favorite."

He had made her an angel.

Talbot, Iowa: December 24, 1933
Your Stars Today: You may find that legal matters and travel
plans demand all of your attention right now.

He woke up to screaming.

The sounds were so violent and piercing they drowned out the old Emerson radio perched on a nearby table. Startled and groggy, the police chief of tiny Talbot, Iowa, lifted his head from the desk and realized he must have dozed off. That meant he was the only one in town who missed Fibber McGee and Molly's special Christmas Eve show.

"Damn, boy, what's that commotion?" he called out to the sole prisoner in a nearby cell.

But the horrible screaming continued.

"You, Kilian! Jack Kilian! I'm talkin' to you!" Now the prisoner was howling.

"That won't do you any good. We're on the outskirts of town. There's no one to hear."

Howling, like some crazed beast.

"Goddamn, Kilian, *what* is your problem?" The chief swiveled around in his chair. "Are you sick or something?"

The howling continued.

"Boy, I'm gonna beat you silly if you don't answer me!"

"The . . . the . . . the . . ."

"Jesus H. Christ!" The sheriff rose with a frustrated shake of his head. Why was it, he wondered, that every time his deputy got sick a crazy landed in town? Not that Talbot attracted many people from the outside, especially on Christmas Eve. And the few who did stumble in were usually lost and always normal. But whenever his deputy got sick and couldn't do night duty at the jail, the crazies appeared and, without fail, did something wrong enough to get locked up. Like this one, who was howling. There had been screamers. There had been shouters. But in his entire twenty-eight years as sheriff there had only been one other howler that he could remember and that one actually might have been a shrieker. But this one was a certified howler. There wasn't even a full moon and he was howling. Damn!

"I warned you, boy. If you're sick, you best tell me right now!"

"There! There!"

"Gonna make me come over, right? OK, boy, you got it." There would be no need for his gun, so he left it on the desk. Still, he took his billy club, just in case. In twenty-eight years, he only had to use a billy club twice. But with a howler, well, with a howler you never knew what to expect. Whatever happened to "all is calm" on Christmas Eve? Come to think of it, whatever happened to "Silent Night"?

In the faint glow of a dangling sixty-watt bulb, the sheriff could see his detainee hunched on the thin bunk mattress in the small cell, cowering and pointing.

"There! There!"

Damn! And Kilian was so quiet when they picked him up and brought him in. Normally they'd just drive him across the line and make him Kansas' problem. God knows, they'd done that enough with gambling cheats. Beat 'em up a bit, then over the border they'd go with a stern warning. But not this time, because of the phony twenty-dollar bills. Cheating's one thing; passing bad money's another. The Feds had to be called in, but there was no telling when the lone overworked agent, stationed in Des Moines, would make his way over.

"There! Over there!"

The sheriff squinted in the dim light as he followed his prisoner's shaking outstretched arm toward the corner of the cell where a book was lying on the floor. "The Bible? Kilian, you tellin' me you're makin' all that racket because of that Bible over there? Damn, boy, you really are loony. Now stop all this foolishness and keep your damn mouth shut."

He was heading back to his desk when he heard something.

"Claude."

The voice was weak, but distinct. "Claude."

The sheriff stomped back to the cell. "Boy, you don't know me good enough to call me by my name and you ain't never gonna know me that good."

"Claude."

His eyes shifted from the prisoner.

"Claude, I forgive you." The voice was coming from the Bible.

"What the . . ."

"It wasn't your fault, Claude." The Bible began to rise.

"What the . . ."

The Bible continued its ascent, first three inches, then five. "It wasn't your fault."

The Bible was now a good foot off the cell floor.

"What the hell?"

Then the Bible crashed to the floor, causing the prisoner to start screaming again.

"Hush your mouth, boy." This time the sheriff spoke softly, his eyes never leaving the Bible.

"Not your fault." The voice was getting weaker as it drifted from the Bible toward the top of the cell. "Going now, Claude. Not your fault." And then it was gone.

"Kilian, you hush now and come over here."

The prisoner didn't move.

"Please, come here."

This time the prisoner did as he was told.

"Now stick your arms through the bars toward me." Again, he did as he was told. "Good." The sheriff uncoupled a pair of handcuffs from his belt and fastened them around the prisoner's wrists. Satisfied that they were secure, the sheriff unlocked the cell door and moved slowly toward the Bible. Kneeling, he cautiously lifted it. The back was wet. He looked at his hand. It was covered with blood.

Breathing more rapidly, the sheriff looked down at the floor where there were traces of something scrawled in blood. He had to put his face almost on the concrete to make it out.

Colos. 1:14.

He tore through the Bible until he reached Paul's "Letter to the Colossians." There, marked with blood, was the fourteenth verse of the first chapter: *In whom we have redemption through his blood, even the forgiveness of sins.* And yet another word was scrawled in blood across the bottom of the page.

Betty.

The sheriff gazed at the book in disbelief, then let it drop from his hands as he backed toward the cell door until his shoulders hit the bars. That's when he remembered his prisoner. He turned his head, but there was nobody there.

He spun around, grabbed the cell door, which was now closed, and tugged on it, to no avail. It was locked. And he realized he was alone.

Slowly the sheriff sank to the bunk and put his head in his hands. A few moments later, he started to howl.

There was no one to hear.

2

North America: June 22, 1942
Your Stars Today: Serious matters command your attention
and may require careful negotiations with authority figures
seeking to delegate responsibilities.

He had been snatched from his Princeton University office by three heavyset men with no mouths, crammed between them in the backseat of a black Packard for a rumbling damn-the-lights ride to the local train station, herded onto a lone car with drawn shades and no other passengers for an eight-hour nonstop ride in virtual silence, shoved into yet another Packard, this one with darkened windows, to endure seventy-five silent minutes of bad roads, then thrust into a closet-sized office painted in drab and decorated in dingy, adorned only by a desk, a few folding bridge chairs, a file cabinet, a broken-shelved bookcase and a smudged sliver of a window that overlooked a large field parched almost the same tan as the room's bare floor.

The day had not been going particularly well for David Walker, Ph.D.

Tired, clammy and confused, he scanned his sparse surroundings, searching for clues, impatient for answers. Unlike the trip, his wait was mercifully short.

The two men who entered the room couldn't have been more different. One was wafer thin, short, bespectacled and nearly bald, dressed formally in a blue suit, white shirt and patterned bow tie. The other, though obviously older, was tall, robust and commanding. Casually clothed in khaki slacks and an open-neck white shirt that accentuated his light tan and rugged good looks, there was determination in his cobalt blue eyes that Walker could read; he knew better than to judge him on outer appearance. The thin, short man spoke first.

"Doktor Walker, sehr gut, Sie zu treffen. Mein Name ist Ulrich Krieger."

An overzealous Ulrich Krieger thrust his hand at him. Walker clasped it halfheartedly, concerned that if he pressed too firmly he might crush Krieger's frail fingers. The other man made no attempt to introduce himself but listened passively as Krieger continued to talk. *"Ich bin mir sicher, dass Sie sehr verwirrt sind, aber der General wird alles erklären."*

"You're right, Mr. Krieger, I *am* confused by what's going on, including why you're speaking German."

"Doktor Walker, würden die Unateraltung bitte auf Deutsche führen? Sie sprechen dock Deutsche, oder nicht?"

"Yes, I know German. I had to learn it for my doctoral studies."

"Doktor Walker, wüden Sie bitte auf Deutsch antworten?"

He had no idea why Krieger was so insistent that he respond in German, but it was apparent that if he didn't play whatever game it was, no answers would be forthcoming. He repeated his answer in German.

"Wie ich schon sagte, der General wird Ihnen alles zu gegebener Zeit erkären."

That was the second time that Krieger said the general would explain things. He assumed the general was the other man, who had settled into a battered black leather swivel chair behind the desk but still hadn't uttered a sound. He saw no reason he should trust him to explain anything and told Krieger so.

Krieger paid him no mind. Instead he smiled at the man at the desk and, at last, began speaking English. "Excellent, General, truly excellent. Not pure Berliner, but rather a mixture of different accents—Bavarian, even a touch of Austrian. Still nothing that would raise any suspicions. Berlin is a cosmopolitan city."

"Entschuldigt mich, aber was."

"Dr. Walker it's all right to use English now, unless you prefer German," Krieger said.

"I prefer not being kept in the dark. What's this talk about Berlin and not raising any suspicions?"

"How about his appearance?" Finally, the general spoke. "Anything that would attract attention?"

Krieger narrowed his small brown eyes to slits and scrutinized Walker. When he finished, he removed his wire-rimmed glasses and poked them like a pointer as he delivered his opinion. "No, I think not. Good average build and height. Strong facial characteristics: nose, chin. They'll like that and the light brown hair. Blue eyes would have been nice, but hazel is fine."

That's it! Enough of being studied as if he were some goddamn lab animal, especially when he was used to being the one calling the shots. "Who will like what?" Walker grabbed Krieger by the bones that were his shoulders and shook him, causing his angular head to bob up and down like a bird dislodging a worm.

"General . . ."

"Mr. Krieger's just doing his job, so please let him go," the general said, and after one more shake Walker released his grip.

"It's all right, Ulrich. I'll take it from here."

With a nod of obvious relief, Krieger quickly left, closing the door behind him.

"Good man, Ulrich. Teaches the boys here German and does translating for us."

"Where's here and who's us?"

"Please sit, Dr. Walker."

"No thanks. I don't plan on staying."

"As you wish. Do you know who I am?"

"Let me guess. You're the general."

"General William Donovan, retired. Late of Wall Street by way of the Fighting Sixty-Ninth and now Director of the United States Office of the Coordination of Information."

"I'm impressed, General. Now why am I here?"

"You tell me." Donovan, who had been fiddling with a capped black fountain pen, pushed it into a thatch of closely cropped white hair, tapping it a couple times against his scalp as if trying to dislodge a thought. "I understand you're quite a good mind reader."

"I'm afraid you've mistaken me for someone else." Walker didn't like the way this was going.

"Really?" Donovan dropped the pen, took a manila folder from the top desk drawer and began reading its contents aloud. "'David Walker. Exceptional college record at Dartmouth. Full graduate scholarship to Harvard. Doctorate with highest honors. Youngest full professor in the history of Princeton's psychology department.'" Donovan closed the folder. "You *are* that David Walker, aren't you?"

Walker *definitely* didn't like the way this was going. He had to keep his cool and get out of there as quickly as he could.

"And do you know what makes your accomplishments all the more amazing?" Donovan continued. "You've been dead for the past six years."

Damn! Walker sat down in one of the folding chairs.

"Perhaps I should qualify that. David Walker's been dead for the last six years. Now if we're talking about . . ." Donovan paused and opened the folder again. "John Matthews. Wasn't that the name you used when you were arrested in Duluth?"

Definitely damn! Walker saw his carefully fabricated life flash before his eyes, crash and roll down the slightly slanted rough pine floor, through a small crack at the bottom of the wall behind Donovan and out into oblivion. "Or was it Mark Adams? No, I think Mark Adams was Beloit, but does it really matter?" Donovan thumbed through a few more pages in the folder. "Of course we could use your given name."

"I *have* no given name." It was an instantaneous, angry reaction and Walker, who prided himself on never tipping his emotions, knew Donovan would jump on it.

"I meant the name the nuns at St. Raphael's Home gave an abandoned baby they took in."

"I have no given name." This time he spoke slowly and emphatically, signaling his determination to take back the advantage Donovan had gained over him.

"I see. Well, then, why don't we stick with Dr. David Walker, in recognition of your being awarded a Ph.D. for completing the fifth grade. Isn't that the extent of your formal schooling?"

"Third grade, actually." It was a small strategic retreat from denial, although Walker was sure Donovan would regard it as surrender. How would the general react to his victory? Would he gloat like Paris, when he dragged Hector's mangled body seven times around the gates of Troy, or be gracious like Grant when he refused to accept Lee's sword at Appomattox?

"We're a young organization. Our information gathering isn't perfect."

So, he was more like Grant. Walker was relieved.

"In any event . . ." Donovan riffled through the papers in the folder. "You ran away from the Home when you were eight, rode the rails and became quite a good little con artist. Now here's the part that fascinates me. You persuaded Houdini to make you his helper when you were what, eleven? Twelve?" Donovan leaned back in the cracked black leather chair, which emitted a loud unoiled creak of protest. "That must have been something, working with Houdini. I assume he gave you expert advice on astrology, tarot and all the other forms of fortune-telling that you're so skilled at. Ironic, isn't it? Houdini used his knowledge to debunk that hokum, but after he died, you used it to swindle people. Seems you had quite a following on the carnival circuit, followed by a colorful career as a revival show preacher. "

"I like to think I helped people."

"Helped them out of a lot of money, you mean. Then, suddenly you just disappeared for years, only to reemerge teaching college with someone else's credentials."

What had prompted Donovan to dredge up all this information? And was he really ignorant about the period between the tent shows and the college teaching? Walker pointed to the folder. "You should have everything there."

"As I said, we're not perfect." Donovan closed the folder and sat up straight again. "There are gaps here and there."

As Donovan spoke, Walker focused on his pupils, measuring them in his mind and watching for even the slightest dilation, which, as Houdini had taught him, was a sure sign of lying. They didn't budge. No, the missing years were still missing, at least from Donovan's dossier.

"However, I'm pretty good at surmising," Donovan said. "Although I doubt I could hold a candle to someone who also spent quite a bit of time with the creator of Sherlock Holmes. Houdini's friend, Sir Arthur Conan Doyle. What an excellent education you must have had, Dr. Walker, even if it wasn't the one you claim."

Godamn it, only a select few people could have told Donovan that, most of whom Walker ruled out immediately.

"Then, somewhere along the line, maybe when you were with one of the carnivals, you found yourself in Nebank, Minnesota, where you saw an obituary for David Walker, a promising young scholar who drowned on vacation in Greece. Since he had no family, it was a perfect opportunity for you to adopt a new life. How are my surmising skills so far, Dr. Walker?"

Well, he had part of it right. "Go ahead."

"You made your way back east and got a job as a night cleaner at Harvard. Once there, it wasn't hard for a man of your unique abilities to change Walker's records from deceased to active, forge a few new recommendations and create a full profile, which you used to apply for a university teaching position. Princeton snapped you up in an instant and here we are. How did I do?"

It was time to go on the offensive. Walker put his palms on the desk and leaned forward so that his face was only inches from Donovan's. "General, just what is it you want? Surely you've got more important things to do than exposing me."

"Exposing you? I have no intention of exposing you. Your department head not only thinks you're a superb teacher, but a genius. He'd hate to lose you, especially after he risked his own professional reputation to hide your past."

"You know Professor Goddard?" Of all the surprises Walker had been hit with, this was the biggest.

"John? I've known him for years. And that's why I know about you."

"I told Dr. Goddard certain things in confidence. I can't believe he would share them with you." Walker was starting to feel decidedly vulnerable.

"He never would have if it wasn't a matter of national urgency and then only because he trusted me. You'll find I'm good at keeping secrets. No, I won't expose you."

Donovan's words didn't put him at ease, but they did open the way for an exit. "Then you won't mind if I leave." He pressed down on his palms and raised himself up.

"You're not even curious about why you're here?"

Of course he was, but every part of him was screaming, Get out! "Write me a letter, General," he said as he turned toward the door.

"Should I address it to Leavenworth?"

That stopped him. He swirled back around. "I'm sorry?"

Donovan walked over to Walker and handed him a piece of paper. "Go ahead. Read it."

He scanned the paper and looked up. "A warrant for the arrest of Jack Kilian."

"Not just any warrant." Donovan took the paper back from him and pointed to some wording. "A *federal* warrant. I believe Jack Kilian was the name you used in Talbot, Iowa, back in 1933 when you were caught passing counterfeit bills."

"I'm no counterfeiter. I won that money in a poker game."

"Yes, I heard you're good at poker, although there's some question about what skills you use."

"I didn't have to cheat that bunch. They were lousy players."

"Whatever the circumstances, this warrant is still active for your arrest and for the unnamed accomplices that busted you out of jail."

"Accomplices? There were no accomplices."

"That's not what the sheriff said."

Walker couldn't help chuckling.

"Want to let me in on the joke?" Donovan asked.

Why not? With all Donovan already knew, one more piece didn't matter. Besides, this was too good not to share. So as a captivated Donovan listened, Walker recounted the story of a small midwestern jail, of a bloody Bible that levitated and of a man who could walk through steel bars. He provided the details, but not the explanations, leaving Donovan to speculate.

"Since I know who your mentor was, the escape part wasn't hard to figure out. It appears Houdini taught you more than fortune-telling techniques."

"A belt buckle makes an excellent pick, especially if someone's foolish enough to handcuff you through jail bars facing forward so the lock's within easy reach."

"I assume the blood was yours."

Walker flopped back down on the bridge chair, pulled off one of his scuffed black loafers and removed a sock. "A slight cut to the fleshy part of the toe, where there are a lot of capillaries, so the blood flows like ink in a pen. The evidence is absorbed by your sock and hidden by your shoe." He dangled the sock in front of Donovan. "The sock also plays another role. If you carefully unravel the thread, you can use it to levitate things like a Bible."

Donovan looked puzzled.

"One of the cell's previous occupants stuck a piece of gum under the bunk," Walker said as he slid his sock back on and forced his foot into his shoe. "A little saliva and it came back to life. I used it to anchor one end of the thread to the wall, draped the Bible over it and controlled the movement by wrapping the other end around my thumb. The lighting was dim enough to make the thread invisible. Besides, the sheriff was distracted."

"By what?"

Before he could answer, a high-pitched voice came from the other side of the room. "Daddy, it's all right."

Donovan's ashen face left no doubt that he had recognized what he heard. It was the voice of his dead daughter.

"Patty?" Visibly unnerved, Donovan swung around in his chair.

"I love you, Daddy, and I miss you." This time the voice came from the window. Donovan swirled around. Sweat started to bead on his forehead.

"No, Daddy, I'm up here." The voice trickled down from the ceiling. "And now I'm here." The voice, slightly muffled, rose from the wooden floor.

"Patty . . ."

"She's not here, General." Walker pressed the tips of his left thumb and forefinger into a pair of lips. "Look, Daddy." And as he flexed his thumb back and forth, the voice came from the makeshift mouth. "I can make her be anywhere you want, but I can't bring her back."

"Ventriloquism! You son of a bitch! You bastard! How dare you make a mockery of my daughter's death!"

"You told me to read your mind, which is constantly on your daughter. You can't forget her, and you can't forgive yourself."

Donovan was radiating anger, the veins in his patrician Irish face and his muscular arms so charged by adrenaline that they looked like they might burst through his skin. In response, Walker braced himself for a physical attack by a man who, though older, obviously could still inflict great harm.

"Goddamn you!" Then the man who had won the Medal of Honor for valor in the Great War slumped back into his chair and bowed his head in defeat. It was a moment before he composed himself to speak. The words came haltingly. "Patty was a student at Georgetown. She was returning to Washington from a weekend away with friends. I was coming in for a business meeting and she wanted to spend some time with me. The weather was bad. Her car skidded and . . ." Donovan stopped, then slowly raised his head and looked at Walker. "How did you know about Patty? Did you read about it? I know you have a total photographic memory. John Goddard said it's beyond anything he's ever encountered and was a major reason you were able to pass yourself off as a Ph.D. You forget nothing, not even the slightest detail. So you must have read about the car crash."

He shook his head. "No, you told me."

"If this is a joke I don't find it funny." Though Donovan was collected, Walker could sense his lingering rage.

"Remember the sheriff? He had fallen into a fitful sleep and kept uttering the name 'Betty.' I didn't care who Betty was or what happened. I just needed that snippet to trigger some uncomfortable memories. The sheriff did all the rest. The same thing here. Your reaction to an innocent phrase told me what I needed to know."

Seeing Donovan was still confused, Walker simplified his explanation. "I looked for something that might have relevance for you. There aren't many personal items in this office, so the few things on display stand out." He made a slow visual sweep around the room. "Like the pictures of a girl at different ages, some with you, some without. It made sense she was your daughter. But why would you carry so many pictures of her around with you? That's behavior usually associated with either a recent or a lingering loss."

"It wasn't recent, but the pain is still there. It's always there."

"Also, this isn't your office."

"We're allies with Canada. We're fighting the same war and we sometimes share personnel. It's my office when I'm here."

So this is Canada. Donovan's first major slip-up! "No matter." Walker swept his right index finger across the desk, and then held it in front of Donovan's face. "See? Dust. The whole room's dusty." He picked up one of the pictures on the desk and wiped it with his left forefinger, which he also showed Donovan. "Nothing. The picture's clean. You don't strike me as a man who would leave things half-done, General. This isn't your office, but all these pictures are yours and you take them everywhere with you."

Donovan lifted the picture Walker had put down and stared at it for a few seconds before setting it back in place. "You could have been wrong."

"So what? I only said, 'Daddy, it's all right.' But your reaction to that statement told me something had happened and, in some way, you felt responsible. I used that information to my advantage. So-called mind readers do it all the time. They toss out some generalities and then trick you into giving them specifics. It's called cold reading and it can be a very effective tool."

For the first time since their conversation began, Donovan actually smiled. "John Goddard was right. You're perfect."

"Perfect for what?"

Donovan got up and gazed out the window "What do you think would happen to Germany if Hitler were removed from the helm?"

"I really haven't given it much thought."

"Well, I have," Donovan said, his back still to Walker. "And I'm not alone. With Hitler gone, Germany and its war effort would be thrown into chaos." The certainty in Donovan's voice belonged to the focused battlefield commander, not the Washington desk jockey.

"Are you saying you intend to get rid of Hitler?"

"No, not me, but somebody very much like me. You."

There was a long quiet stretch as Walker tried to grasp what he had just heard. "You want me to kill Hitler?"

"Of course not." Donovan eased back into his chair, reached for another folder that was already lying on his desk, took a picture from it and handed it to Walker. It was an official Reich portrait of a thin-faced man with a high brow, small mustache and almost nonexistent chin. He was wearing oval glasses, and his military cap, too large for his head, made him look comical. "Heinrich Himmler, the head of the SS and probably the most feared man in Germany."

"You want me to kill Himmler?"

"That wouldn't help, either."

"Then what *do* you want me to do?"

"I want you to convince *Himmler* to kill Hitler."

Maybe it was the matter-of-fact way Donovan said it. No emotion. No theatrics. Just as casual and devoid of danger as *I want you to go to the store and get some bread.*

"Excuse me?"

This time Donovan said it more slowly, but in the same offhanded way. "I want you to go to Berlin and convince Himmler to kill Hitler."

Walker knew several suitable technical terms for Donovan's mental state, but he opted for something easily understood. "General, with all due respect, you're crazy."

"No, Dr. Walker, I'm desperate. Sometimes people confuse the two. You don't know how badly this war's going right now."

"Let's see, the Germans have just driven the British out of Libya and they're pounding away at the Russians in between trying to bomb London into oblivion. I keep up with the news."

"What's reported is bad enough. If you had access to the top-secret communiqués and briefings . . ." Donovan raised his hand and moved his thumb and index finger toward each other until they almost touched. "We're this close to losing Egypt and the whole Middle East and North Africa along with it. We need to do something."

Curiosity overtook Walker's common sense that again was screaming, *Get out!* "If you want Hitler dead, just kill him and be done with it."

"And make him a martyr? That's worse than leaving Hitler alive. No, he has to be killed by someone powerful and credible within the Reich who could take the reins and possibly be forced into a peace."

"Let's pretend that any of this makes sense. Why Himmler?"

"Because Goebbels's too smart and Goering's too stupid. Besides, Himmler could keep the SS in check in the aftermath of Hitler's death. That's a critical factor, as is Himmler's hatred of Russia. He might feel that if he made peace with the United States and Britain, we would join in the fight against Russia. At the very least, with us out of it, he wouldn't have to worry about a two-front war. And it would give the anti-Nazi factions in Germany time to act. That should explain why Himmler."

"But it doesn't explain why me."

"Himmler's obsessed with the occult. He even has an entire SS section, the Ahnenerbe, devoted to it. And he's especially fascinated with astrology."

Walker was now sure that he had fallen down the rabbit hole. "And why's that so important?"

"Astrologers have been banned in Germany, but the elite, including certain high-ranking Reich officials, still consult them. Himmler has a staff of astrologers in the Ahnenerbe and he takes their advice very seriously. We think there's a good chance that a planted astrologer, whose predictions were consistently accurate, could win Himmler's trust. Once he has that—"

"The proper horoscopes could convince Himmler that destiny requires him to get rid of Hitler—"

"So Germany can achieve her true greatness under him. You're a quick study, Dr. Walker."

"And you really are insane, General. Do you know what the chances are that this harebrained scheme will succeed?"

"Conservatively, about a million to one. Can you live with those odds?"

"Those aren't living odds, General. I think I'll take my chances with Leavenworth."

This time when Donovan rose from the desk, he walked to the door and opened it. "You're free to go."

"Don't think I won't. But first, why me? Why not one of your people?"

"I guess we owe you that much." Donovan shut the door. "We had someone. Not ours. An astrologer who was a member of the German underground. He was the linchpin."

"Was?"

"He's dead."

"Killed by the Nazis?"

"Killed by a bus with bad brakes that skidded out of control on a wet street."

"And you had no backup?"

"We were too preoccupied with what could go wrong once the mission started. A mistake, obviously."

"Obviously. Then delay the mission."

"We can't."

"Why not?"

Donovan opened the top drawer of the rusty olive file cabinet, took out another folder and tossed it onto Walker's lap. "Because of this." Walker opened the folder and found a series of newspaper clippings, which he thumbed through.

> *Associated Press, May 27, 1942*
> *Reinhardt Heydrich, Deputy Gestapo Chief and Deputy Reich Protector of German-occupied Bohemia-Moravia, was wounded in an assassination attempt in Prague this afternoon, Berlin radio announced tonight. "There is no danger for his life," the announcement said.*

> *Reuters, May 27, 1942*
> *The condition of Reinhard Heydrich is grave, according to a late report issued by the Vichy news agency.*

> The New York Times, *May 29, 1942*
> *Preliminary reports from usually well-informed German quarters as to exactly how the attack on Reinhardt Heydrich was made indicate that at least two men were involved. One is stated to have*

thrown a bomb at Herr Heydrich's moving automobile, which swerved to avoid being hit. A second man is then reported to have stepped out from concealment with a submachine gun or automatic pistol and to have fired several shots into the automobile as it rolled into the ditch. The assassins are then reported to have escaped by bicycle.

Associated Press, May 29, 1942
According to German radio broadcasts this morning, Reinhardt Heydrich is believed to be hovering between life and death and has been placed under the care of Adolf Hitler's personal physician.

Associated Press, June 4, 1942
German radio this morning reported the death of Reinhardt Heydrich, Deputy Gestapo Chief and Deputy Reich Protector of German-occupied Bohemia-Moravia, who had been wounded in an assassination attempt in Prague on May 27.

Walker put down the folder. "What's the Heydrich assassination have to do with anything?"

"The assassination was the match to the fuse for this whole harebrained scheme as you called it. Now that the fuse has been lit, there's no turning back. Unfortunately, our man caught his bus right after Heydrich was called to Valhalla."

"Am I missing something?"

"Peter Kepler, the astrologer selected by the German underground, sent a horoscope to Himmler predicting that Heydrich would be in mortal danger on May 27. That's the date that we set for the assassination."

"Your group assassinated Heydrich?"

"Not exactly. The Czech government in exile wanted Heydrich killed to boost the morale of its resistance movement and to show the world that it still was in charge. So the British secret service trained a band of Czech freedom fighters, armed them and parachuted them into Czechoslovakia."

"I still don't understand."

"Heydrich had designed the master plan for a new Nazi order and was taking it to Berlin for Hitler's blessing. Had he succeeded, the chances were excellent that Heydrich would have received a major promotion and become Hitler's designated successor. If that happened, there'd be no sense in killing Hitler. Heydrich was every bit as obsessed and every bit as brutal."

"And Kepler, the astrologer?"

"I told you, Himmler only relies on his own astrologers. A chart done by an unknown would have no chance of making it to his desk. The underground relied on that. But after the assassination, the SS started to investigate everything. That's when the chart surfaced. As you can imagine, Nazi officials were extremely interested in finding the person who prepared it."

"And once they checked the obituary records, I'm sure they had no trouble finding Peter Kepler, or his remains."

"They wouldn't have, if Peter Kepler had been run over by the bus."

Just when Walker thought that he had reached the bottom of the rabbit hole, he discovered it was really a ledge and he was just about to tumble off. "What do you mean, *if* Peter Kepler had been run over by the bus?"

"You'll appreciate this. Peter Kepler wasn't the man's real name. It was made up for the mission. The plan would only work with a person who had no past beyond what was created for him, someone totally unknown within the German astrological community. He had to be anonymous until we were ready to bring him into contact with Himmler. So when our astrologer was killed by the bus, he had no identification on him. He became the German equivalent of a John Doe. He was to assume the name Peter Kepler after Heydrich was killed. That way Himmler would be caught by surprise."

"It seems you were the ones caught by surprise."

"A wet street, a bus, a chance accident. Anyway, that's done with. Right now, Peter Kepler has to come into existence. There's a brief window while Himmler reigns supreme next to Hitler. We have no idea how long he can hold that spot. Heydrich had protégés. Eichmann's the most dangerous. If we wait too long, that deadly son of a bitch will step into Heydrich's spot, consolidate power and move against Himmler. And if that happens, we're finished. At least with Himmler, we have a chance."

"You had a chance." Walker got up. "Am I still free to leave?"

Donovan flicked his right hand toward the door. "My men will see that you get back to Princeton. I assume you won't talk about this."

"Do you really think I'd waste my time discussing something so outlandish?"

"If I did, I wouldn't even bother with Leavenworth." Donovan cast a dark look at his guest. "Thank you for your time, Dr. Walker. I guess John Goddard didn't understand you as well as he thought."

The last sentence halted him three steps shy of the door. Goddard again. "He said I'd go along with this foolishness?"

"John recommended you from the start, but it was important that the Germans take the lead in ridding their country of its blight. Now, however, things have changed."

"John Goddard was involved from the start?" So, Goddard wasn't merely a source of background information. He was the damn initiator. Something didn't add up.

"John prepared the psychological work-ups of the Reich leaders and he pinpointed Himmler. He also told us that he knew someone who would be perfect for this assignment, A German order of nuns ran the orphanage, so you spoke German, along with English, practically from birth. Add to that the uncanny ear John says you have for languages. No, John was right. You're ideal. And you spent time in Berlin with Houdini."

"That was years ago. I was a teenager. Berlin's changed."

"Some new buildings and some different street names, but it's still Berlin. John felt you'd want to help the war effort even though you ducked the military."

"I was never called up."

"Dead men don't get drafted. And, of course, if you enlisted, it could have blown your well-prepared cover. Still, John believed there were good reasons why you'd help us."

"Such as?"

"Such as the possibility of ending this war sooner rather than later and perhaps saving millions of lives."

"Keep going."

"Such as saving some very specific lives, underground members who've now put themselves at considerable risk to make this plan work. Those should be two very good reasons."

"I'm no hero."

"Maybe not. I never thought I was, either, but they tell me I am. Besides, you've made it clear what you are. And that brings me to the third reason, which is the chance to pull off the greatest con in the history of the world."

"Was that Dr. Goddard's reason or yours?"

"I think we arrived at it simultaneously. In any event, should I have my men get the car ready?"

He didn't answer. Donovan was right about a few things. It had been easy for him to rationalize not enlisting. Enlisting was a sucker deal. One more soldier wasn't going to make a difference. But what if this plan actually could work? This time maybe one person could make a difference. Then there was the prospect of being the key player in what Donovan said would be the greatest con ever. God, was that tempting. Still, something bothered him. There was a reason missing, one that Goddard would have known, though not shared with Donovan.

"I'm curious. Why didn't Dr. Goddard himself ask me to take this on?"

"I wanted him to, but he wouldn't. He gave me a cryptic answer, something about not influencing a decision that would end your life, even if you succeeded. When I pressed him on why he was so sure you'd be killed, he said that wasn't what he meant. I couldn't get anything more out of him."

There it was: the most important reason. Goddard was giving him the chance, perhaps his last, to stop running from destiny. Yes, if he made it through, he could return to college teaching, but it wouldn't be the same. The classroom would no longer be a hideaway, but simply a place to await his next challenge.

"John remained adamant about not talking to you. In fact, I've told you too much. He said to mention him only if I absolutely had to. He also made me promise that if you said no, nothing was to happen to you. Nothing. That's why you're free to leave. Again, should I have my men get the car ready?"

While Donovan still sounded calm, Walker noticed a slight jerkiness in his shoulders. He had seen that before, when poker bluffers, trying to appear cool and collected, are betrayed by rapid breathing that caused their shoulders to move ever so slightly. Donovan's concealed anxiety said once Walker was out the door the project was finished. Yet if he accepted the mission, he knew his life would no longer be his own. Not that the temptation wasn't there. Donovan was right: he was hardly the type to be consigned to the purgatory of a college classroom. It certainly wasn't a choice Walker had made easily. And now, offered a chance to pull off the greatest con ever, no matter what the cost, and this time for the good . . .

"Dr. Walker, have we lost you?"

No, he couldn't let himself do it. Not when he still had the chance to choose. Obviously John Goddard was hoping he would accept, but John Goddard didn't have to pay the price. Time to leave. Still, Donovan wasn't a bad sort, so why not let him down gently.

"Are you a betting man, General?"

"On occasion."

"This idea of yours is one hundred percent absurd, but I'm willing to give you a fifty percent chance to try it. A coin toss—heads I sign on, tails I don't."

"You're serious?" Donovan's response was part question, part statement. "Who tosses?"

"It's my life we're risking, so I guess I do."

"And use some of your sleight of hand?"

"I'll toss the coin in the air and let it hit the ground. Even I'm not good enough to control it in the air. So, are you up for it?"

"I don't have much choice, do I?"

"Maybe you'll get lucky," Walker said, although he knew luck wouldn't enter into it. "Why don't you select a coin so you know it's not faked."

Donovan fished into his khakis and dropped his cache of coins on the desktop. "Let's see. Why don't we use . . . what the hell?" Donovan picked up a coin, examined it and gave it to Walker. "Damnedest thing. I thought it was a nickel, but instead of a buffalo there's an engraving of three people sitting on the roof of a boxcar. And that's no Indian profile on the other side. It looks more like a Negro. Ever see anything like that?"

Not like it: Walker had seen this exact coin. He had even watched it being made, years ago when he was a boy riding the rails. Now it was his shoulders that were moving up and down as he tried to remain nonchalant. "It's called a hobo nickel, General. Old-time hoboes altered coins with penknives to help pass the time. They especially liked the buffalo nickel because the images were large and gave them a better canvas. A nicely done nickel could be traded for a meal, some groceries or even a place to stay for a night. This one was done by Bertram Wiegand, the best of the hobo artists. Look." He tapped his finger just below the buffalo-turned-boxcar, where the word "Liberty" would normally be. "Wiegand scratched off the *l*, *i* and *y* to get 'bert,' the name everyone knew him by."

"And the face?" Donovan asked.

"Could be anyone," he said, although he knew that face as well as his own. "Friend, stranger, figment of Bert's imagination. Maybe all three run together." Where the hell did this coin come from and why now? he wondered. Coincidence was a stretch, but he wasn't about to admit any other explanation.

"Here's a normal half dollar we can use." Donovan held up a new coin.

Nor was he going to give in to any mystical foolishness. "No, this one will be fine."

Walker had done the move hundreds of times. By starting with the tail side facing up and using a special high toss, he could make it look like the coin was flipping over and over in the air when really it was only rotating. Landing was the tricky part. The coin had to hit at a less-than-forty-degree angle to ensure it came out tails. The wooden floor was dicey, but a small red-and-white oval area rug to the side of Donovan's desk was perfect. "Here we go."

Clasping the coin between his right middle and ring fingers, Walker made a thumb motion as if he were flicking it upward to cover the fact that he actually tossed it upward like a discus. As the coin began its trajectory, Donovan, trying to get a better look, stepped onto the rug, slightly moving and creasing it. The toss had been perfect and the coin would have landed at the necessary angle, falling flat with the tail side up, had it not hit one of the wrinkles in the rug Donovan had caused. Instead it bounced up again, falling back down on its edge and settling with the head side up.

"Well, well." Donovan was beaming. "It must be fate."

Donovan hit it on the head, without realizing it. Shaken but not about to show it, Walker wondered if he had been fooling himself all this time, thinking he really had a say in matters. He picked up the coin and stared at the face. He could hear a voice in his mind, speaking as clearly as it had so long ago: *Do this, son. You always listened to me. Whether you believe or not, you do this and make peace with who you are.* He rubbed his forefinger lightly over the coin. "I will, Delta," he said under his breath. "I will."

"Are you in?" Donovan asked.

"Even con men have codes. I don't welch on wagers."

"Thank you." Donovan reached over and squeezed Walker's shoulder. Walker could feel the sincerity.

"Here's your coin." He picked it up and handed it back to Donovan.

"It seems to mean something to you. Keep it."

"In that case, I'd like you to hold it for safekeeping, until I return."

Donovan nodded his head. "Can I ask you—was the toss really unrigged and did the result actually change your mind?"

He knew Donovan wasn't buying it. "You can ask me, and maybe someday I'll tell you. That is, if I'm around someday. In the meantime, do you want to tell me what part of Canada we're in?"

Donovan's eyes widened. "How did you know you're in Canada?"

"You told me, but you were so wrapped up in things that you didn't realize or remember it. Cold readers play on things like that."

"Remarkable. Anyway, you're just a smidge outside Whitby, a small town near Toronto. This particular property is Camp X, a three-hundred-acre farm that's been converted to a training facility for extremely delicate and dangerous covert operations. The grounds are lovely, but you won't be here long enough to enjoy them. Speaking of which, John is prepared to handle your apartment and any personal matters, along with your classes, if that's acceptable." Walker nodded his head and Donovan continued. "Good. Then let's get started. The code name of this mission is, quite fittingly, Zodiac. From here on out you will be Peter Kepler, not David Walker, though I doubt one more identity will bother you."

"Nice touch." Peter saw Donovan didn't get it. "Kepler. The name means someone who wears a cloak."

"The underground chose it. Going on, you have to be in Berlin by July 2."

"July 2? That's ten days away!"

"We can still get in a cram course on espionage and survival training before you're off to Sweden and, from there, to Denmark. The Nazis control Denmark, but not with their usual iron fist. The Danish resistance has been smuggling Jews out left and right, and they'll get you to Berlin."

"And once I get to Berlin, who do I hook up with?"

"You'll be dealing with the most clandestine of the anti-Nazi underground groups. Only a few people inside Germany know all the players."

"You didn't answer my question."

"I can't answer your question. With no American or British agents in Germany, we're groping in the dark. The only thing I can tell you is that Peter Kepler was in contact with a Nazi SS colonel who uses the code name 'Max.'"

"And how would you suggest I find him? Look under 'Nazi Colonels' in the Berlin phone book?"

"Right after Kepler's death, we received a coded message from Berlin. We don't know who sent it, but it was authentic. It contained a July 2 entry from Kepler's appointment book. *Krähenneste; Oberst Max 20 Uhr.*"

"Crow's nest. Colonel Max at 8 P.M. What's that all about?"

"The Crow's Nest is a bar on Motzstrasse. It appears Kepler was supposed to meet this Colonel Max there on the second. That's how we learned he was the contact. We intend for Kepler to keep that appointment."

"And Hitler's deadly appointment with Himmler."

"That's a little trickier. Since Hitler took power, there have been twenty-three attempts to assassinate him that we know of. Some of these were planned by people close to him. You'll need time to gain Himmler's trust. January 30, 1943, is the tenth anniversary of Hitler becoming Chancellor, a major Nazi milestone. It has to happen before then. Exactly when and where is up to the underground."

"Anything else you don't know that you'd like to share with me?"

"Something I do know. Right now both the Gestapo and the SS are tearing Germany apart looking for Peter Kepler. While we'll teach you as much as we can, you'll really have to rely on what you've been so successful doing all your life—trusting your skills and following your instincts."

"And not getting shot."

"Shot?" Donovan smiled. "You won't get shot. Men like you are born to be hanged."

3

Berlin: June 24, 1942
Your Stars Today: "Big" is the governing word: anything done today should be done in a big and extravagant way. The Sun's interaction with Jupiter produces conditions that favor new proposals and new ventures. Seize the moment!

"Lights back on, please!" Joseph Goebbels, the propaganda minister of the Third Reich, had to shout above the applause. "Can we get some lights on in here, please?" Goebbels rose from a cushioned armchair in the screening room of the Reich Ministry for Public Enlightenment and Propaganda and waited for the room to brighten. "Much better. We wouldn't want people to think we have Poles working here."

Again he waited, this time for the laughter to die down. "But this is a time for rejoicing, not complaining. We have just witnessed a true work of genius." He turned to his still-seated female companion. "Now I'd like you to meet our director, a woman who, in her own way, has done as much as our soldiers to defeat our Russian enemy."

Like the select group of Nazi dignitaries attending the special viewing, she accepted Goebbels' gross exaggerations. After all, wasn't Goebbels himself a gross exaggeration? By rights this man, with a head much too big for his five-four body and a clubfoot anchoring his hundred pounds, should have been eliminated in the New Germany, which worshiped physical superiority. But Goebbels had made himself indispensable to Hitler. And she, in turn, had made herself indispensable to Goebbels.

"*Teuton* is a masterpiece," Goebbels said, and she felt his fingers fish around until he snagged her elbow. "Come, my dear, you can't disappoint your admirers."

As she stood her blond hair fell forward over her shoulders, discreetly landing along the low-cut neckline of a Lucien Lelong gown, fresh from German-occupied Paris. Not content to leave the choice of evening wear to others, she had gone to France herself, where, like a lioness, she carefully stalked her prey among the handful of still-functioning fashion houses.

Jacques Fath, Nina Ricci and Marcel Rochas all proved too staid for her taste, but at the House of Lelong she ended her hunt, pouncing on a masterpiece by his young designer, Christian Dior, which would do perfect justice to her textbook Aryan features. Red-and-ebony silk velvet, the gown—combined with her soft, porcelain white skin—mirrored the colors of the Nazi flag. And it enticingly embraced and traced every contour of her athletic body, unlike the wasted yards of cloth draped over the cow-like figures of the proper Reich wives on display tonight. Of course she'd look better than them, no matter what she wore. More important, she'd look better than their husbands' mistresses. All evening she had felt male eyes tugging at her gown zipper, then drawing back in delight as her bodice unfurled in the hot wind of fantasy. But she could care less what these supermen of the New Germany did to her in their minds. In reality, *she* was in complete control.

"People will praise you and your film throughout the thousand-year history of our Reich." Goebbels kept going on with his tributes, understandable given how much he had staked on *Teuton*. Rankled by the worldwide critical acclaim accorded *Alexander Nevsky,* the Soviet film about heroic thirteenth-century Russians beating back an invading German horde, Goebbels commissioned his own film, showing the same confrontation, but through German eyes. And to direct he gambled on an ambitious young woman who had made some stirring documentaries on Nazi Party rallies. She didn't fail him.

"This is a film that will stoke the fire of patriotism in the German heart," Goebbels continued. "Besides theaters, we'll show it to our soldiers on the Eastern Front. If we had an Iron Cross for the arts, this lovely lady would be wearing it. However, I have something even better." Goebbels reached into his breast pocket and removed a folded piece of paper. "Before the *Führer* left for his field headquarters, he had a private showing of *Teuton* and immediately afterwards, he penned this." Goebbels opened the paper and began to read:

> *My Friends:*
> *You understand why I am not with you on this wonderful occasion. I envy your telling future generations about being present at* Teuton's *exclusive screening.*
>
> *We owe a huge debt of gratitude to the director of this moving epic, which will help Germany emerge victorious in its sacred quest. She has shown herself—along with Jannings, Harlan and Riefenstahl—to be motion picture royalty. Therefore, I have decreed that tonight you*

*are to address her as the Grand Elise, which suits her well-deserved
station.*

"It's signed: *A. Hitler,*" Goebbels said, "with a handwritten postscript
that reads: *Congratulations, Grand Elise.*" Goebbels handed her the note to
another round of applause.

"We're gathered in what used to be the grand palace of Prince Leopold of
Hohenzollern." Goebbels swept his hand in a majestic arc that encompassed
the few vestiges of ornate Rococo trappings allowed to remain when the
interior was redone in a simpler style that emphasized the massiveness of the
building. "It's a fitting setting for our newly anointed cinema sovereign to
hold court. So please join us at a reception in the Ministry Dining Room
where she will receive her adoring subjects."

Ah, a reception. For her it was a taste of the old Nazi Berlin, before the
food and clothing rationing showed that the mighty Third Reich, destined
to rule the future, couldn't control the present. And it wasn't only everyday
citizens who were suffering. A few months ago, she had donated three fur
coats to the winter relief effort for the Eastern Front troops. Not old, shabby
furs, like that dowdy figurehead Gertrud Scholtz-Klink, the Reich Women's
Leader, gave. New furs, including one she hadn't even worn.

No, the old Nazi Berlin, heady with the Reich's many successes, had
been a constant, well-publicized celebration. An art exhibition at the Kunst-
haus gallery extolling the beauty of the naked Nordic body. A musical ode
to German greatness, composed by Richard Strauss and performed by the
Berlin Philharmonic. A museum show documenting Jewish racial and
moral inferiority. A grand dinner at Horcher's, the city's most exclusive
restaurant, marking a great military victory. *That* was the old Nazi Berlin.
But when England and Russia proved tougher opponents than expected,
priorities changed and the social whirl stopped. Tonight was a throwback
to an earlier, better time, before British bombs pockmarked the city and
air-raid sirens replaced Wagner. Tonight was hers and she was going to use
it to her utmost advantage.

"My dear Grand Elise." Something fat and clammy seized the back of
her right hand, jerking it skyward, where it collided with something wet
and spongy. "May I escort you to the festivities?"

She looked at her hand where Reich Marshal Hermann Goering, 320
pounds of insufferable arrogance stuffed into a formal white military uniform, had kissed it. No smudges. Thank God he wasn't wearing lipstick
tonight, just the usual coating of facial powder and the slightest hint of

mascara, making him look more like a drag queen than the head of the Luftwaffe.

Goebbels quickly came to her rescue. "My ministry, my privilege, my friend."

Goering's sigh, like his appearance, was overdone. "Perhaps a dance later."

She saw no escape. "It would be my pleasure."

"Then it's settled. And don't believe anything Goebbels tells you, my dear. He's a compulsive liar."

She watched Goering join the other guests filtering out through fourteen-foot-high oak double doors, and she wondered what Goebbels would do if he knew the truth about some of these pillars of the Reich. Take Count Gottfried von Bismarck-Schönhausen, who now had Goering's flabby arm draped over his shoulder. She could easily imagine how Goebbels, and even Goering, would react to Otto von Bismarck's grandson, an influential legislator, plotting with other German aristocrats to kill his close friend, the *Führer*, and install a new government. His was just the latest conspiracy against Hitler and, like all the others, doomed. That's why she hadn't stopped it.

And there, angling his dwarfish body between people in a rush to the bar, was Walter Funk, the Reich Minister of Economics and Hitler's personal financial adviser. Would Goebbels be more furious over Count Gottfried's treason or Funk's blatant homosexuality? Little matter. Since either transgression meant death, her whisper in Goebbels' ear could send both men to the Plötzensee Prison guillotine. Gottfried and Funk, like so many others, would be shocked if they knew that she knew their deepest secrets. For now, those secrets were safe. For now, but not forever.

"Well, Elie, how do you feel?"

Elie. She hated it when Goebbels used his pet name for her. He did it as a show of dominance, which usually preceded a directive.

"Humbled. Excited. Proud." Aware that she towered over Goebbels by a good five inches, she tried not to look down on this slip of a man decked out in a full dress uniform that would barely fit a Hitler Youth. However, she saw that he cared little about the difference in height, since it brought him eye-to-cleavage with her.

"You should be proud. Your accomplishment is magnificent. And the *Führer's* remarks were lavish. You know, he's not given to praise."

Of course she knew that. That's why she put so much effort into *Teuton*. If the *Führer* liked her work, she would become an undisputed member of the Nazi cultural pantheon, unique for being its only woman. If he didn't—well, that was never an option. She had mapped out everything too carefully, first acting in, then directing those ridiculous low-budget Alpine mountain movies, crammed with scenes of skiing, climbing and hiking that the public—and Hitler—loved so much. She had taken deliberate steps to be noticed, confident that her real talent would one day shine through and be rewarded. Now that day had come. "Should we join the others?" she asked.

"In a moment. There's a matter that we need to discuss before you run into Himmler."

"What's Himmler have to do with anything?" She feigned surprise, even though she was sure where Goebbels was heading.

"It's that damn SS documentary he's been after me to make. Now he's gotten Hitler's support, so there's no putting it off. Despite your relationship he wanted a male director, but after seeing *Teuton,* he wants you."

Excellent! Did she want the Himmler project? Without question. Not for the prestige, which was nice, but for the power, which was essential. And unlike most of Hitler's sniveling lackeys, she would know how to use that power. Tempted to scream, *Yes!* she decided to be coy. "I thought I might take a break from serious film, Joseph. Something light. A romantic comedy or perhaps a musical. The public's wild about them."

"Any semi-competent director can make those. It takes someone with exceptional talent to transform Himmler's flawed vision of a film into my grand reality. Besides, I told you: Himmler's made up his mind."

"Then perhaps I can unmake it at the reception."

"That would be most embarrassing, considering I already told him that you had agreed."

"What! Joseph, how could you do that?"

"I can do it because I'm the propaganda minister of the Reich, Elie, and because, no matter how big you become, your career will always rest in my hands."

She had counted on a such a response. Now to play on his disdain for Himmler. "But, Joseph, work with that chicken shit salesman? Really!"

Goebbels tried to keep his composure, tightening his thin face until it took on the contorted look of a rat sniffing out cheese. "Actually Himmler was a representative for a fertilizer manufacturer." Finally, unable to contain himself any longer, he let out a high-pitched laugh. "All right, a chicken shit salesman, and a failed one at that. But times have changed and so has he."

"Only in position. You know damn well what I've already done for him. You also know he has no appreciation of film, despite his pretensions. You, however, have a true artist's soul. That's why we work so well together."

"You know I wouldn't ask you to do this if it wasn't important."

"Important? Why? Because Himmler wants it done?"

"Do you seriously think I give a damn about what Reichsheine wants?"

Reichsheine. The Asshole of the Reich. A play on Himmler's first name, Heinrich. She had heard high-ranking officials use the derogatory nickname before, but never Goebbels. Was the uneasy accommodation between two of the Reich's most powerful and dangerous men unraveling?

"Reichsheine," Goebbels continued. "You can't even say it with a straight face, which just proves that Himmler's become a joke. Go ahead, try."

She did. He was right. The word lifted the corner of her lips into a slight grin.

"No, I don't give a damn about what Himmler wants." Goebbels was still wound up. "This film's important to *me*." He looked around, double-checking that no stragglers remained. "Look, Elie, we're in a difficult situation right now."

"Joseph, please, our military victories speak for themselves. Rommel's doing brilliantly in North Africa, and, while we've had a few setbacks in the east, the Russians are still on the run."

"Women don't understand war. Yes, Rommel's doing well now, but if we don't find a way to get him supplies more quickly, that will change. As for the Russians—well, our troops don't need another of their brutal winters. That leaves only a few months to complete our conquest. But it's not battlefield matters I'm concerned about."

Goebbels reached into the side pocket of his jacket and took out a pack of cigarettes. He offered her one, which she declined. "It's OK," he said. "Hitler's not around." They both smiled over the ban on smoking in Hitler's presence, particularly painful for the addicted Goebbels, who spent so much time with him.

"No," he said after inhaling deeply and letting the bluish-gray smoke slowly stream out of his lungs. "This is a difficult time because home front morale is down and there's growing grumbling from people who are either too weak or too stupid to understand sacrifice. Imposing more severe rationing is bad enough, but this continual bombing of our cities is taking a toll. Parents are agonizing over having to send their children away to countryside shelters. And Heydrich's assassination showed that even our best leaders aren't safe. Now that idiot Himmler wants a film that glorifies his precious SS. That's not what I need, that's not what the *Führer* needs and that's not what Germany needs. Those films have never stirred the people. Films like *Teuton* stir the people. That's why I committed you to this film."

Rarely was Goebbels so expansive, and so vulnerable, which put him just where she wanted. She paused to remind herself to add to the effect by speaking softly. "Only for you. Not for Himmler or anyone else, Joseph." She put her hand on his cheek. "Only for you, because I respect you." She waited a second for him to take her hand in his and squeeze it. How easy it was for her to manipulate the man who manipulated millions, she thought. How easy and how useful. "I owe you for all my success, Joseph, and now Himmler will owe you as well."

"And I intend to see that he pays dearly. Rest assured, Elie, you'll benefit from this. Remember, not everyone loves you as much as the *Führer* and I."

"It's no secret that I have detractors."

"Please, don't be so modest. You have enemies, not detractors, which is further testimony to how far you've come. It's also a danger. Openly working with Himmler and serving the SS will quiet those enemies for a while."

She didn't reply immediately, and when she did she chose her words carefully. "You're right, as always, Joseph. This will quiet my enemies," she said. And it will also enable me to destroy them.

4

Berlin: June 26, 1942
Your Stars Today: Saturn's current alignment with Neptune can prove distressing, causing serious problems particularly involving government. Those in religious or artistic circles could well encounter chaotic, even desperate conditions and situations.

Watching a street mob kick an old Jewish woman to death delayed his arrival at the synagogue. February's short sun was starting to set when he finally arrived at the small, Moorish-style house of worship, a fixture on Berlin's Linzerstrasse since 1748. Hundreds of people, many armed with heavy sticks and axes, contained by storm troopers, members of the SA, the Nazi security force, were milling in front of the limestone building, One, identified as a captain by the yellow patch on the collar of his brown greatcoat—three diagonal silver pips and two silver stripes—hurried over and extended his right arm in a salute. "Thank God you're here. They're cold and worked up. I don't know how much longer we could have held them back."

He didn't return the salute, just to make sure the captain knew who was really in charge. "That's not my problem. You did as you were told?"

The captain drew back his lips. "Of course I did!" Then, perhaps concerned the abrupt response sounded too much like a reprimand, he quickly repeated his words, this time in a much more subservient tone, adding, "Will you speak to them now?"

"What's your name?"

"Grantz. Albert Grantz."

"All right, Grantz, I'll speak to them now."

"Make him a path!"

The SA men responded immediately to Grantz's bark, pushing people aside until they had cleared a narrow twenty-five-foot-long aisle leading to the synagogue.

"Look, he's arrived!" The cry from someone in the crowd was quickly picked up by others and became a chant. "He's arrived! He's arrived!" As he followed the captain through the passage, people reached out trying to touch him. A few held up children so they might catch a glimpse. He smiled at his well-wishers, but his mind was on other things. He could see from the scattered debris that the gathering had already

been hard at work, ripping out pews and sanctuary trappings. He paused when he reached the base of the five granite steps leading to what was left of the synagogue doors and peered up at rubble piled into a three-foot-high pyre. Grantz was right: they wouldn't have waited much longer.

"Where are the Jews, Grantz?" he asked.

"Over to the side. We've been doing our best to keep them safe, though I don't know why."

"Because you were told to. Now bring them here."

Grantz raised a megaphone to his scowling face. "Get the Jews over here!"

Within moments more storm troopers appeared, shoving men, women and children to the front of the synagogue, where, using hands and rifle butts, the troopers forced them to the ground.

"The congregation, or what we could find of it," Grantz reported.

"Which one's the rabbi?"

Grantz walked along the line of Jews and stopped midway, before an elderly, bearded man in a long black coat and wide-brimmed black hat. "This one, I think."

"Bring him here to me."

Two storm troopers grabbed the old man's arms, yanked him over and dropped him in a heap.

"You're the rabbi?" he asked.

The old man rose, picked up his hat from the ground and put it back on. "I am Rabbi Jacob Lazar," he said, slapping some of the dust from his coat, "and I have led this congregation for thirty-five years."

He put his hand on the rabbi's arm. "Don't be afraid. Come." Still holding the rabbi's arm, he helped him up the steps to the landing, then called down to Grantz, "Where are they?"

"Just inside, to the right, against the entryway wall."

"Stay here, please, Rabbi."

He made his way around the pile of wood and through the doorless frame and returned cradling two parchment scrolls.

"Hold one."

The rabbi carefully took a scroll, kissing and caressing it as if it were an infant.

"Grantz, where are the adornments for the scrolls?"

"Adornments?"

"The silver crown and breastplate and pointer. And the velvet embroidered cover."

"Oh, those. They were taken before my men could intercede. We were barely able to save the damn scrolls."

It was an unsatisfactory answer, but he let it go. Holding a wooden roller in each hand, he lifted the scroll above his head. "Do you know what this is? This is the Torah, the Jews' most sacred object." Slowly he twisted the rollers, revealing Hebrew words on the parchment. "But I say it's nothing more than the Jews' toilet paper, so use it properly!"

With that he heaved the scroll forward. The rabbi looked on in horror as people passed it around, ripping off pieces of parchment. "A broch tsu dir!" The rabbi's voice was clear and strong. "Hitler und bis, yemakh shmoy! Yemakh shmoy ve-zikhroy!"

He turned to the rabbi. "What does that mean?"

The rabbi was silent.

"Who can tell me what this man said?" He directed his question to the Jews, but no one answered.

"You!" Grantz shouted at a boy in his early teens. "What's that gibberish all about?"

Trembling, the boy glanced at the woman next to him.

"I'm talking to you!" Grantz drove the toe of his boot into the boy's ribs. "You don't need her permission. Now I'm going to ask you again what that monkey jabber means." Grantz opened his coat and drew a pistol from its holster. "And if you don't tell me—"

"Tell him, Benjamin!" the woman shrieked.

"Mother—"

"Tell him!"

"It's a curse," the boy said in a halting voice. "A curse, in Yiddish. The rabbi asks that the name of Chancellor Hitler and the man up there be blotted out from the Book of Life and that there be no memory of them."

"Did you hear that?" Grantz asked.

He nodded and turned to the rabbi. "I admire your spirit, but be careful in your curses. Not everyone's as forgiving as I am. By the way, do you smoke?" He pulled a cigar and a small pair of trimming scissors from the inner pocket of his overcoat. "I think everyone's entitled to a few indulgences, don't you?" He snipped off the tapered end of the cigar and put the scissors back in his pocket, exchanging them for a gold lighter engraved with a swastika. He flicked the striker wheel. "And a good cigar is one of mine." He placed the cigar between his lips, dangled it just above the lighter and inhaled, causing the flame to rise and singe the tobacco wrapper.

Slowly he rotated the cigar end in the flame until it was glowing uniformly. "And do you know when I especially like a good cigar?" He moved the lighter away from the cigar and stared at it. "By a nice fire. A really nice fire."

He reached over and held the cigar against the parchment, which caught almost immediately. The rabbi recoiled in horror, backing away until he was pinned against the synagogue's outer wall.

What had been smoldering dry parchment now flared up and in seconds the Torah was ablaze. He clutched the top rollers and wrenched the scroll from the rabbi's hands, quickly tossing it on the altar of rubble, where it proved excellent kindling.

The rabbi, tears in his eyes, jabbed his hands into the fire, trying to pull out the Torah. Then, realizing rescue wasn't possible, he threw his body on top of the scroll. Within seconds the ends of his coat caught fire. The rabbi lifted his head and shouted something in what sounded like Hebrew.

"Grantz, ask the boy what he said."

Grantz grabbed the boy's collar and yanked him up. "You heard him!"

"He's quoting from the Talmud. The Romans were burning a Torah and a rabbi jumped into the fire with it. He said since he was being burned with the Torah scroll, he wasn't worried because God would seek retribution for the insult to the Torah and for him."

"You heard—"

He cut Grantz short and spoke directly to the crowd. "So now you know. The Hebrew God is coming to take vengeance on me for burning the devil's book." There were shouts and screams and laughter, peppered with cries of, "Kill the Jews!"

"The same Hebrew God who demands the blood of Christian children as a sacrifice. Well I trust in our God, the God of the Nordic Race, the God of civilized people." He raised his arms and spread them apart. "You have God's blessing. Perform your sacred duty to Him and to our Führer *by ridding our city of this demons' den."*

The storm troopers waited until he had walked down to the street and out of the way, then broke ranks, allowing the crowd to surge up the steps. Some painted slogans on the outer mortar walls that wouldn't burn: Filthy Jew Bastards *and* Death to the Christ-Killers. *Others heaved kerosene-filled bottle bombs through the door openings.*

By the time he had settled on a good vantage point—the stoop of a nearby apartment house—the final phase of the synagogue's destruction was well underway. The fire, now raging out of control, provided the satisfaction of a job well done but little relief from the penetrating cold. With one hand he drew up his overcoat collar, and with the other he pulled a pewter hip flask from his pant pocket. The fine French brandy inside was warming and welcome. As he took a second swallow, he let his eyes wander from the fire-engulfed synagogue to the spectacular display illuminating the sky. Against the twilight of the night, the smoke, like billowing late-summer clouds, took on shapes. He could make out a dog, which quickly stretched into a horse and then into nothing. He became absorbed with molding the smoke and oblivious to everything else around him: the frenzied screams of the marauders and the sounds of glass windows being shattered in nearby Jew-owned stores.

Now he could detect a large grayish-blue smoke violin, but he didn't want a violin; he wanted a horn, a French horn, and, by concentrating his mind he was able to pull a wisp of stray smoke from here and a tuft from there until he created one, perhaps the most perfect image so far. So perfect, in fact, that he thought he could hear familiar music coming from it: Siegfried's famous horn call from his beloved Ring.

As he listened, the horn of smoke seemed to visually transform into the music it was playing, and he saw Wagner's series of triplets—three different notes joined by a bar across their tops—pulsating with the sound. Then the middle notes disappeared and the music became jarring, causing the still-joined first and third notes to gyrate, revolving, twisting and whirling wildly until they took on the angular appearance of Hebrew letters. At first the letters were separate, then they appeared to clump together to form words he didn't understand but sensed were somehow foreboding. And though he marveled at how the night was playing tricks on him, deep down he felt a gnawing anxiety.

Then, suddenly, as if drawn by some unseen vortex, the words, which had arced across the sky like a grim rainbow, converged, compacting themselves almost to nothingness before erupting into one immense triplet, which again sounded Siegfried's horn call, so loud that he thought his eardrums might burst. He watched as the triplet's middle note began rising above the other two, taking most of the connecting bar with it, which gave it the shape of a giant cross. The remaining bar portions, still attached to the other notes, slid down slightly, creating two smaller crosses.

Now the flames from the burning synagogue intruded into what had been all smoke, leaping high in a brilliant array of yellows and oranges and reds and browns, so vivid that it blinded him momentarily. When he opened his eyes again, he saw that the flames hovering in front of the crosses had themselves taken on shapes. He could make out three human figures, each of which appeared impaled on one of the crosses of smoke: a boy in nightclothes on the left, a girl in a sleeping gown on the right, and between them, on the largest cross, a naked woman who called to him in a voice of thunder: "What has happened? What has happened?"

Suddenly the woman burst free and floated toward him, her arms outstretched as if to embrace him. And as he watched, her naked flesh melted in the heat of the fire that formed it, leaving only a blazing skull and a skeleton. Then, as her arms of burnt bone reached out to gather him in, the skull that had been her face spoke again, not in German but in a language he knew equally well, Church Latin,

"May you be blotted out from the Book of Life and may there be no memory of you."

He awoke, like always, drenched and agitated, and scanned his surroundings. There was no crowd, no synagogue, no brandy, no smoke.

He sat up so he could see out the window. It was still light and the trees were leaf heavy. It was June, not February; 1942, not 1934.

The nightmare had come again. It was always the same.

How many times had it been now? How many times since that day eight years ago? He had lost count. No, that's not true. He had stopped counting. He looked at this watch. Still a half hour left. He could go back to sleep, but the nightmare might return. Sometimes he went weeks without it. Other times it would keep replaying, over and over, night after night. There was no way of knowing. Best not to chance it, not for the sake of thirty more minutes.

So Monsignor Fritz Moeller reluctantly rose from the sofa in his rectory office and began preparing to say mass.

5

Fritz Moeller stood at the altar watching the parishioners slowly file out of the pews. Each day there were fewer, mostly the elderly. The dwindling numbers made the small church seem cavernous. But today there was a young man in his mid-twenties who came in after the Eucharist. He approached the altar.

"Monsignor, a moment please."

Moeller studied him carefully: tall, athletic and blue-eyed, with short brown hair that crowned a narrow, light-skinned face. Thirty years earlier, that could have been him, Moeller thought, except back then his own face already boasted two prominent dueling scars. And while today his hair was long and gray and frown lines had joined the scars, physically Moeller hadn't changed all that much. He was still lean and muscular, more so than most fifty-seven-year-old men, the result of rigorous exercise and moderate diet.

"Do I know you, my son?"

"My name is Hans Eisner."

Moeller continued to study the young man. His posture was back straight and there was no fidgeting. Hans Eisner was obviously military, probably SS, the elite "Black Corps" that produced the Reich's fiercest fighting units. He met all the SS racial requirements that Moeller himself had helped put into place years earlier.

"Eisner? The name isn't familiar. Are you new to the parish?"

"No. I'm from Badenweiler, near the Alps."

Moeller knew the village. "That's a long way from Berlin."

"I came to see you."

"All that way to see a local priest?"

"Not a local priest. Hitler's priest!"

Fritz Moeller lowered his eyes. "I prefer not to be . . ."

"I'm sorry. But the newspapers always called you that and so did my parents. When I was nine they took me to the 1926 Party rally in Munich to hear you. After your opening remarks, the *Führer* embraced you and talked about your heroism in the Great War. He called you a model for all Germans. Do you remember?"

"It's not something easily forgotten."

"And I saw you again in 1933. Hitler had just become Chancellor and you spoke about him at a celebration here in Berlin. You said that he was the right man at the right time. And you predicted the National Socialists would bring Germany back from the humiliation it suffered in 1918. The way you linked everything with God's intent for our great nation was stirring. Now I get to meet you. You see, I'm a soldier, too—SS, like you."

Moeller was growing uneasy. "There was no SS during the Great War."

"No, but you were one of the first SS members back in the thirties. You gave money, wrote pamphlets and helped recruit others. I still think Himmler was wrong to kick the clergy out of the SS."

"Himmler did what he thought best." Moeller's uneasiness was growing into apprehension. "Our responsibility is to support the government, not second-guess it."

Eisner smiled. "See, you're still a good soldier."

Moeller looked at his watch. "I have an appointment, my son. Is there anything more I can do for you?"

"One thing, yes. Would you hear my confession?"

Moeller looked again at his watch and sighed. "Of course, but understand I do have to be elsewhere." He reached into his pocket for his purple confessional stole, which he kissed and draped around his neck, then sat in the front pew. Eisner made the sign of the cross as he slid in next to him. "Bless me, Father, for I have sinned. It's been ten months since my last confession and these are my sins, sins which I have told no one about."

"Go ahead."

"I've killed people."

"You are a soldier, my son."

"No, Father, it's not like you think."

"I know war and what it is to kill." Moeller's voice resonated with traces of memory. "Continue."

Eisner hesitated. "Father, this is still confidential. I mean, even the Gestapo . . ."

"Do you think I would ever violate the sanctity of confession?" Moeller hadn't meant to sound indignant. It just came out that way. The boy's concern was legitimate. These days it could be deadly to trust anyone—priests, family, anyone.

"No, of course not. All right, then. Have you ever heard of the Einsatzgruppen?" Eisner didn't wait for a reply. "They're special SS units that come in after the army has secured a territory." He paused.

"Go on."

"You know the rumors about massacres in the East? Well, they're true, and the Einsatzgruppen carry out the dirty work. I know, because, until they reassigned me to Germany, I was an Einsatzgruppen gunner."

"A gunner?"

"We'd go out to the fields where they brought the undesirables—communists, gypsies and, of course, Jews. They made them strip and get into a large ditch. Then the gunners walked over and shot them. Once we finished a batch, they drove another into the ditch. Then the packers—usually SS Police—forced them to lie facedown on the corpses and knocked any resisters into place. But usually people were too stunned to do anything except obey. You almost felt sorry for them. Anyway, once the packers had everybody properly positioned, we walked along the edge of the ditch and shot them. Even though we took great care, some occasionally remained alive. Normally we didn't waste our time shooting them again. Eventually they'd be smothered by the other groups piled on top of them. And so it went, over and over until the ditch was full."

"I see." Moeller remained emotionless.

"The first few times it troubled me. Not so much the men, but the women and children. I mean they're our enemies, Germany's enemies, but still. So if there was a mother and child together, I always made sure I shot the mother first. No mother should see her child die, not even a Jewess. I tried to show compassion at the start. But after a while it began interfering with my duty. And I was afraid they'd accuse me of being weak. So I stopped. After all, what did it matter? They would all die anyway. No sense jeopardizing myself. I conditioned myself to look but not see. I would do my job, then sit on the edge of the ditch until it was time to shoot some more. Often I could even squeeze in a cigarette between deliveries. But some days there was still bullet smoke in the air as they got the next shipment in place. A thousand, maybe fifteen hundred a day. And even then we were backed up."

Moeller nodded his head but said nothing.

"It got so it didn't bother me. But lately I've been having dreams."

"What sort of dreams?"

"Of ditches and bodies with anguished faces rising out of them. And in these dreams they're not Bolsheviks and Jews; they're just human beings. I never had these dreams while I was there, but . . ." He hesitated. "I never thought what I did was wrong. The commander of our group was a Protestant minister, so how could it be wrong? Now I wonder."

"As I said, you are a soldier."

"Yes, but . . ."

"Our Mother Church condones just war undertaken to protect our people and our state. And our Church hierarchy has determined that this is, indeed, a just war."

"But the mass killings?"

"Catholics understand that communism is the enemy of Christianity."

"And Jews?"

"It's well known that most communists are Jews."

"But not all."

This was becoming increasingly difficult. "Have you forgotten the Jews killed Jesus? Your own local Archbishop recently issued a pastoral letter reminding us that because of their terrible act, the Jews are stained with our Lord's blood throughout all their generations."

"Then they deserve to die?"

"What sentence would you impose on someone who killed our *Führer*?"

"Death, of course!"

"Would you impose a lesser sentence on those who murdered our Lord, Jesus Christ?"

"Then you would have taken part in mass shootings if ordered?"

"I'm a patriotic German who loves the Fatherland."

"But the dreams . . ."

"Postbattle trauma. I had it, too, after Verdun. It's one of the sacrifices we make for doing our duty. It may never pass altogether, but it will lessen."

After a silence, which Moeller thought much longer than it was, Eisner spoke. "And my penance?"

"For what?"

"For my sins."

"Your sins!" Moeller knew what was coming and had decided the safest course would be to sound furious. He had no idea who this Eisner really was, no matter how heartfelt his confession sounded. The Gestapo was always looking to snare priests for treason. Even "Hitler's priest" was fair game. "Do you believe it's a sin to serve your *Führer* and defend the Reich?"

"No, but . . ."

"We all sin in some way, whether we know it or not. Say an Act of Contrition if it will make you feel better."

"Is that all?"

He used his best, no-more-questioning priest's voice, stern and full of authority. "An Act of Contrition."

If Hans Eisner had intended to argue when he opened his mouth, the wrong words came out. "Oh my God, I am heartily sorry for having offended Thee, and I detest all my sins because of Thy just punishments, but most of all because they offend Thee, my God, who art all-good and deserving of all my love. I firmly resolve, with the help of Thy grace, to sin no more and to avoid the near occasions of sin."

Moeller placed his hand on Eisner's head. "God, the Father of mercies, through the death and resurrection of His Son has reconciled the world to Himself and sent the Holy Spirit among us for the forgiveness of sins; through the ministry of the Church may God give you pardon and peace, and I absolve you from your sins in the name of the Father, and of the Son, and of the Holy Spirit. Amen." He made the sign of the cross and rose. "Now to my appointment." He walked Eisner to the door. "Perhaps we'll meet again."

"I'm sure of it. I've been reassigned to Hitler's personal guard. And since you're his friend—"

Moeller cut him off. "Well then, until the next time."

With the sanctuary finally empty, Moeller secured it and headed toward the vestry. As he passed the altar, he bowed his head, then knelt, closed his eyes and whispered.

"Oh my God, I am heartily sorry for having offended Thee, and I detest all my sins because of Thy just punishments, but most of all because they offend Thee, my God, who art all-good and deserving of all my love. I firmly resolve, with the help of Thy grace, to sin no more and to avoid the near occasions of sin."

Fritz Moeller quickly shed his robes in the sacristy. His shirt was sopping with sweat. Was it the heat, the encounter with Hans Eisner or a combination of the two? Whatever the reason, he was already late, so there was no time to change.

He crossed the hallway and opened a broom closet door, shifted around a mound of boxes piled on the floor and then carefully lifted and set aside a half-height wall panel. Moeller had to lie almost flat to work his way through the small opening. He wasn't as agile as he had been in his military days.

Once through and perched on a small platform, he set the panel back in place and locked it with the sliding bolt that had been left open in anticipation of his arrival. He climbed down the steep basement ladder, then tugged the ropes hanging from its last rung upward, waiting until the groaning of rusty springs gave way to the reassuring clang of the ceiling latch locking. Satisfied, Moeller followed a musty scent through a narrow passageway to a large windowless concrete-walled room illuminated by the dim glow from a pair of candles in tarnished silver holders on a small, wooden altar table.

"I see you've already lit them."

An elderly woman nodded, holding a hand to her head to stop a white scarf from falling. "It was time. We also did the blessings welcoming the Sabbath. There are some new arrivals and I wanted them to feel more comfortable."

"Sorry—a last-minute confession." Moeller looked around at the smattering of people, mostly women, a few with young children nestled on their laps, who were sitting in folding chairs about a dozen feet from the table. He recognized most of the faces. Beyond them, in the darkness, he could make out six or seven men, some standing, others sitting on the concrete floor. "How many new ones are there?"

"Three." She pointed to the row of chairs. "A mother and two daughters, five and eight."

"What about the father?"

"Dead, they think. They haven't seen him for days."

Moeller pressed his lips tightly together, accepting the answer as a fact of everyday life in Germany.

"Max brought them and said it'll be a week, maybe more, before it's safe for them to leave," the old woman continued.

"Things are really bad right now." Moeller could tell from the murmuring that he had been heard, so he quickly added, "But Max has good instincts. Anyway, it's out of our hands. Shall we?"

He reached into his jacket pocket, took out his purple monsignor's skullcap and put it on. The old woman looked at him disapprovingly, then reached up and straightened both his cap and his hair.

"You always have to dress me, don't you, Hildie?"

"Now." She handed him a small black book with leather covers flaking from age, and settled into the one remaining empty chair.

Moeller opened the book, placed it on the table between the candles and began to chant, softly, but clearly.

"*Barechu et Adonai hamevorach!* Praise God, to Whom our praise is due!"

Those who were seated rose to their feet, and responded immediately.

"*Baruch Adonai hamevorach le-olam va-ed!* Praised be God, to Whom our praise is due, now and forever!"

Slowly Moeller began rocking back and forth, his eyes closed, as he continued the ancient Hebrew prayer of Creation:

"*Baruch atah Adonai, Eloheinu melech haolam, asher bid'varo ma-ariv aravin.* Praised be the Eternal our God, Ruler of the universe, Whose word brings on the evening."

But even as he heard himself speak this prayer, Moeller heard his mind say another one:

Let us pray and beseech our Lord Jesus Christ, that Blessing he may bless this abode, and all who dwell therein, and give unto them a good Angel for their keeper. . . .

It was a prayer, not of praise but of pleading, consistent with Moeller's feelings at the moment.

May he ward off from them all adverse power.

It was a prayer he said in times of extreme adversity.

May he deliver them from all fear and from all disquiet, and vouchsafe to keep in health them that dwell in this house.

It was a prayer that described a newer and different covenant, sealed on earth and honored in heaven, promising comfort and solace, either in this world or the next.

Amen.

It was a prayer of salvation for those close to death: the Last Rites of the Roman Catholic Church,

Back at last in his study, Fritz Moeller sat at his desk holding a fountain pen over a fresh page in his leather journal. To his right was a snifter of his French brandy; to his left, a cigar resting in a glass ashtray. He paused for a moment, constructing his thoughts. Then, as he had done almost every evening for the past two years, he drew a small cross at the top of the page and began writing:

> *26 June 1942. A mother and her two young daughters came today. That makes eight this week, fifteen in all, counting the seven that haven't been placed yet. Max says they'll all be out in a few days, moved to more permanent hiding places or smuggled across the border, but I'm not sure. It's getting harder and harder. Our limited space makes it impossible to harbor more than another four or five.*

Fridays are the worst for arrivals. The Gestapo's Jew hunters look for secret Sabbath services. Still, we held ours. Everyone we took in this week prayed, except for an elderly man who asked me afterwards how God could allow such evil. I answered as best I could, but my response gave him little comfort. In truth, it gave me little comfort.

Where is God? It always seems to come down to that: where is God?

My mind keeps turning to John 19:31–33. Jesus and the two thieves are crucified on a Friday. The Jews ask Pilate to remove the bodies from their crosses before evening, since it will be both the Sabbath and the start of Passover. He agrees and sends soldiers to Golgotha to break the legs of Jesus and the thieves to hasten their deaths. Jesus is already dead when the soldiers arrive, but they thrust a spear into him to be sure.

In the other Gospels, when we learn that Jesus is dead, we have the centurion immediately affirming him as the Son of God. Having suffered through the agony of the crucifixion, we are spared the agony of doubt. But there's no centurion in John, no affirmation. There is only a dead body. The other Gospels give us hope here, here John gives us a void in the universe with no promise that it will ever be filled. Jesus is but one more crucified Jew. For all we know, God has abandoned both him and the world. The man claiming to be God's son is dead. There's no validation of him or his works, no promise of resurrection.

Where is God in this passage? Where was God when His chosen one was crucified? And where is God today when His chosen people are being exterminated?

In these verses of John the promise stops and reality comes crashing down on us. Jesus is no more. A spear pierces his Sacred Heart and finds it to be human after all. Water spurts out, water and blood. An untransformed sacrament. We witness his all-too-human blood, and, in the absence of God, we fill the emptiness. We become the Jesus who is no longer here to provide for us. We provide for ourselves and for each other.

Why should I believe? Why do I believe? Is the leap of faith the Resurrection or is it the endurance of belief in times such as these? I don't know. I only know that I still believe, perhaps because I want to, perhaps because I need to. I believe and I help. But do I help because I believe or because I'm a priest and it's expected of me?

If I wasn't a priest, would I still help? Would I risk my life? Would others expect it of me? Would God expect it of me? I admit that at times I feel fear. Would I give in to that fear if I wasn't a priest? And what if I lost my faith? Would I still act on behalf of others at my own peril? Would I still fill the void? I only know what I hope I would do, not whether I really would do it.

Enough for the evening. Moeller was weary in mind and body. Exhaustion overcame him. He put down the pen, closed the journal, took a last sip of brandy and poured a little over the cigar to extinguish it. Then he took the journal and walked to the fireplace. He knelt and removed a certain brick from the firewall, which he replaced after putting the journal in the opening. That's when he noticed his cuff had become loose, so with his other hand he rolled his shirtsleeve up to his forearm, revealing something.

A small tattoo just above his left wrist.

6

London: June 27, 1942
Your Stars Today: Because of Mercury's influence on Neptune, communications may be unclear and boundaries vague. Some situations may collapse leaving information lost. Still, perseverance can bring important matters to a close.

Peter had expected an immediate connecting flight to Sweden. Instead Donovan hustled him into a car with a military driver and away from the airport for "a last bit of prepping."

"We couldn't do this on the plane?" Peter asked, but Donovan didn't give him an answer and remained silent for most of the half hour it took to reach their destination, which was gated and heavily guarded. Donovan handed some papers to one of the British soldiers, who scanned, then returned them, saluted sharply and waved the car through.

"Welcome to Bletchley Park," Donovan said, as they made their way along a dirt road woven into a lush country lawn, littered with small wooden huts. "That's where we're headed."

Donovan pointed to a large estate in the distance, a strange combination of Victorian, Dutch Baroque, Tudor and Gothic architecture, all thrown together without any obvious plan.

"Quite a hodgepodge, isn't it? Struck me the same way at first, but it grows on you. The last owner kept expanding the place on whim. When his widow died a few years ago, the government bought it."

"For what?" Peter said. There was no reply.

The car pulled up in front of the white, rounded entry arch cut, where a man was waiting to greet them. Peter judged him to be about Donovan's age, although thinner, with a receding hairline and an ordinary face, given a bit of character by a close-trimmed black mustache. Like Donovan, he had a decided military bearing that showed through his gray flannel pants and rust-and-salt herringbone tweed jacket. Donovan made the introductions.

"Peter Kepler, meet the chief of British secret intelligence, Major General Stewart Menzies, better known as 'C.'"

"C?"

"They called the first secret intelligence chief 'C' and it became the designation for all his successors," Menzies explained with a thick Scottish accent as he escorted them through a pair of rounded oaken doors.

Once inside, Peter's eyes quickly panned a long hallway, then focused on the square oak wall panels, following them up to and across the ceiling, then down the other side where three gold-leafed circular arches opened to a large, ornately decorated alcove.

Meanwhile his ears honed in on a dull, systematic droning coming from an upstairs floor. Peter inhaled slowly, holding his breath so he could concentrate on the air. He detected a faint but distinct oily odor, which could be coming from some sort of engine.

Menzies interrupted Peter's analysis. "The estate itself dates from the eleventh century. It currently consists of this house, several lodges, twenty-eight cottages and some shacks that I'm sure you noticed on the way up."

"What exactly goes on here?" Peter asked.

"Officially we're the British government's code and cipher school. Only we don't teach about codes and ciphers. We break them."

"And they do a damn good job," Donovan added. "The finest Allied intelligence comes out of this building."

"So that's why you have so many machines running." Now some of the things Peter picked up on made sense.

Menzies glared at Donovan. "You told him about the decoding devices?"

"I didn't tell him anything. He's good."

"Let's see how good." Menzies led Peter and Donovan down the hallway and up a richly carved wooden staircase to a room at the end of the second-floor corridor. He knocked on the door. "May we?" There was no response. He knocked harder and repeated the question.

"As you wish."

Peter could hear a pronounced *v* in the word "wish." The muffled voice coming from the room was German.

Menzies fished a key from his pocket, turned it in the lock and slid the door into its side frame. "Go ahead. I'll wait here." When Peter and Donovan had entered, Menzies slid the door shut.

The room was pleasant enough, furnished in late Victorian. Across from the door there was an imposing triptych of windows, magnificently adorned with tulips fashioned out of heavily textured pieces of green, lilac, red and bronze glass that glowed vibrantly as the sunlight streamed through. Directly beneath the windows, seated in a button-back orange-brown leather chair and engrossed in a book, was a meek-looking man in his mid-forties, casually dressed in black trousers and a gray-and-white pullover shirt. He hardly struck Peter as someone who needed to be imprisoned.

"It's General Donovan."

"I know who it is," the man said, never looking up.

"I've brought someone else."

"Another interrogator?" The man turned a page.

"He's an astrologer."

At that the man set the book down on a side table and rose. "How nice, a fellow astrologer." He stared at Peter. "Should I know you?"

"My name is Peter Kepler."

"Ah, *you're* Peter Kepler. What an amazing coincidence. So am I."

Unable to find a single word to express the welter of questions swirling around in his head, Peter settled for four: "Son of a bitch!" Then, glaring at Donovan, he added a fifth: "*You* son of a bitch."

"Peter—"

"Which Peter? Him or me?"

"Actually his name is Horst Jennings. One of the few things we were able to get out of him."

"That's more than I got out of you." Peter didn't try to mask his anger. "What's he doing here?"

"I was kidnapped," Jennings volunteered.

"You weren't kidnapped, Herr Jennings," Donovan said. "You were detained."

"I was kidnapped."

Peter grabbed Donovan's elbow and gave him an emphatic tug. "May I see you outside for a moment?" He glanced at Jennings. "You'll excuse us."

"Over so soon?" Menzies asked when Peter and Donovan emerged.

"That depends on whether I get some answers," Peter replied.

"Not here." Menzies closed and locked the door shut, then guided them to a nearby empty room. The moment he and Donovan settled into chairs, Peter, who preferred to stand, pounced. "Damn you, General! You told me Peter Kepler was dead!" Peter cupped his hand around the wooden arm of Donovan's chair and squeezed it in anger as he lowered himself so the two of them were face-to-face. "You lied to me!"

"I didn't lie to you. I just delayed telling you a part of the story until the proper time."

"What part?" Peter released the chair arm, having finished using it as a substitute for Donovan's neck, and rose to his full height.

"The part about our slight political problem. You see, at a certain point we had to tell the President about the plan."

"Tell the President?" Peter couldn't believe what he just heard. "Roosevelt didn't know from the beginning?"

"We waited until we were sure it might work," Donovan said. "The President loved it. He has a passion for secret operations, no matter how wild. But he didn't trust the German underground. Thinks there are too many uncoordinated factions to be effective. So he insisted *we* provide the astrologer."

"And Churchill agreed?" Peter asked Menzies.

"The Prime Minister has always favored killing Hitler, but, like your President, he had no faith in the resistance carrying it out. He would have argued for one of our people, but no suitable candidate was available. We're already using our best magician elsewhere. Jasper Maskelyne. You may know of him."

"Every magician knows of Maskelyne. His family's been in magic for generations."

"Quite right. One of his ancestors was Queen Elizabeth's Court Astronomer. Now another Maskelyne is serving the Crown. He's in Egypt, baffling the Germans, by turning tanks invisible and making bodies of water vanish. All sorts of amazing stuff."

"Like bringing Peter Kepler back to life after he was run over by a bus?" Peter's fury continued to flow beneath his icy tone.

"Once the German underground decided on their man, they moved him into Switzerland where he'd be safer," Menzies said. "We learned about that when he left Germany and only because we needed to pass on certain information to him."

"The date of Heydrich's assassination," Peter said.

"Exactly," Menzies said. "Coordinating the assassination was our part of the show. After speaking with Roosevelt, the Prime Minister gave the go-ahead for Mr. Jennings to take an extended holiday in England."

"Why not tell him the plan had changed?" Peter asked.

"We couldn't risk a territorial pissing match with the German underground," Donovan added. "But after they were privy to the police accident report that our Swiss friends prepared detailing the circumstances of Horst Jennings' unfortunate death, they had no choice but to accept an emergency substitution."

"They believed you like I did. Then why even bother with this side trip?"

"Jennings may have information that could help you, but he wouldn't tell us anything," Donovan said. "However, you have a way of getting at people's secrets. Considering it's your neck on the block, we thought you might want to have a go at him."

Although Peter still didn't like his London surprise, he had to admit that Donovan made sense.

Menzies looked down at his watch. "We have two hours to get you on the plane for Sweden. Everything's been carefully coordinated, so we need to hit the marks exactly. There's no margin for error."

As Peter got up, Menzies cleared his throat.

"Another little detail?" Peter asked.

"Well, you see, there's a rather complicated system in place to get in touch with Jennings' underground contacts. While we sent out a message about his replacement . . ." His voice trailed off.

Donovan picked up the thread. "We never got a confirmation. You could find yourself alone in the heart of enemy territory, without proper papers, and with no one to turn to."

This time Peter had no trouble finding a single word to express what that meant and, fittingly, it was German.

Kaput!

When Peter returned, Horst Jennings had gone back to reading. "May I interrupt you?" Peter asked in German.

As before, Jennings didn't look up from his book. "Speak English, please. I imagine I'll be here for a while, so I should get used to it."

"I didn't have anything to do with snatching you. I didn't even know you were still alive until a little while ago. I wish they'd let you go right now."

Jennings looked up at Peter. "Then tell them. Let me finish what I started."

"They won't listen. Their minds are made up."

"Then I feel sorry for you," Jennings said, going back to his book. "They're sending you to your death."

"Maybe not, if you tell me what you know about Colonel Max and The Crow's Nest."

"I have already said I know nothing about that," Jennings snapped.

"Didn't you make the appointment?"

Jennings turned a page and read a few lines before responding. "The date book was left at a drop-off spot with the appointment already entered. I was deliberately being kept in the dark until I got to Berlin. Now good-bye."

Thinking fast, Peter went over to a bookcase near the window, scanned the volumes, then removed one. "Now here's a book to read if you haven't." Peter placed it in Jennings' lap. "It's really quite good."

Jennings put down his book and opened to the title page of the new one, which he read aloud. *"His Last Bow: A Reminiscence of Sherlock Holmes by Sir Arthur Conan Doyle."*

"Have you ever read Sherlock Holmes?" Peter asked.

Jennings gave out an exasperated sigh. "I have read Conan Doyle's writings on spiritualism, but not his fiction. Like me, he was a scientist who was not afraid to research things others scoffed at."

That was what Peter needed. "I know. We talked about it a lot."

Again Jennings looked up and turned his attention to Peter. "You knew Conan Doyle?" This time his tone was slightly warmer.

"Fairly well, actually. He was a good friend of my mentor, Harry Houdini."

Jennings's attitude thaw proved only temporary. "Houdini, the great magician." He spat out the words like bad food, then punctuated them by slamming the book onto the table. "Houdini, the great skeptic. Did he mentor you in that, too?"

"He tried, but I was more open-minded. Besides, Sir Arthur also taught me a great deal, especially about observing people." Peter sat down in a red leather easy chair across from Jennings, picked up the book and began flipping through the pages. "He put a lot of himself into Sherlock Holmes. In the title story of this book, Holmes and Watson perform secret wartime undercover work for the British . . ."

"I won't help you."

So much for leveraging Sir Arthur. Peter put the book down. "Why not?"

"Why should I tell you my reasons when I didn't tell the others?"

"Because I'm curious. As a chemist, you appreciate curiosity."

Jennings was taken aback. "I never said I was a chemist."

"You said you were a scientist. The stains on your fingers said you were a chemist."

Jennings looked at his hands and his eyes widened as if he were discovering the yellow, brown and greenish-blue blotches for the first time. "I had a small apothecary. Handling the mixtures does that. You're so used to it, you don't even notice."

At that Jennings got up and made his way to a small mahogany breakfront, removed a bottle and brought it back to his chair, along with two cut-crystal glasses,

"My captors try to keep me happy." Jennings sat, pulled a cork from the bottle and poured about an inch of pale brown liquid into each of the glasses. "Unblended scotch. Some name I can't pronounce." He motioned to Peter. "I don't like to drink alone, although lately I've been making exceptions."

Peter lifted a glass and swirled the scotch, setting off an aroma he identified as peat and iodine with just a hint of ginger. "Are we drinking to something?"

"Yes. To forgetting. But it won't happen." Jennings took a deep swallow of the scotch and grimaced. "Strong, but good." This time he took a sip and fell into a silence that Peter thought best not to interrupt. "Perhaps I should tell you," Jennings finally said, more it seemed to himself than to Peter. "If you know why I accepted this mission, you may understand why I must complete it." He poured himself more scotch before finishing what remained in his glass. "Have you ever heard of *Lebensunwurtes Leben*?"

"Life unworthy of living?" Peter wasn't sure what Jennings was searching for.

"That's an accurate translation. But there's an evil in the phrase that can't be translated. Here, let me show you something." Jennings reached into his back pocket and took out a thin, worn brown leather wallet from which he carefully extracted a small color photograph of a young girl. He handed it to Peter.

"She's very pretty,"

"My sister Ilse." Jennings took the picture back and gazed at it. "As sweet and gentle as she looks. You would never guess she had what they politely call 'special needs.' After my father died, my mother couldn't really provide for her. I tried to help, but with work . . . We sent her to a hospital in Berlin, and though we didn't expect much, she thrived there. The staff said eventually she might even be able to live on her own. It was more than we could have hoped for."

Jennings paused and took a deep breath. The rush of air coursing through his nose produced a faint sandpaper-like rasp, which was followed by a guttural cluck. Peter recognized the sounds of someone on the verge of tears. After a few quiet moments Jennings resumed.

"About a year and a half ago, the Reich ordered institutions to turn over records on patients classified as retarded, even mildly so. A special task force reviewed and color-coded each file. A blue pencil check meant sterilization, while a red pencil check meant . . ." Jennings could no longer contain himself. Tears began welling in his eyes, but he kept talking. "My sister was a red check. They loaded her and the other red checks onto a bus and transported them to Hadamar, a so-called asylum near the town of Koblenz. There they brought her to a large registration room jammed with people, some with mental problems, some with physical deformities, many with both. But that wouldn't have bothered Ilse. She was an outgoing person who would strike up conversations with strangers. She thought well of everyone. No, she was probably fine until the doctors made her undress so they could examine and photograph her. Ilse was a modest girl and would have been terribly embarrassed. Then, when the attendants herded her and the others, still naked, down a corridor and crammed them into a small, enclosed space, she would have been scared, at least until the nurses gave her a scented soap bar. Lavender, perhaps. Ilse loved lavender. 'Are we going to bathe?' Ilse probably asked excitedly and they would have told her, 'No, you're going to shower.' But that was all right, too. So Ilse would have clutched the soap tightly, ready to lather the lavender all over her body when the water started like she so enjoyed doing. But the perforated pipe running through the room didn't spray water. It sprayed carbon monoxide pumped in from the engines of two large diesel trucks parked outside the building."

"How do you know all this?" Peter asked, repulsed by what he was hearing.

"An acquaintance from university days. Also a chemist. He worked at Hadamar, administering the poison. He explained the procedure."

"He saw your sister die?'

Jennings shook his head. "No. He was assigned to the special pediatric killing ward, so he gassed no one over the age of six. He happened across Ilse's records after she had been murdered." Jennings closed his eyes. "Do you know how long it takes for a person to die of carbon monoxide? Sometimes thirty minutes, and each one is filled with agony." Jennings opened his eyes but didn't look at Peter. Instead he stared down intently at the drink he was cradling in his hands as if watching images skimming across its surface. "You can see the pain, frozen on their faces, along with the bright pink blotches. That's how you can tell carbon monoxide poisoning. Bright pink blotches from the gas interacting with hemoglobin."

Peter noticed that the tone of Jennings's account had changed from passionate to clinical. Maybe it was the only way he could go on.

"When it's over, a large fan extracts the gas from the chamber. Then workers take the bodies to the crematorium and stuff them into ovens for incineration. The bones that don't burn are pulverized on special tables and piled up outside with the oven ashes. Once all that's done, the family gets a letter saying their loved one had died suddenly, from a highly contagious disease requiring the immediate destruction of the body."

Jennings looked away from his drink and at Peter. "They told us my sister had contracted meningitis and died. The officials at Hadamar sent a letter, offering to give us an urn with her ashes, provided we paid for the delivery." Jennings went back to studying the glass, tilting and rotating it, then holding it aloft with both hands like a communion chalice. "An urn with her ashes. Only later did I learn they weren't Ilse's remains, but scoopings taken from the top of the ash pile. By then my mother, who wasn't well, had died from grief. They killed her just as sure as they killed Ilse."

Peter was having difficulty keeping his emotions under control, which rarely happened. Absent anything in the American press, Jennings's account was the first Peter had of Nazi atrocities, and it sickened him. Ilse's slaying was depravity of a magnitude he could hardly grasp. If the Nazi leaders routinely murdered the helpless, what else were they doing?

"You know about alchemy?" Jennings asked.

"Yes."

"As a chemist, the attempt to convert one substance into another always fascinated me. And the Nazis have discovered how to do it, how to take any shred of humanity and convert it into evil. Not just evil, but the essence of evil. Pure evil. The Nazis are alchemists of pure evil."

Pure evil. The words unnerved Peter. Before, the mission had concerned him. Now it frightened him. Not because he might die, but because he might live and, as John Goddard had foreseen, have to face the destiny he had been running from for so long. "Wasn't your acquaintance concerned about the authorities finding out he told you this?" he said.

"The asylum's real purpose was supposed to be secret, but everyone living around Hadamar knew what was happening. Staff would go to a local inn for beers and stories would slip out. Even the children knew and taunted one another by saying, 'Be careful or you'll end up in the Hadamar ovens!' So he spoke freely to me."

"Does he still work there?"

"A few months after we talked, Hadamar and the other clinics were closed because some prominent clerics protested. When things quieted down, they reopened, but he had moved on. I heard he was sent to the Eastern Front to use what he learned at Hadamar on Russian prisoners. I moved on, too." Jennings leaned over and brought his face close to Peter's. "You have to understand: I was overjoyed when Hitler took over. Like most, I felt our country was humiliated by the treaty ending the Great War. Hitler made us feel good about being Germans again. But my opinion began to change even before Ilse's murder. Afterwards, I knew I had to do something. Even though I'm not a daring type. I joined the underground, thinking my chemistry skills might be of benefit."

"The underground didn't recruit you as an astrologer?"

"Astrology has been banned in Germany. However, that ban is not enforced for certain astrologers—those who Himmler and other high-ranking Nazis protect. Any others found practicing astrology are imprisoned. I had always kept my interest in astrology private. That's why they chose me. I'm not a professional astrologer. I didn't belong to any societies. And with no close family left, I could easily adopt a new identity. Most importantly, I don't mind dying to repay a debt. That was my motive."

Now Peter understood why Jennings wanted to be the astrologer and why he couldn't be. Not because of Roosevelt, Churchill, Donovan or Menzies, but because of Jennings himself. Maybe Peter's degree in psychology wasn't legitimate, but his knowledge of it was and, no matter what Jennings believed, his stated motive was an oversimplification. Repaying a debt sounded noble. But Jennings was really driven—and blinded—by an all-consuming need for revenge, which yoked him emotionally and made him dangerously unstable. And Peter sensed something else about Jennings from his narrative. Not just what he said, but how he said it—the telling signs in his voice, his facial expressions, his body movements. Jennings was overcome by guilt for not being able to save his sister and his mother; guilt for being alive while both of them were dead. That guilt demanded that he die as well and that, in turn, made him suicidal, prone to taking needless risks, inviting death instead of avoiding it. At this point, Jennings was a greater danger to the resistance movement than Hitler and his regime. But with time running out, how could Peter get Jennings to accept that and offer up any necessary information? Against instinct, Peter resorted to a technique he seldom used when dealing with others: speaking the truth. "So it comes down to revenge."

"It comes down to keeping others from being slaughtered like Ilse was."

"No, for you, it comes down to revenge, about getting even, not killing Hitler. Don't you see you're too emotionally involved and, because of that, you'd make a mess of things? My involvement isn't personal, so I can see and do things differently."

Peter watched Jennings as he let the words sink in. Did they have any impact? That's why Peter hated the truth. You could never predict the outcome. But when Jennings stood, Peter knew the conversation was over.

"Then you will have to do things differently, since you won't have the necessary information, except for this one piece: You are going to die."

Menzies, who had been waiting outside to lock Jennings in and take Peter down to Donovan at the car, held his questions until the three of them were together. "Well, did he tell you anything?"

"He told me I was going to die."

Neither Menzies nor Donovan seemed surprised.

"We're no worse off than we were before." Donovan looked at his watch, then opened the car's rear door. "Still in good shape."

Menzies turned to Peter. "And you, young man. We're extremely—" Menzies was cut short by the sound of crashing glass and something hitting the car's hood. "What the hell?" Menzies looked up at Jennings's room, where there was a large, jagged hole in the decorative tulip window.

Meanwhile Donovan bent over and picked up a bronze lion's head bookend that had bounced off the car to the ground.

"Watch it!" Menzies shouted. "He's throwing something else out!"

All three ducked as the second object missed the car and landed in a small pile of colorful glass shards on the driveway. This time Donovan retrieved a book. He opened it and looked at the title page. "Sherlock Holmes."

"That's the book I suggested to Jennings," Peter said.

"Hold on, there's more. Some kind of bookmark." Donovan pulled out an oversized playing card and handed it to Menzies. "It seems Herr Jennings has a sick sense of humor."

"May I?" Peter said.

Menzies gave Peter the card, which pictured a skeleton in a suit of black armor astride a white horse. Printed at the bottom was a single word: "Death."

Peter dropped the card. "Give me the key to his room."

"There's no time," Menzies said. "We'll deal with Jennings."

"Give me the key!"

"Peter, don't let this foolishness upset you," Donovan said. "Jennings is just trying to reinforce what he already said, that you'll die if you continue with the mission."

Peter shook his head in violent disagreement. "Damn it, you don't understand. Jennings has changed his mind. He's not telling me I'm going to die. Now he's telling me I'm going to live!"

With the key from Menzies and a forty-minute deadline from Donovan, Peter bounded up the circular staircase two steps at a time and rushed down the hallway to Jennings's room. Jennings was waiting and seemed relieved to see him.

"You got my message in time."

"Just," Peter said as he drew the door closed. "And delivered with flair."

"I regret the beautiful stained glass, but they lock the windows."

"And you turned to the tarot for guidance." Peter could have left it at that, but he decided to take a risk. "Even if you did so only because you spilled your drink."

Jennings was shaken. "How could you know that?" His eyes narrowed to slits. "Are they watching me? Can they see what I'm doing in this room?"

"I doubt that." Peter had no idea whether Jennings was being watched, but he didn't want him becoming paranoid and unresponsive.

"Then you're psychic?"

"Just observant, like Sherlock Holmes. I told you I learned a lot from Sir Arthur. Here." Peter went to the side table next to Jennings's chair. A bunch of tarot cards lay facedown. Peter picked up one at random and gave it to Jennings. "Smell it." Jennings gave him a quizzical look, then placed the card to his nostrils and inhaled. "Can you make it out?"

"Iodine?"

"Iodine, peat and just a hint of ginger. Remind you of anything?"

Jennings crinkled his eyebrows, then sudden recognition pushed them apart. "The scotch we had!"

"I smelled it on the Death card. Since I knew there was a tarot deck on the table next to your chair, logic said that you went back to reading, reached for your drink and accidentally knocked it over, spilling the scotch on the deck. You started to dry the cards and that's when you decided to consult them about me. With no time for a full reading, you relied on a single card. Of the seventy-eight cards in a tarot deck, the only one that might convince you to help me is the Magician, because it symbolizes the ability to do the impossible."

"But how could you know I would choose that one?"

"I didn't. I had no idea whether you'd consult the deck at all. But, if the occasion arose, *I* intended to. And I would have used the Magician card to help win you over. So, when you went to get the scotch, I put it on the top of the deck, which is the position for sleight of hand. The spilled drink was a bit of good luck. You probably decided to dry the cards one at a time, starting with the most saturated one, which was on top. You turned it over while blotting it with your handkerchief, saw it was the Magician and took that as a sign. Should I go on?"

"Please. This is fascinating."

"Now that you had your answer, you needed an immediate way of communicating with me. So you used the Death card because, despite what most people think, it means change and new opportunities, not the end of life."

Jennings shook his head in amazement. "The tarot was right. Perhaps you can pull off the impossible even better than I could."

"Possibly, if you tell me what I need to know."

"You've earned an answer. There are several things. All are important, but only one is critical."

"Then let's start with that."

Jennings hesitated, and Peter detected the last-minute doubts of someone at the edge of a high-diving board trying to decide whether to crawl back to the platform or take a deep breath and jump. Then, suddenly, without any theatrics, Jennings took the plunge. "There's a trick to the Heydrich horoscope. Well, not a trick really, but a little-used astrological technique. I gambled that Himmler's astrologers wouldn't catch it right away. But when they did, Himmler would want to find the person who could make such an accurate prediction. So you see, the technique can establish your credibility and help you gain Himmler's confidence. Here, I will show you."

Jennings went to the breakfront and removed a few books, some pencils with different-colored leads, a sheaf of paper, a mapping compass, a protractor and a slide rule. These he placed on a small round wooden dining table off to the side of the room. "They provided some astrological tools. Come."

Peter sat next to Jennings, who had begun writing. "March 7, 1904, is Heydrich's birth date. At 6:12 A.M. in the village of Halle, near Leipzig. Now cast his horoscope for May 27 of this year, the date of his assassination."

As Peter picked up the compass, he wondered if Jennings was testing whether he could pass as an astrologer. He jabbed the sharp metal point of one of the compass' two arms into the center of the top piece of paper and rotated the small pencil in the other arm until he had drawn a large circle. Moving the two arms closer together, he repeated the process, drawing a smaller circle within the first. Then he took the protractor and divided the circles into twelve thirty-degree slices representing the twelve houses of the Zodiac.

"You'll need this." Jennings slid over a green-covered volume with *Phillips World Atlas* printed in gold on the cover.

Peter thumbed through the pages until he found Halle, then jotted down the village's longitude and latitude at the bottom of the paper. Next came the part Peter hated: a series of tedious mathematical calculations. That's why he cast horoscopes only when forced. Palmistry and tarot readings were quickly done and much less demanding. Astrological charts required converting times and locating planets, which meant meticulous operations on the slide rule. It was one big headache.

Although Jennings had said nothing, Peter knew the German was evaluating his every step. Once he finished the basic chart, Peter progressed it—moving it forward from Heydrich's birth to some future date by treating each day as a year. Heydrich was thirty-eight when he was assassinated. Starting with his birth date, Peter counted ahead thirty-eight days to represent thirty-eight years. He used that date—April 7, 1904—to recalculate Heydrich's chart for May 27, 1942, the day Heydrich was shot. When all the details were in place, Peter silently interpreted the various markings and colored lines that he had made, frowning as he did.

"What's the problem?" Jennings asked.

Peter shoved the piece of paper over. "You know damn well what the problem is."

Jennings studied the chart, taking in each detail. "Excellent. Better than I expected. Obviously you reached the same conclusion I did. May 27 is a day of tremendous personal accomplishment for Heydrich, with nothing pointing to a tragedy. Knowing this, I recommended changing the assassination date, but things were too far along. That left no choice but to change one of the chart variables."

Change a variable? The concept went against everything Peter knew about astrology. "What are you talking about? Heydrich was born when he was born. The time, date and place are set in stone."

"The time and date, yes, but not the place. Using Halle is fine if you want to move the chart forward to a day when Heydrich would still be there. But Heydrich wasn't in Halle on May 27, 1942. He wasn't even in Germany. He was in Prague, Czechoslovakia. So I wanted to see what would happen if I treated him as if he were born in Prague, instead of Halle, on the same date and at the same time."

Jennings got up, went back to the breakfront, took another astrological chart out of a drawer, brought it back and placed it on the table. "This chart uses Prague as Heydrich's birthplace. Notice what's happened. We're have the same birth time, so the position of the planets in the signs doesn't change. But they end up in a different Zodiac house, which alters their properties. *Now* interpret the chart."

As Peter examined Jennings' handiwork, occasionally tracing his forefinger over a line that linked one planet to another, his eyes widened.

"You're absolutely brilliant!" Peter reached over and clasped Jenning's shoulders, giving them an approving squeeze.

"Then you see the difference between what the charts foretell," Jennings said, beaming.

"Very clearly." Peter picked up the chart he had prepared and dangled it in the air. "My chart, which any halfway competent astrologer could have drawn, destines Heydrich to great things." He released the piece of paper and it wafted to the floor.

"And my chart?"

Peter grabbed Jennings' chart and waved it around like a victory flag. "And your chart kills him!"

7

Berlin: July 2, 1942
Your Stars Today: Relationships and interpersonal matters face reality now and some situations may become more formalized or cool off significantly. Therefore, diplomacy may be needed.

Just before dawn, ten days after he had been whisked from his Princeton classroom, David Walker, now Peter Kepler, arrived at a remote rural area near Hennigsdorf, a town on the northwest outskirts of Berlin. It was the end of a journey that had taken him by plane from New York to Sweden by way of Canada and London, then by fishing boat to Denmark and finally, hidden behind large wooden barrels of brine-soaked herring, by a truck driven by a hardened Danish underground fighter, here.

Tired and reeking of fish, Peter had wanted to use the darkness and seclusion to treat himself to a bath in a nearby lake. But the Dane wouldn't let him. "Soap is rationed," he explained in German. "One small bar a month for each family. Besides, this is Thursday. Baths are only allowed on Saturdays. Better you stink like everyone else and not arouse suspicions." So after settling for some strategic splashes of cheap Danish cologne, Peter turned to crafting his disguise.

As the Dane kept watch, Peter changed from his slacks and shirt into some secondhand goods smuggled out of one of the Berlin rationing depots that had become the city's clothing shops: a sturdy but well-worn gray flannel suit that nearly fit, a yellowed and slightly frayed white shirt, a black tie with a small deer head stitched in white thread, scuffed black leather shoes that were a half size too large and a still-shapeable homburg hat.

Once dressed, Peter found a suitable tree and plunged a borrowed knife into the trunk until the blade was covered in sap, which he carefully scraped into a small pillbox for later use. Next he bent down behind the truck and rubbed his fingers inside the exhaust pipe, coating them with a blackish discharge that he smoothed under his eyes. Then he clutched the exhaust pipe itself, rolling his palms over it until they were covered with rust. Releasing the pipe, he rubbed his hands together vigorously. The rust and remaining engine residue gave them an aged look. Finally he tried on a pair of black-rimmed glasses with thick lenses ground at Camp X to simulate farsightedness. Satisfied that the glasses had weathered the trip well, he stuffed them in one of his suit jacket pockets.

"Here." The Dane opened a string-tied packet and handed Peter the contents—forged papers, a set of rationing cards color-coded for various products, a cheap silver-plated pocket watch and a wallet and change pouch with enough cash to get him through a few days. "Take these, too," the Dane said, dumping three small packs of French cigarettes from a small linen bag along with a tin of matches into Peter's hands. "For the black market. They are French, the real thing, not the crap they have been selling in Berlin. That makes them better than gold. So, if you are ready," the Dane said, pausing to reach into his pocket for a page ripped from an atlas, "here is where we are." He jabbed his index finger at the top right-hand corner of the map. "And this is the safest path for you to take." He traced a route along the paper. "About twelve or thirteen miles. It is wooded at the start, but then come populated areas all the rest of the way. A bus runs along here." His finger kept darting across the map. "There is also a train once you reach this point, and another one over here." The Dane handed Peter the map. "Study it some more, but do not carry it, in case you are stopped."

There was no need for further study: Peter had tucked the map in his photographic memory seconds after seeing it. He took one of the matches from the tin, struck it and held the flame to the map, which he had placed on the ground. When the small fire died, he rubbed the ashy remains into his hair and beard, giving them a grayish appearance.

The Dane smiled approvingly. "Now I will show you something." He casually turned his head and looked over his right shoulder, then, a second or two later, over the left. "It is called the Berlin glance, to look for Gestapo. Everyone in the city does it. But act natural so as not to draw attention to yourself."

After a brief exchange of thanks and good wishes, the Dane departed and Peter decided to do the same. The rising sun promised a beautiful day. That should make the walk to Berlin easier. Should anyone along the way ask, he was a visitor to the area, seeking the U-Bahn station and a train to Berlin. Who was he visiting? How long had he stayed? Those he'd play by ear. If a con man couldn't talk his way out of any bind, he might as well be a bookkeeper.

So he was ready, but for one thing. Keeping a ritual he always performed before the start of a complicated caper, Peter let out a muted rallying cry that he had stolen from Sir Arthur's Sherlock Holmes just as Sir Arthur had stolen it from Shakespeare's Henry IV. Although Peter was sure no one was around, he used German because the occasion merited it.

"Das Spiel ist im Gáng." "The game is afoot!"

An hour into what was proving to be a pleasant walk, Peter came upon a cemetery, adjacent to the remnants of a stone foundation that, at one time, probably supported a church. He surveyed the thirty or so graves, none of them new. The latest date Peter could find among the few headstones still legible was 1789, inscribed on a plain slab of marble with the name "Hoffmann." Since the first name was worn away and there were few decipherable words, he couldn't tell if Hoffmann was a man or a woman, although it didn't matter for what Peter was about to do.

Peter removed his shoes, knelt beside the grave and, using a large, flat rock as a shovel, dug a four-inch-deep hole. He scooped up some of the softer dirt he had uncovered and threw it into his shoes before putting them back on. Then, after refilling the hole and patting and smoothing it out, he reached for the cash pouch the Dane gave him, found a ten-Reichspfennig coin and placed it on the headstone to thank the spirits. His work in the cemetery was now complete.

But one more task remained. Having gone this far, he might as well go all the way. Besides, this would be easy. The cemetery was carved out of a meadow, and, in an untouched area just beyond the graves, he had already spotted what he needed—a clump of wildflowers, their round purplish-blue blooms bobbing with the breeze.

With the rock he had used for a shovel, Peter tilled the soil around a bunch of the flowers, loosening it enough to gently tug a spray of thin, spiny stems and extract their stubby brown roots, which were about the thickness and shape of a finger with the tip cut off.

"You know why it looks like that, boy?"

"No," Peter involuntarily answered, even though the voice—Delta's voice—existed only in his head.

"God made that plant special and placed it in Paradise to do all kinds of good stuff for man. That made the devil real mad and he bit off a chunk of the plant's root so it couldn't grow no more. But God wouldn't let that happen and fixed it so even with that piece of root missing, the plant would keep flourishing. That's how it got its name—Devil's Bit—and it's still got all the terrible power that God gave it."

All the terrible power . . . Peter broke off three of the roots, wiped away the wet soil and placed them in his pocket. Of course he didn't really believe any of that, or the other foolishness from his past. He was acting out of respect, that's all.

Graveyard dirt and Devil's Bit. Before Peter had been ready.

Now he was armed.

As the day grew hotter and more draining, Peter abandoned his walk and caught a train for Berlin in Schulzendorf, not far from Hennigsdorf. Riding the rails as a boy had given him a lifelong love of trains, so it was an easy decision. Once in Berlin, he knew the perfect place where he could lose himself in the anonymity of the city and spend a few undisturbed hours, perhaps the last he'd have for a while.

The ride itself, which included changing trains at the Friedrichstrasse station, was uneventful. Both times, the female conductors paid him no mind as they collected his ticket, leaving him to watch the urban landscape zip past the window by his seat and marvel at how much Berlin had changed since he was last there. The transformation was even more apparent when Peter stepped onto the platform at the Zoologischer Garten station. Instead of the modifications he expected, he found the old-fashioned, almost quaint terminal building had been replaced by a massive modernistic rectangular hall of steel and glass, which, though impressive, struck him as leaden and sterile.

He was taken more by something outside the station, at the far eastern side of the zoo, which he could see through the wall of clear paneled glass. It looked like a Rhine castle, only much larger, a gigantic window-pocked concrete fortress, which Peter judged to be about as wide as a football field was long and perhaps twelve stories high. On each corner of the roof was a square turret that appeared to have a gun mounting protruding from it. Nobody had mentioned this particular Berlin addition during his briefings.

"Are you looking to book a room?"

On the inside, Peter jumped when he heard the German voice behind him. On the outside, however, he remained unrattled, thanks to years spent expecting the unexpected.

"Sorry?" Peter turned to face his interrogator, a fortyish sausage of a man, encased in worn brown slacks and a short-sleeve shirt more confining than one of Houdini's straitjackets. He seemed innocent, but that could prove a dangerous assumption.

"You were staring at Meyer's Hotel Boom Boom so intently, I thought maybe you were thinking of staying there. They don't take reservations, though. First twenty thousand in, first twenty thousand served."

It had been years since Peter had heard the harsh and jarring Berlin accent, which converted soft consonants into hard and hard constants into soft, while *e*'s were drawn out to breath-exhausting lengths and *r*'s trilled to the point of being unrecognizable. Little wonder other Germans had difficulty understanding Berliners. The man was also using *Berlinische*, a cryptic form of slang littered with irreverent nicknames for well-known Berlin buildings and streets. Once Peter had been adept at *Berlinische,* but new words had entered the dialect. Now he had to quickly piece together why this huge building was called Hotel Boom Boom and who the hell "Meyer" was. The "Boom Boom" part was easy enough. Considering the building's height, the guns on the turrets had to be anti-aircraft. But what about "Hotel"?

"The crowding is worse than the explosives," the man continued. "You can't move and people are fainting on top of you. It's only supposed to hold nine thousand, but when the sirens sound you can get as many as twenty thousand. Twenty thousand people crammed in like twenty thousand sardines."

Crowding and explosives. Thanks to the stranger, Peter had figured out the "Hotel" part. The structure was also a bomb shelter for area residents. "Hotel Boom Boom." Like all Berlin nicknames, it made perfect sense once you knew the code. But "Meyer" still stumped him. Think, damn it, think! A Jew? Maybe. Bombings because of Jews? No. Wrong path. Associate! That's what you did in cold readings, associate things so you looked psychic. Associate! Bombings. Aircraft. Protect. Protect against bombings. Air defenses. Anti-aircraft. German planes. Camaflo—Wait! German planes. Luftwaffe. Goering. Head of the Luftwaffe. Goering."

". . . twenty thousand ripe sardines packed in piss and sweat." The man was still going on.

Come on, Peter! Goering . . . Meyer, Goering . . . Meyer, Goering . . . Mey— Something that Menzies had told him in London. A boast Goering had made. *"If the bombers get through . . . get through . . . get through to the Ruhr River on the west."* That's it! "If the bombers get through to the Ruhr, you can call me Meyer instead of Goering!" Goering's Hotel Boom Boom! Now say something to show you get it. Goering. Big. Fat. Wait. What if this guy is really Gestapo, trying to trick you? Granted, he doesn't feel like Gestapo. Better to give a simple nod. Much safer. Much—ah, screw it! Trust your intuition. Besides, this whole caper's going to rely as much on guts as good sense. Might as well start now!

"Yes, but only ten thousand sardines can fit if Meyer's inside."

The man held up his forefinger in agreement and grinned. "Are you new to Berlin?"

"Why do you ask?"

"You're staring at the hotel, like it's the first time you've seen it."

"Truth is, I haven't been to Berlin in a while. I'm from—" Peter pictured his false papers, which listed the town. "South country, near Kempten im Allgäu, where we have nothing like this there."

"Ah, Kempten im Allgäu—the udder of Germany. No, I expect not. Why would the bombers care about Kempten im Allgäu? Besides, if they ever did come, you could just hide under a cow. So tell me, what do you do near Kempten im Allgäu?"

Peter was ready with his backstory. "Actually, I'm—" He raised his voice to be heard above the sound of an approaching train. "I'm involved in—"

But the stranger turned away from Peter, toward the tracks and the sound and the yellow-and-red electric train approaching. "Sorry. Looks like my ride to work. Four P.M. shift and heaven help you if you're late. You only get two reprimands, and then . . . It's a real haul, but you go wherever the Labor Council sends you for the good of the Fatherland. If you're headed that way, we can continue our conversation."

"No, I'm going to take in the zoo. I visited it once and always promised myself I'd go back."

"Just don't expect it to be the same. Like everything in Berlin, even when it looks the same, it's different." The stranger peeked over his left shoulder. "All the elephants are dead." Then over his right shoulder. "Seems Meyer needed some ready-to-wear lederhosen."

With that he darted into a train car, leaving Peter smiling, not at the joke but at this dose of good old-fashioned *Berliner Schnauze,* a combination of caustic wit and, often, what seemed like rudeness, bound together by traditional Berliners' disdain for authority. Even the Nazis couldn't stifle *Berliner Schnauze.*

Peter exited the station onto Hardenbergplatz. Although there was a zoo entrance directly across the street, he preferred the historic Elephant Gate that he remembered from his youth. So he took a short stroll to Budapester Strasse and, after shelling out ten pfennig for admission, made his way between two sandstone elephants with pillars on their backs holding aloft a gaudy wave-like arch adorned with Oriental carvings and paintings.

The stranger was right. The zoo was different and, Peter thought, better. More species, many of them rare, had been added to an already-excellent collection. And instead of being caged and displayed in ornate buildings, most of the animals roamed freely in specially designed natural habitats.

As he had expected, the zoo was packed, which offered Peter the anonymity he sought. For nearly four hours he became part of a crowd of people as diverse as the wildlife they were viewing. Then, at 4:45 P.M., a voice booming from a loudspeaker told patrons the zoo would be closing in fifteen minutes, earlier than normal, in order to repair bombing damage. That left Peter back out on Budapester Strasse with three more hours remaining until he was due at The Crow's Nest. He took a moment to size up exactly where he was, then headed west on Budapester Strasse for half a block until it cut into Kurfürstendamm Strasse, or Ku'damm as they called it in *Berlinische.*

Ah, Ku'damm, alive with some of the world's greatest—and some of the seediest—nightspots, which featured the best talent in Berlin. Houdini would let Peter wander there, as if he could stop him. "Just be careful you're not taken for a line boy," Houdini cautioned, referring to the boy prostitutes, notorious for frequenting the White Mouse and the other Ku'damm cabarets. "I don't need to be bailing you out of a German jail or identifying your corpse after it's been found on some vomit-coated curb."

Peter smiled at the memory. Ku'damm, where men paraded in front of fashionable boutiques hissing, "*Sssigaretten, Sssigartten,*" a signal that their wares weren't smokes but snorts—envelopes of snowy white cocaine. Ku'damm, where drugs and liquor flowed freely and women danced naked on the stage and later performed sex on leather banquettes in dark booths with anybody, male or female, who had a few marks to spare. Ku'damm, where even day was night and there were no clocks when it came to pleasure.

But the anticipatory excitement Peter felt quickly disappeared after just two blocks. This pallid and stilted street bore no resemblance to the Ku'damm of his youth. The dangerous had become dull. The street was like a once-vibrant old friend now wasting away from some horrible disease. Preferring to remember what Ku'damm used to be rather than what it had become, Peter returned to the train station, where he could blend into the crowds leaving work. Once there, he decided to head back to the Friedrichstrasse station, which was near The Crow's Nest. Only this time he opted to travel underground on the U-Bahn, so he could become familiar with it.

On the train from Hennigsdorf, which wasn't crowded, he could open a window. But the U-Bahn was packed with people and sealed shut. If anything, his Danish driver had understated how overwhelming the stench of the unwashed could be. And Peter's heightened sense of smell made it worse. If he moved his head to the left, he felt as if his nose was cutting through a too-ripe wedge of Limburger cheese. If he moved it to the right, it was as if his nose was a broom sweeping through a fresh pile of horse manure. He tried holding his breath for long periods of time—another skill taught him by Houdini, who could remain underwater for nearly three minutes. But when Peter finally had to take deep, compensatory breaths he gagged and felt he was going to pass out. Finally, admitting defeat, Peter exited a station before his stop and gladly walked ten blocks to Friedrichstrasse.

"Friedrichstrasse is Berlin squeezed into two miles," Sir Arthur once told Peter. "All that's good about Berlin, all that's bad, all that's saintly and all that's sinful—it's all on Friedrichstrasse. If you never get any further than this street, you'll know Berlin!"

When he was in Berlin, Friedrichstrasse, like Ku'damm, had been among Peter's favorite haunts. It could be as tawdry as Ku'damm, but it also had unique surprises, including exciting and innovative architecture that peacefully co-existed with stately old town houses and an occasional estate. He was happy to discover that while the tawdry was now sanitized, the architecture remained, albeit with the unfortunate addition of a few structures executed in the pretentious imperial style favored by Hitler.

Along the way, Peter stopped at a umbrella shop, which still had some goods, and bought a brown Bavarian walking stick with a leaf-carved handle to heighten his elderly appearance. Then, at an outdoor stall, he purchased a handkerchief, and a pack of what passed for cigarettes. He wasn't sure what he would use these items for, if anything. However, the magician in him always felt better having some common props at his disposal, just in case.

From there, he walked what he guessed was nearly a mile down Friedrichstrasse, then another half mile on Motzstrasse until, in one of Berlin's still refreshingly unreconstructed sleazy sections, it intersected with Hamburgstrasse. There, across the street, looking right at home, stood a small, single-story rectangular building, its once-white, cracked concrete exterior blotched with dirt. Above the door, in peeling black paint, were the Gothic-lettered words *Das Krähenneste*—The Crow's Nest.

A single large window faced out onto Motzstrasse, but when he approached Peter found it too grime streaked for him to peer inside. He had better luck with a smaller, slightly cleaner window on Hamburgstrasse where, helped by the dim illumination from some ceiling lights, he could make out the club's interior: a nondescript bar with six stools, a dining area with perhaps a dozen tables, what looked to be a small bandstand, a swinging door that probably led to the kitchen, and some unreadable posters on the walls. Cozy enough for a clandestine meeting, he thought, though not good for a quick exit. Years of experience had taught Peter the importance of carrying out a con on familiar turf. He needed to find a location that worked to his advantage, then steer "Colonel Max" there.

Off to explore, Peter made his way down an unmarked street on the left side of Motzstrasse and discovered it was a narrow L-shaped alleyway that ran behind The Crow's Nest. Even better, from there, three turns, each a block apart, onto other backstreets, and he was on Motzstrasse again. It was viable escape route. Peter retraced his steps, stopping at a short flight of stairs that led to the rear entrance of The Crow's Nest. It was the only door he could see. The windows in the three-floor redbrick building on the other side of the alley were either broken or boarded up. Except for a lone streetlight, the rutted street itself and the fading scent of urine, there was nothing more to the alley. Peter deemed it more suitable for a mugging than a meeting, but it was still better than The Crow's Nest.

His surveillance done, Peter walked on Motzstrasse until he found a small outdoor café that didn't look unhealthily filthy. He settled into a soiled wooden chair by a metal mesh circular table and treated himself to a roll, thinly coated with sausage-speckled margarine, and coffee, which, his sense of taste told him, was nothing more than boiled barley mixed with acorns to give it a strong tannic flavor. As Peter ate, he thought of the full-roasted Berlin he had known, with its freshly baked, heavily seeded *Brötchen* covered with deep yellow butter and topped with generous slices of fine Westphalian smoked ham and the robust Viennese coffee that complemented it.

A previous customer had left a wrinkled newspaper on one of the chairs, so Peter snagged it. The top story was about Field Marshal Rommel and his victory at Algeria's walled city of Tobruk, where more than thirty-three thousand Allied soldiers were captured, tons of supplies taken and British morale crushed. Meanwhile, the paper reported that, on the Eastern Front, after nearly nine months of fierce combat, the German army was on the verge of taking the strategic Crimean city of Sevastopol.

After a second leisurely cup of ersatz coffee, which was worse than the first, Peter put down the paper. Summer's light had enabled him to read almost until 8:00 P.M., gathering little bits and pieces of everyday life needed to pass for German. Now it was time to make his final preparations. The waiter, who was also the café cook, was busy cleaning up inside. There were no other people around, so Peter casually reached into his pocket and took out his pocketknife, the handkerchief, he bought the pillbox with the tree sap in it and a wine cork that he had found outside a restaurant. He carefully sliced off two small pieces from the cork, bored a hole in the center of each and placed them in the handkerchief. Then, while pretending to blow his nose, he inserted one into each nostril. Next Peter coated his fingertips with the sap and rubbed them across his temples. It looked like he was smoothing his hair. Instead he was putting the sap behind his ears, so that when he patted them—the completion of his fake preening—they adhered to his head. Finally, having already touched up his face and hands, courtesy of a car parked on a deserted street, Peter put on the glasses from Camp X and, after a few minutes spent adjusting to the distortion, he was done.

Now Peter concentrated on getting into character, using techniques honed over years of real-world practice to convincingly become a totally different person. He imagined himself an actor and his upcoming meeting as a play. Every word, every action, every aspect of his performance as an actor had to help him realize what Stanislavsky called the play's "super-objective"—its ultimate goal. No matter what the role, Peter's super-objective was always the same: pull off the con and not get caught. Only this time "not get caught" became "not get killed." And to increase the odds in his favor, Peter needed a gesture.

This vital ingredient Peter learned from Michael Chekhov, nephew of the great Russian playwright and Stanislavsky's most brilliant student. So who was this elderly man whose life Peter was now about to live? What was the inner thread that held this person's many pieces together and how could Peter capture, condense and use it so his portrayal rang true? And, the hardest question, what was the experience in Peter's own past that would allow him to connect with this character? Everything hinged on that memory.

Peter slouched in the chair and closed his eyes. Outwardly he was simply an old gent who had nodded off for a few moments. Inwardly he was a young man getting even younger as he sought the key memory. He flew through his early twenties and, after considering them, discarded a few incidents from his teens. Now he was in his preteens, just the terrain he had hoped to avoid. Back, back—wait! Stop! Peter carefully turned the dials on his mind's microscope until something small and blurred became large and clear. A classroom full of students, maybe six, no, seven years old, in hand-me-down uniforms: for the boys, blue slacks, white shirts and blue-and-green plaid ties; for the girls, blue-and-green plaid skirts and white blouses. A nun at the blackboard—he could hear the *click clack* of the chalk and see the white plume of dust surrounding its tip as she wrote *Jesus Saves*, then underlined it, scratching her fingernail on the slate as she did, producing that horrible sound that caused him to shiver even now.

"Jesus saves," she proclaimed, still facing the blackboard.

Then Peter heard somebody answer, "At the downtown bank and trust." It was an old joke, but the other students laughed anyway.

It amazed Peter how fast the nun could turn around, what with that heavy wool tunic and scapular draped over her body to the floor. "Who said that?" Flames shot from her mouth. Suddenly the classroom went quiet. "You don't have to answer. *I* know who said that." She picked up a ruler from her table.

Peter saw the boy lift the top of his wooden desk and thrust his right hand inside.

"Take your hand out of there, stand up and hold it out!" she commanded as she approached.

He did as he was told, extending his arm and his hand, in the form of a fist.

"Open your hand!"

The boy turned his fist so his clenched-white knuckles were directly under the nun's nose, then lowered them a nonthreatening few inches.

"Open it, I said!"

Slowly the boy lifted the tips of his fingers from his palm, then, in a quick spasm, thrust them straight out. Something black and red leapt from his hand to the nun's only exposed part, her face, scurried down her cheek to her bowed white wimple, then, using it as a launching pad, jumped again to her face, landing on her nose. From there it ran down her left nostril and managed to find a small space between the cloth of her coif and her flesh to crawl into.

The nun's screams drowned out the shouts and applause of the students who were delighting in watching her slap her head with the ruler in a frenzy. Finally, she dropped the ruler and ripped off her veil and coif and tore her hands into her barely existent thin brown hair.

"It's a jumping spider," the boy bent down and whispered to the girl next to him while the nun continued frantically rummaging. "They're great."

Finally, the nun's hand found its target and the insect tumbled to the floor, where it lay still. From beneath the nun's tunic came a large black shoe, but before it could strike, the bug, merely stunned, hurled itself through the air again, bounding first to the nun's head and then from there, in a mighty heave, straight through the partially open window.

Immediately all eyes were on the nun, who displayed her rage in silence as she picked up the ruler from the floor. The boy held out his hand without asking and tried not to wince as he felt the first blow against his palm. The second strike brought pain, but he forced a smile and broadened it as the third and fourth smacks caused a deep red welt and the fifth swelling. At the tenth, there were tears in his eyes, but by biting his lower lip he was able to muzzle any cries. It didn't matter what she did to him: he had won. She may have prevailed, but it was on his terms, not hers. He had resisted and, in so doing, had controlled the situation. He had won. She may have had the power to dominate him, but he had won.

Peter opened his eyes and sat up straight in the chair. His character, this vulnerable old man, still had the strength of will to resist even in the face of—well, he didn't need to think about that. He made a fist and stared at it. There it was, his gesture! Whether he made it physically or in his mind, the fist that held the spider was the gesture that would keep him in character. He no longer had to worry about his mannerisms and reactions, knowing they would be immediate and natural. Peter had become his role.

Now he was ready.

Taking hold of the cane, which was resting against his chair, he lifted himself out of the seat, neatened his tie and headed on his way.

He could have made it to The Crow's Nest in five minutes, but he had decided to be late, not wanting to risk arriving ahead of his contact. So he dawdled, then, at 8:25 p.m. he arrived at the entrance to The Crow's Nest, where he was greeted by a familiar sound coming from inside. Jazz! Yet during his Camp X briefings he was told jazz was forbidden in the Reich. He wondered what else he was told that would prove wrong. Too late now. It was time. Peter took a last deep breath, pushed open the hinged Crow's Nest door and poked the tip of his cane through, planting it firmly on the interior floor.

He had passed the point of no return.

As Peter made his way deeper inside The Crow's Nest, the music stopped, and he hoped that wouldn't make his arrival more conspicuous. He turned toward the bar where two men in civilian clothes, talking over pilsners, paid him no notice. Not so the bartender, who immediately began sizing him up like a hunter lining up prey in his rifle sights.

"Is there something you want?"

Peter couldn't tell from the edge in the bartender's voice, which seemed more than the normal Berlin abruptness, whether he meant "Do you want a drink?" or "Just what the hell is your business here?" Peter started to respond, but the bartender shushed him and pointed to the small stage where a debonair man in a tuxedo had stepped up to the microphone, joining a sax, piano and drum trio.

"Listen," the bartender said. "He's excellent."

The man in the tuxedo placed his hands around the microphone stand and tilted it toward his chest. "Did you know Eddie Cantor wrote another version of his famous old song 'Makin' Whoopee' for the Jews of the United

States? Well, Eddie asked me to sing it for all his friends in Germany. So if you good people don't mind, I'm going to switch over to English for this next number."

There was laughter and a burst of applause from diners who by now had filled all the tables. The trio played the opening bars of music and Peter heard the familiar lyrics in his mind. But those weren't the lyrics he heard coming from the platform.

> "Another war, another profit, another Jewish business trick.
> Another season, another reason, for makin' whoopee."

"See, I told you. He's excellent, really funny," said the bartender.

> "A lotta dough, a lotta gold, the British Empire's being sold,
> We're in the money, thanks to Frankie, we're makin' whoopee."

While the loudly laughing patrons were riveted on the performance, Peter gathered more information about his surroundings: an uneven and splintered wooden floor, cracked walls with smoke-darkened beige paint flaking off, a swinging door leading to a kitchen. A strange feeling of familiarity washed over him. The Crow's Nest could easily have been one of the tiny pre-Nazi cabarets where the emphasis was more on the intellectual rather than the sexual. There artists and writers, communists and homosexuals discussed matters of the greatest importance against the background of clever songs that satirized government and the church.

> "Washington is our ghetto, Roosevelt our king.
> Democracy is our motto, think what a war can bring!"

But this was no cabaret, no hotbed of unfettered creativity and comment. This wasn't Weimar Berlin and he wasn't a wide-eyed kid soaking it all in. This was 1942 Berlin and he was Jonah trapped in the belly of the beast.

> "We throw our German names away, we are the kikes of USA,
> You are the goys' folks, we are the boys' folks, we're makin'
> whoopee."

As the audience cheered wildly, Peter inventoried them. Only one was wearing a uniform, and he was also the only person sitting alone at a table.

Peter focused on the man's black dress tunic, adorned with two jagged Sig runes on the right collar and a single gold oak leaf on the left shoulder beneath a strand of gold braid. Everything looked right. The runes were the insignia of the SS, while the eagle and the braid identified the wearer as a colonel. Peter judged him to be in his mid-forties and in excellent shape, a sign that he probably came from a real military background instead of being a Nazi Party hanger-on who had ass-kissed his way to a commission.

Absent others to interact with, the colonel's body language didn't reveal much. He glanced at his watch and tapped the table once or twice, signs he was expecting someone. That was Peter's cue.

Using the cane, Peter took about twenty seconds to reach the table, where he waited another thirty seconds for the colonel to acknowledge him. When that wasn't forthcoming, he pulled out a chair and, using the cane as a pivot, sat down. "Good evening, Colonel. Isn't the entertainment delightful?"

The officer looked up, studied Peter with his hard gray eyes, then crinkled his brow. "Do I know you?"

"You're expecting somebody, aren't you?"

"Excuse me, but I don't see how that's your concern."

Peter could accept the colonel being understandably cautious. He would just have to play him some more. "Oh, but it is."

"My friend, perhaps you've had a little too much to drink. So I think it would be best if you just moved on."

"Are you also sure about that?"

"I'm certain," the colonel said, his voice noticeably sterner. "The first time I ask. The second time—well, you may want to avoid a second time."

"As you wish." Peter pressed down on the cane and lifted himself up. "It's a nice night. I'm going around back to have a smoke and look at the stars. Then I'm leaving. If you change your mind about speaking to me, I'd say you've got about ten minutes."

"I don't think I like your tone. Drunk or not, you're out of line. You realize I could have you arrested immediately."

Peter thought of the clenched fist, then opened it, freeing the spider. "Of course I do. But that would pose a problem for Max."

"Did you say 'Max'?"

"No, Colonel, I said ten minutes, starting now."

8

Peter leaned against the wall of the back-alley building across from The Crow's Nest and lit a cigarette from the pack he'd bought at the kiosk. Usually a bold ploy left him feeling exhilarated, but not this time. He had deliberately acted cocky, instead of simply confident, with the colonel a dangerous move, and he might not have gotten away with it. He let the cigarette burn as long as he could, then put it out and lit another. Is this guy coming or not? And if he does come, will he be alone or will he have some of his SS buddies with him?

With four minutes to spare, a uniformed figure turned the corner into the alley.

"Well, I'm here."

Peter replied by casually tossing his third cigarette to the ground.

"Inside you mentioned Max. What business do you have with Max?"

Peter stubbed out the cigarette with the toe of his shoe and said nothing.

"I asked you what business you have with Max."

Now was the time for words. "The same business you have with Peter Kepler."

"Peter Kepler? I don't know any such person. Am I supposed to?"

The son of a bitch was cool. This called for more prodding. "Look to the stars. Maybe you'll get an answer."

"Again the stars. Listen, I don't like puzzles. And I've spent too much time on . . ." Stopping in mid-sentence, the colonel took a small notebook from his inner breast pocket and flipped it open. "You did say 'Peter Kepler'?"

"I did."

The colonel squinted in the dim light over a few scribbled notes and then looked up. "Peter Kepler the astrologer?"

"The same." Satisfied that matters were on course, Peter stepped out of character, relieved to be able to use his regular voice, instead of straining it to sound older.

"Peter Kepler the astrologer." The colonel couldn't conceal his excitement. "I only know you by reputation. But we were all hoping you would eventually show up."

"Given the circumstances, I got here as fast as I could. Besides, I made it in time for our meeting."

Now it was the colonel who remained silent.

"Look, Colonel, or may I call you Max since we'll be working together?"

"Colonel, are you all right?"

Peter heard another voice. He looked around and saw the bartender standing at the back door.

"Fine, Otto. You brought the rope like I asked?"

The bartender stepped down to the street, dangling a length of sturdy white cord in front of him.

"Good. It looks like I'll need it after all." The colonel reached to his side and drew a Luger from its black leather holster. He pointed it at Peter. "You'll please just stand still and stretch out your hands behind your back."

Wait a minute. Something's wrong here. All right, this isn't the first time you've had problems with a con. The trick is to remain calm and in control of the situation. "If this is some kind of a joke, then . . ."

"Please, also remain quiet." The colonel nodded to Otto. "Tie his hands."

Peter felt the rope cut into his wrists as the bartender drew it tighter before weaving the ends into several secure knots. The colonel came over, rubbed his free hand over the knots and nodded his head.

"Is there anything else?" Otto asked.

"Yes. Call the number I gave you. Tell them I have Peter Kepler, the astrologer from the Heydrich assassination, in custody. Have them send a car and guards for my new friend."

"Immediately." Otto went up the stairs and retreated through the back door.

"Well, Herr Kepler, we have a little time." The colonel returned his Luger to its holster. "Is there anything we should discuss while conditions are pleasant? I can't guarantee that will be the case later."

Something had obviously gone very wrong but Peter wasn't about to figure out what. He needed to concentrate on a more pressing task—freeing his hands. To do that without being too obvious, he had to keep his adversary busy. "I don't know what you're talking about." Peter contorted his wrists as Houdini had taught him. His bindings, which would have held most people, posed no real challenge. He had already undone one knot and was well into the second.

"That's unfortunate. Since you're a fortune-teller, you must know that your immediate future promises to be extremely painful. I had hoped you would want to avoid that."

Read the tone, Peter, read the tone. He's self-assured. And why not? He has the gun. OK, so he's self-assured. A self-assured person thinks he's covered all the angles. That might cause him to lower his guard. And it can leave him unprepared for the unexpected, like your hands now being untied.

"I estimate you have perhaps another ten, maybe fifteen minutes before my associates arrive, Herr Kepler. I do think it will go a lot better for you if we talked before then. I would love to hear about a certain horoscope concerning Heydrich."

"How about a cigarette?" Peter pointed his chin down toward his shirt pocket.

"If it will make you more comfortable." The colonel pulled out the pack of cigarettes from Peter's shirt pocket and grimaced. "Johnnies? Johnnies are terrible cigarettes, even for war rationing. You know what they use for tobacco? Camel dung that Rommel's people ship from North Africa. Here." The colonel shoved the cigarettes back into Peter's pocket, then produced a silver case and flicked it open with the press of a small button. "Have a decent smoke," he said, and held out the case to Peter. "Oh, you seem a little inconvenienced. Allow me." He took a cigarette and placed it between Peter's lips. "And now a light."

Peter watched the colonel slip his right hand into his trouser pocket. There would only be a second or two. Think, damn it, think! They taught you how to kill and maim. You remember everything, so you know how to do this. He'll come close and hold up the lighter with his right hand. When he does, lean toward it, then quickly grab his right hand with your right hand, pull him forward and kick your left leg behind his right leg and force him to the ground.

"Here." As Peter expected, the colonel held up the lighter and rubbed his right index finger over the flint wheel, producing a flame. "Come on, it won't light itself."

Peter bent into the flame and as he did he thrust his right hand out, aiming it directly at the colonel's right wrist, just as he had been shown at Camp X. However, his hand sailed by its target, stopping only when the colonel grabbed and twisted it, doubling Peter's arm and sending him to his knees in agony. Peter knew he had done everything right. It was the damn glasses he was wearing to make him slightly farsighted. It hadn't mattered for distant objects, which was why he could size up the colonel at the table. But short-range objects were a problem, and because Peter's hands were still supposed to be tied behind his back he couldn't get rid of the glasses. He'd factored that in when he made his move, but obviously his calculations were off.

The colonel drew his gun again before releasing Peter. "So, you have a few tricks in your bag. Fortunately, close combat isn't one of them. Get up!"

Now he sounded like an SS officer. Peter quickly complied.

"I should shoot you here and be done with it. One more little stunt and I will. You had your chance to do this easily, but not now."

Peter knew the colonel couldn't shoot him, even if he wanted to. The authorities needed Peter Kepler for interrogation, so the colonel had no choice. But *he* did. He could do nothing, be taken away and, after being tortured, eliminated. Or he could try another escape and count on the colonel not shooting, not to kill, at least. It wasn't a hard decision. The colonel was about a foot away. Close, but in the darkness not close enough to see Peter's lips when he threw his voice. It was worth a try. "I've been waiting," Peter said in his own voice. "What kept you?"

"I beg your pardon?" the colonel answered.

"Not you, Colonel. My friend behind you."

"First you try judo, badly, and now you try this old trick. Did you really think I'd turn?"

"He didn't, but I did."

The voice from behind him caught the colonel by surprise and spun him around. Peter's ploy had worked perfectly, allowing him to move to his left and run as fast as possible, getting about twenty feet away before he crashed into three restaurant garbage cans, hidden in the darkness, that hadn't been there earlier when he plotted his escape route. He didn't fall, but he staggered long enough for the colonel to recover from the ruse and be on him, jabbing him with the revolver barrel before pushing him away.

"I told you what would happen the next time!"

Peter watched the colonel take a few steps back and point the revolver at him. All right, there's still no way he'll shoot. They need to interrogate me, so there's no way he'll—

Peter saw the flash in the corner of his eye. He heard the shot, followed by a sharp pain in his upper chest. Suddenly he felt a tremendous weight crushing him into the pavement. Images began getting dimmer and dimmer.

Then everything went black.

"Idiot! Asshole!"

The words jarred Peter into semi-awareness.

"You stupid, stupid bastard!"

Peter was certain that he had died but unsure whether he had landed in heaven or in hell. Either way, two things were clear: God, or the devil, was a woman and she liked to curse in German.

"Can you at least get up, you old fool? We don't have much time."

With his vision returning Peter looked up at the figure hovering over him. Her delicately featured face was beautifully pale and symmetrical, while her long blond hair was so radiant that its tips glowed as they danced on his chest. Salty language aside, this must be heaven, because he was gazing at an angel.

Reluctantly he diverted his eyes to take in his celestial surroundings and immediately he knew. This wasn't heaven but the same dark alley behind The Crow's Nest, with the heavenly glow coming from the streetlight. And the heaviness that he had felt in his chest, just before he blacked out, wasn't from a bullet but rather the body of the SS colonel, which was now lying across his midsection.

He turned his eyes back to the angel, only now he saw it was actually a woman—an ethereally beautiful woman—and she was holding a gun.

"Didn't you hear me? What do think this is, a vacation?" She reached down, grabbed the colonel's arm and tugged his body away. "Get up, damn it!"

Bracing his palm against the curb, Peter righted himself. "I'm not dead."

"You should be. A few seconds more and you would have been."

"You killed him?" Peter stared at the colonel.

"You can thank me later. How could you have lived so long and be so stupid?"

Peter didn't know how to answer. Nor did he have to. Otto, the bartender who had been the colonel's accomplice, had returned to the stoop outside the back door. "Max, are you all right?"

"Fine, Otto. But we don't have much time. The shot?"

"Nobody heard anything. I made sure the band was playing good and loud."

"Excellent. Now tone them down a little. I want everyone to hear the next sound."

Peter, who was still wobbly, waited until Otto left. "You're Max?"

"That's right, I'm Max."

"I'll be damned." Peter couldn't help chuckling.

"And what's so funny?"

"Your code name. It fooled us. We thought you were a man."

"My code name? Max isn't my code name. It's my *name*. Max, as in Maxine."

Maxine? Nobody thought Maxine. But then nobody thought a woman. Peter looked down at the colonel's body. "Then who's he?"

"He's Helmut Stern, one of the highest-ranking officers in the SS Occult Bureau and an immediate problem."

"So there's no Colonel Max?"

"Colonel Max? Whoever told you there was a Colonel Max?"

"Peter Kepler's appointment book listed this date and place and a Colonel Max. We assumed—"

"There's no time for this now," Max snapped. "Anyone could come walking down this alleyway and a dead SS colonel isn't easy to explain. Once you're out of here, I have to undo some of the damage you've done. Do you know Berlin at all?"

"I can get around."

"When you leave the alley, turn left, go down five blocks, then right, then left again. You'll be on Blumstrasse. Have you got that?"

"Five blocks, left, right, left again—I've got it."

"Midway down Blumstrasse, on the right side, you'll see a movie house. Buy a ticket, go in and sit in the back row to the right. Do you think you can handle that?"

"I'm not a moron."

"That remains to be seen. Here." Max handed Peter the gun.

"What am I supposed to do with this?"

"Before you turn onto Blumstrasse there will be a large pond. Wipe the gun with your shirt, then throw it in there. And try not to be noticed."

"I can do that. Anything else?"

"Yes. Rip my blouse."

"I'm sorry?" It was a wonderful invitation, but this hardly seemed the time or place.

"You have to rip my blouse. You *are* capable of ripping a blouse, aren't you?"

"But why?"

"So it will look like I—" Max kicked the colonel's corpse with the toe of a stylish black leather low-heeled shoe. "Like I was accosted. Now rip my blouse."

She was wearing a sheer white silk blouse with a hint of lace delicately accentuating the collar and cuffs, part of the reason Peter had thought her an angel. He carefully grasped the collar, but she snatched his hand and placed it on the small top blouse button between her breasts. "You fool. When you assault a woman, you don't waste any time." Suddenly she stopped and looked at her own hand, which had slight reddish-black smudges. "What is this, makeup? Shrewd. Maybe you're not that stupid after all."

"I'm—"

"Later!" she commanded, and placed his hand back in place on her blouse. "Now rip! Rip hard, like you have never wanted anything as badly as getting this blouse off me!"

For a moment Peter's fantasy merged with reality. He didn't need to rely on any techniques. This wouldn't be acting. He tore the fabric to the side in a quick jerk. It yielded easily.

"Now the bra. Just tear a strap loose."

This time he willingly did as told. The right side of her bra fell dangling to her navel and for a moment her breast was exposed. Even under these circumstances, Peter couldn't help staring, then smiling as he experienced a pleasant twinge.

"Good." She gathered the torn blouse around her chest. "Now hit me."

"Hit you?"

"Why do you make me say everything twice?" she said, exasperation clipping each of her words. "Slap me on the face, hard enough to cause a bruise."

By now, Peter knew better than to argue.

"You held back! That did nothing, damn it! Don't you understand, this has to look real?"

This time he hit her cheek with more force, and while she said nothing he could hear her throat click as she drew in a short spurt of air. Her lips and eyes both tightened.

"Good." She patted the spot that he had struck. "It's sore. There'll be a nice mark."

"Now what?" Peter asked.

"Now you leave. As soon as you're out of sight, I'm going to scream loudly. Otto and some of the patrons will come rushing out. If there are any police nearby, they'll arrive as well. If not, they'll be called. They'll discover that Colonel Stern was shot in the back by a cowardly assailant who then tried to rape me."

"And you think the police will believe that?

"They'll believe it."

"You're that convincing?"

For the first time, Max offered just the slightest hint of a smile. "There's no need to be convincing if you're Gestapo."

Max's directions were excellent. When he got to the pond, Peter knelt by the edge as if to tie his shoe. He waited for a couple to pass, then pulled out his front shirttail, wiped the gun with it and tossed the gun into the water.

From the pond it was only a short walk to the movie theater. He bought a ticket and settled into a worn seat in the area that Max had specified. He knew theaters, having been in enough of them with Houdini, and this one had seen better days. Its small, run-down interior was refuge to a few scattered patrons whose disheveled appearance made Peter feel he was in a shelter rather than a cinema.

The film was equally dismal, something about a Great War veteran and his family put out on the street by, in the words of a kindly official who befriended them, *"ein diebisch jüdisch Hauswirt,"* a thieving Jewish landlord. Peter found himself drifting between boredom and disgust. Boredom finally won and he dozed off. He awoke to color footage of a medieval battle and a voice-over.

"You know her for so many wonderful films, including her masterpiece *Teuton*. Now this great director is completing her latest work, which tells the story of the SS, the noble descendants of those heroic German knights."

Peter watched as marching SS troops gave a stiff-armed salute before a reviewing stand. The shot cut to the dignitaries who were answering the salute in kind. They were all there, Hitler, Himmler, Goering, Goebbels, with a bunch of heavily decorated military officers. Then the camera panned to the side of the stand, catching a slender blond woman in black slacks and a light brown sweater who was holding a viewing lens to her eye. Suddenly, realizing the tables were turned and she was being filmed, she lowered the lens, smiled and waved to the camera. The screen filled with her smiling face as the commentator continued to praise her in glowing terms: "Heroine of the Reich," "True Daughter of Germany" and "Hitler's Favorite."

Fully awake now, Peter took in the image as the voice-over proclaimed, "She is filmmaking royalty, anointed by our *Führer* as 'The Grand Elise!'"

Peter rubbed his eyes and looked again. He knew that woman. And now, thanks to the unseen commentator, he knew her last name.

Elise.

Maxine Elise.

"Peter Kepler?"

There was no response from the figure slumped in the barely cushioned velvet seat.

"Peter Kepler." This time the words were punctuated by a jostle, which did the trick. Peter moved his head slightly upward, blinked twice, then rubbed his eyes. He was still in the movie theater, but the screen was blank, the lights were on and all the other seats were empty. He turned to his right, where a man, maybe five feet, eight inches tall, stocky but not fat, with a full, smiling face, was standing.

"I know you. You're the bartender at The Crow's Nest."

"Otto Beidecker. I'm a friend of Max."

Max. Maxine. The SS colonel. The shooting. The angel. So much for a bad dream. "A friend of Max? That's good. I wouldn't want to be her enemy."

Otto Beidecker chuckled softly. "No, you wouldn't. But she's really a wonderful person."

Peter was in no mood to argue the point. "What time is it?"

"Early morning. Nearly six A.M. You slept here all night."

"So my back says." Peter straightened up and took a deep breath. "Is that coffee, *real* coffee?"

"Viennese." Otto bent down, picked up a mug that was resting on the worn aisle carpet and handed it to him. "One of the benefits of knowing people who know people, as is this." He dropped a bulging napkin on Peter's lap. "A special treat."

"Strudel!" Peter said as he caught a whiff of the exquisite fragrance coming from the napkin. "Apple strudel!" Ravenous, he would have settled for anything. But fresh strudel! He carefully removed the pastry, not wanting to crush its delicate, flaky layers, and admired it as he might a work of art, then bit off a small piece, closing his eyes as he savored it. "Magnificent!" he proclaimed, then proceeded to take larger bites, washing them down with hearty gulps of coffee. In between, he managed to get in a question. "Wasn't Max supposed to come here last night?"

"Max went to Gestapo headquarters to file a report. Himmler was notified and he came and brought her to his house—"

"His house?"

"The one he shares with his wife and children when in Berlin. He keeps his mistress elsewhere."

"I wasn't implying—"

"It's all right. Now I'm sure you'd like to freshen up. The projectionist is a friend. He has a small apartment upstairs where you can bathe. I brought you a change of clothes. Come." Otto helped Peter out of the seat. "Hot water can work wonders."

So, too, can a razor, which Peter found in the bathroom. When he emerged, a towel draped around his waist, his beard was gone, as was the gray in his hair.

"Quite a transformation," Otto said. "I wouldn't be able to recognize you. And I tied you up." Otto pointed to the bed. "The clothes are there."

Peter lifted a pair of black trousers and a real white shirt. Unlike the suit, these were more his size. They certainly didn't come from Otto, who was at least five inches shorter. "Use them now. Later I'll bring you a good suit. Meanwhile, there's food in the icebox and the radio works. I should be back before seven to pick you up."

"Where are we going? Not back to The Crow's Nest?"

"Not tonight. Tonight we're going to the other extreme. Tonight we're going to church. Max wants you to meet Father Fritz."

"*Father* Fritz? Sorry, but priests aren't among my favorite people."

"No matter. It's important that you meet him."

"So he can load me down with the Holy Spirit?"

"So he can help you summon some unholy ones."

9

Wannsee: July 3, 1942
Your Stars Today: Approach matters in a novel way and you'll find that embracing the unusual will bring you success.

Even *he* had to admit the women were beautiful, but he wanted a man. A very special man: Werner Ebling.

That's why he came to this popular recreational area on the outskirts of Berlin. He knew Ebling was among the high-ranking Nazi officials staying at Villa Marlier, the SS resort house, which overlooked the Grosse Wannsee, perhaps Berlin's most beautiful lake. There, over the best of food and wine, they were finalizing plans to exterminate Europe's Jews.

Ebling had been at Villa Marlier in January when Heydrich had unveiled the initial draft of those plans to top Nazi leaders. But it was too cold then for Ebling to start the day with a swim, one of his great pleasures. Now the weather was warm, and he knew Ebling would seize the opportunity to walk the short distance from the guesthouse to the lake and indulge. So, just before dawn, he staked out an inconspicuous spot on the shore and waited.

His patience was rewarded. Within a half hour Ebling arrived, stripped off his robe and immediately ran a few steps from the shore into the water, plunging in headfirst. He watched as Ebling, propelled by a powerful backstroke that belied his portly physique, swam a good distance from shore, then turned over to float on his back.

Keeping Ebling clearly in sight, he slowly waded into the lake until the water just covered his shoulders. At this early hour there were only a handful of people around—a few men, but mostly wives and children of lower-ranking officers who were staying in modest SS vacation bungalows—and he spent a few innocent minutes just treading water and blending in. Those who glanced his way would see another anonymous frolicker. What they wouldn't see was his right hand reaching under the side fabric of his bathing suit, just above the knee, and carefully sliding a slender three-inch piece of hollow wood from a piece of elastic tied around his thigh.

Turning his back to the shore, he lifted the wood partly out of the water, clasped some corking that covered one end between his thumb and forefinger and tugged, exposing a point with an opening at its tip. Holding the wooden shaft upright so the tip remained dry, he moved toward Ebling, who had drifted a few more feet away from him. Soon the water neared the top of his neck. Another couple of steps and he would lose all footing. That would make the task much more difficult but much more invigorating. He continued.

Now the water was just over his chin, causing him to hold the shaft even higher and threatening his leverage. He closed his eyes momentarily and imagined himself Wagner's immortal Siegfried, armed with his father's great sword, Nothung, and facing Fafner the Giant, who has taken the form of a fierce dragon. Wagner's words, which he knew by heart, flooded his mind.

Come, Fafner, come and teach me fear. You cannot escape me! Wotan the Father, the great protector of the Germanic people, will deliver you to me!

He opened his eyes and saw Wotan, in the form of a small wave, had turned Werner Ebling's floating body slightly and brought it closer, almost within striking distance.

So, Fafner, you decide to face me.

Now the words were his own, uttered in his mind since the water was over his mouth. But he only needed one more step.

Wait! This is no giant! This is no dragon. This is Mime, the duplicitous dwarf! The ugly gnome who once claimed he was Siegfried's father! How could his deformed flesh produce a true German! He insults our people by pretending he belongs!

Moving his right arm parallel to his body, he took aim at a patch of Werner Ebling's flesh, just below the ribs, that was above water.

Treacherous Mime.

As his right arm lunged, his right hand pointed the shaft toward its target.

Face me, Fafner! Face Siegfried, your better!

The momentum drove the point of the hollow shaft through Werner Ebling's skin, where it remained long enough for its contents—a small dose of curare—to drain.

Face me and die like all misfits who defile our heritage and our race!

He heard Werner Ebling make a small, startled noise and he watched him try to move his hand toward his side as if to swat an insect that had stung him. But the hand jerked to a sudden stop and remained immobile, as did his lips, frozen around some word he was trying to say.

No other swimmers were close enough to notice the bluish hue coating Werner Ebling's face, which meant his lungs had seized up and his heart was failing. Slowly Ebling's head sank beneath the water, followed by the rest of his paralyzed body.

About twenty feet away, a hand reached to the lake bottom and deposited a wooden needle beneath a rock where it would probably never be found. And even if it was, it would be taken for a lake reed. Some fifteen minutes later, in a changing-room stall, the same hand finished fastening the belt on a pair of trousers. Outside there was commotion. Obviously Werner Ebling's body had been discovered. There would be an autopsy, revealing nothing, and the death would be attributed to natural causes. It was so much neater that way.

He had placed little in the changing-room locker: a wallet, a pen and a watch, which he loosely strapped on so he could slide and rotate it to just the right position.

Finally he pulled the strap tight, satisfied the watch's face was perfectly in place, completely concealing a small tattoo just above his left wrist.

Hildie Rausch answered the knock at the side door of the redbrick rectory and cautiously checked the two men standing on the stoop. One she knew; one she didn't.

"Max said you were coming, Otto. She didn't mention someone else."

"Then Max is here?"

"She's in Father Fritz's study. So, who's your friend?"

"As you said, a friend. May we?"

She gave him a shrug. "You know the way. Father will be a little late. He's cleaning up after his excursion."

"Excursion?"

"I insisted he take a day trip to the woods for a little relaxation. A walk. A swim. A nice lunch in the open air. He needed some time away."

"It's good you pushed him. He's lucky to have you."

"No, we're lucky to have *him*."

When they entered the spacious study, Peter's eyes involuntarily gravitated to Max, seated at a leather-inlaid pedestal desk. Peter couldn't resist. "If priests looked like you, I just might go back to church."

There was no reaction. So much for getting off to a fresh start. Peter looked around the room. There were several comfortable chairs scattered about, but instead he selected a stark straight-backed wood and wicker one, which was light enough to swing around so it was facing Max.

"Father Fritz took a day off?" Otto opted for an overstuffed club chair across the room, and Peter watched with amusement as his small body sank deep into the soft, thick burgundy padding, leaving only his head visible.

"His last for a while," Max said. "The next few weeks are going to be nonstop." She nodded toward Peter, her first acknowledgment of him. "That is, if *he* can produce."

"I take it that I'm the 'he,'" Peter said.

She continued to talk right through him. "Otherwise, we might as well call it all off right now before lives are lost."

"It'll work, Max," Otto said. "I have a good feeling about Peter."

"Feelings are dangerous, Otto. From what I've already seen, he's dangerous. I don't have the time to babysit him and neither do you."

Again, Peter felt invisible. "If you want to talk about me, fine, but at least pretend I'm here!"

Max turned toward him. "I don't have to pretend. You have a way of making your presence known."

"I believe in lasting first impressions," Peter said, and Max smiled, but not at him. "Father Fritz." Max started to get up,

"Stay put, Max. Please." A figure in slacks and a short-sleeve shirt standing behind Peter eased her back down with the motion of his hands and grabbed a second straight-backed chair, which he pulled next to Peter. "And who's this you brought?"

"Our new Peter Kepler, such as he is," Max said.

"Father Fritz Moeller. I'm glad to meet you." He patted Peter lightly on the back as he sat down.

"Don't make a hasty judgment, Father," Max replied.

"And why is our Max so smitten with you?" Father Fritz asked.

Finally, someone was speaking to him. "It probably has something to do with her shooting an SS colonel who captured me."

"I heard about that. Unfortunate, but nothing can be done. Let it go, Max. We've got a lot to do. Have you reformulated the plan?"

"Yes, and I'm not convinced he can pull it off. It's more complicated, riskier."

With difficulty Otto lifted himself out of his chair. "Max, we can't just call everything off!" He took a few paces on the red Turkish area rug that covered the walnut wooden floor before flopping down again. "We just can't."

"Otto's right, Max," Father Fritz said. "Not after getting this far. What have you come up with?"

"It's a gamble." Max twisted a heart-shaped locket that hung around her neck with her right hand as she spoke. "We're going to have to work on Himmler directly. No intermediaries."

"That's not riskier, Max, that's disastrous!" Otto registered his opinion even more strongly than before, although this time he didn't try to get up.

"You're the one who said we can't call it off! What do you propose?"

"Children, please!" Father Fritz looked at Peter. "Young man, how good are you at what you do?"

"I'm the best."

Father Fritz grinned. "You wouldn't lie to a priest, would you?"

"A priest is the first person I'd lie to."

"I see. You're Catholic?"

"I don't see how that's relevant, priest."

"The priest has a name!" an indignant Max reminded him.

"So do I!" Peter was equally indignant. "And if you start using mine, I'll start using his. Agreed?"

"Agreed," Max reluctantly answered.

"Anyway, Father Moeller—"

"Father Fritz," Max said. "We call him Father Fritz."

"Anyway, Father Fritz, I thought I was here to help the German underground, not to join the Legion of Mary."

"My apologies. Religion is of no matter to your mission, although some of us believe that this New Germany violates all the principles we adhere to. Not just Catholics. Max and Otto are Protestants. From your feelings toward my collar, I assumed you are, or were, Catholic."

"I'm nothing. I'm too good at fooling people to let myself be fooled by humbug."

"How dare you talk to Father Fritz that way!" Max's eyes flashed hot with each syllable.

"It's all right, Max," Father Fritz said. "Our only concern is whether Peter can pass Himmler's scrutiny."

Max was adamant. "Himmler's scrutiny? I doubt he could pass our scrutiny."

Peter had finally had enough. It was time to take control and put a stop to this nonsense. He stood and dragged his chair to the side of the desk. As he sat back down, he reached over and pulled Max's hand away from her locket. "Is this the hand you write with?"

She was too startled to say anything but, "Yes."

"Fine." Peter held her right hand in his left so her palm faced up. "Maybe it'll speak to me, even if you won't." With that Peter began gently stroking Max's palm with his right forefinger. "Such a soft hand for such a hard woman." He was quick not to give Max a chance to respond. "These areas right here—the elevations at the base of your fingers—are called mounts. They're named for various planets and they—"

"Is this going to take forever?" Max demanded.

If Max wanted a fight, Peter was prepared to unleash Armageddon. "Tell you what: I'll speed things up, although without a thorough reading I might not be as accurate."

"See, he's already making excuses." Max started to pull her hand away, but Peter's grip remained firm.

"Not so fast. Why not let me make a fool of myself?"

Max seemed satisfied with that prospect, so Peter continued. "Very interesting. See right here. This is your life line." He pressed his finger on a crease running the length of Max's palm. "There's a second line that runs parallel to it all the way to the end. That means you're living two separate lives, each with its own course, but related."

"Amazing. The lines reveal something about me that you already know. I'm sure Himmler will be impressed when you read his palm and tell him that he's head of the SS."

"You mean I'm supposed to tell you something that I don't already know?" Peter again tried a little levity, and again watched as it was batted away.

"This is a waste of everyone's time." Again Max tried to draw back her hand only to have Peter continue to hold it tightly.

"Hmmm. Something I don't know. Well, I could look at this line. . . ." He began tracing a crevice that started between Max's first and second fingers. "It's the heart line and, because it's red and prominent, I could say that deep down you're a romantic, even passionate person. Now certainly there's no way *I* could know that."

"First old news and now generalities! You're a worse fraud than I thought!"

"You want specifics, which is impossible." As Peter spoke, he ran his forefinger over Max's life line. "No one could know from this line that you hide that passionate nature, not just from me, but all men, because something traumatic happened to you when, let's see—ah, here it is. This little mark that crosses the life line just below your thumb. Something traumatic happened to you when you were four or five. But of course nothing did."

Max was silent for once.

"You're thinking even that's too general. But how could I possibly look at your palm and, for example, know that when you were that age, your father abandoned you and your mother, which is why you have a problem getting close to men, even though you want to. You don't trust men. Even the ones you know well you have lingering doubts about." Peter looked across the room. "Sorry, Otto." Peter looked back at Max. "But Father Fritz is all right. He's probably the only man you completely trust, but then he's a priest, not a man. So if I wasn't a fraud, that's the kind of message I could read in your palm."

With a sudden yank Max finally wrenched her palm from Peter's hand and, in a sweeping arc, smashed it across his left cheek. "And in case you can't read the message in that palm, it's stick to business and don't ever pry into my personal life!"

Peter winced and rubbed his fingers against a welt that was slowly rising on his face. "This *is* business, damn it. You doubted I could handle the assignment. Well, do you doubt it now?"

She looked at Peter. He had expected a glare, but he was wrong. "Nobody but Father Fritz knows about that part of my life. Not Otto. Nobody. How could you?"

"I have mystical powers."

"Don't play games with me."

"I have mystical powers. Can you offer a better explanation?" There was no answer. "Otto? Father Fritz? Can either of you?" They remained quiet. He looked at Max. "Will Himmler be able to? More importantly, will he want to? We usually believe what we want to believe." Peter turned to Father Fritz. "No matter how outlandish."

"I'd really like to know," Max said. "Please."

Please? She hadn't said please to him before this. "You helped. When I held your palm, you told me things. Not the lines, but your pulse and the slight muscle movements in your wrist. It's called contact reading. One of the best practitioners, Alex Hellstrom, was a German magician. I learned the basics from him when he came to America. The rest was practice. I asked you some leading questions and your body gave me the answers."

"I still don't understand."

"Do you remember playing with your locket?"

"Not really."

"I didn't think so. It seemed like a nervous habit that you weren't aware of. Well, at one point the locket opened for a moment—"

"You were that observant of me?"

"Don't be flattered. Con artists are always on the lookout for something they can exploit. Eventually I knew you'd reveal something. And you did. The locket had a picture of a woman and a child. I assumed it was you and your mother."

Instinctively Max caressed the locket.

"But it wasn't a perfect picture. Part of it was torn away as if someone else was deliberately removed. Since the picture appeared to be a professionally taken family portrait, your father should also have been in it."

"It could have been a brother or sister," Max said.

"Possible, but unlikely. Besides, Otto already told me that you were an only child, one of the few bits he knew about your family. And you were guiding me. As I closed in on my revelation, your body clues said I was on the right path."

"But for argument's sake say you had been wrong," Father Fritz said.

"Then I'd have to talk my way out of it," Peter said, his eyes still fixed on Max. "A con artist's life hangs by his tongue. Most children have something happen to them at four or five. Maybe it's falling down and breaking an arm. Or a family pet dies. Whatever it is, it may seem like nothing when you're an adult. But when you're that age, it's traumatic and it leaves a mark. I probably would have drawn that out of you and then found a way to link it to my statement about men."

"You're very good." Max's words were barely audible.

"I'm sorry, I didn't hear you," Peter said.

"I don't know if you're the best, like you boast, but you really are very good." This time Max's voice was strong.

"Thank you. I know that took a lot. By the way, your mother must have been quite something."

"Why do you say that?" Max asked.

"Had I continued to do the reading, I could have told you about her, again using your reactions. Instead, I'll simply surmise. She never remarried, a combination of things, including her own hurt. So she raised you herself and what she went through gave you your strength and determination."

"Not a bad surmise," Father Fritz said, and Max nodded in agreement. "But that wasn't the con artist speaking."

"No, the bogus professor of psychology. That's my dark secret, as long as we're all being honest. I've spent the past few years passing as a professor of psychology at Princeton, though I actually never even made it through grade school."

"That's a remarkable feat," Father Fritz said.

"Not really. In our own ways, all of us pretend to be what we're not, some more openly than others. What about you, Father? Who are you pretending to be?"

Max gave Peter an icy stare, which told Peter she had come back from the past and had reclaimed her feisty self.

"Forgive me, Max, I know that Father Fritz means a lot to you, especially since your mother is dead."

"How did you know her mother is dead?" Otto asked.

"Precisely because of the closeness Max feels for Father Fritz. And she's an only child. So she probably wouldn't be taking all these risks if she still was responsible for a mother who did so much for her."

"You're very good, but not perfect," Max said.

"Your mother's alive?" Peter said.

"No, you were right about that. But even if she was alive, I'd still be taking these same risks."

"Why?" Peter asked.

"Why? You can't be serious. Why are you here?"

"It's a long story," Peter said.

"Well, mine isn't," Max said. "I'm here because I love my country and I hate what's happening to it and to innocent people because of it."

"The Jews," Peter said.

"The Jews, the gypsies, the mentally deficient—anyone who's different from Hitler's idea of a German. So if my mother was alive, I couldn't face her if I wasn't doing what I'm doing. What's more, I couldn't face myself."

Now Peter was silent.

"Different reasons don't matter as long as we have the same objective." Father Fritz looked at Peter. "I don't think there's any question about your abilities. The OSS didn't let us down." Next he looked at Max. "I think we should arrange a meeting with Himmler as quickly as possible." Finally he looked at Otto. "Since Peter will be staying with you, bring him back tomorrow so he can study."

"What am I studying?" Peter asked.

"How well versed are you in the occult?" Father Fritz replied.

"It's a staple in my line of work."

"This isn't run-of-the-mill occult. Himmler is involved in the dark and dangerous."

Peter could handle that, too, but chose not to say so, not yet at least. Instead he tossed off another flippant remark. "They sound like Catholics."

"They are," Father Fritz said, giving the biting remark credence. "Like Hitler and many others in leadership positions, Himmler was born a Catholic. It's no secret that he used the Jesuit Order as his model for structuring the SS."

"Touché," Peter said. "Back to studying."

"You might profit by browsing through my library, which includes an extensive collection of works on occultism and on old Germanic ways. I'm sure you'll find some of the material useful. I'll only make one recommendation: the *Bhagavad Gita,* the famous ancient Hindu work on justice and spirituality. Himmler's intrigued with Indian culture, especially the Gita. He always keeps a copy with him, so you'd do well to become very familiar with it."

"Tomorrow, as you said," Peter said, rising, as did Otto.

"You two go ahead," Max said. "Father Fritz and I need to discuss a few things."

Father Fritz walked Otto and Peter to the door. He extended his hand to Peter, who reluctantly took it and held it a few seconds before letting go. "Fascinating."

"What's that?" Father Fritz asked.

"Your hand. Any accomplished palm reader would see it right away. Look at your right thumb. Notice the thick, rounded tip and the short nail that make it look like a club."

Father Fritz rotated his hand so he could view his thumb from different angles. "I guess you could say so, yes."

"The old-timers believed a thumb shaped like that unmistakably marked a certain type of person."

"Really? What type?"

"A murderer."

For Fritz Moeller it had been an exhausting string of days. He was almost too tired to tend to his daily diary. Usually he paid attention to style. But tonight he just wanted to get the words out, as if he were exorcising demons. Pressing the gold nib of his Montblanc Meisterstück to the top of the journal page, Father Fritz drew a short horizontal line, followed by an intersecting vertical line, to form a cross, then entered the date—3 July 1942—and began to write.

> *"Do not render evil for evil"—"Let him refrain his tongue from evil"—"Let him turn away from evil"—"But the face of the Lord is against those who do evil."*
>
> *I am surrounded by evil—in my faith, in my country, in my life. And I am part of that evil, still caught in the vortex of such terrible doings. Are the words from First Peter for me or about me? "Why does God allow evil?" people ask, but the question is really why does man allow it? Satan is the tempter, but man gives in. Satan tests and man passes or fails. Satan no more causes evil than God does. Our deeds define evil. To look elsewhere is to lie.*
>
> *Matthew says: "Whoever shall murder shall be liable to judgment." Murder, both the physical act and the intent. "But I say to you that everyone who is angry with his brother shall be liable to judgment." We are most of us murderers, some in act, some in spirit and some in both. Individuals are accountable for their actions, both good*

*and bad. To say or do nothing when an individual or a state commits
murder is the same as to commit it yourself.*

*And where then is forgiveness? Are we ever to be forgiven? Am I
ever to be forgiven?*

Done, Father Fritz took a long sip of his customary brandy, closed the
journal and exchanged it for a scrapbook, filled with newspaper clippings.
Then he daubed some thick white library paste from a small ceramic pot on
the back of an article he had trimmed earlier and pushed it firmly in place
on an empty page.

An article reporting the death of Werner Ebling.

It only took a few seconds for Werner Ebling to die.

It took a lot longer to bury him.

First there was the dispute that began soon after Ebling's body was discovered. Himmler wanted Ebling's remains to rest in a central location along
with those of other top-ranking SS officers. Normally that would have been
the end of the story. But Ebling's widow wanted him buried with the rest of
his family. She prevailed on Himmler and finally, in deference to her, and
perhaps also to the fact that her father controlled one of Germany's largest
banks, he struck a compromise.

So on the morning of Sunday, July 5, the body of Werner Ebling was
brought to the Mosaic Hall of the Reich Chancellery in Berlin, where it lay
in state for public viewing. The next day an elaborate funeral ceremony,
presided over by the Reich's government and military leaders and attended
by thousands, was held outside the Reich Chancellery. Hitler hailed Werner Ebling as "one of the greatest of the National Socialists," and Himmler
extolled him as "the staunchest defender of the Reich and the fiercest adversary of its enemies." Following nearly two hours of oratory, Ebling's coffin
was placed on a gun carriage towed by six black horses and transported to a
special train, which carried him to his family plot in Münsterberg for a private interment.

His right hand, complete with the SS Death's Head ring on the forefinger, didn't make the trip. Instead, pending Himmler's further instructions,
it remained in Berlin, watched by a special SS Honor Guard.

That was the compromise.

10

Berlin: July 14, 1942
Your Stars Today: This is a perfect time for expressing your artistic ability through unique creations, which can have a significant impact.

In his cramped apartment on Austerstrasse, Hans Reiber, fists clenched and elbows resting on the breakfast table he had fashioned from a butcher block, sat staring at a cup of lukewarm tea, a roll coated with a thin slice of local cheese, the morning newspaper and five cured rat skins.

He didn't have much of an appetite, so he retrieved one of the skins, which he spread out, brown fur down, on the newspaper. After taking an unenthusiastic sip of tea, he positioned the cup so the handle held the rat's head in place. The skins weren't bad, better than the last batch, which weren't treated properly and had tended to curl. These lay flat and that made his job much easier.

With the rat skin secure, he reached over and lifted a medium-sized ceramic bowl and an elongated metal box from one of the kitchen chairs and set them on the table. Dipping his hand into the bowl, he extracted a glob of thick, gelatinous material, slopped it onto the middle of the rat skin and, with his fingertips, spread it into a thick layer extending eight inches from the rat's neck to the base of its tail. Then he opened the metal box. Inside were five pencil-like objects, each about five inches long and encircled with a thin band of a different color. Hans Reiber deliberated: The white band would be too long—nearly an hour and a half. On the other hand, the black band would be too short—only ten minutes. He settled on the red band—nineteen minutes, a reasonable compromise.

Reiber drew his choice from the box and studied it. Time pencils never ceased to amaze him. So deceptively simple: one end brass, the other soft copper containing a glass capsule of acid. With a good squeeze on the copper casing the glass would break, sending the acid onto a fine copper wire. Once eaten through, the wire would release a spring-loaded striker onto a cap and detonator, exploding the main charge. The color band represented the wire width. The thicker the wire, the longer the acid took to work.

Carefully he pressed the pencil timer into the gel. When he was satisfied it was properly in place, he covered it with more gel from the bowl and made the layer thinner so it would respond better to touch. His nose crinkled at the gel's pleasant almond scent. It reminded him of the sweets shop he enjoyed visiting as a boy.

One more step remained. He took a last box from the chair, this one filled with sewing supplies. Breaking off a long strand of pinkish thread that closely matched the color of the rat's belly, he poked it through the eye of a needle extracted from the round green cushion in the box and began stitching. Within a matter of minutes, he had a whole rat ready to go.

Hans Reiber examined his handiwork. An excellent job if he did say so himself. Clasping the rat by the end of its tail, he gently lowered it into an empty cardboard carton by the table leg. One down, four to go. Finally he succumbed and took a nibble of the roll.

Then he reached for another rat.

Seated at Father Fritz's desk, lost in an ancient volume on the occult, Peter didn't hear the first knock. But at the second, louder one he swiveled his chair around to find Max standing in the open doorway, dressed in black slacks, a simple white blouse and black loafers, her long blond hair gathered into a chignon. "Am I interrupting?" she asked.

"Not at all." Peter quickly rose. "Come sit down."

"This isn't a social call," Max said, but accepted his invitation anyway and headed for one of the armchairs. "I have to tell you something that affects the mission."

"So that's why you have your work clothes on." Peter walked around the desk and sat down in an armchair facing Max, who looked confused. "I saw a clip of you on location and you were dressed like that. Are you as good a director as they made you out to be?"

"Better, when I make the films I choose and not *Teuton* or some other propaganda piece. But I'm not here to talk about cinema. We've discussed it and settled on a date for the assassination. January 6. That's the—"

"Wait a minute. Why wasn't I part of this discussion?"

"Because you would have added nothing. And because it's not your decision, so be quiet and listen. On January 6, 1929, Hitler appointed Himmler to take charge of the SS, which then consisted of only two hundred eighty members. Today there are over half a million. Each year on January 6, the staff at SS headquarters in Berlin holds a gathering to commemorate Himmler's accomplishments. The leaders of the SS make it a point to be there.

And, since the war started, Hitler also stops by briefly. It's the perfect opportunity, but you lose nearly a month of preparation."

"I'll be ready," Peter answered without hesitation, but his confident reply couldn't pierce Max's skeptical look.

"We'll see. In the meantime, concentrate on being ready to accompany me a week from Saturday. Himmler's entertaining some of his big-money supporters at Wewelsburg that evening."

Peter checked the German atlas he had committed to memory and came up blank. "Where's Wewelsburg?"

"It's a what, not a where—a medieval castle in Paderborn that supposedly stands on a sacred spot. Himmler's been renovating it for nearly a decade. He's made it a center for research on ancient Germany, but he and his intimate circle also conduct their mystical ceremonies there. That makes it the perfect place for you to win Himmler's confidence."

"And you expect me to do that at our first meeting?"

"No, but you can grab his attention by revealing some deep secret through seemingly supernatural means." Max reached into her back pocket and drew out a slip of paper, which she waved at Peter.

"So what's this?" Peter snatched the paper from her hand, unfolded it and read the contents aloud. "A-one-nine-one-two-seven-two-oh." He was bewildered. "Is this the deep secret?"

"Yes. And before you ask, I have no idea what it means. I only know if you pass it on to Himmler it'll make a major impression."

Peter looked at the scrap of paper again. "A-one-nine-one-two-seven-two-oh. A code of some sort."

Max shrugged her shoulders. "Oh, and there's something else. When you reveal the code, or whatever it is, you've must work in the phrase 'avenge the blood.'"

"'Avenge the blood'? A little melodramatic, isn't it?"

"Just make sure you use the phrase."

"Who gave this stuff to you?"

"An utterly reliable source. That's all you need to know."

Peter pressed his front teeth into his lower lip and kept them there, so when he said, "Fine," it came out with the proper measure of contempt.

"Good." Max rose from the chair. "A week from Saturday then."

"Funny, isn't it?" Peter said, not bothering to stand. "A month ago, the closest I got to this war was the front page of *The New York Times*. Now I'm about to be Himmler's guest at some swank reception."

"Guest?" Max crinkled her face. "Don't flatter yourself. Have you forgotten the Heydrich horoscope? You're still wanted by the SS, which this man heads. You're not going to be Himmler's guest, Peter. You're going to be his gift."

"Des Juden Israel Geldgier Ist Unsere Unglück!"

The headline screamed from the front page of the current week's issue of *Der Stürmer,* the Reich's most inflammatory anti-Semitic newspaper: "The Jew Israel Money-Grubber Is Our Misfortune!" Beneath the headline was a finely inked caricature of a man, his exaggerated rodent-like face, bulging eyes and oversized hooked nose framed by curly strands of hair that drooped along the front of his ears well past the lobes. The accompanying caption read: *Defiler of our Sacred Heritage,* while the article chronicled "the terrorist acts and desecrations a bunch of brigand Jews and Jew lovers have committed against the Reich."

Wilhelm Strauss stared into a cracked mirror hanging on the basement wall of an abandoned building on Kaiserstrasse, then looked again at the newspaper he was holding in his hand. "I don't think I look like that."

"What are you ranting about?"

Strauss tossed the newspaper to his companion, who was sitting in a tattered-cloth–covered easy chair. "They continue to use that vile drawing, even when writing about me and my so-called band of vigilantes. Why, soon the German people might actually start believing that all Jews look alike. Now I ask you—does that resemble me in any way?"

Hans Reiber, normally expressionless, smiled. "Other than your normal nose, deep-set eyes, square-jawed face and close-cut hair, I'd say it was a perfect likeness."

"Of you, perhaps, but I'm much prettier."

"Write the editor a letter, then. Or send him your picture and ask that he publish it. That way every Nazi in Germany can be on the lookout for you."

"A picture. That's not a bad idea. Perhaps I could get Hitler's personal photographer to snap it."

"Only if you were dangling at the end of a rope." Reiber looked at his watch. "Come on, Wilhelm, it's nearly seven. They'll be shutting down in an hour."

"Relax. It takes no time to get there. Besides, the others won't be arriving for another twenty minutes or so."

"I like to be on time."

"It's the soldier in you," Strauss said.

Reiber's reply was caustic. "Back when a Jew could be a soldier."

"Back when a Jew could be a German. Well, tonight you can be both, my friend." Strauss grabbed two raincoats from a table near the mirror and tossed one to Reiber.

"Do you think the Jew catchers will be out, looking to turn in their own?" Reiber asked as he struggled into his raincoat.

"The Jew catchers are always out, though they haven't had much luck with us. But that's about to change. Tonight they'll be a lot of Jewish vermin to get their hands on. Come on. Let's not disappoint them."

The black letters on the red banner draped over the entrance to Berlin's Museum of Natural and Social Sciences touted its new exhibition, *Deutschlands prachtvolle Vergangenheit*—Germany's Glorious Past.

The museum, which opened in 1941, had been stocked largely with conventionally displayed pieces the SS had looted from collections in conquered countries. This exhibit, spanning from the earliest known history of the Germans to their stand against Roman invaders, was its first major event. Himmler himself had designed and supervised its every aspect, from the dioramas depicting battles, domestic life and religious ceremonies to the thick catalog jammed with photographs, drawings, maps and historical propaganda. Glass cases were filled with newly excavated artifacts, carefully selected by Ahnenerbe researchers to prove Germany gave birth to Western culture and civilization.

That's the point Goebbels seized on. Despite his dislike of Himmler, Goebbels saw the propaganda possibilities of the exhibit, so he relentlessly exhorted "all good Germans" to "perform your patriotic duty by going to this magnificent display and appreciating your ancestors' gifts to the world."

Whether it was Goebbels's push, curiosity or because the war had curtailed so many leisure-time options, thousands of people had flocked to the museum since the exhibit opened at the start of July, and they kept coming. Today their number included Wilhelm Strauss, Hans Reiber and a few of their closest associates.

At 7:35 P.M., as attendees packed the cavernous main exhibition hall, a young woman, part of a crowd gathered around a display of spearheads from Germany's Saxony region, dropped her handbag. She knelt down to retrieve it, and as she did she flipped up the clasp and hit the bag's side with the back of her hand, emptying its contents onto the red swirled marble floor. Then she bolted up, screaming, "Rat! Rat!"

Eyes turned toward her, then followed the large grayish-brown object as it darted between feet. Meanwhile, a man, taking advantage of the distraction, opened his attaché case and released a second rat.

"Damn, another one!" he shouted, and as he did a third rat was set loose in a different area of the main exhibit floor. Women scooped up children and headed toward the exits, pushing past museum guards who were trying to keep the crowd calm.

As Hans Reiber watched, he stuck his right hand inside his raincoat pocket and poked at its specially sewn seam, which broke apart easily. Then he bent down to deposit one more rat on the floor.

A dead rat with a bomb inside.

"Here's another one!" Reiber stomped on it with his foot, breaking the seal on the nineteen-minute pencil fuse and starting the bomb detonation sequence. "Jesus, it's an infestation!" He kicked the rat across the room, adding to the growing panic.

The head of the museum guards, a burly man in drab brown quasi-military dress, began shouting orders. "Out, out! Everyone out of the museum! The exhibition is closed for the evening!"

Away from the confusion and unobserved, Hans Reiber headed away from the jammed exits and ducked into a men's lavatory. He scanned his surroundings. It was safe. "Wilhelm?"

Wilhelm Strauss emerged from a stall. "I hear the noise. It worked well then?"

"Perfectly. They're streaming out. Another few minutes and they should all be gone."

"The other bombs?"

Reiber looked at his watch. "By now, they should be in place and activated."

"Then it's time for the coup de grâce." Strauss drew a dead rat from his coat pocket and pressed its stomach. He could hear the glass crack, releasing the acid in the fuse. "Your ten-minute rat, Hans," he said, tossing it into a corner. "The most powerful." He grabbed a wastebasket by the sink and emptied its contents onto the rat. "Good kindling."

Reiber started to speak but was interrupted by the restroom door being pushed open. He was somewhat hidden by the door, but Wilhelm Strauss was in full view. He held his breath.

"Out, out!" Only the profile of the guard's face was visible. "If anyone's in there, get the hell out, right now!" The door started to swing back, muffling the guard's final warning.

"Wilhelm, we've got to get away from here!" Reiber said.

"In a moment, my friend, in a moment."

"Please, it's too dangerous!"

But Strauss paid him no mind. "I'm tired of not getting any credit for all my hard work." He reached into his other raincoat pocket and took out a stubby broad brush and a small tin of black paint. "And I certainly wouldn't want Streicher to blame poor Israel Geldgieriger for this."

He pried open the tin with a key and dipped the brush into the paint. Then he slapped the brush against the whitewashed wall, over and over, until he was finally satisfied. "Now we can go."

Exactly ten minutes after Wilhelm Strauss pressed the stomach of a long-dead rat and four minutes after he and Hans Reiber left the museum, there was a series of explosions, followed by a fire that raged for five hours. When it was finally extinguished, the entire exhibition had been destroyed and the museum severely damaged.

The next day, the cleanup crew entered the area that had been a men's lavatory and came across a crumbling portion of wall on which a Jewish star had been painted. Beneath the star were some words:

Der Jude Wilhelm Strauss ist Himmler's unglück. The Jew Wilhelm Strauss is Himmler's misfortune.

11

Wewelsburg: July 25, 1942
Your Stars Today: This is a time for elaborate, celebratory events, infused with great feelings of confidence. You may well find yourself having to resort to quick and innovative thinking when demonstrating your willingness to accept unusual conditions.

A day before the reception, Max took off for Wewelsburg on a flight that Himmler arranged, leaving Peter to make the three-hundred-mile jaunt in a 1938 Lancia Astura convertible with Otto at the wheel. The car, specially designed in the Nazi colors—red for the exterior and black for the leather interior—was a gift from Mussolini to Hitler. However, Hitler preferred his armor-plated Mercedes-Benz, so he let Max use the Lancia whenever she was in Berlin.

"Almost there," Otto said when they reached the Westphalian city of Paderborn. "We just have to pick up Max."

"She's not staying at Wewelsburg?" Peter asked.

"She has in the past, but she doesn't like it," Otto said as he navigated the narrow streets past tall, steeply pitched buildings with imposing bay windows and lavishly decorated façades. "This is more her style."

They passed a quaint moated palace, which Otto said had been home to the region's bishopric princes since the seventeenth century, then went another half mile down the road and pulled over in front of a small, half-timbered cottage, that looked like it might once have been part of the royal property. "Belongs to a friend of hers," Otto said, and honked twice.

Within seconds Max came bounding down the walk, looking refreshingly natural in a simple summer blue-and-white-flowered frock and a rose-colored lightweight sweater. "Otto explained about the letter and the horoscope?" she asked after settling into the backseat.

"Before leaving Berlin you gave me a letter of introduction to Himmler explaining why I was sending the horoscope," Peter said. "But you only said it was important. You had no idea it was Heydrich's and what it portended. Did I pass?"

"I won't be the one grading you. Just be convincing. Himmler may look like a man, but don't be fooled. You'll be dealing with the devil."

Not true. Peter had already dealt with the devil and it wasn't Himmler. But Peter understood Himmler's lack of regard for human life and his capacity for evil. Ilse Jennings' horrible death by gassing had brought that home to him. "Believe me, I won't underestimate Himmler."

Otto was right. It was a short trip to Wewelsburg Castle, a triangular stone structure with three massive round towers, two of them domed, set high on a mountainside. The car made its way across a bridge and stopped at the arched entrance to the castle. Two SS guards helped Max and Peter from the car and directed Otto to the parking area. Then, without saying a word, the guards pulled open an oak double door inlaid with swastikas and runes, revealing an SS lieutenant in a summer white uniform stationed just inside.

"Fräulein Elise, on behalf of the *Reichsführer,* may I welcome you and . . ." The lieutenant looked at Peter.

"And guest," Max said.

"Yes, of course. And your guest to Wewelsburg Castle. If you would." With that he escorted Max and Peter down a short corridor into a great entrance hall dominated by a magnificent hand-carved oak spiral staircase and a white-marble eight-foot-high fireplace that took up nearly two-thirds of a wall.

"Thank you, Lieutenant. I'll take it from here." Heinrich Himmler obviously had been on the lookout for Max. "As lovely as ever." He kissed her warmly on her right cheek.

"Oh, Heinrich, I'm afraid I didn't dress for the occasion," Max said as she surveyed the other female guests. "How embarrassing."

"My dear Max, remember—the more understated the vase, the more prominent the flowers." Like the words, Himmler's high-pitched delivery was clumsy.

So this was Himmler. Peter took in the figure who looked more like a clerk at a costume party than Hitler's second in command. While Himmler's black SS dress uniform gave his slight frame some false heft, his chicken-like chest seemed barely able to support the array of medals weighing down the left side of his tunic. Himmler's chinless face was pale, with a nondescript moustache beneath a thin, beak-like nose, which was a perch for a pair of owl-eyed oval glasses. Amazing, Peter thought, that this unprepossessing individual, with his flabby neck and an inverted bowl of black hair balanced on closely cropped temples, should be the leader of an elite corps of soldiers hailed as the epitome of German manhood.

"Heinrich, for a man of such integrity, you lie divinely," Max said.

"I don't believe I've met your escort." Himmler stepped back and extended a delicate, almost girlish hand, his blue veins clearly showing beneath translucent flesh.

"Allow me to introduce Peter Kepler."

"Peter Kepler!" Himmler's demeanor immediately changed and he quickly withdrew his welcoming gesture before it could be accepted. "Max, do you realize who you have here?"

"A fine astrologer, a talented writer and an authority on early German mysticism. I told you that in the letter."

"What letter? I don't recall any letter."

"The letter of introduction I wrote to accompany the horoscope Peter prepared. Right before I left Berlin to film in Poland. Don't tell me that one of your clerks lost it. Now that's troubling."

"What exactly did Herr Kepler tell you about the horoscope?"

"Just that he felt you should see it."

"He didn't tell you the horoscope predicted Heydrich's death?"

"Heydrich's death?" As planned, Max, looked convincingly astonished.

"No, I can see he didn't." Himmler gave Max a solicitous pat on the wrist. " But now you know why we're so interested in Herr Kepler."

"Peter, I can't believe you didn't say something to me."

"In any event . . ." Himmler gave Peter an icy stare. "Your chart for *Obergruppenführer* Heydrich was fascinating, Herr Kepler. It didn't conform to any of the normal methods. I'm sure the Ahnenerbe astrologers would like to know exactly what mysterious technique you used."

"Not mysterious, *Reichsführer*, logical. Heydrich may have been born in Germany, but he was stationed in Czechoslovakia. And, as its Protector, his fate had become intertwined with that country. I simply used Prague as his place of birth, prepared his natal chart and progressed it. Have your people try it. They'll find the results very interesting."

Himmler was obviously intrigued. "I've never heard of that being done. I'll have them look into it. Still, there are many other things I need to know about you, Herr Kepler."

"Why not let him do your chart, Heinrich. Once you see just how phenomenal he is, all your qualms will disappear."

"Perhaps at some point. But as I'm sure Herr Kepler has explained to you, drawing up an accurate chart is not a quick matter, and since tonight is a social occasion and tomorrow I'm off to—"

"Or perhaps he could read your palm." Max pried open another door, one that Peter wished she hadn't. "I can attest that he's quite good. He read my palm the other day and—"

"Palm reading? Is Herr Kepler also a strolling cabaret trickster?"

Damn it, Max, why couldn't you just let it go? Peter thought as he pre-pared to jump into the fray. If Himmler really believed, as Father Fritz said, that India was the wellspring of the Aryan race, then any connection between it and the mystical should command his attention.

"You're right, *Reichsführer.* There are many fake palm readers. But as you know, palmistry is an ancient science handed down to us from India, where it's considered to be on an equal footing with astrology. Then there was our own countryman, Carl Gustav Carus, royal physician to the King of Saxony, who, during the last century, helped place palmistry on a strict scientific footing."

"You're extremely knowledgeable, Herr Kepler. Does your skill match that knowledge?"

"Judge for yourself, Heinrich," Max said. "Let him read your palm."

But Himmler was distracted by an aide who whispered something in his ear.

Max tried again once the aide had left. "Heinrich? Won't you let him read your palm?"

"Later, perhaps. But now there's a call I must take, so if you two will excuse me. Please, try some of the Champagne. A gift from our good friends in France."

With Himmler out of earshot Peter gave Max an angry look. "Not palm-istry, Max. Did you see the way he reacted?"

"And you recovered very nicely. Besides, he wasn't biting on astrology, and it's essential that you pass on that code I gave you."

"Just steer him back to astrology. He obviously dotes on you. Meanwhile, I'm going to find a waiter and liberate some of that French Champagne. I have a feeling we're going to need it before the night's over."

It took only a few steps for Peter to figure out why, despite the pleasantly warm evening, officers far outnumbered civilians in Wewelsburg's large, triangular courtyard. Unlike the stiff, cushioned bottoms of German mili-tary boots, the soft leather soles of regular shoes offered little protection from the hard cobblestones.

"Champagne, *mein Herr*?"

Reacting to the voice behind him, Peter swung around, and his elbow hit a tray of crystal flutes being carried by a waiter. The resultant torrent of champagne doused Peter's white shirt, his tie and, most heavily, his beige jacket before trickling onto his grayish-blue slacks.

"Please, *mein Herr*, I was so clumsy." The waiter set the tray on the ground and began daubing Peter's jacket with a cloth that had been draped over his arm. "I apologize profusely. I should have been more careful."

"What has happened here?" One of the officers grabbed the waiter's arm and pulled him away from Peter.

"It was my fault," Peter said. "You see I—"

But the officer continued to reprimand the waiter. "Don't you know how to treat the *Reichführers* guests? Go inside and wait. This will be dealt with." The officer pushed him toward one of the castle's many courtyard entrances, throwing him off balance and causing him to fall. "Get up and get out of here!" the officer commanded.

The waiter managed to balance himself on his palms and toes and, not bothering to rise, scampered as best he could on all fours out of sight. Finally the officer acknowledged Peter. "I apologize for this inexcusable behavior. I hope you won't take offense."

"Really, it wasn't his fault." Peter looked at the insignia on the officer's uniform—four pips on a black field. That meant he was a *Sturmbannführer*. "It was mine, Major. I knocked into him."

"Still, he should have been more careful. Rest assured, it will be handled. Your coat is all right?"

Peter patted the wet fabric with his right hand. "My coat's fine. There's no reason to—"

"Then you should have some Champagne to drink, not wear." The major snapped his fingers and motioned to a young girl in a plain black skirt and white blouse. "She will take care of you properly. They should only use women for this anyway."

"And the man?"

"I will address the matter later. You have my word."

Arguing would be useless, so Peter gave the major a nod, which sent him on his way.

"Your champagne, *mein Herr.*"

Peter took a flute and the opportunity to study the slim, plain-looking young woman who offered it. He guessed she was in her mid-twenties, even though her heavily wrinkled face made her look older. Otherwise, her only distinguishing feature was a small mole just beneath the right side of her lower lip. More noticeable was the purple triangle sewn breast high on the left side of her blouse. Peter made a quick mental search of Nazi color triangles, the system used to classify concentration camp prisoners: pink for homosexuals, red for communists and other political enemies, green for career criminals, purple for—purple for *Bibelforscher,* Jehovah's Witnesses, dissenters imprisoned because they refused to join the military, take part in air-raid drills or even utter, *"Heil Hitler."*

"You're a Jehovah's Witness. Is there a camp near here?"

The girl bent her head down, hiding her mouth behind the tops of the flutes. "Right here," she whispered. "Niederhagen. You can see it from the road. A few women, but mostly men, who either do building or maintain the castle and the officers' houses."

"And the waiter—do you know him?"

She began to tremble. "He is my husband. Please, sir, if there is nothing more, I must attend to the others."

She was terrified and, after witnessing how an innocent incident could turn deadly, Peter knew she should be. "Only this." He took another flute of Champagne for Max.

"Then if I may be excused." With that, she gave a slight bow and hurried off.

He had read the reports and had heard the stories, but over the last five minutes Peter had had his first personal encounter with gratuitous Nazi brutality and he found it difficult to fully comprehend. What was it Jung said about understanding evil? It's not a cure but a help, because you can cope with a comprehensible darkness. For the mission to succeed, Peter would have to hone his coping skills. And, as Max warned, be extremely careful while doing so.

Peter returned to the great hall, only to run into Himmler almost immediately. "Herr Kepler, I was just coming for you." He looked at Peter's damp jacket. "An accident?"

"I knocked into a waiter."

"One of the Witnesses. Excellent workers and even better prisoners. Never think of escaping. They'd make fine soldiers if we could ever get them to give up their foolish beliefs."

"Yes, well, I would appreciate it if he wasn't punished. It was my fault."

Himmler didn't hesitate. "For a friend of Max, of course. You have my word on it. Now perhaps you can do me a favor. I've been thinking about our earlier conversation and believe a palm reading might prove productive."

So much for selling him on astrology. "Allow me to bring this to Max." Peter held up one of the Champagne flutes. "Then, if there's a quiet area with no others about, preferably with some chairs, I'll be more than happy to read your palm and—"

"Oh no, Herr Kepler, not *my* palm. One of my associates'."

"Of course. Is your associate here already?"

"In a manner of speaking."

"And his name?"

"His name is Werner Ebling."

"Werner Ebling? *Gruppenführer* Werner Ebling?"

Alone in a corner with Max, Peter gauged her reaction as being midway between astonishment and disbelief. "He didn't mention rank. Anyway, soldier or civilian, what's the difference? It's not like we have a choice in the matter."

"Peter, Werner Ebling is dead."

"What are you talking about?" Peter didn't try to pretend he wasn't startled.

"Ebling was one of Himmler's most trusted officers. He died of a heart attack the same day you first met Father Fritz."

"Then it can't be the same person."

"It's the same person. Himmler intends to test you by having you read a dead man's palm. This is a step beyond, even for him."

"It's bizarre, but it's do-able." Peter was determined not to seem concerned. "A hand's a hand, living or dead. It still has lines. Or it should, if it hasn't decomposed too badly. They must have preserved it in something."

"They buried it."

"Then they dug it up. How should I know? They're your friends, not mine."

"They're nobody's friends. Don't you understand what's going on here and how dangerous this is? Our whole plan could end tonight, right here in this creaking pile of stone."

"This isn't our game, Max—it's Himmler's. He sets the rules. What am I supposed to do, tell him I don't feel like playing?"

"Shhh! He's back. Over there, by the window." Max smiled and gave Himmler a little wave, which he took as an invitation.

"Herr Kepler, please," Himmler said as he approached. "I know Max is a lovely woman, but you mustn't monopolize her. You'll make enemies of every other man here, and these are not enemies you want to have."

"I was just recounting our conversation, *Reichsführer*. But there I think I might have missed something."

"No, I don't think you missed anything, Herr Kepler. However, with all the distractions, I could have neglected to mention one or two details. If so, I'm sure Max has provided them."

"Heinrich, I said he was gifted, but there are limits," Max said.

"For some, perhaps, but you told me that Herr Kepler has extraordinary abilities, which go beyond astrology. Now I am ready to be convinced."

"I'll be more than happy to read Herr Ebling's palm," Peter said, seeking to put the matter to rest. "Although I believe we already know what his future is."

"It's not his future I'm concerned with, Herr Kepler. I want to see what his palm has to say about Germany's future." Himmler turned to Max. "I'm certain you'll want to join us."

Max clamped her lips tightly together, then opened them just slightly to speak. "Peter, would you give us a moment alone, please."

"Why don't I get myself another glass of Champagne," Peter said, feeling his jacket. "I seem to be almost dry."

"Heinrich, this is madness," an agitated Max said when she was sure Peter was gone. "This isn't one of your inner-order initiates. He's not prepared for this."

"And what *is* he prepared for, Max, taking advantage of you?"

"That's unwarranted, Heinrich! I'm having him consult for the SS documentary and also work on the narrative. I told you he's quite an accomplished writer. Of course, I had him thoroughly checked out. His purity papers are ready to be filed with the propaganda ministry when I return to Berlin. You can review them whenever you like."

"And I will. I can't simply let Heydrich's assassination and Kepler's possible involvement pass."

"What do you think Peter did? Plan Heydrich's murder just to impress you!"

As Max's tone grew more indignant, Himmler's became more solicitous. "Max, I know you mean well. You're a brilliant filmmaker. And the Reich has benefited greatly from your Gestapo work. But the hidden realm isn't familiar territory for you. There are those who are excellent at pretending they possess special abilities. They can deceive even the best, so there's no shame in being fooled. You've put a lot of trust in this fellow. I merely want to see if it's justified. If he turns out to be a charlatan, I won't blame you. And at least we'll stop any further embarrassment."

"Heinrich—"

"Our conversation is over, Max. If need be, I'll give you some people from the Ahnenerbe to help with the documentary. That's where you should have looked first." Himmler signaled to Peter, who had returned, waiting in view but out of earshot. "Herr Kepler, we're ready if you are."

"Where's Ebling's body, Heinrich?" Max asked.

"Still in the ground, I should imagine."

"Then how—?"

Himmler put the tip of his right forefinger on her lips. "Everything will be answered in the North Tower."

Peter arrived in time to see the color draining from Max's face and to hear the apprehension in her voice when she repeated, "The North Tower?"

"Why, yes, of course, Max. You know that special events like this take place in the North Tower. You've been in the North Tower, but not to this part. You see, we're going to visit Valhalla."

Himmler waited a few seconds for that to sink in. "Now if you'll excuse me for a moment, I'll make certain everything is ready."

With Himmler gone Peter asked Max, "How bad is it?"

"You know about Valhalla?"

"The mythological dwelling place for slain Teutonic warriors?"

"This isn't mythology. Here Valhalla is where the remains of the dead SS heroes reside. It's also where the most secret SS rites take place. I've even heard stories of human sacrifices, and while I don't put much stock in them, I believe Himmler's capable of anything."

"So what are you telling me?"

"That your testing is going to be much more rigorous than any of us imagined. That you may not be up to it. That I may be forced to denounce you as a fraud, admit that I've been duped and demand that Himmler take care of you."

"You mean do away with me."

"They'll torture you first, which will endanger the whole operation."

"If I don't pass muster, the operation's over anyway."

"That's not the operation. It's just one part. There's much more involved. Rescuing the Jews. The other resistance work. Everything could be at risk. You know too much. And if they break you, they break us."

"You knew that when we started."

"Yes, but you've shown you're resourceful. That's why I have confidence you'll be able to find a way."

"A way to withstand the torture?"

"A way to kill yourself before it starts."

Carrying a lit candelabra, Himmler led Max and Peter down a dark flight of stairs in the north tower to Valhalla, a vast underground chamber beneath the castle's great "Hall of the Generals."

"I prefer not to use electric lighting down here given the solemnity." Himmler slowly waved the candelabra around as they entered the cavernous circular room, "During the day, the sun provides natural light. During the evening, we use the candles."

With his vision unaffected by the dim light, Peter could clearly make out twelve short pedestals spaced at regular intervals along a circular wall and, above them, high arched windows pointing to a golden-hued false dome designed like a swastika. Directly beneath, in the center of the floor, a marble altar rose from a small, sunken circle. It was here that Himmler took them, after first pausing to gently remove a black ceramic urn from a niche carved into one of the wall columns.

"Are you ready for the reading, Herr Kepler?" Himmler asked as he handed Max the candelabra and carefully placed the urn on the altar.

"At your convenience, *Reichsführer*."

"Good." Himmler removed the lid, set it on the floor beside the base of the altar and pointed to the interior of the urn. "Then here is Werner Ebling's hand."

Peter peered into the mouth of the urn and squinted. "Ashes?"

"The early Germans often burned the bodies of their fallen heroes. Because Ebling's widow wasn't cooperative, we had to settle for his hand."

"With all due respect, *Reichsführer*, it may be difficult to find lines on this particular hand."

"But surely a man of your skill and learning will be able to read the ashes much as our ancestors did. Wasn't that one of their main methods of divining the future?"

Peter shot a quick what-have-you-gotten-me-into glance at Max, who remained expressionless. He wasn't going to be able to talk his way out of this. "True, *Reichsführer*. But the readings were nearer to the event. For example, ashes from sacrificial offerings were read immediately."

"This wasn't a sacrificial offering, but rather the disposing of earthly remains so the eternal spirit of a modern-day German warrior could soar to its true home. Surely the right person could use these ashes to connect to that spirit,"

Peter was caught in a rare moment of not knowing how to respond.

"Herr Kepler? Have we lost you?" Himmler asked.

"No, *Reichsführer*. I was simply"—he had to get some quiet time to think—"concentrating to better focus my energies."

"And how long must we wait while you focus your energies?"

"A few minutes of solitary contemplation is all I need. However, if the request is . . ."

"Reasonable, since we know how important it is that you make contact." Himmler took the candelabra back from Max, then signaled for her and

Peter to follow him toward an arched opening in the perimeter wall. "There." He stopped and thrust the candelabra forward, lighting up a small alcove. "We use this area to prepare for ceremonies."

Edging past Himmler into the alcove, Peter jostled him ever so slightly. As he did, he delicately put the tips of his thumb and first two fingers of his right hand into Himmler's rear pocket, withdrawing a handkerchief, which he pinched before quickly concealing it. The stickiness said it had been used. Exactly what he needed, should the occasion arise.

"My pardon, *Reichsführer*. I'm still getting accustomed to the dim light."

"Here." Himmler removed one of the three candles in the candelabra and stuck it into an iron holder on a small table. "I trust this will be suitable for you."

Looking around, Peter saw, besides the table, a pair of stools and a few cabinets with strange markings, which brought to mind Max's comment about human sacrifices. Could there possibly be—

"Herr Kepler, have we lost you again?"

"I apologize, *Reichsführer*. I was taken by my surroundings and the overwhelming sense of history."

Max placed her hand on Himmler's wrist. "Heinrich, perhaps we should let Peter have those few moments of solitude," she said, and drew him back to the altar.

Peter waited until Max and Himmler were a safe distance away, then took stock of the alcove but found nothing that might be useful. He sat on the stool and considered his next move. There had to be a solution. There was always a solution.

"Have you had enough time, Herr Kepler?"

Peter ignored Himmler's impatient shout and focused on the candle's flame as a way of blocking out any further distractions. There had to be a solution. What was he overlooking? As he mulled that over, his eyes shifted from the candle's flame to a slow-moving stream of wax making its way down its side. What was he—Yes! Like always, there *was* a solution!

"Herr Kepler?" The edge to Himmler's voice told Peter his tolerance was exhausted.

"I'm almost done," Peter said, and hurriedly prepared. In less than a minute, he took the candle and started to leave, then stopped abruptly and inhaled deeply. He couldn't be sure, but on the off chance he decided to check it out. This time he anticipated Himmler. "Just allow me to say a brief prayer to the Gods, *Reichsführer*."

With that Peter set down the candle, went to the right rear corner of the alcove and knelt, placing his hands on the floor. In a few seconds, he bolted up and went to the table, where he spread out Himmler's handkerchief and poured some graveyard dirt from his shoe into it. Folding it neatly, he exchanged it with his own breast pocket handkerchief.

One detail remained. Taking out his knife, Peter hurriedly etched Himmler's name into the candle, as close to the top as he could. When he was done, he grabbed the candle and made his way back to Max and Himmler.

"At last we are ready," Himmler said, clearly exasperated.

"Bring me a plate."

Himmler stiffened at the command. But Peter had decided that since everything was on the line, he might as well go all out. "Preferably unadorned gold; however, I will settle for sterling or pewter."

"Herr Kepler—"

"I am prepared to bridge the realms. Any delay will weaken the connection that's been established."

"And I wouldn't want that to happen." Himmler headed over to the niche that had held the urn, reached in and grabbed something. "Will this do?" He handed Peter a large ceramic tile emblazoned with a coat of arms. "It was Ebling's SS heritage plaque, designed by Wiligut himself."

"Given the circumstances, and its creator, it will suffice." Peter turned to Max. "Please lift the urn from the altar." Once she had, Peter placed the tile on the altar where the urn had been. "*Reichsführer,* if you would lay the back of your right hand on the tile." Despite his skeptical look, Himmler complied.

"And now, Max, if you would tip the urn and let the ashes slowly run over the *Reichführer's* hand."

"Herr Kepler, what are you—?"

"Quiet!" As loud as Himmler's aborted question was, Peter's reply was louder, and it resulted in a stunned silence, which he quickly broke. "No one is to talk but me during this ceremony! Another outburst and we will end this here and now! Max, please do as I asked."

As gray, white and black ashes streamed from the urn, Peter recited repeatedly, "Let what is gathered be scattered," until the urn was empty. "Now, *Reichsführer,* please lift your hand about an inch and turn it over." Himmler's action left a small, broad mound of ashes on the pile. "Good. Now, please press your hand firmly into the ashes. Excellent." Peter placed his hand on top of Himmler's. "Let what is scattered be gathered."

When he removed his hand, Peter knelt down before Himmler and said, "Place your right hand on my forehead." Then he closed his eyes. "Gods of the German People, who have guided their course across the centuries to this great moment of destiny, who have created a race of men capable of perceiving and accomplishing your sacred will here on earth and who have blessed us with our savior, Adolf Hitler, I entreat thee to send forth the spirit of thy servant Werner Ebling. May he speak through me to his brother-in-arms, *Reichsführer* Heinrich Himmler, and, in so doing, guide his beloved Fatherland. So be it." Finished, Peter let out a scream and fell backward to the floor.

"Peter!" Max shouted. "Peter, are you all right?"

Slowly Peter rose to his feet. "Werner Ebling has spoken."

"I heard nothing," Himmler said.

Peter took one of the candelabras and held it close to his face so that, in the flickering light, Himmler and Max could make out something on his forehead.

A1912720, written in ashes.

The first gasp was from Himmler; the second, Max. Only Peter, who was anxiously holding his breath, made no noise.

"This can't be." Himmler, still startled, stared at the writing on Peter's forehead. "There's no way."

"What do you see?" Peter asked.

Max set the urn on the floor and took a compact from her purse, flipped it open and handed it to Peter. She waited until he had a chance to hold the mirror at an angle so it reflected the ash message. "What's it mean, Peter?" When Peter shook his head, she turned to Himmler. "Heinrich?"

However, Himmler avoided her question. "Do you have a pencil and paper in that purse?"

"Yes."

"Please write down the message."

Max did as Himmler asked and gave him the paper. He glanced at it, then peered directly into Peter's eyes. "There's no way you could—and yet." Himmler looked back at the paper. "These jottings mean nothing."

Well, that sounded ominous enough, Peter thought. Was the secret information Max gave him bogus? Or was Himmler trying to hide the effect it had on him? Either way, Peter knew he'd better act quickly.

"We must seek clarification, *Reichsführer.* To do this, I'll need something with the emblem of the Reich on it," Peter said and lifted the urn from the floor back onto the altar. "Your armband will do."

Himmler hesitated, then removed his red armband with its black swastika set off against a circle of white, which Peter dropped into the urn. Then Peter pulled the handkerchief he had stolen from Himmler from his breast pocket and, keeping it folded so none of the graveyard dirt fell out, he gently blotted his forehead. When he finished, he placed the handkerchief in the urn, draping one of its ends over the lip. "Werner Ebling, we ask you to provide guidance in interpreting the sign that you have given," he said, and turned to Himmler. "*Reichsführer,* for the guidance we seek, we must re-store the integrity of Werner Ebling's remains so his spirit might rest." Pe-ter took the candle from the floor, gave it to Himmler and pointed to the exposed portion of the handkerchief.

Himmler touched the flame to the fabric and a deep red flare suddenly shot up, then settled into a steady yellowish-blue burn. Within a minute or two, the fire died out.

"There. Did you see it?" Peter asked.

"See what?" Max said.

"The blood-colored flash and the sword-like pattern in the flame. The message was clear."

"And what was that message, Herr Kepler?" Himmler asked.

"The ancient Germans used a special weapon to extract vengeance—a blood sword. That's the message: avenge the blood."

There was no gasp this time. Instead. Himmler was visibly transported to some other place, far from the cellar of a renovated twelfth-century cas-tle. When he returned, his mood was different. Any skepticism that Peter had detected had given way to quiet acceptance. "Have the rites now ended, Herr Kepler?"

"Almost. Please hold the candle over the urn, and under no circum-stances move it." Then Peter, his head bowed and his eyes closed, began speaking solemnly. "Let the scattered now be gathered. Gods of the German People, we give thanks for allowing us this brief time with the spirit of Werner Ebling. Now we commend that spirit back to you as we reflect on the knowledge imparted which will strengthen our blessed Fatherland."

Opening his eyes, Peter saw that the letters he had scratched on the candle were now part of the rivulets of wax dripping into the urn. Just as he hoped—Himmler himself had used candle wax bearing his name to seal his body fluid on the handkerchief onto graveyard dirt. According to the folk teaching Peter had learned as a boy, that act also sealed Himmler's fate. Not that Peter believed it, but he appreciated the symbolism.

"You may put the urn back in its place of honor now if you wish, *Reichs-führer,*" he said, but Himmler appeared too preoccupied.

"Heinrich, are you all right?" Max asked.

"Few people could have sent the sign and message revealed here tonight," Himmler said. "One was Werner Ebling. We'll know soon enough if this was the case. Meanwhile, I would like Herr Kepler to enjoy my hospitality for a few days. Being so schooled in the old ways, I'm sure he'll find Wewelsburg's library and research facilities impressive. Is that acceptable, Herr Kepler?"

How many German words are there for "no"? Peter wondered. And would Himmler understand any of them? Max's concerned look gave him the answer.

"Max had wanted me with her in Paris, but if she can make do, I'd be honored to accept your invitation, *Reichsführer*."

"Excellent. It's settled. Now we should rejoin the festivities. I've been remiss as a host. And don't worry, Max. If Herr Kepler's message is accurate, he'll be brought to you in Paris immediately."

"And if it's not?" Max asked.

"Then there will be nothing left to bring!"

12

Berlin: July 28, 1942
Your Stars Today: Stimulated by spiritual idealism and optimism, you look to actions that will bring about purification and healing.

Earlier it had rained, but by day's end it stopped, giving way to unpleasantly high humidity. Was it more unbearable inside the crowded concert hall, he wondered, or outside, where he and others were lingering during the intermission? It was one of the rare times in the past three years he had gone to a concert. How nice it was not to have to rely on memory for the nuances of Beethoven. That's why he was so enjoying tonight's concert, despite the reason he was there. . . .

"Do you smell one yet?" half of a stunning Aryan couple nearby whispered as they awaited the bell summoning them back to the auditorium.

"No, not yet," the woman replied with a laugh. "Do Gestapo members really believe a Jew can smell another Jew?"

"Some do. What difference does it make, Helga? Smell them, spot them, feel them. As long as you point them out."

"But I thought we all look alike," she said playfully. " You should be able to find them yourselves. Wouldn't you know right off that I'm a Jew?"

"You look more German than my sister."

"I *am* German."

"In a manner of speaking."

"I was German enough for you last night."

"Anything?" he asked, disregarding her remark.

She looked away from him, her eyes darting first here, then there. "Nothing."

"So we can enjoy the rest of the music and do another look around afterwards. The evening's not over. Perhaps we'll get lucky."

"Wait." She looked ahead some ten feet. "I know her. She's a Jew."

"Anyone with her?"

She scanned the area. "No, just her. Out to hear the music."

"Let her go. She's of no value. Besides, we'll find her again."

He lit a cigarette and thought about the profound spirituality of Beethoven's

Violin Concerto in D, part of the night's program. Do the Nazis even hear the music, or do they perform Beethoven simply because he's German? It must be because he's German: they couldn't possibly hear the concerto and condone and commit atrocities. He always wished he could play the concerto, but its demands were beyond him. Still, he yearned to hold a violin again, if only to play the simplest of scales. Back to reality. He looked at his watch. Ten more minutes, then back for something dreadful by Richard Strauss, composed to please his Nazi masters. Ten more minutes. Maybe he should move to a different location, since you can never tell where the Jew catchers might be lurking.

"Are you sure the information was correct?" Helga asked her Gestapo escort.

"The higher-ups were convinced. That's why they wanted Helga Kantor, the best Jew catcher in Berlin."

It wasn't an exaggeration. In the fourteen months since the Gestapo "turned her," Helga had sunk more "U-boats," the common name for Jews hiding underground, than anyone. In fact, the U-boats had taken to calling the boxcars that transported Jews to the concentration camps Helgas because she filled so many of them.

Usually she worked alone, signaling when she had sighted her prey, then leaving the messy details to others, although occasionally she had to block a door or a turnstile to keep a Jew from escaping. In return for her services, she received money, extra rations, a place to live, the ability to move about freely and, of course, her life. It seemed a fair exchange.

He made his way around to the side of the concert hall where more patrons were milling. Beneath his jacket, his shirt stuck to his body. He pulled the saturated cotton away, hoping a wisp of air might sweep up and cool him. It didn't.

"God, it's hot!" Helga Kantor tugged at her dress. "We should have gotten a cold drink."

"There was no time. You know the plan: out quickly and start watching."

"We could have spared the time for a cold—" She stopped short.

"What is it? Do you see someone?"

"I don't know. I thought so. A moment ago. Behind those people, over there." She nodded to a group near the side entrance. But I don't see anybody now. Maybe it was nothing. I'm not sure. You wait here. I'll check."

Helga! Helga Kantor! He knew her immediately. His informer said she would be here tonight and there she was. Less than a foot away, staring right at him, and yet, for all her repute, she obviously couldn't tell he was a Jew. It didn't matter. All that mattered was the plan.

He took two quick steps forward, thrust out his left hand, and he yanked her long auburn hair sharply, jerking her head back. Taking something metallic from his vest pocket, he pressed a sharp edge against the left side of her exposed throat.

For a moment he hesitated. This was a Jew. Despite what she had done, did he have the right to kill her? The question clouded his mind. He could feel her struggle, even if she couldn't feel his struggle. Did he have the right? A murderer could be killed. Under Jewish law, was she a murderer? She may not have physically committed murder, but she assisted. Without her, how many more would still be alive? And if she lived, how many more would die? Under German law—but there was no German law, anymore. What would a rabbi say? It didn't matter. There was no more time.

He pushed down hard on the metallic object and it ripped through her left jugular. There was a scream that quickly turned into a gurgle. He continued pulling the object under and around her chin until it tore through her right jugular, stopping just at her ear. Red droplets in an arc spewed wildly, drenching both of them. He had done what he set out to do and he had done it well. He dropped her and she fell limp to the street. Only then was he aware of the shouts from the crowd.

He had already decided that they wouldn't take him. He wasn't going to give them the satisfaction of a sham show trial. He removed a capsule from his pocket, put it in his mouth and bit down on it. He could taste the slight bitterness on his tongue. He swallowed and immediately knew they were right: the effects were almost instantaneous. Managing to muster breath enough for one last utterance, he forced it to be as loud as possible. He wanted his words to be heard.

"Free Germany!"

Gestapo agents were swarming all over. "Get up!" one commanded, but there was no response. "I said get up!" He gave a hard kick to the ribs for emphasis, but there was still no response. The agent knelt and felt for a pulse but found none. Frustrated, he rose and drew his Luger, firing three shots into the body. Then he knelt again, this time to pick up a small metallic object near a lifeless hand. It was an Iron Cross, First Class, Germany's highest honor, and one of its edges was coated with the blood of Helga Kantor. He turned the medal over and read the inscription: *For Heroic Valor* followed by a date: *August 27, 1917.* There was also a name:

Captain Wilhelm Strauss.

13

Paris: July 29, 1942
Your Stars Today: Hard as it may be, put your ego aside to
get the job done. Take practical considerations into account
and be especially aware of time. Stick to a specific task and
you'll make headway.

Peter didn't officially know he had been a prisoner until he had been re-leased.

Oh, he *knew*, of course, but during his stay at Wewelsburg he continued to act like the guest Himmler said he was. It wasn't hard. The accommodations were excellent, as were the food and drink, the service impeccable and the niceties, including several changes of clothes, abundant. There was even intellectual stimulation. Some of the archeologists discussed their research with him. As promised, he had full access to Himmler's extensive library, filled with historical and occult material. Even the ever-present SS soldiers were cordial. No, he never felt like a prisoner.

However, on his fourth day at the castle an SS officer woke Peter before dawn. "Please dress," he said. "You'll be leaving shortly."

"Leaving for where?" Peter asked, wondering in his still-half-asleep state if it was to an SS prison in Berlin and the torture Max had warned him about.

"A plane trip—"

Oh shit!

"To Paris. I understand you're to assist Fräulein Elise, who's filming our great success in France."

So there it was—liberation . . . and Max! God, he hadn't thought about her for, let's see—it must have been last night, right before he drifted off. And now they were taking him to see her. Oh yes, he understood. The mission. Strictly business. But maybe she'd be different. And even if not, well, it would still be good to see her.

The trip was short and silent. Peter was the only passenger in the small two-engine plane. They had given him a newspaper to read, but he had dozed off. The first time he had a chance to look at it was in the backseat of the SS staff car taking him from the airport to the Eiffel Tower, where Max and her crew were on location. Well, what's this? he thought as he scanned the latest events. Appears the Gestapo boys have been busy. Pretty grisly photo. Wonder what that's all about. Says that . . . that—

"Hey!" Peter shouted at the SS driver. "How far are we from the Tower?"

"Not far. You'll be there soon."

"How soon?"

The driver looked around. "Please, I'll get you there as fast as I can. We try not to speed down the streets here. It's a friendly gesture toward the French."

Knowing he was being escorted under Himmler's personal protection, Peter didn't accept the answer. "I don't give a good goddamn about the French! Get me to the Tower, now!"

The sudden acceleration pushed Peter back in his seat while a sharp turn sent him slamming into the right door. He latched on to the door handle as the car continued to accelerate, his heart pounding in sync with the clump of the tires, which were bouncing over rough Paris pavement and setting the beat for the wailing siren the driver had activated. Through the window, against a backdrop of buildings that appeared to be bobbing up and down, Peter could see a blur of people, some jumping back in fright from the street to the curb. Suddenly everything stopped moving—the people, the buildings and the car—as a loud screech drowned out the siren's wail and sent Peter's head into the back of the passenger's seat and his body sprawling on the car's rear floor.

"Fast enough for you now?"

But Peter, who could hear the smirk in the driver's voice, was preoccupied with finding the door handle again and pushing it up and open. Successful, he barely managed to tumble out on his hands and knees before the driver gunned the engine and, this time without urging, tore off, leaving tire marks and Peter on the street.

"Peter, over here!"

The familiar voice rose above the laughter of the SS Tower guards that greeted Peter's dramatic arrival.

"Otto, what the hell are you doing here?" Peter stood and dusted himself off.

"Himmler's people called ahead and let us know you were on your way. I've been waiting. You made an impressive entrance." Otto motioned at the guards to let Peter pass.

"I thought you were a bartender."

Otto smiled. "Like you, I'm many things. I often accompany Max on shoots, helping her keep track of schedules and handling various incidentals."

"Well, right now one of the incidentals is eager to speak to her. Where is she?"

"Up there."

Peter's eyes slowly swept the 108 stories from the beige base of the Eiffel Tower to the top. Somehow the height looked even more forbidding than when as a youngster he had visited Paris with Houdini. Peter had refused to go to the top then, despite the urgings of his mentor, who thought nothing of hanging upside down from the edge of a skyscraper while wiggling out of a straitjacket.

"We're all scared of something," Houdini finally said, letting the matter drop. "Just never let people know you're afraid or you'll lose the upper hand and the magic will be gone. And don't worry—if it's important enough, you'll face your fears."

Remembering that didn't make the tower seem any smaller. "Up there?" Peter said.

"She's doing a panorama shot," Otto explained. "The weather's good, so we've got about forty-five or fifty miles of clear sight today. Come on, I'll take you to her."

"Why don't you bring her to me instead?"

Otto chuckled. "You obviously haven't learned much about Max. She spent three straight days and nights camped out on the deck just waiting for the right morning light. If I dared suggest she come down she'd have my head. She can get angry when she's working."

She can get angry. Peter couldn't restrain himself. "Goddamn it, Otto, she hasn't seen anger yet!"

Peter sensed the change in Otto's mood even before his words confirmed it. "Maybe it's better I don't take you to see her. Not right now, anyway."

If it's important enough. "No, Otto, I think right now is the perfect time."

"Why not tell me what the matter is, Peter?"

"This is the matter!" Peter took the newspaper from his jacket pocket and thrust it into Otto's hand. Otto unfolded it and scanned the front page. Strewn across the top was a headline: "Vicious Jew Terrorist Wilhelm Strauss Meets His End!" Beneath it was a three-column picture of a blood-soaked body lying in the street surrounded by a group of men the caption described as *Brave Gestapo*. Otto handed the paper back to Peter.

"You didn't read the story."

"I didn't have to."

"That's what I thought. So everyone was in on this—you, her, that damn priest. Funny, I was actually starting to trust all of you. I guess I'm not as good at reading people as I thought."

"Look, why don't we talk a bit before—"

But Peter cut him short. "I'm tired of talking, especially when most of it's double-talking. Take me up to her now!"

"That's not the place for a discussion, Peter."

"There's no discussion, Otto. I just need to tell her something."

"And what's that?"

"Good-bye."

Peter wasn't happy about the prospect of taking an open elevator to the top of the Tower. He was considerably less happy when he found out the elevators weren't working.

"French saboteurs," Otto explained. "They cut the cables and screwed up the electrical system. Supposedly, because of the war, no one can get the necessary parts. Did it right before Hitler came over so he'd have to walk the steps to the top, but he refused."

"Smart man." Peter gazed up through the latticed iron frame, which seemed to soar forever. "About how many steps are there?"

"There's no 'about.' I've been up and down them so many times I can give you an exact count. One thousand, seven hundred and ten—three hundred and forty-seven to the first level, three hundred and twenty-seven more to the second level and one thousand and thirty-six more to the third. Not too bad as long as you're in halfway decent shape. Besides, it gives you the opportunity to pause whenever you want and enjoy the view. Because everything's so open, it's like you're floating in the air. Taking the elevator just isn't the same."

Otto paused and stared at Peter, who knew he was noticeably changing color.

"You're not afraid of heights, are you, Peter?"

"Of course not!" It was a quick response, brimming with false bravado. "I'm just not particularly partial to them."

"If you'd rather not . . ."

Peter shook his head weakly, but it was still a "no."

"Listen, here's all you have to do. Don't let the crisscrossed iron steps fool you. All that open space makes them look flimsy, but they're not. We've hauled heavy equipment up them just fine. If you start to feel uneasy, don't look down. The sight of the ground getting further and further away will make it worse. Just hold on tight and let one foot follow the other without thinking about it. Also, it'll get a little windy as you get higher, so expect that."

"Not flimsy. Don't look down. Wind. Got it."

"OK, if you're ready, follow me."

Otto bounded up the first nine or ten steps, then looked over his shoulder at Peter, who was right behind him. "See—nothing to it."

Peter made a noise somewhere between a throat clearing and a grunt, which was the best he could manage. But by then Otto had already climbed another eight steps, successfully challenging Peter to put aside any fears and keep up with him. The competition continued until they reached the first level, where both paused to catch their breath.

"Peter, come here!" Otto was at the edge of the platform, his forearms resting on a large red banner draped over the rail with black lettering that read: *Der Sieg für Deutschland Bedeutet Frieden für Paris*—"Victory for Germany Means Peace for Paris."

Peter eased his way over, trying not to look too tentative as he followed Otto's finger.

"See, there—that's the Seine. Those large green fields, those are the Trocadéro Gardens, a wonderful place to just sit and relax. Then the large building between them—see where the gardens end—that's the Palais de Chaillot. It was built about five years ago for some big exhibition. Really something grand, even from this far. And it's even more spectacular from the higher levels."

"I can hardly wait," Peter said, his earlier hesitation replaced by resignation.

"Then shall we?"

Otto moved like a compass point around the circular stairs, pointing at the different perspectives of Paris each turn offered. And while Peter was more concerned about the steps getting progressively smaller and jutting out nearer to the tower's edge, even he couldn't resist an occasional quick peek as he listened to Otto's continuous narrative.

They reached the tower's second platform in just under six minutes, about the same time it had taken them to climb to the first level. Although they were nearly four hundred feet above the ground, as Peter looked up toward their ultimate destination he realized they had only completed about 40 percent of the climb.

Otto looked at his watch. "Hey, we're making good time. We could set a record if you want."

But Peter demurred. "If we make it in one piece, that'll be accomplishment enough for me."

The final leg took more than twenty minutes. Otto, who this time refrained from calling attention to any "breathtaking" views, also slowed the pace, without offering what both knew was the obvious reason. In fact, Otto didn't speak at all until he and Peter were firmly planted on the third-level platform.

"Good for you," Otto said as Peter retreated to the part of the platform farthest from the edge. "You've conquered Mount Eiffel."

After composing himself, Peter looked around. He saw what he assumed were a few bored-looking film crew members and some scattered pieces of equipment but no Max. "Where is she?" he asked Otto.

Otto's eyes turned skyward. "Up there."

"Up there? Otto, there is no more up there! We *are* up there!" Peter wasn't amused.

"On the antenna deck," Otto said, holding his hand high above his head.

"I see a small deck, but I don't see any stairs."

"There." Otto nodded.

"Otto, that's a ladder, an unenclosed ladder! Nothing but rungs and space."

"Peter!"

The voice was unmistakable.

"Peter! Up here!" The sound led to Max's face. "Come up, Peter!"

"No, Max, come down!"

Max cupped her hand around her ear. "I can't hear you! The wind!"

She didn't have to tell him that. Along with a noticeable drop in temperature Peter could swear he felt the Tower sway. "Come down!"

Instead, Max waved him toward her.

"Look at it this way," said Otto. "You've come this far. And if you should fall, you'd probably land here instead of the ground."

Otto's words didn't give Peter much comfort. Still, would he want Max to think him a coward? Wait. Where did that come from? What the hell did he care what Max thought of him? He had something to tell her and then he'd probably never see her again. Otto was right: he had come this far and if it was the last thing he did—and it could well be—he was going to have this out with Max.

Peter looked at the ladder again, but he didn't see it. Instead, he saw a black-and-chrome steamer chest in the corner of Houdini's study, not plastered with foreign stickers like the others Houdini owned. Peter had never thought much about the chest until one day Houdini pulled it into the center of the room.

"Remember how frightened you were at the Eiffel Tower?" he asked Peter, who answered with an embarrassed nod. "Well, this is my Eiffel Tower." With that Houdini swung the trunk open, got inside and ordered it shut and locked.

Peter waited, expecting Houdini to emerge within a matter of minutes. But when nearly a half hour passed and no sounds came from the trunk, Peter began to worry. Finally, after another ten minutes or so, his worry turned to desperation and he did the unthinkable—he unlocked the chest and swung the top open. There he saw Houdini, alive but sweating profusely.

"Why did you open it?" Slowly Houdini lifted himself out, and Peter could see his entire body was drenched.

"I was getting really concerned." Peter prepared himself for a severe tongue-lashing.

But Houdini merely asked, "How much time has elapsed?"

"Forty-five, maybe fifty minutes."

"I'm usually in there for an hour." Houdini closed the lid. "It's my special chest," he said, sliding it back out of the way.

"Because you can't get out of it?"

"Oh, I can get out of it. It's special because I won't get out of it."

Peter didn't pretend to understand.

"I'm going to share something few people know. I'm terrified of enclosed spaces. They call it claustrophobia. I call it my worst nightmare. Pretty funny for someone who spends so much time in cells and crates, isn't it?"

Now Peter *really* didn't understand.

"I've taught myself to face my fears," Houdini continued. "And I work at it all the time. That's what you've got to do. Train yourself never to be scared, even when you are. If you panic, it's over."

"Did you ever panic?"

"A few times," Houdini said with a smile that quickly changed to a frown. "Once, in California, when I was bound and buried alive. I had no problem getting out of the handcuffs and leg restraints. But then something happened. I don't know—maybe it was realizing I was literally six feet under, just like a corpse. That's when I panicked. I started gasping, using up precious breath, and clawing and ripping at the dirt, which felt like an iron lid on top of me. Each time I managed to open a pathway, it would fill right back in. I felt so sure I was going to die I even screamed for help, something I had never done when performing an escape. Even now, I can't tell you how I managed to break through to the surface. But I can tell you I've never been that frightened in my life. Not from being buried, but from giving in to my fears and losing control of the situation. I have never let that happen again. And neither can you. Whenever you're performing a dangerous stunt, you can never let yourself be afraid, even when you are. And that takes constant training. You may never lose your fear of heights, but you have to seize every opportunity to confront it, hard as that may be. Most people won't confront their fears and that's why you'll have an advantage over them. Show confidence, whether you feel it or not, and you immediately get the upper hand. Show fear and you're dead."

"Well, Peter, are you coming up?" Max's voice broke through Houdini's words—*show confidence, whether you feel it or not*—still echoing in his head. "Of course I'm coming up."

So, with a deep breath and a "damn," Peter clutched a ladder rung and began to climb.

In Peter's mind, it took longer to scale twenty feet than it had taken to climb ninety stories. Part of the problem was trying to pry his hands from a rung each time he had to reach for a higher one, part was not knowing whether he should look up or straight ahead, since down was definitely not an option. Finally he pulled himself onto the open deck that was the base for the radio antenna. Only a knee-high perimeter rail stood between him and the streets of Paris. He crawled a few feet, then unsteadily maneuvered into a sitting position. His eyes were the only part of his body he felt comfortable moving. As they swept the deck, they gathered images of Max flanked by motion picture cameras and tripods.

"Isn't it beautiful?" Max walked beyond Peter to the edge of the deck. "The view is spectacular."

"I'll take your word for it."

"You're missing one of the most magnificent sights in the world."

Actually Peter thought his view was pretty good. Radiant, free-flowing Max, in her characteristic work garb, floppy trousers, a blouse and a baggy sweater: she wore frump like a Paris gown. But he wasn't about to be distracted. "I'm not here to sightsee, Max."

"No, of course not." She turned, came over and sat down beside him. "We have work to do. But let it go for a few moments. This is Paris."

Peter looked around. Next to the radio antenna was a large Nazi flag, which could be seen for miles from the ground. "This isn't Paris. This is Berlin with better wine."

"This is still Paris. Even Hitler can't crush its spirit."

"In case you haven't noticed, Max, those are German troops in the streets, not French."

"The real French troops are underground, part of a resistance movement that's been fiercely battling the Germans. It's also been helping us smuggle Jews out of Europe."

Out of Europe. That was the opening Peter needed to have it out with Max, get down from this damn tower and get far away from this mess. "Can they smuggle me back to America?"

"When the time comes."

"The time may have come."

"What prompted this?" Max answered too quickly.

"Here, read all about it." Peter drew the newspaper out of his pocket only to have a gust of wind catch it and send it sailing. Max jumped up to retrieve it, dashing precariously close to the edge. Without thinking, Peter bounded up and rushed toward Max, grabbing her arm and jerking her back. Only then did he remember where he was. Max watched as the newspaper wafted over Paris while Peter, in a cold sweat, released her arm and retreated to the center of the deck.

"What did you think you were doing?" Max yelled.

"Trying to keep you from killing yourself." Peter sat down again, which made him feel slightly more secure.

"Keep *me*?" Max broke out laughing as she joined him. "Peter, I ski the Alps. I climb mountains. I'm not afraid of heights, but they obviously petrify you." Peter's face, still sheet white, answered for him.

"That was very brave of you. Stupid, but very brave." Max threaded her arm through Peter's, but he pulled away.

"So, you try to save my life, but you want nothing to do with me. Just what did you want me to see in that newspaper?"

"An account of a Gestapo street shooting in Berlin."

"Which happens regularly."

"The victim's name was Wilhelm Strauss."

"Go on." Max was suddenly less animated than she had been.

"The authorities said that Strauss was a—let me get the words right—a 'Jew Terrorist' who had sabotaged a museum show on German prehistory."

"Good for him."

"Apparently not good for him. Did you know Wilhelm Strauss, Max?"

Max said nothing.

"Himmler made an interesting comment after the shooting. He said, 'The blood has been avenged.' Recognize that, Max?"

"Peter—"

"The newspaper credited the Gestapo's extensive investigative work for bringing Strauss to justice. But maybe that wasn't the case. Maybe the Gestapo had some secret information. Secret coded information from Himmler himself, courtesy of me."

"Peter, please—"

"The hell with 'please,' Max! You set me up better than I set Himmler up. You set me up to send a man to his death. Was this another of those unimportant little details that wasn't necessary to share with me?"

"There's more to it. But can't we discuss this later, back on the ground? We could have some dinner and—"

"You still don't get it. There's not going to be any later. I've had it. I'm finished. And don't hand me any honor-and-duty crap. What you made me do wasn't part of the deal."

This time Max was determined to be heard. "Oh yes, it was very much a part of the deal. And Wilhelm Strauss was a part of the deal as well. A big part, right from the start. When we determined that we would have to do something dramatic to prove that Peter Kepler was legitimate, something that would be meaningful to Himmler, Wilhelm Strauss came up with the idea."

"You still set me—"

"Let me finish, Peter. This was all planned well before you entered the picture. Your predecessor was going to feed Himmler the information. No matter what, the German-heritage show would have been blown up and Wilhelm Strauss would have been caught."

"And shot? The newspaper showed his body covered in blood from Gestapo bullets."

"Lying bastards."

"Who?"

"The Gestapo. They didn't kill Wilhelm Strauss. They shot him after he was dead. Better press propaganda if it looks like they killed him."

"How do you know that?" Peter asked, then quickly added, "Oh, I forgot."

"That I'm Gestapo? You're right. I know how it operates and I know how Goebbels operates."

"Then what happened to Strauss?"

"He took cyanide."

"Strauss committed suicide?"

"That was also part of the plan. The Gestapo wanted him alive so there could be a show trial and a public execution. That wasn't going to happen."

Max stopped momentarily, as if allowing Peter time to absorb what she said, then resumed. "Would it help if I told you that Strauss volunteered for this because the Nazis killed his wife and son?"

"It wouldn't excuse things, but it might make them a little more understandable."

"Well, they didn't. Wilhelm Strauss wasn't married. He didn't die for vengeance. That would be easy. Instead he died for something he believed in."

Peter, who had been staring intently at Max, looked away.

"Can't you accept that? In war, people undertake missions knowing they'll never return. Isn't that what you're doing?"

"I'm returning!"

"Maybe. But Wilhelm Strauss knew *he* wasn't and it didn't bother him. He was a martyr for Germany—a Jewish martyr. That's why the Gestapo had to discredit him. Jews aren't supposed to be capable of heroic acts like martyrdom."

Peter turned around so he was again facing Max. "Martyrdom isn't heroic. It's stupid. Damn it, you still should have told me."

"I was afraid you might balk. Would you?"

"I don't know."

"Well, I couldn't take the chance. I talked it over with Wilhelm and he agreed. I'm sorry, but it was important, especially to him."

"I thought we were done with secrets."

"Never again, no matter what." Max her hand on his arm. "I promise."

"You promise." Peter jerked free of her touch. " Should I believe you?"

"I hope you do."

There she was again, the vulnerable Max he had encountered briefly after reading her palm. But experience told him the old Max usually came right back. It was time to test her. "Who gave you the code?"

"What?"

"The code I passed to Himmler that allowed his henchmen to find Strauss. Who gave it to you?"

Max waited before answering, and when she did her voice barely rose above a whisper. "Father Fritz."

"Father Fritz?" That was unexpected. "And where did he get it?"

"Peter, I swear to you I don't know, any more than I knew what it meant. Wait, I knew what it meant. It gave the time, date and location of where Wilhelm would be. But I don't know *how* it meant that. Father Fritz said it had something to do with the early days of the Nazi Party and that only a few of the highest officials would be able to decipher it. He wouldn't say where he got it and I didn't press the issue."

"He wouldn't say and you didn't press? Jesus Christ, Max, how would a Catholic priest be privy to information that only a few top Nazis would understand?"

Max turned defensive. "A lot of Catholic clergy backed Hitler early on. People called them *Braune Pfarrer*—Brown Priests. Some, like Father Fritz, even joined the Nazi Party. And like most clergymen, Catholic or Protestant, Father Fritz still keeps on the Party's good side. Only in his case it's so he can do his other work without suspicion."

"You didn't answer my question. Besides, I'm not talking about an ordinary Nazi Party member. I'm taking about somebody who was high enough to know its deepest secrets. Put that together for me."

Max turned away and stared at the sky, which had lost its misty early-morning veil and was now radiant in its darker and purer blue.

"I'm waiting."

"It's the past, Peter," she said, still not facing him. "It's not important. What's important is—"

"It's not important? Goddamn it, Max, it's vital!" Peter bolted up. He realized his temper was soaring with each word, but he didn't care. "You know next to nothing about this man, yet you give him every benefit of the doubt."

Now Max stood, her eyes ablaze. "From the start you've repeatedly let everyone know how much you hate religion, especially Catholicism. Well, that's your problem, Peter. Deal with it and stop using Father Fritz as an excuse to get out of something you never wanted to be involved with."

"What I'm dealing with is someone who blocks out anything she doesn't want to face. Who's to say that your saintly Father Fritz isn't one of the monsters he condemns?"

"Father Fritz never denied his Nazi past. He hasn't spent his life pretending to be someone he's not. Just because you're a fraud doesn't mean everyone is."

Peter had been called a fraud many times and it never bothered him. But for some reason, coming from Max, it stung. "Is that what you really think of me?"

"Isn't that what you are?"

"I guess you could say that, which is why I can spot a fellow fraud."

"Well, you're wrong about Father Fritz." Max had taken her tone down a few notches.

"No, I'm certain about him."

"And what's that supposed to mean?" Max asked.

"It means I should get out of here."

"You're giving up the mission?" Max was back to shouting.

"Not the mission, damn it! This place! Here! You!" Peter took four long strides, which brought him near the edge of the platform, knelt down and took hold of the ladder. "Suddenly I'm more bothered by the atmosphere than the height." Ire sparked Peter's false bravado, but he was determined not to show his fear as he backed his feet down onto the third rung from the ladder's top.

"Peter!"

But he had vanished, leaving only the fading sound of his voice: "Either I'm in on the decision making or I'm gone. Make the right choice and Otto will know how to find me. Make the wrong choice and no one, including your goddamn Gestapo buddies, will ever know how to find me."

14

Paris: July 30, 1942
Your Stars Today: Powerful and persuasive words are spoken now. Agendas are announced and there may be news about intelligence-gathering operations and other secret matters.

Compared with the six art-deco passenger elevators with their gold doors and wood-paneled interiors operated by attendants in crisp blue-and-white uniforms, the two self-service freight elevators in the Hôtel des Artistes, well hidden from the guests, were as dilapidated as their richer cousins were decadent. One of them was reserved for the maids and bellboys who served the hotel's occupants. The other was used solely for routine maintenance work—usually transporting furniture into and out of the sub-basement and hauling repairmen and their equipment up and down the hotel's eighteen floors.

Most of the more demanding upkeep was done during the day when guests were out. But at times it lasted into the late-evening and early-morning hours. So it wouldn't have been strange for two men—one burly, one slight—to be walking down the hotel's fifteenth-floor corridor just past midnight, each with an end of a ten-foot-long rolled carpet resting on his shoulder. When the men reached the maintenance service elevator, they angled the rug into the car and steadied it against one of the padded walls.

"We're good, Philippe," the burly worker said, and his companion pushed and held a button until two dented metal doors, each with a small wire-mesh window, pulled out of their side sleeves and slammed shut. He pushed and held another button, which sent the car jerking slowly downward.

"Do you see anything yet, Philippe?"

"Quiet, André." Philippe pressed his face against one of the door windows. "Don't distract me."

The two remained silent as the car made it way past the shaft doors for the different floors: twelve, eleven, ten. When the number 9 appeared and vanished in the window, Philippe pulled his finger from the button and the car jolted to a stop. "Now. Quickly, André."

André reached up and pushed against a three-foot-square metal trap embedded in the elevator-car ceiling, raising it up and moving it to the side. "Done."

"Good." Philippe knelt on the car's floor and formed a stirrup with his hands. "Careful."

"Don't worry." André placed his right foot in Philippe's palms, stuck his hands through the open trap and, using the roof for support, lifted himself out of the car. "Next."

Philippe rose and rotated the carpet. When one end was under the trap, André reached down and grabbed the rope wrapped around it. "Got it."

Philippe, on his knees again, put his hands under the other end of the carpet and, with a grunt, boosted it up a few inches. Still balancing it in his hands, Philippe started to stand as André kept pulling.

"It's fine right there," André said. "I can handle it." Philippe watched the carpet disappear through the trap. "Now you. Put your hands up." Reaching down again, André grabbed Philippe's wrists and pulled him through the hatch, depositing him on the car roof next to the rug. "Perfect."

Philippe flicked on a flashlight, put it down and slid the trap cover back into place. "The screws?"

André handed a bunch of two-inch-long screws to Philippe, who inserted them into the holes along the perimeter of the hatch and tightened them with a penknife. In the meantime, André pushed against the brick wall of the shaft.

"Find it?" Philippe asked.

"Not yet, But I think . . . Wait. Ahhhh." André turned and showed Philippe his prize: a dirty, yellowish brick. "Jackpot! Now stand there while I hand you the bricks."

Within minutes, Philippe had lined up thirty bricks in a pile. "Any more?"

"No. The rest are anchored."

"Can you make it OK?"

"We'll see." Hunched over, André stepped from the roof of the elevator car and over a foot-high lip of bricks, first one leg, then the other. "No problem. Roll the rug a little and careful not to hit the bricks."

"They're well out of the way." Philippe did as André asked.

"That's good." André reached over, again grabbing the rug by one of its ropes, and tugged it through the opening in the wall. "Now the bricks."

One by one, Philippe passed the thirty bricks through the opening to André, then took the flashlight and made his way across the lip.

"What's the time?" André asked as he began putting the bricks back in place.

Philippe looked at his watch. "Twelve twenty-six—ten minutes ahead of schedule."

"Excellent." André sealed the hole and lifted one end of the rug onto his shoulder. "Shall we?"

Philippe lifted the other end of the rug. "How does it look?"

André held up the flashlight. "Straight, maybe ten meters, then an incline. At that point, we should start to smell the sewers."

"Paris perfume. And tonight, nothing is sweeter."

At 12:30 A.M. a busboy at the Hôtel des Artistes headed down the stairs to the darkened sub-basement and edged his way along the wall until he felt the indentation for the first service elevator and then, a few feet farther along, for the second. He rubbed his hand against the metal frame stopping when he reached a single button, which he pushed hard. Then he waited. When he heard the sound of cables whirling as the elevator car headed down he quietly retraced his steps and at 12:35 A.M. began clearing his last dinner table.

He was smiling and, under his breath, he was singing, *"Allons enfants de la Patrie, le jour de gloire est arrivé!"*

General Carl Oberg, chief of SS and German police forces in France, stood facing the window, his back to the two men frozen in place by his desk, and stared out at the deadened dark of a blacked-out Paris

It was 1:15 A.M. when Oberg summoned the Paris-based heads of Germany's two espionage organizations—SS *Sturmbannführer* Karl Boemelburg of the civilian Gestapo and Colonel Friedrich Rudolf of the military Abwehr—to his office at 57 Boulevard Lannes, one of the more fashionable addresses in the wealthy Sixteenth Arrondissement. The time, and the fact that the two officials had no use for each other, gave them notice of the seriousness of the situation at hand. Oberg's studied indifference to them was his way of showing just how furious he was. When he did finally turn toward them, his frown seemed to extend from his plump face all the way across his bald head.

As if on cue, both men nervously shuffled their feet, obviously expecting the worst from the man Hitler handpicked and sent to France a few months earlier to wipe out resistance efforts that had flourished under the lax policies of Military Commander SS general Otto von Stülpnagel. By contrast, Oberg's actions, including mass killings, were so swift and severe that the French quickly dubbed him "the Butcher of Paris," a title he wore as proudly as the gaudy SS decorations on the tan tunic draped over his flabby chest and corpulent belly. The military commander might govern in France, but there was no doubt that Oberg, his subordinate, ruled.

"Sit!" Oberg barked, and as the two fell into chairs he reached for a piece of paper on his desk. "I want you to hear something." He proceeded to read aloud from the paper, his tone shifting from stern to angry as he did. "Mademoiselle Maxine Elise is now in the hands of the patriotic French who will drive the German occupiers from their land."

Oberg paused to gauge their reaction, which was a subtle mixture of astonishment, disbelief and fearful dismay. These two idiots really don't know what's going on, he thought as he continued. "For her safe return, the following must be released from German detention within the next forty-eight hours: Avril LaCroix, Cesar Perinne, Gervais Lefebvre, Emile Dubois, Gascon Fournier, Colette Braud, Genevieve Roux, Auguste Gaudet, Girard Bertrand, Luc Leveque. Unless these people are transferred to Geneva and placed in the custody of the Free French Embassy there by the deadline set, Mademoiselle Elise will be killed. This demand will not be negotiated. *Vive la France!*"

"So there you are." Oberg turned again to the window. "Snatched from her hotel room under the very noses of your people. From her own hotel room and smuggled out into the night." He whirled around suddenly. "How could Fräulein Elise be snatched from her own hotel room? Snatched from the Hôtel des Rêves! From the goddamn Hôtel des Rêves! Goering stays at the Hôtel des Rêves when he's in Paris and yet they can snatch and smuggle her out! How do you explain that?"

"Do we know which of the resistance groups took her?" Boemelburg asked.

"Do we know? Do we know?" An enraged Oberg crushed the letter and rolled it into a ball, which he heaved over his desk at Boemelburg. Oberg started to reach for the inkwell but thought better of it. "No, we don't know because the Gestapo and the Abwehr, with all their wonderful informants inside the resistance, haven't told us yet. Nor have they told us where she is. So right now the only thing we do know is that we are to set free some of the most dangerous resistance leaders and undo all our hard work in capturing them. Three of these prisoners are in camps in Germany. One has already been executed, although that has not leaked out yet. Wait, we also know one more thing. If we don't comply with this ridiculous ultimatum we will have the pleasure of informing the *Führer* and Himmler and Goebbels that one of their favorites has been murdered because of the incompetence of your agencies." Finished, Oberg finally sat and waited. This time it was Rudolf who spoke.

"Herr General. I appreciate the gravity of this situation. But you understand that the Abwehr is not under your authority."

"When it comes to the organization chart, you are absolutely right." For the first time, Oberg sounded calm. He even managed a slight smile, which he immediately contorted into a snarl to suit his ensuing shout. "Do I look like a goddamn organization chart to you? Do I? This is Paris, not Berlin. You answer to me when I say you do." With a violent sweep of his arm Oberg shot the telephone to the edge of the desk, where it just missed dropping in Rudolf's lap. "Would you like to waste time by calling the Commander to verify that? I'm sure he'll appreciate being awakened in the middle of the night just to confirm what I've said. Well, Colonel Rudolf, what is your pleasure?"

"I await your orders, *General*."

"Good. Then I ask again, how did this happen?"

They didn't answer, nor did he expect them to. Their uneasy silence was exactly the response he wanted. They knew he meant business.

"Let me tell you how. As usual, your two organizations were spending more time spying on each other than on our enemies, fighting over who should handle this and who should get credit for that. So which one wants the credit for Maxine Elise being held captive? It's the same foolishness that goes on between the Gestapo and the Abwehr in Berlin. Well, let me repeat: this is not Berlin. I will not hear excuses, nor will I tolerate any more squabbling. You will find Maxine Elise immediately or I promise you'll suffer a worse fate than hers. Do I make myself clear?"

And while still silent, this time the two men nodded their heads.

"In three days Fräulein Elise is to receive a special award at the Paris opening of *Teuton*." He peered over the top of his glasses as if addressing delinquent schoolboys. "She will appear or you both will disappear. In the meantime, there is to be no official word of this incident. Is that also clear?"

There was no response.

Oberg pounded his fist on the desk, sending a stack of books crashing to the floor. "Is that clear?"

"*Jawohl, General*," the two replied in spontaneous unison.

"Then get out of my sight and don't return without Maxine Elise and her abductors."

Boemelburg and Rudolf shot up to attention and gave the Hitler salute, which Oberg reluctantly returned. "Forty-eight hours or the next time I salute you, you will be in your caskets."

Otto's 3:30 A.M. pounding brought a half-asleep Peter to his hotel room door. The news of Max's abduction jolted him awake "The authorities only know that one of the French resistance groups took Max in an attempt to force an unacceptable prisoner swap."

"Will they find her?" Peter asked after Otto detailed the massive search operation now underway.

"I doubt in time, if at all." He explained about the forty-eight-hour deadline, adding that he was convinced Max's captors would really kill her if their demands weren't met.

"Can we find her?"

"Perhaps," Otto said, which told Peter that he was already working on something. "But finding and freeing are two different things."

"Then we'll split them up. You handle the first and I'll handle the second."

At 9:35 A.M., Otto returned to Peter's hotel room.

"Do you know where she is?" Peter asked.

"No. But someone else may. Come."

Peter said nothing during their brisk five-block walk that ended on Rue des Artistes, in front of a small, shabby bookshop with a faded sign that read: Boulant et Fils.

"It's been around since the Revolution and the same family still owns it," Otto said. "Proust was a regular. So was Balzac. And Joyce, too, when he was working on *Ulysses*."

Peter brushed away Otto's historical asides. "And these booksellers know where Max is?"

"Wait." Otto opened the door to the shop, ushered Peter in. "Monsieur Boulant," he softly called out.

A rotund, baldheaded man sporting a thick, drooping white moustache, who struck Peter as some kind of superannuated walrus, looked up from a newspaper crammed between two stacks of volumes on a cluttered counter. "And how are you this morning?"

"Old. Old with a lazy son who will never learn this business." Boulant glanced at Peter. "He looks bright enough. Does he want a job?"

"I'm afraid he has a none-too-pleasant one already, Monsieur Boulant. Has your guest arrived?"

"Go downstairs. Sit. Wait. You young people are too impatient."

"*Merci*, Monsieur Boulant." Otto tapped Peter's arm and led him down a narrow circular staircase to a musty, shelf-filled room carpeted with books, save for a few small gaps that revealed spots of floor. Like a seasoned path-finder, Otto blazed the way through the thicket, stepping over and on scattered volumes until he and Peter reached a clearing of sorts with a table and a few chairs.

"Upstairs is organized." Otto sat down and prompted Peter to do the same. "But down here is reserved for the adventurous, a place to mine for gold."

"I'm interested in this so-called guest, not gold," Peter said. "When is he coming?"

"He's here."

It wasn't Otto speaking. Peter looked around and saw no one.

"Otto, my old friend, it is good to see you." A figure casually attired in a short-sleeve shirt and slacks emerged from a dark aisle of shelving and embraced Otto. As he did, Peter took stock of him: late thirties, average height, slender with a plain but pleasant clean-shaven oval face. Nothing exceptional, but then it was his information, not his looks, that was important.

"Peter, allow me to introduce Gilbert Renault, better known as Colonel Rémy, perhaps the most eagerly sought resistance leader."

Peter started to rise, but Rémy thrust his hand downward, telling him to stay put. "I understand that you are a critical part of the special project Otto and Max are working on."

"You know about that, Colonel?"

He sat down next to Peter. "Please. Rémy. Or Gilbert, if you wish. I answer to a lot of names."

"I know how that is," Peter said.

"Anyway, to answer your question. Yes, I am among a very select few who are also part of that project. When Hitler is disposed of, France and other occupied countries must take immediate action. Still, there are more fingers in this room than there are people outside Germany who know what is going on."

"Nothing is going on if we don't get Max back," Otto said.

"This is a serious problem," Rémy said. "Perhaps an impossible one."

"Why?" Peter asked. "Otto just said that you're one of the resistance leaders. Have her released."

"Easy to do if the resistance was unified. But it is not. There are many groups, many interests: nationalists, communists, socialists—even monarchists. Some believe in negotiation, some in violence and some in both, depending on the moment."

"But all of them look up to Colonel Rémy," Otto said.

"Look up to, perhaps. Sometimes even listen to. But act is a different story. Besides, it is more complicated. I cannot help Max without revealing her anti-Nazi involvement, and that information would quickly find its way to the Gestapo's infiltrators."

"Can't you find some other means?" Peter asked.

"I have tried. Through intermediaries I have warned them not to harm such a famous person, since retaliation would surely be swift and brutal, causing many innocent people to suffer. But Max was abducted by a faction of the Francs-Tireurs Partisans, which is the largest of our groups. They are communists, so completely committed to violence against the Nazis that they disregard anything else. And the more prominent the victims the better."

"If there's no maneuvering room, I'll have to free her myself," Peter said.

"That is foolishness," Rémy said, then tightened his lips and put his hand on his chin. "Foolishness. Yet something must be done, so I will not waste time trying to reason with you. I just hope you realize the dangers involved."

"Enough to wish you *could* reason with me. Do you have any other information?"

"I have heard there are at least two men guarding her. I do not know who they are, but they have to be very high-level and very skilled to have this responsibility. Keep in mind, to us these men are French citizens who love their country, not criminals. I am Max's friend and I know what she is doing. Were it otherwise, I would quietly rejoice that a jewel of the Reich— one of Hitler's favorites—has been snatched right out from under him. In any event, these men are extremely dangerous, so they will probably kill you before you can kill them. And even if you did manage to kill them, as I have said, their deaths would be a loss."

"I don't intend to kill anyone."

"You don't intend?" Rémy burst out laughing. "You don't intend! You are an army then. At least you go into this with a sense of humor."

"No, but I still promise you I'll try not to kill them."

Rémy just shook his head, "Whatever you say, *mon ami,* whatever you say."

"So where they're keeping her?"

"They have moved her again. I received this just before coming here." Rémy handed Peter a slip of paper with a bunch of numbers scribbled on it.

"Eight–twenty-four–twenty-four–sixteen–sixteen–eighteen–twenty- one–two–eleven–twenty-five–six–two–twenty-six." A bewildered Peter read off the numbers, an uncomfortable reminder of the code he fed to Himmler. "You understand this?"

"So will you." Rémy took a small pad and a pencil from his pocket.

Opening the pad, he wrote the word "Teuton" across one of the pages. Then, down the left side of the page, he wrote the twenty-six letters of the alphabet in order, from *a* to *z*. Finally he drew lines first down the page, separating each letter in "Teuton," then across the page, separating each letter of the alphabet.

"Now we are ready," he said, showing Peter the grid. "A very simple system, but impossible to break without knowing the key word, which always changes. This time, given the mission and the person, it is 'Teuton.' Now we fill in the grid. We start with the *t* in 'Teuton' and go down the first column until we find the matching *t*. In that box we put the number 'one.' Once we have that we continue putting the numbers in order in each of the successive boxes of the column. So 'two' goes in the *u* box, 'three' in the *v* box and so on. At the end of the column, we go back up to the top and continue. So in the *a* box we put the number 'eight' like this and continue until we put the number 'twenty-six' in the *s* box. Now that column is complete and we move over to the next one—the *e* column. We find where the two *e*'s intersect, put the number 'one' there and go through the same process. Then on to the third, fourth, fifth and sixth column."

Rémy's hand flew across the grid until all the boxes were filled. "And now we can decipher the message. What is the first number on the paper I gave you?"

"Eight," Peter said.

"That's the first letter of the message, so we start in the first column and look for the number eight." Rémy scanned the paper. "Here. It is in the *a* box, so the first letter of the message is *a*. And the second number?"

"Twenty-four."

"Second number, second column. Twenty-four is in the *b* box, so that is our second letter. Next."

Peter kept reading off the numbers and Rémy kept jotting down the letters. When they reached "twenty-one"—the seventh number—they went back to the first column and again proceeded in order from there until they had matched a letter to each of the thirteen numbers.

"So here it is—a-b-r-i-d-e-n-f-e-r-t-o-s."

Peter watched Rémy blanch. "What's the matter?"

Without answering, Rémy plucked the paper with the numbers from Peter's hand and stared at it, then at the grid, his eyes moving up, down and across like digits on a mechanical calculator. Finally he threw the paper on the table and Peter retrieved it.

"Denfert shelter bone? They're keeping Max in some kind of shelter on Rue Denfert?"

"Not on. Under. They are smart. It is the perfect way to hide her. It also explains how they got her out of the hotel."

"Hey, remember me?" Peter had no idea what Rémy was going on about.

Rémy rose and disappeared within the book stacks, only to re-emerge a few minutes later with a slim green volume, which he threw on the desk, dislodging a cloud of dust from its cover. "Have you read *The Phantom of the Opera*?" he asked as he sat.

"And also saw the Lon Chaney movie."

"Then you know about the Catacombs."

"The underground caverns where the Phantom kept the singer captive?"

"More than that. Much more." Rémy opened the book and thumbed through it until he found a map that spread across two pages. "Look." Peter arched his neck so he could see the entire map. "Not just caverns, but tunnels and quarries—over three hundred kilometers of them, like a city under the city. Hundreds of years ago they tossed bodies down there. Tens of thousands of bodies that are now just bones."

As Rémy took a breath, Peter cut in. "That explains 'bone.'"

"In part. Four years ago, a defense shelter was built under Rue Denfert to protect the technical people who work nearby managing Paris's water and sewer system. It is quite elaborate—like a subterranean hotel, with showers, lavatories and private rooms."

"So that's where Max is?"

"Not in the shelter itself. It would be too dangerous. The shelter is only a marker, as is the word 'bone.' She is in an area somewhere between the shelter and the ossuary, the place where millions of bones are stacked in neat piles."

"Will they move her again?" Peter asked.

"This location is safe and secure. No, I think they will remain there. It is far enough away from where the Germans have settled in. And if they need—"

"Wait. The Germans are down there?"

"They have a shelter as well, also very elaborate I understand. Here." Rémy pointed to a location on the map.

"Do they know about the Denfert shelter?"

"Perhaps. But they do not bother mucking around in the Catacombs. There is a type of agreement—unwritten, unspoken, just followed. We leave them alone, they leave us alone. Now, for your entry point. Here, see. The tunnels correspond to the streets. Not perfectly, but close enough. However, this map is nearly thirty years old. Things change underground. Cave-ins, some caused by construction, some by the earth shifting. What I am saying is that a route may not necessarily be clear. An obstruction can force you off course. That is just another reason why it can be so dangerous even for those who know the Catacombs well, let alone a novice."

"We have no choice," Peter reminded him.

"Which is why I'm helping you. They will kill her. So you have to be prepared. Here." Rémy moved his forefinger over the map. "In certain places, there are parallel paths. The problem is they are not completely parallel. Like this one." Rémy pressed his finger down and started to trace. "Notice it goes along fine until . . ." He tapped his finger twice. "Poof, it is gone. Now there used to be a small opening in the wall that would lead all the way over to here." This time Rémy moved his finger a few inches to the right. "It may still be there, but even so, it may not be clear all the way. You could crawl halfway through, then nothing, and you are not able to get back out. You understand?"

"Unfortunately."

"Hope for the best, assume the worst and take things as you find them."

Rémy had just summarized Peter's life.

"Here, take this and study it." Rémy slid the book to Peter.

"Are there other maps in it?"

"No, just the one, but as I said, it is the best we have."

Peter slid the book back. "Then I already have everything I need."

"Do not be stupid!" Rémy snapped. "Rip out the map and keep it. Max's life is at stake."

Peter picked up the pad and pencil and scribbled furiously for about thirty seconds, then handed the result to Rémy. "The basics of the map. If you'd like, I can give you every detail."

Rémy took a long breath and exhaled. "Otto said you were an unusual man."

"He was too kind to say 'lunatic.'"

"Lunatic." Rémy put his index finger to his temple and twisted it. "Lunatic. Not just you. Me, Max. All lunatics. Otto. The members of the resistance, here, in Germany, in Poland. All of us—lunatics. The Nazis are sane ones, the logical ones. That is how they see themselves—the rational future of mankind. Yes, lunatics. The whole lot of us. And maybe that is just what the world needs right now if it is to survive—a bunch of lunatics."

The rest of Peter's morning was busy and productive. For two hours he roamed Le Bois de Boulogne, the sprawling forest in the east of Paris, stuffing plants into a burlap bag. Then he caught the Metro, which brought him back to Rue des Artistes and Boulant et Fils.

"Back so soon." Monsieur Boulant was still hunched over his newspaper. "And with a bag of goodies as well."

"Fresh greens. I was looking for a book on preparing them."

"Yes. It is important to prepare greens properly. But I have something better than a book." Monsieur Boulant fumbled around the debris piled on the counter. "Yes, here." He handed Peter a scrap of brown wrapping paper. "I knew I had jotted it down somewhere. An excellent recipe for greens. Take it."

Peter glanced at the paper. It was the address of a vacant apartment Rémy had secured. "I hope it turns out well," Boulant said.

"I guarantee, Monsieur Boulant, it will truly be a dish to die for."

The apartment—a kitchen, a common area and a tiny bedroom—was on the top floor of a four-story building near Rue du Château-des-Rentiers, the main street of Paris's most notorious slum.

"Everyone minds their own business around here," Otto, who had already arrived, assured Peter. "It's the best way to stay alive."

"Is there electricity and gas?" Peter asked.

"I told Rémy you needed that, so his people rearranged some wires and piping. By the time it's discovered, you'll be gone."

"Running water?"

"See." Otto went over to the sink and turned a knob, releasing a spurt of rusty liquid from the faucet. "Another bit of rigging. There's a bathroom down one floor, but hold your nose."

"Where did this come from?" Peter pointed to a cracked wooden table and two semi-stable wooden dining chairs.

Otto shrugged his shoulders. "Left here, I guess. Also, a foul-looking mattress on the floor in the other room, bedbugs included, in case you get tired."

"I won't have time to get tired. And the other stuff?"

Otto slid a wooden crate over from against a wall, stuck his hand in and pulled out a smaller sack, which he emptied on the table. "Scalpel, surgical mask and gloves, a mortar and pestle, tweezers, a tin of matches and a cheap watch." He reached in again and retrieved two more items. "Max's portable hair dryer and a baking pan." He placed them on the table as well, along with two packs of Lucky Strikes, which he had in his pant pocket. "Top brand, real tobacco," he said. "And, oh yes. . . ." He fished in the crate once more. "Another large burlap bag."

"The clothes?"

"Ragged and putrid, scented with sewer. They're on the mattress, which is bound to make them even more rank."

Peter shook his head. "How do you do it, Otto?"

"We each have our talents. And so, what did you bring to add to the soup?"

Peter spread a newspaper he had bought on the remaining table space and carefully dumped his trove of wild plants. Otto reached over to examine them, but Peter quickly slapped his hand away. "They're highly toxic. Some have poisons that can seep through skin at a touch."

Otto stepped back, distancing himself from the plants. "I'll be careful."

"You won't be here."

"But, Peter—"

"Even I'm in danger working with these plants, and I've been doing this for a long time."

"Then can't I help in some other way? Max is very special to me."

Peter clasped Otto's shoulder. "Of course you can help, just not here. Find a café or some public place with a view of the building. Make sure this apartment is as safe as it seems."

"That I can do."

"Good. Come back in the early evening. Most of what you brought will be contaminated. You'll find it bundled up in the large burlap bag. Bury the bag in an isolated spot, away from people. Just be careful handling it."

"I understand." Otto smiled at Peter. "And you take care handling what you find in the Catacombs. We don't need to be burying you."

Once Otto left, Peter wasted no time. After opening the two windows in the room and donning the surgical mask and gloves, he took the tweezers and removed the seeds from some of the plants, placing them in the baking pan. Then, with the scalpel, he cut the leaves and roots from other plants into small pieces and put them in the pan as well, making sure to spread everything out in an even layer. Finally he plugged in the brown Bakelite hair dryer and held the nozzle so the heat blew against his palm. When he judged that the temperature was right, Peter held the hair dryer about an inch from the pan and swept it back and forth, being careful not to singe the contents. After a half hour of tediously going through this process, he lit the oven, set it on low and placed the pan on a middle rack. Since this part would take at least three hours, he went into the bedroom, opened its lone window and inspected the clothes, which were as grubby as Otto had said. Avoiding the mattress, Peter sat on the floor and, leaning against a wall, began reading what remained of the newspaper.

At 7:15 P.M. Peter opened the oven door and, deeming the plants done, removed his shirt, which he used as a mitt to set the hot pan on the table. Another treatment with the hair dryer made the plants brittle enough to work with. Tweezers in hand, Peter carefully plucked pieces from the leaves and roots, along with some seeds, and deposited them in the mortar so he could grind them into a fine powder. While not the most dangerous, the last part of the process was the most delicate. Drawing on a technique he often used with marked cards, Peter opened one of the cigarette packs in a way that would enable him to reseal it without any sign of tampering. Then he laid the cigarettes on the table, lifted one and, using the tweezers, extracted a small core of tobacco, poked some of the powder into the hollow and plugged the tobacco back in. He repeated the painstaking process until all but four of the cigarettes had been altered. One pack he filled completely and closed. He placed the remaining sixteen altered cigarettes in the other pack, kept one of the four unaltered ones and discarded the rest.

But Peter wasn't finished. The plant parts and seeds left in the baking pan he ground into another powder. He removed the matches from the tin Otto had brought and poured in enough powder to layer the bottom. Then Peter replaced the matches and closed the tin tight. The preparations were done. All that remained was to clean up.

Peter stripped naked and placed his clothes and the materials he used to make the powders in the burlap bag, which he tied and placed on the floor next to the table. Next he washed himself thoroughly in the kitchen sink and went to the bedroom, where he put on the ragged clothes. Having already decided to forego makeup and rely completely on costume and character, once he was dressed Peter was ready for a night on the town.

And then under the city.

For nearly three hours Peter roamed Paris' Latin Quarter, the final resting place for famous French citizens such as Voltaire, Rousseau, Victor Hugo and Émile Zola and the gathering place for seedier ones such as whores, thieves, tramps and, just for tonight, Peter.

Peter had taken great pains to fit in. His near obsession with looking and feeling the part went back twenty years, to his first meeting with Konstantin Stanislavsky, the great Russian director. Through theater contacts, Houdini arranged for Peter to have early-morning tea with Stanislavsky, who was visiting New York. Peter arrived at the Biltmore Hotel, full of questions about Stanislavsky's revolutionary theory of acting. But each time Peter asked one—through an interpreter since Stanislavsky neither spoke nor read English—the old man rebuffed him, giving a perfunctory, unenlightening reply. After fifteen minutes, Stanislavsky excused himself, saying he had promised to observe a rehearsal and, it being a nice day, he wanted to take a leisurely walk to the theater. Never shy, Peter asked if he might walk along. With a shrug and a sigh Stanislavsky agreed, but only if Peter acted as a guide, pointing out sights worth seeing.

For the first few blocks, interpreter in tow, they strolled 42nd Street in silence. When they went through Bryant Park, behind the library, Stanislavsky spied a derelict rising from his makeshift bed of bench and newspapers and he said something, as if thinking aloud.

"But don't you teach that motivation is more important than appearance in creating a role?" Even though the untranslated remark wasn't meant for him, Peter responded in Russian.

Stanislavsky stopped, snapped his head toward Peter and stared.

"If our first impression of someone is his appearance . . ." Peter, still in the moment, pointed to the man, and continued in Russian. "His clothes, his disheveled look, then what about motivation?" Only then did he remember the interpreter and realize what he had done.

Speaking directly to Peter, Stanislavsky asked how it was that he understood Russian. It was less a question than a demand for an explanation.

"I learned it a few years ago, from the same person who introduced me to your acting techniques," Peter replied, also in Russian. "I have sort of a knack for languages." Then, aware he had revealed more than he intended and not anxious to revisit that part of his life, Peter quickly tried to change the subject. "But I'm really rusty, so I was embarrassed to use it at the hotel."

That was partially true: Peter hadn't used Russian in a long time and had no desire to. However, because of his unique memory he had forgotten none of it. He drifted back a few feet so as not to further annoy Stanislavsky, still hoping the matter would be dropped. But Stanislavsky summoned him and sent the interpreter ahead to the theater.

"Now we talk in Russian, young man, and we will scrape off some of the rust. About your question. Our first impression of that fellow comes from his shabby clothes, his slovenly appearance. Only when we observe him further, through his actions, can we start to tell what sort of person he really is. See how he folds the newspaper that had been spread over him? He seems orderly. Perhaps a successful businessman once, fallen on hard times. When he reveals his little habits, when he starts to interact, that is when we can tell what drives him. Until then, we are just aware of his looks. It is the same on the stage."

Stanislavsky turned from the derelict and faced Peter. "When an actor applies his makeup, he must do so with an attitude of great respect, affection and attention. It must not be laid on mechanically but with psychology while he broods over the soul and life of his part. Then the slightest wrinkle will acquire its inner basis from something in life that produced it. In this way, a touch of the makeup brush on an actor's face can serve to open the flower of his role."

"And what about costumes?" Peter asked as they resumed walking.

"The same is true of costumes. An actor must know how to put on and wear a costume. He must know the customs, the manners, of the times or the place, the ways of greeting people, the use of a cane, hat, handkerchief. He can only do all this when he feels himself in his part and his part in himself. That is when a costume ceases to be a simple material thing and acquires a kind of sanctity. Outer and inner become one."

Peter's questions kept coming and Stanislavsky kept answering. What began with an innocent slip into Russian became a three-hour master class in acting. The lessons Peter learned he would later use to his advantage as a con man. Wiling away the evening in the Latin Quarter, he focused on making his outer and inner become one. Already his appearance and his actions made him seem *bourré*—"blotto"—to anyone who bothered looking, a lost soul reeling from too much cheap red wine and staggering between being amusing and obnoxious. But he had also been taking in the sound of the distinctive Parisian slang to spice his lower-class French and the exaggerated hand and body gestures to spark it. For a final touch, Peter deliberately tumbled into a curbside puddle of still-warm vomit and urine, making sure that he coated the groin of his trousers with enough of the vile mixture to be offensive. At that moment he clearly understood what it meant to suffer for art.

Then, satisfied that he was ready enough, Peter headed south to the Rue de Revolution and its manhole entry to the Catacombs. Crowds of people anxious to get home before the curfew gave him cover as he scouted out and settled on a place near enough to the manhole—the narrow doorway of an abandoned building—to wait until the lights were turned off and Paris was plunged into darkness.

Exactly at 11:00 P.M., the street poles exhaled in unison and extinguished their lights, followed by a less coordinated and more reluctant darkening of apartments and, last, of bars and bistros. Still Peter lingered until the clouds, which had begun drifting in, had thickened. In the meantime, he unrolled a towel he had filched from a bar, on which he placed a tightly corked, partially emptied bottle of wine, the two packs of Lucky Strikes and the match tin. He wrapped the towel tightly around the items three times for cushioning and secured each end with a length of rope from a junk pile. *Voilà!* He now had a backpack!

Then, when he felt that conditions were about as good as they were going to get, he carefully made his way down about half a block to the manhole. With one last glance for any onlookers he crouched low to the ground and took twelve short steps to his destination.

Quickly he fell to his knees, placed his hands in the recesses of two nodes on the perimeter of the solid manhole cover and yanked. The cover was loose, as Rémy had said it would be, but it was also heavy. Removing it proved more difficult than Peter expected. Bracing himself to get as much leverage as possible, he continued to tug until he was able to pry the lip of the cover out of its fitting and partially onto the street. That done, he slid his hands beneath the cover and, with a vigorous jerk, hoisted it upward.

This time Peter used too much force and the cover righted itself on its edge at a sixty-degree angle and started to roll. Instinctively he thrust out his arm and pushed against the iron wheel, knocking it off course. He watched as it spun around like a gigantic coin before striking the pavement with a loud clang, followed, seconds later, by the shrill sound of a nearby whistle, which sent him sprawling to the ground. Lying flat, Peter began concocting an explanation for the German-controlled French police on the prowl for curfew violators. He heard the whistle again, drawing closer, and prepared for the worst. Then the whistle changed direction and grew fainter. The police—or the Nazis—were after someone or something else. But the next time it could be him. Best to disappear quickly. So he peered down into the manhole. It was too dark to see anything except the rise of a ladder attached to the wall a few inches below the opening. Peter maneuvered his legs around and slowly lowered his feet into the shaft. When they hit the ladder's top rung, he pressed firmly until he could feel the slender metal rod dig through the spots where the bottoms of his beat-up work shoes had been resoled—one with thin rubber, the other with pleated straw—and into his arches. Then, grasping the ladder rail with his left hand, he draped his right forearm over the manhole cover and, with his fingers pressed against its edge, pulled until it started to move slowly toward the opening. With each strained heave Peter stepped down another rung so he was completely out of the way when the cover, yielding to one last ferocious jerk, dropped into its recessed base. There was no clang this time, only a dull thud.

Like the lid of a casket slamming shut.

15

Peter looked up but could see nothing. The dim light of the night sky had vanished, which meant the cover was properly seated and wouldn't attract any attention. With his hands tightly wrapped around a rung he reluctantly looked down, but sharp as his eyes were, they couldn't pierce the black that lay beneath him. Rémy had told him the ladder was 120 feet—twelve stories—but, whether because of the darkness or his worry over Max, Peter wasn't bothered by the height. Still, he knew his fear could erupt at any moment. The sooner he was on solid ground, the better, so he started descending, gauging his progress by the intensity of the slightly putrid smell coming from what he assumed was stagnant water waiting below to greet him.

Peter had gone about a third of the way when suddenly his right foot plunged into empty space, startling but not frightening him. Probably just missed a rung, he reasoned, and stretched his leg so he could feel around with his free hanging foot.

There was no rung.

Holding on more tightly, Peter cast his foot into the void again, moving it from side to side and then along the wall.

Nothing. No rung and no evidence of a ladder.

Now neither the dark nor Max made a difference. Peter's hands were clenched so tightly they hurt. His mind began swimming as spasms of panic coursed up his spine, shooting out to his shoulders and arms and making them shake. Peter felt his heart would stop if it weren't pounding so rapidly. With anxiety-induced paralysis fighting for control of his body Peter struggled to draw his foot, which seemed coated with cement and encased in lead, up and back into place. Without thinking he quickly took a step up the ladder, back toward the security of the street.

You can never let yourself be afraid, even when you are. Show confidence,

whether you have it or not, and you immediately get the upper hand. Show fear
and you're dead.

Houdini was in his head again, popping up just like he did at the Eiffel
Tower, with the same old tired pep talk.

"I understand you can't show fear in front of others." Peter didn't care
that he was responding aloud to words that existed only in his mind. "But
what if there's no one around to see your fear? What about then?"

Not waiting, Peter answered his own question. Not don't *feel* fear—don't
show fear. Show fear and you're dead.

"Show fear and you're dead." Peter repeated it several times as he nervously stepped back down to the rung he had just been on, ending the
conversation. Then, prying his right hand away from the rung, he reached
in his pocket for an old prewar Rayovac flashlight, flicked it on and, lower-
ing his head, forced himself to gaze down along the wall. The beam hit
what appeared to be another portion of ladder, but he was unable to tell just
how far away it was. So Peter had to look elsewhere for the answer.

Toledo, Ohio.

There, during the 1920s, while working as a fortune-teller in yet another
carnival, he met the Amazing Carlinis, a troupe of acrobats who taught
him some trapeze tricks. Given his fear of heights, Peter never ascended
more than twenty feet, and even that was painful. But he endured, learning
the basic hangs and swings, which was good enough for him. Whether it
would be good enough for what he now had to do was a different story.

Uneasily stomping the rusty rung he was standing on, Peter detected no
give and concluded it would do as a makeshift trapeze bar. He poked his
hand between the rung and the wall to measure the space. Slightly more
than four fingers—enough for a hang, but that was all. Making sure his
pack was tightly bound around his waist, Peter kicked off his shoes and
waited for what seemed an eternity until he heard them hit the ground, one
more reminder of how high up he was. If things went as planned, he could
retrieve the shoes when he reached bottom. If not, he wouldn't need them.

Finally he took off his belt and used it to lash the flashlight to his left
forearm. With everything in place he was ready to get into position. There
was enough back space for him to hunker down and partially sit on the
rung. Relaxing his legs, he let them dangle as he moved first one hand,
then the other to the rung he was perched on, grasping it firmly. Then, taking a couple of deep breaths—but being careful not to hyperventilate—he
moved his body off the rung and, flexing his arm muscles to prevent a sudden jerk, lowered himself into a fully extended hang.

Suspended in space, with his sense of freedom temporarily overcoming his fright, Peter let himself sway ever so gently for a few seconds while he indulged in a few memories, one of which was of Nikki Carlini, who performed with her parents and her brothers. Nikki was the reason he attached himself to the Carlinis and learned the trapeze techniques. She was also the reason he left the carnival rather hurriedly. Ah, Max!

Max? How the hell did Max get into Nikki's moment? Oh shit, Max! Peter snapped back to the present, flexed his shoulder muscles and began pulling with all his might, hoping he judged the strength of the rung right. As he pulled, he lifted his legs up and over his head, then thrust his feet forward and lowered them until he could feel the rung cutting into them at the point where they met and formed a right angle with his legs.

Now for the tricky part.

Releasing his hands, Peter kept his chest and back muscles taut, which allowed him to better control the extension of his body. Not bad, he thought as his head passed beneath his hips. Not bad at all. Some things you never—

Peter's momentary distraction broke both his concentration and his rhythm, causing his left foot to slide off the rung. Instinct immediately kicked in and Peter flexed his right foot, creating a sharper angle and giving him a more secure grip.

Steadied, but precariously, with his entire weight pulling on his right ankle, Peter felt the strain in his calf muscle and he knew it would soon cramp or tear. He reached out and, pressing his hands flat against the limestone wall, he rubbed the surface in all directions, seeking something to take hold of. Finding a fissure to his left side about six inches below his chin, he pressed his fingers over the crack and tried inserting them, but the opening was too small and shallow. The best he could do was to jam his pinky in as far as the first knuckle and a bit of his ring finger. Still it was enough to give him a slight anchor. He placed his right hand over his left to secure it even more, relieving some of the pressure on his ankle.

Funny what races through the mind during a crisis. For Peter it was Sir Arthur giving him advice, indirectly, through Sherlock Holmes. The slip of Peter's foot jolted "The Five Orange Pips" free from memory and flipped it open to a page where a passage stood out: *"Tut! Tut!" cried Sherlock Holmes. "You must act, man, or you are lost. Nothing but energy can save you. This is no time for despair."*

"This is no time for despair." Peter could see the words clearly. *"Act, man, or you are lost."*

All right, he told himself, this isn't too bad. You've done a single-foot hang before. Refocus, lift your right leg and place the foot back over the rung. Good. Now get the top of the foot back in position. Perfect. You're back in a double-foot hang and now your body's extended—not quite according to plan, but extended nonetheless.

Peter moved the flashlight on his forearm back and forth. This time he could clearly make out another rung, three or four feet beyond his reach. Now it was clear: a section of ladder *had* broken away from the wall, but there was a good chance the rest was intact. All he had to do was reach it by falling and catching hold of the rung as he passed by it. What seemed straightforward was in fact a death-defying—or death-inviting—stunt. Done right, it would certainly be a great crowd-pleaser. Here, however, there would be no cheers if he succeeded.

And only one scream if he failed.

Peter knew he could catch the rung. He had been catching ladder rungs since running away from the orphanage. Fastened to boxcars, they were his train tickets to every part of the country. Once he learned the technique, he never missed. He wouldn't miss now. The problem was the fall itself. In his carnival days, he had seen horrifying examples of the tremendous momentum a falling human body builds before it lands and splatters. The greater the distance, the greater the impact, although even a few feet can generate enough force to break a metal rung. He'd have to keep his fall as short as possible. Hanging by his hands and dropping would certainly be easier, but his extended arms and body would add eight more feet before he could reach for the rung. Dropping from the position he was already in would shorten that distance considerably, provided Peter had enough trust in his ability to take the risk.

Since that wasn't in question, and seeing no sense in stalling, Peter flexed his hands a few times, rubbed them against the wall to coat them with grit, spread them into a wide cup-like shape and, concentrating on the rung below, pointed his feet upward.

Instantly in free fall, he grabbed at the rung with both hands, flexing his upper body the moment they made contact to slow the forward thrust of his legs. Peter caught the rung perfectly, but the impact pulled it away from the left side of the ladder, throwing his body off balance and causing his legs to jut downward with a wrenching force. Literally holding his life in his hands, Peter clung to the partially detached bar—which he realized could snap completely off at any moment. Quickly he released his left hand and snatched the next rung and, as soon as he did, he moved his right hand from the broken rung to the ladder's side post. Then, with as much muscle as he could muster, he pulled his body up into a diagonal and eased the tension. He grimaced as his shins slammed into the ladder, but kept a tight hold, quickly working his feet around until they were secure on a rung a few feet below. Within moments he maneuvered himself back into a climbing position, his initial feeling of relief giving way to a flush of self-satisfaction, the kind he usually experienced after pulling off an impossible con.

Peter allowed himself a few moments to regroup before starting down the new stretch of ladder. With the exception of two more broken rungs the remainder of his descent was uneventful. When he set foot in the pool of fetid water he had smelled earlier, he was just thankful to reach ground. Besides, his shoes, which he had tossed down earlier, had landed in a nearly dry area. Peter put them back on and turned his attention to navigating the maze of tunnels, many of which led to dead ends or potentially deadly drop-offs that Rémy had warned him about.

"Even those who think they know the place well can get trapped," Rémy had said. "Philibert Aspairit back in 1793 was the most famous. He had explored the Catacombs many times and even had keys to get in and out. He went down with a candle and disappeared. They found him—or his remains—eleven years later just meters from an exit. He's buried on that same spot."

Determined not to be the newest Philibert Aspairit, Peter removed the flashlight from his arm and swung it, first like a censer, upward and outward away from him, then like a golf putter, downward and from side to side. He repeated the motions turning his body until he had completed a full rotation. Then, closing his eyes, he mentally unfolded the map he had memorized and rechecked his course.

Rémy said that, for the most part, the underground passages mirrored the streets above them. Considering where he entered, on paper he should be less than a mile from his destination—a fairly straight initial stretch, followed by a right turn and then, after a bit, a left and another right. Of course "on paper" was perfect, but "in reality" could get messy.

To Peter's surprise the first two hundred yards or so were nearly obstacle free. The mound of large boulders that blocked almost the entire path at one point didn't count since Peter was able to squeeze his way through by turning sideways and contracting his stomach muscles. And, just as the map indicated, there was another corridor to the right, which Peter took, going fifty yards more without incident. Then he felt water, seeping through his porous patchwork shoes, which had earlier been spared a soaking. One more thing to contend with, Peter thought. At least this water didn't reek and, since it didn't even reach his ankles, it only ranked as an annoyance, so he sloshed on.

However when the water level rose, as it seemed to with every few steps, so did Peter's concern. Positioning a foot on some small rock outcroppings near the bottom of each of the walls and straddling the stream, he was able to move a few more yards. When the corridor began widening, he was still able to continue by bringing both feet together on the left wall ledge and then bending over and pressing his hands against the right wall. Finally, though, the corridor grew too wide for him to bridge and he slipped into the water, which now was almost to his knees. At this rate, he knew it wouldn't be long before he was waist, if not neck, deep in what now seemed a river and there would be no guarantee he could keep the special cigarettes in his towel-pack dry. Reluctantly, he turned and headed back.

On the main path again, Peter took stock. He had maintained a constant stride and kept track of his steps, so he could calculate how far he had traveled. And, if the map was correct, the corridor to the right—the one he had just been in—was where it should be, give or take a few feet. No sense going crazy: It is what it is, he told himself, and trudged on ahead.

By his count he had only gone another forty feet when he saw a second corridor to the right. But he hadn't seen a second corridor on the map and this was much farther along. Maybe the map was wrong or maybe . . .

Peter entered the second corridor, which, like the main one, had no obstructions. Even better, walking had squeezed enough water from Peter's shoes that they stopped their irritating squeaking. Best of all, his next turn soon appeared on the left and, from the partially blocked opening to his right, Peter knew it was the same cross corridor that connected to the flooded passageway. The map wasn't wrong, just outdated. Obviously the side corridor passage it showed had become unusable and a second parallel passage was either found or created. But the rest of the directions should hold up. So Peter turned left, as indicated, and continued.

This passage was rougher, a downward-sloping combination of holes and overhangs with the potential to shatter legs and crack heads. The tricky terrain forced Peter to beam his flashlight on first the ceiling and then the ground every three or four steps and, even with that, he stumbled twice. Keeping to this time-consuming routine was bad enough without it ending, not with his final turn, as he had expected, but rather a solid wall of stone. Besides the turn, the map clearly showed that the current corridor continued on to a major limestone extraction area. Perhaps it did, once, but not now. And from the look of the corridor ceiling, the formation of the wall now facing him and the debris on the ground, Peter knew why.

The quarry had collapsed.

It was inevitable, of course. Things had been going too smoothly. Well, so much for that. This time Peter had but one option: rummage through the rubble where the turn was supposed to be and search for an opening with no guarantee he'd find one. So for thirty-five hard minutes he pried away rocks, labor that finally produced a small result. Very small: a jagged rectangle, maybe two feet wide and ten inches high, located three feet above the quarry floor. Peter looked through the opening and waved the tip of his flashlight around but saw only darkness. Did the tunnel curve, he wondered, or was it so long that its exit was beyond the flashlight's beam? Or was there no exit at all? He took another mental scan of the Catacombs map, which, despite being out-of-date, still provided an overview. He saw that taking a complicated route to work his way around the blockage could consume hours he didn't have. The opening offered the only chance of reaching Max before the deadline to kill her.

Peter had been warned not to try working his way through collapse holes—unstable passageways through the rubble of fallen rocks—lest he get trapped. Normally he wouldn't need any such warning. Of course, normally he wouldn't be deep beneath Paris fighting the clock, most likely in a bid to commit suicide. Damn! This was over and above what Donovan had asked of him.

Peter licked his fingers and, instead of the flashlight, thrust his hand into the hole. He thought he could feel a faint ripple of flowing air, which would indicate there was indeed an exit point. Should he trust that? His senses had always served him well, but . . . He placed his hand in again. This time he felt nothing. But he was sure it was there before. Was that because he *wanted* to feel it? What the hell! Done with speculating, Peter braced himself by grasping the bottom edge of rock and lifted his right leg, then his left into the hole,

He had made his decision.

From what Peter could tell, this passage also sloped downward. Crawling through belly down and feetfirst would make it easier to pull himself up the incline if he had to turn back. He grabbed his pack by its rope strap, drew it into the hole and worked his body into the proper position. Ready as he was ever going to be, Peter placed both palms on the ground and thrust himself into the unknown.

Except for the dirt that managed to slip through Peter's clenched lips, the first thirty feet or so posed little problem. Then suddenly the passage narrowed sharply, compressing Peter's movement from feet into inches and threatening to stop it entirely. Peter probed the passage floor until he located two suitable holds—one a jutting rock, the other a hole. If the bottleneck was debris, a strong shove might clear it. If not, he'd still need the extra burst of power to get through the smaller space. With his hands anchored, Peter pulled himself slightly forward, tightened his arm and shoulder muscles, then released them in a violent push that sent him lunging ahead.

He didn't travel quite a foot, but Peter was satisfied. His progress also indicated no unusual amount of debris, so he'd just have to cope with this snug section and hope it was short. Again Peter felt the ground and found another two holds, not as good as the last pair but better than nothing. Hands in place, he repeated the process of drawing forward, then pushing away with all his might. This time, though, he only moved about six inches. In fact, he moved so little, he was still able to place his hands on the same holds. Determined to use even more strength this go-around, Peter pulled on the holds, but nothing happened. He pulled again, but still nothing. Why wasn't he moving?. The upper rocks were barely rubbing the top of his head, so, unless the opening clamped severely just a foot or two farther along, there was room. But the best his legs could manage was a wiggle that accomplished nothing. He backed up and tried again, this time angling his lower body a little, but it didn't help. After a third failed attempt, he accepted the obvious: he was stuck.

Never Panic. Peter found Houdini's number one rule particularly relevant: panic could cause parts of the body to swell and make escaping from tight quarters impossible. Peter didn't panic, but he did push, pull and squirm to no avail. By inhaling deeply and holding his stomach and chest muscles taut, he gained some upper-body room, but compressing his lower body was the problem. *This is no different than any other escape,* Peter told himself, then, channeling all his energy to his right foot, he tried to position his heel against either the side or back of his left shoe. Each foot twist hurt, but Peter kept raking with his heel, exploiting any contact, no matter how slight.

Persistence paid off, and finally Peter was able to slide his left shoe from his foot and then, using the same method, his right. With one hurdle overcome, he forced his hands under his stomach and loosened his trousers. This was it—all or nothing. He drew his hands free and reached forward again for the rocks that served as handles. Closing his eyes shut until they hurt, he took one deep gasp of air and yanked with every fiber of muscle.

Sharp stones tore into his face, but since he moved backward six or seven inches the warm drops of blood Peter sensed trickling onto his lips felt wonderful! Clothes might not have made the man, but they made a difference. It meant he might be able to work his way forward again, pushing along his pants, which he had now wiggled out of, and his shoes with his feet. But when he tried, he ended up stuck in almost the same spot. Now what was the matter? His shoes were off and so were his trousers, so . . .

Wait! His trousers! Maybe the fraction of an inch they added wasn't the problem after all.

Once more Peter pulled himself back and, with his toes, which, thanks to Houdini's training, he could use almost as effectively as fingers, grabbed the trousers and jiggled and tugged them, but they barely budged. And for good reason, as Peter discovered when he maneuvered his right foot under the trousers and felt the raised rock.

He was snagged!

This time using his toes as pliers, Peter cinched the trousers near the point they were caught but couldn't lift them off the rock. Resorting to a more direct approach, he jerked the trousers to his left side and ripped them loose. With the obstruction removed, Peter grasped his rock handles, flexed his arm muscles and propelled himself forward. The rock that had hooked his trousers gashed his right calf just below the knee as he passed by. But Peter ignored the pain and, encouraged by actually making progress, continued to push, using his toes to pat down his trousers and prevent any further catching or clogging.

He was back!

Peter's euphoria was short-lived. After an hour of strenuous labor during which he had traveled only five hundred feet, he felt his shoes and trousers bunch up against something solid and immovable. He stretched his toes upward as best he could and rubbed them over what was certainly stone.

With thoughts of another collapse racing through his mind, Peter moved his left foot to the side of the passage and poked, stubbing his toes against more stone. He tried his right foot, and while it, too, struck stone on its side of the passage, there was some yield, enough for Peter to push through to an opening. Slowly he worked his left foot until it went through the opening as well. Peter knew that by lying on his left side instead of his stomach he could get his entire body through the opening. He raised his head and almost immediately struck the roof. From that Peter estimated that the passageway was only eight or nine inches high, not nearly enough room to allow him to turn. There was, however, an alternative.

"Try bending over backward and picking up a pin with your teeth from the floor."

That was the first thing Houdini taught him about becoming an escape artist. Houdini used the skills he developed during his early career as a contortionist to get out of straitjackets and chains. And though Peter lacked his teacher's almost super-human flexibility, he learned Houdini's body manipulation techniques well enough to twist, turn and stretch his way free from any restraint. But he had never tried what carnies called enterology—the ability to squeeze into incredibly small places—although he understood how it should be done. Peter had once worked a sideshow with "King Brawn," a master of the art who could pass his body through a four-and-one-half-inch-by-eight-inch keyhole-shaped cutout in a wooden plank. "The same basic body-contorting techniques can get you in or out of anything," King Brawn said, and gave a few demonstrations. Now Peter was about to find out if that was really true.

Drawing his left leg up about an inch off the ground, Peter visualized it pointing at 6 on a clock and started moving it as far to the right as he could. An untrained person could reach the 7:30 point and maybe 8:30 with exercise. However, with his rigorous physical conditioning Peter could hit 9:30 with no difficulty and, with exertion, 10:30. He kept inching his body ahead until he sensed he could go no farther, then strained to move his right leg as close as possible to his left.

The movements wrenched at his midsection and Peter's upper teeth, which were pressed against his lower lip, registered the pain, sinking deeper with each spasm. But King Brawn was right: by contorting his legs and tightening his stomach and gluteal muscles, Peter managed to angle his hips into the hole, although the intense agony from turning them so severely made him worry that he had ripped a joint from its socket.

Once he had overcome that part of the ordeal, getting the rest of his body through was relatively easy, and when Peter was finally inside the new space he found he could actually bend his legs toward his back and extend his elbows out to his sides. In contrast to the passage from hell, Peter encountered no hindrances as he pushed his way through these spacious surroundings. And when, after about a hundred yards, he stopped, it wasn't because his feet hit rock but because they ran out of ground.

After crawling for so long, Peter now had to adjust to dangling. He had reached the end of something but didn't know what, so he kept moving ahead until his waist reached the end of the drop-off and he could probe with his legs, which hung over the edge. But despite repeated attempts Peter couldn't determine how far a drop it was from the passage's end to the ground. Going back wasn't an option, so he'd have to rely on trial and, he hoped, nonfatal error.

Carefully he lowered more of his body over the side, trying to keep it as close to the wall as possible, so at least he might have something to grab onto in case of a steep fall. By the time his shoulders reached the edge, Peter, who had been holding on by grinding his palms into the passage floor, knew he could no longer fight gravity. Relaxing his body, he lifted his hands an inch and let nature take its course.

Peter hit the ground hard, and he felt sharp stabbing pain in different parts of his body, especially in his still-bare legs. And he had no doubt about what was causing his pain.

Broken bones.

Tibiae, fibulae, ribs and skulls. There had to be thousands, maybe tens of thousands, some forming haphazard hills, others randomly strewn throughout the large, semi-circular chamber, their rest disturbed first by Peter's fall, then by his flashlight's beam. These were hardly the well-organized and neatly stacked bones Rémy had described.

Peter swept away the shards from the bones he'd shattered on impact and which retaliated by cutting into his flesh with their splintered edges. He thought of Delta, who made sure Peter showed proper respect for the dead when gathering materials from graveyards. So desecrating human bones, even unintentionally, upset him. True, Peter knew how to use an evildoer's bones to counteract harmful spells or to control enemies, but here the bones of the bad and the good were co-mingled. As Rémy said, "Princes, prelates and prostitutes—they all share a common grave."

Peter slid back into his trousers, put on his shoes, then eased himself up and surveyed the chamber. Across from where he stood was an opening, the only one in the chamber, and it looked large enough to enter standing. Reconciled that he would damage more remains, Peter made his way toward it. Some of the bones beneath his feet easily rolled aside when he gently nudged them. Others—those that were more brittle—cracked under his weight like dry leaves or twigs in a late-fall forest, and he cringed at the sound.

Midway through the chamber, Peter paused before a heap of skulls. Maybe his eyes were playing tricks on him, deceived by the dim illumination the flashlight created, but it wouldn't hurt to check. Setting the flashlight down, he removed one of the skulls and rubbed his finger over the crown, which was coated with a green-colored growth. He transferred a little of the substance from his finger to his tongue. Just as he thought: moss! *Moss from a skull make the flesh whole.* Those were the words Delta had recited as he applied the moss to nine-year-old Peter's back, covering the deep gash from a bad boxcar jump. Almost immediately Peter had felt a drawing in the wet, bloody wound. Within minutes both the bleeding and throbbing had stopped. If it worked then . . .

Peter rubbed the fingers of his right hand on the skull, gathering as much moss as he could. There wasn't a lot, so he'd have to use it sparingly.

He started with his face, identifying the blood-moist areas with the dry fingers of his left hand. He dabbed some of the moss off the ones he found and, within seconds, they turned from moist to sticky. Soon they would only appear to be small scratches, adding another touch of realism to his disguise.

Peter put the rest of the moss on a large gouge in his right leg and then took the skull in both hands and lifted it over his head. "Then thank that soul for what you stole." Delta had said that after using the moss, so Peter expressed his gratitude with the same words, then gently placed the skull back among the others and went on to the other side of the chamber.

The opening was the entrance to one more passageway, which wasn't high enough for him to stand completely upright, but which he could still negotiate comfortably by hunching his shoulders like a bear.

Although Peter was still unsure of his location, the chamber of bones had suggested he was on the right track. The pinpoint of light that greeted him when, after maybe two hundred straight yards, the passage curved to the right was the most welcome sight he'd seen since he'd descended to this godforsaken place. Frozen in place by the tiny yellow spot, like a forest animal picking up on a potential danger, Peter felt his senses kick into high alert and he let the information they gathered flow into his brain unfiltered. Then, after a few seconds, he began analyzing it. His taste, touch and vision had provided nothing of worth and Peter attributed the few unfamiliar odors to his immediate surroundings. However, he was getting some vague yet familiar auditory sensations and, acting on these, Peter took a few very quiet confirming steps forward. Yes, that's what they were.

Voices!

They were so faint that even with his exceptional hearing Peter couldn't make out what was being said. But they were definitely voices. Flicking off his flashlight and placing one hand on the passage wall for guidance, Peter made his way toward the light, which grew larger even while the intermittent voices remained indistinct, which meant they were coming from beyond the passageway's exit area. Still Peter moved cautiously. When he reached the end of the passageway he pressed his body flat against the wall and took a hard look at what he was about to walk into. The light, which had seemed so bright at a distance, was much dimmer, trickling into the small, triangular room from one of two full-sized corridors, which was also the source of the voices. Certain he was on the last leg of his journey, Peter entered the room. Using the tarnished chrome barrel of the flashlight as a mirror, he saw that his tunneling ordeal had made him look scruffier than when he started. Satisfied, Peter reached into his left pant pocket, took out a small slice of onion and a clove of garlic, bit off a piece of each and chewed them into an odorous paste, which, with his tongue, he brushed across his upper and lower gums. Cupping his hands to his mouth, he blew and in-haled. Something was missing. He unrolled his pack and grabbed the wine bottle by its neck, yanked out the cork and took a slug, swishing it between his teeth like mouthwash before spitting it out. He set down the wine bot-tle, cupped his hands to his mouth again, blew, inhaled and gagged. Now the noxious smell was perfect.

Where others might have been terrified, Peter was exhilarated. The ex-citement of a really big con about to go down easily outweighed the life-and-death stakes. After the whole Strauss incident and his confrontation with Max, Peter finally felt in control again. Only the ritual he reserved for special cons remained. He lifted the wine bottle as if toasting, then, in a hushed, but no less exuberant voice, proclaimed *"La partie reprend!* The game is afoot!"

Bottle in hand, Peter headed toward the voices and, as he did, he started to sing. For the occasion, he chose one of France's most familiar and popu-lar drinking songs, "Chevaliers de la Table Ronde"—"Knights of the Table Round." He began loud and built to louder, slurring his raucous off-key telling of tasting and testing wine.

> *"Chevaliers de la Table Ronde,*
> *Goûtons voir si le vin est bon."*

When he got to the rollicking chorus, he really poured it on, screaming out the opening words, *"Goûtons voir*—Let us taste and see!"

> *"Goûtons voir, oui oui oui.*
> *Goûtons voir, non non non.*
> *Goûtons voir si le vin est bon."*

Peter was certain he had been heard, perhaps even by some of the 8 mil-lion souls whose bodies had been unceremoniously deposited in the Cata-combs. But he also wanted to make sure he was seen, so as he continued his screeching he waved the wine bottle in his left hand and the flashlight in his right, taking pains to demonstrate no sense of rhythm.

"Goûtons voir, oui oui oui. . . ." Peter hit the flashlight against the passage wall, being careful not to damage his Catacombs lifeline. *"Goûtons voir, non non non. . . ."* He hit the wall again. *"Goûtons voir si le vin—"*

"Hey!"

This voice was clear, although Peter couldn't see its source. He continued to sing.

"Hey, you—Maurice Chevalier! Enough. Come over here!"

Now Peter could see a light, much stronger than his, swinging in an arc about seventy-five feet away.

"Ah, an audience!" Peter shouted, and burst back into song.

"I said to stop the singing and come here!"

"Who are you to tell me not to sing?" Peter could now make out a figure with a rifle. He had found his prey. "You are in my house, not yours."

"This is the house of the dead, which *will* be your house if you don't shut your mouth and get over here like I say."

Staggering closer, Peter took a better look at the man. About his height, but heavier, wearing beige slacks and a white patterned shirt. Thick black hair and two days of stubble framed a Gallic face with its dark eyes, and its aquiline nose wedged between cheeks that were full but not fat. French enough except for the rifle, a Mexican-made Mondragón, which was standard German army issue and so probably captured.

"Reporting for duty, *mon capitan*." Peter raised his flashlight to his forehead. The man answered Peter's salute by shoving him against a wall and frisking him.

"Hey, hey, watch yourself, you pig! I'm no Moulin Rouge girl."

The man wheeled Peter around so that they were face-to-face. "I don't know who you are, but we're going to find out."

"Find out? What do you hope to find out?" Peter carefully selected words that allowed him to exhale forcefully as he said them, making his captor blanch and turn away from the blasts of stale breath. That gave Peter enough time to peer over the man's shoulder, where he saw what looked like an alcove cut into the opposite wall.

"Ah, you stink." Regaining his senses, the man shoved Peter's face away. "Your breath . . ." He looked down at Peter's dress. "Your clothes. And that stench! My God, you've vomited on yourself."

Peter looked down at the dull blotches and streaks on his trousers. "That's not mine," he said, lifting his bottle and shaking it. "I can hold my wine."

With a nod of disgust the man grabbed Peter's arm, jerked him forward and pushed him into the alcove.

The alcove opened into a larger kerosene lantern–lit chamber, which, except for the limestone walls and floor, resembled a squalid Paris garret, functionally furnished with a few dilapidated chairs and a table with some meager provisions on it. A second man was seated at the table playing solitaire. A few feet back was a rusted iron cot covered by a worn rug in lieu of a mattress. And there, atop the mattress, sat Max, chained to the cot's frame.

"Well, André, what have you brought?" The man at the table looked up from his game.

"Our troubadour, Philippe." He thrust Peter into one of the chairs. "A smelly one at that."

So, André and Philippe. Not that their names mattered. Sizing them up was more important. Peter's first impression of André proved right in the brighter light, except his arms were more muscular. In contrast, Philippe, attired in black slacks and a red pullover shirt with horizontal black stripes. was short and scrawny, with a thin moustache and even thinner hair. Older than André, he struck Peter as perhaps a minor government official involved with the resistance. On the table in front of him, next to some chipped coffee cups and bread, was an ashtray but very few butts, a stark contrast to the mound of spent cigarettes Peter had seen outside the chamber when André was manhandling him. That could be a bad sign.

Even worse were some of the other items lying on the table: a ten-inch-long .35-caliber Webley Mk IV revolver and a double-edged, foil-grip Fairbairn-Sykes Fighting Knife. At Camp X, Major William Fairbairn, who developed the knife, taught Peter and the other trainees innovative ways to use it for dispatching enemies. The weapon was so deadly and effective that it became known simply as "the Fairbairn Killing Knife." Both the knife and the revolver had probably belonged to a British SOE operative working behind the lines with the resistance. "So, is this what they have sent to rescue you?" Philippe looked over his shoulder at Max, who remained silent.

Philippe wasn't the only one looking at Max. So was Peter, and he concluded that, because of the light and the disguise, she had no idea who he was. So much the better for the moment.

"No, I don't think this is your hero." Philippe turned to André. "Well, what do you make of him? Is he what he seems?"

"Maybe. But better to be sure." André leaned his rifle against the table. "You used all the chains?"

"It doesn't matter. He had no weapons, right?"

"Nothing."

"Then I think we can handle him."

While they were talking, Peter rose and started walking unsteadily around the perimeter of the chamber. "Nice place. Much nicer than where I stay down here." He paused in front of Max, who still didn't recognize him. "I don't have one of these, either. Who is she, your own private whore?"

"Hey, you, shut up and get back in that chair!" André shouted.

"Easy, easy. I meant no offense. Just . . ." He poked Max, who glared at him.

"Fiery, this one." Peter winked, and when he saw Max's brow furrow slightly he smiled and made a barely audible shushing sound. Max's eyes widened. "Just wanted to tell her that if she wants a real man—"

André grabbed the revolver from the table and pointed it at Peter. "I said sit down."

"Easy, please." Peter raised the wine bottle he was still clutching. "Have some wine and cool down."

André snatched the bottle from Peter and slammed it on the table, then rammed his left hand, complete with gun, into Peter's breastbone, propelling him into the chair.

Once he caught the breath André had forced out of him, Peter resumed his singing. "*Goûtons voir, oui oui oui. Goûtons voir, non non non. Goûtons voir si le vin—*"

"Will you stop that damn fool!" Philippe implored, and André again aimed the revolver at Peter.

"I am here against my will. I cannot drink my wine, I cannot sing my songs. Am I allowed perhaps . . ." Peter reached into his shirt pocket and pulled out a prepared pack of Luckys. "To smoke my cigarettes." He shook the unaltered one out and put the pack back into his pocket, pretending to fumble, thereby drawing more attention to his action.

"Give me those," Philippe demanded.

"Forgive me. I should have offered you one."

Philippe took the pack Peter held out, studied it and then gave it to André, who turned it around in his hands a few times before handing it back.

"Where did you get American cigarettes?" Philippe asked.

"I have my ways. You want them? Keep them. There's more." Peter pulled the second pack of Luckys from his pant pocket and Philippe, reaching over the table, grabbed it from him.

"Once more, where did you get them?"

"*Goûtons voir, non non non,*" Peter softly sang, then stopped abruptly. "I got them down here, all right? There are many places in the Catacombs where black marketers hide goods. If you know your way around, and aren't greedy, you can gather a few crumbs."

"What do you think?" André asked.

Philippe held up the pack. "Look at the tax stamp. Spain. They still have American cigarettes in Spain. Probably smuggled in. The Germans love American cigarettes. It's illegal to smoke them, but still. Somebody's making a fortune. One pack would command a small ransom."

"And so now we all share in the spoils." Peter snatched a box of matches from the table and lit the cigarette he had kept for himself. "Go ahead. They're fresh and they're free."

"I don't smoke," Philippe volunteered with a sneer, and slid the ashtray toward him. "And neither do you while you're with me."

Peter held back for a few seconds, then, making a show of his disdain, tossed away the cigarette. Wonderful. The only person over the age of five in France who didn't smoke had to be this guy. That could be a problem.

"Here." Philippe slapped the pack into André's hands. "Better you enjoy them than the Germans."

André tore the foil, eagerly retrieved a cigarette and started to light it, but Philippe stopped him.

"Hey, hey, come on. We agreed. Outside. Please."

"You are such an old woman," André grumbled, the unlit cigarette dangling from his mouth.

Well, here we are, Peter thought. One smoker who, of course, was the heavier one. His weight could affect how rapidly the additive in the cigarettes hit him, if it hit him at all. There had been no way for Peter to test whether he had properly prepared the adulterated tobacco. Too heavy a hand would ruin the taste and the plan. Too light and the effects would be minimal. And how would he know, with André smoking out of view?

"Now, back, André. We still aren't sure about this one. If we're wrong, he probably has friends. You watch for them. I'll look after him."

With a grunt of agreement André grabbed the rifle he had set against the table and lumbered out of the chamber. Philippe turned to Peter and tapped the blade of the Fairbairn Killing Knife with his fingers. "You. No more songs."

"The wine is singing now. It's telling me to just lie down and listen." Peter rose from the chair, made his way unsteadily to the cot and yanked the torn, soiled pillow that Max had been resting on. "Bury my head in this pillow. . . ." Concerned that some cigarette smoke might drift into the chamber, he emphasized the words and hoped Max got the message. Just to be sure, he repeated them. "Bury my head in this pillow. . . ." This time, when he finished he placed his face in the pillow so that it was completely covered.

"Hey, get your dirty face out of the pillow and sit down!"

"As you wish," Peter grumbled. He tossed the pillow back on the cot and took two steps toward the table before stumbling to the floor, his head knocking against the chair. "Ah, this is just as comfortable. He rubbed his body against the limestone as if he were snuggling into a feather bed. "I should piss, I suppose." His words were partially obscured by a yawn. "But when one is so cozy . . ."

"Remember—I'll be watching you."

Drawing his eyelids tight enough to seem closed but open enough to make out general images, Peter began formulating a backup plan. Long before Camp X, Peter had mastered handling a knife. But getting his hands on the Fairbairn wouldn't be easy: Philippe, who had resumed his solitaire game, still glanced up every few moments to check on him. Moreover, Peter was physically drained and that would eventually take its toll on staying alert. Obviously, he couldn't afford to sleep, but he could refresh both body and mind another way.

Peter could use hypnotism.

Not stage-variety hypnotism but the kind he had used when he was one of Manhattan's leading—and most handsomely rewarded—psychoanalysts. Of course he had no real credentials for practicing psychoanalysis, any more than he did for teaching college. For Peter, confidence always trumped credentials.

Peter figured he could rest for twenty minutes. Then, if the cigarettes still hadn't done their job, he would try to distract Philippe and secure the knife. He began silently taking deep breaths, releasing the tension in his body as he exhaled by focusing on a soothing, beautiful image.

He focused on Max.

After a minute or so, Peter altered his pattern. As he breathed in, he told himself that he had twenty minutes to spend in a semi-conscious state and that when he emerged he would be energized. Then, as he breathed out, he told himself that his eyelids were glued together and that nothing could unglue them until twenty minutes had passed.

As he kept silently repeating the pattern, he could feel himself drifting and his eyelids adhering more strongly to each other. Soon nothing would be able to pry them apart them until twenty minutes had passed.

Nothing except the two blasts from a Mexican-made Mondragón rifle.

"André?" Philippe shouted out, and another rifle shot answered him. "André, what is it?" Philippe bolted up, seized the revolver and sped to the cot.

Peter, jolted out of his trance, eased his way up from the floor and, being careful to keep in character, rubbed his eyes and asked, "What the hell's going on?"

"Quiet!" Philippe was holding the revolver to the side of Max's head. "André, are they coming?"

There was a third shot, heralding an agitated André who backed his way into the chamber, his rifle still at the ready. "You didn't hear them? They're all around!"

"I heard nothing but three shots."

"I killed two of the search dogs they sent first. You must have heard the dogs."

"Dogs? André, I heard no dogs."

André swirled around. "Are you deaf? The dogs. And the whistles. The whistles of the damn police working with the Germans."

The doctored cigarettes had taken hold. André was growing more paranoid and incoherent by the second and his instability was making him extremely dangerous.

"Shoot her, Philippe! Shoot her now! If we die, she dies."

"André, get a grip on yourself. There's no one out there."

"No one? Go out and you'll see! Then you'll know we must kill her now! Go! You'll see!"

"This is ridiculous, but if it will bring you to your senses . . . You do nothing until I'm back. Nothing. Do you promise?"

"Just hurry. We're running out of time."

"What's going on?" Peter asked again.

"Shut up, you!" André swirled around and waved the barrel of the Mondragón. "I have more than enough bullets for you and for her. And even if she lives, I think I'll kill you."

Peter held his palms up in front of his chest and pressed his lips tightly together, although he wasn't sure exactly whether André was seeing him or some threatening hallucination that should be immediately eliminated. And while she was trying to remain collected, Peter could sense Max's anxiety over André's deteriorating mental state.

"There is nothing there," Philippe said as he reentered the chamber. "Nothing. No dogs. No police. No Germans. But there's no telling who your shots may have aroused. Come, we must move to another location quickly."

"How can you say that?" André stared at Philippe, who was gathering some papers from the table. "You were just out there. How can you say there's nothing? I know you saw and heard them."

"You're crazy, and we have no time for you to be crazy. Unchain the girl, kill the drunk and let's go."

"Kill the drunk" wasn't exactly what Peter wanted to hear. He began calculating the distance between him and the knife. But even if he got to it, he could only handle one of them. No, he would have to use—

"Unchain the girl? I told you, Philippe—if we die, she dies." André lifted his rifle and pushed its tip against Max's temple. "In fact, she dies now."

This was it. Peter could only distract André for a moment, but since he wasn't about to let him shoot Max, it would have to do. "No, you die now!" he shouted.

A startled André turned as Peter leapt for the table with as much force as possible, his arms outstretched, attempting to get his hands on first Philippe and then the knife. As Peter's head and upper body slid over the table's edge, he reached for Philippe, trying to catch hold of a piece of his clothing, anything.

But there was nothing.

Instead Philippe was by the cot, Webley in hand, evidently more concerned with André than Peter. "Turn the rifle away!" Philippe shouted, tugging on André's arm with his free hand.

"She's leading them here! She's sending them signals! She has to die! That will stop them." He lowered the rifle from Max's head and pointed it at the pillow. "See, she has a transmitter!"

Philippe raised the Webley and hammered the butt hard against the back of André's skull. André started to turn and Philippe hit him again with the gun, this time sending him crashing to the floor.

During the commotion, Peter had grabbed the knife. Philippe was holding the revolver in his right hand, so Peter held the knife with his left, clasping it just below the hilt with his thumb and forefinger and wrapping his middle finger around the bulge in the handle. Fairbairn had drilled the grip into them at Camp X, then showed them all the ways it could be used to quickly kill an opponent. Like Philippe

But Peter had promised Rémy that, if possible, he wouldn't kill any of the resistance members. That meant slashing rather than plunging with the knife and relying on his dexterity to control the blade's cut.

Peter was ready, and as soon as Philippe bent over to remove the rifle from André's hands he acted, bounding toward the cot with a loud shout. Philippe looked up and, seeing Peter, tried to point the Webley, exposing his arm. With the same lightness that he'd used so often to snatch a wallet Peter swung the knife in a horizontal arc, catching and tearing through Philippe's shirt at the base of his right biceps.

If Philippe had intended to shoot, he didn't. Nor did he drop the gun. Instead he let it loosely dangle in his hand as he looked at his arm. He seemed more dazed than hurt. Before Philippe had a chance to absorb what had happened, Peter attacked again, this time using the edge of his open, extended right hand to strike Philippe's right wrist hard enough to make him release the gun. That was one of Fairbairn's special maiming techniques and, from Philippe's scream, Peter assumed the blow broke a few bones.

For good measure Peter delivered a good old-fashioned uppercut to the jaw, which sent Philippe sprawling to the floor, where he lay motionless. After nudging the body with the toe of his shoe and getting no reaction, Peter stooped down and placed his hand on Philippe's chest. He could feel a slight rise and fall, which meant Philippe wasn't dead, merely cold-cocked.

"Peter!" Max was sitting on the cot, tugging on a small padlock that secured her chains. "I don't know where the key is."

"Right here." Peter came over, sat next to her and plucked a pin from her hair. "This will do just as well." He grabbed the padlock and studied it for a moment. Then, holding it with his left hand, he inserted the point of the point into the cylinder and jiggled it around.

"I don't scare easily, Peter. I never have. But I was afraid. They weren't bluffing."

"I know. But it's over now." Peter heard a faint click. "And so is this." He tugged on the lock and watched as the U-shaped metal shackle popped up. "Voilà!"

"No, bravo!" Max leaned over and tried to kiss him on the cheek, but Peter bolted up.

"I'm afraid my costume is a bit aromatic and you've obviously been dis-comforted enough. So I'll claim my reward later, if that's all right."

"It's an open offer." Max got up and stretched her shoulders and legs. "Besides, I would adore a bath myself. I have a million questions."

"And later I'll answer all of them." As he spoke, Peter dragged Philippe closer to André and, taking the chains he had removed from Max, bound the two men together. "There's no telling when they'll start to come to."

Peter secured the chains with the padlock and jammed the hairpin he had used as a pick back into the cylinder, wiggling it back and forth until it snapped. "Even if they can get to the key, it'll be useless. Up for a walk?"

"I'm up for anything that'll get me out of here."

Rémy had identified a few different portals to the Catacombs, and, from what Peter could tell from the map he had memorized, one of them—a boarded-up mausoleum in the southeast end of Montparnasse Cemetery—was nearby.

"I think we're good." Peter retrieved his flashlight from the table, flicked it on, took Max's hand and led her out of the chamber. After one false turn Peter located the corridor matching the map, and he and Max followed it to a stone staircase that rose to a wooden planked ceiling. Peter climbed the fifteen steps alone and pushed on the ceiling boards with both hands, dis-lodging a four-foot-square panel. He lifted himself through the opening, then beamed the flashlight down so Max could see to walk up the steps. When she reached the top, he grabbed her wrists and pulled her out.

Although it was small and confining, after his experiences in the Catacombs Peter found the mausoleum spacious. Any crypts it once held had long since disappeared, and the flashlight revealed large chunks of masonry had fallen from the walls, just one of many obvious signs of neglect and decay. The mausoleum's metal doors were heavily dented, and when Peter pushed against them they easily gave way, admitting a rush of warm, fresh early-morning Paris air. He took Max's hand again, releasing it when they were safely outside, and then only to shut the mausoleum doors.

He and Max had risen from the dead.

16

"Well, well, well—have the ghosts come out to play? If so, that is a mistake. Ghosts are not exempt from the curfew."

A startled Max turned to find a stocky man in dark trousers and a dark shirt approaching, speaking gruff street French and holding a flashlight in one hand and a gun pointed at Peter in the other.

As the man drew closer Max observed him with a director's eye. He had Edward G. Robinson's menacing sneer, although he was much taller than Robinson and solid rather than squat, while his face was more harshly lived in, marked by a nose obviously broken more than once.

"Now what is so important that you risk arrest by being in this cemetery after curfew?" The stranger beamed the light directly in Peter's eyes, forcing him to squint and look away. "See, you even act guilty."

Not sure who they were dealing with, Max let Peter take the lead.

"And who are you to ask?" Peter said.

"I am the man with a gun in your face. Now, shall I repeat the question?"

"That won't be necessary," Peter said, and placed his arm around Max. "How can I put this delicately? There are reasons for us to meet secretly. Madam is married to a ne'er-do-well who treats her badly. Tonight she left the house for her own safety and sought me out for comfort and protection." Peter winked. "As a man of the world you understand how such things are."

"I understand very well and so normally I might let it go at that. But there is one thing I don't understand." The man swept Peter with the light, flicked it toward Max, then back to Peter. "Why would a lovely woman take up with filthy scum like you? You look like a pig and stink worse."

"You know the heart," Peter said.

"I also know something else." The man stuck the flashlight under his arm while he fished a folded paper from his pocket and shook it open. "I know I have a picture of this woman. A strange coincidence, no? Here, see."

Peter took the paper, a hastily put-together flyer from Gestapo headquarters with a picture and a description of Max. When he reached out to return it, the man grabbed Peter's wrist and swung him around so both arms were behind his back. Snatching handcuffs from his belt, he slapped them on Peter, then shoved him face-first to the ground. With Peter secure, the man turned to Max and made a slight bow.

"Allow me to properly introduce myself. I am Pierre Lecourt of the Gestapo and it is an honor to be in your presence, Mademoiselle Elise."

He's Gestapo? And what was he doing here? Luck or a leak? Max looked at Peter on the ground. Five minutes ago she was quietly celebrating her rescue. How quickly the situation had changed. Best to go along and let matters unfold, or unravel, as now seemed more likely.

"I am just thankful that I was here when I was," Lecourt continued. "Because of that, you are free."

"No, I'm the one who's thankful. I believe they really would have killed me."

"Is this where they were hiding you, in the cemetery?"

Think fast, Max. "They had me in a different location until two or three hours ago. But they were afraid that someone had tipped off the authorities. So they had the one called Pierre . . . ," she said, pointing to Peter, "bring me here to wait for them. We had been in the mausoleum, but I needed some air, and that's when you appeared."

"So, then, you—"

Max cut him off. "Please don't think me rude, but it's been such a trying ordeal. And I'm afraid the others may come soon."

"Indeed. "How thoughtless of me." Lecourt bowed more deeply this time. "I'll take you somewhere safe and send for the authorities. Like a champion of old, I will see that you are not harmed, my lady."

Lecourt's ridiculous attempts to imitate upper-class French and his clumsy display of manners marked him as a pretentious—and dangerous—fool of gargantuan proportions and for now Max knew it would be best if she catered to his illusions. "And him?" She kicked Peter in the ribs.

"He will come with us." Lecourt seized Peter's forearm and jerked him up. "But do not worry about your friends who are to meet you here, Pierre. I guarantee they will be greeted properly when they arrive."

———

What was supposed to be a knock sounded like a hammer pounding away at the wooden bistro door, sending flakes of red paint flying. "Hey, are you dead in there?" Lecourt's ham fists kept battering until Max didn't know whether the door or her eardrums would burst first. "Marcel, you son of a whore, I know you're in there. I give you another thirty seconds to open or I'll kick this goddamn door in and blow your fucking brains out!"

So this is my self-proclaimed knight in shining armor. Max shook her head in disgust as she watched Lecourt shed his previous genteel posturing and revert to type.

"What is the matter with you?" A pudgy, florid face peered through the partly opened door. "Do you know what time . . . ?" There was an audible gasp as the door swung fully open. "Lecourt. I didn't recognize your voice. I was upstairs. I didn't—"

"I'm not interested in your explanations. Now get out of the way." Holding Peter by the back of his collar, Lecourt beckoned Max inside with a sweep of his free hand, Then, shoving Peter like a battering ram, Lecourt entered and slammed the door shut with his heel.

"Please, Monsieur Lecourt, may I—" The bistro keeper quickly placed the chairs that were tilted against the edge of a small, round table firmly on the floor. "You know that no matter the hour, you are always welcome here."

Lecourt didn't reply; he pulled Peter to the table and plunked him into one of the chairs, then drew another back for Max. "Marcel!" he bellowed after sitting down himself. Max saw that the bistro owner was shaking. "You will bring us a bottle of wine—a decent bottle, not that swill you pour."

"*Oui*, of course."

"And some cheese and bread. Bethmale. Cow, not goat. And don't tell me you have none, because I know you do."

"Of course, of course. The Bethmale you so generously sold me. And wine. A nice Jurançon that you made available—"

Lecourt slammed his palm down on the table. "Red! Bring us some real red wine!"

"Of course. A red wine. A Collioure, perhaps. Your people were not around, so I had to get—"

"Spare me the details. Just bring it."

"Of course, Monsieur Lecourt." Marcel backed away from the table. "Immediately. You'll excuse me."

"Really not a bad fellow, Marcel. Just not too smart. But he understands authority. Many do not. Not like Germany, eh, Mademoiselle Elise?"

Max managed a wan smile. From the bistro owner's timid utterances she had pieced together Lecourt. He was a common criminal, whose power came from controlling the French black market. That's where Marcel got his cheese and wine. But those were only crumbs: the best goods were reserved for the German occupation leaders. Besides luxuries, Lecourt and his kind supplied them with something more important.

Dead bodies.

The SS, which found cold-blooded killers like Lecourt useful, dubbed them "the French Gestapo" and gave them some quasi-authority along with immunity from arrest. That explained the Gestapo remark. However, the real Gestapo wanted her abductors alive. That's why Lecourt didn't kill Peter in the cemetery, although it would have been a merciful end. Max shivered at the thought of what Peter now faced.

"You are cold?" Lecourt asked. "Or still just a little frightened. Do not worry. . . ." He reached over the table and gripped Peter's chin with his hand and wrenched it toward Max. "He can no longer hurt you." Lecourt released Peter and pounded again on the table. "Marcel, where are you with the food and drink?"

As if on cue, the bistro owner scrambled in, a tray with rattling glasses and plates in one hand, a bottle in the other, both of which he hurriedly set on the table. Then he retreated, quickly returning with a platter bearing bread and cheese. "What may I do for you now, Monsieur Lecourt?" he asked, placing the platter down.

"You can take your miserable self upstairs and call the Gestapo. Tell them I am here with Mademoiselle Maxine Elise and one of her captors. Tell them to come immediately. Then you stay in your quarters unless I call for you."

"Of course. Of course. I will do that immediately." Marcel bowed awkwardly to Max as he backed away, then turned and exited through a doorway. She could hear the sound of his shoes hitting against stairs and then the loud closing of a door.

Meanwhile Lecourt, who had taken the plates from the tray, was busy cutting the rind from a large wedge of cheese. "The treasure is buried inside." He held up an ivory-colored slice studded with oval holes, which he had extracted, and sniffed it, "Not too pungent, so it is not that old. But its taste . . . Well, you tell me." Lecourt hacked a piece of bread from a long loaf, placed the cheese on it and gave it to Max. Though she was hungry, Max had little desire to eat Lecourt's offering, but to avoid angering him she took it and bit off a portion. He was right. It was delicious—creamy with hints of spice. She put the rest in her mouth.

"Not like those things you call cheese in Germany. *This* is cheese. Bethmale was the favorite of King Louis the Sixth, a cheese for royalty." Lecourt cut some bread and cheese for himself and devoured it in a gulp.

"Do I get to taste?"

It was the first time Peter had spoken since being handcuffed, and Max took it as a sign that he had worked out a plan.

"What did you say?" Lecourt squinted at Peter, as if his eyes were trying to validate his ears.

"Am I allowed a little something to eat?"

"Something to eat?" Lecourt turned to Max. "Did you hear that? He wants something to eat." He turned back to Peter and burst out laughing. "Who do you think you are, a guest here? Something to eat. The idea. Wait. You want something to eat?" Lecourt chopped off another piece of cheese and some bread, then rolled them both in his hands and, as if he were shooting dice, tossed them onto the table before Peter. "There is your food. Now eat like the pig you are."

Max, who was growing ever more uneasy, watched as Peter bent over and, in clumsy fashion, plucked up the morsels with his mouth.

"Bravo, pig!" Lecourt's contemptuous laughter echoed through the room. "Bravo!" He grabbed the wine, poured some for Max and himself and lifted his glass. "To your rescue." Max took her glass and clanked it against his. Before she could put it down, Lecourt hit it again. "And to a delightful evening. Wine, food and now even entertainment. What more could we ask?"

"I could ask for some wine," Peter said.

"You could ask for—" Lecourt again began to laugh. "Now he wants some wine. Can you believe the nerve?"

"There won't be any wine for me where I'm going. A last sip then." With that Peter began to sing, the same ditty from the Catacombs. *"Goûtons voir, oui oui oui, Goûtons voir, non non non. Goûtons voir si le vin est bon. Goûtons voir, oui—"*

"And he even sings! Here." Lecourt shoved his wineglass toward Peter. "Anything to keep you quiet. Besides, you should toast your capture at my hands."

"Are you crazy?" Peter said.

Lecourt drew the glass back. "Then I guess you are not all that thirsty."

"Wait. I'll toast."

"I thought so. Mademoiselle, would you do me the honor of going over to him and lifting the glass?"

Now Max was certain Peter had come up with something. She stood up, moved next to him and held up the glass Lecourt had pushed over.

"Well, go ahead," Lecourt said to Peter.

"Monsieur Lecourt, I salute your—"

"Louder!"

"Monsieur Lecourt, I salute your skill and great courage in capturing one of those who abducted Mademoiselle Elise and your gallant efforts in freeing her."

"You say it, but you're thinking it is bullshit, right?"

Peter said nothing.

"What do I care if it is bullshit? The taste is in your mouth, not mine. Me, I taste no bullshit. I only taste good wine and hear the sweet words of defeat." He leaned over and tapped the glass Max was holding. "Now you may give him a drink. Do not be afraid."

"I'm not afraid with you here." Max continued stroking Lecourt's ego, hoping it might make him lower his guard. As she spoke, she bent down and placed the rim of the glass between Peter's lips. Peter moved his head back slightly, prompting her to tilt the glass diagonally until the wine began to stream into his mouth. Suddenly Peter plunged his head forward, clenching his teeth around the glass lip and snapping off a large piece. He swung his head back again and opened his mouth, allowing the piece to drop in.

Max's unfaked shriek was followed by loud crunching and she watched in horror as Peter chewed the glass.

"What are you doing?" shouted Lecourt, who appeared momentarily stunned.

"I'm not going to be tortured by the Gestapo." Peter swallowed and coughed, then began chewing again, the crunching giving way to a grinding.

"You idiot!" Bolting up, Lecourt was on Peter in an instant, tugging at his jaw until he finally pried his mouth open, but there was no glass. "Idiot!" Lecourt began bellowing for Marcel, the bistro owner. Again Max heard shoes on the stairs. But Lecourt didn't wait for Marcel to emerge. "Go back! Call the Gestapo again! Have them send a doctor! Now!"

Peter started making jerking motions and Max saw blood flowing from his mouth. The motions became more violent, sending him from the chair to the floor.

"He's convulsing!" she screamed.

"*Merde!* Marcel call! Now! Now!"

Kneeling next to Peter's twitching body, Max put her head on his chest and listened. "His heartbeat's erratic!" The words made her nauseous. Damn you, Peter! This was your plan? To kill yourself! Even in Gestapo hands, there might have been a chance! Damn you! "Do something! Where is the doctor?"

"Move over!" Lecourt shoved Max aside and placed his ear on Peter's chest. "This is crazy. His heart is faint. He seems to have no—"

It happened so fast that Max wasn't sure whether she really saw Peter's right hand thrust until Lecourt rolled away, an inch-long shining sliver of glass protruding from his neck.

"You fucking son of a bitch!" Lecourt raised his hand to his neck and plucked out the glass. "I don't know how you got free, but if you think this will stop me . . ." He threw the glass at Peter, who was now standing. "I was startled, but now . . ." Lecourt was having difficulty getting up. He took his gun from his pocket and he targeted Peter. "I should shoot you and be done with it, but I'd rather savor the agony of your Gestapo interrogation."

"You won't live that long," Peter said. "You'll be dead in less than five minutes. So you really should shoot me now, although I doubt you have enough feeling in your hand to pull the trigger. Go ahead, try."

But the gun had fallen from Lecourt's grip before Peter finished speaking. "What's going on?" he asked, his speech heavy and slurred.

"Paralysis is setting in and your body is shutting down."

"Tha . . . Tha . . ." Lecourt couldn't get the words out.

"See."

But the only thing Lecourt could see was the bistro ceiling. As he was unable to support himself in a sitting position, his upper body collapsed with a thud.

"It'll be over very soon."

"Peter, in God's name, tell me what's happening," Max said.

"Shhh." Peter stood silently. "Hear it?"

"What?"

"Faint sirens. The Gestapo." Peter reached down, picked up the gun and fired three shots into Lecourt's body. "That's for Wilhelm Strauss." He turned to Max. "Lecourt was already dead, just like Strauss. "Now give one of your best screams, like you did outside The Crow's Nest."

"Peter!"

"Quickly!" Peter grabbed Max's arm and started to pull her. "And afterwards shout for the bistro owner."

Max screamed, then yelled, "Monsieur Marcel! Marcel!"

"Excellent. Now when he comes, tell him I killed Lecourt and tried to take you again."

Marcel came rushing through the entrance and Peter loosened his grip on Max. Seeing Lecourt lying motionless on the floor, Marcel grabbed a butcher's knife from behind the bar and Peter fired a shot at him, deliberately missing, then fled from the bistro. Cautiously Marcel went to the door, stepped outside and then quickly back in. "He's off into the night."

"He killed Lecourt and tried to drag me away again."

"Please." Marcel helped Max to a chair. "Believe me, he won't get far. Listen."

The weak sirens Peter had heard were louder and more piercing.

"The Gestapo, mademoiselle. They'll be here any moment. They will get him. And you will let them know I helped you, yes?"

Max nodded her head and smiled weakly, even as she was beaming inside. She had never met anyone quite like Peter and he intrigued her. Despite her earlier reservations, Max was now confident she could trust him to do what he had been sent to do. But Peter was still a man, and while Max wanted to believe he wouldn't hurt her, she wasn't willing to trust him beyond the mission.

For now.

17

It was either a late breakfast or a brunch, not that it mattered. Peter's only concern was that it included hot coffee and Max, not necessarily in that order. Admittedly, he was still tired after the events in the Catacombs and the bistro, but Max, as always, looked fresh and radiant.

"Peter!" She smiled and waved him over. There was something about the smile he hadn't detected before. He couldn't quite put his finger on it, but somehow it was different. That he was sure of.

"Slacks, shirt, colorful sweater—you look very dapper," Max said as Peter joined her at the table. "Coffee?"

"Desperately." Peter unfolded the crisp napkin and placed it on his lap.

Max lifted a white porcelain carafe. "So, did you get some sleep?"

"A little." Peter lifted his cup as soon as Max stopped pouring and took a long sip. "Wonderfully strong. Paris coffee reminds me of the jungles."

"Jungles?"

"Hobo jungles. Camps near rail yards where hoboes would gather and share food and stories."

"Were you a hobo?"

That wasn't something Peter wanted to get into. He was surprised he even had mentioned it.

"I've been a lot of things." He took another sip of coffee. "It was a long time ago."

"Then how about something closer at hand, like a few hours ago? Otto already told me about Rémy."

"Interesting guy." Peter broke a croissant in half and dabbed on some sweet country butter. "He was in film, I understand."

"Never in a big way. He dabbled in producing without much success. Still, we hit it off and he introduced me to some of the top filmmakers in France. Hitler's rise and his monstrous designs for Europe drew us closer."

"Well, I like Rémy and he was a big help to me."

"Otto also told me about the plants and the cigarettes. Why didn't the poison kill André, the one who smoked?"

"I promised Rémy I'd try not to kill anyone. I only used enough of the plant mixture to produce hallucinations, not death."

"But how did you know how much to put in the cigarettes?" Max refreshed Peter's coffee and poured some more for herself.

"Instinct and practice. Besides, I learned from the best."

"Who would be?"

Another question Peter had no desire to answer right now. "Again, it was a long time ago and it doesn't really matter. It worked." Now *he* changed the subject. "Was Lecourt really Gestapo?"

"No. Just one of the lowlifes who help their German masters in return for privileges and protection. I found out Lecourt was a murderer and one of the most feared black marketers in Paris. That's why the bistro owner was so terrified. You should get the Legion of Honor for getting rid of that vermin. But I have so much to ask about that."

"Like?"

"Like the glass I saw you chew and swallow. I know you could open the handcuffs but the glass."

"Want to see me do it again?" He lifted his water goblet, but Max took hold of his hand.

"No, please, just tell me."

"It's an old carnival trick. I manipulated the chunk of glass in my mouth with my teeth and tongue and broke a piece off that I crunched and ground with my molars. Pulverized glass is harmless. You can swallow it."

"And the other piece."

"I used that to cut the underside of my tongue so I could make it look like I was coughing up blood."

"But Lecourt examined your mouth and found nothing there."

"That's because there was nothing there."

"You're not making sense."

Peter could tell Max was getting a little irritated, but he was having fun toying with her. Oh well. "Remember the bread bits Lecourt threw on the table for me? I kept them in my mouth and once I finished cutting myself I worked the glass into them. So when I swallowed that glass it was cushioned. But it never made it to my stomach. I used muscle control to hold it in the top of my esophagus, just beyond my larynx, and then bring it back up again when I needed it." As he spoke, Peter moved his right forefinger over his throat to illustrate his points. "Houdini taught me how to do that.

It's one of the ways he hid keys and picks. I practiced the technique the same way he did, by putting a piece of cooked chicken on a string and partially swallowing it, then pulling it back up. That trains you to get over your natural gag reflex. Some human ostriches can even—"

"What in the world is a human ostrich?"

"Sorry. A human ostrich is a sideshow performer who can swallow all sorts of things—money, keys, rings, watches, even live animals like frogs and mice—and then bring them back up in any order you want."

Max made a face. "It sounds disgusting."

"You'd be surprised how many people pay to watch it done. Anyway, that's what happened to the glass. It was in the back of my throat. When I pretended to fall from the table, I brought it back up, spit it out and rolled over so my lower back was resting on it. That way it was ready and reachable when I freed myself from the handcuffs. Does that answer everything?"

"But how did you know you'd be able to hit Lecourt in just the right spot with the glass and with enough force to kill him?"

"The glass didn't kill Lecourt. The poison that was on the glass killed him."

"The poison you put in the cigarettes?"

"That was Datura. This poison was made from Black Henbane, which is much more deadly. Ancient warriors put it on their spears and arrows to kill enemies. I brought it along as a precaution, not knowing what to expect from your captors. I had it in a match tin in my back pocket. When I faked going into convulsions, I opened the tin, found a part of the glass that was point-like and stuck it into the powder. If I had merely scratched Lecourt, he would still have been a dead man. It just would have taken longer for the poison to act. By plunging the glass, I was able to get the poison deeper into his system, where it worked faster. Pretty simple, really."

Max shook her head. "You're amazing."

"I thank you." Peter made a slight bow. "As they say on the midway, if you liked the show, we'll be repeating it again in two hours."

"I never want to repeat that show." Max turned serious. "And now you know what it's like to kill somebody. Ending a life isn't a decision taken lightly, even when it's necessary."

"You're right. But the crucial word is 'decision.' I had no part in the decision involving Wilhelm Strauss. I didn't even know about it, yet I was a key player."

"You made that clear the other day, Peter," Max said. "I swear to you I will never hide anything again. I don't know what else I can do to make you forgive me."

There was a very slight, almost imperceptible catch in Max's voice, but

Peter heard it and, more than her words, it spoke to her sincerity. He was going to let her know he had already forgiven her. But now she had opened the way for him to add a condition.

"You can take me for that dinner you offered when we were atop the tower."

"What?"

"That's the price of peace. Dinner. Tonight at seven. A place of your choosing, since you're more familiar with Paris."

"That's it? No negotiations?"

"None."

"Very well. If those are your treaty terms . . ." Max lifted the napkin from her lap and waved it in the air. "Then this German willingly surrenders."

For dinner, Max selected the Left Bank's legendary *La Tour d'Argent*—The Silver Tower—on the Quai de la Tournelle near the juncture of St. Germain and Henri IV boulevards. Opened in 1582, *La Tour d'Argent*, Paris's first restaurant, took its name from an earlier occupant of the site, a twelfth-century military tower whose mica-embedded stone roof "glistened like silver in the sunlight."

Even under German occupation, *La Tour d'Argent* remained popular. Members of the Nazi elite ate there so often that the restaurant printed a special set of menus in German to accommodate them.

However, the maître d' chose French to greet Max, proclaiming her beauty and his establishment's pride in hosting "Europe's greatest director." Max, responding in French, thanked him and introduced Peter as a consultant on her new film.

The maître d' bowed to Peter from the waist and, switching to German, told him he was the luckiest man in the world to be working with Max.

Peter however, used French to tell the surprised maître d' that he was the luckiest man in the world just to be dining with Max.

"Another surprise," Max said as she and Peter followed the maître d' through a plush parlor, its walls jammed with signed celebrity photographs. "You speak French, and much better than I do."

"It comes from working with circus folk," Peter explained as they entered a small manned elevator, which then lurched its way up seven stories to the main dining room. "They come from all over the world and speak every language imaginable."

"Well, in France, food is a language, and *La Tour d'Argent* speaks it perfectly." Max stepped out of the elevator onto a maroon carpet patterned with gold laurel sprigs that complemented the warm wood tones of the room.

Following her, Peter caught an enticing whiff of real butter, fresh garlic and salt from a sizzling pan delicately being rocked by a server in white tie and tails. "So it seems," Peter said. "I just caught part of a conversation."

The maître d' led them across the crowded room to an intimate window seating. Max surveyed the gold silk table draping, impeccably set with over-sized Havilland Limoges floral-themed porcelain plates framed by scrolled-handled Puiforcat sterling silver flatware.

"These are their finest pieces," Max said while the headwaiter pulled back her chair. "They date from the mid-nineteenth-century reign of the Emperor Napoléon the Third." She turned to the maître d'. "Louis, you didn't bring these out just for us?"

"Unfortunately I had to cast the same settings before swine so they wouldn't get jealous." He subtly turned his eyes toward a larger table where two SS generals were growing tipsy with their giggling Parisian escorts. "But you did say you wanted to make this a special evening."

"You wanted to make this a special evening?" Peter asked once the maître d' had left. "And why's that?"

"Because for a little bit, at least, I want to make believe there's no war going on, and that we're just a man and a woman in Paris together. For a few hours, I want to forget those hungry children we saw in the street outside searching the gutters for scraps. I want to forget the endless slaughter and how powerless and ineffective I feel, despite my efforts. It's a selfish indulgence, I know, but I'm not a saint, Peter. I never wanted to be and I never pretended to be."

More like a Madonna, Peter thought. An understandably tired and frustrated Madonna; he wanted to reach out and embrace the vulnerability that for the moment was Max. But before he could do anything, Max, her mood transformed, popped up and peered out the window, pressing the glass with the forefinger of her right hand.

"Peter, there! Across the Seine on the Ile de la Cité. The Cathedral of Notre Dame. And there. See how the slate roofs of the houses shatter the fading sunlight into pebbles and skim them along the surface of the river. Isn't it spectacular?"

"Breathtaking." Peter rose, pretending to look, but his gaze never left Max, attired in a simple black velvet cocktail dress and a single strand of pearls. Max wasn't just *in* Paris; she *was* Paris. "Absolutely breathtaking."

Peter sat back down, facing the room, and he noticed how many German officers, in their crisp white summer uniforms, were commanding the discreetly separated tables. "Isn't this a little conspicuous, given our dining companions?" he said.

"The more conspicuous, the better. Hide in plain sight, remember? Besides, you have Himmler's pardon and now you're on the verge of having his blessing."

Peter wasn't sure what Max meant by that, nor was he sure he wanted to know, but he asked anyway.

"Not now," Max said. "Let's have that nice meal and relax. Afterwards is time enough."

As if to make sure Peter dropped the matter, Max suddenly exclaimed, "Oh, look!" and drew his attention to a high flame dancing in a pan on a rolling serving table. "Crêpes suzette! It's always so wonderful to watch them being prepared. Only the orange flame isn't nearly as dramatic as the red one you produced at Wewelsburg. Was that just an accident?"

"Accident?" Peter said with mock indignation. "That flame was the product of great planning!"

"Then you should teach the waiters here. It would make their presentation even more spectacular."

"They would have to use a very special ingredient."

"A very special ingredient?" Max clapped her hands together. "Tell me, tell me!"

Peter leaned over the table and signaled for Max to do the same. When her right ear was so near to his lips they almost touched, he whispered something.

A startled Max recoiled with a snap. "Ants?"

"Damn, now everyone knows the secret."

"You used ants to produce that red flame?"

"In a way. Do you really want to know?"

Max's widened eyes said, *Yes!*

"While I was in the alcove working out how to fool Himmler, I detected a familiar odor. It was coming from some white powder spread on the floor in one of the corners."

"What was it?"

"Boric acid, commonly used to get rid of insects. Wewelsburg may or may not have spirits, but it definitely has ants. I took the handkerchief I was going to burn and rubbed it in the powder. Boric acid gives off a brilliant red flame when set on fire. Added a little more flair, don't you think?"

Max shook her head. "You really are amazing. And I'm famished. Shall we?"

They started with a glass of Champagne, because Max said it wouldn't be Paris without Champagne, followed by a traditional appetizer, coquilles Saint-Jacques. For an entrée Max suggested the house specialty—duck done as two courses: roasted breasts with a special sauce and grilled legs and thighs with béarnaise sauce.

"La Tour d'Argent is famous for its duck," Max said. "They record each one served in a registry and give you a certificate with the number."

"Wonderful," Peter said, though he saw no reason why he would want a dead duck's number.

After they had ordered, the sommelier approached with a bottle of red wine. "Compliments of the owner, Mademoiselle Elise," he said, showing the label to Max, then Peter.

"Excellent," Max proclaimed.

Having her approval, the sommelier opened the wine and handed the cork to Peter who pressed it between his thumb and forefinger. Nodding for the sommelier to pour a small amount. Peter lifted the glass and swirled the wine to let it aerate, then held it to his nose, inhaled and finally took a sip, breathing deeply to draw air over the liquid on his tongue. He nodded again and the sommelier poured Max half a glass, then filled Peter's to the same level.

"Why was he smiling?" Peter asked once the sommelier had left. "Did I make a fool of myself?"

"On the contrary. I think it was the cork. You felt it to see if the wine had been stored properly on its side. Germans usually sniff the corks, pretending to be sophisticated, not realizing that sniffing says nothing about the wine. And your tasting technique was classic. I see Houdini taught you more than magic."

"Sir Arthur, actually. Houdini, growing up in Wisconsin, liked beer."

"Well, I think he would have liked this burgundy."

Peter reached for the bottle and examined the label again. "I'm afraid I haven't paid much attention to recent vintages. Was 1936 a good year?"

"No, it was a dreadful year. One of the worst. Unfortunately Goering looted the best wines from all the top restaurants. La Tour d'Argent was particularly hard hit. Once it had the finest cellar in France. Now there's nothing."

"Then I did make a fool of myself. I thought the wine was superb."

"It should be." Max lowered her voice to a whisper. "It's an 1867 burgundy, one of the greatest vintages ever."

"I thought Goering took the best wine."

"But not the *very* best. Certain restaurants, usually with ties to the resistance, hid them. Here the wine is behind a fake stone wall in the basement.

Claude Terrail, the owner's son, even brought in spiders to spin cobwebs so the wall would look older. But a few bottles, with phony labels, were left accessible for certain people."

"Are you going to tell me why you're one of those certain people?"

"Maybe one day."

Peter lifted his glass. "Here's to one day."

Max followed suit and, with a clink, added, "And here's to Paris."

Peter watched her sip the wine and envied her glass. God, what was this city doing to him?

Max, however, expressed what he couldn't—or wouldn't. "Paris always makes me feel so giddy. Even with the horrors of war around us, it's special. Sometimes I feel I'm an old French soul trapped in a German body."

Peter was tempted to say something about that body. But he had already decided not to complicate his mission by becoming involved with a woman, especially a woman he had to work with. Was he attracted to Max? Why wouldn't he be? She was stunning, smart and spirited. Under different circumstances, he would welcome a casual relationship, like those he previously had. Nothing binding. A good time and then a good-bye. But since these weren't different circumstances, Peter would simply enjoy a beautiful woman's company and a fine dinner. His resolve reaffirmed, Peter looked past Max to where an older man in a tuxedo was turning what appeared to be a two-foot-high silver corkscrew mounted on a pedestal. "What's he doing over there?"

"Preparing our duck," Max said after taking a look. "He's already removed the skin and the breast fillets and placed them in a special reduction. Now he's crushing the carcass to extract the blood. That's what's flowing into the silver bowl. When it's all drained, he'll add it to the sauce with the duck's liver, cognac and some other ingredients. If you want, we can go over and watch."

"No, thanks." Peter was emphatic. "It's enough I'm eating duck served in blood. You never mentioned that to me."

"I thought it best not to. But why not reserve judgment until after you've tried it?"

It was wise advice. Once Peter had savored the tender, rare meat, its gaminess muted nicely by the pleasantly pungent sauce, his qualms quickly passed. The crisp legs and thighs were equally satisfying. But best of all was the table talk with Max, which, as agreed on, included no mention of the war.

"I envy the French directors," Max confessed as she and Peter enjoyed the last of their wine over a platter of richly creamed cheeses and fresh fruit. "They have such magnificent settings for romantic scenes. See how beautifully Notre Dame is silhouetted now that the moon is up. What a wonderful backdrop: the cathedral protecting the river and giving its blessing to strolling lovers. Have you ever been to Notre Dame, Peter?"

"Once. With Houdini, when I was young. He was scouting it out for an escape. I went along hoping to catch a glimpse of the hunchback. Today I'd be looking for Esmeralda."

"So you like the wild gypsy types. Well, that . . . Damn! Gypsies! I nearly forgot!"

"Forgot what?" Peter watched Max fish around in her purse.

"This."

Peter's eyes narrowed as she removed a small red flannel bag cinched with black drawstrings. It can't be, he thought as she pulled the top edges of the bag apart. It's merely a coincidence.

"Someone must have used this with sachet. It has such a lovely smell." Max reached over and held the bag to Peter's nose. "I don't know what it is, but it's intoxicating."

Inhaling cautiously, Peter used his trained sense of smell, and knowledge acquired long ago, to identify what Max couldn't: Queen Elizabeth root, cardamom, coriander and dill seeds, cubeb berries, lavender buds, lemongrass, cinnamon and—he inhaled again, this time more deeply—probably a smattering of elecampane, verbena and mistletoe, all finely ground and blended for a specific purpose. This complex mixture was no coincidence. What Max had was a conjure bag, used to hold magical materials, often for casting spells. This particular bag contained remnants of a powder so powerful that a mere trace was potent enough to achieve its purpose.

This powder was meant to capture a heart.

"There's still a little of the powder left, but here's what's really exceptional." From the bag Max pulled out a strangely hued blue string, which held a rusted iron carpenter's nail twisted into a cross dangling from it.

Suddenly Peter felt all the air rush from his body. "Where did you get that?" he asked, trying to maintain his composure.

"From an old gypsy woman, this afternoon, as I was leaving the Eiffel Tower." Max placed the piece on the table, then unclasped her pearls and placed them in her purse. "I don't know why she was out in the open like that. The authorities were sure to grab her and send her off to one of the camps. But there she was, selling all types of jewelry—gold, silver." She picked up the piece and waved it gently in front of Peter's eyes. "This was hidden beneath everything, but somehow I found it. Or maybe it found me. Anyway, for some reason I was completely taken with it. Strange, because it's not what you'd think of as jewelry at all. More like a talisman. Initially I think the string attracted me. Such an unusual shade of blue—I've never seen anything like it." She spread the string, placed it over her head and lowered it until it fell around her neck. "There, how's that?"

But Peter pursued his own line of questioning. "What did this gypsy look like?"

"Like an old woman. I don't know. A bandanna over her hair. Wrinkled. Colorful clothes. Why are you so interested in a gypsy?"

Not a gypsy. *The* Gypsy. Easy, Peter. Concentrate on acting nonchalant. "When I worked the carnivals, there were always gypsies around. They fascinated me. Maybe it was their sham magic." There. That sounded plausible, he thought.

"Well, for some reason this piece called out to me." Max rubbed the nail between her thumb and forefinger. "But the gypsy would only sell it if I promised to wear it tonight. I told her I had a dinner engagement and wasn't sure it would be appropriate, but she was adamant. Isn't that weird?"

"Very." Peter felt like he was going to wear a hole in the silk napkin with his fingers.

"So I promised her I would, but I forgot about it until you mentioned Esmeralda. Funny, isn't it?"

Anything but funny, and right now Peter desperately wanted to block the necklace from his mind.

"Peter, are you all right?" Max asked. "You look a little pale."

"Do I? Maybe it's the duck blood catching up with me. And I know just the cure. An Armagnac."

"Ah, the brandy of D'Artagnan. You really can be quite worldly when you want, can't you?"

"Does it make you think more of me?"

"It doesn't make me think less."

"I'll settle for that."

Even as they lingered over the Armagnac, the necklace kept telling Peter he had to break the mood. Reluctantly, he yielded. "About Himmler and his blessing."

"So, time to stop pretending." Max sighed. "Well, it was sweet while it lasted, but you're right: dinner's over and we both know why we're really here together. Shall we walk by the Seine? It's such a lovely evening and the moon is bright enough to light our way. Please. It'll be quieter."

Clearly Max was about to ask for something teetering on the impossible and preferred not to have an audience. And impossible or not, whatever she asked, Peter would have to find a way to do it. The Gypsy sent the necklace to remind him of that.

But the Gypsy also sent him a message. By placing the necklace in the conjure bag with such a powerful powder she finally answered the question Peter had asked her years earlier in a Mississippi graveyard at midnight.

The Gypsy said Maxine Elise would be the one great love of his life.

There was a touch of coolness in the night air, enough that a woman might welcome a man's arm around her shoulder. That's what Peter was hoping. He reached across Max's back, gently clasped her and leaned in so his face was close to hers. "Just keep walking," he whispered. "We're being followed."

Instead Max stopped abruptly. "How romantic!" she said. Breaking free of Peter, she began to laugh.

"After what you went through you find being followed funny?"

"I'm sorry. We're being followed *because* of what I went through." She turned and called out, "Come on. Show yourselves. It's all right!"

A pair of uniformed German soldiers emerged from the shadows. Max waved to them and turned back to Peter. "My bodyguards. Oberg insisted."

"They've been with us all night?" Peter asked.

"They've tried to be discreet. Most people wouldn't have noticed them. Of course, you're not most people. So is that why you put your arm around me? To sound an alert?"

"I just thought—"

Max was laughing again. "Never mind." She took his hand. "They really won't bother us. Let's continue our walk for at least a few more minutes. Just a man and a woman in Paris."

"With two Nazi chaperones."

Gently he squeezed her hand, and they walked quietly, first along the Seine, then on the Pont de l'Archevêché, one of the twenty-eight bridges that crossed it, and finally a short distance to a small park behind Notre Dame. Max was right: The moon's brightness defeated the government's mandatory blackout and guided them to a granite bench. There they sat facing the great cathedral, its magnificent stained-glass windows replaced by canvas sheets and its awe-inspiring stonework taking on a corpse-like bluish-gray tone in the cold, natural night light.

"So?" Peter said.

"So?"

"Himmler's blessing."

Max sighed. "You're right. No sense avoiding it any longer. Maybe that's why I was supposed to wear the gypsy's necklace tonight. Maybe it's my new good-luck charm. We'll see when I tell you." She put her hand to her chest, then suddenly slid it down, feeling around the scoop of her dress. "Peter, it's gone! The necklace is gone!"

Of course it's gone, Peter thought. It served its purpose. Now it would only be a distraction.

"I can't believe it." Max paused and stared at Peter. "You didn't take it, did you? This wasn't some of your sleight of hand."

"Believe me, Max, that necklace is the last thing on earth I want to put my hands on. The string probably broke. It looked pretty flimsy."

Max seemed to accept that. Certainly better than telling her the string was unbreakable. There's no way she would have believed that, even if it was the truth. Though after all these years Peter still wasn't sure he accepted that himself.

"And it was such a perfect evening until now."

"Because you lost a cheap gypsy necklace that nobody would find attractive?" Peter said.

"No, of course not. Well, maybe a little, but only because I'm not looking forward to the conversation we're about to have and losing the necklace may be symbolic."

"I'm harder to lose, so why not just tell me and get it over with."

"You tell me something first. At Wewelsburg, when Himmler used the ashes to make the code appear on your forehead. You fooled him completely and he wasn't the only one. How did you do it?"

"An old family formula, guaranteed to dazzle."

"Please, Peter, please."

This wasn't the desperate Max in Father Fritz's study, wanting to know how he discovered and pulled the scab off a deep personal wound. This was the little girl in Max, filled with the wonder of the sideshow, wanting to know how all the impossible things were done. "Sorry, Max. Magicians take an oath never to reveal their methods."

"Please, Peter."

"However, there have been exceptions. Now promise you won't tell."

Max raised her right hand. "Promise."

"Remember I asked for time to meditate. That was a stall: I had no idea what I was going to do. Then, while I was sitting in the alcove gazing at the candles, an old trick came back to me. I dabbed my finger into the melting candle wax, then lightly traced the code on my forehead. When Himmler pressed my brow, the ashes on his hand adhered to the wax."

"But wouldn't Himmler feel the wax?"

"Kiss me."

"What?"

"Kiss me—on the forehead."

Though obviously confused, Max obliged.

"Good." Peter took out a cigarette, lit it, took a few puffs, then grabbed Max's hand and gently knocked the ashes into her palm. "Now press your palm against my forehead, then take it away."

Again, Max did as asked.

"Feel anything?"

"No."

"Look." Peter angled his face. "Is there enough moonlight for you to make it out?"

Max stared intently. "There's a faint impression of a pair of lips!"

"Because the skin on the palm is thick, it isn't that sensitive to begin with. Coat it with some ashes and it becomes even less so. You put more lipstick on before we left the restaurant, so there was enough wax for the ashes to adhere to." Peter rubbed the ashes and lipstick from his forehead. "Voilà, the evidence is gone. The rest, as you know, was just a little dramatic license."

This time the kiss was on his cheek and Peter didn't wipe it away. "What was that for?"

"For doubting you when we first met. For giving you a hard time. For what I'm about to say."

Finally. "Himmler's blessing."

Max smiled, but it was a tight smile, an exactly-how-should-I-tell-you-this? smile. Again Peter helped her out. "Go ahead, We'll figure out how to deal with it."

Max responded in a single breath. "Himmler wants you to predict a major military victory for him."

Or maybe we won't figure it out. "What?"

"We're finally into astrology, and Himmler wants you to do some charts and tell him when and where Germany will achieve a major military victory in the next few weeks."

"For Christ's sake, Max, I'm not a goddamn battle seer. Sure, I can talk my way around birth charts and make some vague predictions, but victories are pretty absolute."

"This is how you'll gain his confidence. Himmler fancies himself a brilliant military strategist, but he's never been able to convince Hitler."

"So you expect me to help this fool look like Alexander the Great, Julius Caesar and Napoléon all rolled into one?"

"Peter, it's the opportunity we've been waiting for."

"Opportunity? Himmler just erased his name from my death warrant and now you want me to hand him a pen so he can sign it again. Predict a military victory. Do you realize what you're asking?"

"You agreed to this mission."

"But I didn't agree to commit suicide just because some crazy woman asks."

He regretted saying "crazy," even though it fit at the moment, so Peter braced himself for an angry response. Again, Max surprised him.

"You can do it."

"Can isn't the issue. *Should* is."

"I already told Himmler you'd do it."

"You already told—I *hate* it when somebody makes decisions for me! Why did you do a stupid thing like that? Haven't you learned anything at all about me?"

"Yes. I learned that I trust you."

"Well, that's a poor— What did you say?"

Max was silent.

"Max, what did you say?"

She turned her face away, still not responding.

"Damn it, Max!" Peter placed his hand on her shoulders and forced her to look at him. "What did you say?"

"This." She put her arms over his shoulders and pulled him forward until his lips met hers. By the time Peter realized what was happening, it was over. "I trust you. I trust you and I believe in you, Peter. I know you can pull it off."

It was time to become the old confident, unflappable Peter and lie. "There's no question I can pull it off."

"I'm not trying to pressure you. But the sooner you do . . ."

"How about now? Is that soon enough?"

"Are you serious?"

"Absolutely," Peter said, knowing he should have said, "Are you kidding? No, I'm not serious. I just shot off my mouth to impress you." Now he had to come up with something quick. Peter's mind began rapidly tossing around bits of information, which collided with each other. Himmler. Military. War fronts. Eastern. Russia? No, not now. No connections. Europe? No, that's quiet. Africa? What did Donovan say? Allies are on the verge of losing? But things are going back and forth—one day Rommel, one day the British. The British? The British. Wait. London. Bletchley Park. Menzies. Something Menzies tossed out. Did he know? Yes, of course he did. That's it! The particulars don't matter. Just make contact and he'll provide what I need to make Himmler look like the most—

"I can't believe you came up with a plan this quickly."

Now be calm and smooth, no matter how pleased you are with yourself. "You don't have to believe. You just have to do one thing and I'll handle the rest."

"What's that?" she asked.

"Get me to Cairo."

18

Algeria, August 9, 1942
Your Stars Today: Mars and Saturn are creating abrasive conditions that can easily lead to tension and conflict. Take special care on this day of potential dangers, especially when traveling.

When Peter asked Max to get him to Cairo, he assumed it would be easy. Maybe not to Cairo itself, but close—German field marshal Erwin Rommel's headquarters near El Alamein. From there, he'd find a way to get across the remaining 150 miles of desert to the city.

"Just say you're shooting a segment on Rommel's Afrika Korps for the SS documentary and like always I'll be part of the film crew," Peter said, only to have Max tell him that Rommel considered SS soldiers "stupid and worthless" and refused to use them.

That didn't change things: Peter still needed to get to Cairo; otherwise he couldn't cast the predictive military charts Himmler was expecting, Finally Otto came up with a way, which he explained in a word.

"Rémy."

"Rémy may not be able to get you to Egypt directly," Otto continued. "but I know he can get you out of France and into North Africa. And I'm sure he'll have some ideas about how to handle the rest."

"The rest," as Otto casually referred to it, would mean a trek across thousands of miles of unforgiving terrain where, absent the cover of Max's film crew, Peter would be in danger from both the Axis and the Allies. It was a fool's errand and Peter let Otto know that.

Right before he asked him to arrange the meeting with Rémy.

Otto was right. Rémy did get Peter out of France—personally escorting him over unguarded routes to the port city of Marseilles. There the small twin-diesel vessel Minna was waiting to take him on a brief voyage to a location near the Algerian port of Oran, in Vichy-controlled Algeria. Under the cloak of night, two crewmen brought Peter by motorboat to a point about five hundred feet from shore and tossed a pack into the water. The pack automatically spread open on impact, forming a small dinghy made of canvas and wooden stretchers, which one of the crewmen used to row Peter to shore, leaving him to continue his journey alone.

Rémy's instructions were simple: make your way to La Gare d'Oran, the city's central railway station, take the early-morning train to Algiers and then go to the offices of Floc-Av, an oatmeal manufacturer and distributor.

"Ask for Rygor Slowikowski," Rémy said. "He's the boss. He's also a Polish army officer and a spy. Rygor created Floc-Av as a cover for his intelligence-gathering organization and staffed all its North African offices with spies. He's a fascinating man. You'll enjoy meeting him."

If the Minna captain's information was correct, the first train to Algiers left in just over four hours, at 8:15 A.M., and supposedly Peter was less than five miles from the station. Plenty of time, especially since he was traveling light: just the clothes he had on—an open-necked cotton shirt, light-colored linen slacks, a slightly darker linen jacket, shoes and socks, a sun-shielding hat, and some local currency, a pocket notepad and forged identity papers. He was now Pierre Dugard, a businessman trying to sell Floc-Av his supply of Moroccan oats. According to the map he had memorized on the Minna, the route to La Gare d'Oran wasn't complicated, so he wouldn't be hindered by the dark. Besides, he would rather reach his destination before the sun rose; it would make it easier for him to blend in. With the hat and his facial growth, now several days along, Peter felt confident that his lightly tanned skin wouldn't be a problem, especially if he subtly concealed his hands. All set, except one last thing, which, for Peter, was always the first thing when starting on an unpredictable venture—the rallying cry, sounded aloud but low, just in case someone was listening.

"The game is afoot!"

La Gare d'Oran seemed more mosque than train station, a sprawling white rectangular structure, with a triple set of arched entrance doors leading to a magnificently tiled domed interior. In fact, Peter mistook the station's high, imposing tower for a minaret until he was near enough to see the clock on its face. With time to kill, he bought some coffee and a hunk of warm bread slathered with butter and jam from an outdoors seller. The bread, an Algerian breakfast staple, was delicious, but the coffee was salty from the seawater that, Rémy had told him, continually seeped into Oran's wells.

Peter bought his ticket without a hitch. He decided on second class—not as plush as first class, but more comfortable than third class. A reasonable compromise and the least conspicuous option. Before boarding, he purchased several French newspapers to get him through a seven-hour trip. Diversion aside, holding up a newspaper would help conceal his face.

Since he had boarded early, Peter had his choice of seats, all of which faced forward and were fairly roomy. He selected one by a window, settled in and opened a newspaper. The train took off almost exactly on schedule and made only four station stops along the way. When it pulled out of Blida, the last of these, Peter felt more relaxed. Only 3:12 P.M., and Algiers was a mere forty miles away, which meant he should be on the street heading to Floc-Av by 4:00 P.M., give or take a few minutes.

No sooner had the train worked its way up to full speed than it slowed back down and stopped. Within seconds, a man dressed in a white suit and holding high an impressive-looking badge boarded and, offering no explanation, ordered the passengers off the train. They obeyed without so much as a question. Peter could smell their fear. As he made his way to the door, he heard some passengers muttering in French and mentioning the name "Achiary."

"Excuse me, but do you know that man?" he asked one of them.

"Achiary? Not personally, and that's how I'd want to keep it." Then, seeing Peter's blank look, he elaborated. "André Achiary—the Vichy Commissioner of Counter-Espionage for Algeria. From what I've heard, you don't want to run afoul of him."

The Commissioner of Counter-Espionage. Wonderful. Just what he needed. And almost at Algiers. So near. So damn near!

"Please hurry," Achiary said as the passengers filed out. "I want to inconvenience you as little as possible. This should not take long."

Peter walked down the car steps onto the hot, sandy ground and lined up with the other passengers. He noticed two men in white shirts and beige slacks leaning against a sleek black Citroën Traction Avant. The moment Achiary emerged from the train, the two straightened up, drew pistols from their hip holsters and moved away from the vehicle, trying to look as menacing as possible.

"Please have your papers ready," Achiary said.

Maybe they're looking for somebody else, Peter considered, then dismissed the possibility, certain they wanted him.

"I will be quick. I promise." Achiary began examining each passenger's paper while the two other men stood guard. There were four people ahead of Peter in the line, but, true to his word, Achiary was moving swiftly, and was only two passengers away from Peter when he broke stride. "Madame, I asked that papers be ready," Achiary snapped. "You will now hold everyone up."

The flustered woman tore through her purse until she found her papers. "At last." Achiary snatched them from her hand. "I thought perhaps we would have to set up camp here."

Would have to set up camp here. Peter detected the trace of an accent, one he had recently heard. Where was it? He closed his eyes and concentrated. It was on the way to Marseilles and . . . wait . . . yes! A farmer, one of Rémy's men, had the same accent, only more pronounced, and he was—

"Monsieur, your papers, please."

Basque! That's it! Achiary is Basque. Peter scanned his memory. The Basque population was clustered in . . . in the Pyrenees, especially the southwest region.

"Monsieur, your papers please."

Now what had Rémy said about the Basques? Proud. Highly independent. Extremely anti-fascist. Good friends of the resistance.

"Hey, are you sleeping standing, like a horse? Open your eyes." Achiary jostled Peter's shoulder. "We are not playing here, you know. Now for the last time—your papers."

Peter had been paying more attention to Achiary's accent than to Achiary and was caught by surprise. *"Pardon."* He reached into his right inner jacket pocket and withdrew the forged identity documents Rémy had given him. *"Ici."*

"Good. Then we will not have to shoot you." Achiary laughed as he flipped open the papers, but Peter wasn't amused.

"Or maybe we will," Achiary stared hard at the document. "Pierre Dugard, correct?"

Peter nodded his head.

"Come with me, please."

This was ridiculous. Rémy had assured Peter the papers were perfect. "There must be a mistake of some sort. I'm a businessman traveling to Algiers to make a sale."

"And do you know who I am?"

"You are Commissioner Achiary."

"Then you know I do not make mistakes." Achiary took a few steps back and put his hands to his mouth like a megaphone. *"Alors.* Everyone, please, go back to the train. I appreciate your cooperation and I hope the remainder of your ride is pleasant."

Peter watched the passengers, perhaps afraid that Achiary might change his mind, rush to the railcar and then bunch into a shoving mass on the steps trying to board.

"Shall we?" Achiary walked back to Peter and motioned toward the Citroën.

As if he had a choice. Now what else did he remember about Rémy's Basque farmer that might be useful? Peter focused on finding a very small fragment somewhere in his photographic memory.

"Monsieur, don't you hear?" Achiary reached inside his suit jacket, pulled out a pistol and tapped Peter on the shoulder with it.

"I still have no idea what you want with me." Peter continued to search as he spoke.

"You will soon enough." Achiary whistled loudly, then shouted to his subordinates, "Come, finish up there. We must go!"

Whistling. That's right. The farmer liked to whistle. Two tunes, neither of which Peter had recognized, over and over again.

Achiary turned back to Peter. "Well?"

He needed another few seconds to locate those tunes. "I don't suppose you can tell me where we're going?"

"I can tell you where we are not going: to Floc-Av."

Shit! He knows everything. But where was the leak? And who else has been compromised? OK, it is what it is. Just go to the car and . . . wait! There's one of the tunes. Whistle it on the way to the car and see what happens. "Then let's go. I love surprises."

"Not this one, I think," Achiary said.

Peter began whistling the first tune, but Achiary didn't react. Then, while waiting for the two guards to finish getting everyone on the train, Peter managed to grab snippets of the second tune. Rather than continuing to search for the whole tune, Peter decided to go with what he had and began whistling again, trying to link the disjointed bits and pieces in some musically coherent fashion.

"What is that you are whistling?" Achiary asked.

"I don't know." Peter wasn't sure Achiary would respond at all, let alone this quickly, and hadn't fully fleshed out his plan. "Something that's stuck with me . . ." He spoke slowly, dragging out his words and crafting something plausible to say. "From when I was very young. My grandmother used to sing it. I can't remember the words, but I vaguely recall them being strange."

"*Bonbolontena, nere laztana, Ez egin lorik basuan. Aizteritxuak eamango zailu. Erbiya zeralakuan. Bo!* The words are Basque, part of a traditional lullaby. However, your tune is not quite right." Achiary began singing very softly. "*Bonbolontena, nere laztana, Ez egin lorik basuan. Aizteritxuak eamango zailu. Erbiya zeralakuan. Bo!* That is the way it is supposed to sound." He resumed singing. this time in French "Bonbolontena, my darling, don't sleep in the woods. The little hunter will take you, mistaking you for a hare. Sleep!"

"Yes," Peter said. "That's it."

"Then you are Basque?"

"Not that I know, although when I was a young child my grandmother did live . . ." In his mind, Peter unfolded the map of France and selected a place in the Pyrenees that was on the fringe of the Basque region. "In Lourdes."

"Lourdes?" Achiary smiled. "I am originally from Tarbes, very near Lourdes. Have you been to the Pyrenees?"

"Regretfully, no, but I have heard it's beautiful."

"'Beautiful' is not the word. I could tell you things . . . but unfortunately we must go." Achiary, who had started to drift, was back at anchor. "Are you two ever coming?" he shouted at his men, who were speaking to the engineer.

"You can tell me later, when we get to Algiers," Peter said, still seeking to stall.

"There is no need for you to go to Algiers. Whatever would be done there can be done here."

Achiary's men had returned and one reported that "the engineer understands to wait until we have left."

"Good." Achiary poked Peter in the ribs with his pistol. "Take him."

The men grabbed Peter by his upper arms and partly carried, partly dragged him around to the other side of the car.

"Back a little." Achiary rubbed his fingers across the Citroën's shiny black hood. "Cleaning sand off the finish is one thing, blood another."

"I'm certain that if you would just bring me to Algiers—"

"Would you like a cigarette?" Achiary asked, disregarding Peter's plea.

Looking beyond Achiary and over the car, Peter could see the train windows blocked by curtains of human faces fascinated by the drama outside and relieved that they weren't part of it. "No."

"Very well. Is there anything more you wish to say?"

"Bring me to Algiers."

"I will take that to mean you have nothing more to say." Achiary motioned to his men. "Both of you step a little to the side, but hold him tight by the elbows."

Was it the heat that was making Peter weak or the realization that he had run out of options? He couldn't talk his way out of this and the Camp X fighting techniques didn't cover this kind of situation. Besides, he was growing weaker.

"Let this be a warning." Achiary spoke loudly enough to be heard by those watching from the train cars. "Algeria does not tolerate spies. It does not waste time with them. Instead it dispenses justice." He raised his pistol to eye level. "Swiftly." He squeezed the trigger. A shot rang out. Peter slumped forward and, when Achiary's men released their hold, he crumpled to the ground. Achiary made his way to the body, bent down, pointed the pistol at Peter's head and fired again. "And with finality."

One of the men opened the car trunk, took out a large white sheet, and wrapped Peter's body in it. Then he and the other man lifted the sagging package, which now showed red stains, heaved it into the trunk and slammed it shut. Almost simultaneously, with three warning whistle blasts and the crunch of engaging gears, the 8:40 A.M. train to Algiers pulled away. Once it was out of sight, Achiary climbed into the back of the car. One of the two men slipped into the passenger's seat, while the other, who was already behind the wheel, started the ignition, shifted into gear and took off, leaving nothing behind but the sun, the heat and some bloodstained patches of sand where Peter's body had been.

At 4:50 P.M., eighty minutes and sixty-one often bumpy miles after leaving the outskirts of Blida, the Citroën rumbled to a stop. Achiary stepped out and opened the trunk. "Ah, you *are* alive," he said.

"Are you pleased or disappointed?" Sweat-drenched and confused, his voice parched to a rasp, Peter lifted his upper body and shook it free from the sheet.

"I was concerned." Achiary motioned and one of the men held out an earthen jug filled with water. Peter grabbed it and took a long swig. The water was tepid but not laced with salt like it was in Oran. He drank some more, then poured the rest over his head. Revived although still groggy, he eased his way out of the trunk and leaned against the side of the car.

"We ventilated the trunk so you would not cook. Still, I am sure it was an uncomfortable ride."

"The gun?"

Achiary took the pistol from his shoulder holster, held it to his own right temple and fired. "Blanks."

"But the drug was real enough." Peter rubbed the back of his neck. "I felt a prick when your men were hauling me. I thought it was an insect bite, until I started to pass out. Only a barbiturate would work that fast."

"Sodium thiopental, fast acting, but not long lasting."

Sodium thiopental! Christ! No wonder Achiary was concerned. A miscalculated dose would have been as deadly as bullets.

"I apologize if you have a headache from it," Achiary continued. "But Rémy and I agreed that everything must be convincing."

Rémy? Rémy was in on this elaborately staged sham? Or did Achiary drop his name as part of a setup to get information about the resistance? "Who's Rémy?" Peter asked, playing it safe.

"Unlike you, I have never met him. But we have ways of communicating when it is absolutely necessary."

If this was turning into a fishing match, then Achiary had no chance. "So where are we?"

"Not the place we need to be, so we must go." Achiary opened the left rear door. "This time you will ride in the back with me and I will do my best to explain."

Achiary went around to the car's other rear door and got in. "Remember we have to be there by five thirty P.M.," he said to the driver, then leaned toward Peter as the car began to move. "There is a schedule we must keep. But we do not need to keep up any pretense, Major Baker."

This wasn't good. Achiary knew the identity Peter would be using in Egypt. "Baker? I told you, my name is Pierre Dugard."

"Your name is Peter Baker and you are a British officer whose travel to Egypt was coordinated by Gilbert Renault. Oh, I am sorry—by Colonel Rémy of the resistance."

Despite Achiary knowing who Rémy really was, Peter wouldn't yield. "I don't know who told you such a ridiculous story."

"Rygor Slowikowski, the man you were going to Algiers to see, told me when he asked for my assistance. Surprised?"

That was an understatement.

"Rygor and I share the same hatred for the Nazis and for the puppet Vichy regime they put in place," Achiary continued. "I have, on occasion, used my position to protect him and Floc-Av. The Allies could ill afford to lose such a valuable espionage network. Now what more must I say before you accept that I am here to help you, Major Baker?"

"I might need to know why you just didn't let me get to Algiers."

"Concern over an Allied invasion has caused security in Algiers to be tightened. Even I am being watched. It would have been too dangerous for you there, so the plan Rémy told you about was changed and we would now intercept you before you reached Algiers. Stopping a train for a search is a common occurrence these days and would not cause suspicion. However, too many people would see me take you into custody. One of them might say something to the wrong person and I would have to explain why you

were not taken back to Algiers. Killing you was the best solution. Fear of
retaliation would silence mouths. Besides, such summary executions often
happen."

"On your part?" Peter asked.

When Achiary didn't answer, Peter tried another question. "Couldn't
your men have told me to collapse when I heard a shot?"

"I considered that, but had no guarantee you could do it convincingly.
Medicating you would be sure to make it look authentic."

"The bloody sheet was a nice touch."

"Two small vials of beef blood, broken when you were being wrapped. A
bit dramatic, perhaps, but effective."

"And now?"

"And now you should eat something." Achiary opened a straw basket
that was on the seat and took out a small feast: slices of roast lamb and
khobz, the ubiquitous Algerian flat bread, to put it on, along with mari-
nated olives, fresh figs, a selection of dried fruit and some *Makroud el Louse*—
flourless almond cookies. Peter, who was famished, didn't resist and Achiary
seemed to take pleasure in watching him eat so heartily.

"Here. Something to wash it down with." Achiary produced an unla-
beled bottle of dark red wine, which was already open, and handed it to
Peter. "A friend has a fine vineyard in Coteaux de Mascara, near Oran. The
region produces magnificent wine."

Peter hesitated and Achiary laughed. "I see you have had the water from
Oran. But this wine is as good as the water is bad." He took the bottle
back, pulled out the cork and drank. "Delicious. Here."

This time Peter drank some. Achiary was right—the wine was excellent.
When he finished eating, Peter again asked Achiary where they were going. But Achiary was more interested in talking about the war, especially
the prospect of the Free French storming North Africa to drive out "the
Vichy pigs." Eventually Peter was able to steer the conversation to Libya and
Rommel. Once there, Achiary was more than willing to share what he
termed "informed gossip."

Achiary's driver was better than his word, getting to wherever it was
they were going fifteen minutes ahead of schedule.

"Excellent!" A delighted Achiary hopped out of the car and Peter followed, looking around at his new surroundings.

"I am afraid there is nothing worth seeing," Achiary said. "Besides, you
will only be here a few minutes."

"That's worth seeing." Peter pointed to a plane about four hundred yards
away, at the end of a long strip of concrete.

"Ah, the Bloch MB. 81." Achiary started walking toward the plane, talking as he did. "A fine example of French ingenuity. Worth seeing indeed, and you, Major Baker, will be seeing a lot of it over the next few hours."

The small single-engine plane didn't spark the same degree of enthusiasm in Peter, although he said nothing until saw a single seat in the cockpit. He turned to Achiary. "I'm not a pilot."

"But Henri is."

"Henri?"

"Forgive me." Achiary looked embarrassed." I never introduced you to my companions. This is Rafe. . . ." He gestured at the man who drove the car. "And this is Henri."

After some quick, muttered greetings were exchanged, Peter mentioned the sole seat.

"It will be fine. Henri will sit there and you will be in here." Achiary ran his hand across the portion of the fuselage between the cockpit and the engine.

Peter squinted. "In there? What kind of plane is this?"

"An ambulance plane." Achiary grabbed a handle on the fuselage, twisted and lifted it up revealing a compartment, about ten feet long, four feet wide and six feet high. "One that can take off and land in extremely close quarters. Normally it would carry a stretcher in this compartment and perhaps another one or two strapped to its wings. It will get you safely to your destination."

"And where might that be?"

Achiary took a shrub branch and drew an inverted pyramid in the sandy soil. "This is Tunisia. And this is where you are going." He stuck the branch point just below the triangle's tip and slightly to the left. "The plane is taking you to another airstrip, this one near Bordj Messouda, which is still in Algeria but very near Libya. Bordj Messouda is a convenient entry point for the Sahara Desert, if you know what you are doing."

"Which I don't," Peter said.

"Someone will contact you there, using the code Rémy provided. He will take you to wherever it is you are going. And now . . ." Achiary swept his hand across the open compartment space. "The entire trip will take maybe six hours. You were drugged while in the car trunk, but now you will not be, so I hope small spaces do not make you anxious."

"I think I'll survive," Peter said. He couldn't help thinking about how traumatized Houdini would be at the prospect of spending six hours in such cramped quarters.

"Then I think we should not delay any longer." Achiary shook Peter's hand. "I have done what I can. Soon you will be in other hands. I can only wish you well."

"I'm sure you'll eventually find out, one way or the other." Peter put his hands on Achiary's shoulders and smiled. "Thank you for killing me and for everything else."

"It was my pleasure. And so, Rafe, Henri . . ."

Achiary's men hoisted Peter and helped him into the compartment. Actually the space wasn't all that confining and there was a pillow and an adequate supply of water. Hardly all the comforts of home, but enough to make the flight bearable. Peter tightened the safety strap around his waist and flashed a thumbs-up sign.

"Remember Bonbolontena," Achiary said. "Don't sleep in the woods. *Bon*, and bon voyage." With that Achiary closed the compartment hatch and locked it.

Peter heard Henri climbing into the cockpit. Two or three minutes later Peter's feet, which were facing the engine, began quivering from its vibrations. The vibrations grew more intense as the plane began to taxi and he was bounced up and down as the wheels struck the pocked concrete. Before he could adjust to that, Peter was swept by the sensation of being lifted into the air. The plane swayed slightly from side to side as it continued its climb, then leveled off and maintained a steady cruising speed. Meanwhile, Peter thought about how to spend the next six hours, but his body decided for him. Within minutes, he was fast asleep.

19

The impact of the plane wheels touching ground jarred Peter awake. Moments later, he heard footsteps above the din of the still-running engine, followed by some rustling on the side of the fuselage. Then the compartment hatch swung out and up, letting the fading daylight rush in.

"We have arrived." Henri took Peter's arm and helped him down. "I must leave you here alone, but this location was chosen with great care. You will be safe."

Henri gave Peter a cloth bundle containing some more fruit and the remainder of the wine and the two said their good-byes. Peter watched the plane take off, then sat on the sand. Given how efficient the operation had been so far, he assumed his next contact would be along shortly. However, an hour of waiting proved otherwise. To combat the boredom, Peter occupied himself with some logic puzzles created by Cambridge professor Charles Dodgson, a brilliant mathematician better known for the children's books he wrote as Lewis Carroll.

"Master the machinery of symbolic logic and you will have a mental occupation of absorbing interest always at hand, one that will be of real use to you in any subject you may take up." That, Sir Arthur told Peter, was what Dodgson advised. Sir Arthur had great respect for Dodgson, perhaps because the two had much in common. Both were scientists and highly imaginative writers and they traveled in the same psychic circles, although Dodgson, also a skilled magician, was more interested in the occult than in spiritualism.

The fact that Dodgson and Sir Arthur could keep their equilibrium while teetering between the rational and the speculative intrigued Peter. Unlike them, he chose sides, living by logic and skeptical of anything that dared defy it. Yet Peter could never completely break free of Delta's influence. Perhaps one day he would find his own balancing points.

But not today, as a wide yawn reminded Peter. The second yawn warned him. Determined that there not be a third, Peter plunged into puzzles.

"And I suppose you are the minnow?"

The sand had muted any footsteps, so Peter was taken by surprise by the mammoth man in flowing white Bedouin robes towering over him like a mountain covered with snow and glowering.

"You certainly look like a minnow," the newcomer growled.

Peter certainly felt like one by comparison. Rémy said the code question would include the word "minnow"—a play on "Minna"—and that it would be asked in English. But Rémy didn't mention a German accent.

"I am waiting. Must I ask again?"

"*Vraion.*" Peter gave the required answer—a play on *vairon*, French for "minnow," and *vrai*, French for "true": *vraion*, true minnow.

"Well, come on."

That was the wrong response to *vraion*. Peter didn't budge.

"I said come on. Must I repeat everyth— Oh, of course. Excuse me for being more concerned with staying alive. Fool, you butcher the language. There. Is that what you were waiting for?"

"Yes, with the exception of 'fool,'" Peter said, sounding like the British officer that he was supposed to be.

"Hmmm, hardly what I expected."

"Nor you." Peter lifted himself out of the sand. "You're German?"

Either the man didn't hear or he chose not to acknowledge Peter's question.

"I asked if you were German."

He heard it that time and acknowledged it by placing his right hand firmly on Peter's shoulder and turning his head so that they were face-to-face. "I am a member of the Thirteenth Demi-Brigade of the Foreign Legion, fighting for Free France. That's all you need to know about me." He moved his hand from Peter's shoulder to his shirt collar, which he clutched tightly. "I should tell you that in the Legion it is considered bad manners to ask too many questions about a man. It can quickly lead to death." He released Peter's collar and patted him on the back. "Now we understand each other, right?"

"Perfectly," Peter rasped, rubbing his fingers across his bruised throat. "I'm Baker. Major Peter Baker. Is there something I can call you without getting myself killed?"

It wasn't a grin exactly—more like a lesser scowl. "Call me Johnny. You know the wonderful Brecht and Weill song 'Surabaya Johnny'? I heard it at Brecht's house when they first wrote it. Weill's wife, Lotte Lenya, sang it and he played the piano." He started to hum some of the songs.

Surabaya Johnny? Bertolt Brecht and Kurt Weill? This thuggish figure hobnobbed with some of Weimar Germany's most creative people?

"Yes, I always liked that song. It speaks to me. But even before, I liked the name Johnny."

"Then Johnny it is," Peter said. "And I'm happy to see you. I was getting concerned."

"Arranging for our transportation took longer than I thought it would. But everything is fine now, so let us leave before it gets light and company arrives."

Johnny signaled for Peter to follow as he made his way through the sand to a grassy area about a quarter mile away, where two camels were tethered to a post. "Those are?" Peter asked, despite a gnawing feeling that he already knew the answer.

"Our transportation," Johnny said, rubbing each camel's chin in turn. "Won in a backgammon game. Unfortunately, the loser decided he didn't want to part with them." Johnny took a knife from his robe belt and stared at it. "Ultimately, however, he saw the wisdom of honoring his obligations."

As if to emphasize his point, Johnny tossed the knife, which missed Peter's face by less than an inch and ended up embedded in the trunk of a slender palm tree. "That's for you to carry. And this is for you to wear." Johnny yanked a bag from the back of one of the camels and tossed it to Peter. Inside was white clothing similar to Johnny's.

"Well, what are you waiting for? Undress!"

Peter stripped down to his undershorts and stopped. "These, too?"

"Unless you enjoy camel crotch."

"Camel crotch?"

"The undershorts will hold in your sweat and after hours of riding a camel the pain from the chafing between your legs will be as intense as any you have ever experienced."

Undershorts gone, Peter put on the robes and, after scrutinizing him, Johnny bellowed his approval. "We are now members of the same tribe. Brothers."

"Perhaps. But I doubt anyone will take us for natives."

"The clothing is protection from the desert, not a disguise, although from a distance it will hide your pale skin. And you will be in Cairo before the Sahara can bake you brown. This is what lies ahead."

Johnny dug his heel into the soft oasis earth and dragged it around until he had sketched out a rough, ragged rectangle. "We are here." He tapped a spot with the toe of his sandal. "There is where you need to be." He drew his toe across the rectangle and made another spot. "Cairo. Now straight from here to there is maybe thirteen hundred miles, nearly a month's travel by camel."

"I don't have a month."

"You do not need it." Johnny kicked a point in the sand near their starting point. "We are only going to here. Then the rest of the trip will be much faster."

"Why is that?"

"The sooner we start, the sooner you will find out. So tell me, brother, have you ever ridden a camel?"

Peter weighed saying he had and shocking the shit out of Johnny. While it was only a couple of times around a circus ring to please an animal trainer's daughter, Peter had gotten the general idea. But it was unlikely that Major Baker would have any camel-riding skills, so Peter resisted the temptation. "No."

"Then you better be a fast learner, because there is no time to baby you."

"Nor a need. As an expert horseman, I shall easily master the basics." Keeping to character, Peter added a touch of arrogance to his British indignation.

"We will see. A camel is no horse and it takes more than a Brit's sense of superiority to control one. That one is yours."

Johnny pointed to a brownish-white creature that, Peter estimated, weighed close to six hundred pounds, all of it stuffed into ten feet of undulating curves, not counting another two feet of rope-like tail, perched on four slender legs and rising some nine feet in the air at the top of its hump.

"Be careful," Johnny warned. "I do not really know them yet, but with any luck it will like you."

Peter knew what would happen if the camel didn't like him. It would spit. On him, not the ground. Foul spit. Like desert skunk. Best to try starting off on good terms.

"Do the camels have names?" Peter asked.

"Do the camels have names?" In disbelief, Johnny repeated the question while choking on his laughter. "They are fucking camels! Beast and other beast!"

"Then I'll name mine. That will make it much more convenient when we have to refer to her."

"By all means." Johnny's words still quivered from leftover laughter.

"And what about yours? It doesn't seem quite fair for only one to have a name."

"I'm not naming the goddamn camel."

"May I do the honors for us both, then?"

"I could care less. Just get it over with." Hands in the air, Johnny sounded more weary than angry.

"First I need to check gender."

"Let me save you the trouble. Female. Both of them."

"Excellent." Peter crept over to his camel and held out his hand so she could see and smell it. "Then I have the perfect names, and you helped, Johnny." Peter touched the camel's forehead. "From this point on you shall be known as Lotte."

"What the—"

"And you . . ." Peter swung back to the second camel, which wasn't as accepting of his hand, so he dubbed her with a wave. "You shall now be known as Lenya." Peter turned toward Johnny. "So now we have Surabaya Johnny and Lotte Lenya reunited."

"And you think that is funny?"

"Actually, yes."

"No, I will show you funny." Johnny walked over to Peter's camel and laid his right hand on her neck. *"Koosh,"* he commanded, and the camel dropped her front knees to the ground and then her back knees, finally settling down on top of them completely prone. "Now she—"

"Lotte," Peter corrected him.

"She awaits."

Lotte already on the ground put Peter one step ahead. Her saddle, however, might set him two steps behind. Unlike an ornate circus saddle, it was little more than a pitched wooden frame with a post jutting up at each end, precariously perched in front of Lotte's hump. A thin blanket was spread over the saddle, a halfhearted attempt to provide a modicum of comfort.

Since the saddle had no stirrups, Peter tested the sand to make sure it was solid. Satisfied, he caught hold of the dangling reins, which were attached to a peg in Lotte's nose, and gently pulled her head slightly to the right, just enough to make it awkward for her to suddenly stand while he was in mid-mount. That little touch, which he had learned from painful experience, wasn't lost on Johnny.

"I thought you had never ridden a camel."

"We British read a lot of travel accounts," Peter said.

Even with the positioning of her head, Lotte was restive, giving indications that she was going to do what she wanted—including bolt up—if she wanted.

"You have a strong-willed one," Johnny said.

"Strong-willed can be an admirable trait."

"Not if it costs you your balls."

"Understood." Holding the front saddle post, Peter flexed and threw his leg over Lotte's hump, then quickly pulled himself up and into position.

Johnny grunted and gave another unintelligible camel command. Suddenly Lotte's hind legs shot up, catapulting Peter toward her head. In desperation Peter wrapped his arms around Lotte's neck and held tight. He was secure, but only for an instant.

Her rear legs in place, Lotte lifted her front legs, and the jolt broke Peter's hold, hurling him back toward her tail. Acting on reflex, Peter maneuvered his legs so that this time he could lock them around Lotte's neck. The move kept him from falling but left his body dangling over the side with his head six inches from the sand.

"Now *that* is funny!" Johnny exclaimed as Peter struggled to right himself and settle back in the saddle. Lean back when a camel starts to get up, then lean forward. There it was: what he was searching for from his circus days. Peter's memory hadn't failed him—it never failed him. Timing, however, was another matter.

"I hope you slept while you were waiting for me. We will go until midmorning." Johnny shouted another command and both camels started to move. Only Lotte spurted instead of strode.

"That is good," Johnny said as Peter passed him. "You are in a hurry to get there."

Hurry, my ass. Johnny knew damn well the camel was out of control. "Stop her."

"Her?" Johnny said indignantly. "She has a name. Do not hurt Lotte's feelings."

"Would you please stop her!" Peter, who was getting farther from Johnny, yelled.

"Just hang on!" Johnny shouted back, convulsed with laughter. "She will come around on her own or you will get shot by a Berber band. Either way, the problem will take care of itself!"

At first, Peter thought it was exhaustion, the result of riding for eighteen hours with only two painfully short rest breaks. Then he thought it might be the heat, which despite his protective robe was brutal. But when he realized it was neither, he halted his camel and called out to Johnny.

"Jesus Christ, what the hell are you doing?" Johnny, who had been riding ahead, turned his head around and shouted. "We have three hours until the sun starts to set, so we can cover a good distance before we rest. Now move!"

But Peter didn't.

"What the fuck?"

"What's that?" Peter said, pointing into the distance.

"What? I see nothing."

Peter had wondered if the desert would affect his senses, but his vision was as acute as ever. "You will. Watch."

"Watch for what?"

"Dots."

"Dots? You stopped because you saw dots?"

"Only when they grew larger."

"Listen, the desert can do strange things, especially if you are not used to it." Johnny sounded concerned. "Maybe we *should* rest for a short while."

"No, I'm all right. Just watch."

"Name the camels. Stare at nothing. The next time I get talked into— Hello. What is this?" Johnny's eyes narrowed. "Now I see your dots."

"Only they're not dots." With his keener eyesight Peter could make out the shapes Johnny couldn't. "They're camels."

"You can see that?"

"Camels . . . with riders . . . three, no, four of them."

"The desert has many travelers, so it's probably nothing," Johnny said, but his tone didn't support his words. "We will wait until I can make them out more clearly."

"Which will be soon. They're riding faster and coming toward us."

But Johnny said nothing until the men were close enough to hear. Then he raised his hands in a friendly gesture. *"As-salaam alaykum."*

One of the men took a rifle from his shoulder, and bolted it and shouted something which Peter didn't understand, but the tone was clear.

"He is ordering us off our camels." Johnny kept his hands raised. "I will try again."

Johnny uttered a few more sentences, only to receive the same responses.

"They do not care that we are peaceful travelers," Johnny said.

"So what do we do?" Peter asked.

"What they say."

Peter and Johnny had brought their camels to a resting position and dismounted. Johnny made a last appeal, saying they had nothing of value, to
no avail. "Then they will take what we do have." Johnny removed his robe
as he translated for Peter. "The camels, all our supplies . . ."

"Even our clothes?"

"Everything."

Peter removed his garments and tossed them on top of Johnny's while the
men pointed and laughed.

"They find your pale skin funny." Johnny picked up the clothing and
shoved it into one of the bags hanging from Lenya's saddle.

In contrast, Johnny's body was a palette of earth tones—umber here,
sepia there and all over gradations of burnt sienna and Indian red. Besides
being more colorful, it was a body better able to resist the heat, although
that would be a very short-lived advantage.

"Kush. Kush." At Johnny's prodding the camels rose. He put their reins
together and handed them to the leader, who nodded to his men. Then,
with Lotte and Lenya in tow, the four slowly rode off.

"Why didn't they just kill us?" Peter asked when the men were far enough
away.

"Why bother when they can let the desert do it? Shooting is quick and
easy. But this . . ." Johnny spat on the sand and then shouted at the distant
figures, *"At'abak ta'b an-namla!"*

"What's that all about?"

"A Bedouin saying: 'I will tire you till you are tired as an ant.' It means
you will pursue those who have done you wrong without stop or mercy."

"Provided you're alive. We're naked in the middle of the desert, Johnny.
Do the Bedouins have a saying for that?"

"They do, but there is a better Legion saying."

"Which is?"

"March or die."

Johnny set out the basic rules: breathe through the nose, don't talk to pre-
serve water and walk slowly to minimize sweating. Then, two hours into
their trek, he added one more. "From now on, we walk in the night. The
cold will be better than the heat." He got down on the sand and scooped
out a trench, about six feet long and a foot deep. He motioned for Peter to
do the same. When done, Johnny lay down on his back in the trench and
covered himself with the sand, rolling his head to one side to minimize his
face's exposure. Peter mimicked his moves.

"This will shield us some. Now sleep and try not to suffocate yourself."

Although certain he wouldn't be able to sleep under these conditions, Peter did, and soundly, until Johnny woke him up.

"Come. If we are to survive, we must find a part of the desert that is not all sand."

Before setting out, Johnny set down another rule. "When you must piss, you piss into your hands." He put his hands together at the little fingers and formed a bowl. "Keep as much as possible from spilling and quickly drink it. In the desert, any liquid that is not poison is gold."

"More yellow than gold in this case," Peter quipped, and Johnny couldn't resist a smile.

So they set off, and as they journeyed the desert night grew colder, diving below freezing. During their brief rest periods, Peter and Johnny nestled together, pooling their body heat to help keep warm. Morning came, but the terrain hadn't changed. Walking and water loss had left them both weak. Peter's urine was still light yellow while Johnny's was darker, an indication that he was dehydrating faster. Hunger had set in, but they hadn't looked for nocturnal desert life to eat, since digesting food would have wasted energy needed for other tasks.

They continued to walk, albeit ever more slowly, until the sun reached its high point in the sky, the signal for them to dig and retreat to their trench shelters and sleep. At sunset, they started out once more, hoping to find a rocky stretch of desert, where there might be water and plants. But dawn found them still surrounded by sand and in worse physical shape. Besides dry mouths, they now were suffering from throbbing headaches and lethargy had supplanted fatigue. Their urine, which was little more than a trickle, had changed color: Peter's was now deep yellow and Johnny's a yellowish brown. Speaking was difficult and draining, so they tried to avoid it.

The possibility of finding water made them more determined, but by daylight their efforts had produced no success. Determination gave way to desperation as they now stumbled along, trying to maintain balance, afraid that should they fall, they would never get up. Nor did they dig their trenches during the early afternoon, knowing that they would probably become their graves. "Better to keep moving and die trying," Johnny said less than an hour before dropping to the ground.

Peter didn't attempt to help Johnny up; he could barely maintain his own balance. Instead he prodded by example. "Come on, Johnny, come." Peter's words, like his parched lips, stuck together. He managed a few more steps in the sand and then fell to his knees. He looked over to Johnny and, as he did, saw some low-lying shapes on the sand about a hundred yards away. They didn't appear to be rocks, but he knew how deceptive the desert could be.

"Johnny, over there!" he weakly called out.

Johnny mumbled something but didn't move. Peter forced himself to stand and walk half the distance to the forms, then fell once more, this time face-down and flat. Rather than expend energy on getting up, Peter crawled until he was close enough to make out what he had seen. Despite the desert heat, he chilled at the sight.

Bodies.

"Hello!" Peter strained to be heard. "Hello!" He waited a few seconds, then called out again. "Hear me?"

Still receiving no reply, Peter continued crawling until he reached one of the the robed figures who was lying on his back, his lifeless eyes open to the sky.

"What do we have?" Johnny had found the strength to inch through the sand on his belly and join Peter.

"Our bandits."

"Cocksuckers!" Johnny weakly pounded the corpse with his fists.

"Didn't get far."

"Not going far." Johnny's voice sounded just slightly stronger and Peter wondered if the sight of the dead bandits had momentarily revived him. "Could not see them, but they see us. Enjoy our suffering. Wagered on who die first, never thought it be them."

"Blood on the robe." Words were hard to get out. Peter looked more closely. "Bullet wound. Other bandits?"

"Do not know. But one thing sure: they be back."

Too weak to continue, they had no choice but to stay with the bodies and if those responsible returned so be it. All of the bandits' possessions were gone except for the robes they had been wearing. Peter and Johnny each put on a robe and knotted the other two into a covering. Then they dug a single, slightly larger trench. Each handful of sand drained their dwindling pool of energy until, when they finished, nothing remained. Yet they managed to drag the bodies over the sand, using them to anchor the covering over the trench. Finished, Peter and Johnny slipped into their shelter to rest and to wait.

Water was still their major concern. "Think on it, go mad. Sleep. Not wake up, not know." Johnny's speech was growing more slurred and fragmented from dehydration, as was Peter's, but they had learned to interpret each other's verbal shorthand.

Don't go crazy dwelling on water. Get some sleep. If you sleep and don't wake up, you won't know. Peter found a logic of sorts in the advice that Johnny offered, then followed: within ten minutes, the sound of his snoring filled the trench. Loud as it was, it couldn't keep Peter from yielding to the inevitable, and he soon drifted off as well.

To Peter it seemed like only minutes since his eyes had closed, although when they bolted open he could tell from the difference in light seeping under the covering that it had been hours. His sensitive hearing had detected distant sounds, which jarred him awake. Johnny was still sleeping soundly and there was no reason to wake him yet. Peter pushed the covering up with his head and peered out. Something was moving toward the trench. Something strange. Something . . . Peter blinked, but there was no moisture to wash his eyes. Something very strange.

Something blue.

Was this a mirage, the sky's color being refracted by the surface heat of the sand? Peter considered the possibility. That would account for the blue but not the brown, which he could now distinguish. No, this wasn't a mirage. These were people, probably dressed in blue, on camels—brown camels— and, although in no rush, they were heading for the trench. Now it was time to wake Johnny, which Peter did with a sharp poke to the ribs.

"What the—"

Peter moved his hand over Johnny's mouth and whispered, "More men."

"What color men?"

What color are the men? Why would Johnny ask a stupid question like that unless he already suspected the answer? "Blue. Robes. Turbans."

"Move shlow?"

"Yes."

"Cover, bodies—cautious. Could attack."

So the riders were being cautious because of the covering and the bodies. Peter was all right with that. But not with the prospect of them attacking. "Who?"

"Tuareg."

Tuareg? Peter's memory search came up blank.

"We greet them."

"Kill us?" Peter asked.

"Possible. Desert kill certain. Go possible."

This new band might kill them, but the desert definitely would kill them, so it was better to gamble on the possible. Johnny's thinking was clear even if his speech wasn't.

"Follow. Shay nothing." With that Johnny squirmed out of the trench and looked up at the seven men clad entirely in indigo. *"Alxer Ras!"* he said, then lay still in the sand. As instructed, Peter wriggled next to Johnny and, as he did, he cast a surreptitious glance at the Tuareg. He had hoped to read their expressions but couldn't. Blue veils covered their necks and faces and then, wrapped into turbans, their heads, leaving only narrow slits for their eyes.

"Ma dar tolad?" Johnny raised his head again and very slowly and deliberately formed each word.

"Alxer Ras." Finally. One of the men spoke. *"Ma dar tolad?"*

"Alxer Ras," Johnny said, and Peter, guided by instinct, repeated the phrase. *"Aytedamnadarosssss."* Frustrated, Johnny tried again. *"Aytedam-nawan mad-arolaaaaa."* The Tuareg looked at one another and Peter didn't want to even speculate on what they might be thinking. One of them dismounted, walked over and stood gazing down at Peter and Johnny. Then he placed his right hand on the handle of a long, slender sword secured in his robe belt.

"Now," Johnny said. "Live, die."

After a moment of hesitation, the man moved his hand from the sword to a leather flask, which he unfastened and placed on the sand in front of Johnny's face. *"Alxer Ras. Aytedam-nawan ma dar olan."*

"Live." Johnny pushed the flask to Peter. "Drink."

Not about to be noble, Peter pressed the flask against his parched lips, letting some of the water trickle over them before taking a deep swig and passing the precious liquid to Johnny.

"Good you know language," Peter said, finding that his words were coming a little easier.

"Greeting ritual. Scattered words. No more."

Meanwhile all the Tuareg had dismounted and were gathered around Peter and Johnny. The Tuareg who gave them the water said something, then sat down in the sand. "Arabic," Johnny said to Peter. "They speak. We talk."

This time Peter had a face to read—Johnny's—and it brightened the longer his halting conversation with the Tuareg went on. When it ended, Johnny said the Tuareg would take the two of them to their rendezvous point.

"Spend night their camp," Johnny said. "Weak, ride with Tuareg."

In contrast to Johnny's halting words, the Tuareg took swift action. Two of them lifted Peter and Johnny from the sand and onto their kneeling camels, securing them to the back part of the saddles. They repeated the process with Peter. Then draped blankets over them to block out sun, although having seen nothing but sand for days, Peter was even happier that they had blocked out the desert. But after a half hour or so, Peter caught a whiff of something and poked his head out from under the blanket. Yes, vegetation! Peter watched the variety of plants and shrubs that shot up from gravelly soil become more abundant as they approached the Tuareg camp where children were darting all around, women were preparing food over open fires and men were sitting on the ground conversing over tea. All about were tents—strips of goatskin sewn together and stretched over wooden poles—and through their open entrances Peter saw decorative mats used for flooring. Set off to one side camels and goats grazed near a pile of saddles in various stages of construction or repair.

The Tuareg led Peter and Johnny from the camels to a tent, removed the two with cool water and coated their faces and bodies with a salve. Covering themselves with sand during the day had paid off: though both were sunburned, they were only slightly blistered, and the curative effects of aloe and marigold—natural burn balms that Peter smelled in the salve— began working immediately. Once Peter and Johnny had dressed in clean robes, they sat on cots and ate a light meal of sand-baked bread and broth, followed by highly sugared tea, which Johnny said was the Tuareg liquid of life.

Peter thought he detected something other than sugar in the tea, which could account for why both he and Johnny suddenly felt an overwhelming urge to sleep. Yielding, they slept for eighteen hours, awakening in the late afternoon refreshed, if not pain-free. After another application of salve and a light meal of millet porridge, they wandered around outside. Although their muscles were still sore, their speech was almost back to normal, enabling Peter to ask Johnny about their hosts.

"The Tuareg are nomads who have ruled the Sahara forever, it seems," Johnny explained. "Once they controlled the trade routes, providing protection for a price. They are a proud people and fierce when need be, much feared by others. However, these days they are mostly peaceful. Some Tuareg have moved to the cities, but others, such as these families who travel together, call houses the graves of the living. They could never live in one place, so eventually they will pack up and go elsewhere in the desert. The Tuareg who found us were protecting the camp. They came back to make sure the men they killed were not part of a bigger band."

"Why do they wear blue?"

"They do not just wear blue—they are blue." Johnny put his hand up just as Peter opened his mouth. "The Tuareg believe that indigo has many magical powers, including the ability to ward off evil. They pound powder into their clothing to dye it indigo, but the powder also permanently stains their skin. You'd never know though. A Tuareg man would suffer great shame if a stranger saw his mouth or nose. So he only removes his *tagelmust*, the thirty feet of wrapped indigo cloth that's both veil and turban, when he's alone or with close family."

Rest had rekindled Peter's curiosity and he was teeming with questions that he would have asked if he hadn't been barraged by sounds and smells that were still beyond the range of Johnny's senses. "Come on," Peter said, breaking away from Johnny.

"Hey, slow down. Your muscles can still cramp."

Undeterred, Peter's brisk steps soon brought him to the area where the Tuareg kept their small herds: goats, sheep, donkeys and camels.

"There!" Peter wove through the animals. "Lotte!"

One of the camels bellowed and Peter excitedly called out to Johnny, who still hadn't caught up. "And look over there! Lenya!"

"I told you before, they're just fucking camels and they'll still be there tomorrow." Johnny caught Peter's arm that was waving at the camels and led him away.

Supper, which Peter and Johnny again ate in their tent, consisted of more substantial fare. Besides the porridge, there was milk and cheese, bread with a dipping sauce and even some goat meat. "Prepared in our honor," Johnny said. "The Tuareg rarely eat meat." Later, Peter and Johnny were invited outside to join the men who were gathered around a fire drinking tea and talking. Out of consideration for their guests, the men spoke Arabic, but Peter was still shut out. So, after drinking what Johnny explained were the customary three glasses of progressively sweetened tea—the strong and bitter tea of death, then the sweeter tea of life and finally the extremely sweet tea of love—Peter retired to the tent. Johnny came in about an hour later with news.

"The Tuareg have agreed to escort us to our meeting place tomorrow. We leave at dawn. They wanted us to rest another day, but I explained we had to make up time."

"And in return?"

"They keep the camels."

"That's it?"

"The Tuareg consider it a matter of honor to show hospitality to strangers," Johnny explained. "Or to slaughter them."

20

Saharan Libya: August 15, 1942
Your Stars Today: You are likely to find relations strained,
and participation and your cooperation forced or coerced.
This is a difficult time for open talks, trust, and sharing.

The camels began braying just before dawn.

It was a loud, harsh sound, more felt than heard, and impossible to ignore.

"Jesus Christ, somebody shut up those fucking *beasts*!" Jolted out of a sound sleep, Johnny rolled over on his mat and opened his eyes.

"Your special alarm clock." Peter was already dressed in his white robe and headgear. "I was up. The camels started a few minutes ago when the Tuareg put their saddles on."

"That means it will be dawn soon," said Johnny, yawning. "The Tuareg will want to leave at light and ride straight through until dark, when the djinns come out."

"Djinns?"

"The spirits of the desert." Johnny stood up, stretched his shoulders and arms and grabbed his clothing. "The Tuareg will not travel when the djinns are active."

"Personally I would have welcomed a djinn or two when we were stumbling around the desert at night."

"No stumbling today," Johnny said as he finished dressing. "Today we go in style. First class. Come."

Tea and bread were waiting when they emerged from the tent. They ate quickly, and once they finished the Tuareg gave them daggers with ornately tooled wooden handles to place in their belts. Johnny, speaking in Arabic, expressed their thanks and farewells. Then, with the courtesies concluded, Peter mounted Lotte and Johnny, Lenya. The camels rose.

"Well, look at this." Johnny lifted up a rifle hanging on the saddle and stroked it gently, as he might a lover. "Do you know what this is?"

"A rifle," Peter said.

"This is not a rifle. This is an old and faithful friend, a Fusil 1886

/M93—eight rounds, eight millimeter. Standard Legion issue. You have one, too. They must have belonged to fallen comrades."

He didn't mean fallen: he meant killed by the Tuareg. Peter wondered whether Johnny had told the Tuareg he was a Legionnaire.

"Now we are certainly ready," Johnny continued. "With these rifles and three Tuareg warriors we can face a hundred enemies before needing reinforcements."

Oh shit—that's right. Johnny thought he was accompanying a British officer, able to skillfully handle a rifle. Peter knew how to handle a rifle, but the "skillfully" part was a problem.

"Part of me hopes we do not have to use this and part of me does." Johnny hung the rifle back on his saddle. "I know you understand, Major Baker."

"Perfectly," Peter said. Before Johnny could bring up any other military-related matters, Peter tugged on Lotte's reins and shouted, *"Kush!"* effectively ending the conversation.

By Johnny's reckoning, it would take four days to reach the small, isolated oasis he and his comrades often used as a safe rendezvous point. But the Tuareg's superior knowledge of desert routes cut out a day. The journey itself was uneventful: death stalker scorpions, dung beetles, some scraggly desert shrubs and a few birds were the only forms of life they encountered. The oasis, however, provided more varied company: monitor lizards, sand vipers, gerbils, desert hares, jerboas and sand larks living among assorted grasses and cypress, olive and date palm trees.

But no humans.

"I thought you said your friends would be waiting for us," Peter said to Johnny.

"They will be here," Johnny assured him. "Unless they cannot be here. Like we almost couldn't be here."

"What about our other friends?" Peter looked at the Tuareg. "I doubt they want to stay and wait."

"Let me find out." Johnny rode over to the Tuareg, exchanged a few words in Arabic, then came back. "It will be dark soon. They will stay until morning and then we can return with them to the camp or remain here. Either way, the camels are theirs. We will decide when the time comes. For now, we will brew some tea and relax."

Peter and Johnny tethered and tended to the camels while the Tuareg prepared the tea. The Tuareg also brought out some bread and soft goat cheese, which was an unexpected treat, and all five sat on the ground around the teapot, eager to relax after their ride.

Their tranquility was short-lived, shattered by the shot that sent a bullet whistling past their heads and into a date palm tree that was providing shade. The Tuareg dropped their tea glasses and grabbed their rifles as Peter and Johnny flung themselves to the ground. Johnny shouted for the Tuareg to get down, but they paid no attention and instead crouched in defensive positions. There was another shot and this time the bullet came from a different direction.

"More bandits?" Peter shouted to Johnny.

"More dangerous. These are—"

A barrage of shots in rapid succession interrupted Johnny and sent him, Peter and the Tuareg sprawling facedown on the sand.

"A Thompson .45 sub-machine gun," Johnny said. "And worse to come."

"Lucky they're terrible shots," Peter said.

"They are excellent shots, only they are not trying to kill us—yet." Johnny leapt up and, tearing off his turban, jogged into the open, waving his arms and shouting, *"Ne tiree plus! Cesserle feu! Je ne suis pas un Tuareg! Je suis Johnny!"*

But despite Johnny's plea, the shooting didn't stop and the next volley sent him to his knees in self-protection. *"Non!"* he yelled at one of the Tuareg who was crawling toward him. *"Rentrez! Ils sontimes amis! Ce sera bien!"*

Johnny gave his directive to get back and let him handle things in French, not Arabic, yet the Tuareg did as told. That surprised and disturbed Peter. If the Tuareg understood French, why hadn't Johnny used it all along, enabling Peter to take part?

"Arrêtez de tirer, salauds!" Johnny, still on his knees, called out to the attackers. *"Tous ne me reconnaissez pas? C'est moi, Johnny! Johnny!"*

"Johnny?" Finally there was a response.

"Oui!" Johnny stood up. *"Restez où vous êtes jusqu'à ce que je vous dis!"*

"What the hell is going on?" Peter said when Johnny returned.

"There will be no more shooting for the moment. Now I must speak to the Tuareg before we have a war within the war."

No longer bothering with Arabic, Johnny spoke in French, explaining that his comrades had fired the shots and that they, like him, were Legionnaires. The disclosures led to a loud and heated exchange during which Peter learned that the Legion and the Tuareg had a long and bitter history of attacking—and massacring—each other. Despite their finally declaring a truce, festering animosities still led to occasional violent encounters. No wonder Johnny hadn't wanted to use French, any more than he had wanted to tell the Tuareg that he was a Legionnaire. After ten minutes of bickering and bargaining, the Tuareg agreed not to use their weapons unless the

Legionnaires threatened them, in which case they would respond by first killing Johnny and Peter. Satisfied, Johnny returned to the open area and summoned his troops.

There was a distant crank and hum of engines, heralding the arrival of
three garishly painted vehicles carrying three men.

And one woman.

Peter looked at her and then at Johnny. "She is Susan," Johnny said.
"And she is unique."

"I would say so to travel with Legionnaires."

"She travels with Legionnaires because she *is* a Legionnaire."

That caught Peter off guard. It was common knowledge that the French
Foreign Legion only allowed men to join. Most often, men with a past.
Men like Johnny.

"I will explain later," Johnny promised. "Now I must keep the two sides
from killing one another. And Susan will be the hardest to restrain."

Proving Johnny right, Susan jumped from the jeep and spat on the sand.
"Tuareg dogs, you stink up the desert!" she shouted, first in English, with a
pronounced British accent, then in French.

"No, Susan," Johnny said as Peter heard the Tuareg, who were gathered
behind him, bolt their rifles. "It is in the past. These are good men. I owe
them my life and we owe them our mission."

"I owe them nothing but a bullet. Each of them and any other Tuareg
within sight of my gun."

"You will not harm these men." Johnny's voice turned frighteningly firm,
leaving no doubt that the penalty for disobeying would be both severe and
gender blind.

"So you've forgotten. So soon and you've forgotten."

"So soon? It was years ago. And forgotten? It is one of many things I can
never forget. Still I go on."

"You go on with slime." Susan glared at the Tuareg.

"There will be no more of this talk. These men are now my guests and
they will be treated as such."

"Not by me," Susan said.

"By you, by them . . ." Johnny pointed to the men in the vehicles. "By us all."

Susan's eyes shot two rounds directly at Johnny, before she stormed away.

"She will be fine," Johnny said to Peter. "The story is not pretty. But she
will be fine."

Johnny spoke again to the Tuareg, who were packing their camels, then
to Peter. "They will not be staying. They will ride a good distance and make
camp."

"But it will be dark," Peter said.

"They say they would rather risk djinns than trust Legionnaires. It is probably better." Then Johnny shouted to the men in the vehicles, "Get out and leave your rifles until the Tuareg have departed!"

"And her?" Peter said, looking at Susan, who had found a solitary spot where she sat, more stone statue than person.

"When the Tuareg are no longer here, I will handle Susan," Johnny said.

The Tuareg loaded the last of their gear and mounted their camels, ready to leave. Johnny handed back the rifles they had given him and Peter and tried to return the daggers as well, but the Tuareg said they were gifts and wouldn't take them.

"Give me a few moments with them," Johnny said, and Peter and the Legionnaires moved out of earshot. The conversation was short, and when it concluded and the Tuareg rode off Johnny took Peter aside. "The others will not care, but you should know that we parted on good terms. Not perfect, but good."

"I could hear laughing at one point."

"When I apologized for Susan's remarks, I used an old desert saying: 'better a broken leg than a sharp tongue.' That is why they laughed. Just before they left, one of the Tuareg said that, in life, it is always possible to reach agreement, as we did. He also said that when the music changes, then the rhythm of the dance must change also."

Peter got the sense that beyond just translating, Johnny was repeating things for his own benefit, reinforcing some lessons it might have taken him a while to learn.

"And now I must attend to Susan," Johnny said.

"What do you intend to do?"

"Whistle a new tune and teach her to dance."

Although Johnny's desert squadron had no qualms about traveling at night, they decided to stay at the oasis and start fresh in the morning.

"How did it go with teaching Susan to dance?" Peter asked when he had a few minutes alone with Johnny over the sparse fare that passed for breakfast.

"That woman has two left feet. But at least she made the effort. It would be hard for me as well if someone killed my fiancé. But I believe eventually she will get over it."

"Wait," Peter said. "Go back. The Tuareg killed her fiancé?"

"It was years ago. Susan had left England for Algeria and found a job

doing nonmilitary secretarial work in the Legion's Algiers office. That is
where she met my friend Jean and they fell in love. But Jean was no desk
Legionnaire. We served together, patrolling the desert. The Tuareg and the
French had already officially made peace, but that did not mean that all
the hostilities had ceased. It was night and three of us were out on a scouting expedition, leaving the other thirty-seven men at the camp. While we
searched in one direction, the Tuareg came from another. I do not know
how many, but when we returned the thirty-seven were dead. Butchered.
One of them was Jean. The three of us spent hours burying what was left of
their bodies. Then filled with foolish bravado, we set out for revenge, but
the Tuareg had disappeared into the desert. For a long time thereafter, I
was like Susan. If I saw a Tuareg, at a bazaar, anywhere, I wanted to kill
him. God knows, I pounded many nearly to death with my fists."

"But you changed?"

"Like the music and the rhythm, yes, but more slowly and in bits so
small that I did not even realize I had changed until it was all done. Susan?
She never healed. She never forgot. She never forgave."

"And about joining the Legion?"

"It was either a fluke or meant to be. Susan returned to England, but
Jean's memory was too strong and it called her to the Legion life. She returned to Algiers before the war and applied; however, she never put her
gender on the form. One of the men on that scouting mission with me,
Michel, had been reassigned to processing Legion applications, and he took
care of Susan. Then came the war, Vichy, all the confusion, and nobody
cared. She was a driver, but she also fought in the field. When the opportunity arose, she joined our group behind the lines."

More than merely information, Johnny's story gave Peter a deeper in-
sight into Susan, and he felt for the sorrow she bore. That was part of his
own change, and although it, too, was occurring in "small bits," he was aware
of it. Since he met Max, Peter had begun to allow himself to experience
emotions he had avoided for as long as he could remember, but expressing
them still didn't come easily. As Johnny said, "small bits."

Once everyone had eaten and the gear was packed and loaded, Johnny
positioned himself in the driver's seat of one of the jeeps and motioned for
Peter to sit beside him. "These jeeps will take anything the desert can
throw at them. They were abandoned by your British Special Air Service.
But I personally fixed them. Everything. My work."

"Except for the color scheme, I imagine," Peter said, referring to the pink,
green and yellow paint on the jeeps. "That definitely looks like a woman's
touch."

"It's an effective camouflage scheme, so I don't give a damn what it looks like," Susan, who had overheard the remark, snapped. "Now for important matters. Johnny, you are behind my lead jeep, with Marcel at the rear. I assume that's acceptable."

Johnny grunted.

"Good," Susan said, and headed for her jeep. "Then we're off."

During the first day's drive, to Peter's delight, Johnny told a stream of stories about Legion life, pausing only once to praise Susan's navigational genius for making an unexpected turn. "She never uses instruments," Johnny said. "Looks at the maps and relies on her hunches. I think maybe she was the child of a camel and a homing pigeon."

On the second day, Johnny's jeep got stuck in the sand. After deflating the tires, the group dug trenches on a slight incline between the front and back wheels and placed steel strips into them, tucking one end just under the rear tires. Then they put wood and cloth sand mats beneath the front tires. When all was ready, Susan released the clutch and the men pushed the jeep over the mats and strips until it gained enough velocity to shoot free. For the rest of the trip, neither Peter nor Susan let Johnny live the incident down.

The same day a late-afternoon sandstorm struck without warning. "The sirocco," Johnny told Peter. "It pushes north from the deep desert. This one is not too bad. Sometimes the winds can exceed fifty knots." Still, the stinging sand, which pelted their faces and any uncovered skin and even seemed to penetrate their clothing, forced them to stop.

"Get under the jeeps!" Susan shouted into the gritty wind. When Peter jumped out of the car and stood, he found that the blinding sandstorm swirled only as high as his upper chest: his neck and head were clear of the storm, and above was blue sky. After they had covered their jeep with a tarp and crawled beneath it, he asked Johnny about that.

"Out here, the sand never rises above six feet in a storm," Johnny said. "Only during the first few minutes does the sand blow high and cover everything. Near the coast, where you get a mixture of sand and many other things, the plumes are much higher and more dangerous. Those storms can last days. So can these, sometimes, but this one, I think not."

Johnny was right. In less than two hours the storm had died down completely, allowing them to resume their journey.

On the third day, Johnny spotted aircraft, which were either German or Italian. Following a preplanned strategy, Marcel stopped the rear jeep, then Johnny stopped his jeep 150 yards away from Marcel's, and finally Susan 150 yards from Johnny's.

"Because we are not heavily loaded we did not generate a lot of dust," Johnny said to Peter as they waited. "That makes us less noticeable."

Soon the planes were directly overhead. There were six and Peter could make out swastikas on two. But instead of starting strafing runs, the planes made no alterations in their flight pattern and soon were out of sight.

"The pink, yellow and green paint is a pretty good camouflage," Johnny said.

Peter agreed, and when they broke for dinner and rest he apologized to Susan for doubting her.

If the desert crossing had dangers—including Italian and German patrols, which Susan seemed to sense and avoid—it also had distractions. The diversity of the terrain—from sand to rocks to mountains—fascinated Peter. Then there were the dunes. Some looked like crescent moons; others, with radiating arms, like stars. There were linear dunes, domed dunes and even parabolic, or u-shaped, dunes.

At times traveling up and over the dunes was the most direct route. "Try to keep your teeth in your mouth, and please do not throw up on me," Johnny said the first time, then increased the jeep's speed and started scaling the wall of sand. Peter could feel the car tipping backward and, despite Johnny's request, his meager breakfast lurching forward. Then, suddenly, the labored vibrations of the engine ceased and Peter's queasiness turned to calm as the jeep appeared to be floating in air. His ease ended, however, when the jeep reached the top of the dune, its hood jutting over the edge into nothingness, ready to plunge.

At that moment Peter was back in 1925, at Coney Island, eighty-six feet in the air in a car atop the Thunderbolt, the brand-new wooden roller coaster. That car also seemed at the point of being propelled forward into space. Then, at the last possible moment, it changed direction, tilting nose first onto the ride's downward track, then plummeting to the bottom so fast that the force threatened to push Peter's stomach through his back, leaving it splattered on the leather of the seat he was strapped into. Now, seventeen years later and five thousand miles away, Peter was braced to relive that terrifying, but thrilling experience.

Johnny dropped the car into a lower gear and sent it over the side of the dune. With no roller-coaster rails to keep the car on course, Peter felt like they were negotiating a sheet of ice, sliding first one way, then another, while an exhilarated Johnny shouted jubilantly, turning the vehicle into each skid, and keeping their speed and their motion constant by deftly manipulating the accelerator.

"I could have come down at an angle instead of straight," Johnny said when they reached the bottom of the dune. "Safer, but not as much fun."

Sensing that Johnny was still trying to redeem himself after getting stuck, Peter replied, "I would have been disappointed if you had." In truth, Peter enjoyed the experience and, from then on, he welcomed each opportunity to "hop a dune."

On August 17, two days after they started out, the convoy arrived at its destination, a large oasis in the Great Sand Sea. As they neared the green, Peter asked about the group of men who began waving when they saw the cars approach, but Johnny's mind was elsewhere.

"What the fuck is that?" Eyes bulging, he stopped the car, leapt out and stood, looking.

"You've been out in the desert too long, Johnny," a nearby voice said. "It's a plane."

"I know it is a plane, Giles, you idiot. But what is it doing here?"

"Waiting to transport you on the final leg of your journey," Giles said.

"Magnificent, Giles! It is magnificent!" Johnny wrapped his arm around Peter's shoulder and squeezed. "Do you see what they secured for us?"

By his rough calculations, Peter saw a twenty-two-foot, tear-shaped fuse-lage with sixty-foot-long wings that were perched on its roof about eight feet from its bulbous nose. The cockpit canopy was directly in front of the wings, while beneath them, at least on the port side visible to Peter, was a small glass door. What Peter didn't see was a propeller or anything that might suggest an engine, which meant this so-called plane was really a glider.

"Truly magnificent, Giles," Johnny kept repeating as he walked around the glider, admiring it. "Where did it come from?"

"We borrowed it from our German neighbors," Giles said. "They had it on a strip about two hundred miles from here that they probably used for recreational flying. They had a few other gliders there, but they were pilot only. This one will take two people."

"They left the planes unguarded?"

"No," Giles said. "There were three soldiers around."

"And they said you could borrow this?"

"They said nothing once we shot them."

Johnny clasped Giles' bearded cheeks and kissed him on the forehead. "Peter, come and meet Giles, the greatest procurement officer in the French Foreign Legion. A genius. No one else could have gotten this for us."

Peter wandered over to the plane.

"Giles, this is Major Peter Baker of the British Army, the package we are to deliver." Johnny released Giles, which allowed him to shake hands with Peter. "Giles' gift will enable us to travel above the desert instead of on it."

"You can pilot this?" Peter asked.

"I can pilot anything that flies," Johnny said.

Peter wasn't greatly comforted by the answer. "Then you've flown this type of glider."

"Like this one, no," Johnny admitted. "But others, yes. Besides, it is all the same. You find some rising air to lift the plane up and give you altitude, then you glide downward through the still air for a distance. At a certain point you find some more rising air and you repeat the process."

Peter, who understood the aerodynamics, persisted. "Just out of curiosity, when did you last fly a glider?"

"Ten, maybe fifteen years ago. Before the Legion anyway." When Johnny saw the look on Peter's face, he added, "Do not worry. Getting you to Cairo is my mission, and in the Legion's Code of Honor a mission is sacred. A Legionnaire must accomplish it at all costs. I will teach you something else about the Legion. *Démerdez-vous*. Take care of it. That is our unofficial motto. Use what you have available and manage it. If we had only skis, then we would find a way to use them and get to Cairo. If we had only a boat, then we would find a way to use it and get to Cairo. But instead we have this." Johnny lovingly rubbed his hand across the fuselage, as if it were the soft flesh of a woman's inner thigh and not metal covered with canvas. "This is what we will use to get to Cairo and we will arrive in style. Remember I told you that in the Legion we say, 'March or die'? Now we will 'fly or die.' A good change, is it not?"

Peter bobbed his head in agreement, although he couldn't care less what Johnny changed the saying to, as long as it wasn't "fly *and* die."

Edible food, decent drink, a bath of sorts, a tent with a cot and a real breakfast waiting when he woke kept Peter from dwelling on the impending glider flight. Johnny worked until late morning with Giles, familiarizing himself with the plane and its controls; then they joined Peter at a table set up in the shade of some desert trees. "I have figured out most of the controls," Johnny said. "The rest I will not bother with." Johnny smiled at Peter, then looked at Giles. "Only one problem remains, although surely you have addressed it. Since I see no tow plane, how will we get the glider airborne?"

"*Démerdez-vous*," Peter said.

Giles reached over and slapped Peter on the back. "He learns fast, Johnny. Yes, Major, we will indeed use what we have at hand. The Great Sand Sea is filled with enormous dunes, some of them more than two hundred feet high. We drag the glider up one of those giant dunes and push it off. So, Johnny, do you think that will provide the lift you need?"

"We won't know unless we try. What is it you British say, Major Baker? Are you game?"

"Certainly I'm game." Peter suspected he was the butt of a joke. Still, with Johnny he couldn't be sure.

"There is another way, but it won't provide the same thrills," Giles said. "Would you care to see?"

"Why not?" Johnny said.

They left the shelter of the trees for the open area where the glider was kept, but something had been added: a jeep with its rear end jacked up and chocks behind the front wheels. Secured to the left wheel with bolts was a winding drum for a winch, which already had a few turns of three-eighth-inch rope wrapped around it. Beneath the rear axle was a support with an extension a guide that enabled the rope to be fed to and uniformly wound on the drum. The remainder of the rope lay coiled on the sand.

"I do not believe it!" Johnny looked at the contraption in awe. "Giles, you truly are a genius! It is brilliant. Our own homemade ground launcher, using simple items."

Peter agreed, now that he saw Giles' actual solution to getting the glider aloft. "*Démerdez-vous!*" The admiration in his voice said he understood the full meaning of the expression.

"Let's head back." Giles picked up the rope and let it uncoil as he walked. "You both should get some rest while you can. It will be your last for a while."

They followed Giles' advice and, as usual, Johnny was out in seconds, contentedly snoring away, while Peter stayed awake, planning for contingencies. As solid a sleeper as Johnny was, at the sound of Giles rustling the tent flap when he came to fetch them he leapt up and grabbed his knife from under his pillow. "Giles, you idiot, never do that!" Johnny bellowed. "I might have killed you without even looking at who it was!"

"Before I'm a genius, now I'm an idiot. It will be good to get you out of here. Conditions are right. The heat has built enough to produce fine thermals."

Thermals. The famous Sahara thermals. Those currents of warm air rising from heated ground would be their ticket to Egypt. If Johnny's flying skills were as good as his boasts, he could use the thermals to lift the glider to a high altitude, let the aircraft glide to gain distance, then repeat the process.

"We must go immediately," Johnny said. "The afternoon thermals can take us most of the way. After dark we can glide low, beneath the radar, and land in a remote spot inside Cairo. From there . . ." Johnny looked at Peter. *"Démerdez-vous."*

The rope was already attached to the hook on the glider's nose when Peter, Johnny and Giles arrived and the launching crew was in place. "So, Giles, prepared as always." Johnny placed his hand on his friend's back.

"As I said, I just want to be rid of you."

"You will never be rid of me. That is your curse." Johnny turned and faced the crew around the winch. *"Mes amis."* He raised his voice to be heard. "Thank you as always. You are ready no matter what the challenge. There are none better then you."

"Have you finished your bullshit?" Giles asked.

"You are such a sentimentalist." Johnny pinched Giles' cheek.

"Then put this on." Giles picked up a packed parachute and shoved it into Johnny's hands, then picked up a second one and tossed it to Peter. "You, too, Major. Standard precaution."

Within seconds Peter had accessed a diagram in his memory for strapping on a parachute and managed to follow it closely enough to look like a military man.

"Good, now we are ready." Johnny hugged Giles, then climbed onto the glider's wing and into the cockpit. Peter boarded the glider through the glass door and took his seat, which was behind and considerably lower than Johnny's.

"Are you fastened in?" Johnny asked, and Peter said he was. "Then we go." Johnny flashed his right thumb in the air for Giles to see.

"Ready!" Giles yelled, and within seconds the winch drum started to revolve, slowly drawing in the rope and moving the plane forward.

"Take up the slack and step the speed up gradually!" Giles shouted, and as the drum accelerated in small increments he watched the plane gain momentum until it lifted off the ground.

"It's at thirty-five miles per hour, Giles," the winch operator said.

"Hold it at that speed."

The glider began rising, its nose pointed at a fifteen-degree angle. As it gained more height, the angle increased to thirty-five degrees.

"Come on, Johnny, a little bit more," Giles urged from the ground. "No stalls now."

The glider kept climbing and then, when it was nearly four hundred feet in the air, the rope suddenly fell free of the nose hook.

"He's up and on his own!" Giles cried as the others cheered. "The bastard hasn't lost his touch."

Aboard the glider, Johnny was also elated. "Jesus Christ, it worked!"

"Did you have any doubts?" Peter asked.

"More than you want to know." Johnny caught a current, sailed high into the sky, stayed there for a bit, then swooped down and grabbed another current, like a falcon taking its prey in midair. "It is necessary to test it out," he explained, although Peter knew he was having a grand time playing with his new toy.

After the late-afternoon thermals had weakened, Johnny began gliding longer at lower altitudes, which made for a smoother flight, enough so that when it grew dark Peter considered a nap. Besides, there wasn't much to see anymore: some stars, the moon, some clouds . . . and a rainbow of blinding lights that appeared suddenly, filling the sky and showing no sign of leaving.

"Fuck!" Johnny cried. "Tracers! Ahead of us!"

Peter watched as exploding magnesium and phosphorus from special bullets, used to sight targets, put on a fireworks display while the glider headed for front-row seats.

"I thought we were flying under the radar!" Peter shouted over what sounded like large hailstones striking the fuselage.

"We are," Johnny said as he tried desperately to set the glider on a different course.

A rush of air swept over Peter. He reached up with his left hand and immediately put it back down. "There are holes in the fuselage, Johnny, and they sure as hell didn't come from moths!"

"Shut up! I am doing what I can to get us away!"

Peter could feel the plane turn. "Good, Johnny. You've got it!"

"Not yet, but close. Are you hit?"

"No. What about—"

Although it seemed instantaneous, there was a tiny time gap between the sound of glass shattering and the shards that went flying, enough for Peter to shield his face with his hands. "That was no bullet, Johnny!" Peter edged up in his seat and saw that there was little left of the front canopy. "Johnny, are you all right?" He waited a few seconds. "Johnny?"

"I am still here."

Relieved to receive a response, Peter asked, "What the hell happened?"

"A large piece of debris. This is not a combat plane with glass made to withstand impact."

"Debris? From what? Aren't they firing at us?" Peter looked behind him. He still could see tracers, some sailing up into the sky, some soaring down from the sky. But the glider was well clear of the area.

"No. I do not think they knew we were up here."

"Who are *they*? We're flying over a damn desert."

"Probably a British patrol shooting at German planes back from a bombing run and heading our way but at a higher altitude. We flew over the patrol just as they began firing anti-aircraft weapons and before the German planes started a strafing run. The bullets that hit us were from a smaller-caliber machine gun, the kind the Long Range Desert Group carries. But also they carry captured Italian Breda machine guns, which can punch holes the size of your fist through metal. That is what they probably used to hit the plane the shrapnel came from. We could not have survived even one shot from that gun. As it is, we have problems."

Bad as "we have problems" was, Peter heard something more troubling. There was the sound of mucus in Johnny's voice and his speech was becoming more labored and his breathing more rapid. "Johnny, are you sure you're all right?"

"Be concerned with the glider, not me. The stick control is not responding like it should. It may have been damaged by the shrapnel or by a bullet underneath. I can use the other controls to compensate but not forever."

Several times while speaking, Johnny coughed up phlegm, which gave Peter a good idea of what was happening. Despite the lack of light, if he could get a look at Johnny he'd know for sure, but the arrangement of their seats made that impossible.

Instead, Peter closed his eyes to block out distractions and drew on some of Sir Arthur's medical tricks, listening carefully to Johnny's body for something he hoped not to detect. But there it was—a distinct sucking sound when Johnny inhaled, caused by air rushing through a chest wound and collecting in the lung cavity. From the sound's volume Peter could tell that the wound was large and needed to be dressed immediately to stop the air from entering Johnny's chest cavity. Meanwhile, the mucus was continuing to accumulate in Johnny's trachea, pushing his physical condition beyond bad. There was a chance Peter could do something, but only if they were on the ground. "Johnny, can you land this thing?"

"Land? I am trying to get the plane up higher."

"Higher? For God's sake, Johnny, why higher? Get it down on the ground!"

"We will crash if I try." Johnny was pausing between every few words and straining for breath. "I must get it to rise so you can jump."

"Jump? Are you out of your mind? Johnny, you have to land. I know you're injured. Get us down and let me help you."

"Injured. Please, do not insult me or you and let us not make this into a cheap cinema melodrama. I hate melodrama."

"What happened?"

"The shrapnel that struck us and shattered the glass was metal. A sharp edge penetrated my midsection. It is partially in and partially out, but the result will be the same."

"Johnny—"

"Fuck Johnny. Johnny will soon be dead. But Stéphane . . . That is the name I was born with and will die with. Stéphane Neidecker. You have wondered about me since we met. Well, now I will satisfy you. Stéphane Neidecker. A Berlin-born musician of great promise, close friends with Weimar's best, such as Weill and Brecht." The gurgled words fought their way through the heavy mucus clogging his throat. "And, ever since killing a man over an unworthy woman and fleeing, a member of the French Foreign Legion."

Peter thought of the story of Surabaya Johnny about a ne'er-do-well who mesmerized an innocent young girl with his rakish charm, then treated her like dirt. Only here the roles were reversed. Now Peter understood why the song, written by two men who really *were* his friends, spoke to Johnny.

Johnny's voice trailed off, and it seemed as if he was talking to someone other than Peter in German. "*Die Liebe führt uns und ich folge, es gibt keine andere Wahl als zu gehorchen. Richtig oder falsch, gewinnen oder verlieren Es macht keinen Sinn. Mein Herz wird nicht zurückweichen.*"

"Love leads, and I follow, choiceless but to obey." Peter softly repeated Johnny's words in English. "Right or wrong, win or lose, it makes no matter. My heart will not retreat."

"Brecht." Johnny's voice grew somewhat stronger as he turned his attention back to Peter. "From a poem never published. Funny, is it not. Love can destroy a life, but without love there is no life. Love is the better gamble, although maybe not for me. Still I would gamble again if I could."

Although he wanted to say something, Peter found he couldn't.

"Enough of this," Johnny continued. "We are lucky. There is a small draft we can ride. Another two hundred feet and we will be good for you to jump, Major Baker."

Suddenly Peter could speak. "Not Major Baker and not British. Almost everything I told you was a lie. I'm sorry, but it had to be because of the one thing that's true. I'm here to kill Hitler."

"Kill Hitler? They have sent you on a fool's errand, although a noble one. Remember . . ." Johnny was slipping into extreme distress. "Remember the Legion Code. Complete your mission even at the cost of your life. Are you prepared to do that?"

"Yes." Peter was surprised by his own response. Sometimes, he realized, he knew more about others than he knew about himself.

"As I am prepared to complete mine." The rumbling in Johnny's chest cavity competed with his words. "What is the condition of your cockpit portion?"

"It wasn't damaged."

"It is designed to be removed. There is . . ." Each word became heavier. "There is a small lever behind your head. Lift it and the canopy will detach."

Peter pulled the lever and pushed up on the canopy, sending it over the side of the plane. "Done."

"Good. Even if you are not Major Peter Baker, have you used a parachute before?"

"I can get through it." That wasn't a lie, either, as long as the cord was where the diagram in his mind showed. Peter unfastened the seat's safety straps and edged himself up until he was sitting on the lip of the cockpit. Just like when he entered the Paris Catacombs, the dark and the inability to see the ground below calmed his fear of heights.

"Then go and . . ." The rumbling had grown thunderous. "Go and complete your mission. Put an end to that motherfucker."

"It's *our* mission," Peter said. "Without you I couldn't complete it." There was a catch in his voice and he paused for it to pass. It wouldn't. Leaving was difficult, but Peter knew if he didn't do it now, he might die with Johnny. It was time. *"Démerdez-vous!"* he shouted, his hands ready to push against the plane and send him hurling.

"Non! Démerdes-tu!"

Peter turned back one last time. Johnny was sending him off using the familiar form—the one reserved for friends, for soldiers-in-arms—letting him know he had proven himself. He was now truly a Legionnaire. With that in his mind, Johnny's words in his ears, pride and sadness in his heart, a questionable parachute on his back, a falling plane under his ass and no idea of what lay ahead, Peter took a deep breath, shouted, "The game is afoot!" to the heavens and plunged into the unknown.

21

Outside Burg al Arab: August 19, 1942
Your Stars Today: Problem-solving activities increase in intensity now. Success will depend on your power to supply ready answers when challenged and to effectively convince others to accept them.

Peter was convinced he was dreaming, so he disregarded the sounds of machinery and the voices shouting coarse commands in very bad German.

But being poked in the ribs with some kind of blunt object actually seemed real enough to hurt and, even in a dream, demanded some kind of response.

"Verpiss dich," he said, and felt another jab.

"Schiesse!" A groggy Peter stuck his head out through the folds of the parachute, which he had wrapped himself in like a cocoon to keep warm. *"Verpiss dich!"* He opened his eyes and was immediately blinded by truck lights.

"What's he saying, Sarge?"

"'Piss yourself away'. Best I can tell that's 'fuck off' in kraut."

Christ, it really wasn't a dream! Those were soldiers surrounding him, the blunt object poking him was a rifle, and Sarge, the guy holding it, had an Australian accent. This was probably the Long Range Desert patrol that earlier had been shooting at the Axis aircraft.

"G'day, Fritz. How ya goin'? Now that we done the formalities, lift your ass, you bloody fuckwit."

"Wait!" Peter raised his hands. Sarge grabbed them and yanked him up.

"See, Fritz, this is what 'lift your ass' means!" Sarge held Peter while one of the other soldiers slapped on a pair of handcuffs, then released him. "We found your boxhead buddy a few miles back, all mashed up in glider wreckage. Left him for the jackals and I'm thinking we should do the same with you."

Not even a burial for Johnny. Damn, how did it come to this? "Listen, you don't understand. We're on the same side. I'm Peter Baker, a major in the British Army."

"Pretty good accent for a kraut, Sarge," the soldier who handcuffed Peter remarked.

"They teach their agents well, but he's no fair-dinkum Brit. No, I'll bet Fritz here and the other Herr Heine were preparing to pay Churchill a little surprise visit so they could chew the fat."

Churchill? What the hell did Churchill have to do with anything? "I'm telling the truth. How can I convince you?"

"Not us," Sarge said. "It's the shiny arses at Field HQ you have to convince. Good on ya, Fritz. You'll be getting where you were going anyway, courtesy of me and my Digger Darlan's. What ya think, boys—won't Winnie be goin' all hooly dooley when Fritz here lobs in to yabber?"

Sarge's question produced peals of laughter.

"Enough," Sarge said. "Time we threw the cactus in the back of a truck and headed home."

"Cactus?" Peter said.

"Oh, sorry, Fritz. I forgot for a moment that you're a Brit so you wouldn't know strine lingo. Well, no problem. Translated into the King's English, 'you're cactus' simply means 'you're fucked.'"

Under different circumstances, Peter might have enjoyed Burg al Arab, the Egyptian coastal village thirty miles southwest of Alexandria. With lush fig groves bordering on stretches of snow-white sand that abruptly burst into the cool blue hues of the ocean, the village seemed more suitable for a luxury resort than for a military headquarters.

But, as with everything he did, General Bernard Law Montgomery, the newly named Commander of the British Eighth Army, was very deliberate in his choice. Unlike his predecessor, Sir Claude Auchinleck—sacked for not getting the better of Rommel—Montgomery didn't believe in living like his men. However, he didn't mind his men living a little like him by enjoying Burg al Arab's amenities in between their dangerous desert duties. That didn't include men claiming to be British officers who arrived at his headquarters cuffed and tucked into the back of a patrol truck.

Sarge and his crew stopped their vehicles in front of Montgomery's caravan, a travel trailer captured from the Italians that served as his bedroom, map room and office. "Brought Monty a gift," Sarge said.

"Better if you had brought him the food Churchill ordered from Shepheard's Hotel," one of two soldiers on guard said. "It still hasn't arrived from Cairo and if it's not get here by lunch, the PM's sure to bite into Monty's head."

"Not my problem, mate. And either is he anymore." At Sarge's signal his men pulled Peter from the truck.

"What's all this commotion?" A dashing man in his early forties, militarily slim and tanned, with slicked-back black hair and a carefully cropped full moustache, emerged from a smaller caravan, walked over to Peter and sized him up.

"A special prisoner, sir." Sarge hopped from the truck. "Found him wrapped in a parachute asleep near a wrecked Nazi glider. We rousted him awake and he starts jabbering in German, then switches to English when he sees who we were. Claims he's a British officer, but what's a British officer doing sneaking under the radar in a German glider and heading toward where Mr. Churchill's at?"

"Young man, I'm Brigadier General Francis Wilfred de Guingand, General Montgomery's Chief of Staff. And you are?"

"Major Peter Baker, sir."

"I see. And were you indeed aboard a German glider that crashed, as the sergeant said?"

"Sir, is the Prime Minister here today?" Peter knew he would be put under lock and key no matter how he responded.

"I'm the one asking the questions. Now, were you on that glider?"

"Sir, if I could speak to Mr. Churchill briefly, it would avoid a lot of trouble."

"Did you hear that?" Sarge said to his men. "Speak to the PM. Next he'll ask to borrow a gun."

De Guingand shot Sarge a look that prompted an immediate "Sorry, sir," then turned back to Peter. "That's not about to happen. But I promise you'll have plenty of time to explain your side of things."

"That's just it, sir. I don't have plenty of time."

"And why's that?"

"I can't say, sir. Not here. Not now."

"Would you like us to deliver him to the confinement tent, General?" Sarge asked.

"Absolutely not. I want him more solidly secured and far away from others. Nigel!"

"Sir?" one of the soldiers standing guard responded.

"Nigel, keep this man handcuffed at all times and lock him in my sleeping quarters. You stay in the front compartment and keep watch. Basil!" A second solider stepped forward. "You'll continue to stand watch out here, just in case."

"But, General, if he's not an assassin he might be a spy," Sarge said.

"I assure you, there's nothing in my sleeping quarters of interest to a spy, or anyone else for that matter. As for you, Major Baker or whoever you are, you've obviously had a go of it and, for the moment, I don't intend to make it worse. Feel free to nap on my bed if you wish. I'll have something to eat sent up. Later, we'll see about a more permanent holding spot while we sort things out. I trust you won't give my men any trouble."

"I won't, sir." Lying wasn't a problem for Peter, who had already begun formulating a plan. His problem was securing something very valuable he had noticed outside of de Guingand's caravan.

"That being the case, I'm off to make sure lunch with the PM doesn't turn into a disaster."

"You won't be needing us," Sarge said as de Guingand walked away. "So it's some food and sleep and back to the desert where we belong."

Nigel took Peter by the arm. "Come on. Let's get this done then."

Peter watched the patrol drive off. "Seems like a nice fellow, your General de Guingand."

"Him?" Nigel said. "He's a keeper all right. A real gentleman. He'll treat you fair, he will, but that don't mean he can't be tough. So if you're really a kraut, don't play games with him. It'll go better for you."

As they neared the caravan steps, Peter's ankle suddenly twisted and he fell out of Nigel's grasp, face forward, into a thick clump of plants.

"Here, what's this?" Basil, rifle pointed, was there in an instant.

"A little weak and fatigued, I'm afraid." Peter rustled on the ground for a few seconds until Nigel helped him up.

"You all right?"

"I'm fine," Peter said. What he didn't say was that soon Nigel might not be.

De Guingand's sleeping quarters were small but comfortably appointed: a bed, wardrobe, washbasin and bath. They were also Peter's prison, and for Peter a prison was simply a place to escape from. What he needed, and soon, was an opening. Getting free of the handcuffs would be easy, as would picking the lock on the door. That left Nigel, seated at a desk in the front compartment facing the door. Peter considered the small windows on either side of the quarters as an alternative. He could fit through them by contorting his body, but that would surely bring Basil. Instead Peter had to hope that de Guingand really would send him some food, and he began preparing accordingly. He reached under his shirt and retrieved a branch he had snapped off the bottom portion of a shrub during his staged fall. It was actually quite attractive with its palm-shaped leaves and yellow flowers. But Peter was only interested in the grayish-brown seeds, which he extracted from its prickly red pods and placed under each of his shirt cuffs. When he finished, he sat on the bed and waited.

Opportunity, in the form of Nigel, soon knocked.

"They've delivered you some food!" Nigel called out, then unlocked and opened the door. "You'll eat it out here, then back in." He pointed to the desk with his pistol. "Come on and shut the door behind you."

Nigel stepped back, allowing Peter entrance to the front compartment.

"Go ahead, put it there." Nigel pointed the pistol at the desk chair.

As Peter sat, he took stock of the food: a platter of fruit—dates, plums, pears, apples and oranges—an assortment of nuts and from the scent, a pot of the perfect tea for what he had in mind. "It's a little awkward with these." Peter motioned to the handcuffs with his chin, keeping his forearms bent to hold the seeds in place. Then he lowered his hands to his lap, letting the seeds fall to the hard floor.

"You heard the general's orders same as me. They stay on." Nigel settled into an office chair opposite Peter, placed his pistol on the desk, but close at hand, and reached for the teapot. "I'll pour you some."

That was the opening Peter needed. "I don't fancy any." While he spoke, Peter placed his right foot over the seeds and began grinding them with the heel of his shoe.

"What? Don't fancy tea?" Nigel gave him a strange look. "This is the good stuff, not like we get. Earl Grey, probably made up for Churchill's lunch."

"The smell puts me off," Peter said, referring to the distinctive aroma of bergamot and orange. "Has since I was a lad. Have it if you'd like."

"Don't mind if I do." Nigel reached for a small pitcher of milk, added some to the cup, then poured the tea and dropped in two teaspoons of sugar from a bowl. "Be a sin to let it go to waste."

"Enjoy it." Peter reached over with his bound hands, took a date and plopped it into his mouth. "Fruit's good. Have some."

"The tea's enough for me. By rights I shouldn't even have that."

"I wonder . . ." With his right hand Peter took two oranges, tossed one about two feet in the air, then, as it started to fall, he tossed the second one up and caught the first.

"Here, what's going on?" Nigel asked.

"You broke my concentration," Peter said, letting the oranges fall to his feet. He bent over to retrieve them, along with them some of the pulverized seeds, which he hid in his left hand. "I used to be quite good at this, but I never tried it while handcuffed."

Peter added one more orange and with his left hand carefully arranged all three in various positions between the fingers and thumb of his right hand. "Let's see, shall we." He tossed up one orange and, just before it reached its turning point, he tossed the second. Then, when the first orange was two inches from his right hand and the second almost at the top of its arc, he tossed the third and caught the first. Peter repeated the process of catching and tossing over and over, speeding it up by cutting down on the height. "I think it's coming back to me. Peter leaned in closer to Nigel, who was fixated on the oranges circling in dizzying fashion, and slipped the powdered seeds into the teacup.

"Bravo!" Nigel exclaimed as Peter leaned back and ended the performance. "Good show." He lifted the teacup in a mock toast and took a sip.

"Yes, I must say I'm rather proud of myself." Peter dropped the oranges on the table, hoisted a water glass and clinked it against the teacup. "Cheers!" Peter downed the entire glass and Nigel did the same with the tea.

"Tea and a show," Nigel said. "More than I expected when the day started."

Unfortunately for Nigel, there was more to come. Peter didn't relish what lay ahead for his keeper, but it was unavoidable. Although Nigel might feel otherwise for a bit, he'd live. Peter was sure of that, even though he relied on touch to measure the powder in Nigel's tea.

"Do you want more of the food?" Nigel asked. Peter said no and Nigel took his pistol and rose. "Then up and off you go." He directed Peter to open the door and back through it. Once he did, Nigel closed the door and locked it.

Secured again in the sleeping area, Peter opened his handcuffs with a sturdy paper clip de Guingand had been using as a bookmark, moved a chair next to the door and listened. Nearly a half hour passed before he heard the first groan, and with that he began to pick the door lock with the paper clip.

The groans grew louder and more frequent. Peter cracked open the door and peeked out. Nigel was hunched over the desk, clutching his stomach with both hands. Suddenly he vomited and fell to the floor, where he lay on his side, shivering and shouting for Basil. Peter raced from the sleeping quarters, grabbed the pistol that Nigel in his agony had dropped, and stood behind the door, waiting.

Basil burst into the caravan seconds later and when he saw Nigel writhing in pain he hesitated just long enough for Peter to club him on the head with the pistol butt and knock him out. Quickly Peter stripped off Basil's uniform and put it on. Nigel's uniform would have been a better fit, but it had vomit on the shirt and diarrhea stains on the trousers. Besides, Nigel was still conscious, although unable to do anything but moan.

"I'm terribly sorry," Peter said. "I'll make sure you're tended to, but I really must leave. It's growing late and it would be bad form to keep the Prime Minister waiting."

Peter didn't care that his stolen uniform was too big. He wouldn't be wearing it for long. But while he did, it served its purpose, allowing him to move freely through camp and locate the large fly screen–shielded tent where Churchill was lunching with the Eighth Army command. Peter sized up the situation. Guards were strategically stationed around the tent, but the formally dressed caterers from Shepheard's went in and out as they pleased. Now that he knew the lay of the land, Peter set off to find the nearest latrine and wait for the inevitable.

The Shepheard's waiter entered the latrine twenty minutes after Peter and stepped up to the pissing trench. Peter had heard him coming and was already there, pretending to zip his fly. This was the fourth time he had gone through this routine. On each of the other three occasions, a soldier had come in to relieve himself. Now Peter had what he needed.

"Looks like quite a spread you brought," Peter remarked.

"Mr. Churchill only likes the finest. What do they generally serve you chaps for lunch?"

A sharp chop to the neck from the edge of Peter's open hand was undoubtedly not the response the waiter expected. Alert to someone else entering, Peter quickly swapped clothes. He pulled his soldier's trousers only to the waiter's knees and yanked the man's boxer shorts down to meet them. Then he propped the waiter on a toilet and manipulated his arms so that his hands were balancing his slouched head. Peter knew his hastily sculpted creation wouldn't last long, but he only needed two or three minutes. By then, the guards would be more concerned with him than with his ruse.

Leaving the latrine, Peter adopted the proper mien of a Shepheard's employee and, without even giving the guards a glance, strode into the tent. Inside, two men, dressed like him, were removing plates from a long table while the ten diners were engaged in conversation.

Peter, his head lowered to hide his face, joined in picking up the luncheon dishes, working his way around the table until he reached his target. "Mr. Prime Minister, I must talk to you!"

Peter's remark startled the rotund figure encased in what had become his customary clothing, a one-piece zippered garment called a siren suit, which resembled a toddler's rompers.

Some of Churchill's luncheon companions sprang up and wrestled Peter

to the ground and held him for the short time before two of the outside
guards responded to the commotion, The guards lifted Peter to his feet and
began dragging him from the tent.

"Please, sir, just a few moments!" Peter shouted as he tussled with the
guards. "It's a matter of the utmost urgency!"

Churchill raised his hand, signaling the guards to stop. Then he reached
toward the silver pagoda-shaped ashtray that always traveled with him, lifted
his sepia-colored Romeo y Julieta cigar, smoked down to four inches from
its initial seven, and thrust it, no longer lit, into his mouth. He seemed perfectly content to chew on the already-frayed end while considering Peter's
request.

In the meantime, de Guingand, who recognized Peter, ordered the guards
to search him, which they did, though they found nothing. "Mr. Prime Minister, this man was brought in earlier today. Although he claims to be a
British officer, there's every indication that he is actually either a German
assassin or a German spy. He was under lock and key, or he was supposed
to be." De Guingand glared at Peter. "What happened to the men who were
watching you?"

"Both are in your caravan, sir. One was struck on the head with a pistol;
the other ingested some ground castor plant seeds and will need medical
attention."

"A castor plant?"

"They're a common plant in Egypt, sir. The seeds have been used since ancient times as a poison and as a medicine. Castor oil is made from it. The seeds
contain something called ricin. Too much of it in your system can be fatal.
But the amount your man swallowed will only make him sick. Have the
medics pump his stomach, then give him activated charcoal. That will bind
any remaining ricin. And keep him hydrated. In a few days he'll be fine. If
he asks, tell him it was the tea."

Before de Guingand could continue his questioning, Churchill, who had
been listening intently while making a futile attempt to revive his cigar using
a candle placed on the table expressly for that purpose, issued his ruling.
"Set him loose, but stay where you are," he said to the guards. And you . . ."
Churchill pointed the dead cigar at Peter. "You are certainly not in the
employ of Shepheard's. So who exactly are you and what is so important
that you've risked your life to tell me?"

"Please, sir, I am Peter Baker, a major in the British Army, and I must
speak to you in private."

"Considering your situation, you're hardly in a position to be making
demands," Churchill thundered, then resumed chewing on the end of the

cigar, working it to shreds before announcing, "I will dismiss the guards, but understand they shall be right outside."

"The others as well, sir."

"Good Lord! You expect me to send out my generals and the members of my senior staff?"

In for a penny, in for a pound. "Yes, sir," Peter said.

Churchill was biting the cigar so hard that Peter thought he was going to devour it. "You've managed to engage my curiosity, Major Baker, or whoever you are." Churchill stopped chomping and looked around. "With my deep apologies, I must ask all of you to leave. But don't stray. I expect this shan't take very long."

The scattered protests, which Churchill halted, were followed by some disgruntled muttering as the room emptied.

"Well, it appears that only we two remain."

"Thank you, sir. Perhaps I might—"

"Not yet, young man. If I am to be entertained, I prefer to be in the proper mood." Churchill took the cigar he had been fiddling with and tossed it to the ground, replacing it with a fresh one that was on the table. Then from a pocket sewn onto the left breast of his siren suit he retrieved a narrow strip of brownish paper and wrapped it around the end of the cigar. "I devised this. A little glue holds it in place. Keeps the end from getting too moist." Churchill took a spent wooden match from the candleholder base and punctured the cigar with it. "Much cleaner than cutting." He drew the candle near enough to poke the cigar into the flame and inhaled deeply until it began burning. Satisfied, he pointed to a bottle of Hine brandy on the table. "Fetch that and . . ." He swung his hand around and pointed to his empty snifter. "Fill this."

Peter did as told. Churchill removed the cigar from his mouth and lifted the glass. "I adhere to certain sacred rituals. One is that the smoking of cigars and the drinking of alcohol must only be done before, after and, if deemed necessary, during meals." With that he took a swallow of brandy. "Only sip when it runs low. Go ahead, take some. It may well be your last."

As Churchill watched, Peter poured an inch of the mahogany liquid into a water glass and, from there, into his mouth. Hints of fruit and flower tingled on his tongue, mildly at first, then more aggressively.

"Young, but balanced, with a decent aftertaste," Churchill noted. "Excellent in this beastly heat. Now for your few moments."

Peter cleared his throat, which was still tingling from the brandy. "Sir, I must see Jasper Maskelyne."

"Maskelyne? The magician?"

"Yes, sir."

"Maskelyne. Where do you think you are, Baker? This is Egypt, not the Hippodrome."

"I know he's here, sir, working on deceptions for the military."

Churchill took a very long drag on his cigar and held it a good ten seconds before ejecting the smoke from his mouth in a violent puff, which, to Peter, was a sign that he had hit pay dirt.

"Deceptions for the military? You're babbling, Baker, and I have no idea what you're babbling about."

"The Zodiac mission, sir. Himmler killing Hitler."

Churchill emptied his snifter and slammed it on the table. "Now I understand why you burst in here. The sun has taken charge of your brain and made you mad. Himmler killing Hitler. Utter nonsense of the highest order. We need to summon back the guards." Churchill rose from the table.

"Please, sir, not yet. I need Maskelyne to help make some astrological predictions come true, and very soon."

"The only thing that needs to be done very soon is to get you some professional care." Churchill grabbed the brandy bottle, refilled his own glass and took a generous mouthful. "Let's suppose I actually were to believe any of this. How do I know you really are who you say? De Guingand suspects you're a German and I know the Germans are very good at this sort of thing."

"C will vouch for me."

"C?" Churchill seemed determined to play dumb.

"Sir Stewart Menzies, the head of MI6."

"What have you to do with Menzies?"

"The Zodiac mission, sir. Wild Bill Donovan brought me to Bletchley Park and C introduced me to the man I'm replacing."

"Wild Bill Donovan? Bletchley Park? Sheer foolishness, which I intend to end right now by cabling Menzies in London."

"No, you can't do that. It's not safe."

"Nonsense. We code all cables."

"And they have to be decoded. Sir, this mission is highly secret, known to only a few people, of which you're one, no matter what you say. You have to personally give C a message."

"Have you forgotten to whom you are speaking?" Churchill's anger, which he had momentarily suspended, returned in full force and his eyes were glowing more fiercely than his cigar. "How dare you presume to tell me what I must do!"

"Sir, I—"

Peter was cut short by the intrusion of a shoot of a man, thin moustached, with a hairline that began in the middle of his crown and didn't extend much farther, who crouched down and started whispering in Churchill's ear. He was the same man who had been seated next to Churchill at lunch. He was also the same man whose photograph had been in one of the newspapers Peter read on the train from Oran to Algiers. Alan . . . it was right there . . . Alan . . . Alan Brooke. Field Marshal Alan Brooke, chief of the Imperial General Staff and, as such, in command of the entire British Army. No wonder he had Churchill's ear.

But not anymore. Brooke finished whatever he had to say to Churchill, and the Prime Minister didn't whisper his reply. He roared it. "Now I have a fuller picture. Apparently, *Major Baker*, you were picked up after the crash of a German military plane."

"Mr. Prime Minister, please, you can confirm—"

But Churchill would have none of it. "This discussion is over. Guards!"

The two soldiers sent from the room reappeared.

"Take this man and place him under a much more rigid watch. He seems to have bypassed our normal procedures. In the morning he is to be interrogated, then confined with the other prisoners of war. Should he escape again between now and then, the two of you will be sent there instead. I assume I have made myself clear. And as for you." Churchill fixed his eyes on Peter. "I have never underestimated our German enemy. Apparently we are not accorded the same respect. That proved costly when your planes attacked Britain and it will prove costly here as well—to Rommel, to his army and to you personally." Churchill's cold gaze shifted back to the guards. "Now get him out of my sight and tell the others to return. And have them bring more brandy. I suspect this may well be a very long day."

Nearly five hours after they had secured him according to Churchill's orders, the same two guards came for Peter. They began walking and soon Peter's sight confirmed what his ears and nose had already detected. Before him lay the majestic Mediterranean Sea, the light from the setting sun on its surface fractured by soldiers frolicking naked in the water. Not everybody was in the water. The guards brought Peter to an area on the beach and saluted the small gathering of men, casually dressed but still reeking of rank, and two others Peter recognized from the lunch. And, from pictures, he also recognized General Montgomery, who hadn't been there. Peter had no idea who the rest were, although given the company, they had to be important.

"The Prime Minister wants to see you," Brooke said to Peter once the guards dropped back.

What was this all about? Had Churchill contacted C anyway, despite being warned of the danger to the mission? "Of course, sir. When will he be arriving?"

"Over there." Brooke pointed to a rotund figure splashing about in the water. "And you are to join him."

In the water? From Donovan, Peter knew about Churchill's peculiarities, those little quirks that endeared him to the British people. So an in-water meeting really wasn't surprising to Peter, although it could be for Churchill. Putting Peter in water was like returning a fish to its natural habitat and, for an instant, he imagined himself swimming off, leaving an astonished Churchill in his wake. Swimming off to Cairo—now that would really be something. Could he do it? Probably, but not all at once. He'd need rest breaks that he couldn't afford to take. Shame—it would be a good challenge.

Still, he certainly could break away by swimming underwater without surfacing. He hadn't practiced, but even so, Peter was sure he could do 150 yards. That would put him well out of sight and allow him to take a breath. Repeat it a few times and soon he'd be far enough away from the camp to go ashore. Then it would be all bets off.

"The Prime Minister is waiting," Brooke said.

And obviously having a good time while doing so. Churchill had taken to performing an awkward somersault in the water, and as his legs broke the surface they spread apart in a limp but still-recognizable V. Was he intentionally flashing his famous "Victory" symbol or simply flailing? Peter wondered as he took off his shirt, then loosened his pants and let them drop to the sand alongside Churchill's siren suit.

"Will you be joining us, sir?"

"The Prime Minister prefers to see you alone," Brooke replied. "However, I shall . . . *we* shall be watching."

Then watch this, Peter thought as he dropped his shorts, stepped out of them and walked toward the water, taking his time and allowing his swaggering bare backside to send a message.

The warmth of the water embraced Peter's ankles as he waded in from the beach. It felt wonderful and since he hadn't bathed since leaving the Tuareg camp—and that was simply a sponging—he silently thanked Churchill for this particular peculiarity. Not one to be tentative, Peter backed out of the water onto the beach, then rushed forward and dove, completely submerging himself. When he lifted his head above the surface, he saw Churchill waving at him. Once more Peter disappeared, and this time when he emerged he was face-to-face with the Prime Minister.

"It appears you enjoy a good swim as much as I do, Major Baker."

"Yes, sir, I certainly do." Churchill seemed in a much better mood than at lunch.

"Shall we start by agreeing on one thing, that you are in fact not Major Baker?"

"I am not Major Baker, sir."

"Are you at least British?"

"No, sir. I'm an American."

"As was my mother." Churchill gazed down at his own flabby body, then lifted and ran his eyes over Peter's body, chuckling at the contrast. "Since we find ourselves in a position that lends itself to complete exposure, could you now tell me just who you are?"

"Peter Kepler, sir. That's the who that C knows."

"C again. You realize I put very little credence in your story."

That was progress. At lunch, Churchill had put no credence in his story. "Yes, sir."

"But out of curiosity, what had you wanted me to tell him that couldn't be sent by cable?"

There it was, Peter thought: Churchill's admission that he knew about Zodiac. "That you ran into Peter Kepler at The Crow's Nest and he said Sherlock Holmes still fancies the Death card and wondered if the window's been repaired."

"'Crow's Nest,' 'Sherlock Holmes', 'Death card,' 'window.' What is this gibberish?"

Go easy. Don't spook him. Churchill hadn't repeated the words merely to make a pronouncement about them. He wanted to make sure he didn't forget them. "Just that, sir—gibberish."

"Complete." Churchill nodded his head and all of his chins quivered in agreement. Then he moved slightly to the left side of Peter and shouted, "Brooke, Montgomery—may we have the pleasure of your company!"

The two, who had been watching intently from the beach, looked confused.

"Here. In the water with us. At your earliest convenience, which I would hope is immediately."

Now it was their turn to shed clothes. Churchill couldn't help laughing at Montgomery's expense. "I thought his knees pitifully pale, but now that I see the rest— Compared to him, Brooke looks like a bronze Adonis!"

Hardly, although Churchill was right about the difference in coloration, much of it probably due to genes rather than exposure to the sun. Instead of swimming, the two waded to where Peter and Churchill were standing.

"Listen carefully, Montgomery," Churchill said as soon as they arrived. "Shortly you will receive a call from me. Until then, Major Baker is to be kept here, confined but comfortable. When I call, I shall personally give you a one-word message. If that word is 'yes' you are to release Major Baker. At that time he will tell you everything." Churchill shot Peter an authoritative glance. "Everything. And you, Montgomery, will not share that information with another soul. You will also cooperate with Major Baker fully. Whatever he needs to know, you are to tell him."

"Mr. Prime Minister—"

"Did I not make myself clear, General?" Then Churchill shed his gruffness. "Cheer up, Monty. If the word is 'no,' which it will most likely be, you are to consider Major Baker a highly dangerous spy or worse. Therefore, in the name of the Crown, you are to dispense with any and all formalities and discussions, march him out to the trooping area and, in front of all assembled, shoot him. I trust you had no difficulty understanding that."

"No, Prime Minister," Montgomery said.

"Excellent. And now, since we all understand each other . . ." Churchill looked at Peter. "And we all do understand each other, correct?" Heads bobbed. "Then shall we bask a few more minutes in the water?" Churchill again took in his own flabby body and Montgomery's scrawny one. "Monty, do you think the two of us should have a photograph taken au naturel here in the water?"

"A photograph?"

"A photograph. One we can send to Rommel. If we can't kill the bastard with our tanks and guns, perhaps we can make him die from laughing."

At 8:00 P.M. on August 19, upon returning to Cairo from Montgomery's headquarters, Churchill dispatched his most trusted aide to London. There, on August 21, in a private meeting at the Prime Minister's War Headquarters beneath the Parliament Building, the aide delivered a memorized message involving Sherlock Holmes, the tarot and a window to Sir Stuart Menzies. Immediately Menzies telephoned Churchill and, as he had been instructed, said one word. Minutes later the Prime Minister repeated that word in a call to Montgomery.

"Yes."

Fifteen minutes later, Peter was sitting in Montgomery's caravan, listening to the general give a quick, but comprehensive overview on how he planned to overtake and defeat Rommel. Twenty minutes after that, Peter was sitting in the front seat of a black sedan next to a soldier dressed like a civilian.

"Are you taking me to Maskelyne?" Peter asked the guard as they headed out of the camp.

"Maskelyne? Hell, no! I'm taking you to a whorehouse!"

22

Cairo: August 21, 1942
Your Stars Today: Amorous urges predominate and you may
find yourself abandoning old romantic patterns for something different.

The well-kept but otherwise nondescript apartment building at Cairo's 6
Kir al Salam Street existed to fulfill fantasies: most of them sexual, a few of
them military, all of them secret.

Years earlier, the building had been converted into a brothel. Unlike the
squalid styes that cluttered Wagh El Birket, Cairo's notorious red-light district, it was clean, elegant and discreet, as befitted its regular clientele: army
officers, government officials and others of prominence.

Recently, however, Dudley Clarke, a mysterious moneyed British gentleman, had rented the entire premises, his offer being too generous for the
owner to refuse.

But Clarke proved generous in other respects as well. Finding the street
level sufficient space for his needs, he allowed the women to use the upstairs
floors to conduct business. And while the two factions shared the quarters,
respecting each other's boundaries and privacy, the women weren't above
trying to entice Clarke's occasional male visitors.

Visitors like Peter, who, after being dropped off in front of the building
in late afternoon, stood in its empty lobby, deciding on which of several
closed doors he should knock.

"Anta wasiim. Hana'mil Hafla. Hal ladayka raghba?"

The woman at the head of the stairs hadn't been there a few seconds ago.

Neither had the man who materialized next to Peter. "Sorry, Kiya, I'm
afraid he's mine."

"Honest mistake," she replied in Egyptian-accented English. "He looked
lost, so I thought maybe I could help." She smiled at Peter. "Perhaps later."
With that she vanished through a curtain of beads.

"She was asking if you were up for some fun," the man volunteered.
"Kiya manages the upstairs establishment, which I'm sure you've heard

about. In rather dull contrast, I'm Dudley Clarke, consigned and resigned to these lower realms, and the man I believe you seek."

He appeared a genial fellow, this short-statured Dudley Clarke, with his prototypical high-browed, elongated British face, darting dark eyes that overshadowed a partially cut-off left ear and a certain bounciness he exuded through his calm.

"Major Peter Baker." The two clasped hands.

"I'm afraid I have the advantage, Major Baker. Montgomery sent a messenger on ahead, so I know more about you than you do about me."

That wasn't quite the case. Montgomery had briefed Peter on Colonel Dudley Clarke, a career officer with "a genius for deception." Two years earlier, following the humiliating British defeat at Dunkirk, Clarke devised a way to bolster sagging morale. With Churchill's blessing, Clarke formed the Commandos, a guerrilla warfare unit that wreaked havoc with the German forces in France and in the process cost Clarke a chunk of his ear.

After that, Clarke's military career soared, bolstered by an impressive record of accomplishments and by the kind of audacity that led him to burst unannounced into a high-level strategy session and convince his superiors to appoint him head of all British espionage operations in Egypt and North Africa. For that Peter liked Clarke before they even met.

"Shall we move to a more private setting?" Clarke said, and showed Peter into one of the rooms, which would have been cramped even without its sparse office furnishings. "Sorry about the quarters. This is actually a converted bathroom. It could have been worse; we were considering a closet. Come, have a seat."

A converted bathroom. By comparison, Donovan's Camp X office was palatial. For a man who, Montgomery said, liked only the finest in food, wine, clothing and women Clarke's surroundings were deceptive, which made them perfect.

"Let's start with some tea. How do you take it??"

"Just lemon, if you have it."

Clark opened a tin on a neatly organized desk, scooped some leaves into a perforated metal tea ball and dropped it into a cup. "Hardly the Ritz." He took a kettle from a hot plate resting atop a file cabinet, poured water into the cup, then added a slice of lemon from a plate on the desk. "But it serves its purpose." He handed the cup to Peter, then took his own from the desk and sat down. "Sorry, but we ate all the biscuits yesterday and I haven't had time to replace them. So, Major Baker—"

"Peter, please, Colonel."

"Peter it is then. And hang rank. Dudley. So, I understand you need some deceptions created, for reasons that weren't explained. My orders are to comply completely and without question. Correct so far?"

Obviously, Montgomery was following Churchill's directive to the letter. Peter nodded.

"Then there's this Maskelyne thing, which, I have to admit, caught me by surprise. Montgomery said the LCS sent you, but both he and they know that I'm responsible for the deception operations here, not Maskelyne."

The crunch Peter heard came from toes being stepped on. During their sit-down, Montgomery *had* told him about the newly created London Controlling Section, which oversaw all strategic military deception. But this new group didn't know about Zodiac, so neither did Clarke. "Only because what I need will involve some principles of stage magic and Maskelyne is a master of those." There. That sounded convincing enough.

"I see. And you're able to judge that because you have a familiarity with magic?"

"I dabble in it now and then."

"I knew we'd hit it off. It so happens that I do as well. Of course, I'm not all that good, but still . . ." Clarke got up and retrieved a deck of cards from one of the desk drawers. "More to amuse myself." He sat and handed Peter the cards to shuffle, then set them facedown on the small tea table. "Now look at this top card." Clarke turned it over, displayed the Queen of Diamonds and put it back facedown on the deck. "Take the card off and stick it anywhere in the deck you want." Peter did, yet when Clarke turned over the deck's top card the Queen of Diamonds had returned.

"That's astounding!" Peter exclaimed, even though it really wasn't. The trick, called the ambitious card, was at least a hundred years old and had dozens of variations, one of which even fooled Houdini. Magicians used it as a test of skill. For an amateur Clarke was good.

"To a layman, yes. But of course you know how it's done." Clarke handed the cards to Peter. "Your turn."

Peter wasn't about to accept the challenge and leave Clarke staring in real disbelief. "I can't follow that up, Dudley, Too bloody devastating. Did you teach yourself magic?"

"Actually I had a very fine teacher in my uncle Sidney. He was a barrister by profession, but loved magic and hobnobbed with the greatest, even Houdini himself."

Uncle Sidney? Peter inventoried British magicians named Sidney. Sidney Lansford? Doubtful. Sidney Welles? No, Clarke's not old enough. Clarke's not . . . wait. Clarke. Sidney Clarke! A prominent member of London's prestigious Magic Circle and the author of many well-respected books and articles on magic. That *must* be Uncle Sidney. "I recall reading some interesting pieces in *Conjurer's Journal* by a Sidney Clarke."

"One and the same. Uncle Sidney left us two years ago. I still miss him. He was my best audience. Each time I tried a new effect, he gave me sterling advice on how to make it better. So you see, deceiving people runs in my family as well as in Maskelyne's."

Again Clarke implied that Maskelyne was more a rival than an ally, and Peter trod more carefully to avoid a land mine. "Had I known that . . . Listen, Dudley, perhaps I should work only with you."

"I wouldn't hear of it. Besides being good at what he does, Maskelyne's name and reputation increase our credibility with the High Command. True, he occasionally requires guidance, but Maskelyne and I get along famously."

Sure. And when I'm not busy being a British major I really am a German astrologer who can foresee the results of military campaigns. Still, Peter looked to wiggle free from a sticky and possibly dysfunctional situation. "Then that settles it. The three of us will work together."

"No need. Maskelyne will handle everything in fine fashion."

"Sorry, Dudley, but I'm afraid you have no say in this. I'm to have whatever I want and this is what I want."

"I very well can't disobey orders, agree with them or not. So if you insist, then the three of us it shall be. We can discuss deceptions tomorrow when we're all together, if that's suitable. No sense doing it now and repeating it. However, if there are any questions you might have that don't require Maskelyne's participation."

"Yes, actually. Why did the military establish offices in a brothel and what goes on here?"

"About the brothel." Clarke couldn't conceal his delight in having a rare *sanctioned* opportunity to explain his operation. "Where better for men, even those in uniform, to be seen coming and going without attracting attention?"

"Brilliant!" Peter said, and meant it.

"Now the meat of your question. Besides being a house of pleasure, this modest building is also the Advance Headquarters of A Force."

"A Force?" Montgomery hadn't said anything about an A Force. "As in Airborne?"

Dudley nodded. "And, like you, those nosing about have undoubtedly arrived at the same conclusion, especially when their surveillance showed the massive array of planes belonging to A Force's various companies."

"But we would be wrong."

"Totally, since there is no bloody A Force, except here." Clarke tapped his right forefinger against his forehead. "It's notional."

"You're getting ahead of me, Dudley."

"Sorry about the jargon. A notional person or thing is imaginary, although to the enemy it's real. Take the planes. Despite what Goering's boys think when they take their aerial photographs, there are no planes, only very convincing wood and canvas decoys."

"A bit of legerdemain."

"Yes, but not the most important bit. First you need to create a mental impression. Once that's in place, the physical props verify that impression. So before we even resorted to carpentry and paint, we planted snippets about this mysterious new military force being based in Cairo in advance of an Allied invasion. Credible enough, given all the Jerry concern about the Allies coming into North Africa and taking out Rommel. We used our rather extensive network of double agents to get all this disinformation into the right ears. Add a scattering of boys in British uniforms with strange patches and soon the Berlin brass is spinning. Now put those decoys in place and you've batted a century."

Either Clarke really knew his stuff or he talked a good game, and Peter had to find out which if he hoped to dupe Rommel. "With all due respect, you're convinced that it's working."

Clarke smiled. "A legitimate question. My gut says yes and so do the Germans."

"They've told you so," Peter said, trying not to sound sarcastic.

"Matter of fact, they did, only they don't realize it. Can you imagine how many heads would roll if they knew?"

"That they told you?"

"That we broke their code."

Broke their code! Goddamn Montgomery! Why didn't he say anything about breaking the German code! What was with these people? First the German resistance. Then the British Army. Did these fucking people want to win this war or what?

"Of course you knew about that."

"Yes, but I had to wait until you brought it up." Peter regrouped quickly and smoothly.

"Smart lad." Clarke looked at his watch. "It seems the day's near end and the sun's been lingering over the yardarm far too long. Shall we get out of here?"

"A fine idea, By the way, where will I be staying?"

Clarke rose, took the cups and set them on the file cabinet. "We'll get to that in due time. Say over a fine dinner at Shepheard's."

Peter wasn't going to argue. The morning at Montgomery's headquarters had been too rushed for anything more than a cup of tea and a slice of toast, so he could do with some food.

"I need just a few more moments here, so why don't you meet me out front and we'll be off."

"Out front it is," Peter said.

"And see if you can fetch us a cab while you're out there," Clarke said as Peter was leaving.

"Is there a special way that—" Peter was cut off by the door closing. He shook his head: then, accompanied by some muted sounds from the upper-floor rooms, which he recognized as squeals and moans, he exited.

"*Ai ta'mili hagat wiskha ma'aya?*"

The singsong Arabic caught Peter as soon as he set foot on the upper stoop.

"You, English! Can't you hear?"

Looking down and to the right of the four steps leading to the sidewalk, Peter saw a woman, her face almost completely concealed behind a veil and her body hidden by a loose-fitting dark blue galabiya, the traditional single-piece Egyptian garment.

"Don't pretend. All English know some Arabic. Important Arabic. *Aiyz temus?* Good, I promise."

At a loss, Peter was saved by Dudley Clarke, who was standing at the door to the building and laughing. "She asked if you wanted to do naughty things with her."

"I assumed as much." The desert and now this: Peter really had to take a few days and learn Arabic.

"You must be quite a ladies' man, Peter. Two offers in one day. The next shift must be coming in from an afternoon off. Come on, there's a taxi." Clarke signaled with one hand and grabbed Peter's arm with the other, leading him down the stairs.

"Really good time, English." The woman was persistent.

"I'm sure he doesn't know what he's missing, but we really have to go," Clarke said as he brushed past her. With that he opened the rear door, ushered Peter into the taxi and then joined him.

"Don't worry, English!" the woman shouted as Clarke shut the rear door and the taxi took off. "Maybe you will have another chance to find out!"

Unlike Peter's last experience with Shepheard's, this one was quite pleasant and uncomplicated: he actually got to try the food and he didn't have to knock out any of the staff.

He and Clarke dined for three hours, partly because of the restaurant's infamous slow service but mostly because Clarke proved a well-versed conversationalist. But the long day, more than the constantly flowing wine, was taking its toll and Peter didn't object when, shortly after 10:00 P.M., Clarke suggested "we should really see to your accommodations."

Peter had assumed that, like other British officers, he would be billeted at Shepheard's or one of the other better hotels in Cairo, but Clarke said those rooms were fully occupied, although he assured Peter that he would be "extremely satisfied with the arrangements."

So they walked out into the smoldering Cairo night and through the city's still lively streets, which quickly went from the elegant to the squalid, and Peter wondered if Clarke was going to put him up in Cairo's underbelly, perhaps in retaliation for intruding on his domain of deception.

Their sojourn continued and soon brought another change, from the sordid to the simply seedy, where somewhat respectable looking people—mainly men—were going in and out of nightclubs.

All the while Clarke said nothing, content to let the surroundings speak for themselves. Now he stopped and broke his silence. "Do you know what lies just beyond here?"

"Tell me," Peter said, since he wasn't sure which direction Clarke meant by "beyond."

"I'll do better. I'll show you." Clarke led Peter through a long, narrow alley, made a left turn into a much shorter alley and then pointed and proclaimed, "The Nile! Magnificent, isn't it?" For a few seconds Clarke simply stared in awe at the river. "I never tire of it. And I hope you won't, either, since you'll be seeing quite a bit of it over the next few days. See those lights across the water? They're coming from the palatial dwellings on Gizara Island, Cairo's most exclusive area. Somewhat like Richmond upon Thames back home."

"Really, Dudley, you needn't have gone to all that trouble," Peter joked. "I'm a simple man, requiring only a modest mansion with a butler, two or three maids and a groundskeeper. No need to smother me in luxury."

"No worry there. Still, considering you're a soldier in the middle of a brutal war, I'd say you've fared rather nicely." Dudley started walking again, this time along a long row of shrubbery that buffered the road from the river.

"Dudley." Peter caught up with him and placed a hand on his shoulder, drawing him to a halt. "Christ, Dudley, must you be so damn tight-lipped? After all, I'm not one of the Jerries."

"Do you know what this city lacks? Theater. I miss the theater in London."

Ah, the theater. "Yes, I can imagine. I'm quite fond of it myself. However, you, at least, have the ability to create your own."

"How so?" Clarke said, then thought about it for a few moments. "Oh, you mean the deceptions? I never considered that theater, but then, what with so many of the crew taken from the stage and from the cinema—"

"'All the world's a stage and all the men and women merely players.'" Peter recited the famous line from *As You Like It*. "And on this stage, in this particular part of the world, you, Dudley, are the stage manager, overseeing exits and entrances."

"What a clever and tidy way to look at it," Clarke said. "The stage manager. I rather like that."

Clarke was acting light-headed, but Peter was convinced that it was just that: acting. True, they had both slightly overindulged at Shepheard's, but Peter could handle his drink and he had to believe that, given his position, Clarke could as well. "Well, my Lord Stage Manager, could you help this poor, confused actor find the entrance to his temporary abode?"

"Since you put it that way." Clarke went another twenty feet or so and waved his hand at some shrubs and a plain metal gate. "There it is. An oasis in Cairo and it's all yours."

Not that Peter was an authority on oases, but from the few that he had encountered recently this hardly qualified. "Dudley, your oasis is a bunch of bushes and a rusty gate."

"Of course it is. But in theater, there are wondrous things behind the scenes that the audience never sees." The gate groaned as Clarke lifted the latch and swung it open. "Do mind the stairs. Only a few, but they can still trip you up."

The short descent led to a three-foot-wide path of carefully placed stones that cut through clusters of well-tended trees and floral plantings, which Peter easily identified by scent: lotus, jasmine, chrysanthemum, poppy, dragonwort. The sloping path continued to the riverbank, where it gave way to a narrow gangplank linking the land to what seemed the roof of a long shed set atop an even longer barge.

"Behold the *Samak*. That's Arabic for 'fish.' Not very original, I'm afraid." Clarke edged past Peter and walked across the gangplank. "Don't worry, Major. She's securely tethered to the shore."

Curiosity, not safety, caused Peter to hesitate. He was looking at the other houseboats that lined the Nile, all of them much grander in scale and design. "Seems the *Samak* is a fish out of water," he said when he finally boarded.

"Fish out of water." Clarke chuckled. "That's very good. And true in a way. The Egyptians call those other boats *dahabiehs*. Years ago, when they were summer residences for the well-to-do, their outside walls had to be painted gold, and *dahab* is the Egyptian word for 'gold.' Smaller, less luxurious boats like the *Samak* were used for servants. But that's all changed. A few of the wealthy still have *dahabiehs*, but more often the occupants are mistresses, prostitutes—"

"British soldiers."

"Once the war got going, some of the *dahabiehs* were pressed into service. The larger ones became convalescent quarters for the wounded, for example, while the smaller ones, like the *Samak*, were fine for emergency officers' lodgings. It may not be opulent, but the *Samak* should suit you quite nicely. Come. I'll show you."

With Peter behind him, Clarke climbed down a short ladder to the *Samak*'s foredeck and pushed open a door to living quarters. "Your salon, complete with a sofa, a table and some chairs. Over there at the rear, just to the right of the curtain, is a small fridge, stove and sink. And beyond the curtain you'll find four berths, a loo and, at the aft, an actual stateroom, with a bureau and a bed."

"Certainly not what I was expecting," Peter said.

"And now for the best part of the *Samak* yet." Clarke led Peter out the door, up the ladder and over the gangplank back onto the street.

"I thought you said the best part of the boat."

"I did." Clarke took off again, retracing their path, only this time he went two blocks farther down the street and stopped in front of a nightclub with a garish sign that read *Kairo Kanteen*.

"What's this?" Peter asked.

"The finest place in the city to forget about why you're in the city to begin with."

"And this is the best thing about the houseboat."

"Absolutely." Clarke grabbed Peter's arm and escorted him to the door. "After you've had a good time here, the *Samak*'s close enough for you to pass out there instead of in the street."

Passing out sounded very inviting to Peter. "Dudley, it's been a long day."

"And now it's night, your first in Cairo. Don't tell me you shrivel up when the sun goes down?"

"Not normally."

"Then let's be at it," Clarke said, and continued to talk as he went in. "You'll get to see Cairo at its liveliest."

The Kanteen's interior wasn't what Peter expected from its tacky exterior. The crowded bar area didn't create a great first impression, but he had seen worse, and the patrons were surprisingly quiet. The bar itself offered a view of the dining room, which looked like a mid-scale Manhattan nightclub, with thirty or so occupied tables, all of them facing a large elevated stage.

And on the stage beautiful women in colorful sequined bras and skirts with waistbands below their navels were undulating to music played on Egyptian instruments by six men.

"Drat!" Clarke looked at his watch. "It's the tail end of this performance, but there's an even better one within the hour. Meantime, let's sit and enjoy what little is left."

"In case you haven't noticed, Dudley, the bar is full. And so are the tables, except for one." Peter pointed to a table directly in front of the stage. "But some people are waiting."

"That's easy enough to remedy." Clarke, with Peter in tow, approached a burly man in a tuxedo who was watching over the room, and in a quiet but authoritative tone announced, "I finally made it."

"We were wondering, Mr. Clarke," the man said.

"And as you can see, I've brought a friend. He's never been here."

"Well, I am certain he will enjoy himself." With that the man detached one end of the red velvet rope strung between two low brass poles to restrict entrance to the dining room. "I will summon a waiter to escort you."

"Not necessary. Instead tell a waiter to fetch a bottle of Champagne for us. Well, Peter, shall we sit?"

Peter looked again at the empty table, obviously the best in the house. "Very sneaky, Dudley. You made a reservation."

"I did nothing of the sort. The Kanteen doesn't take reservations. Now follow me and mind your step. Try not to trip over anything while eyeing the girls."

Easy to say. Peter had seen his share of carnival belly dancers, but none were like these. Their music, their moves, even their costumes—skimpy but classy—were entirely different. This wasn't bump-and-grind for the chicken farmers who wanted a visual taste of the dangerous. This was art.

As Peter and Dudley took their seats, the music changed, the tempo becoming faster; the dancers responded with enthusiastic shimmying and shaking.

"It's a variant on something called *Fellahy*, which is, shall we say, a very provocative rhythm," Clarke explained as one of the women drew close to Peter and bent backward so that her midsection was almost beneath his chin, her gyrating hips moving from one side to the other.

The dancer lingered for a few more seconds, and Peter saw that her face and body were covered with a thin layer of sweat. "And quite athletic, it seems."

"Damn exhausting. In a complete routine, a Fellahy is simply one of many rhythmic transitions—*Maqsoum, Masmoudi, Malfouf*—each of which determines the dance. You'll see later on. For now, concentrate on the women."

Although he was tired, Peter wasn't *that* tired and had no problem doing as Clarke said. After another five minutes and a round of loud applause, the dancers gracefully departed the stage. The bar, which had been so quiet, grew noisy and Peter, hearing the clamor, looked over his shoulder. When he and Clarke had arrived, the bar was jammed with men. Now one of them had surrendered his seat to a light-skinned Egyptian woman in a black skirt and black pumps, her dark hair flowing freely over the shoulders of a simple red blouse.

"You seem intrigued with that woman," Clarke said.

Peter realized he had been gawking. "Beyond the fact that she's stunning?" Peter looked back at the bar. The woman was conversing with the man next to her. Then it clicked. "I've seen her before, Dudley. And so have you. Outside your building, when we were leaving, she was arriving. The woman who tried to pick me up."

Clarke stared at the woman again. "What makes you so sure that's the one? She was all but hidden by her clothing."

"I have a feel for these things."

"I think it might be more fantasizing than feeling, not that I'd blame you."

"Strange, seeing her here," Peter said.

"Cairo's the city of strange. As for her being here, sometimes Kiya's girls do a little work on their own. Kiya tolerates it in moderation. She feels it's good promotion. Anyway, seems our young lady is leaving and by herself. Now that is strange, even for Cairo. A looker like her should have had no problem finding suitable company."

True enough. Besides the man she had been speaking with, who was still at the bar, Peter had noticed one or two other potential clients approach, only to be turned down with a smile. Maybe she had changed her mind about a little extra work. Maybe, like him, she was tired and had opted for sleep rather than sex. Whatever the reason, Dudley was right: she was gone.

However, someone else had arrived. "I come bearing Champagne."

Peter and Dudley both rose to greet a striking woman in her late forties who appeared as trim and graceful as the dancers. Indeed, her clothing resembled theirs—a long lavender-and-silver lamé skirt and matching bra, both emblazoned with purple and silver sequins.

"We are in the presence of royalty," Clarke said, and bowed. "Major Peter Baker, allow me to introduce Madame Adiba, the queen of this marvelous realm."

"*Enchanté.*" Peter leaned over, took Adiba's hand and kissed it.

"Another charmer like your friend Dudley, are you not, Major Baker? Please, sit." They did and she joined them. "So Dudley, I see you have again taken the King's table."

"King Farouk," Clarke said to Peter as he removed the wire from the Champagne and started wiggling the cork back and forth. "He's very much a party person. Every club in Cairo keeps a table open for him."

"And what if he should show up here tonight?" Peter asked.

"Adiba would probably throw him out."

"No, his money is good," Adiba said. "He was here once, but never again. He prefers a different type of establishment."

"But you still keep a table for him," Peter said.

"Custom. Besides, certain of my friends, such as Dudley, are not shy about putting the table to use."

"Britain is a democratic monarchy, not a dictatorship," Clarke explained. "Should His Majesty King George come into the Kanteen, I would allow him to share the table with us. I would, of course, extend the same courtesy to King Farouk." With that he pushed the cork one last time and it shot from the bottle. "We're being fired upon. Quick, let's discharge the weapon." He poured Champagne for the three of them and lifted his glass. "To you, Madam Adiba, for bringing a modicum of civilized decadence to this old city." They clinked glasses and drank.

"And now . . ." Adiba got up from the table.

"You're not leaving us," Clarke protested as he and Peter stood up.

"I will return, but at the moment I must make sure everything is ready for the final show."

"We won't drink it all," Clarke promised.

"You most certainly will, and be on your next bottle, or perhaps even the one after that, when I am back."

"She knows you well, Dudley," Peter said.

She flashed a dazzling smile. "And I hope to know you better as well, Major Baker."

"Quite a woman," Peter said when he and Dudley took their seats.

"That's somewhat of an understatement. Among her many accomplishments was bringing *raks sharki*—real belly dancing—to Egypt. Because of her it's in every Cairo cabaret."

"She was a belly dancer?"

"The best. She still dances occasionally and she's lost none of her skills. She's also a gifted teacher. Some of her most accomplished protégés, Samia Gamal and Tahia Carioca, for example, opened up their own places or strayed into the movies. I suspect that will happen with a few of the girls you just saw." Clarke refilled the glasses. "In any event, she's a good person to know, especially since the Nazis hate her."

"Why so?"

"Originally they tried to win her over and get her to do some spying. Bad enough she refused, but then the Kanteen began putting on some screamingly funny parodies of Hitler. It really got to the Jerries, so their sympathizers pumped out the propaganda, calling her a traitor and accusing her of working with us."

"And is she?"

"I'm not sure that information is relevant to your mission."

Touché. Clarke's way of reminding Peter he was miffed at not knowing everything about the mission. After pausing to make sure his jibe had sunk in, Clarke continued. "Let's just say that if Rommel makes it into Cairo, she's a goner for any number of reasons, provided they can catch her, which is unlikely. But should they, guaranteed she'll take a few of them with her. Carries a gun, you see, and can use it quite effectively if need be."

"Obviously a talented lady."

"And perceptive." Clarke lifted the Champagne bottle. "We will indeed need another round, unless you'd rather switch to some Egyptian beer, strong but very drinkable."

"I'd rather switch to sleep. No, let me correct myself. I *have* to switch to sleep."

"Nonsense."

"Which is exactly what I'll be reduced to if I don't sleep. It would take a superhuman to keep up with you, Dudley. I, unfortunately, am but a *mere* human, puny and, therefore, in need of rest."

"Adiba will be greatly disappointed."

"I'm sure your company will more than compensate for my loss."

"Well, if you must, you must. Pity, though. Positive you don't mind me not joining you?"

It was an obligatory question, a show of good manners. Clarke wasn't about to leave, no matter what Peter answered. "I'd be offended if you did."

"Then ta until tomorrow."

With that Peter weaved a path through the still-filled tables, crossed the bar area and exited onto the street. Though warm, the night air was a refreshing contrast to the crowded club, and after a few breaths Peter felt revived. Despite appearances, he had drunk much less than Clarke, although Peter would be a poor con man if he couldn't make it look like he was matching glass for glass. He *was* exhausted, however, and appreciated Dudley's point about the *Samak* being so near the Kanteen.

It kept him from passing out in the street.

23

Maybe the *Samak* was only a second-class houseboat, but to a weary Peter it was the *Queen Mary* and he had a first-class booking.

Within five minutes, he was standing on the *Samak*'s foredeck, enjoying a slight breeze and a last look at the Nile before retiring. Relaxed by the night waves that gently rocked the *Samak*, Peter let his mind drift to another river, the fierce Mississippi, and to another time, when, as a boy, he rode the rails through the Deep South.

> *Mississippi River she got a hold on me*
> *I I'll come for you baby if I ever get free.*

From across the years Peter could hear the world-weary voices of dockhands, sharecroppers, chain gangs, barrelhouse whores—anyone who, as Delta said, "got Mississippi River water for blood"—singing about hardship, oppression and, most often, love lost or gone bad, in laments called the blues.

No one knew more about the blues than Delta; no one could sing the blues like Delta. He was a legend. Long ago Delta told Peter, "You don't sing the blues 'cause you want to. You sing the blues 'cause you has to. You sing the blues to get rid of them, but it don't last. See, boy, you can sing the blues out of your system, but never out of your soul."

As Peter thought about Delta, about how he missed his calm wisdom, snippets of songs filled his head.

> *Dreamed I seen my woman*
> *Lying there cross my bed.*
> *But then I opened my eyes*
> *And seen the blues there instead*

Instinctively Peter reached into his pocket, but the old beat-up harmonica he always carried as a boy, the one that Delta gave him, wasn't there; it hadn't been for years. No matter how much you grasped at the past, you always ended up with a handful of the present.

The Nile's spell was broken and the voices gone, but Peter continued to gaze at the faint flickers of light from the night sky that skimmed the river's surface. It reminded him of the Seine the night he and Max dined at La Tour d'Argent. At that point Peter had already decided his relationship with Max would be strictly "professional," defined by the mission, and he wasn't going to let romantic Paris or some gypsy's wild prattle change that. A cross made from a twisted nail that seemingly vanished of its own accord? With time to think Peter had dismissed it as merely a combination of coincidence and carelessness.

So why couldn't he let it go? He had thought about that, too, but couldn't come up with a satisfactory answer. Was it because Max said she trusted him? And what did she mean by that? Did she trust him to complete the mission? Or, more worrisome, did she trust him not to hurt her, just like a woman he loved had trusted him nearly a decade ago? Only Peter had hurt that other woman badly. Hurting her was the only way to save her, but the emotional impact of his actions devastated them both. Peter would never let that happen again. Since then, he had steered clear of love, Besides, Peter hadn't met anyone else he felt he could love, so it wasn't hard. When he met Max, though, she caught him off balance.

Peter hadn't expected "Colonel Max" to be a beautiful woman, a breathtakingly beautiful woman. He wasn't surprised that she was wary of him at first. It would have been strange if, growing up as she had, in the uncertainty of Germany after World War One, knowing her father had abandoned her and her mother, she'd felt differently about Peter. But she no longer distrusted him, and that made him more determined to protect her. By living her double life she was risking as much as he was risking. It was a damned good thing he was determined to keep their relationship focused on the mission. It was proving hard enough to do what he had to do in order to gull Himmler. If Peter was foolish enough to get involved with Max, it could jeopardize the plan he had formulated. Besides, Johnny was right: love could destroy a life. Funny, this was the first time Peter had really thought about Johnny since the glider crash. Although they weren't really friends, Peter felt they were kindred spirits. Did Johnny sense that as well? he wondered. And if so, were his dying remarks about there being no life without love a message for Peter?

Die Lieb führt uns und ich folge. Damn, he missed Max!

Well, never mind. There was more than one use for a bed.

———

Peter's acute hearing jolted him awake.

After a few seconds to focus, he analyzed the auditory input: light steps on the *Samak*'s deck and the faint sounds of Egyptian music. A robber or an assailant would probably have gone inside by now. And if these were fun seekers who, as Dudley mentioned, sometimes partied on seemingly empty houseboats, it would be noisier. That suggested no more than two people who wouldn't look out of place on the boat after dark.

Done with speculating, Peter slipped on his pants, made his way to the salon and, with his night-adjusted vision, surveyed the dark room. It was empty and everything appeared normal. A few silent steps brought Peter to the deck door. He cracked it open and peeked out, not knowing what to expect.

"What the . . . ?" Peter threw the door open and stared. A woman wearing a red bra and a long skirt, its waistband secured beneath her navel with a tasseled belt, was dancing to music from a small hand-cranked phonograph placed on a deck chair. Draped over her head was a rectangular strip of red gauze with silver sequins, and she held one end so that it covered her face just below her eyes. After a few seconds to get over his surprise, Peter walked onto the deck and lifted the phonograph's tone arm from the record.

"Ah, finally." Still in step, despite the lack of music, the woman worked her way closer to Peter. Just as he thought. "You're the one I saw on Kira Street and at the Kanteen."

"If you prefer, I can be someone else," she said, emphasizing her willingness with a provocative sway of her hips. "I can be whoever you want, whatever you want."

"How about your real self?"

"That is not as exciting."

Even so, it might help Peter understand why a nearly naked woman was sharing a houseboat with him at—he glanced at his watch—nearly 1:30 in the morning. "Look, I don't mean to sound rude, but I really wasn't expecting company. So perhaps you could explain why you're here?"

"I am here because I know what you want."

Although that response begged for elaboration, Peter had a more immediate question. "How did you know where to find me?"

"When you left the Kanteen I followed. After, I went back and borrowed these from a friend who dances there." The woman cupped her bra suggestively and then slid her hands down her stomach to her skirt, pulling it a little lower in the process of showing it off. "I saw how you watched the Kanteen dancing girls. And I saw how you looked at me. Now you have me as a dancing girl." She reached out and slid her fingers across Peter's cheek. "Are you pleased?"

He was skeptical. "Why go to all this bother? There were men falling all over you at the bar."

"When I am at the house on Kira Street, I take who I am given. When I am on my own, I decide who I want. You have a nice face."

Peter wasn't satisfied by the explanation. Granted, she could be telling the truth. Dudley had said that in Cairo the unexpected was the norm. But she could also have something other than sex in mind. Had there been a leak? Did others now know about the mission? Was she here to compromise it in some way? Peter needed to test her and find out. "I'm sure you have a nice face as well, but can't tell. Perhaps if you removed the veil."

"Sure. You pay and I remove the veil, the belt—whatever you desire."

"It's an inviting offer, and a wasted effort, I'm afraid. I suggest you gather your belongings and leave. Even at this hour, there are bound to be other men out there with nice faces and less than nice ideas."

"What is the matter? You don't like women?" She plunked down in one of the chairs.

"I definitely like women."

"Then what is wrong? You are married? I am friends with many married men."

"No, not married."

"A girlfriend, then, maybe here in Cairo."

How did she become the interrogator? "Not really a girlfriend and not in Cairo."

"Then what is the problem? You do not have urges?"

"We British have great self-control."

"There are better ways to handle urges. So, what do you say?" She stood up and turned around, allowing Peter to better appreciate what was being offered. "You, me—we can have some fun."

Whatever the woman's true intent, there was something else about her that Peter couldn't quite pin down. "Just as a matter of curiosity, what would a—that is, were I to . . ."

"Fifty British pounds."

"Fifty pounds! Are you mad?"

"I am good. Better than good. Fifty pounds and I will stay with you until light. Many hours for many things. The best money you have spent in a long time. I promise."

What was it about her? From the first time he saw her, she had intrigued him. He had to keep the conversation going. "Twenty-five pounds."

"Now you are the one who is mad. Fifty pounds and I will teach you magic—Egyptian magic—to bring home and make your Englishwomen very happy."

"Thirty-five pounds. Final."

"Forty pounds. Final."

Where was the missing piece Peter needed to solve the puzzle? He felt he was getting close. Why couldn't he find it?

"So, what do you say? Forty."

This time she rubbed her shoulder against his and cocked her head so she could see his face. And when she did, something clicked in Peter's brain. That's it! It has to be. It would certainly explain a lot. But Peter had to be sure. It was too important. "Done. Forty pounds."

"Excellent!' She stepped back from him and did a celebratory twirl. "You understand, the money first."

"My wallet's below in the bedroom."

"And that is where we are heading." The woman started toward the deck door.

"Could we stay out here a little longer? It's s a lovely night. You'll get your money. I promise."

"If that is what you want. I trust you."

Damn! It would have been better if she hadn't mentioned trust, but Peter let it pass. "By the way, since we're about to get better acquainted, my name is . . ." He ran through some possibilities. "Harry. What should I call you?"

"Anything you want."

"Let's see. What about Fatima?"

"Fatima. Fine. Very original." She started to remove her veil, but Peter stopped her. "No, no, please. Keep it on a little longer. I find it exotic and curiously stimulating. However, your decorative bra—that has to go."

"As you wish." She positioned the veil on her head so that her entire face was hidden beneath a red gauze tent. Then she put her hands behind her back to unfasten her bra.

"Wait!" Peter commanded, and she immediately dropped her arms. "Come here. Let me teach you something in return for what you're going to teach me. Only my lesson will be free of charge. Isn't that refreshing?"

She approached, and when her body was almost touching his Peter reached over her shoulders. "I learned this from an expert." He slid his hands down the curve of her back, enjoying the feel of her soft skin. "Quite an unusual method." His fingers wrapped around the bra's hook and catch, ready to separate them. "However, I think you'll be impressed." All of a sudden Peter's right hand flew up and over her shoulder, clutched the front of her bra and ripped it down. She shrieked and dropped her veil, but before she could do anything else Peter spoke:

"Hello, Max."

"Bastard!"

Peter was laughing too hard to respond.

"Bastard!" Max slapped Peter, which only made him laugh harder.

"Hey, I was supposed to do the slapping, once I ripped your bra off. Don't you remember our first date in the alley behind the Crow's Nest? You gave me a gun, and I didn't even think to bring you flowers."

"Bastard!" Max raised her hand again, but instead of striking Peter, she went past his cheek, grasped the back of his neck and pulled his face to hers.

"Sorry about doing that to you, but I couldn't resist," Peter said. "Am I forgiven?"

Max's long and passionate kiss caught Peter by surprise, but he didn't resist. "What prompted that?" he asked afterwards, still mystified.

"Ladies first. When did you know it was me?"

"The moment I unfastened your bra."

"What?" Max pushed him away. "Peter!"

"No more slaps." Peter raised his hands in surrender, then took Max's head scarf and placed it around her shoulders so that it covered her bare breasts. "There. That's much less distracting. Let's sit. We both have a lot of questions."

"My question's still out there," Max said as they settled into deck chairs. "Answer it first."

"When did I know it was you? Only at the very end and that's why I agreed to pay for your services."

"Then I really fooled you?" Like a delighted child, Max clapped her hands together rapidly.

"You really did. Here, at the bar, outside the brothel."

"What finally gave me away?"

"Your eyes."

"My eyes?" Max was crestfallen. "That can't be. I took such great pains to disguise them, which, thankfully, I no longer have to do."

With that Max bent over, placed her fingers to her eyes and poked and pulled. "Ouch! Damn!" When she finally looked up, her eyes had turned from brown back to their normal blue. "Here." She dropped two circular pieces of translucent brown glass in Peter's hand. "My secret."

"Colored lenses." Peter studied them more carefully. "Ingenious."

"They're just starting to be used in color films, and I wasn't kidding about going to great pains. Those damn lenses take forever to insert and hurt like hell. But a blue-eyed Egyptian would draw more attention than I wanted, even though King Farouk has blue eyes."

"These are a refinement of an old technique." Peter continued to be intrigued by the lenses. "I'd sometimes put eggshell membranes over my eyes to fake blindness, like Lon Chaney did in *The Hunchback of Notre Dame*—"

"Ah, Notre Dame. Paris. The Seine. Do you ever think about that, Peter?"

Best to casually brush this aside. "Now and then. Mostly about the duck blood." Max scowled, as she usually did when Peter countered serious with flippant. "Anyway, the colored lenses were very effective."

"Not if you could tell it was me."

"Any decent mentalist knows your eyes never change even if their color does. Once I had a chance to really look into them, everything else—the hair dye, the body makeup—came together and there you were. But the how and the why weren't. Want to fill in the gaps?"

"I'm sure your journey to Cairo was more interesting than mine."

Let's see: Oran; Algiers; the train; Achiery; Johnny; the camels; the Sahara; the bandits; the Tuareg; the glider; Churchill; Monty; Dudley. Yes, it probably was. But if Max managed to make it to Cairo, why couldn't she help him get there? "Come on, Max. Just the highlights."

"If I must," Max sighed. "I had filming to do in Greece for Himmler's documentary and, with you gone, I decided to get it over with. Once in Greece, I wasn't terribly far from Egypt, and no one really was keeping watch over me. Otto could handle any film matters and make excuses should anyone ask my whereabouts. Father Fritz had given me a letter of introduction for an acquaintance in Greece who, he said, would help in an emergency. It turns out the acquaintance was the Archbishop of Turkey and Greece and although he lived in Istanbul, he traveled regularly to Athens. I contacted him and after he read my letter from Father Fritz he offered to get me into Turkey unnoticed. He dressed me in a nun's habit and then personally took me to Istanbul in—and you'll enjoy this part—the official plane of the German ambassador to Turkey. Seems the ambassador's a devout Catholic. He counts the Archbishop among his close friends and lets him use the plane for church-related travel."

"And the Turkish authorities at the Istanbul airport?"

"Because it was a diplomatic plane, it took off and landed in a special area, with no checks. There were Nazi guards, however. So I put on a long raincoat and some slacks, bunched my hair under a hat and went with the Archbishop to his waiting car. He let me stay at his residence while I figured out how to sneak into Cairo."

"I take it the resourceful Archbishop had no ideas."

"He would have come up with something, I'm sure. But, within a day, I found what I needed advertised in an English-language newspaper. Taheya Gamal, one of Adiba's former star dancers, was giving her last performance at the Orient Club."

"Whoa! Back up a moment. You know Adiba?"

"I've known her for years. Before the war, I'd occasionally visit friends in the Egyptian film industry. We'd often go to the Cairo Camera, a popular gathering place for actors and directors that Adiba ran before the Kanteen. That's how I met her and Taheya. Taheya and I always got along well, but I hadn't seen her since 1939. While I had no idea what she could or would do for me, she was my best hope. So, with the help of hair dye, dark body and facial makeup and those horrible lenses, I transformed myself into an Egyptian and called on her. Obviously she was surprised to see me, but also pleased. When I explained that I had to see Adiba on an urgent private matter, Taheya suggested I pose as a member of her troupe, which was leaving for Cairo by train the next morning." Max rose and shook her hips. "I guess I looked the part."

"And do the Egyptian officials at the Cairo train station extend diplomatic privileges to belly dancers?"

"No, but belly dancers sometimes extend certain privileges to the Egyptian officials at the Cairo train station." Max lifted and dropped her hips more slowly this time, then stopped abruptly. "And it's not what you're thinking, you naughty boy. Taheya gave them free passes for her show. In return, they waved her and the troupe through."

So in Paris Max hadn't held anything back. She was in Cairo thanks to a series of fortunate events. But instead of relief, Peter felt pangs of guilt, which, for a con man, was always dangerous and potentially fatal. Peter hadn't experienced guilt in so long, he thought he was immune. Why did it hit him now? Because he wondered how Max got to Cairo? That was merely his usual wariness, certainly nothing for him to feel guilty about.

Max sat back down and continued. "Taheya's driver brought me to Adiba. I told her I came to Cairo to meet someone. That was sufficient. Like the Archbishop, Adiba didn't press me. She has too many secrets of her own.

She gave me a room above the Kanteen and that's where I've been staying. The rest you know."

"Do I?"

"You said the highlights. Now I suppose you want to know why."

Peter could sense Max's mood shifting. The alluring belly dancer was gone. "It doesn't have to be now."

"Actually it does." Max rose again and, head tilted downward, walked to the deck rail. Peter got up to join her, but she stopped him. "Just give me a few moments," she said, and looked out over the water.

"Max, are you—"

"Please." Max raised her right hand and slowly turned around. "Peter, realize this isn't easy for me to talk about. So don't do anything, don't say anything—just listen." She paused and drew a deep breath. "That time in Father Fritz's study when you read my palm and said my father had hurt me. I wouldn't—couldn't—admit it then, but you were right." Max put her hand to her neck, then quickly withdrew it. "See. Still reaching for my locket, even when it's not there." She took another deep breath. "My father abandoned us when I was six. With no marketable skills and a child to provide for, my mother took menial jobs when she could find them. When she couldn't—well, she did whatever she had to do. Growing up watching my mother suffer because of my father only deepened my resolve never to let a man hurt me again. Don't get me wrong. I enjoy a man's company, but I always ended a relationship before I became too attached. I just couldn't expose myself to being abandoned again and experiencing that pain . . ."

"That's nice enough for you." Peter broke into Max's pause.

"Back to playing the psychology professor." Max almost smiled. "Was there anguish for the men? Yes, sometimes, I suppose, but so what? They all soon found another woman. That's the way men are. Now it's my turn to play the psychology professor. No, better—the mind reader. You're wondering if I enjoyed making a man suffer, aren't you? You're wondering whether I was getting revenge for what my father did."

"You're not going to put me out of business, but you're pretty good."

"Only because I considered that possibility, then dismissed it. It wasn't important. It was only important that I not get hurt, that I not suffer. Sounds horrible, doesn't it?"

"No." Peter got up and walked over to Max. He gently took her hands in his. "It sounds honest."

"There's more."

"It can wait." Peter's uneasiness grew as he realized his earlier inkling was becoming a certainty.

"I've come this far. Let me finish. Unlike you, I'm capable of losing my nerve."

Peter squeezed her hands tighter. "You give me too much credit."

"More than you realize. Would you like to hear something funny? After what you did at Wewelsburg and in Paris, I started to believe you were some kind of invincible miracle man, able to find a way out of the most hopeless situations. Then you didn't arrive at your rendezvous point. . . ."

"How did you know that?"

"Shhhh." Max pulled her right hand from Peter's and gently placed it over his mouth. "Otto stayed in Paris with Rémy, monitoring your progress. He came to Greece to tell me that you had simply disappeared. Suddenly I had to face the possibility of not seeing you again. I had never considered that . . ."

"You were worried about the mission." Peter offered Max an out.

"That's what I told myself: No Peter, no mission. Poof! All our work—for nothing. But resistance plans had fallen apart before and we always came up with another. This would be no different. I told myself all those things, and even though I believed them, I couldn't shake my anxiety and depression. That wasn't me. I'm a film director, accustomed to being in control of everything—actors, technician, cameras, lighting, everything. Even my own feelings. Yet when you went missing—and this is going to sound like a bad movie line—it was as if some of me went missing as well. Finally I fully understood how my mother must have felt when my father walked out. I was afraid."

"I didn't walk out," Peter said. "I didn't want to go; I had to go."

"You were still gone. All I could do was wait, and I wanted to do that in Cairo. And that's what I did when I got there—stayed in my room, not knowing what might happen next. Then an anonymous message was left for Adiba at the Kanteen, probably from one of Rémy's people in Syria. It consisted of two Arabic words—*Buruj Yawm*, 'Zodiac Today'—and the Kira Street address, which, Adiba said, was a high-class brothel. She also said that the British used a small portion of the building and wouldn't take kindly to a German intruder. I assured her I'd be careful and, again making myself up as an Egyptian, set out for Kira Street. I found an outdoor café with a view of the building, so I sat there sipping many cups of coffee until you finally showed up. I left the café and positioned myself to greet you when you came out. Later, I described the man you left with to Adiba. She smiled and guaranteed he'd bring you to the Kanteen tonight."

"And now I do know the rest."

"Almost. I said before I was afraid. My mother loved my father so completely—she invested her whole self in loving him. And even when he was gone, she never stopped loving him. He was her life. If I felt even a small part of what my mother felt, then I knew it was for the same reason. That's why I was afraid. I was afraid that I might be in love with you. There. I said it. I don't care if you think me silly. I had to say it, no matter what the consequence."

Might be in love with you.

"It was silly, wasn't it?" Max said.

"Not silly at all. It's just that I wasn't expecting this."

"Well, don't worry. I can't say for sure that love threw me off balance. Since I've never let myself fall in love, I could only judge by my mother. So you tell me, Peter: is what I described love?"

This time Peter responded quickly and truthfully. "I'm not the best person to ask."

"Don't tell me you've never been in love, either."

"No, I was in love once." That was also the truth.

"Only once?"

"Maybe twice."

"You didn't know for sure?"

He gave a nonanswer. "It's complicated."

"I see." Max pulled her hands from his. "Well, you certainly don't need me to make it more complicated. But you do need me to explain. This feeling I had—love, or whatever it was—I thought maybe you— I assumed— That is, I . . ." Max paused to collect herself. "I apologize for rambling. Usually I'm better at handling the unexpected. You see, my best efforts aside, I found myself growing interested in you and I needed time to think that through. But then you went missing, and I realized we don't control time. Right time, wrong time, enough time—it all means nothing. We can only be sure of the moment we live in. And I resolved not to waste that moment if we were reunited. But I also thought you might be . . . receptive, and that's my fault. I obviously misread certain things you said and did. I took them as signals of what you were feeling, and I ended up putting both of us in an uncomfortable position. I'm sorry for that. But maybe it's best that we cleared the air. Other than having more faith in each other, nothing's changed between us."

Earlier Peter had given Max an out. Now she had returned the favor. A nod, maybe a smile and a simple "Why don't we both get some rest?" and it was over. Done. "Nothing's changed between us? *Everything's* changed between us. You talk about time? Let me tell you something about time. You can't reset the clock just by saying so, Max, and even if you could, I wish you wouldn't."

So much for "done." This was new territory. Peter could always imagine he was playing a role and put on a convincing show. It wouldn't exactly be a scam and Max probably wouldn't know the difference. What would be so terrible? Why couldn't he— Peter's train of thought was abruptly derailed by another bit of blues:

> *Woman you done ruined me, and the life is led.*
> *If you ever think I'm lyin', want you to shoot me dead.*

Peter heard a voice reminding him that *the blues are the compass of the soul 'cause they tell if you're headin' where you supposed to be goin'.* It was Delta, giving Peter his bearings as he had so often in the past. Taking Max by the hand, Peter led her back to the chairs. He asked her to sit, but he remained standing. "The things you said, about Paris, signals—you were right about all of that, about my feelings for you. I've always thought you were special, from the very beginning, lying in that alleyway half-dazed and gazing up at you—I honestly thought you were an angel."

"I'm no angel, Peter."

"Shhhh." Peter leaned over and, as Max had done to him, pressed his fingers to her lips. "My turn to talk; your turn to listen." In one continuous motion, he pulled back his hand and ran it through his hair, then across his cheek and finally, semi-cupped, over his mouth before. "Then I began to appreciate that you were an angel not because of your looks, but your deeds. Of course, that didn't stop my envisioning us engaged in very un-angel-like activities. True, you took an instant dislike to me, but I knew you'd weaken. And once you gave me the slightest hint, I was ready to— well, you get the picture. Then, that night in Paris, when the hint came, the desire had gone."

"I don't understand." Max appeared more taken aback than confused.

"Not my desire for you. Christ, no! I wanted you more than ever. What I didn't want was a casual fling. I thought I did, initially, but by the time I got to Paris, that changed. I didn't want anything between us to be casual. And that's why there can never be anything between us."

"Peter, you're talking nonsense."

He was, but only to himself. "When I said I had been in love once—the woman ended up getting hurt."

"By you?"

"She got hurt because I loved her." Peter winced as he said the words; the pain was still there. "And I won't let the same thing happen to you. No matter how crazy it sounds, hurt happens to people I love."

"And you've concluded this from one instance. What about the second woman?"

"The second woman?"

"You said you've only been in love once, maybe twice."

"Haven't you already figured that out?"

"I'm still waiting for you to tell me."

"Tell you what, Max? That I can't let myself fall in love with you? Is that what you want me to tell you?"

"That tells me enough." Max stood up and looked at Peter, then walked past him. "And, like everything else you set your mind to, I assume you've been successful." She scooped up her bra from the deck and examined it. "You broke the hooks," she said, and tossed it overboard.

"Damn it, Max! Would you please . . ."

Max was moving again, this time toward the boarding plank. "I'll be at Adiba's. Later in the day, we can discuss how to proceed with the mission. Pleasant dreams, Peter."

In poker, Peter was always prepared if somebody called his bluff. But this wasn't poker. "Max, I think I love you."

She stopped short and then wheeled around and stared at him. "Again."

"I think I love you."

"There. You told me and, see, nothing bad's happened."

"Don't joke about it, Max."

Max went back to where Peter was standing and draped her arms over his shoulders. "I still don't really understand what you meant before, beyond wanting to protect me from being hurt. I'd rather take my chances and, as I hope I made clear, I'm ready to."

"But not with me, Max." Peter removed her arms. "My life is all illusion. I use artifice to trick people and take their money."

"Sounds a lot like making movies, so who better than you?" Max chuckled. "Aren't we the pathetic pair? Two decisive people, turned tentative. How many risks have we taken without a thought since beginning this mission? Yet this one paralyzes us. And why? Because each of us is trying to avoid hurt, just coming at it from different directions. Well maybe we should just forget all that, close our eyes and jump."

"*Démerdez-vous,*" Peter said, then, realizing the words were probably lost on Max, added, "I'm talking to myself."

"It's all right. I'm nearly done. You know, it's possible that, no matter what we think, we're not in love with each other. There's only one way to find out for sure. I've made my decision, but it's meaningless without yours. And you're the one who said nothing between us should be meaningless."

Bitten in the ass by his own words and faced with a situation that he had adeptly skirted for so many years, Peter was forced to reflect. When he asked Max how she got to Cairo, was he actually hoping she'd give him an excuse to avoid commitment? He honestly didn't know. And all the unusual happenings that began when he was eight and first met the Gypsy? Usually the skeptic in him prevailed. But sometimes, when the skeptic wasn't looking, he wondered whether there really might be forces that neither he nor anyone else could explain. Graveyard dirt in his shoe, moss on a skull— those he justified by saying he was just respecting Delta's memory. Was that all, or did Peter actually believe in them? And if he did, even a little, was the familiar twisted nail Max wore that night in Paris warning him to steer clear so she wouldn't be hurt? Or was it telling him that she would be the love of his life? Which? As Max said, he had to decide.

"How would you suggest we start?"

"Are you asking Maxine Elise, the great German director, to set the scene?" Suddenly Max was beaming. "I think that can be arranged. Let's see." Max did a panoramic sweep of the surroundings and then placed a deck chair directly across from Peter. "Main camera with wide-angle lens right about here for our establishing shot. That way we'll get our actors, the boat rail and enough of the Nile for atmosphere. Next." Max moved another deck chair. "Our key spot, rigged for medium to low illumination since it's a nice, bright night. Now don't move, Peter, and continue to look straight at the camera. I'll be on your right side, only looking away from the camera, toward the river." Max took her place. "I think we can use a long shot for the whole scene, assuming it's brief. And now for the actors' instructions. Even if you've been trained in other methods, this is my set and you are to follow my directions. I play Fatima, a lady for hire. I've been bought and paid for by a randy British officer—that's you—who I want to satisfy, since it could lead to more business. You, on the other hand, want to make sure you get your money's worth. Pleasure is your main motivation."

"Pleasure doesn't motivate you at all?" Peter asked.

"Maybe a little. It's a hazard of the profession. Are you ready?"

"I've been ready for ages."

"Good. Then places! And action!"

The moment Max was back in position, Peter turned and moved behind her, then swirled her around and lifted her in his arms.

"So, you British have some passion after all. What do you have in mind?"

"Give me a second," Peter said as he walked away from the rail. "We went over this earlier. Ah, yes. My line is—" He jerked his leg, pressed his heel against the bottom of the slightly ajar deck door and pulled it open. "I think you get the picture."

And with that they were gone.

24

Egypt: August 22, 1942
Your Stars Today: Mars transiting Jupiter makes this a good
time for outdoor initiatives and quick, decisive decisions, all
of which are likely to turn out positive.

So far, it had been a flawless run.

Yet despite a reputation for daring and a Knight's Cross of the Iron Cross with Oak Leaves, Swords and Diamonds to back it up, Oberst Werner Becker took nothing for granted. True, the British had cut back on engaging the Luftwaffe in the air lately, relying more on ground-based anti-aircraft weapons. Still Becker prepared as if the entire RAF would be up and out to get him and the planes, which, as mission leader, he was responsible for.

Becker shifted around in his seat to keep from tightening up, but the JU-88 bomber didn't give him much room to wiggle. He and the three others on board—a navigator, a radio operator and a bombardier, all of them JU-88 regulars—had been shoehorned into the tiny cockpit. The super-minds of the Luftwaffe thought closeness would encourage camaraderie. Instead it encouraged cramps. Becker yearned to be back in his one-man Messerschmitt, dive-bombing the enemy.

However, the JU-88 was the right plane for level bombing missions like this one. Becker disliked level bombing—staying at a constant altitude and delivering your load. Yes, it took out more targets in a larger area, but it made you easy prey. You had to get in and out fast or you were a goner. Challenging in its own way, but lacking the offensive excitement that Becker craved.

If this mission had been less important, not requiring the very best, someone else would be in the pilot's seat. That Becker was there just showed how much faith his superiors placed in him. Becker would give them what they wanted: there was no way he'd let himself be killed in a "clunker" by ground fire. Luftwaffe aces didn't go out that way.

"Captain, I have confirmed bearings from Pharos." Becker's bombardier had locked on to the powerful beam coming from a lighthouse near the target.

"Do we have a confirm?" Becker waited for his radio operator to check with the other JU-88s flying with them. The squadron had deliberately been kept small in hopes of preventing an early detection and the kind of large in-air defense that worried Becker. Even the number of smaller attack planes had been reduced, leaving the squadron "not naked but in our underwear," as Becker told the members of the mission before its start.

"They are good, Captain," the radio operator said.

"I can see the lights." Becker had already been decreasing altitude. Now he brought the plane down to six thousand feet, which, while good for level bombing, made them dangerously vulnerable. Becker turned to his navigator, who doubled as the front gunner. "Ready?"

"Let them come."

Suddenly the night sky, which had been growing bright, turned black. "They've shut down the light," Becker said. "They're about to greet us." He listened, then shouted, "Here we go!" as the fire from anti-aircraft weapons shook the plane and set the sky ablaze.

"A few seconds more!" the bombardier yelled. "Three, two, one—bye-bye, boys!"

"Look, Werner!" The navigator was so excited as he looked through the plane's glass nose, he dropped formalities. "Look down. It's all aflame!"

The bombs—both 1100- and 550-pounders—had returned the British greeting and brought along gifts.

"The others?" Becker asked.

"They report all bombs on target," the radio operator, who had been maintaining contact with the other planes, said.

"Excellent! Damage?"

"Very light, Captain. The escort bombers must be keeping them busy."

"Or they could be scrambling their planes. Let's not press our luck."

Becker pushed the throttle forward and the plane responded immediately. One thing he did appreciate about the JU-88 was its speed, especially when it was six thousand bomb pounds lighter. "Now let's get to a more comfortable place." Becker pulled the wheel back and the plane angled upwards. "The more altitude, the better. I don't particularly like flying on the ground."

Having put height and distance between the plane and the target, Becker smiled for the first time all evening. "You have done well," he said, adding for the benefit of his crew, "and this plane has done well."

Knowing how Becker felt about flying the JU-88, the crew greeted his "conversion" with a cheer. It felt good. And he had to admit that the mission wasn't as bad as he had thought it would be. Since the war began, Becker had scored more than two hundred aerial kills flying solo in his Messerschmitt.

But tonight he won over his first crew.

"Baker! Peter Baker! Damn it, man, it's dawn. Don't tell me you're still sleeping!"

A shouting Dudley Clarke barged through the closed bedroom door.

"Up, man, up!" Clarke waited as first one and then another naked body emerged from beneath a white cotton sheet. The second body was female, which changed Clarke's eyes from piercing to bulging.

"What the hell is this, Baker?" he demanded.

"If I remember correctly, it's a woman." Peter reached to his right and rubbed his open hand from Max's face to her navel, where he caught the edge of the sheet and drew it back up to her neck. "Most definitely a woman." He yawned the words. "For God's sake, Dudley, haven't you heard of knocking?"

"What woman?" Clarke was still livid.

"Why does it matter? Christ, Dudley, stop being such a prude. Remember, you're the one who works in a whorehouse."

"Yes, but I don't bring my work home with me." Clarke was near the sputtering point. "And I don't expect you to, either. Now get that tramp out of here, Major!"

The urge to deck Clarke was strong, but good judgment finally prevailed. Better that Clarke think of Max as nothing more than an insignificant streetwalker.

"Oh, so we've reverted to rank, have we," Peter said, further diverting Clarke's attention from Max. "In that case . . ." Peter tossed off his portion of sheet, slung his feet over the edge of the bed, rose and stood facing Clarke. "Major Peter Baker reporting for duty, Colonel, sir." He snapped his right hand to his forehead in a crisp salute. "Do I pass muster?"

"Good Lord, Baker, would you kindly put on some bloody clothes?"

Peter fished around on the bed until he located his boxer shorts, which he slipped on, followed by a pair of tan khaki pants that were lying on the floor. "Sufficient?"

"Shirt, too. We need to get going."

"Where?"

"You'll see."

"No, Dudley, no more 'you'll see.' We exhausted that last night. Where are we headed for?"

Clarke shot Max a look.

"Oh, you're right. I do see." Peter reached into his back pocket, took out a wallet and threw some bills on the bed. "This should more than cover your services. And may I say you were delightful. Should you ever need a recommendation—"

This time the killing look from Max was a quite convincing one. Then, with the sheet wrapped around her, she got up and gathered her clothes.

"Be a good girl, will you, and dress out there in the garden," Peter said. "No one will see you, and even if they did, you're hardly shy. You could even drum up some business."

As she already had killed Peter with her eyes, this look buried him.

"*Yaa l-'aahira!*" And with that Max stomped out of the room, over the gangplank and into a clump of garden bushes.

"Do you understand what she said?" Peter asked Clarke.

"My Arabic's far from perfect, but I believe she called you a bastard. Wasn't she the girl at the bar last night? You know—at Adiba's."

Peter nodded. Come on, Dudley, get your mind off the girl.

"Thought so. Perhaps I better have her checked out."

"I told you, she's one of Kiya's girls, which you said made her OK."

"Still, can't be too safe. Did you at least get her name along with her goodies?"

Fine. You don't want to get off of your own accord, I'll pull you off. "Fatima."

"Ah, one of the hundreds of Cairo working girls named Fatima. The others are named Isis. And I suppose you didn't catch her last name." Clarke immediately thrust his hand in the air. "Never mind. Even if you did, it would be false."

"Dudley, I appreciate your caution, but really," Peter tried again. This son of a bitch was tenacious. "Don't tell me all the members of your team are chaste."

"Sorry. Normally I wouldn't be such a prig. But I have reason to dislike whores on houseboats, and it has nothing to do with morality." Clarke sat on the edge of the bed and continued to speak while Peter finished dressing. "Rather it has to do with breaking the German code."

This showed signs of being good. "Go ahead," Peter said.

"I had intended to explain all this during our drive this morning."

Peter snatched up his shoes and socks, sat next to Clarke on the bed and began putting them on. "I'm listening."

"A few months ago the Germans smuggled two spies into Cairo to gather intelligence. The spies linked up with Hekmat Fahmy, a well-known belly dancer. Fahmy was already providing secret information to anti-British Egyptian groups, so she had no qualms about doing the same for the Germans, for a price of course."

"Of course." Peter bent over to tie his shoelaces. "And she got her information from?"

"Her paramour. A fellow British major, I'm sorry to say, whom we refer to only as 'Smith.' Fahmy entertained Smith on her houseboat. He would come directly from work, bringing his briefcase stuffed with secret documents."

"Stolen?"

"No. He had clearance. Sad part is Smith had no idea that Fahmy was pumping him in more than one way. Or rather her German friends were. While Smith was in the bedroom having his way with her, the Germans came aboard and had their way with his briefcase, which he always left in the sitting area."

"That explains how the Germans got our secrets, not how we got theirs."

"One of the spies—John Eppler—picked up this woman named Yvette at a bar and brought her back to his lodgings for the night. Only it turns out that Yvette was a spy for the Jewish Agency, a group that wants Palestine to become a Jewish state. While I won't bother you with the reasons, Yvette came to suspect Eppler was also a spy, only for the Germans. So she told the Agency, and because the Agency was cooperating with MI6, it shared the information. At the right moment, we arrested the lot of them and also retrieved their transmitter for sending messages to Rommel. A pro-Nazi priest had hidden it in the pulpit of his church."

Involuntarily Father Fritz's face flashed into Peter's mind.

"But we couldn't find any clues as to the code the spies were using," Clarke continued. "Then Yvette told us that one night she was straightening up while Eppler was asleep and noticed a book, *Rebecca* by Daphne du Maurier."

"So? It's a popular book. I've read it and you probably have as well."

"As a matter of fact, I have. And, like you, I normally wouldn't give it a second thought. But inside the book Yvette found notepaper with hand-drawn grids, the type used for ciphers, and letter groupings. She made a copy, and noted the pages of the book that appeared to be turned to most often."

Peter rose to put on his shirt. "Why didn't she report this right off?"

"Because the Egyptian police, unaware of Yvette's connection with MI6, picked her up the same night. By the time we finally found out, we had already rounded up the buggers and gotten ahold of the receiver. But it doesn't matter: we have the code now and we've already begun using it. Herr Field Marshal Rommel still believes his dispatches are coming fresh from Cairo."

So the German code was broken not by prowess but by lust, some stupidity and a stroke of luck. Still, Peter wished Montgomery or someone had told him. Having the code to manipulate Rommel would make creating false horoscopes a lot easier.

"So, now that I look proper, where are we off to, tea?"

"When we arrive."

"We won't be arriving unless you tell me where we're going. I thought I made that clear."

Clarke sighed. "We're off to Alexandria."

"I thought we were going to see Maskelyne today."

"That's where he is, waiting to celebrate something that occurred last night."

"And what happened last night?"

"The Germans bombed Alexandria Harbor to smithereens."

Only one thing kept the German bombs from completely destroying Alexandria Harbor.

They never hit it.

Yet as they entered Alexandria, Peter saw heaps of rubble along the sides of streets and bricks strewn everywhere, evidence of the devastation Clarke had finely detailed during their 150-mile drive from Cairo. Peter also saw buildings, supposedly the source of that rubble, still standing, some with canvas paintings of bomb craters strung between them.

"Damn!" Clark slowed down the car to an idle and pointed to a clump of bricks blocking the roadway. "Be a good fellow and toss those out of the way."

Peter got out, picked up a brick, then, in a moment of recognition, hurled it at the windshield and watched it bounce off and back onto the street. "Bloody hell!" He stamped his foot on another brick, crushing it flat. "They're papier-mâché."

"If they can fool you up close, think of the Jerries in the sky," Clarke said as Peter got back in.

"All of this—the rubble, the street craters—decoys?"

"The Nazi reconnaissance planes always take pictures as soon as it's light. We didn't want to disappoint them."

"There wasn't a bombing?"

"Oh, there was a bombing, all right. It just wasn't a bombing of Alexandria Harbor. Let's go have a look."

The trip along the coast was short, hardly more than a mile, and it ended in a phalanx of soldiers guarding a cordoned-off area. They immediately recognized Clarke and waved him on.

"Are those hammers and saws?" Peter asked.

"You can hear that at this distance?" Clarke sped up and soon clusters of men, making sham buildings from plywood, came into view. "British navy construction crews. When they finish, they'll rig those phony buildings with explosives, which we'll set off so the Germans think their bombs struck. See those men over there to the right trucking sand? They're covering the remains of the so-called buildings that the Germans hit last night. Out with the old, in with the new."

"I bow to you, Dudley," Peter said, admiring both the creation of the effects and the coordination of the overall effort. "You would have made a fine stage illusionist."

"Wait. The best part is still some five hundred yards away." As Clarke drove, Peter saw other construction crews assembling fake ships from canvas and wood and hanging lights on them. Clarke stopped the car by the water where men on real boats were anchoring wooden stakes with lights on the top.

"Enlarging the fleet," Clarke quipped. "From the air it will look like a very potent presence. Come, let's get out."

"What is this place?"

"Maryut Bay, which, by a stroke of good fortune has geological features that are strikingly similar to Alexandria Harbor. We only needed to add a few touches to make it complete."

Peter shook his head in wonderment. He had pulled off some high-stake scams that required him to transform rooms, houses, even larger buildings. But Clarke and his team had taken the game to a different level.

"I'll show you the maps later on and you'll see for yourself. As for our immediate priority . . ." Clarke cupped his hands to his mouth. "Jasper!"

Responding to the shout, a stick of a man draped in an ill-fitting tan work shirt and shorts emerged from the gaggle of workers. Although Jasper Maskelyne had lost both weight and hair and gained a moustache, Peter recognized him immediately. But would Maskelyne recognize him? They had crossed paths only once, briefly, when Peter was twelve. Hopefully Maskelyne wouldn't remember and blow his cover.

"Jasper, over here!" Clarke signaled with his arm, continuing to speak as Maskelyne made his way over. "A brilliant job, Jasper. Fooled them completely."

"But will they buy tickets for an encore performance?" Maskelyne smiled at Clarke, who patted him on the shoulder, then turned to Peter. "And you are?"

"Major Peter Baker, allow me to introduce Major Jasper Maskelyne, our resident miracle worker."

Considering Clarke's true opinion of Maskelyne, Peter thought he did a commendable job of sucking it up and stroking some ego. "Major." Peter clasped Maskelyne's hand, then let it go. But Maskelyne still kept hold of Peter with his eyes.

"Forgive me for staring," Maskelyne said. "And forgive me even more for an old line, which I'm not accustomed to using with men, but have we met before?"

Well, here it comes . . . maybe. "I've seen you perform."

"Yes, I'm sure you have," Maskelyne said, displaying the same sense of self-importance that Peter remembered from twenty years earlier. "But so have tens of thousands of people, none of whom I remember. Yet you look familiar."

"Now if I might use an old line, I certainly would have recalled meeting you," Peter said. So far, so good.

"Yes, I imagine you would. Well, in any event, what brings you here, Peter is it?"

"Major Baker has similar interests to ours, Jasper," Clarke answered.

"Ah, fancy a good ruse do you?"

"Very much so."

"Then you've surely come to the right place. Has Dudley explained our operation?"

"He has an overview," Clarke said. "But I thought some field experience might prove more valuable."

"Indeed it would." Maskelyne looked at the sky. "Going to be another beastly day and we're already running behind. We started right after the Germans did their dawn flyover, but the extra effort needed to hide some of the previous damage has created a fair amount of havoc. Fortunately, the lighthouse is still intact. That's the masterpiece. Re-creating it would be a nightmare."

"The lighthouse on Pharos Island that overlooks Alexandria Harbor," Clarke said before Peter asked. "It's the Luftwaffe's welcoming light. Jasper and the boys built a replica here."

"For God's sake, don't tell him," Maskelyne said. "Show him the damn thing."

"An artist's temperament," Clarke quipped. "But point well taken. Let's."

Clarke led the short charge through a maze of decoys in progress to the edge of the bay where a battery of truck searchlights mounted on a plywood platform stood supported by six stilt-like legs.

"That's the lighthouse?" Peter said without considering how Maskelyne might react.

"Awfully sorry we didn't have the leisure to fabricate an exact model to size, Major Baker, all thirty-one bloody stories." Maskelyne made sure every drop of spewed sarcasm hit its mark. "Very unsporting of the Germans to impose a time constraint."

"From the altitude they fly at, the German bombers can't determine an object's height." Clarke the diplomat tried to broker a peace. "So this replica fits the bill. But the real genius is the inside, not the outside. Jasper, would you mind?"

Maskelyne sighed and made an "if I must" face. "The Germans use the beam to get their bearings. The lights on the fake lighthouse are connected to a timer that switches them on and off, giving the impression that the platform—our beam—is rotating. We control the whole shebang remotely from a console in the real Pharos. Once the Germans get into range, we shut the Pharos beam down and switch this one on. Then, as the planes near our dummy location, we kill the fake beam, flick on the search lights and commence the anti-aircraft fire."

"We transported the searchlights and the anti-aircraft weapons from the actual harbor," Clarke added. "The brass weren't especially keen on that, but we prevailed."

"We had to make it appear authentic," Maskelyne picked up the account again. "That's why we needed the right mixture of the real and the sham."

"Well, it seems to have worked brilliantly," Peter said.

"We'll know better if they come back tonight for a return engagement," Clarke said. "That's why we're setting all this up again."

"I understand from our message monitoring that Berlin's been informed of the successful bombing," Maskelyne said. "So they must have bought a penny's worth if not a pound. Now, if you'll excuse me, I have to oversee the remainder of the work. Evening will be here soon enough."

"I'm afraid they're going to have to do without you a little longer, Jasper. We have some matters to discuss."

"Which can wait," Maskelyne said.

"Only with the PM's permission. So if you'd care to ring him up . . ."

"The PM? What's so damn important to discuss that the PM's got his nose stuck in it?"

"The sooner we sit down and start, the sooner you'll find out." Clarke was clearly containing his temper.

Maskelyne took a long, slow breath, which he held. When he released it, there were words tacked on. "The Field Command Hut."

"Perfect," Clarke said. "I knew you'd come around."

With Peter and Clarke following, Maskelyne headed for what was indeed a hut, containing a table, six chairs, a small desk with a phone and some radio gear and little more. He plopped into a chair and waited for the others to do the same before starting the discussion with a curt, "Well?"

Brusque. Peter could play brusque. "Well, I want to know everything about the deceptions you're preparing for Montgomery's El Alamein offensive."

"What?" Maskelyne leapt up. "See here, Dudley, this is absurd. I have no intention of talking about deep tactics with this fellow."

"Sit down, Jasper!" Clarke snapped, indicating his patience had as well. "Your intentions carry no weight in this matter. Major Baker knows about Operation Lightfoot."

The fact that Clarke used the code name for Montgomery's offensive unnerved Maskelyne. "Knows? Knows how?"

"Knows from Montgomery himself," Peter said. "So can we drop all the posturing and get down to it?"

"A brief recap of the plan is in order." Clarke rose and went to a large map of Egypt hanging on a wall. "This, gentlemen, is the Alamein line." He placed his right forefinger against a point on the Mediterranean coast and moved down the map to an area of the Sahara Desert known as the Qattara Depression. "All forty miles of it." For emphasis Clarke jabbed his finger on the two boundaries of the line, one after the other. "Here water and here soft, impassable sand. So a flanking attack is impossible. Meanwhile, all along key penetration points . . ." Clarke brushed his hand over the imaginary line. "Rommel's laid a massive defensive barrier of barbed wire and land mines. Despite this, Monty will focus his attack on the northern portion of the line and attempt to cut two corridors through the minefields here and here." Clarke illustrated his statement by making two short parallel horizontal sweeps in the upper portion of the map. "He will be relying on Operation Bertram to make this possible." Clarke returned to his seat. "And now, Major Maskelyne, please provide us with the key points of Operation Bertram."

"In short, Operation Bertram consists of various well-integrated ploys to make Rommel believe that Montgomery's attack will be coming from the south." Maskelyne, who apparently had accepted the inevitable, went about his explanation in an even, unemotional voice. "Therefore, we're employing a selection of our best deceptions at the southern portion of the line. For example, we've placed two thousand fake tanks there rigged with the necessary pyrotechnics and we've been generating an ongoing stream of fake construction sounds. We've even been constructing a fake water pipeline, very slowly, and extending it far south. Our hope is that the Germans will tie our attack to the pipeline's completion and misjudge the date and location."

"In the meantime, we've also been sneaking in real tanks along the northern portion of the line by disguising them as trucks," Clarke said.

"Nicely done," Peter said. "Good old-fashioned misdirection, the magician's staple. Make them think something's happening in one place, while it's really happening in another. Keep watching my right hand, while my left hand hides the card."

"And we've been hiding a great many cards," Maskelyne said.

"Jasper's right," Clarke said. "There's more, but I'm sure you can fill in the gaps. Nevertheless, I'll set up another meeting in a day or so and bring in some others who've been working on this." He glanced at Maskelyne, who weakly shook his head in agreement.

"Then it's settled." Clarke rose from his seat. "Jasper, you're free to attend to your other matters. I'm going to spend a little more map time with Major Baker. Of course, stay if you wish."

"Good to meet you, Baker." Maskelyne was half out the door already. "Until the next time."

"Must be a chore keeping him reined in," Peter said as Maskelyne slammed the door shut behind him.

"I often wonder if it's worth the effort," Clarke confessed. "But then he comes up with a smashing idea that reaffirms how useful he can be. The useful outweighs the insufferable."

"With him gone, would you care to explain why we really stayed behind?"

"On to me, are you? I really did want to point out some things to you on the map."

"Things Maskelyne knows nothing about?"

"Precisely." Clarke walked back over to the map. "And you wouldn't, either, but for the PM and Monty," he said testily. "Look here." Clarke circled an area southeast of El Alamein.

"'Alam Halfa Ridge,'" Peter read the map wording aloud.

"This is where, in eight days, Rommel will capitalize on what he believes is Monty's greatest fear, by attacking the poorly defended ridge and gaining a tremendous toehold from which to deal a death blow to the Eighth Army. Then it's on to Cairo."

"Rommel's putting great stock in his information. Do you know where it came from and whether it's reliable?"

"It came from us and it's totally unreliable. But Rommel has no idea."

"The Rebecca code."

"We used it to plant information that Rommel believes is coming from trustworthy sources. In fact, according to a recent message we intercepted, he's put his chief Cairo spy in for an Iron Cross. We, however, have already put that same spy in a jail cell."

"And I imagine that when Rommel attacks the ridge he's going to find more guns and tanks than he thought existed."

"Wait, it gets better. This entire section around the forward part of the ridge is soft sand, hungry to swallow tank treads. Trying to dislodge the tanks will take a heavy toll on Rommel's dwindling petrol supply."

"Surely Rommel knows the terrain."

"It hasn't been well charted. Rommel's relying on an old map taken from the satchel of a British courier killed when his desert vehicle struck a German land mine.

"A phony map."

Clarke smiled.

"You smuggled a car into German territory planted with a fake map and a dead body."

"The body was quite alive when it set out," Clarke said matter-of-factly.

Peter, however, was less sanguine. "Do you mean to say you sent one of your men on a suicide mission?"

"Oh, he wasn't just one of our men, Major. Remember last evening, the British officer I told you about who had dalliances on a houseboat belonging to spies, leaving his briefcase unguarded for them to poke through?"

"You sent him." Peter shook his head. "Did he know?"

Clarke smiled again and glanced at his watch. "I thought a late lunch in Alexandria before we head off and the Germans head in, now that you're completely up-to-date on all our plans. Of course I still haven't the foggiest about what you intend to do with them."

Because Clarke was such a dedicated fisherman Peter felt he deserved at least one catch. "I'll tell you exactly what I intend to do with the plans, Dudley. I intend to give them to the German Military High Command in Berlin."

Then Peter smiled.

———

It was nearly midnight when Peter returned to the houseboat, but Max was in the salon waiting for him with wine, cheese and questions.

"He's not with you, is he?"

"Who, Dudley? No, he went straight off to the nightclubs. The man is unbelievable."

"I don't like him."

"I never would have guessed."

Max handed Peter a glass and poured him some wine. "I got it from Adiba." Peter took a sip and nodded approvingly. "And the cheese is very much like Feta." She spread some on a cracker and popped it into his mouth. "So, should I put a change of clothes in the garden or do you think we're done with early-morning callers?"

"I'm really sorry about that." If Max was still annoyed, even though she understood the situation, wait until she heard what he now had to tell her. "And I'm sorrier about this. You don't know how sorry." No sense putting it off. Peter braced himself. "You have to get back to Berlin."

"What?" Max seemed stunned.

"Believe me, it's not what I want."

"Peter, please, I really won't be in danger. If you're afraid—"

"That's not it. You have to give Himmler something right away. It's important."

"Spending a little time exploring what happened last night, our feelings toward each other, that's important, too. Would a few days really make that much of a difference?"

"Yes." That was hard enough to say, but what came next was even more difficult. "Max, we both understood that what we have to do could strain a relationship that's still developing."

"Are you saying we made a mistake?"

"Not at all. I'm only saying we have to learn to accept that. We'll have our time, I promise, just not now. Any delay could throw off the entire mission."

"You're right, of course."

While Peter had certainly seen Max angry, he had never seen her cry. He wiped the moisture from her cheek and embraced her. "I know."

"At least tell me what's so urgent?" Max pulled away from him, sniffling.

"What Himmler wanted: a predictive horoscope for the upcoming battle."

"Are the British planning an attack?"

No secrets. Peter was the one who insisted on that. "No, Rommel is."

"Rommel? How do you know?"

"Rommel told me, just like he told me that, unless something major happens, the attack will start in just five days, on August 31."

"Are you crazy? You've never even met Rommel." Max paused. "Have you?"

"No, never. Here, come sit with me." Peter took Max's hand and led her to the couch. "Actually Rommel told Montgomery who told Clarke who told me."

"You *are* crazy! There's no way Montgomery could know what—" Suddenly the confusion vanished from Max's face and her eyes widened. "They broke Rommel's code!"

"Not just Rommel's code, but the machine used to encrypt and decrypt all the codes."

Max gasped. "Enigma?"

Peter figured Max would know about the Germans' top-secret device. By all rights, she shouldn't, but then this was Max. "Enigma."

"Impossible." Max was still reeling. "Enigma is unbreakable."

"And you believe that?"

"Not just me. Everyone who knows about it, from Hitler on down."

"Take it from me, Max—there's nothing closed that can't be opened. It was just a matter of time. Enigma was broken nearly two years ago."

Max astonishment escalated. "Are you serious?"

"Very. The machine's design was—and is—brilliant. But 'brilliant' doesn't mean 'unbreakable.' And once the basic structure was known, it was relatively easy to adjust to any changes that were made."

"Montgomery told you about this?"

That's what Peter was afraid of. Max was much too thorough to leave things at face value. "No," he said, knowing that she wouldn't let it rest there. "Montgomery told me about the specific code Rommel was using with Enigma."

"Then when? Did you know about this when you came to Berlin?"

Total truth time had arrived. "I found out about it in England, on my way to Berlin."

"And you didn't tell me?"

"We didn't tell each other a lot of things then. Now isn't then."

"Nearly two years." Peter watched Max's hair swing from side to side as she shook her head in disbelief. He still had difficulty getting used to her being a brunette. When the shaking stopped, she started to laugh. "Two years. I would love to see Hitler's face when he finds Germans' unbreakable coding machine is providing Churchill and Roosevelt with bedtime reading."

"Yes, but he can never find out. No one can know what I told you. Not Father Fritz, not Otto, no one. And no one can suspect that you know. It's much too dangerous."

"I can handle myself, as you've found out. But your concern is nice." Max leaned over, put her right hand behind Peter's head and drew him close enough to give him a long and passionate kiss, then followed it with a question. "This horoscope. What does it say?"

"I'll show you." Peter got up and retrieved a document from his jacket hanging on a rack. He sat down next to Max again and unfolded it. "I roughed out a sketch in the car on the way back here. I'll do a finished chart later."

"I have no idea what it means." Max returned the paper.

"That's exactly what you're to tell Himmler when you give it to him. You're simply a courier. Make sure he understands that."

"He's going to wonder why I have the chart. Why can't we return together and you give it to him?"

"I'm not finished here. If he asks, tell him anything. Tell him I was in Greece with you and fell ill and was unable to travel. But I insisted he have the chart. You'll come up with something."

"And what will Himmler see in this all-important chart?"

"Little, if anything. He can't handle a detailed chart, so he'll have his Ahnenerbe astrologers read it. They'll report that, according to the chart, Rommel shouldn't open a new North African offensive during the next few weeks."

"A new offensive? Even if one's being planned, I doubt Himmler knows about it. Hitler rarely includes him in the High Command's daily military briefings."

"It doesn't matter. Himmler wouldn't mention the chart. If it's wrong, he would be a laughingstock. If it's not, he'd want credit for his fine military reasoning, not for relying on the esoteric. No, he'll keep the chart to himself and wait to see what happens."

"If your information is correct, Himmler will have his proof."

"Exactly. So how soon can you get out of Cairo?"

"Possibly later today. Have you ever heard of an Egyptian businessman named Talaat Pasha Harb?"

"No."

"He founded the country's largest bank and scores of companies, including a commercial airline and a major movie studio. I've never met him, but Adiba knows him well. She told me one of my very close friends is directing a film for Talaat Pasha Harb and has a plane available for location work. So the pieces are in place for me to get into Istanbul. Then I'll ask Father Fritz's friend to get me to Greece and my location plane."

As Max was talking Peter was calculating distances in his head. "That's roughly twenty-one hundred miles of travel."

"So? It won't be the first time I'm tired. The important thing is it can be done."

Now Peter calculated average air speeds, built-in delays, weather and unknowns. "Yes, it can. I'll have Clarke prepare the necessary papers. He'll grumble, especially when I don't tell him who they're for, but he'll come through."

"When will you be returning?"

"As soon as possible. A few more days at the most."

"Well, when you do, you'll need these." Max got up, fetched some paper and a pencil and jotted a few things down, which she gave to Peter. "I assume you'll be able to get to Istanbul. If I use my director friend now, I don't want him to make another trip there so soon. People might grow suspicious."

"I'll find a way to get to Istanbul."

"Once there, call that phone number. Father Fritz's friend expected to get us to Greece together. I'll tell him about the change in plans. When you get to Athens, go to that address. Otto will be waiting. Don't lose that." No sooner had she said it than Max smiled. "Never mind—I forgot that you never do."

"Just to be sure . . ." Peter ripped up the paper. "Now I won't lose it. Don't worry—when it comes to getting back to you, I'm a homing pigeon."

"I'm not worried." Max reached over and embraced Peter again. "I'm frightened. Not for me—for you. Staying here and leaving here is still dangerous. And what happens if the chart is wrong? Himmler won't blame the courier."

"Hey, I can handle myself, as you've found out," Peter said, throwing Max's words back at her. "Besides, it has to be done and we have to do it. We both made that choice."

"Yes, we did. For different reasons."

"But I've changed mine."

"And what's your reason now?" Max asked.

"My reason is to end this goddamn war as quickly as possible, single-handedly if necessary, so I can see if our experiment will work or not, free from any distractions."

"I like your reason." Max started to unbutton Peter's shirt. "I like it a lot."

"What happened to your concerns about Himmler?" Peter put his hand on hers before she could get to the next button.

Refusing to be thwarted, Max pulled her hand from under his and undid the next button, then the one after that. "Screw Himmler."

Peter heard the words, but as Max undid the final button, then started on his belt, he got the distinct impression that Himmler wasn't quite who she had in mind.

25

Berlin: August 25, 1942
Your Stars Today: With the Sun squaring Uranus conditions are ripe for disruptions and disputes to flourish and for authorities to struggle. You feel the need to take action but have no idea what that action should be.

Citizens of Berlin, this is Kobo, the voice of Germany. I am broadcasting to you not from England, not from one of the allied or neutral nations, but from within your own city, right under the noses of Hitler and the others who are destroying our great nation.

I am calling on all those who love Germany to take action. Together we can liberate our country. Together we can pry open the iron grip of tyranny that is strangling the life from our Fatherland.

Over the next week you will witness how ordinary actions by ordinary people can break oppression's yoke. And you will witness how the powerful masters of the Reich will be rendered helpless, unable to do anything.

My enemies, your enemies, Germany's enemies, will not be able to silence me, though they will try. Join with me and together we will prevail against the evil that has blanketed our nation.

Remember who Germany really is. Not Hitler nor any of his henchmen. You are Germany. We are Germany.

Joseph Goebbels switched off the wire recorder with such force that the lever went flying. Even Himmler was taken aback, not by the propaganda minister's anger, which he had often witnessed, but by its physical expression. This was not going to be a cordial discussion, and maybe that was better. Since he and Goebbels hated each other, pretense made little sense.

"You heard that?"

"Of course I heard that. I have my own recordings of Kobo's first broadcast and every other one since."

"But what you and your fucking elite Gestapo boys don't have is Kobo!"

Best to let him rage, Himmler thought. He was going to anyway. Let him wear himself out.

"Kobo! Do you realize what problems this prick is causing?"

Dragging his clubbed left foot, Goebbels did an ersatz stomp from his desk to the chair where Himmler was sitting, then back. "This Kobo, the voice of Germany." Goebbels mocked the words with disdain.

Himmler couldn't resist baiting him. "I thought you were supposed to be the Voice of Germany."

"You joke, but with little reason. Kobo made good on his promise of disruptions despite your vaunted security forces. And he continues to do so!"

Himmler shot up from his chair. Bad enough he agreed to come to the propaganda ministry this morning, but now to suffer a barrage of insults? "My security forces have kept things well in check, not just in Berlin, but throughout Germany and all the countries under the Reich's control."

"Poor Heinrich, you really believe that, don't you?" Goebbels sat. "I'll grant you some of the success, but only some. Fear controls people. Pure fear. Your men are very good at reinforcing fear, but they didn't create it. *I* created it! The Gestapo, the SS—you may have formed them, but I made them into forces of fear. Their reach, their methods, their exploits—all embellished and disseminated by me. Fear! Fear keeps people from becoming saboteurs. The fear *I* created. But do you know what happens when someone acts because he's no longer afraid of the consequences? People take notice. And if he gets away with his actions, people become more emboldened. Some start to emulate him. Soon it doesn't matter whether you destroy him. He's no longer needed. Freedom from fear has spread too far and too deep. And when it reaches that point, nothing you or I do can change it."

"Even if I accepted what you say completely, and I do not, we're nowhere near that point."

"That shows the strength of our shield. But unless we stop this Kobo—"

"You think I haven't been concerned with this." Now Himmler did the stomping, to and past Goebbels' desk, right up to his ferret-like face. "You think I don't find it puzzling that the man who controls the airways, the man who has the best radio equipment and engineers available to him, can't find a simple medium-power transmitter?"

Up again so fast the top of his head almost struck what little there was of Himmler's receding chin, Goebbels tried to bellow, but his high-pitched voice made it a shriek. "That is not our job! That is your job! If you would like me to ask Hitler to let me do your job because you cannot, then say so!"

Veins bulging from the midpoint of his high forehead clear back to the back of his rapidly balding scalp, Himmler responded in kind. "I advise you not to make Hitler choose between the two of us, Joseph! You will not like the outcome."

It wasn't a truce, just a pause allowing each of them to take a deep breath.

But it was as close to a truce as they were going to get, and since Goebbels initiated it Himmler went along, withdrawing to his chair.

"Heinrich, this is not helping either of us," Goebbels said, breaking the silence. "It is unbecoming and unproductive. And I'm to blame for my inflammatory start."

Turning on his charming self, Himmler thought as Goebbels settled back into his own chair. And the bastard can do that—out-charm the best of them when he wants to. That was one of the only traits Himmler admired in Goebbels, wishing that he, too, could play up to people and have it come across as genuine instead of forced. Bastard! "I did my part as well, Joseph. We both share a passionate commitment to the *Führer* and the Reich, but I daresay we've had so many other matters to deal with that this Kobo concern may have slipped to the bottom of the pile. So let's restack that pile and place Kobo on the top."

"Then we are in total agreement. Kobo has taken enough advantage of our distractions. Today we have signed his death warrant." Goebbels punched a button on small desk console.

"Ja, Herr Reichsminister."

"Please have the folders brought in."

"Immediately, *Herr Reichsminister.*"

Within seconds there was a knock, then the door to the office opened and a man took a few tentative steps inside, handed Goebbels two folders, and left.

"I took the liberty of compiling for you." Goebbels tossed Himmler one of the folders. "Just so we would have the same materials in front of us when we talked. It's our files on Kobo, no doubt very similar to your own."

Himmler thumbed quickly through the many pages. "Basically, yes, it seems so."

"I will, of course, give you our latest thinking, but I'm curious what your analysts have concluded about Kobo."

Of course he's curious. Goebbels's people have come up with nothing, despite all their so-called thinking. Himmler had enough dealings with him to know that. He also knew that Goebbels's feelings about him didn't necessarily extend to his staff, and it was their opinion Goebbels was after.

"Our view hasn't changed," Himmler said. "Indeed, every new incident is just further confirmation. This is one person working alone to—"

"You still hold to that?"

Snapping at Goebbels for interrupting him would do no good. "Yes. Were others involved, we would have caught them by now. The secret could not have been kept from us this long."

"Even by youth groups? Their members can be extremely closemouthed."

"And also extremely careless. We have informers in every major youth group throughout Germany—the Edelweiss Pirates, the Swing Youth, the Leipzig Meuten—along with others you don't even know exist. The Hitler Youth have been particularly useful in this regard."

"You still give them too much leeway," Goebbels said.

"Some, but never too much. Remember, we have taken harsh action against those who stray too far. Need I remind you of the hangings? Your public justifications for why fifteen- and sixteen-year-olds were being executed were especially convincing."

"And will be again, whenever and as often as is necessary."

"But that will not be necessary with Kobo."

Goebbels nodded his head. "I'm sure you can anticipate my other question."

Of course Himmler could, in part because he shared Goebbels's concern. "Communists. Obviously I never completely rule them out. You were at the briefing. Within the next week or two, we will have broken the back of a major communist presence, a highly organized group that is sending secrets back to Stalin. But that is espionage, not sabotage, and many of those involved in this conspiracy against the Reich aren't even German. True, our home-grown communists were often saboteurs and provocateurs, but they have been rooted out and destroyed. No, if Kobo is a communist, he's a communist without credentials, acting on his own."

"Still, he must have help in transmitting his messages."

"Why? Surely you know better than I that not very much is needed if the intent is just unadorned information."

Goebbels had a way of crinkling up his face when he heard something that he didn't like, almost as if he had just gotten a whiff of an especially vile fart. It always amused Himmler when this happened; when he was the cause, it delighted him.

"Possible, yes, but also highly difficult."

"Come, Goebbels, I think we would both concede that this is an extremely intelligent and resourceful person. He's able to make much out of little. Look at how he disrupted the morning train traffic. Nothing fancy—or conspicuous—like explosives. Simply some salt and a weather forecast. Choose a morning when rain is predicted. Pour the salt on and around an important switch point while it's still dark, before the rain—and the first train—arrives. As soon as the salt is soaked, the signal shorts out and people spend hours waiting to get to work. Critical factory production goes down and Kobo's reputation goes up."

"And after each incident, there is more graffiti calling for the overthrow of the Reich, more pamphlets left around detailing the government's abuses."

"Pull out your files on the Wilhelm Strauss Gang, which was much more dangerous. Have you forgotten the museum bombing and everything that preceded it? Pull out the files and look at the picture of the dead Jew on the ground who was Strauss."

"And my picture of Kobo?"

Himmler rose and tossed his copy of the Kobo file on Goebbels's desk. "Save some room. You'll have one to put in there very soon."

"He might be more useful alive. I haven't decided yet."

"A decision that's not yours to make. However, if possible we will confer. At the very least, I will have his apprehension well documented so it can be used any way you see fit."

"Shall I count on that?"

It was the way Goebbels raised his eyes, like questioning a subordinate—or giving him a masked order. Either way, Himmler had had enough for one session. The next time they met, it would be on his turf, where he would have the pleasure of shoving Kobo up Goebbels's tight ass. For the moment, the hint of a grin would be sufficient. *"Reichsminister."*

"Reichsführer." Goebbels was forced by protocol to respond in kind, using Himmler's higher rank. Himmler could envision him trying hard not to gag while saying it. Goebbels may have had the last word, but Himmler had the victory.

Ever since its premiere in mid-June, it was *the* movie in Berlin, the kind Max told Goebbels she'd like to make as part of her ploy to ensure he "forced" the SS saga on her. The lines at the ticket office never grew any smaller, in part because of the people who came back to see it again and again.

Die Grosse Liebe (The Great Love)—an upbeat, feel-good musical about a popular singer and a wounded Luftwaffe officer who fall in love, starred Zarah Leander, the beautiful Swede who had become Germany's favorite actress and Goebbels's favorite mistress. Just as Goebbels had planned, hearing her sing *"Davon geht die Welt nicht Unter"* It Isn't the End of the World" and *"Ich weiss, es wird einmal ein Wunder Gescheh'n"* I Know One Day a Miracle Will Happen"—reignited some of the public's cooling hope, and kept it going for at least ninety minutes.

But this night most of the audience had stormed out of the theater before either song was sung. It wasn't a protest. It was itching powder from bags inconspicuously planted at various spots in the ceiling. The bags had been rigged with harmless time charges that did little more than rip them apart.

And scatter the powder all over the moviegoers, irritating and inflaming their skin on contact.

Goebbels made sure nothing appeared in the newspapers, but accounts of the "attack" spread from person to person.

Kobo—the itch that neither Goebbels nor Himmler could scratch—had struck again.

26

Istanbul: August 29, 1942
Your Stars Today: This is a time for you to show cool headed diplomacy. Mars in conjunction with Neptune enhances your sense of timing and leads to decisive, dramatic action, often accompanied by the theatrical, which cloaks your true intentions.

Much to Peter's relief, getting out of Egypt was much easier than getting into Egypt. Months earlier Dudley Clark had traveled to Turkey, where he established the channels for extending the flow of disinformation beyond Egypt and North Africa. Little did Clarke realize his efforts would also play a part in the greatest deception ever attempted.

So when Peter said he had to get to Istanbul, Clarke, who by now knew better than to ask why, arranged for the necessary air and train connections and for the appropriate papers to forestall any difficulties crossing between countries. The result was a smooth four-day journey that left Peter at Istanbul's huge Haydarpasa Terminal, its five stories teeming with morning traffic. After placing a deliberately cryptic phone call, Peter made his way to a modest white brick residence at 82 Ölçek Street, the Papal shield above its arched double doors the only indication that it housed the Vatican's Apostolic Delegation to Turkey and Greece and its head, Archbishop Angelo Roncalli. There he was courteously received by Msgr. Vittorio Ugo Righi, Roncalli's secretary, who had been waiting for him.

"You found us without any difficulty?" Righi's English lilted with Milanese.

"Your directions were excellent," Peter said. "And I've brought the communion wafers you ordered."

Righi laughed. "As you said you would when you called. Supposedly the Istanbul police stopped monitoring our phones after Archbishop Roncalli charmed the governor over a few bottles of raki. One of his first official acts. Still, you never know. Istanbul is an unusual city—British, Germans, Italians, most of them spies, each watching the other, and the Turkish officials watching them all. Best to assume that everyone—including the Vatican—is suspect and act with caution. Just as you are at the moment."

"I'm sorry."

"You've been staring at me since we met, I think because of these." Righi brushed his hands over his Western business attire. "You were expecting a cassock and perhaps are wondering if I'm really a priest. Am I right?"

"I didn't realize I was so obvious."

"Priests are trained to be good watchers as well as listeners. You won't see any cassocks in Turkey, or habits or any Muslim religious dress, either, even though it's the dominant religion. The government has banned the wearing of religious clothing, part of an effort to rid the country of clerical-ism. But when you consider that the Mexican government has ordered the killing of priests, this isn't so bad."

Being in a country that put religion in its proper place made Peter more comfortable. "Thank you. That clears it up."

"Then if you're ready, he's expecting you. Follow me, please."

Roncalli's study was just off the reception room. Righi knocked on the door, which prompted a hearty, *"È aperto. Entrato per favore."*

"The Archbishop speaks several languages, but English isn't one of them," Righi said. "I'll be glad to translate."

"Thank you, but it won't be necessary. I speak Italian." Peter preferred that Righi not know why he had come, if Roncalli hadn't already told him.

"Good. That will make the Archbishop very happy." Righi pushed the door open. A figure in his early sixties, nearly as round as he was tall, was already standing in anticipation, his chubby hands on his goodly belly and a benevolent smile on his moon-shaped face. Despite the thin layer of un-tonsured white hair and a suit that was a decade behind the times, he re-minded Peter of a jovial medieval friar.

"You are Peter Baker?"

"I am, Your Excellency."

As Righi predicted, a smile stretched across Roncalli's plump face when he heard Peter answer in Italian. He whispered something in Righi's ear. Righi nodded, whispered a response and left the room.

"Please, sit." Roncalli patted a chair in front of his Spartan-neat desk, its only accoutrements a Philco radio on one end and a telephone on the other. With a little difficulty Roncalli wedged himself in his desk chair. "I think that they make these desk chairs for demi-bishops, not archbishops. Will you have some tea?"

"Thank you, but I'm fine."

"Let me commend you on your very impressive Italian. Do I detect a bit of Napolitano in it?"

"Yes, Your Excellency." Roncalli had a good ear. While perfectly capable of speaking standard Italian, Peter often fell into the dialect of the strolling singers he had encountered in small music halls during his teen travels.

"And do you speak German equally well with my dear friend Father Fritz?"

"I try, Excellency."

"Does he call you Mr. Baker?"

"He calls me Peter, Excellency."

"Then I will exercise my apostolic authority and demand that Father Fritz and I be treated equally. I will call you Peter and you will call me Father Angelo." Roncalli patted his stomach. "Besides, do I look like an Excellency to you?"

Before Peter could craft a response, Roncalli absolved him.

"They try to make me diet. Coffee and fruit in the morning. Coffee and soup in the evening. But in midday I insist on eating like a real person. Three courses and wine. They tell me inside this body is a thin man, but I think inside this body there is still a fat man. No matter, fat or thin, as long as he is a Christian man."

Garrulous and slightly self-deprecating, yet with a confidence that came from his solid beliefs: Peter could see how Roncalli had charmed the Governor of Istanbul and, undoubtedly, many others.

"But you haven't come for a lesson in nutrition," Roncalli continued. "You have come because of a request Father Fritz made through Monsignor Montini. For some unknown reason you need to get to Greece right away."

Here we go again. Peter anticipated another Clarke situation, where he would be pumped for an explanation.

"I assume it involves a diplomatic or political matter. Many in Rome believe I have no head for such things, that I am too naïve. Montini knows differently, just as he knows I leave such dealings to him and the others in the Curia and content myself with my mission here. Christ came to minister to the people. I imagine some thought him naïve as well. Anyway, Montini doesn't bother me with the whys. If it becomes necessary, he will tell me. In the meantime, I will get you to Greece."

With a potential problem resolved Peter asked, "When might that be possible?"

"Late this afternoon, if everything goes well. You see, there is one other matter."

One other matter? No one told Peter about one other matter.

"Again through Montini, Father Fritz asked that you speak with Demir Medov, my other guest."

Demir Medov. Peter processed the name. Medov's Russian and Demir's Turkish. "He's a Soviet Turk?"

Roncalli was taken aback. "Yes, a Tartar. Very astute. Officially, he is the Soviet press attaché here in Istanbul. In reality he is a lieutenant colonel in Soviet military intelligence who recruits agents throughout occupied Europe and runs several important Soviet spy networks."

"And this Demir Medov is a friend of yours?" Peter's disbelief was evident.

"I met him a few days ago when he came to see me."

"So this top Soviet operative just came by for a chat."

"No, he came by to defect."

Even for a con man used to sudden twists, this one was pretty good. Still, Peter concealed his surprise and focused on putting together some pieces. Father Fritz must think Demir Medov had information that could help the mission. But how did Father Fritz know about Medov? OK, that was easy: Roncalli told Montini who told Father Fritz. But did Medov really defect and, if so, why to a Catholic archbishop? Or was this a Russian ruse to gain access to a Vatican network, using a cleric with little interest in politics? By Roncalli's own admission, many considered him naïve. Father Fritz, however, was anything but naïve and, from what Max said, neither was Montini. Medov had much to explain and Peter would have to separate the truth from the lies. "And where is this Medov?"

"I asked Monsignor Righi to bring him to the parlor. Shall we join him there? Perhaps I can convince you to have some of that tea. It comes from the Rize Province of Turkey, on the Black Sea, and is really quite refreshing. Besides, it will give me an excuse to have a few biscuits." Roncalli gave Peter a sly wink. "One must make sacrifices to be polite with company."

Roncalli rose and led Peter from the office down a hallway to the parlor. There, seated at a small round table—Roncalli's promised tea and treats at its center—was a short, solidly built man in his early forties, his clean-shaven face strong featured, his black hair slicked back from a high forehead. Like Roncalli he wore a suit, which, while more modern, was still Soviet sturdy rather than stylish.

"Sit," Roncalli said before Demir Medov had a chance to rise. "I'm afraid my Russian is almost as nonexistent as my English. Fortunately, we all speak Italian, so if no one objects, we will use that. Demir, this is Peter Baker, the man I told you about." He put his arm around Peter and steered him to a chair next to Medov. "And that leaves one chair for me." Roncalli settled in and pulled a tea glass toward him. "Are you sure, Peter?"

"One must make sacrifices to be polite with company," Peter said, noticing that Medov already had a glass. "Please."

"Very good." Roncalli chuckled as he poured some tea and passed it to Peter. "Every priest loves to hear his words repeated and acted upon. Now I have explained to Demir that you have questions, some of which may be very detailed, and he has agreed to answer them honestly. Is that correct?"

"To the best I can." Medov's Italian was awkward but still comprehensible.

"Peter, I have also explained that while you are not a member of the British military, you work very closely with them. Is that correct?"

"Yes." Because they had been so rare over the years, Peter relished those instances where he could answer succinctly and without lying.

"And because of that, Peter, you will arrange for Demir to receive political asylum and protection from the British once you have finished speaking with him."

Son of a bitch! *Archbishop* son of a bitch! No head for politics, my ass! Peter conveyed his thoughts through his eyes and, from Roncalli's slight impish grin, he knew they had been understood.

"Correct." Peter gave the only acceptable answer.

"Now for the last matter. Demir has asked that I remain in the room while he talks with you. Does that pose a problem, Peter?"

"Not at all."

"Good. In that case . . ." Roncalli reached over to snatch a few biscuits and placed one on Peter's plate, the rest on his own. "Shall we begin?"

"Indeed, and I'd like to begin by asking Demir—may I call you Demir?"

"Please."

"By asking Demir why such a high-ranking and trusted Soviet operative is defecting."

"You are quite right." Medov responded without hesitation as if he'd been anticipating the question. I have served the Soviet Union faithfully in many capacities since late boyhood, gradually rising in rank and responsibility. Being sent to Istanbul to coordinate espionage efforts showed how much my abilities were respected. I wanted my wife, Nina, to join me here but was told that the war made it impossible. Too much red tape. So we wrote constantly, although her responses to my letters became less frequent. Then, in one of those responses—the last one, as it turned out—Nina said she had been moved from our Moscow dwelling to a remote place in the Ural Mountains, supposedly for her safety. She also wrote about her parents. We had a code. If at any time she mentioned her parents it meant she no longer wanted to join me: she *needed* to join me, needed to get out of the Soviet Union."

Medov grew quiet. There were no tears, but lines of hurt formed on his face along the path tears might have trickled down. Then he resumed. "A few weeks later I was summoned to the ambassador's office here." Medov pulled a piece of paper from his suit jacket pocket. "The ambassador was glum faced as he handed me this. It is in Russian, so I will translate."

Peter shook his head "no" and took the paper, a decoded cable that read: *Your wife died suddenly. Hope you will work even harder for the Motherland. Director.*

"You know about this, I assume," Peter said to Roncalli.

"Yes."

"Why didn't they send this directly to you?" Peter handed the cable back to Medov, who tossed it on the table.

"That is the same question I asked later, when some of the grief had lessened. The ambassador said he did not know, any more than he knew any further details of Nina's death. But I knew. I knew my poor Nina didn't die suddenly. They murdered her. Murdered her because she was Jewish. Part of Stalin's ongoing purges."

Either Medov was telling the truth or he was a good enough actor to evoke emotions in his audience. Until Peter found out which, he would tread softly, yet firmly, on what might be sensitive ground. "I'm sorry for your loss, so please forgive me, but are you certain she was killed?"

"The word is 'murdered' and, yes, I am certain. If you spend as many years in the Soviet intelligence apparatus as I have, you learn how to read what isn't printed. . . ." Medov picked up the cable, shook it and threw it back down. "To hear what isn't said."

"So that was why you defected?"

"Nina was my last personal tie to the Soviet Union. We had no children and all of my family was killed during the Revolution. Her being gone was—how do the logicians say it?—it was a necessary factor but not yet a sufficient one."

Another piece was forthcoming and Peter hoped that this one would give him what he needed. He said nothing, letting Medov resume when he was ready.

"Soon thereafter, I was ordered back to Moscow. For my safety, they said, the same words they used for Nina. The truth is, I had been set up to take the blame for a botched assassination attempt."

"Whose assassination?" Peter asked.

When Medov hesitated, Roncalli stepped into the silence. "Franz von Papen, Germany's ambassador to Turkey."

Franz von Papen, Hitler's predecessor as Chancellor. The man who brought him into the government hoping to control him and who later briefly served as his Vice Chancellor. Max had only referred to von Papen by position—Roncalli's ambassador friend with a plane—not by name, so Peter didn't realize he was stationed in Istanbul. Why was he put there? Von Papen was a skilled diplomat, who, as ambassador to Austria, eased the way for Germany to annex it. What was he expected to accomplish in Turkey? Rather than wonder, Peter asked, and, again, it was Roncalli who answered.

"Von Papen has only one task: keep Turkey out of Soviet hands, preferably by forging an alliance with Germany. Failing that, he is to make sure Turkey remains neutral. So there is good reason for the Soviets to want him killed, but without it being linked to them. That would only inflame Turkey's historical animosity toward Russia and could push it into allying with Germany." Roncalli placed his hand on Medov's forearm. "Go ahead," he said, and Medov picked up the account.

"The assassination was planned to make it appear that Germany actually eliminated its own ambassador and was falsely blaming the Russians to prevent an alliance with Turkey. I was to make that story believable and circulate it. Moscow put its most accomplished and ruthless butcher, Leonid Naumov, in charge of the mission. It was Naumov who assassinated Trotsky, so who better? Only this time Naumov chose an idiot to do the dirty work—a Yugoslav student who had been a member of the Communist Party there. His assignment was to wait until von Papen was walking to work, then shoot him and explode a bomb to cover his exit. This so-called student was too dumb to understand that, for him, there would be no exit. Not that it mattered. Somehow he got confused and set off the bomb, which he was holding, too early."

Roncalli broke in. "Von Papen suffered a broken eardrum and a large cleaning bill for removal of the blood and body fragments that covered his clothes. It was major news here for weeks. Rooting out all the intricacies became a matter of national pride for the Turkish officials. Finally they discovered enough to lay the blame on the Soviets."

"And while they were investigating, I was still being urged to spread the rumor that the Germans themselves were the perpetrators," Medov said. "There is more, but this is the heart of it. Needless to say, Naumov and the Soviet hierarchy needed a way to cover their own incompetence. So they claimed that von Papen had been warned of the plot. Not only von Papen, but the Turkish authorities and others."

"Warned by you," Peter said.

"That is why I was ordered back to Moscow. But I would never arrive there alive. Once over the border, bang! Justice, Stalin-style."

So far, Medov was showing no sign that he was trying to hide something. But Peter still wasn't satisfied. "Even if I accept everything you've said, why did you come here instead of going directly to a consulate to seek asylum?"

"I tried the British, but they told me they could do nothing. I think they were afraid of angering Moscow. The Turkish authorities? This is Istanbul, where one doesn't know whom to trust so no one trusts anyone. Certainly not anyone in government."

Medov looked at Roncalli, who took the cue. "If I might. Here in Turkey I am responsible for and minister to thirty-five thousand Catholics. As of a few days ago that number became thirty-five thousand and one."

"So you're Catholic," Peter said matter-of-factly. He had considered that possibility, but the odds were against it.

"My mother was Catholic. My father was Russian Orthodox by birth, atheist by belief. I, too, am an atheist. Still my mother's early teachings claimed a place in my heart if not my intellect. There was a practical reason as well. When I was preparing for my assignment here, I learned something about the Archbishop's efforts in Bulgaria."

"Before coming to Turkey, I was the papal representative there for nearly ten years," Roncalli said, filling in the gap for Peter. "The Vatican didn't know what to do with me, so it sent me there to get me out of its hair."

"I discovered that the Archbishop was a man concerned not with politics but with the welfare of others, a man who took considerable risks to assist those in need, and not just Catholics," Medov said. "In this nest of vipers that is Istanbul, I felt this was a man, if any, I could trust. I was right. He welcomed me, despite any possible dangers."

"And those dangers could be considerable," Peter noted.

"I am, as you have observed, a big boy," Roncalli said.

Denials aside, Peter again saw that Roncalli was much more astute politically than he let on. He was also impossible not to like—even if he was a priest. "The Russians don't know where you are?" Peter pressed Medov.

"I took extreme care coming here. I gave my people no reason to suspect that I wouldn't return to Moscow and only asked for a few days to set my affairs here in order. However, those few days have now passed and I am sure they have begun to search for me. Because their spies in foreign embassies have not reported a defection, they are almost certainly looking beyond Istanbul or even beyond Turkey. Eventually, though, they will figure matters out."

"And by that time you will be under British protection, isn't that right, Peter?" Roncalli said. Instead of waiting for a response, he reminded Peter of his pending "afternoon appointment" and suggested he might want to focus on some "other areas." Peter followed his advice.

"Demir, about Russia's use of intelligence in formulating its military strategy—"

"I thought you were not in the military," Medov said.

"But I work with the British military, as the Archbishop has explained."

"Then you should ask the British. They spy on us as much as we spy on them, so I am sure they can answer that question."

Nice answer. Peter gave Roncalli a "why don't we just leave now?" look.

"Demir, you are expecting something very important from Peter," Roncalli said. "Perhaps you might consider being a bit more helpful in return."

Medov drew his lips tightly together, then slowly opened them, adding drama to his ensuing words. "Please forgive me, but I have led most of my life making sure that I never divulged what you are asking. Even with my allegiance no longer to Moscow, it is not easy."

"I understand, but we're on the same side right now, fighting the same enemy," Peter said.

"Never believe that!" Medov finally showed some passion. "Never! Stalin is thinking far ahead. He never lets us forget that the real enemy of the Soviet Union is the United States, the epitome of capitalist evil. It is the United States that Moscow must eventually bring to its knees. The United States and its capitalist allies like Britain. Whatever I might say could one day be used against Russia."

Peter wasn't pleased with Medov's stall. "To protect a country you say you want to be your new home."

"I want freedom."

"Then you have to decide where you can find it."

"I have already decided. That's why I am here."

"And you know why I'm here," Peter said.

Medov's lips tightened again, but this time the corners of his mouth rose slightly in what was either a smile or a smirk. "Tell me, Peter Baker, do you like the theater?"

"Demir . . ." Roncalli seemed ready to admonish him again, but Peter had a hunch that this seemingly extraneous remark might lead somewhere.

"It's all right. Yes, I do. Very much."

"I don't, or didn't, probably because when I was young I had little opportunity to experience it. My ignorance was shared by many in military intelligence. But I forced myself to become acquainted with theater. We all did, to curry favor with Stalin and to survive."

"I wasn't aware that Stalin was that big a fan of the theater," Peter said.

"He learned a great deal from the theater and from Stanislavsky in particular. Of course you know of Stanislavsky."

"Of course." For once Peter's British understatement wasn't feigned.

"Everybody praises Stanislavsky for his theories, which he employed so brilliantly, especially when directing Chekhov. But the best examples of his theories were not on the stage. They were in the courtrooms of Moscow during the 1930s, when the Old Bolsheviks were put on trial. Stanislavsky and his protégés taught Stalin's henchmen how to run those trials. They even coached the defendants into believing they actually were guilty of the false charges brought against them. For that the defendants received not applause but a bullet in the back of the head."

Stanislavsky trained actors to believe they really were the characters they portrayed, so Peter understood how the Master's same methods could be effectively used as Medov described. But Peter didn't understand why Stanislavsky would let them—and himself—be used that way. "Fascinating, but what has this to do with military strategy?"

"It has to do with why *maskirovka* is one of the core principles of Soviet military strategy."

"Camouflage?" Peter knew the meaning of *maskirovka*, but, from what Medov said, there seemed to be more to it. "Camouflage is a key part of every nation's military strategy."

"Beyond camouflage. For the Soviets, *maskirovka* has become a highly developed system of tactical deception, combining concealment, imitation, misleading maneuvers and disinformation. Yes, the military of every nation builds these elements into their strategies, to varying degrees, but for the Soviets they have become an art form. We are trained to believe our own deceptions, so that our enemies believe it, just as an actor believes so fully in the reality of his role that the audience believes it."

"And Stanislavsky personally approved this?" Peter asked.

"He was old, ill and destitute. Some of his family had been interned or killed, victims of the purges. Stalin provided for him, gave him a house, paid his expenses, showed leniency to his remaining family members. He also kept the Moscow Art Theater alive and made Stanislavsky's teachings the official Soviet standard for theater."

Stanislavsky was one of the few people Peter had ever looked up to. To see his work, which emphasized truth and authenticity, so corrupted was painful. True, Peter used Stanislavsky's methods to pull off scams, but his victims only lost money, not lives. Peter could live with that distinction, for now. "Let's go back to *maskirovka,* which doesn't seem to be working against the Germans at Stalingrad."

"I told you that *maskirovka* was very complex. Look at the calendar. Winter will soon arrive. In terms of the theater, the stage has yet to be set."

"And for Stanislavsky the stage setting can stimulate the emotions, both the actor's and, by extension, the audience's," Peter said.

Medov was startled. "You have more than heard of Stanislavsky, it seems."

"So when the stage is set, how will *maskirovka* be used against the Germans at Stalingrad?"

"You expect me to know? It's enough that I had access to this much. I am not one of Skrobat's inner circle. They're the only ones—"

"Who?"

"Of course. You would know nothing of Skrobat. He is a closely guarded secret."

"That's his name—Skrobat?" Thoughts began racing haphazardly through Peter's mind, trying to form a pattern.

"I assume it is his nom de guerre, adopted during the Revolution. It was a common practice. Afterwards, some kept the names. Vladimir Ilyich Ulyanov continued to use 'Lenin,' from the river Lena, where the Tsar's troops massacred striking gold miners. It was the last of his more than a hundred pseudonyms. And, of course, Iosf Vissarionovich Dzhugashvili is Stalin—the Man of Steel—a name he took for obvious reasons."

"And Skrobat?" Peter's thinking had automatically switched from English to Russian, seeking anything that might hold a clue.

"I have no idea. It is not a real word in Russian, but it must have meaning for Skrobat. To me it is just nonsense."

Nonsense. That triggered something else and Peter's mind kicked into overdrive, furiously playing with letters, moving them around with lightning speed and making conversation difficult.

"And you have no clue about this man's background, nothing?" The motion in Peter's head had slowed, but now he felt pressure building.

"Please, I have told you everything. Can we now stop talking about Skrobat?"

"I'm sorry. . . ." The pressure was getting worse, causing Peter to become distracted.

"Peter, are you all right?" Roncalli asked.

"I'm fine; it's only—" Then Peter's brain burst, so violently that he wondered if Roncalli and Medov had heard the explosion. He took a sip of the now tepid tea and collected himself. "Really, I'm fine."

"Then we can go on to other things?" Medov asked.

What the hell. Nothing lost in being wrong, so Peter decided to give it a shot.

"That depends on what I say next."

"What are you talking about?" Medov said. "You are speaking nonsense."

"Yes, nonsense again. Thank you for that. I'm going to say one word, Demir, and that will determine whether we keep going or end things right now."

"I do not understand this at all," Medov said.

"Maybe you will when I say the word. Are you ready?"

"I am ready." Medov sounded as if he were humoring a madman.

"Then here's the word: Greshnekov."

Medov's eyes suddenly popped open, so wide that they seemed to touch his hairline. "What did you say?"

"Greshnekov, as in Tolya Greshnekov."

"What is Tolya Greshnekov?" Roncalli asked.

"Not what, who." Peter looked at Medov, who was slouched over the table and sweating profusely. "Would you like to tell him, Demir?"

"Would *somebody* please tell me?" Roncalli said.

Medov looked up, his pale face drenched, unable to speak.

"I will, since he won't or can't." Peter said. "Tolya Greshnekov is Skrobat."

Medov's years of training and experience in espionage had suddenly crumbled. Unflappable cool had become frozen fear, stiffening his body and face and leaving him looking like Roncalli should give him last rites. Then, slowly, Medov's lips began to move. "How do you know that name?"

Peter countered with his own question. "I thought you didn't know Skrobat's real name."

But Medov wasn't about to yield. "Who are you working for really?" he asked, his voice trembling. "Has Naumov sent you? Has he sent you here to kill me?"

"We've gone through this. Naumov didn't send me and I'm not here to kill you."

"Then Skrobat sent you directly. You are a *biryut,* a lone wolf, one of his elite corps of murderers who act without any organizational controls. They have been taught to never abandon an assigned mission, no matter who tells them to. Even Skrobat, himself, cannot call off a *biryut* once he has been given an order. Like a chess pawn, a *biryut* only moves forward until he has completed his task."

"I'm not a *biryut,* and as for Skrobat. I don't know him. If he was sitting across the table from us, I wouldn't recognize him."

"Then how did *you* know his real name?"

"A lucky guess."

"Liar!" Medov erupted. "You are playing games with me! Games with my life!"

"I said I don't know him. And as for liars, perhaps you'd like to explain why you denied knowing Skrobat's real name."

Still visibly shaken and uncertain, Medov turned to Roncalli. "Father?"

"I do not believe he is here to harm you in any way."

"You are sure?"

Roncalli nodded. "I am sure."

"I only heard it once, by accident." Medov shook his head as if he were about to commit a grave crime. "The men who were talking did not know I heard it. That is why I am still alive. To admit knowing Skrobat's true identity is to sign your own death warrant. Do you understand that?"

Peter nodded his head. "Tell me more about Greshnekov."

"What can I tell you about Greshnekov? Greshnekov is the head of nothing and of everything." Medov's voice dropped and Peter and Roncalli both strained to hear him. "He has no title, but Greshnekov directs every aspect of subduing our enemies, internal and external. The others who have titles, they come and go. Who is officially in charge of what—Berzen, Beria, Proskurov, Golikov, Panfilov, the GRU, the NKVD—makes no difference. Behind the scenes it is Greshnekov and, since Stalin took control, it always has been Greshnekov. The Stavka—"

"The what?" Roncalli asked.

"The Stavka—the Soviet Supreme Military Command," Medov said. "It makes decisions on the war, but they are only carried out if Greshnekov agrees with them. You ask about Stalingrad? Greshnekov will make the final decision on what is done."

"Not Stalin?" Peter said.

"On major matters, Greshnekov and Stalin come to an agreement. Greshnekov alone can argue with Stalin—even argue him down—and not suffer punishment or death. He is the only one that Stalin completely trusts. Supposedly they have been good friends going back to the time before Stalin was Stalin. I cannot say for sure if that is true, but it would make sense. Stalin places the most faith in those from his early days."

"What else do you know about Greshnekov?"

"I told you. It is said he and Stalin are very old friends, though that may be rumor. So much about Greshnekov is rumor. Or myth. Once a very informed person told me that when he was young, Skrobat was in the circus. Can you imagine—in the circus! Skrobat. I have no idea where these things come from. None at all."

"Anything else?" Peter said.

Medov spread his hands apart, palms up, and shrugged.

"No more rumors, no more myths?"

"I think I said this, but maybe not. If I did, let me say again: one does not talk about Skrobat; one does not ask about Skrobat. There are already too many ways to die in the Soviet Union."

Peter nodded and looked at his watch, then at Roncalli. "That afternoon meeting, Father."

Roncalli looked at his own watch. "Yes, yes indeed. Thank you for keeping track of the time." Roncalli rose, as did Peter.

"Father?" Medov remained seated.

"You will be fine here. I will be back tomorrow. Until then, Monsignor Righi can handle anything that needs handling."

"And the British, Father?"

Roncalli glanced at Peter. "Yes, of course, the British."

"Can we make a stop on the way to our appointment?" Peter asked, and Roncalli nodded that they could. "Then former Comrade Medov, I suggest you spend the next day or so preparing for the prospect of overcooked beef and warm beer."

Roncalli drove.

· "They assigned a priest to drive me, but a priest belongs in a church, not a car, so that is where I put him," Roncalli explained. "Besides, I enjoy driving."

Peter wasn't sure anyone else on the road enjoyed Roncalli's driving, but somehow they made it to the British Embassy. Peter went in alone. Roncalli warned that the ambassador—Sir Hughe Montgomery Knatchbull-Hugessen—could be "a bit fussy," so Peter adopted a simple strategy: he would begin by being brusque and become downright rude if necessary.

Peter was escorted into the embassy and taken to a secretary who told him that Sir Hughe was "indisposed."

"Then unindispose him, please." Peter was tired, rushed and not about to put up with a runaround. "Inform him that Dudley Clarke has arrived."

"I really can't—"

"Inform him! Please."

The secretary picked up the phone, buzzed and, after a ten-second wait, delivered the information. When she hung up, she led Peter to the ambassador's office, knocked on the door and then opened it.

"Dudley." The man at the desk got up without even looking and walked toward them. "I'm honored. Your first visit to my—" He stopped short as soon as he realized that he wasn't speaking to Clarke. "What's the meaning of this?" he demanded, then looked at the secretary. "This isn't Dudley Clarke. Fetch the guards."

"Yes, fetch the guards," Peter said. "Then fetch the movers, because you will soon be getting a call, not from Dudley but from C in London and then from the PM and finally from your replacement telling you to leave the keys." That was ballsy and Peter loved ballsy.

"Who the devil are you?" the ambassador asked.

"Major Peter Baker and I'm late, so I won't be social, nor will I answer questions." Peter hadn't played the old authoritative role in a while, but he hadn't lost his touch. He turned to the secretary. "You. Go. Now. Please."

"Sir Hughe, shall I get the guards?"

Pete watched as the ambassador, overwhelmed and confused, pondered the question,

"Sir Hughe?"

"Go ahead back to your desk. I'll be fine."

Peter slammed the door the moment she had stepped away from it. "Now listen to me. I am working with Clarke and Montgomery with the specific authorization of Churchill. Clarke will confirm that. You are to send your men immediately to the Archbishop's residence. There you will put a Russian defector named Demir Medov under British protection and bring him here. He is to be granted political asylum and safely transported to London. Do you understand me?"

"I've never—just who do you think you are to give me orders?"

"I've told you who I am. Clarke will tell you who I am. Monty will tell you who I am. And the PM will tell you who I am. And if this is not done, you will really find out who I am and you won't like it."

"But—"

"This is not a discussion. Make your calls and then do what I said *now*." Peter opened the door. "Thank you, Ambassador. It's been a pleasure."

On his way to the embassy front door, Peter paused by the secretary. "Perhaps you should fetch Sir Hughe a cup of tea. I suspect he's having a bad day."

"Well?" Roncalli asked when Peter got back in the car.

"The ambassador was extremely accommodating," Peter said as he prepared himself for round two of Roncalli behind the wheel. "It may take a few hours, but I doubt Demir will be there when you return."

"Thank you." Roncalli started the car and pulled out onto the street. After a few minutes of tempting fate, he turned to Peter. "This Skrobat or Greshnekov or whatever he calls himself. You really don't know him?"

"No." Peter was going to leave it there, but he liked Roncalli and it didn't compromise the mission, so what the hell. "Not personally. But I know how he thinks. I know how he plans. And I know what he's likely to do."

"How?"

"By using 'slithy' and 'mimsy.'"

Peter didn't blame Roncalli for looking at him as if he were mad. "If you watch the road I'll explain."

"You doubt my driving?" Roncalli sighed and turned away from Peter.

"Have you read the Alice books by Lewis Carroll?"

"In Italian years ago, when I was young."

"Do you remember 'Jabberwocky'?"

"The poem with all the silly nonsense words?"

"Like 'slithy' and 'mimsy.' Medov called Skrobat a nonsense word, and that set off things in my mind. When Humpty Dumpty explained 'Jabberwocky' to Alice, he said some of the so-called nonsense words in it were like a portmanteau."

"Like a suitcase?" Roncalli was trying to follow Peter.

"Exactly, but instead of holding different items of clothing, these words hold different sounds and meanings. I had a hunch 'Skrobat' might be a portmanteau, a blend of sounds and meanings from other words, so I played around with it and it paid off."

"But how did you even think of that and then how did you ultimately get the name?"

"'Skrobat' sounded familiar. It reminded me of an old circus term, *shtrabat*, which refers to the surprise ending of an aerial or acrobatic act. You know—the performer swings from one trapeze to another and misses, only to catch a safety rope at the last minute, right before hitting the ground. The audience expects one thing, but gets another. That's *shtrabat*. The circus is made up of many nationalities, so its vocabulary includes words from all different languages. *Shtrabat*'s Russian, but everyone in the circus uses it."

"How do you know circus terms?"

Though the question was innocent, Peter didn't want to get into any details. "For a time I was interested in circuses and would attend them whenever I could. I became friendly with some of the performers, including a circus family named Greshnekov, who escaped Russia at the start of the Revolution. Besides the parents, there were two sons and a daughter. There had been a third son, Anatoli, whom the family always called Tolya. He was known for his death-defying feats that fooled the audience."

"*Shtrabat?*"

"Very good. Anyway, Tolya loved both the circus and the stage and always hoped to combine them in some way. So he left his family to study acting in Moscow. He was killed by the Bolsheviks, about a month before his family fled."

"And that gave you the name?"

"When I played with 'Skrobat' some more, I saw it was made up of two Russian words—*akrobat* and *aktor*—Tolya's two passions. A portmanteau word, with an *s* thrown in to make it sound like *shtrabat*. Skrobat—an agile actor who takes extraordinary chances to accomplish extraordinary feats. There were just too many coincidences. So I tossed Medov the name Tolya Greshnekov. I only risked getting a quizzical look if I was wrong."

"Brilliant. But I still don't understand how you worked all that out so rapidly."

"Neither do I. It's just something I've always been able to do. Some kind of mental abnormality I suppose."

His questions answered, for the remainder of the drive Roncalli regaled Peter with stories. When they finally arrived at the airport, Peter asked, "Are you sure the plane is still here?"

"Here and waiting to fly the Archbishop of Greece and a member of his staff who is to conduct a special clerical project in Athens."

"Von Papen's plane."

"Von Papen. Yes, he is a very devout Catholic. His assistance has made my duties easier. He has also helped me save a number of Jewish lives, behind the scenes of course. He is a Nazi, but a conflicted Nazi. We are complex beings, we humans. I always wonder if that's really the way God intended us to be."

Peter turned the talk back to the plane trip. "Do I have a name should anyone ask?"

"Yes, of course. A fine one. Your name is Father Peter."

Athens was only 350 miles from Istanbul, so it was a quick flight. The German guards, who knew Roncalli from past visits, greeted him warmly. There was no need for papers.

"That was easy enough," Peter said as they walked to a nearby area where Roncalli kept a car.

"I said there would be no problem. You must have faith, at least while you are a priest."

A priest. Peter had assumed many identities, including ministers, but a priest? What would the nuns at the orphanage think? he wondered.

"I will take you to where you are to meet your friend," Roncalli said. "Or are you still concerned about my driving?"

"I have faith." Peter grinned, got into the car and prepared for the worst. Twenty minutes later they arrived intact at the rendezvous site, a small tavern.

"Are you sure your friend will come?" Roncalli asked, and Peter assured him he would. "Then we say good-bye." Roncalli reached over and placed his hand on Peter's head. "Bless you, my son. Go with God."

For some reason, Peter found Roncalli's farewell strangely comforting. Not the religious part, but when Roncalli touched him Peter sensed an energy flowing from the man, an energy that he saw as a light when it reached his brain. There was something special about Roncalli and Peter had a feeling that one day they would cross paths again.

"Thank you for your help," Peter said.

"Please. There may come a day when I will need *your* help."

"And I will be happy to provide it."

"I hope that you still feel that way should the time come. And if it does, perhaps you will tell me who you *really* are."

Peter opened the car door. "Perhaps by then I'll know."

27

Your Stars Today: Your sharp mind and potentially sharper
and very persuasive tongue can be put to good use today,
provided you don't fall prey to distractions.

An empty bottle of Dom Perignon stood on the nightstand near a Limoges plate that earlier had held Leonidas chocolate truffles. Rumpled satin sheets were strewn on the double bed, their wrinkles satisfied smiles, while the unbleached French hand-crocheted spread and its matching pillows lay bunched on the floor.

Peter, lying on his stomach with his eyes still shut, inched his left hand across the mattress and felt the warmth of a recently risen body. Max was up and about and, from the rustling he could hear, already busy.

It had been two weeks since Peter had come back from Istanbul, time spent with Max, working on the SS documentary and making up for Cairo by exploring their new relationship. It was a "honeymoon," absent the rings, and they put it to good use.

"It's getting late." Max entered the room with coffee and buns on a tray.

"What time is it?"

"Nearly six A.M."

"Six A.M.!" Peter groaned.

"Yes, six A.M. Do you intend to sleep all day?"

"Depends on who I'm sleeping with."

"I see." Max tried to set the tray on the nightstand, but the remnants of romance prevented it. She placed it on the bed, instead, and sat down on the edge. Peter reached for the coffee, but his hand landed on Max's sheer white satin robe and the breast beneath.

"Hey!" Max slapped his hand away. "You know we have to get going. No more lounging."

"Why? You're nearly done with the Munich filming. Let's just have a fun day and go see all the Nazi sights: the Beer Hall, the SS Barracks, Dachau—"

"Hitler himself. Now up. You know they're expecting us at the Berghof and we have a long drive ahead."

"Hobnobbing with Hitler at his retreat. Sounds thrilling."

"And promises to be productive. Himmler's left us alone, so we've had a lovely interlude. But the clock's ticking down to January 6 and I'd feel much better if I knew we had more things in place."

"By 'we' you mean me."

"Peter, I have no doubts. I really don't. Just humor me. Please. This weekend can prove extremely productive. Now come on!"

"I love it when you're Teutonic."

"Peter!"

"Jawohl!" Peter thrust his right arm out in a limp Hitler salute.

"That's not funny, Peter, not at all."

"Just practicing. I wouldn't want to embarrass you. Did I do it right?"

"You know very well you didn't."

"Then show me how."

"I'll do no such thing."

"Show me how and I promise I'll get up."

"What am I to do with you?" Max shook her head and sighed. "Very well. Like this." She shot her arm out, straight and rigid and easy for Peter to grab hold of and drag her onto the bed.

"What are you doing?" Max struggled for a second or two, then surrendered. Peter slipped her robe off her shoulders and arms and gave it a slight tug, drawing it off her body and onto his.

"Keeping my promise." Peter tossed aside Max's robe and pulled her on top of him.

"You promised you'd get up."

"And I kept my promise."

Max's hand slid down Peter's side to his thigh, then turned and journeyed inward. "So I see. Congratulations. At least part of you knows how to give a proper Nazi salute."

Max called it right.

The drive to the Berghof, Hitler's Alpine hideaway near the Austrian border, took nearly five hours, too short for Peter's liking. That idyllic period when he and Max could be themselves, alone in each other's company, would end with this trip, and Peter wanted to stretch it out as long as possible. But they were already late and Max drove the final fifty miles as if she were competing in the Grand Prix, slowing only when a guardhouse came into view. "Get ready. We're at the driveway to the Berghof." Max stopped the car, spoke briefly to a soldier who'd approached. He smiled and opened the gate, allowing her access.

As they neared the main house, Peter saw a small group of people. "I see they have a welcoming party."

"Herbert Döhring, who manages the Berghof, and some of the staff. Döhring was sent here in the mid-thirties when the Berghof was being built and here's where he's stayed." As soon as Max pulled up in front of the house, Döhring opened the door and escorted her out while one of the staff attended to Peter.

"Good afternoon, Fräulein Elise. So good to have you visit once again." He bowed and kissed her hand.

"Thank you, Herbert. And it's so good to be back here. I've missed it—and you."

"How kind. This must be Herr Kepler."

"It is indeed," Max said.

Döhring clasped Peter's extended hand. "It is a pleasure to meet you, Herr Kepler."

Peter smiled and nodded, deciding that the less he said the better. This was Max's territory and he would follow her lead.

"Where is he?" Max asked Döhring, then took a peek at her watch and answered her own question. "Of course. He's at the Teahouse with Eva and the guests."

"Yes, but Fräulein Braun didn't go. She wanted to wait for you."

"Max!" Almost on cue, there was a scream as a lithe female figure, up-raised arms shaking frenetically and brown hair bobbing wildly, rapidly descended the stone stairs from the Berghof's main entrance to the driveway and collapsed on Max with a tight hug.

"Max!" she exclaimed again, not loosening her hold.

"Evie!" Max leaned her head back and smiled. "You look so good!"

Eva Braun did look good, much better than the photos, which couldn't properly capture her simple prettiness. Peter had seen the photos, even if most of the German people hadn't. Goebbels had been especially careful to suppress anything suggesting that the *Führer* was seriously involved with a woman. There was no time for that: the *Führer's* passion was for Germany alone. Besides, what woman could possibly be worthy of him? No pictures, no stories, no appearances, nothing, except, of course, gossip.

But Eva Braun's OSS file was full of photos—including one showing her sunbathing in the nude—along with whatever biographical information could be found. There wasn't much. She had been an assistant and model for

Heinrich Hoffmann, Hitler's personal photographer. That's how, in 1929 when she was seventeen, she met the future *Führer*. Two years later, they began seeing each other on a regular basis. Then, in 1936, a captivated Hitler moved her into the Berghof, where, isolated in luxury, she had stayed for the past six years.

Tongues wagged about Eva Braun, and about the suicides of two other Hitler paramours during the early 1930s: his niece Geli Raubal, and the actress Renata Müller. Tongues wagged about Eva Braun's own two attempts to kill herself, once with a pistol, once with poison. Tongues wagged about Eva Braun deliberately botching her second suicide try so that Hitler would move her to the Berghof, which he did soon after she recovered. But though tongues wagged, the public never knew for sure.

Neither did the OSS, and neither did Max, although she told Peter she thought Eva certainly capable of such a ploy.

"Your drive was good?" Eva finally separated herself from Max.

"It was fine. Autumn here is so beautiful, how could it not be fine?"

"And this is Herr Kepler you told us about?"

"I'm Peter, please."

Eva moved closer to Peter and gently pressed his outstretched hand. "It's so nice to have you here. I understand you are quite the authority on German antiquity."

"I don't know about that."

"Peter's so annoyingly modest, Evie," Max said. "Actually, 'authority' is too weak a word. You know how demanding I am. But I can assure you that Peter completely satisfies me."

The double meaning wasn't lost on Peter and, from her slight facial movements, he saw it wasn't lost on Eva, either.

"That is quite a compliment." Eva turned to Max. "Would you like to freshen up or go right to the Teahouse? He's been anxious to see you. He was so disappointed that you weren't here for lunch."

"So was I, but it couldn't be helped. I needed the Munich morning light for one of the sequences in the SS documentary, and I got it. Now I can enjoy tonight and tomorrow without worry. As for freshening up, I'm fine, though I must look a mess."

"You can never look a mess," Eva said, and brushed her hand across Max's face. "If this is what hard work does, then I need to throw out all my fancy creams and lotions and take immediately to finding myself employment."

"I'm sure Max can always use a beautiful woman in her films," Peter blurted out, then thought the better of it. Rumors aside, Peter had to assume this was the woman Hitler had claim to.

"Why, Max, how charming your Peter Kepler is." She turned back to Peter. "I'm afraid I'm spoken for, but Max—"

"Is ready to head for the Teahouse." With that Max took a few steps along a pine-lined path, halted and turned back to Eva and Peter. "To sin with gin is passe," she said in a melodic voice. "And sipping scotch won't make my day. I don't consider wine divine. And beer well I simply decline."

"She's going to sing," Eva said. "It's always the same whenever she comes here. She sings this silly American ditty from the Follies, written by a Jew no less, while she does a Negro dance. Once the *Führer* even caught her. You know what he did?"

No, but since Max was still here Peter knew what the *Führer* didn't do.

"He smiled and then he applauded. Applauded. Can you imagine that?"

Where Max was involved, he could imagine anything. "In any event, she seems to have stopped."

"She's done no such thing. She's just waiting for me. Wait. I'll show you." Eva called out to Max. "And tea, Max. What about tea?"

"Ah, tea! That's a different story, because, you see . . ." And suddenly, as Eva predicted, Max burst into song and began shaking her shoulders and hips. "I shake my shimmy on tea. Tea makes a wild woman out of me."

"Max, I forbid it!"

Eva's words only encouraged Max to shake more vigorously. "I get a reeling feeling when I sip Darjeeling . . ." She stopped and crooked her finger at Eva. "Come on Evie. You want to. You know you do."

"See," Eva sighed. "This brazen woman now tries to corrupt me." She motioned to Döhring. "Have the bags brought in." Then, picking up the song, she headed for Max. "And Pekoe makes me carry on so, Earl Grey can have his way with me, you see, because I shake my shimmy on tea!"

Eva also started shaking, but from a bout of uncontrollable giggles, which quickly spread to Max. Finally gaining her composure, Eva looked over at Peter. "Come on, Peter Kepler, join us." Then she and Max resumed their singing, skipping along the path and pausing every few seconds to shake.

No way was Peter going to sing, and he definitely wasn't about to dance his way into Hitler's presence. Instead, he waved and walked but deliberately stayed a few feet behind them. Not that the women cared. They were somewhere else, and wherever that was, they were totally enjoying being there. The innocence of the moment set Peter wondering. Max, who spoke with Eva often, said she knew more than she let on. Did that include the full extent of the atrocities and the depravations brought about by the man she had chosen to love? Given the opportunity, it wouldn't take Peter long to find out. A few minutes of directed conversation and he could draw out the truth. The only hitch was that Peter would have been shot dead by the time he did. Forget truth. Speculation would be fine.

They were schoolgirls now, Max and Eva, no longer dancing but skipping. It was rare to see Max so frivolous, even if it was feigned. Peter knew Max had carefully cultivated her relationship with Eva Braun because it might prove valuable to the resistance efforts. But Peter had learned acting from the best: feigned or not, a bit of the real Max had been caught up in the moment. The giddiness wasn't pretense: Max really *was* having fun. As Stanislavsky would have said, she had become the role. It wouldn't last. But while it did, Peter could feel her joyful spontaneity and he was happy for her. It was a strange sensation, another of those emotional experiences that he had avoided for so long.

Damn you, Max! Why did you have to screw everything up?

Hitler was snoring.

Not heavily, but enough to be heard by his guests still inside the Teahouse, who were engaged in hushed conversation around a long, snack-laden wooden table that commanded most of the space in the large circular room. The marble walls were inlaid with gold, save for one portion that was cluttered with windows. The other guests had fled outdoors, where they could enjoy the smoke that Hitler forbade in his presence.

So there he was, the ruler of the Reich, slumped in an armchair upholstered in green, his favorite color, the glasses, which he never wore in public, askew on his drawn face, before him a half-drunk cup of apple-peel tea and a barely touched portion of baked apple cake and behind him an array of windows affording a majestic view of the multi-hued majesty that was the Bavarian Alps. At his feet, Blondi, the German shepherd he loved and Eva hated, was peacefully sprawled on a rug.

"I was afraid of this," Eva whispered to Max as they stood at the door peering in. "He dozes off more frequently these days. All the long hours, from late at night to early morning, working. It's taking a toll."

"He sacrifices for Germany," Max said.

"The people don't appreciate how much," Eva said.

"The people idolize him. But you love him, so you see things differently. You see things the people can't. Besides, he will never change."

"It's his cross." Pride showed through Eva's resignation. She was still the First Lady of the Reich, and as long as she knew that, nobody else mattered. "Here, let me wake him."

"No." Max put her hand on Eva's arm. "He should rest."

"If I don't, he'll sleep until it's time to leave for dinner."

"And that's when I shall see him. Besides, now I feel some of the trip. A bath would be lovely."

"Yes, of course," Eva said, adding hesitantly, "I should stay here, however. He'll look for me when he awakens. He's so used to having me there." She pointed to another armchair to Hitler's left.

"Please. Peter and I can walk back and enjoy the views."

"No, you will be driven back. I insist. Come."

Max and Peter followed Eva through the anteroom, where she stopped to summon a car, then outside. "It will only take a minute," Eva assured them. "We keep cars here. He never walks back, either. "

The wait allowed Peter a better look at this refuge to which Hitler always retreated after lunch. The exterior could easily be taken for a silo—an oversized silo, since any building associated with Hitler had to be built on an outsize scale. Other than that, there was a small, rectangular appendage, which Peter figured housed the kitchen and areas for the staff and guards. Overall, he wasn't particularly impressed.

"See, I told you. Here it is."

Peter turned and saw a guard opening the rear left door of a black Volkswagen Cabriolet for Max.

"You're sure?" Max said.

"Positive. The ride will be quick. Besides, there's an armored Mercedes on hand if need be. He usually prefers that anyway. Now go." Eva kissed Max on the cheek. "Come, Peter, don't keep a lady waiting."

Peter got into the right rear seat and another guard, who had held that door open, shut it firmly. Eva waved her right hand first from side the side, a signal for the driver to get going, and then up and down, a farewell to Max and Peter.

"Just to be in the presence of such greatness," Max said.

"Overwhelming," Peter replied, playing to the driver, as was Max.

"I've had the privilege so many times, and yet it still has such an impact on me."

Stanislavsky might have disapproved, but Peter refused to continue playing a Hitler sycophant in a five-minute performance. Max would have to make it a monologue. Or maybe not.

"Forgive me, Fräulein Elise," came the stammer from the front. "I realize this is very inappropriate of me, but I have to tell you how much I admire your films."

"Isn't that sweet." Max placed her hand on the driver's shoulder.

"Yes. *Teuton* was truly inspiring. I saw it three times."

"Three times! I don't think I've seen it all the way through three times."

"It was shown to our unit here on a number of occasions. I took advantage of that."

"And what unit are you? I'm afraid I can't see your insignia from back here."

"SS Sturm Five/Thirty-One."

"Sturm Five/Thirty-One." Max screwed her face in thought. "Sturm 5/31. I think I've heard Himmler mention your unit."

"Really?"

"I can't be sure, but I think so. And very favorably."

Heard Himmler mention your unit? Peter bit his tongue as Max continued to lead the driver on.

"Are you here only when the *Führer* stays?"

"No, Fräulein, we are here all the time. We have a barracks beneath the guardhouse you saw when you arrived."

"Such an important job, protecting the *Führer*, and such an honor. What is your name?"

"Gunther, Fräulein. Gunther Apel."

"And you are a . . . ?"

"*Unterscharführer-SS, Fräulein.*"

"*Unterscharführer-SS!* So young to be a sergeant. You must be an exceptional soldier."

If Apel was stammering before, he was spluttering now, trying to utter words that wouldn't form. Peter had to keep from applauding Max's performance. She had already charmed the pants off Apel and now she was going for his shorts.

"Well, *Unterscharführer*-Gunther Apel, I shall ask Himmler about the Sturm Five/Thirty-One and I shall certainly mention you."

The Volkswagen stopped abruptly and Peter put his left arm in front of Max to keep her from flying forward. The driver, meanwhile, began spewing apologies so rapidly that they jammed one another and became incoherent.

The poor kid was in a dither and Peter felt for him. Max had messed with his mind, like a cat playing with a captured bird, then tossing it aside, not quite dead but quivering and maimed.

"I don't know what happened. Please, I have never—"

"I see we are here." Max again put her hand on his shoulder. "And it was a wonderful ride. You were delightful company, *Unterscharführer*-Apel."

"What happened?" An agitated Herbert Döhring, who had dashed down the stairs, opened the door and leaned over Max. "Are you all right?"

"I'm perfectly fine," Max said as Döhring helped her out.

"What did you do, you fool?" Döhring leaned back in and looked as though he was about to rip Apel from the front through the rear and onto the ground. "Are you crazy?"

"No, he's gallant. Please, Herr Döhring, it was my fault."

Döhring backed away from the car and stood facing Max.

"You see, I thought I saw something in the road, a squirrel probably, and instinctively I shouted to stop. Like the good soldier he is, *Unterscharführer*-Apel immediately obeyed my order. I'm sorry if my silly reaction caused you worry. That is why women are not soldiers."

"Completely understandable, Fräulein." As quickly as he was angry, Döhring was calm. "Obviously there was no harm done."

Peter marveled at the seemingly effortless way Max consistently defused difficult and dangerous situations. With the right mentor she could become a wonderful con artist, right up there with the best of them. Peter was sure of that. Hadn't he known one of the greatest women con artists and hadn't she—

"Peter, the car may prove a little cramped for changing. Why don't we let Herr Döhring show us to our rooms instead?"

"Yes, of course. Forgive me. I've been entranced by our surroundings and by the thought that I shall soon be dining with the *Führer*." Back to portraying the awestruck admirer, Peter climbed out of the car. Max had put on a fine show for him, so tonight, before the toughest of audiences, he would return the favor.

And then some.

"Good, I see we have all assembled," Hitler said when he entered the ante-room. He was dressed much the same as when Peter saw him in the Teahouse—black slacks, white shirt and black tie—the only difference being his double-breasted jacket, which was now charcoal rather than brown. Eva Braun, however, who stood just behind him, had transformed herself from country girl to sophisticated woman. No frock for her now. Instead a belted tangerine silk evening gown, one of the many designer dresses, usually from Paris or Florence, she insisted upon buying, over Hitler's objections.

In contrast, Max's evening dress was simpler: pale blue patterned with floral sprigs, it flared from the hips and had a fishtail back. Both women wore their hair down: Max because Hitler liked that style, Eva because Hitler insisted on that style. Max, however, had placed two small blue gardenias in her hair as a subtle complement to her dress.

Hitler made his way over to Max, bowed slightly, lifted her right hand and pressed his lips against the back. "May I have the honor of escorting you to the dining hall?"

"The honor is mine, my *Führer*." Max locked her arm in his.

"Since I seem to have sacrificed my companion to the Reich . . ." Peter offered his arm to Eva Braun, but it was Martin Bormann, Hitler's powerful Reich Secretary, who responded.

"Generally I have that privilege. However, since this is your first time here, you couldn't know that."

But I could know you're a pompous prick, Peter thought. "I am really so very sorry. Of course, I had no idea."

"How kind of you to ask me, Herr Kepler," Eva Braun said, glaring at Bormann. "It would be my pleasure."

From experience Peter knew the ensuing silence usually signaled that something was mere inches from the fan and traveling fast.

All eyes were on Hitler, waiting to see if he would intercede. The answer came quickly. "Well, now that the matter has been settled. However, I must ask you a favor, Herr Kepler. You see, the table settings have already been arranged and the staff has become used to certain protocols, such as *Reichsleiter* Bormann sitting to the left of Fräulein Braun. So if you wouldn't mind—"

Hitler stopped and Peter responded only when he was certain that Hitler had said all he was going to say. "I would certainly want *Reichsleiter* Bormann put in his proper place, my *Führer*." Peter said it as innocently as possible, and while Max's eyebrows shot up, the remark seemed to sail right past Hitler.

But not Bormann, and now it was his turn to glare. Peter took stock: in the space of seconds he had made both a social faux pas and a dangerous enemy. He also had discovered, without trying, that Eva Braun despised Bormann and that the feeling was mutual. That could be useful. All in all, Peter deemed it a worthwhile trade-off and an extremely stimulating aperitif. With Eva on his arm, he triumphantly followed Hitler into the dining room.

Once inside, the men stood around the long wooden table while servers held chairs for the women. Discounting the quick Teahouse peek at a Hitler slumped in sleep, this was Peter's first real opportunity to observe him at close range. Moderate height—five feet ten at the most—mainly head and paunchy trunk resting on a pair of disproportionately short bowed legs. Offsetting his pasty, pebbled skin were his signature hair wisp, which limply dangled over his forehead, and his truncated moustache, wedged between a large nose and a mean mouth. His dark-ringed, sunken eyes, mottled with tinges of green and blue, were easily his best feature.

Eva Braun sat on Hitler's left, Max on his right, and although Peter would have normally have sat next to Max, as a new guest he was given the place of honor—directly across from the *Führer*. On his right was Margarete Speer, beside her husband, Albert, the architect responsible for Berlin's redesign, who now held the powerful and much-coveted position of Reich armaments minister. On his left was Eva Braun's sister Gretl, her constant Berghof companion.

When everyone had settled in, Hitler turned to Max. "Your dress is so lovely, and the flowers in your hair. I tell Eva simple is the best, but she is a slave to clothing. I have just had to accept that."

"All women are slaves to clothing, including me, Wolf." Max was one of the very few allowed to use Hitler's nickname. "It's a weakness we are born with. You may be able to change the world, but you can never change that."

As they spoke, the servers arrived—SS enlisted men wearing short white double-breasted dinner jackets with wide lapels, white formal shirts, black bow ties and black trousers—carrying plates of food, which they placed before the guests: ham, potatoes and a variety of vegetables. Hitler's plate, however, consisted entirely of raw, stewed and mulched vegetables, cottage cheese and boiled apples, which he attacked as soon as it arrived, not waiting for the others.

"You have gotten so thin, Max," Hitler said at one point, between bites. "Like a boy. Women and men are different. Why are curves on a woman frowned upon today? It didn't used to be that way. It's not good and it's not healthy. You must eat more." Leading by example, Hitler plunged his fork into the pile of broiled tomatoes, speared a batch and thrust them into his mouth. "You cannot starve yourself."

"I eat." In contrast, Max sliced into a hunk of roasted ham and placed a chunk between her teeth. "See," she said, letting the ham roll back onto her tongue. "I always take your advice, my *Führer*." She followed her words with exaggerated chewing.

"You are mocking me." Hitler's stone face shattered into a smile. "And you are also amusing me. You always know how to amuse me, Max. You are a smart woman and that is your problem. I fear you will never find a match. A smart and successful man must choose a stupid woman for a wife, never one such as you. So you will just have to share my lot, Max, and be satisfied with being married to Germany."

Hitler glanced over the table at Peter, who was grinning. "See, Herr Kepler is grinning. He agrees with me."

Sure, I'm grinning, asshole, Peter thought. Grinning at how pissed you'd be to know that Max *has* found her match and how much more pissed if you knew who that match really was and what he intended to do.

Hitler spent the next few minutes shoveling another heap of food from plate to palate. Then, releasing his silverware, he placed his hands on the edge of the table and leaned forward. "Herr Kepler."

Peter, who had just taken a sip of water, quickly placed the crystal glass down and bent his head to better hear Hitler. At last he was being brought into the conversation.

"My *Führer*?"

"Herr Kepler, do you know what a volt and an ampere are?"

Shit! That was Peter's reaction, not to Hitler's strange question but to his deadly breath. Shit! That's what it smelled like—horse shit, only worse. Max had warned Peter about Hitler's flatulence but not about his breath. Had the blast really taken away the surface layer of Peter's facial skin when it hit him full force, or had it just felt that way? From the corner of his left eye Peter saw Max's straight face, but he could hear her guffawing inside, pleased with herself and her nasty little trick. Really nasty, worse than the dreaded camel spit Peter had dodged in the desert.

"Herr Kepler?"

Of course—Hitler *had* to overaspirate his *h*'s! Maybe a quick answer to his question, which had nothing to do with anything being talked about, would mercifully end matters. It was worth a try. *Anything* was worth a try. "If I remember correctly, my *Führer*, a volt measures an electric current's force and an ampere measures its strength."

Peter's attempt to withdraw from the danger zone was thwarted when Hitler kept going.

"Congratulations, Herr Kepler. Your memory is very good. Now can you tell me what a Goebbels and a Goering are?"

Again a rancid wind scorched Peter's face and he placed his hand over his mouth, as if he were thinking rather than hiding his uncontrollable wincing. Hitler's mouth was partially open, revealing an aerial ammo dump of crooked yellow-and-brown teeth, some of which were part of a badly made lower front bridge anchored to a base of blackened gums. Peter removed his cloaking hand and fluttered it in the air, trying to wave away any lingering odor while indicating he had no answer. He glanced to his left, seeking possible assistance from Goering, who was too preoccupied with gorging himself on ham to notice.

"Don't bother," Hitler said. "The only thing you can learn at this moment by looking at Goering is that pigs are the only species that eat their own."

Where did that come from? Peter wondered, making a note to ask Max about the caustic remark.

"Since you seem have no answer, let me provide it," Hitler continued. "Like the volt and the amp, both are measures. A Goebbels measures the amount of nonsense a man can speak in an hour and a Goering measures the amount of metal that can be pinned on a man's breast."

A joke! Hitler was trying to prove that he had a sense of humor by telling a joke. Ears perked, Peter listened for the room's reaction. Max immediately started to laugh and Eva Braun followed. Then even Goering, one of the cheeks of the joke's butt, broke away from his food and, in his typical way of exaggerating everything, began roaring. That's when Peter joined in. Actually the joke wasn't bad, considering its source. One more reminder that these "monsters" were still human, which made their acts all the more despicable, but which also made *the* perpetrators all the more vulnerable.

Hitler slouched over and concentrated on his food once more, tossing etiquette aside as he shoveled, stabbed, smacked and slurped. How he could marshal such gusto for gruel was a mystery to Peter, yet within minutes the proof was in the plates: those of the other diners were still nearly full—Goering was on his second portion—while Hitler's was empty.

Sated, Hitler swallowed a burp, then drew nearer to Max. "Did you go to the exhibition while in Munich?" he asked.

"There wasn't time. Besides, I've seen it already."

"And what about your friend?" Hitler leaned over. "Surely an educated man such as Herr Kepler must have an interest in our great cultural heritage."

Here we go again, but this time Peter had time to brace himself for the barrage of bad breath. That was probably why he detected a garlic-like odor that had been masked by the stench. It could have come from the food Hitler had consumed or it could have come from something else—seeds from the *Strychnos nux vomica* tree, which were commonly used in folk remedies for gas. And if not the seeds themselves, perhaps their deadly derivative—strychnine, enough to generate a smell. Peter looked beyond Hitler to another guest—Theodor Morell, Hitler's longtime personal physician, a rotund, slovenly man whose medical credentials and credibility were both suspect. Yet Hitler would trust no one else. Was Morell treating Hitler with some strychnine compound? That would explain other things

Peter had noticed about Hitler's appearance, especially the yellowish tinge of his skin.

"Herr Kepler, have you been to the exhibition at the House of German Art?"

"Not yet, my *Führer*, though it is certainly something I want to do."

"You must. The great artists of our Reich are on view: von Grützner, Böcklin, von Stuck, Ziegler. You know some of them?"

Peter knew none of them. "I must confess that I am not very well versed in art."

"But you do know what you like and dislike."

"Yes, my *Führer*, I certainly know that."

"See, that is the important thing." Hitler, who seemed pleased with Peter's response, now directed his remarks to the entire table. "Not some critic telling people what they must like, making the choice for them. Artists create for the people, not for themselves. That is why we have provided an artistic environment in which the people are called in to judge their art. The people know when an artist thinks them stupid, painting a field blue instead of green and then faulting them when they do not like it. I tell you that if artists do see fields blue, they are deranged, and should go to an asylum. If they only pretend to see them blue, they are criminals, and should go to prison. Likewise the people know it is not the mission of art to wallow in filth for filth's sake, to paint the human being only in a state of putrefaction, to draw cretins as symbols of motherhood or to present deformed idiots as representatives of manly strength. That is why I have forbidden these degenerate artists to force their so-called experiences upon the public. That is why I have purged our nation of them. Art must be the handmaiden of sublimity and beauty and thus promote whatever is natural and healthy. Of course, this is a broad charge with much room for disagreement. Consider Goering, for example."

Another mention of his name by Hitler forced Goering to lower his fork.

"Goering has a keen appreciation of fine art, as do I. And usually we are in agreement. But there are divergences. For some reason he retains a passion for Gothic art, which I consider devoid of any redeeming aesthetic value. Fortunately, Speer is my architect and he shares my love of the classical and Renaissance styles and has found magnificent ways to adapt their essence to our times."

It was Speer's turn to put down his fork, although it wasn't as wrenching an experience for him as for Goering. "You are too modest, my *Führer*. I have always considered the Reich buildings a collaboration. Indeed, your ideas are much more in evidence than my own."

Speer showed himself to be as obsequious under fire, as Max had said.

"I should have liked to be an architect." Hitler made no effort to counter Speer's claim. "History and circumstances chose otherwise."

"You could also have been a fine painter, my *Führer*." If Goering had to stop eating momentarily, he was at least determined to get a word in.

"Perhaps. But I don't know how much would appeal to you if I had. Certainly I would not have followed the path of your favorite, Dürer. I still cannot understand what you see in him." Hitler turned again to Peter. "What are your feelings about Dürer, Herr Kepler?"

"I tend to favor Michelangelo and Rembrandt, my *Führer*." Peter hoped those choices would be safe enough.

"That is just the kind of—" Suddenly a look of agony washed Hitler's face and his upper body stiffened as if jolted by lightning. His lower body, while unseen, was not unheard, producing a high-pitched sound, which was followed by several deeper and louder bursts. Ashen, Hitler bolted up and stormed out of the room while his guests continued dining as if nothing had happened.

Speer leaned over to Peter. "This frequently occurs. An indisposition brought about by the stress of leading the nation. Those of us who dine with him regularly have become accustomed to it."

"I completely understand," Peter said, trying to rid his nostrils of the smell of sulphur. But Hitler wasn't simply indisposed, Peter suspected he was chronically ill, probably suffering from a form of meteorism. That would explain the strychnine on Hitler's breath: Morell was using it to treat Hitler's uncontrollable flatulence. Perhaps "misusing" was more like it, from Hitler's appearance. And why did Morell allow Hitler's fiber-intensive diet, which would worsen the accumulation of excess gas in the gastrointestinal tract? Important questions, but not for now.

For the next hour, during the remaining supper courses, Peter engaged in small talk, much of it with Speer, whom he found to be highly intelligent. As he had been cautioned, Peter carefully avoided referring to the war, save in the most benign generalities; Speer did the same.

Finally Morell, who had followed Hitler when the Führer suddenly left supper, reappeared and whispered something in Eva Braun's ear. She, in turn, addressed the guests. "While I know that it's customary to join the *Führer* for informal discussion at midnight, following his final military briefings, I fear we will have to forego that this evening. Dr. Morell has given strict orders that he must rest. I apologize for any disappointment."

A collective sigh of relief greeted her announcement. Max had warned Peter about these sessions, during which Hitler kept his guests captive for hours as he stuffed himself with sweet cakes and rambled nonstop on any topic that grabbed his fancy. It was the punishment for privilege.

"Since the *Führer* is regrettably unavailable, let me invite all of you to my house for an after-dinner drink," Bormann said, stepping into the void. His offer was eagerly snapped up by most of the company, who eagerly started to leave the dining room.

"Am I expected at this?" Peter asked Max.

"Given how well you and Bormann hit it off, I would suggest you stay behind. I'll convey your regrets with some plausible excuse."

"You're going?"

"Not because I want to. Bormann's 'after-dinner drink' usually turns out to be hours of partying, as uninhibited as Hitler's sessions are staid. But I would be missed. Besides, I might be able to pick up some helpful tidbits." Max gave Peter a peck on the cheek. "Sweet dreams."

"Of you?"

"I prefer you think of me always, not just when you're asleep."

"Then of what?"

"Killing Hitler."

28

Berchtesgaden: September 13, 1942
Your Stars Today: This is a good time for careful negotiations and patience in bringing matters to completion. Authority figures may need to make decisions and engage in serious communications.

Peter had been up since six, slightly later than the Berghof morning staff but considerably earlier than any of the other guests. Having the luxury of time, he did some stretching and flexibility exercises before enjoying a leisurely bath. Once dressed, he remained in his room, taking a last look at the astrological charts and preparing for his meeting with Himmler. Just after eight Peter heard water running through the pipes in the adjacent room. Max was awake. He waited another twenty minutes, then went out to the corridor, gently knocked twice on her door, then made his way down the stairs to the main floor where some staff members were bustling about.

"May I do something for you, sir?" a member of the household staff, still wearing formal serving livery, asked with a slight bow of his head.

"It seems a lovely day, so I thought I might go onto the terrace if that's all right."

"Of course it is, sir. Simply through those doors on your left." The man pointed the way. "The terrace will be straight ahead. May I bring you some coffee there?"

"That would be very nice."

The man bowed his head again and he and Peter headed off in their respective directions. Peter, however, was stopped short of his destination by the sounds of loud arguing that thundered through the open terrace door.

"I hired her. You have no right to fire her without informing me."

"I told you to do the firing and you refused."

"Because there was no good reason to fire her."

"The fact that I told you was all the reason necessary. You seem to forget that while you may manage here, you are not in charge."

"I cannot manage if you keep interfering."

"This talk is over. If you feel that strongly about this woman's firing, I suggest you explain the situation to the *Führer*. But I would consider the consequences of that and of any further questioning of my decisions. Now I wish to finish my coffee in peace."

Döhring came storming into the Berghof. "Choke on it, pig," he muttered, knowing that his words couldn't be heard outside but realizing, once he saw Peter, that they were clearly audible inside. He began to stammer. "Herr Kepler, I'm afraid that I—"

"Was outside taking a few breaths of fresh mountain air before your day gets any more hectic."

"Yes," he said, relieved at what now need not be said. "Thank you. Exactly. If I had been informed that you were an early riser, I would have made the proper preparations. The *Führer* and Fräulein Braun generally don't come down until after eleven. It is rare to have guests stay here overnight. Usually they are accommodated at the chalets below."

"It's quite all right. I would have slept later myself, but the noises of the country woke me. Those of us who dwell in the city aren't used to them."

"I had the same problem when I first arrived. May I get you coffee and pastry?"

"One of your excellent staff is already taking care of that, thank you."

"Then if you don't mind, there's always much to be done and it is my job to see that it is. The *Führer* expects everything to be in perfect order when he comes down. And he can spot the least little thing—a chair out of place, a picture slightly off-kilter. He is amazing."

"Please, don't let me take you from your duties. I'll just take your place out there and enjoy the morning views."

"They are indeed magnificent. But careful, Herr Kepler. The insects are out this morning and they are biting."

With a knowing nod Peter stopped out onto the granite of the terrace. He had recognized the second, more strident voice, arguing with Döhring, so he was prepared when it greeted him.

"Ah, Herr Kepler." Martin Bormann rose from the circular table. "Such a pleasure to see you again."

"And you, Reichsleiter Bormann."

"I regret that you couldn't join us after supper last night, but Max explained. You're feeling better, it seems."

"Yes, thank you. Probably just fatigue. About last night—you must let me apologize once more."

"Nonsense. An honest mistake. Please." He motioned to the table and Peter sat and, as if planned, the moment he did the steward arrived. He set down the pastries, poured Peter a cup of coffee, then, with a slight bow, withdrew into the house. Peter took a sip of the coffee and pronounced it "excellent."

"I'm still able to get some from Guatemala, even though all the German coffee-growing plantations there have been seized. But soon I may have to look elsewhere."

"You secure the coffee for the Berghof?" Peter already knew the answer. After last night's supper, Max had explained how Bormann controlled everything at the Berghof, including Döhring. Even Eva Braun, who despised Bormann, had to defer to him, making her nothing more than the titular mistress of Berghof.

"The coffee, the food, the help, the paving stones in the walk . . . it all falls to me." If it weren't said in such a boastful manner, Bormann's answer might have been mistaken for a complaint.

"It must be quite difficult handling every aspect of the Berghof." What sounded like sincerity was really a setup, which Peter had conceived while listening to the tail end of the Bormann–Döhring contretemps.

"Let's just say that I work as hard as a horse to ensure that at all times the Berghof is a refuge truly befitting the *Führer*. Harder than a horse, actually, since a horse has Sundays off and its night's sleep."

Bormann was probably anticipating laughter and Peter obliged before zinging him again. "Then imagine having to handle all those things, not for one place, but for the entire nation. The thought is overwhelming. Fortunately, we have Reichsminister Speer for that. Last night at supper he was good enough to give me a brief overview of all he must do as head of Armaments and War Production. I tell you it was overwhelming, and yet he is able to accomplish everything so effectively. The *Führer* must be extremely proud of such a brilliant manager."

Peter lifted his cup, holding it in the air for a moment so that the anger radiating from Bormann's face could warm the coffee.

"Yes, well, I derive my satisfaction from the *Führer's* satisfaction," Bormann said. "It is enough to know he need not bother himself with a thousand daily matters that I can dispose of."

Bormann was seething, but Peter wasn't ready to go in for the kill yet. "Of course. How I envy you, being able to work so closely with the *Führer*. Not only him, but the leaders of the Reich, the men our Führer holds in such high esteem."

Bormann cocked his head until it was almost resting on his left shoulder, making it easier for Peter to see his shaved temple and monitor changes in his pulse rate.

"*Reichsführer* Himmler, for example, whose amazing mind gave Germany the SS. Is it any wonder that the *Führer* relies on Himmler—his Loyal Heinrich, as he so often calls him—to carry out his most important directives? In fact, I understand the *Reichsführer* is arriving today, so we'll have the pleasure of his company and his thoughts."

The throbbing in Bormann's temple was growing more pronounced as Peter continued his litany of praise.

"And *Reich Marshall* Goering. What a thrill it was to meet him last evening. How I recall his exploits during the last war, his aerial daring. More than two decades later, all of Germany still hails him as one of our greatest heroes."

That was it. Bormann's face confirmed that Peter had succeeded in pushing him over the line.

"Yes, and when Goering dies, he will have rows of cushioned seats filled with his decorations!" Bormann snapped. "That is not what I want. And why should I? This may be difficult for you to fully understand, Herr Kepler, but the person who holds the *Führer's* confidence needs neither rank nor title nor decorations."

"Please, *Reichsleiter*, I never intended to minimize the importance of what you do. If that is how you interpreted my statements, then I owe you yet another apology. I was merely noting that should the time ever come, Goering will make an excellent successor to our great *Führer*, don't you agree?"

Bormann could no longer control the temper that he had shown earlier when arguing with Döhring. "You dare to rank Goering on the same level as the *Führer*, believing that he could accomplish for Germany even an iota of what the *Führer* has?"

Got him! Peter had saved the best for last. So, as Peter had suspected and this outburst confirmed, Bormann was positioning himself to replace Hitler. That was extremely valuable information. Now to put an end to things. "*Reichsleiter*, I would never suggest such things had the *Führer* himself not named Goering to lead our nation if he could not. My boldness is but a reflection of the *Führer's* own estimation of the *Reich Marshal*."

Peter lifted a breakfast pastry from the tray and bit into it. It was sweet, but not nearly as sweet as watching Bormann digest what had just happened. Gaining control over a controlling person was difficult, but this was too easy. Bormann wasn't very complicated; he was nothing more than a crude bully.

A crude bully who last night disliked Peter and this morning hated him.

"I hope you two are playing nicely."

It was a classic Max entrance, an offhand yet trenchant remark, wrapped up in a beautiful package. Peter and Bormann sprang to their feet.

"Martin, good morning. What a nice surprise to come out and find you here." Max gave him a brush kiss on the cheek, greeted Peter with a smile and a "Morning," then sat and motioned for them to do the same. Bormann, however, continued to stand.

"I only came by to address a minor problem," he said. "There are others elsewhere that require my attention."

"Such a shame that you won't be breakfasting with us, Martin. It would allow you and Peter to get to know each other better."

"I believe we know each other quite well enough." Bormann's eyes never left Max. "Will I see you at lunch?"

"Unfortunately, no. I also have things that require attention, so we'll be returning to Munich and rejoining our film crew."

"Then until the next time, Max. Herr Kepler."

"*Reichsleiter.* I look forward to continuing our conversation." Bormann, apparently struggling for a proper reply, finally gave up and left without saying anything more.

"Well, that appeared pleasant," Max said.

"He may have been the most disagreeable of the lot I've met so far."

"And, in some ways, the most dangerous of enemies." Max took a sip of coffee from Peter's cup. "As the information and access conduit to Hitler, he can shape things to suit his purposes. Goering, Speer, Goebbels—none of the top leaders can stand him, but they're also afraid of him. He's able to turn Hitler against them. I suspect he's currently doing that with Goering. But the others will be next. Himmler's about as close to an ally as he has, and even that relationship is becoming strained. Speaking of Himmler, I ran into him when I came down. He'll be here as soon as he finishes a call."

"Which means I can give him the information he wants and we can take off even sooner."

Max shook her head. "Not until we say good-bye to Hitler and Eva. Even I can't get away with that. Hitler doesn't usually rise until after eleven, and then he takes some time to read the morning reports. So it'll be noon at the earliest. But that should give you more than enough time with Himmler."

"Just what I want—more time with Himmler and less time with you." Peter put his hand on top of Max's, but she drew it away.

"Not here. I told you. You and I work together. Nothing more. You are my consultant and my writer, but also my subordinate."

"And you think they buy that?"

"Pretense is one of the pillars of the Reich. They're comfortable living and believing lies. It's truth they react badly to. Besides, if Hitler found out you're screwing his favorite director, one of the Reich's public icons, there's no telling what could happen."

"Screwing his favorite filmmaker? What about if he found out I'm in love with his favorite director?"

"He's another one who can't understand love. But he can understand screwing."

"What about Eva Braun?"

"That's an interesting story. If it were a screenplay, it—"

"My apologies. The call took longer than I expected."

Peter, who had only seen Himmler in an SS uniform, was surprised by his simple single-breasted gray suit, white shirt, solid green tie and plain black laced shoes. For once this man who oversaw the murder of millions really did look like the nondescript manure salesman he had been.

"Max I have greeted, but how are you this morning, Peter?"

"Fine, *Reichsführer*. The Berghof seems to agree with me."

"It agrees with everyone." Himmler sat down and waited until the server, who had reappeared, placed more cups on the table and poured coffee, then left. "A tonic. And a much better one than those the *Führer* is receiving from his Dr. Morell."

"Morell is no doctor, Heinrich," Max said. "He's a dangerous charlatan who's going to end up killing the *Führer* with his so-called remedies. I can't believe that Morell is still allowed to attend to him. "

"We've tried to stop him, Max, but the *Führer* will hear none of it, not even from Eva Braun. He swears by Morell. Those black pills Morell gives him—he must take as many as fifty a day. And who knows what Morell is injecting him with. It's unnatural."

The strychnine smell. The arm tremor. The gastrointestinal problems. Himmler's concerns. Peter's mind was rushing. The bits and pieces of information were starting to come together. Now he just needed to draw Himmler out some more.

"Frankly, I'm a firm believer in homeopathic treatments," Peter volunteered. "But I'm sure you already know that from things I've said."

"No, I didn't know that at all."

True, but that didn't matter. All that mattered was what *Peter* knew: Himmler was fascinated by homeopathic medicine, part of his preoccupation with old Germanic folkways. His wife, Margarete, from whom he was separated, had run a homeopathic clinic before they were married. "Definitely," Peter continued. "All the medications we use today are nothing but variations of natural remedies that we've known about for centuries. These remedies haven't lost their usefulness. Rather, we have lost the skills to use them properly. Take the *Führer*'s stomach problems. I wonder if he has ever tried asafoetida?"

"I've never heard of that," Himmler said.

"I'm sure you have, but you probably called it by its common name, *Teufelsdreck*,"

"Ah, Devil's Dung. Vile stuff. Isn't it used to ward off evil spirits?"

"Your intellect never ceases to amaze me, *Reichsführer*." Peter took a gulp of coffee, giving him a moment to search his memory for some medieval grimoire famous enough that even Himmler had heard of it. "You are undoubtedly referring to *The Key of Solomon the King*, where the magus uses asafoetida to evoke daemonic forces and to protect himself while he binds them. But asafoetida is also is a very effective stomach calmant that relieves gas. And you're right—it *is* vile, but only when uncooked. When prepared properly it's no more overwhelming than a mild onion."

"Fascinating. You must tell me more."

"But of course, *Reichsführer*. However, I understand that our time is short today and . . ."

Himmler raised his hand. "And we have other, more pressing issues to discuss. You are quite right." Himmler didn't try to hide his disappointment.

"Issues that have no need for me." Max pushed her chair back, and rose, followed by Peter and Himmler. "You two finish your business so I can come back out here and enjoy your company."

"Max, you're not leaving, are you?"

Everything stopped at the appearance of Eva Braun, dressed like a Bavarian in a bodice, blouse, full skirt and apron.

"Evie, what a beautiful dirndl." Max stepped back to take it in, and a willing Eva swirled around to give her a better view.

"Adolf loves them," Eva said. "He says they're so much better than highly styled clothing, but I think his opinion is shaped more by price than look. You weren't leaving?'

"I didn't expect you up so early. So I thought I'd fetch a magazine or two and lounge on a chaise until you came down."

"Oh, I rise much earlier than Adolf," Eva said, then giggled. "But I must confess that often I roll over and go back to sleep. This, however, is a historic day. The *Führer* is up before ten. What's more, he's bathed and dressed and nearly finished his briefing papers. Which means he'll be down shortly to join us. And you, Max, are the reason. The *Führer* knew you had to get back to Munich and wanted to spend more time together. So he left orders to be awakened. The poor SS guard who got the assignment feared for his life. Now come." Eva Braun caught Max's hand and led her back to the table. "All of us, let's sit and enjoy each other's company."

As they took their seats, Peter shot a concerned look, first at Max and then at Himmler, who was equally perplexed.

"Now, what do you think we should do this morning?" Eva asked Max. "We can only linger over breakfast for so long."

"I don't know. I didn't—" She halted abruptly. "Well, yes, I did. Since Peter has never been to Obersaltzberg, I thought it might be nice to show him the Eagle's Nest."

Eva's face fell. "The Eagle's Nest?"

"Yes. It'll be fun. Don't tell me it's no longer one of your favorite places."

"No, that's not it. I love the Eagle's Nest as much as ever and still go up there quite often. But the *Führer*. You remember, Max. He hates it. He says it's because the air is too thin, but you know how he feels about heights."

"Heights?" Now Peter's face fell. Not heights. Peter thought about the platform atop the Eiffel Tower, and started to get queasy.

"Of course you're right, Evie. No, the *Führer* would never agree. Such a shame, since I would so like Peter to see it."

Peter tried signaling Max to indicate that he could live without seeing the Eagle's Nest, but to no avail. Then he realized her insistence had a deeper purpose.

"You could take him yourself, I suppose," Eva said. "Though that would cut into the time Adolf and I wanted to share with you."

"Don't be silly. I wouldn't . . . wait. Maybe we can get everything done." Max turned to Himmler. "Heinrich, would you possibly consider taking Peter to the Eagle's Nest? It would be such a favor."

Peter looked at Himmler and saw that he had reached the same conclusion: Max was brilliant.

"I would be glad to," Himmler said. "But I don't know how the *Führer* would take to my not being here."

"Good, loyal Heinrich," Eva said. "Commendable, but I assure you that the *Führer* will survive an hour without you."

Everyone, including Himmler, chuckled at the remark. "Well, if you're sure."

"Fly off to the Eagle's Nest, you and Herr Kepler," Eva said. "Go, now, both of you."

"Your wish is our command," Himmler said as he rose. "Come, Peter."

"I'm right behind you." Peter got up and, as he did, flashed Max a quick wink for a job well done: helping turn Eva Braun into an unwitting conspirator.

Having crossed the desert with Susan's patrol, Peter shrugged off Himmler's warning about the four-mile stretch of road leading to the Eagle's Nest being a "precarious ride."

"The first time, it can make you nervous," Himmler said as he climbed into the driver's side backseat of his black BMW staff car. "Even after the first time, it can make you nervous."

"I'm prepared," said Peter, joining Himmler in the rear of the car.

Himmler tapped his driver on the shoulder. "Not too fast. Good as you are, it's still dangerous."

As the car rolled away from Hitler's Berghof home, Himmler looked out the window, commenting for Peter's benefit, "This road is an astonishing feat of engineering, taking us through what was once solid rock. Bormann, of course, claims the credit, but he had nothing to do with the methods devised to make the road possible. The whole thing took only thirteen months. Can you imagine—thirteen months? It also took eight lives, including Bormann's own driver, just to get it done so fast. Forget deutsche marks: that was the real cost. Not that I blame Bormann, you understand. Things like that happen. Still, if there had been less of a rush, perhaps they never would have died. I feel for lives needlessly lost."

Lives needlessly lost? What about the thousands of lives needlessly lost each day because of your racial policies? Peter wanted to ask. And what about *Lebenswurtes Leben*—lives not worthy of living—lives like that of Horst Jennings's sister Ilsa? That was something else Peter wanted to ask. But even if he could, there was little chance Himmler would understand the questions or, if he did, care.

"Enough unpleasantries," Himmler said. "I'll let you enjoy the ride."

After twelve minutes, five tunnels and one turn that redefined "hairpin," the car halted in front of an arched entrance to the Kehlstein, the Eagles' Nest's mountain perch. As Peter figured, the ride, while slightly harrowing, didn't come close to Johnny's negotiating a sand dune. But, purely for Himmler's benefit, he sighed a relieved, "Thank God."

"See, I warned you. Now we walk." Himmler got out of the car and pointed to a rectangle in the sky. "That's it, up there."

Up there? By Peter's calculations, they were already nearly a half mile higher than the Berghof. He stared at their ultimate target, then, seeing what he was in for, wished his vision was less keen. That rectangle, which was resting on a wisp of land, was a house of sorts with three of its sides bordered by sheer vertical slopes. Just as he had feared, it was the Eiffel Tower all over again, except higher. Much higher.

"Are we hiking up?" Peter tried to sound casual.

"Would you like to?" Himmler replied.

"The choice is entirely yours, *Reichsführer*."

"In that case, we'll take the inner scenic view rather than the outer." Himmler signaled to the two SS guards on duty and each took hold of one of the lion-shaped handles on the bronze doors and pulled them open. Beyond there was a long tunnel that, Himmler explained, had been bored through the granite of the mountain.

"Another marvel of engineering. But there's better to come."

The tunnel, which Peter gauged as being slightly longer than a football field, led to a circular room, its walls and domed ceiling made from the same reddish Bavarian marble used for the floor of Hitler's Reich Chancellery office.

"The elevator." Himmler pointed to an open door, then led Peter into its enormous car, which had green leather benches set flush against three highly polished brass walls, each of them adorned with a large, round Venetian mirror. "You can fit fifty people in here." Once he and Peter were seated the SS soldier operating the elevator closed the door and rotated a lever, setting the car in motion.

"How far up is it?" Peter asked.

"Four hundred feet—as high as the tunnel is long. The elevator lets us off directly in the main house. Beneath this car is another one for transporting supplies that opens into the basement for easy unloading."

"Impressive."

"A Bormann creation, like everything here. He commissioned this mountaintop house as a gift for Hitler's fiftieth birthday. The irony, of course, is that the Führer can't stand the place. Besides being uncomfortable with heights, he doesn't take well to confined spaces. So you can imagine how he feels about walking through the tunnel and then getting into the elevator."

Another shot at Bormann and another valuable piece of information for Peter to tuck away.

The elevator slowed to a stop and Himmler rose. "We're here," he said as the operator slid back the door. "Let me give you a quick look around."

Himmler stepped into an entrance hall and Peter followed him past the staff members standing in wait and through a door on the room's right side into a huge wood-paneled hall. On one wall three windows overlooked a sun terrace, its arched openings offering a spectacular view of the mountains and of Lake Königssee nestled among them.

"The dining area." Himmler swept his right arm, taking in a long table with thirty-two green leather chairs—fourteen on each side and two at either end.

"This is quite something," Peter said.

"Yes. What a shame it's never used. The same is true of almost every room. If the *Führer* has been up here half a dozen times it would be a lot. There is, however, one room that is more to his liking. I'll show you."

This time Himmler led Peter through a door and up six steps that ended in a gigantic hexagonal hall. "This is the great room. On rare occasions, Hitler has held a meeting with foreign dignitaries here."

Peter could see why Hitler might favor the room: it was more in keeping with the Berghof Teahouse, complete with a ridiculously oversized round table, ringed with alternating wooden chairs and overstuffed armchairs. There were also some smaller tables with chairs scattered around. But the true showpiece lay behind the mammoth table—a commanding red-and-bronze tiled Carrara marble fireplace.

"It was a gift from Mussolini." Himmler rubbed his hand over the marble. "And this magnificent carpet we're standing on was a gift from Emperor Hirohito of Japan. But here's a secret for you: most of the furniture was designed by Paul László, the Hungarian Jew architect. Speer was like a lunatic when he found out. Obviously we don't make much mention of this."

"You can rely on me," Peter said, in between a few feigned chuckles. The idea of Jewish furniture somehow being at the seat, if not the heart, of the Reich was just absurd enough to fit right in.

"And now to business. It's a lovely day, and the view is grand, so why don't we enjoy the sun terrace? It will also afford us the most privacy."

Himmler didn't wait for Peter's approval but instead headed down a short flight of stairs at the west side of the hall and cut through a small, Swiss pine–paneled room where, he noted, Eva Braun held teas and out onto the sun terrace.

"You'll see what I mean by the view." Himmler, standing at one of the arched openings, motioned for Peter, who reluctantly came over.

"On his visit here, the French ambassador said the building seemed to be floating in space." If Himmler thought that would impress Peter, it didn't. Floating in space wasn't the most enticing prospect for someone afraid of heights. "You must come closer and look. You will never see a view like this."

Which would be fine for Peter. Still, he edged closer to the arch. There was a base wall of sorts beneath the arch, but, since it only reached to his knees, it did nothing to lessen his queasiness.

"Here, look down at the dairy below."

As he peered down, Peter pressed his hand against the stone of the arch, hoping it would help him fight the feeling of being pulled over the edge, but it didn't. "Over to your right is a beautiful meadow. You may have to poke your head out a bit more to truly appreciate it."

Peter lowered his head and thrust it forward, hoping Himmler didn't notice that his eyes were shut. "It is in truth quite a beautiful sight, *Reichsführer*. I certainly wouldn't have wanted to miss that."

"Would you believe the *Führer* has never seen it, because of his concern about heights?"

"Very unfortunate," Peter said, thinking more of the fact that he and Hitler had something in common.

"Look closely. Do you see the cows there?"

Just in case Himmler was testing him, Peter opened his eyes. With his acute vision he easily saw the cows. He also saw himself tumbling through the air to the ground and joining the herd if he didn't step back from the wall. "Yes, I see them." Peter turned after answering and walked away from the ledge.

"Did you know we've had some great success in reintroducing the aurochs?" Himmler asked.

Aurochs? What the hell is an aurochs? Peter opened one of the dictionaries in his photographic memory: *Aurochs (Bos primigenius)—an extinct (1627), long-horned wild ox; the ancestor of domestic cattle in Europe and other parts of the world.* Now ready to respond, Peter widened his eyes for effect. "That's amazing. It's been extinct for hundreds of years, hasn't it?"

"The last one, a female, died in a Polish forest in 1627." Himmler appeared pleased with his display of knowledge. "But soon they will again roam the land, their strength and power symbolizing our Reich. That fool Goering has been a big supporter of this project, but for the wrong reason. Bringing back the aurochs will further prove the validity of the process of scientific selection and breeding through which we will create the Master Race. But Goering only cares about using the aurochs to stock massive hunting preserves after we win the war. That's the extent of his vision. Well, enough about that. I really just wanted you to enjoy some of the unique aspects of the Eagle's Nest."

"I can see now why Bormann named it that."

"Bormann didn't name it. In truth he gets upset when anyone calls it that. No, Bormann is very insistent. For him, it is always Kehlsteinhaus—the house on Kehlstein Mountain. The French ambassador, the one who had talked about floating in space, referred to the house as being perched like an eagle's nest. So was born the Eagle's Nest, and the name stuck. But you're quite correct: the name is fitting. You know that eagles all sorts of interesting items to construct their nests. Did you bring any interesting items to our Eagle's Nest?"

"I have this." Peter reached into his inside left breast jacket pocket and produced a packet of folded papers. Opening and smoothing them out, he gave a sheet to Himmler, who pretended to study it before rendering judgment.

"A fairly standard astrological forecast using transits to determine what lies ahead in North Africa for the third week of October. I had my Ahnenerbe astrologers prepare a similar chart."

Just as Peter anticipated. "And it shows nothing extraordinary for Rommel in North Africa during October?"

"Not according to them."

"And of course your astrologers relocated Rommel's birthplace from Germany to his current location."

"Yes, just as you did with Heydrich's horoscope."

"In that case, may I?" With a slight tug Peter removed the paper from Himmler's hand and, with a few exaggerated motions, tore it to pieces. "Worthless."

"Because?" a puzzled Himmler asked.

"Because it uses Rommel as its reference point. Rommel may symbolize the Afrika Korps, but they aren't the same. Just like Rommel, the Afrika Korps has its own unique birth date—February 19, 1941, the date the *Führer* sent an expeditionary force under Rommel's command to assist the Italians in Libya. The Afrika Korps, not Rommel, must be relocated, from Berlin, where it was created, to Libya."

"Yes, that makes sense. Go on."

"Look at this." Peter gave Himmler a second chart for October, with Afrika Korps on it instead of Rommel. When Himmler stared at it too long for Peter's comfort, he stepped in to guide him.

"As you can see, this chart indicates a potentially disastrous event befalling the Afrika Korps during the last part of October."

Himmler stared at the chart again. "Strange. What do you make of it?"

"I didn't know quite what to make of it, *Reichsführer*—until I prepared a chart for the British Eighth Army, Montgomery's command." Peter handed Himmler a third chart. "Using its formation date and applying the appropriate relocation information resulted in the latter part of October being a very fortuitous time."

Himmler looked up from the chart. "However, there is no reason to believe the British will initiate any offensive actions during October. Even if they wanted to, our intelligence clearly indicates that they lack the resources and won't have them in place until mid-November at the earliest."

"Your intelligence might be wrong, *Reichsführer.*"

"So might your charts!" Himmler snapped.

"They might, but they've been correct in the past, as I believe you know, including the one last month I sent back from Egypt."

"I'm very well aware of your abilities, Peter."

"*Reichsführer,* please, I've done what you wanted. I only ask that you think on what I've shown you."

Himmler nodded and placed his hand on Peter's shoulder. "I will. I promise you. And if I was a little short, forgive me. I'm afraid the war has strained even the strongest of us."

Peter found the mention of strain interesting and wondered what might come out if he used some cold reading and tossed a general statement Himmler's way. "Please, there's no need to apologize. But if I may be frank, I have been getting a definite impression of something more immediate that's weighing on your mind."

"I should know that nothing escapes your psychic sense, Peter. Actually I've been considering asking for your assistance. You've heard about Kobo, I'm sure."

Pan for gold and sometimes you find it. "Indeed I have, *Reichsführer.*"

"So has everyone else in Berlin. But I have also heard about Kobo from Goebbels. Continually, and I'm growing weary of his yammering about the ineptitude of my people because they can't apprehend Kobo. Perhaps you can use your skills to help us hone in on him."

"Of course." Peter kicked himself for not letting well enough alone. Now Himmler expected him to find a resistance operative who'd been able to elude the Gestapo and SS with ease.

"As soon as I return to Berlin, I'll have the files on Kobo brought to you. I would appreciate it if you could give this your immediate attention."

"I'll start as soon as the files arrive."

"Thank you. I don't know how I can repay you."

No, you don't, Peter agreed. But very soon you will.

29

Berlin: September 19, 1942
Your Stars Today: Important communications on matters of concern for many are at issue now. Moral, philosophical or religious issues may be raised and debated.

Find Kobo.

Himmler didn't say that exactly, but Peter knew what he meant. And that he had better succeed.

So as soon as he was back in Berlin, Peter turned to Father Fritz for guidance. Father Fritz, however, had nothing immediate to offer except to suggest that Peter, Max and Otto meet with him at week's end after he had a chance to think. It wasn't much, but it was better than nothing.

On the designated day the three arrived at the rectory just after 7:00 P.M. and Hildie directed them to the study. The door was closed.

"He's probably working on his sermon." Max knocked and a familiar voice said, "Come in."

Father Fritz, nestled in his reading chair, was scribbling notes on some sort of leaflet while four teenagers—three boys and one girl—sat facing him.

"Seems we barged into a youth group meeting," Peter said.

Like Father Fritz, the three boys rose, but the girl continued to sit. "You don't know what you barged into, so why venture an opinion?" she barked, her attitude hovering somewhere between anger and annoyance.

"Ingrid, please, can you try being a little more civil to our guests?" Father Fritz said. He was about to make the introductions when one of the boys blurted out, "Maxine Elise. You really are Maxine Elise, aren't you?"

"Since this is a church house, I'll confess. Yes, I really am Maxine Elise." She flashed him a warm smile. "But please, call me Max."

"Max." Beaming, the boy turned to his friends. "Can you believe? Maxine Elise, here, with us."

"But why would Hitler's favorite director be here?" another boy asked.

"We'll get to that," Father Fritz said, regaining control of the conversation. "So this is Max, this is Otto and this is Peter. Now, the other way."

Father Fritz put his hand on Ingrid's shoulder. "This, as you may have guessed, is Ingrid. And here we have . . ." He turned to the boys, pointing as he named them. "Eric, Johan and Ammon." Each nodded in turn. "Now let me finish one last piece of business before we go on."

Father Fritz picked up the leaflet from his chair. "Again I commend you, Ingrid. This is excellent. Perhaps the best one yet."

"Thank you, Father." As Ingrid reached for the sheets her fountain pen rolled from the pad on her lap to the floor. Peter retrieved it and handed it back to her.

"A homework assignment?" he asked.

"It's really none of your concern."

"All right," Father Fritz said. "We're at that point: either I bid you all good-bye or we have some more of Hildie's wonderful refreshments and talk." He swept his eyes across the four young faces. "Last chance. Yes or no?"

Peter glanced at Max, who raised her shoulders slightly, indicating she, too, didn't know what Father Fritz was referring to. Johan, who had been dazzled by Max's presence, responded first with a firm "Yes," quickly followed by Ammon and Eric, who also said, "Yes." Then there was silence.

"We agreed it has to be unanimous," Father Fritz said.

"We know nothing about these people," Ingrid said.

"We know about Max," Johan said. "Everyone knows about her."

"Everyone knows about her films," Ingrid shot back. "The only thing I know about *her* is that she's one of Hitler's favorites."

"We know that Father Fritz trusts her," Ammon said.

"And we're being asked to trust him and agree to something without knowing what it is," Ingrid said.

"Stop it, Ingrid." Eric's lips tightened around his words. "We have always trusted Father Fritz, and with good reason. And we all know that he wouldn't ask for our help unless it was essential."

All eyes were now on Ingrid. "So it's up to me."

Peter had refrained long enough. "Can I ask what's going on?"

"No, you can't!" Ingrid flared. "This isn't your concern, yet, so just keep out of it!"

"You can spend some more time being rude, Ingrid, or you can give us your answer," Father Fritz said.

"Fine. If everyone wants to march blindly I won't be the one to stop you. My answer is yes, since I obviously can't save you from yourselves."

"If you start saving people, I'll be out of a job," Father Fritz said, and everyone, except Ingrid, laughed at his remark. "That's it, then. No turning back. In that case, Max, Peter, Otto, let me introduce my friends here."

"But you already have, Father," Otto reminded him.

"I introduced you to Ingrid, Eric, Ammon and Johan. Now let me introduce you to Kobo."

Unlike the first introduction, this one took some time to sink in. Max's and Otto's expressions said that, like Peter, they were caught by surprise. The revelation was another example of how far Father Fritz's reach extended. It also continued to feed Peter's suspicion that there was another, darker side to the priest, which he would eventually have to confront if the mission was going to succeed. But for now Peter needed to learn about Kobo.

"This is Kobo—four kids?" Peter's remark was both question and statement.

"We're not kids!" Ingrid was defiant. "How dare you come here and pass judgment."

"Whoa, easy." Peter put his hands in the air, taken aback by Ingrid's belligerence. "That's a fact, not a judgment. I mean, how old are you, fifteen?"

"Sixteen."

"In two months." Johan corrected her.

"Sixteen!" Ingrid was more emphatic. "Almost."

"And what about the others?""

"Ammon and I are seventeen, but I'm about to turn eighteen, in two weeks, not two months like some others." Eric didn't acknowledge Ingrid's dirty look. "Johan is sixteen."

"That's what I said, kids." Peter looked at Father Fritz. "I can't understand why you would drag them into danger."

"He didn't drag us anywhere!"

Ingrid was getting more fired up, but Eric jumped in before she could launch a tirade. "Father Fritz had nothing to do with Kobo. The four of us formed it. As for being kids, I wish we could be. But there are no kids in Germany anymore, only commodities, owned by the Reich, by Hitler. What used to be childhood is now a phase of ongoing indoctrination in how to serve the *Führer* without questioning. Children, adults—all are servants of the State, whether willing or not."

"But some of us resist that," Johan said.

"At the risk of your lives," Peter said.

Johan shrugged his shoulders. "Life at any age is cheap in Germany. We've seen some of our friends taken away by the Gestapo, never to return."

"Young people of all ages die in Germany every day," Ammon added. "Most have no say. At least if we die, we'll have had a say. If we die, it'll be for something."

"Which is?" Peter asked.

"Let me." Eric claimed the question. "We want to be remembered. Not for who we were, but for what we did. This is our country and our war as well. Eventually the story of what really happened in Germany will be told. There will be an accounting. In our own small way we want people to know not all German youth accepted Hitler and his horrors. It's important that this is remembered, even if it's only in a footnote."

"And so Kobo was born," Max said.

"We took the name from the Kobolds, mischievous shape-shifting spirits who help humans, but also torment them with tricks," Eric explained. "They're harmless."

"Not always." Peter said. "What about Goldemar?"

"Goldemar?" Eric asked.

This was good: Eric's curiosity, which the others visibly shared, meant Peter was on the verge of winning over his audience, although he still wasn't sure to what end.

"You've never heard of Goldemar, the Kobold King, who preferred to remain invisible? One curious fellow scattered ashes on the ground, hoping to see Goldemar's footprints. Goldemar was furious. He chopped up the man, roasted the pieces, boiled the head and legs and then ate it all, enjoying every bite."

"Maybe we could introduce him to Hitler," Ammon said.

"That's not a bad idea," Peter said. "Goldemar could be very helpful, as long as you didn't get on his wrong side. He had many useful powers, including the ability to see the secret sins of the clergy."

Just as Peter intended, all eyes shifted to Father Fritz, who countered by quipping, "In my case, Goldemar would need very big eyes."

"You seem to know a lot about Kobolds," said Ingrid.

So, Ingrid was still alive. Of course Peter knew a lot about Kobolds. Kobolds were part of the fairy family. And if Sir Arthur, who believed in the existence of fairies, was your mentor, you learned everything about them. Everything.

"Maybe it's because you've been ordered to devote a lot of time to Kobolds," Ingrid continued. "Maybe you've fooled Father Fritz. Maybe you're not who you pretend to be."

Not only still alive, Ingrid was still kicking. And Peter was her sole target. Granted she was partly right on the pretending.

"And who am I pretending to be?"

"Why don't you tell us?" Ingrid said.

"I know Father Fritz vouches for you," Eric said. "But Ingrid has a point. We really know nothing about you."

It was just so easy, Peter thought. So easy. Like some rube handing over a wad of bills and begging Peter to con him. OK, folks, if that's the way you want it, welcome to my world. "That's true, you don't and it's not fair, since I know so much about all of you."

Having been through it numerous times, Max, Otto and Father Fritz could tell what was coming, but the four youths were confused.

"You told him about us?" Eric said to Father Fritz.

"You know better."

"Then what is it you think you know about us?" Eric asked Peter.

"I'm not sure you want me to talk about some of it."

Eric persisted. "Go ahead, please."

"You're sure you want Father Fritz to know his former altar boy, the person who told him about Kobo, has been flirting with communism, even while he's the poster boy for the Hitler Youth, an elite member holding its highest rank?"

Peter's response left Eric openmouthed but unable to speak.

Strike one, as Peter prepared to deliver his next pitch. "And Eric's not the only one with other interests, is he, Johan? Except being a member of the Swing Kids is more about rebellion than politics, right? Wearing a zoot suit instead of the slacks and sweater you have on now, dancing to forbidden American swing music and listening to hot jazz with a bunch of others."

Johan turned his head this way and that. "Did one of you tell him?"

"Don't be stupid," Ammon said. "We just met him."

Strike two and Peter was hot. One more to go. "Right you are, Ammon. Just like they didn't tell me you're a devoted Mormon."

"How did you know that?" Johan asked.

"Magic."

"No, please, really," Johan pressed. "How did you know?"

"So you don't believe in magic. Then how about this: Ammon told me. Just like you and Eric told me about yourselves. Only you didn't realize it."

"Peter, stop torturing them," Max said.

"Anything for you, my lady." Peter blew her a kiss. "Let's start with you, Eric. I've been admiring your Himmler haircut—the sides shaved nearly bald and the top respectfully long and neatly trimmed. It's a giveaway. And your ring. You do a very good job of keeping its face hidden, but you slipped once or twice, so I saw the eagle clutching the sword and hammer and the swastika in a central wreath. I've seen this ring before, at a reception. A Hitler Youth was proudly showing it off, bragging that it was awarded to a special few who demonstrated outstanding leadership skills."

"And you remembered that?" Johan said.

"He remembers everything," Otto said. *"Everything!"*

"Actually, Eric, even when you were a youngster, your face radiated the confidence of a leader," Peter said. "I noticed that immediately in one of the pictures hanging in the rectory hallway. You and three other boys were attired in altar robes."

"And you recognized me?" Eric asked. "I was only ten."

"You have very strong facial features. I meant it when I called you a Hitler Youth poster boy: blond, blue-eyed, rectangular face, strong, jutting jaw. You're a living promotion for a better Germany through eugenics."

"But the communist group. Certainly my face didn't reveal that."

"No, your speech did. When you talked about the Reich treating people as commodities, you sounded exactly like a young Karl Marx. You've picked up a bit of communist jargon from your association. Better be careful."

"And me—what about me?" Johann asked enthusiastically. "How did you know I was a Swing Kid?"

"You smelled like one."

Johann's eyes narrowed, but Peter put him at ease. "Not your body—your hair. It's much longer than Eric's, even though it's unkempt now, not slicked back as it was yesterday when you were at a Swing Kid gathering. That's the thing about using brilliantine—it's hard to wash out, even if you could get your hands on soap and shampoo. Sugar water works just as well, but then sugar's rationed, too."

Johann grew defensive. "That doesn't mean I'm a Swing Kid. Maybe I'm just a nonconformist."

"A nonconformist with an excellent grasp of complex rhythms. I suspected you might be a Swing Kid, but I wanted to make sure. You probably weren't consciously aware of my humming while we were waiting for Father Fritz and Ingrid, but your subconscious was. You were tapping on the arm of your chair. My seemingly mindless humming was actually a swing rhythm—pairs of eighth notes played like triplets. The first eighth note is accented and held a fraction longer than the second. Then I stopped humming, but you kept tapping out the rhythm, going beyond my simple four-four time to nine-eight time. That's not easy unless you know what you're doing. No, you're a Swing Kid."

"And what did I do to indicate I belong to the Church of Jesus Christ of Latter-Day Saints?" Ammon asked.

"Calling the religion by its proper name only confirms what I surmised. Actually, what you didn't do, not what you did, said you were a Mormon. You're the only one who didn't have coffee—real coffee—with Hildie's

delicious pastries and cakes. No tea, either. Of course, that doesn't necessarily mean anything, unless your name is Ammon. Ammon's not a very
common first name in Germany, except among Mormons. According to the
Book of Mormon, Ammon was a great missionary in ancient America."

"Circus tricks." Ingrid scorned Peter's explanations. "You want our help
with circus tricks? But you avoided saying anything about me. Have you
run out of circus tricks?"

"Don't worry—I won't reveal your secrets," Peter said.

"You mean you can't reveal my secrets." Ingrid appealed to the rest of the
room. "Don't you see what a fraud this man is? Oh, I'll admit he's clever. A
clever fraud. A con man." She looked at Peter. "Do you deny it?"

"Being a con man? No."

"Sweetheart, he's not what you think," Max came to Peter's defense, but
Ingrid would have none of it.

"Then go ahead. Prove me wrong. Tell them something about me nobody knows. I give you permission. If it's accurate, I'll say so."

"Don't make me do this." Peter was sincere. Earlier he'd wanted to set
up Ingrid for this moment. But now he realized the possible consequences
and, uncharacteristically, he drew back.

"I insist. Otherwise, I leave now."

"Ingrid, we all agreed," Eric said.

"Or I leave now." Ingrid was even more defiant. "Well, Mr. Circus Con
Man?"

Peter took a deep breath. "You asked for it, then."

"This should be good," Ingrid said.

"I think not," Peter replied. "You see Eric, Ammon and Johan are members of Kobo because of moral and religious convictions. But you have a
very personal reason for being involved, don't you?"

"I have no idea what you're talking about." In contrast to her earlier out-
bursts, Ingrid's response was firm but calm.

"*You* do, but your friends don't. Unlike them, you helped create Kobo so
you could get personal revenge."

"What kind of revenge?" Ingrid's voice was a little weaker.

"Revenge for your boyfriend."

"Ingrid doesn't have a boyfriend!" Johann shouted out. "Who would want
to be her boyfriend?"

"Shut up, you ass!" Ingrid snapped.

"I can stop now," Peter said.

"No, go on, since it's clear you have no idea what you're talking about."
Despite being tentative, it was a dare, and Peter loved dares.

"I'm talking about the boy who was your childhood friend and became something more when you both grew older. I'm talking about the boy who was your first love, who produced emotions you never felt before. I'm talking about the boy the Nazis hauled off to a concentration camp because, unlike you, he was a Jew. I'm talking about Abraham. I'm talking about the dead."

Just like that, Ingrid broke, slouching and then sliding to the floor, as if all the life had been suddenly sucked from her body.

But Peter didn't stop. "And now I'm talking about a girl who grew up in privilege and wants life to always go her way, a girl who thought it was so daring to be involved with a Jew and who's reveling in her new status as a martyr, a girl who doesn't want to be bothered distinguishing between friend and foe, so she avoids honesty. I'm talking about you, Ingrid. I'm talking about you. So, Ingrid, tell me: how do you like my circus tricks now?"

With her curled up on the floor Ingrid's pathetic moaning filled a room numbed by Peter's disclosures. Max dropped to her knees, lifted Ingrid's limp body and held it close to her own. "How could you be so unfeeling?" she demanded of Peter. "How could you be so cruel?"

"Do you really think this is what I wanted, that I take any joy in it? Here's a more important question: do you think Himmler's goons would show more compassion if they had Ingrid in their grasp? So far it's all been about whether I pass muster. Well, what about Kobo? Do its members pass muster or will they threaten what we're trying to do? You know what word you never see on a gravestone, Max? 'Bravado,' yet it's killed an awful lot of people. These kids are loaded with bravado and I don't want it killing them *or* me."

"He's right, Max," Father Fritz said. "Peter was harsher than I would have liked, although I understand why. It's not about what he did, but why he did it."

"I'm sorry for that." Peter crouched down and took Ingrid in his arms, placing her back in the chair. "Some tea perhaps?"

Otto, already a step ahead of Peter, was there almost immediately with a cup and saucer. He placed it on the chair's wooden arm and retreated. Ingrid was bent over, lump-like. Peter lifted her head gently, then took the cup and pressed it to her lips, tilting it so a little of the tea trickled into her mouth. As soon as he released her she slumped over again.

"I hope eventually you'll forgive me, Ingrid. Until then, I hope you'll at least believe Father Fritz when he says what I did was important. May I just ask you one more thing: did Ammon, Eric and Johan know about Abraham?"

When Ingrid didn't respond, Peter turned to the others. "Did you know?" The three answered, with either a shake of the head or a muted "no."

He turned back to Ingrid. "Don't you see how important that information was for them? I'll bet you knew that Ammon was a Mormon, that Johan was a Swing Kid and that Eric—well, that Eric was and is a lot of things, didn't you?"

"We thought we knew all about each other," Eric said. "Ingrid told us she lost a friend to the Nazis and that convinced her to take decisive measures. But she never really explained the extent of it."

Saying nothing more, Peter started back to his chair, but Ingrid reached out and caught the leg of his trousers. "Please. How did you know? How did you know everything? I never said—how did you know?"

"Circus tricks," Peter said.

"Please. Don't joke with me. Don't throw it back in my face. Don't make me beg you, though I will. How did you really know? Is there a file somewhere?"

"There's no file. It really was circus tricks. Just a little more refined."

"Tell them, Peter," Max said. "I'm sure they realize by now how extraordinary you are."

Ingrid was still hunched up, nestled on a diagonal in her chair. "Please."

"It's the same as with the others. You told me, both directly and through some of your possessions. The first giveaway was your pen. When I picked it up from the floor, I studied it."

"But you only had it a few seconds," Ingrid said.

"Believe me, that's all he needs," Otto said.

"I know about pens and I could tell right away that it wasn't yours. You're right-handed. But look at the pen nib."

Ingrid took the pen from the table and held the tip close to her eyes, squinting as she examined it.

"Do you see how it's been cut to produce a slight oblique angle to the edge?"

"I never noticed that before."

"That's done to make the pen easier for a left-handed writer to use. You'll also see that the nib wasn't made by Montblanc. It has none of the company's telltale markings. It was custom crafted, which can be costly. There are other, even more significant clues. May I have it for a moment?"

Ingrid gave Peter the pen, and he ran his eyes over it more slowly than he had initially. "It's magnificent. I like pens, but Father Fritz is passionate about them. You've seen it?"

"Seen and envied it," Father Fritz said.

"It's an early-model Montblanc, isn't it, Father?"

"Nineteen thirteen. The first model to have Montblanc's white snow-flake symbol on the cap."

"Which, I believe, is the same year that Abraham's father received it. These are his initials here." Peter rubbed his finger over the cap of the pen. "It was a bar mitzvah gift from his father, who had it engraved. The second set of initials is Abraham's." Peter held the pen up and pointed to them. "His father had them engraved when he passed the pen on."

"But how did you know his name was Abraham?" Eric asked.

"From the first letter of the initials, an *A*."

"Many names, including mine, start with an *A*," Ammon said.

"Which is why I used the science of guessing."

"Guessing isn't a science," Johan said.

"It is the way he does it," Otto offered.

"By tradition, a bar mitzvah fountain pen is passed on to the firstborn son. Abraham was the first patriarch, the father of the Jews as well as the Christians and the Muslims. First patriarch equals first son equals Abraham."

"But it could have been Adam, who was the first man," Eric noted

"But not the first Jew," Peter said. "Abraham was. That's why Abraham is a common Jewish name. And since in Judaism it's customary to name a child after a deceased relative, there was a high probability that there had been an Abraham in the family."

If Peter's audience was captivated before, they were now enthralled. Even Ingrid.

"But what if you were wrong?" Eric asked.

Again Otto supplied the answer. "He would have figured something out right on the spot. He always does."

"There's also a third set of initials on the pen cap," Peter said. "The initials belonging to Abraham and his father are beautifully engraved and done by the same person. The style is unmistakable. But the third set is totally different. The engraving is crude—a do-it-yourself job. And instead of three letters—which represent the owners first, middle and last names—there are four: *bsrt*. Those letters don't represent a blood relation."

"They stand for me!" Ingrid's cry was filled with emotion not anger.

"I know they do," Peter said, trying his best to console her.

"How can they?" Ammon asked. "No part of your full name starts with one of those letters."

"The letters don't stand for a person," Peter said. "They stand for a word—*beshert*."

"What kind of word is *beshert*?" Eric asked, speaking for the others in the room.

"Yiddish," said Peter, who learned the language from Houdini, a fluent speaker. "It means 'soul mate,' the person who's meant for you."

"I still don't understand," Johan said.

"According to Jewish legend, each soul has a partner. Forty days before a child is born, the angels shout out the name of that partner. Later, when those two souls meet on earth, they recognize each other, fall in love and become as one." Peter looked at Max. Was she his soul mate? Was that what the Gypsy meant when she said he'd meet the love of his life? He turned back to Ingrid. "Abraham told you the legend and you engraved the third set of letters."

"And I've lost my soul mate," Ingrid said, her voice catching. Max, who hadn't left Ingrid's side, again embraced her.

Father Fritz rose, took a few steps and knelt down next to Max and Ingrid. "It's only a legend, you know. Very beautiful, but still a legend. There's another Jewish legend that says we have many soul mates. Besides a soul mate for marriage, there are soul mates, for example, who teach us important things about life and help us grow as human beings. I've always liked this legend better, perhaps because there's a part of me that believes it. So, yes, Abraham was your soul mate, but that doesn't mean that the two of you were destined to be man and wife. Perhaps he was the soul mate meant to teach you about love and about loss, to teach you about resiliency and about courage."

Ingrid dug her fingers into Max's back, clinging more tightly as Father Fritz spoke. She was still crying and so was Max.

"And, yes, your two souls were and are intertwined and always will be, in this life and in the life to come," Father Fritz continued.

Ingrid broke loose from Max and placed her hands on Father Fritz's shoulders. "Why did God take him from me?"

"God didn't; Hitler did. God gives us the ability to choose our actions and the responsibility to answer for our choices. If God directed our every move, then God would be a dictator, no better than Hitler. It's all right to be angry with God. It's even all right to hate God when the hurt is so bad. But if you really want to set things straight, then God isn't the target. Neither is Peter. The Reich leaders are. We have to make them answer for their choices. And if you work with Peter and the rest of us, that's what I hope we'll be able to do."

There was no denying it—this guy was good, Peter thought. Father Fritz could have brought in a fortune at revival meetings by convincing the lame they could walk and the blind they could see. For the moment, it was enough that Ingrid bought what he said and was now sitting straight in her chair and sobbing less. Still, Peter felt an urge to say something more to her, which he did as he gave back the pen. "You understand Abraham would never have given this to anyone except—"

"His own son." The tears began welling again in Ingrid's eyes.

"As a bar mitzvah gift, just like his father gave the pen to him. But he gave the pen to you because he sensed the Nazis would take him and that he would never have a son, or a daughter or a wife. You were the one person outside of his family whom he cared deeply about and he gave you this pen because he knew you would use it to keep his memory alive."

"But I can't." Ingrid put the pen on the table. "You were right: I'm spoiled and selfish."

"So am I, sometimes. But only sometimes." Peter took the pen and put it back in her hand. "Abraham could see the real Ingrid, the one who was writing something with that pen when we arrived. Would you mind letting me see that?"

Ingrid reached down to the floor on the left side of the chair and caught hold of the paper. "Here."

"Kobo's next radio broadcast," Peter said after glancing at the sheet. "Perfect. Father Fritz, tell me, when you write something, say a letter or sermon, how do you start?"

"How do I start? Usually 'Dear' and the name of the person I'm writing to, or 'Brothers and Sisters in Christ.'"

"Before that."

"Before that?" Father Fritz thought for a moment. "You mean the cross?"

"Exactly. Priests and very observant Catholics will often draw a cross at the top of the page before they start writing. Let me show you something, Ingrid." Peter placed the paper on the table. "I want you to draw a stick figure right here. . . ." He pointed to the top of the page. "With its legs spread apart and its arms outstretched and bent at the elbows so the hands are raised toward the heavens. Can you do that for me?" Although clearly puzzled, Ingrid nodded her head up and down, then leaned over, picked up her pen and did as Peter asked. "Excellent," Peter said when she finished and held the paper up for all to see, then put it back on the table. "Now scratch it out."

Ingrid's puzzlement visibly changed to confusion, but again she did as told.

"Good." Once more, Peter lifted the paper, showed it to the others and returned it to the table. "You have now performed a variant on the old Jewish custom of testing a pen by writing the name Amalek in Hebrew."

"Who?" Johan said.

"Amalek was an ancient genocidal anti-Semite." Father Fritz opened a Bible that was on the table and thumbed through it. "Here we are. *Deuteronomy Twenty-five, verses seventeen through nineteen: Remember what Amalek did to you on your journey after you left Egypt—how, undeterred by fear of God, he surprised you on the march, when you were famished and weary, and cut down all the stragglers in your rear . . . You shall blot out the memory of Amalek from under heaven. Do not forget!*"

Strange. Father Fritz appeared to be reading, but Peter could tell he was reciting from memory. Why, he wondered, then Peter resumed his explanation. "So, you write the name Amalek in Hebrew with the pen and then scratch it out. If the pen doesn't skip, then it's good. Today Amalek is Hitler and what you drew was the ancient Hebrew pictograph for the letter *H*. Kind of resembles Hitler making one of his speeches, doesn't it?"

For the first time Ingrid smiled.

"And now you have obliterated him. Tell me, Ingrid, is the pen good?"

"The pen is excellent!" she buoyantly proclaimed.

"Then each time you write an anti-Nazi piece, start by drawing and striking out the symbol. By blotting out Hitler, you'll be honoring Abraham's memory and using the pen as he intended."

"Thank you," Ingrid said softly. Then she stood up. "My vote is 'Yes.'"

"You already said that," Ammon reminded her.

"My vote is 'Yes' with one condition."

"Here we go again," Ammon sighed.

"Will you ever learn to hold your tongue, Ammon?" The scowl Ingrid gave Ammon was gone when she faced Peter. "About what you're involved in—"

"Please, Ingrid, I'm sure Father Fritz has explained that I can't give you any details."

"I wanted to ask if I'll have a lot of opportunities to practice drawing stick figures."

"I guarantee it."

"Then my vote is 'Yes' with no conditions and no hesitation."

As Ingrid sat, Father Fritz rose. "Thank God, finally it's done. You have a fine team to assist you, Peter. Ingrid writes strong pieces, which Eric, Kobo's leader, reads, his voice disguised by a device that Ammon created, just as he did the transmitter. Ammon's a genius at inventing. And Johan? Johan's smart and fearless, a valuable combination. He sets everything up— itching powder in movie houses, salt on railroad tracks. So, with a nod to your mentor, Sir Arthur—" Father Fritz lifted his coffee cup in a toast and everyone stood to join him. "Here's to our version of Das Freikorps aus der *Bakerstrasse*. Although they're not exactly street urchins, may they prove as helpful to you in Berlin as the Baker Street Irregulars were to Sherlock Holmes in London!"

Although he realized that by being Kobo Ingrid, Eric, Johan and Ammon already had put themselves in serious danger, Peter still felt uneasy about using them. He also realized that without their help the mission could suffer a serious setback. And their arguments had made sense. So he accepted Father Fritz's pronouncement. It was indeed done.

"A fine toast, Father, which needs one small addition." Peter lifted his cup. "As of this moment, *das Spiel ist im Gange*"—the game is afoot!"

30

Erkner: September 25, 1942
Your Stars Today: The Sun's influence on Uranus makes this
a dynamic period, one in which taking advantage of unusual or unconventional opportunities may reap rewards.

It was raining in Berlin's wealthy Grunewald district, a soaking morning rain that forced people leaving this bucolic setting for the city's crowded center to seek refuge in the rustic—and dry—train station.

But not everyone was headed to Berlin.

Down a flight of stairs, in an adjacent yard, the train had already arrived at Platform 17. Normally it would be loaded with commercial goods, but today there would be passengers—more than two hundred of them, young and old, who had spent hours outside waiting for SS guards to cram them into four cattle cars.

They were headed for Auschwitz.

The train to Berlin came and went, but still the train to Auschwitz was running behind schedule. The SS hadn't anticipated this many Jews, and packing them posed problems. Even with five cars it would have been difficult; with four it was almost impossible.

But the SS guards were used to making freight fit, ramming people continuously with spare railroad ties, smacking down the little ones and shoving them into tiny spaces—a slight opening between some legs, a minuscule gap between floor slats. It wasn't pretty, but it worked. Besides, the situation would right itself at the first water tower stop when the SS guards opened the cars and had the living toss out the dead. That was always good for a 10 to 20 percent cargo reduction. The only bad part was the stink of sweat and excrement that whooshed out like air in a vacuum can when the doors opened.

War was hell.

Finally finished, the SS guards went down the line, sliding the doors shut, inevitably mangling a resistant arm or leg in the process. The locks were the last step, allowing the impatient engineer, slightly hungover and angry over losing so much time, to sound the whistle and slowly roll out of the yard, building up speed as he prepared to "run the Ring," the railway line that circled Berlin. It wasn't a full run: he only had to pass through three of the Ring's many stations, but at each one there was the possibility of track delays because of higher-priority Wehrmacht trains carrying soldiers or war supplies.

Since the war on the Eastern Front had intensified, these delays had been more frequent. The last time, he waited for five hours at the Putzlitz-brücke station, while the captive Jews shouted and screamed and wedged notes pleading for help through crevices in the car walls. People gathered to gawk—at the station, along the roads and atop the bridges. It was exactly the type of spectacle the SS wanted to avoid when they chose sleepy Grunewald as a Jew staging area.

But this time the engineer was lucky. Not only was the Putzlitzbrücke station clear, but Gesundbrunnen as well. With no audience, let the Jews make all the noise they wanted. He could care less. He just wanted to make good time to Auschwitz, where he and a certain female guard would be sharing her "bonus" for effectively disciplining inmates: three days at Solahütte, the nearby SS resort on the Sola River, where he could wash away the Jew stink.

Don't mess me up now! he prayed silently but fervently as he slowed into Rummelsburg, the last station. Please don't mess me up now!

Somebody answered his prayer. His track was empty, so once he was through the station the chances of further holdups lessened considerably. He could already visualize her—his Auschwitz guard—out of uniform and in a skirt and blouse and, later, in nothing. The images stayed and played with him as he rubbed, then pulled down on the throttle and, oblivious to the rain, sped toward Erkner, just outside of Berlin. The rain limited visibility, but the route was straightforward from here to Frankfurt and then into Poland, and he knew it well.

The engineer glanced outside at the signal light, its faint green glow a haze against the sheets of water. That was his go-ahead and he accelerated to 70 mph, just a notch above proper for the long stretch of track ahead.

But much too fast for the construction spur tracks that suddenly appeared.

There was no signal! he screamed in his mind, when he saw them and yanked up on the throttle, making matters worse. The locomotive veered sharply to the right, catching the rails for a second or two, then wildly careening off, skating on a sixty-degree angle and then flipping on its side, still moving by momentum until nature's brakes—the rocks and trees it crashed into—took hold.

The weight of the rear cars pushed them forward with tremendous force, squeezing them together like the bellows of an accordion and producing loud, discordant sounds from the human reeds and valves inside, some damaged beyond repair. Like the locomotive, the cars, too, jumped the tracks, the first rolling from side to side on its wooden skin, stopping only when the other cars piled onto it, creating a mangled mountain.

The impact shattered the cars, resulting in an avalanche of bodies, alive and not, Jew and Nazi, and those too maimed to tell. Some were snagged by rubble as they rolled from the doors; others made it made it all the way to the ground, where they lay dazed or dead.

Next, those who weren't thrown out by the crash and could move emerged, seeking footholds for a descent. A few simply took their chances and jumped. Others remained in the cars, refusing to abandon the severely injured, whether family, friends or strangers.

Amid the chaos, groups of Jews took off into the dense forest, the strong helping the weak, while the SS guards who were still able tried to regroup. A band of five started after the Jews but halted abruptly when they heard their commander, able to shout but not walk.

"Forget the fucking Jews! They'll die in the woods or be captured when they come out! We have injured here! Get back and help them! Help the ones trapped in the cars!"

Turning back, the guards were suddenly set upon by a pack of younger Jews, bearing makeshift weapons: sticks, rocks and wreckage remains. The Jews struck before the guards could draw their pistols.

It was over quickly and now the Jews, armed with those pistols, headed toward the fifteen or so guards scattered on the ground. The first shots came, in different directions, from those Nazis who, despite their wounds and limited mobility, could still fire a gun well enough to score three deadly hits before the Jews could fan out and respond in kind. With the immediate threat removed the Jews quickly killed the guards on the ground, starting with the commander, then disappeared among the trees.

And through it all, the engineer lay lifeless, crushed in his cab, while five hundred miles away a certain female concentration camp guard, rewarded for her part in keeping Jews captive, prepared for three days of fun, blissfully unaware of her part in setting Jews free.

Berlin: September 29, 1942
Your Stars Today: Concentrate on research and investigations right now and be on the lookout for opportunities to gain power.

No. 8 Prinz-Albrecht-Strasse was the most dreaded address in Berlin. Once it was the location of a fine art museum and people would freely flock to it.

However, since 1933, when it became the headquarters of the Gestapo, most people went there only if forced. Peter was the exception. Having been summoned by Himmler, Peter was treated like a visiting dignitary from the moment he walked into the palatial arched entrance hall. Subjected to a cursory and cordial screening, he received a "guided tour" while being escorted to Himmler's office. Peter was, however, keenly aware that beneath him, in the bowels of the building, people were being brutally interrogated and that any who survived would be confined to one of the thirty-nine cellar cells to await transfer to a concentration camp.

After more pleasant greetings from the staff attending to Himmler's outer chambers, Peter was ushered into the inner sanctum, which, like those of all the top Nazis, was a study in excess. Large and cold, appointed with artifacts more political than personal, Himmler's office was neat and organized, befitting a man whose OSS psychological profile characterized him as being "obsessed with order and detail" and "compulsive in completing tasks." When Himmler was a schoolboy, his classmates would say, *"Der Heini macht es schön* Heini will take care of it," and Heini—now Heinrich— still did, whether the "it" was creating the SS or exterminating the Jews.

"Herr Kepler . . . Peter." Himmler rose from a desk that seemed to swallow him. "I noticed your interest in Heydrich's death mask on the shelf. Death masks are tolerable only at certain times and on special occasions, either as a memory or as an example. Here it's both." He made his way to the front of the desk. "It was good of you to come on such short notice. I hope I didn't cause you too much inconvenience."

"Not at all, *Reichsführer.* I was actually taking a few days away from the documentary to concentrate on your special project."

"That's very interesting." Himmler walked over to a couch. "Please, come join me here. Much better for conversation."

So this was to be a conversation. Peter was already certain of the topic. He simply didn't know how Himmler would frame it. Now he did.

"You have seen the newspapers about the sabotaged train."

There was no way to avoid seeing them. Goebbels decided he could use the crash to turn people against Kobo and perhaps shake loose some information. "Tragic."

"Good German soldiers—SS men—murdered. I called their families. It tore at my heart. What sort of world are we living in?"

"One that the *Führer* will make better, with your assistance."

"Yes, but unfortunately that will not happen tomorrow or the day after tomorrow, which makes bringing Kobo to justice essential. He has risen to a new level. Before it was resistance broadcasts and pranks designed to cause chaos. That has now changed. There's no telling what this deranged beast will do next."

The deranged beast would do whatever Peter needed done. As Himmler said, previously Kobo had committed acts of annoyance, disruptive but not deadly. But Kobo had assured Peter they were capable of more if necessary, as they proved when he asked them to sabotage the train. Salting the track switch to short it out required rain, which was beyond Kobo's control. So they rewired the signal light, ensuring that the train would be routed onto the siding. All of them—Peter, Max, Father Fritz, Otto, the four youths— knew there would be injuries and probably deaths; they had debated this at length and concluded that most of the train's "cargo" would die anyway, if not that day, then at Auschwitz. As it turned out, the crash was a gift of life for many, which only put more pressure on Himmler and set him up perfectly for Peter.

"There must not be another next, which is why I am channeling all my efforts and abilities into finding Kobo for you, *Reichsführer*. But there is so little to go on, even when using less conventional investigative methods."

Himmler thought for a moment. "Do you suppose it would be worth it for you to look at the items found near the altered track switch that caused the train crash?"

He was playing right into Peter's plan. "Perhaps. It's certainly worth trying."

Himmler stood, went to his desk and pressed a button on his intercom. "Have the evidence from the latest Kobo incident brought to my office immediately."

"At once, *Reichsführer*," came the slightly crackled response.

"You understand that my people have carefully examined these objects and found no clues," Himmler said, and rejoined Peter on the sofa. "I can't believe that they missed anything."

"Possibly not. Or possibly they didn't use the right examination technique. We shall see."

"Do you have something in mind?"

Peter had an idea but wasn't yet sure of it. Thinking on his feet always inspired him. "Respectfully, *Reichsführer*, it would be better if I explain while I demonstrate."

"Then we'll wait," Himmler said, and for the next ten minutes engaged Peter in small talk, although, like a child eager to unwrap a present, he kept looking at the door, as if his gaze would make the evidence arrive faster. When the knock finally came, Himmler bolted up and opened the door himself, surprising the box-toting underling who had expected to hear "Enter."

"Set it on the table in front of the sofa," Himmler directed, "then leave us."

As soon as they were alone again, Himmler sat next to Peter and removed the box lid. "This is what they found."

"Have you gone through it yourself?" Peter asked.

"To what purpose? We have highly trained people for this sort of work. I trust their abilities. That's why I don't know what you hope to discover."

"Maybe nothing." Peter began rummaging through the objects in the box. "No. No." He lifted out a slab of plaster, the cast of a heel mark, studied it and put it back. "No. It just may be that . . . what's this?" Peter fished out a small, tarnished silver lighter. He flicked up the top with his thumb and turned the flint wheel, which resulted in an inch-high flame. "This may fill the bill." Peter closed the top over the flame.

"How?" Himmler took the lighter from Peter's hand. "It's a cheap Myflam lighter. People all over Germany use one. There were no fingerprints, or I would have been informed. This is worthless." Himmler tossed the lighter on the table.

"Not necessarily." Peter picked up the lighter and placed it into the outstretched palm of his left hand.

"Do you see something?"

"I'm not looking for something."

Although silent, Himmler rubbed his fingers against the back of his neck for a few seconds and then crossed his arms on his lap, the warning signs of frustration about to turn into exasperation. Peter loved the rush that came from bringing a mark right to the brink. But Himmler wasn't just any mark, and any mistake in timing could have an unpredictable and unwelcome result. So Peter quickly moved on. "What I will, however, be doing . . ." Peter pressed his index and forefinger against the lighter. "Is feeling for something."

"Feeling for what?"

"Energy, transmitted through vibrations. As you know, *Reichsführer,* energy may be converted into different forms, but it can never be destroyed. Who we are is conveyed through the energy in our individual aura. That aura, in turn, permeates everything within a certain range of it—our psychic territory—and is retained. That's the reason we can communicate with the souls of those who came before us. Think of your own experiences, *Reichsführer,* for example when you slept on the tomb that bears the mortal remains of Henry the Fowler, your previous self. Didn't you feel the connection?"

"I did indeed. It was very mystical." Himmler was intrigued.

"And yet very scientific. One day the entire world will appreciate how advanced the work of the Ahnenerbe researchers really is, when compared to the more conventional thinking, much of it put forth by Jews like Einstein." Peter continued to spew nonsense and watch Himmler agree with it. He was definitely hooked. "*Reichsführer*, could I ask you to turn off all the lights and other electrical sources in the office. It's possible to distinguish between residual energy contained in objects, but artificial energy can make it impossible to focus on that residual energy."

Peter had spouted more gibberish, but it must have sounded good to Himmler. He was scurrying around shutting things off.

"Better?" Himmler asked when he was done.

"Let's find out." Peter placed the lighter, which he had set down, back in the palm of his left hand and again pressed his fingers against it. "I'm getting some weak vibrations. Are you certain everything is off?"

"Quite certain."

"Then it could be— Wait!" Peter rose and, as if in a semi-trance, made his way to and then behind Himmler's desk. He crouched down and a moment later bounded up, some wires in his hand. "You had neglected these."

"You just pulled out the phone wires!" Himmler exclaimed.

"Because they were causing interference. Getting new phones is easy, unlike getting Kobo. Now let's see what happens." Peter sat, put the lighter in has palm, positioned his fingers and, after a few seconds, closed his eyes.

"Peter, do you—"

"Quiet!" Boy, did that feel good. Not only didn't Himmler make another noise, but Peter could hear him trying to take softer breaths. He *really* wanted Kobo. "I need to concentrate." And Peter's furrowed brow gave the impression that he was indeed trying to tap into the lighter's energy. In reality he was thinking about what he would have done if Himmler's cracker jack agents hadn't found the lighter, which Kobo had deliberately planted. But here it was and Peter was ready to give Himmler a great show, broken up into little chunks, like spurts of energy, each of them power packed.

"Old. No, not old. Older. A man. An older man. In his fifties. Mid-fifties, maybe. No, mid-sixties. Rough hands. A worker. No, a builder. No, not a builder, a worker. A skilled worker. A factory. Other places. Many other places. But always the factory. Isolated. Alone. A lot of artificial energy. Aura fluctuating. Parts destroyed. Tubes. Batteries. Obscured. Gone."

Peter kept his eyes shut for nearly a minute, letting his words and their effect sink in. Then he opened and closed them repeatedly, as if to make sure any contact was broken. "You can turn the lights back on if you wish, *Reichsführer.*"

But Himmler was too engrossed in what had just happened to bother. "Fascinating."

"It was a fragmented energy field, I'm afraid. This lighter has spent too long near high artificial-energy sources, which corrupted the aura."

"Sources like radio transmission equipment?"

"Certainly that has to be considered. A man in his mid-fifties, who is probably skilled in many areas, including electricity. He moves around a lot, but his base seems to be a factory."

"You said 'isolated.'"

"It could be the factory, it could be him or it could be both."

"How certain are you of what you read from the lighter?"

"Gathering information in this way has a long history of verification. In any event, you have a busy schedule, *Reichsführer,* and I'm anxious to get back and resume working with this new information."

"Then what you learned will help you?"

"It already has helped me, *Reichsführer.*" Coupled with Himmler's reactions, it had helped Peter decide what Kobo would do next.

Die.

31

Berlin: October 6, 1942
Your Stars Today: With the Sun in conjunction with Mars,
make your actions speak louder than your words. But exercise caution: strained relations with others can lead to violent incidents.

The glow was barely visible through the grime-tinted windows, but it was definitely there, coming from the ninth floor of the abandoned factory, on the river side of the building, where only a sliver of land separated brick from water that was notorious for its swift and unpredictable currents. The factory was in a part of Berlin where sensible people rarely ventured, and certainly never at night. The block it was on was completely dark. The street-lights had stopped functioning years ago and the city government hadn't bothered to fix them. As a location for matters best kept secret, only one thing kept it from being perfect.

Hitler Youth.

Not just any Hitler Youth, but the most obedient, ambitious and ruth-less. The Reich Security Administration, having stretched its normal avail-able patrol resources to their limits and placing little trust in the regular Berlin police service, turned to members of the *Streifendienst,* the Hitler Youth's internal police force, giving them power and guns and assigning them to keep watch over various sections of the city. Those who performed well became members of the Gestapo when they turned eighteen. Those who didn't were sent to the Eastern Front.

With so much at stake, little wonder that Klaus was thrilled when Eric showed him the flicker in the window. Klaus never would have noticed it himself, but Eric would have, even if he hadn't known in advance that it would be there. As smart and perceptive as Eric was, Klaus was dumb and oblivious. However, he was also obedient, fawning and devoid of any moral compass, qualities he openly displayed in hopes that the Gestapo officials would take notice. Eric, who had been teamed with Klaus before, certainly did, which was why he made sure they were assigned to work together this particular week. "Do you think someone's up there?" Klaus stared at the window and then shone his flashlight on his watch. "At eleven o'clock?"

"Turn off that light!" Eric barked. "If someone *is* up there, you don't want him seeing us. There was nothing last night when we patrolled. There has to be a reason for the change."

"What do you think we should do?"

"Let's go around to the door and check it."

"Yes, good idea. Let's check the door."

As they walked around the building, Eric drew Klaus' attention to the remnants of a fire escape, part of it still attached to the brick wall, part of it on the ground.

"I nearly tripped on that yesterday while you were over by the river taking a leak," Eric said. Klaus thanked him for the warning.

When they reached the entrance to the building, Klaus jiggled the door handle and pushed. "Look. The door's not bolted. Do you think Kobo did this?"

"Maybe. Or it could have been someone else. These deserted buildings attract a lot of derelicts."

But Klaus had already started constructing what he wanted to be the case. "Well, I think it was Kobo, unless he used that fire escape and then destroyed it so no one could follow."

Just like Eric was having trouble following Klaus' thinking. "No, I think the fire escape has been damaged for a while. Probably neglect and vandals."

"Then he had to use the door or perhaps he scaled up with a rope."

"With radio-transmitting equipment?"

"He could have been holding another rope attached to the equipment and once he was secure, he could have hauled it up."

Eric got the feeling Klaus' speculations would go on forever. "No—you were right the first time. I now agree with you. It's the only logical answer. He came through the door."

"Yes, he had to come through the door." Klaus sounded very pleased with Eric's acknowledgment of his deductive abilities. "We should call the Gestapo."

As Eric had anticipated, Klaus, in search of commendation, would want to report the sighting immediately. "Not yet. Let's check one more thing, just to be sure," Eric said, and stepped inside the building.

"What are we looking for?" Klaus, tagging along behind him, sounded impatient.

"Shhh." Eric put his fingers on Klaus' lips. "There could be someone down here."

GARY KRISS

Klaus immediately drew his pistol. "I'm ready if there is."

Excellent, Eric thought. The Klaus he needed was the Klaus who showed up. The Klaus who was the Hitler Youth's enforcer of choice to physically discipline wayward members. The Klaus who, in lieu of considering options, always defaulted to violence as a solution to any problem. "Now what do we do?" Klaus whispered.

"Keep your gun out," Eric said, "and put your other hand on my back. I'm going to make my way to the stairwell."

Eric knew exactly where the stairwell was but made a production out of finding it. "Now we can use the flashlights." Eric flicked his on and went down the steps with Klaus close behind. "I'm certain the power to the building has been shut off, but just in case." After a few minutes of searching, they found the electrical box and saw that the master switch was in the off position. Eric shook his head. "Whoever's up there has to be drawing power from somewhere."

"Maybe he's using a battery," Klaus offered.

"If it's Kobo, a battery wouldn't be strong enough for him to broadcast very far. No, he would need a regular power source to reach the distances he does. To be thorough, we should go back outside and investigate more closely."

"Yes, the Gestapo would certainly want us to be thorough," Klaus said.

Eric sighed. "I agree. We definitely should." Once out of the building Eric led Klaus to a spot where some overhead power lines were clustered. "This is a possible location," Eric said, belaboring the obvious, which was often necessary with Klaus.

"Power lines. Yes, we should investigate this area very carefully."

"We're in luck," Eric said. "Some of the clouds have broken up, so we have a little moonlight. It will make our task easier." Eric waited nearly a minute, then asked Klaus if he saw anything.

"Nothing? And you?"

"The same," Eric said, his neck still craned. "Nothing. Not a single . . . Hold on."

"What? Do you see something?"

"There. Up there." Eric pointed to one of the electric poles. "That line running down and around and into the window on the river side. Come on."

They walked to the back of the building, hardly able to keep their balance on the tiny strip of land by the river. "Look at the line and follow it," Eric said. "It's threaded through the window fan."

"But how is it drawing from the power source?" Klaus asked.

"That's what we need to find out."

They returned to the electric pole and tilted their heads back, focusing on the overhead lines. Unlike Klaus, Eric, who had kept watch before when Johan completed this part of the plan, knew exactly where to look. "There appears to be something securing the line." Eric squinted until his eyes were almost completely closed. "Very hard to tell, but it looks like . . . it is. I think it really is. Look closely to where I'm pointing, Klaus, and tell me if I'm wrong. That's a meat hook."

"You're right," Klaus said after staring intently for a few seconds. Now that the image and the location had been planted in his mind, he, too, could see it. "The power cord is attached to a plain meat hook that's been slung onto the overhead transmission line. That's how he's getting the electricity."

"Whoever's in there is either very smart or very lucky. Unless you know exactly what you're doing, the voltage running through that transmission line will kill you in an instant."

"Now what?" Klaus asked.

"*Now* we contact the Gestapo." Eric placed his hand on his holster. "I'll wait here and make sure no one leaves the building. You go, find a phone and tell them what we've observed. Tell them the main switch to the building is off and suggest that they may want to have the power turned back on. That way, when their men arrive, they can trigger the building's electricity and surprise whoever's in there."

"It's a very good idea," Klaus said. "I'll tell them."

Eric watched Klaus leave. Yes, Klaus would tell them and when they said they liked the suggestion he would claim it as his own. So predictable. With only a few minutes before Klaus would be returning, Eric reentered the building, turned on his flashlight, went back to the stairwell and dashed up to the ninth floor. He knocked three times on the locked door, waited, then knocked three more times. When he heard the same signal coming from the other side of the door, he quickly made his way back down and out. Good timing. Four minutes later, Klaus reappeared.

"They're coming," Klaus said. "Even as I was talking, they had someone get in touch with the power company. It was indeed a very good suggestion. They were really pleased. This will certainly be noted in our records."

"That's welcome news. So now we just stand guard until they arrive. You keep an eye on the main door and I'll stay here and watch the window."

"Yes, a wise move, Eric. That way the Gestapo will see how we take everything into account." Klaus slapped Eric on the back. "This is going to be a fine evening for us, my friend. Why, the Gestapo might even bring us on board before we turn eighteen. They make exceptions in special circumstances and certainly catching Kobo would be a special circumstance."

"Let's not get too excited yet, Klaus. We still don't know that it's Kobo in there."

"Oh, it's Kobo. I can feel it. I have a sense for these things."

Poor Klaus. The Gestapo probably would snatch him up and put him on tasks requiring a totally dispensable agent. Poor, stupid Klaus. "I'm sure you're right. Either way, we'll soon find out."

Again Klaus took off, leaving Eric free to agonize over the many things that could go wrong once the next part of the plan unfolded. When he had expressed his concerns Peter told him not to worry, but he worried anyway. That's who he was. And Eric wondered whether Peter, despite brushing the danger aside, worried as well, since he was the only one with something to lose should the plan fail.

His life.

"They're here!"

Immersed in his thoughts, Eric had lost track of time.

"Eric, I said they're here!" Klaus' excitement was boiling over. "There are ten of them. They parked some blocks away so as not to spook our friend."

Ten of them! Ten more things that could go wrong. "Did they say how they were going to proceed?"

"It's very straightforward. There will be two men at the entrance to the building, one at each of the two street sides, two at the bottom of the stairwell and four to enter the ninth floor. They agreed with me about the fire escape."

They agreed with *him*. Well, it takes a fool. That's all right. Let Klaus make all the points he wants. "Sounds like everything is covered."

"More than everything."

"What do you mean by that?"

Klaus pointed toward the dark water. "There is a Gestapo boat, with its lights out. Just in case Kobo has some friends that could arrive that way. Smart thinking, right?"

"Right," Eric weakly replied. He didn't remember any mention of a boat when they were working out the plan. That could be trouble.

"And here's the fantastic part," Klaus said. "We get to go with the agents to the ninth floor. It's a reward. We'll be right in the thick of the action! They can't help but take us into the organization after that!"

"That's wonderful!" Hard as it was, Eric forced himself to feign enthusiasm.

"Well then, come on. We can't blow our big chance." Off Klaus went, half-walking and half-running, anxious to report back to duty and too caught up in the moment to notice that Eric was sharing neither his pace nor his eagerness. When he was within a few feet of the Gestapo agents, all of them clad in long black leather coats and black hats, Klaus stopped and stood silently. Finally, one—the leader—broke away and acknowledged him.

"Your companion, where is he?"

"Right behind me, sir."

"Lagging behind, you mean." The leader waited as Eric approached. "Nice that you could join us."

"Sorry, sir. I was just checking one or two last things."

"Don't you believe we can handle matters?"

Eric noted Klaus' disapproving look. "Yes, sir. I was merely doing what they teach us in the Hitler Youth."

"For the moment you are Gestapo and you will do what we teach you, not the Hitler Youth. Do you understand?"

"Yes, sir," Eric said.

"Good." The Gestapo leader nodded and then walked back to where the others were milling around. "Get ready!" he barked. Immediately everyone dispersed, save the three men who would be going with him to the ninth floor.

"Sir?"

The agent turned around and glowered at Klaus, who had followed him like a puppy, leaving Eric behind. "What?"

"Will we still be allowed to go with you?"

"I said you would. Do you doubt my word?"

"No, sir. Of course not, sir."

"I would hope not. Listen to me carefully. You two will stay behind us and keep your mouths shut." The agent looked at the pistol holstered at Klaus' waist. "Did they give you bullets for that, or is it all for show?"

"No, sir, it has a fully loaded magazine."

"And the two of you know how to shoot, I assume."

"We both have marksman medals, sir." Klaus' answer sounded like a boast.

"Yes, well, this won't be paper targets. Have you ever killed anyone?"

Klaus turned slightly ashen at the matter-of-fact question. "No, sir, not yet."

"The first time is special, but tonight is not that time. We have orders to bring Kobo in alive. You may draw your gun, but you are not to fire unless I tell you to. Even if the others do, you will not. Unlike you, my men understand how to aim to maim. Am I perfectly clear?"

"Yes, sir, you are." Klaus seemed pleased that he and Eric would at least be able to have their guns in hand.

"Then I charge you with making that perfectly clear to the other one. I'll give you thirty seconds and then we're off to the entrance."

Klaus swiveled around and hurried back to Eric. He quickly explained the rules, then the two caught up with the procession, which was almost at the building entrance.

"This is it," the Gestapo leader said as the small group assembled around him. "Once we enter, we will have three minutes before the power switch is flipped on. When it is, be prepared to crash through the door and take anyone in there by surprise. Remember, the space is a large open room. We don't know what it contains and there may be more than one person. But whoever is in there must be taken alive, so do not shoot to kill. Any mistakes regarding this will be costly, I assure you."

With that the leader went through the door to the stairwell and began snaking his way up to the ninth floor, with three other agents and Eric and Klaus close behind. Because of the need to work quietly, it took them longer than normal to reach their destination, leaving less than a minute before the power was switched on.

The leader clutched the handle of the door that opened onto the ninth-floor workspace and slowly turned it. As expected, the door was locked. He stepped back, drew his pistol and aimed it at the handle. Then he glanced at his watch and mouthed a countdown of the time remaining. When he got to ten, the others also drew their pistols and Eric and Klaus followed suit. At the count of five the little beads of sweat that had been forming on Klaus' brow began to trickle down. At three Eric noticed Klaus' gun hand slightly shaking. At one Klaus' face was shaking as well.

Zero!

With power restored a sudden rush of light filled the stairwell, and the moment it did the leader fired two pistol blasts, shattering the lock and sending his contingent bursting through the door and into the massive work-room.

Dropping their flashlights, which were no longer needed, the agents formed a defensive circle, scouring the area for people, but there was only one—an older man, perhaps in his mid-sixties, hunched over a long table near a grimy window with an industrial fan. On the table, between two lit candles that had been supplying illumination, was a shortwave transmitter, the size of a milk box, which had been connected to the outside line until the power was restored and the restarted fan blades sliced through it.

"Stop what you are doing and put your hands on the table!" the leader shouted as the others turned toward the table, backing him up. You can see there is no escape for you. The only thing is to—" A loud crash coming from the right side of the door chopped off the leader's sentence.

"What's that? What's that?" Eric punctuated his startled words by pushing a jittery Klaus. Now, would he or not?

Klaus whirled around. "I see him! I'll get him!" He began firing his pistol and the others turned and did likewise.

"Stop, you fools, stop!" The leader tried to be heard above the clamor. "There is no one there! Stop!"

As soon as they did, Eric shouted, "Watch out! Over here!" He pointed to the table. The man who had been sitting there was standing. "He's going to do something."

"No, he's not!" Klaus screamed, and began firing at the man. The others did as well, but the man had already dropped to the ground.

"Stop! You imbeciles—you'll kill him!" The frantic leader fought to gain control and finally prevailed. Through the blue-gray haze of smoke, two hands arose from beneath the table and grasped its edge. Next an unsteady body appeared, stood briefly, then slumped forward, crashing on the table-top and sliding from there back to the floor taking the candles and the electronic equipment, which was throwing off large sparks, down with him. Within seconds the space around the table was ablaze.

"He's got some sort of booby trap there so we don't get his equipment!" the leader cried. "We have to get to him before he's incinerated along with it."

"Wait, he's moving!" one of the agents yelled, as a figure, his arms engulfed by flames, stumbled toward the window.

"He's on fire!" The leader was beside himself. "Get him before there's nothing left!"

But before any of the agents could act, the man collapsed onto the fan, his burning arms thrust into the blades. To the accompaniment of sickening thuds, shards of charred and bloody skin, muscle and bone shot out across the room. The fan casing, unable to withstand the weight, began vibrating wildly in all directions until it finally broke loose from the window and plunged into the powerful current of the river, taking what was left of the mangled, flaming man with it.

"Get out!" the leader commanded as the fire spread. "Get out while there's still a path."

The panicked agents fled and, once he was sure all of them were gone, so did the leader. When he came down, they were waiting outside watching the fire jump to other floors and nervously anticipating him jumping on them. The Fire Protection Police would soon arrive, so time was short. The leader went immediately to Klaus, yanked the pistol from the boy's holster and sniffed the barrel before smacking him across the face with it. "Didn't I tell you not to fire?" the leader demanded.

Klaus tried to answer, but all that came out was an unintelligible stammer.

The leader turned to Eric. "And what about you?"

Eric took out his pistol and handed it to him. The leader smelled the pistol and returned it. "So, you kept your head."

"You told me not to shoot, sir."

The leader seemed satisfied with that answer. "And the rest of you? You don't know better? Did anyone else besides me and the boy hold their fire?"

A single hand went up.

"One person. Only one." The leader shook his head in disgust. "Now listen. We have worked together many times. I don't have to tell you what we're in for. Our only hope is to stick together. So this is it: I will provide the explanation and all of you will back me up. Those who were not with us upstairs will say nothing at all. Kobo fired at us, not with a pistol, but with a repeating weapon. He left us no choice. And he booby-trapped the room so he could not possibly be taken alive. Then he made a desperate attempt to flee, but we killed him and ended his illegal activities. As for the body, what happened, happened. When shot he fell and became tangled in the fan and fell from the window. The river is too swift for them to immediately find his remains. If and when they ever do, it will be too late to determine anything other than what has been reported. And you had better not mess this up. The higher-ups won't discriminate. Not just me but every one of you will be dealt with severely if the truth comes out."

No response was necessary: all of the assembled knew that what the leader said about retaliation was true.

"And you two . . ." He motioned for the boys to come forward and he put his hand on Eric's shoulder and spoke to him directly. "I may have been harsh on you when we first met, but your actions changed my mind. I will be recommending you for the Gestapo."

"Thank you, sir." Eric was actually pleased. Being Gestapo could help his resistance efforts.

"And me?" Klaus asked.

"Ah, yes—you. You are a hero."

"A hero, sir?"

"Yes, a hero. Look at the burning building behind you."

When Klaus turned, the leader drew his pistol and shot him in the back of the head, killing him instantly. The leader put his pistol back and signaled for the other agents to come forward. Without him explaining, they knew what to do. Each passed by Klaus' body, which was lying facedown on the ground, and fired a shot into it—his back, his leg, his shoulder. When they finished, the leader signaled to Eric, who knew he could show no reluctance. Drawing his pistol, he fired a bullet into Klaus' neck.

"Yes, a hero." The leader took out his lighter and set its flame to various parts of Klaus' clothing. He let the fire continue for three or four minutes and then took off his coat and began to slap it out. Again without needing to be told, two of the agents did the same.

"It was a foolish move, but a brave one," the leader said when the fire had been extinguished. "You didn't ask but took off after Kobo during the exchange of gunshots. It happened so fast that nothing could be done. We couldn't help hitting you with bullets, but it was probably better since you were so badly burned. The best we could do was pull you out so you could be laid to rest with honors. Isn't that right?"

Everyone nodded in agreement.

"You came to us a Hitler Youth . . ." The leader gazed down at Klaus' body. "But you died the Gestapo way."

Soaked, exhausted, but alive.

By Peter's reckoning, it could have been worse.

He had suffered no injuries of any consequence that he could find. Some bruises, which he expected, and an annoying headache, not unusual when diving into cold water from nine stories up. Otherwise, he was fine.

And the deception? Well, that was about as close to perfect as Peter could ask. The vest filled with crushed glass and broken tile blocked the few bullets that struck him, while the alcohol-based solution that he placed on his hands when he "fell" from the table prevented burns when they caught fire.

The human arm that Peter, under the cover of smoke, thrust into the blades when he collapsed on the fan was a lovely touch, giving the impression that his own body parts were being shredded. He didn't know the whole story of how the resourceful Otto got the arm from the mortuary, but somehow the man always came through.

The fan itself, with its blades mounted on a swivel joint, was pure genius, both Peter's concept and Ammon's execution. The secondary control hub Ammon crafted was a thing of beauty. When pushed into place, the hub locked the blades, enabling them to slice anything that came between them—like an arm—while they rotated. With the flip of a hidden switch the hub retracted, pulling out locking pins, so that the blades pivoted out of the way of anything in their path.

With the fan mounting already loosened ahead of time, the rest was a lark. Peter merely had to fall slightly into the fan when its blades were disengaged and his weight would send it plummeting. But instead of being jammed in the fan, he rode down on top of it, jumping away the instant it hit the river's surface and swimming underwater from the scene. The water was restorative, washing away Peter's makeup and with it some thirty years.

A perfect deception. Peter's only regret was not being there to appreciate the "audience" reaction. Even the Gestapo, which specialized in blood and gore, had to be impressed. Hell, anyone would have been impressed. But the Gestapo! That was a tough crowd, but guaranteed—they were wowed. Sometimes Peter managed to amaze even himself. This was one of those times.

Unfortunately, basking in his accomplishment didn't ward off a night chill that penetrated his wet clothing. Peter's mind moved to the post-performance phase: getting to his preestablished safe location where he could change and rest until morning. Then he could blend in with the crowds going to work. Considering when he began his little charade and taking everything else into account, Peter figured that it wasn't quite midnight. Patrols would still be out—patrols were always out—but he had planned his route carefully with that in mind. There should be no problem, although, as always, he had built in some alternatives just in case.

It turned out they weren't needed. Given the hour, the local Berlin police weren't going out of their way to look for trouble. That was fine, since Peter wasn't about to give them any. Besides, he had caused enough havoc for one day, maybe even a month.

And there it was: home, at least for the next eight hours or so. The Church of Saint Gertrude, where the priest was one of Father Fritz's underground allies. What did Father Fritz say about Saint Gertrude? That she was never formally canonized. Instead one of the popes just said, "Poof, she's a saint," and she was. Oh, they gave the process some fancy name—equipotent canonization—but it still came down to "poof." Peter could identify with that. Donovan said "poof" and made him a German astrologer. Then Rémy said "poof" and made him a British major. And even before that, for most of his life, Peter himself had said "poof" and become whoever he wanted. Yes, he liked Gertrude. No three-miracles crap. No committee of sanctimonious clerics hoisting up her habit, looking for any little transgression. Just "poof." Maybe she had conned them. Wouldn't that be something? And, to top it off, Gertrude was also an orphan. Walking up the steps of the run-down wooden structure as tired looking as the neighborhood it served, Peter felt the urge to genuflect, his way of saying, "No matter how you did it, Gertrude, well done." Instead he smiled and nodded. Then, with his homage completed, Peter opened the door and quietly entered the church.

Inside, the only light came from a wall of votive candles, most of them burned out, in a small alcove to the right of the entrance. Peter picked up an unlit candle and stuck the wick in one of the five still-flickering flames. With his tiny torch in hand he went back to the entrance where a small stoup, the vessel containing holy water, was set on a wooden table along with a beat-up missal, which had been opened. Peter had no intention of blessing himself with holy water; he would save that nonsense for Father Fritz and his friends. But the drawer, if it was anything like the one in the stoup table at the orphanage, might have something Peter could use. He opened it and drew out a tightly tied white linen bag about the size of a grapefruit. He knew by the feel that he had found what he was looking for. He loosened the bag and shook some white substance out onto the pages of the missal, then retied the bag and returned it to its drawer. The good old consistent Catholic Church had provided what he needed.

Not salvation, but salt.

Most parishioners weren't aware that the salt, which was blessed by a priest, was added to the water in the stoup to make it holy. But former altar boys like Peter knew, just as he knew some salt might prove useful. Peter closed the missal and took it with him to the sanctuary.

"Unimposing" would be the kind way to describe the interior of St. Gertrude's; "falling apart" would be more accurate. There was some evidence of minor bomb damage. The financial deprivations of war being felt by every segment of German society had done more damage. Yet St. Gertrude's moral fabric hadn't been diminished. Its sole priest—there had previously been three—didn't hesitate when Father Fritz asked him to shelter Peter for the night. But that was nothing for a man regularly entrusted with a parcel of Father Fritz's most precious possessions: the remaining Jews of Berlin who had to be hidden in hopes of being smuggled out of the city.

Peter would have liked meeting the priest, but Father Fritz had already said that he would probably not be there when Peter arrived, away on "other business." There was no need to ask what that might be.

So Peter went directly to his designated spot—the last of four confessional booths, more than the church needed at this point in its history. The prie-dieu in the penitent's compartment was unfastened, allowing Peter to easily lift it out and remove a loose floorboard, which concealed the dry clothes that had been left for him. He also discovered some thick slices of

Bavarian ham and rich pumpernickel bread, a small thermos of coffee and even a bottle of beer. The provisions were unexpected but welcome and, once he had changed and added a pinch of his purloined salt to the coffee to make it less bitter, Peter enjoyed them all.

When he finished, Peter placed the thermos, the beer bottle and the food's paper wrapping under the floorboard along with his wet clothes, then put the floor board and the prie-dieu back. He considered stretching out on one of the pews but decided it would be better to remain out of sight. It really didn't matter: he was so worn-out that he could sleep anywhere, including the cramped confessional compartment, although, with a few contortions, he was able to use the prie-dieu as a makeshift chair and its cushioned kneeler as a pillow.

It took about fifteen minutes for Peter to adjust to his unnatural position. Once he did, he opened the missal again and poured the salt into his palm. Some of it he transferred to the breast pocket of his shirt. The rest he placed on the top of his head. A folk healer Peter had met while playing a carnival in North Carolina told him that a handful of salt on the top of the head would "draw out the pain." Peter was sure his teacher, Delta, wouldn't put any stock in that. He didn't himself, but what the hell—it certainly wouldn't make things worse. Then he closed his eyes and soon fell asleep, waking only twice. The first time was when he turned and slammed his head against the wooden wall of the confessional.

The second time was when the wooden door of the confessional flew open and three Gestapo agents hauled him out.

"Well, well, isn't this convenient, a confessional," one of the three said while the other two held Peter. "Unfortunately, there is no priest. However, I will be glad to hear your confession."

The bastard's gloating didn't make it any easier for Peter to contain himself, even though he was convinced this had nothing to do with the factory incident. "The church door was open. I merely came in to seek some warmth. That is all I have done."

He had resorted to his best deferential German and, mentally, Peter, as Stanislavsky taught, imagined himself small and meek, letting those thoughts radiate as controlled tension through his muscles where they could be sensed by the hands that were clasped around his arms.

"That is all you have done? Seek shelter?"

"Yes, sir."

"Then perhaps you can still help us. How long have you been here?"

"I don't know. A few hours certainly."

"And during that time, did you happen to see any Jew runners?"

So that was it. They were searching for people like Father Fritz, who smuggled Jews out of Germany. Somebody must have tipped them off about this church. Wonderful timing.

"Jew runners, sir?"

"Yes, Jew runners. The ones who run this Jew Depot. You haven't seen any?"

"I wouldn't know what a Jew runner looks like, sir."

"Maybe I can help you." The Gestapo agent edged his way into the confessional and looked around. "They come in all varieties, which makes it tricky." Using his palms, he pushed up against the ceiling and then against the walls. "Very good at disguises as well." He glanced down at the floor and then stepped out of the booth. "Very good." Kneeling down, he felt the bare wood and stopped. "They tuck them in all sorts of places. . . ." With that he lifted the prie-dieu from the floor and tossed it from the confessional. "That way they can change quickly."

Peter knew the loose board was visible and he could feel the agent gloating again, this time in anticipation of what he might find. There was an interminable wait and then, "For example, from wet to dry clothing." The agent stood up and heaved the clothing at Peter. "I don't recall it raining."

"My clothing is dry, sir, and was before I came here."

"Really." He drew his face close to Peter's. "And the garbage."

Peter knew what was coming and remained silent.

"I said 'the garbage'!" The agent slapped Peter hard across the face, forcing him to exhale, much as he tried not to. "Beer? Were you drinking beer in your dry clothing before you came here?"

"A little, perhaps."

"Enough of this. I have tried to be polite, to be a gentleman, to no avail. I think we should now leave and see if the night air and a trip to headquarters makes you think more clearly."

That was all the other two needed to drag Peter from the church, down the stairs to the street where a black Mercedes 260D, the Gestapo's car of choice, was parked. As they forced him into the back, Peter glanced at the bottom of his shoes. He could neither see nor smell anything, yet he knew for sure.

Somehow he had managed to step in shit.

32

Berlin: October 7, 1942
Your Stars Today: Venus is beginning an interesting alignment with Uranus that will produce changes, some of them
startling, and result in you doing things differently.

This would be Peter's second visit to Gestapo headquarters and he knew his reception would be very different. Instead of a cordial welcome, perfunctory screening and escorted tour, he could expect a grueling interrogation, involving repeated near drownings in basins of ice-cold water, electric shocks to the genitals and beatings with pipes and rubber nightsticks.

Peter also knew that if he entered the rambling building at 8 Prinz-Albrecht-Strasse he would never leave. Worse, Peter knew that when Himmler found out about the arrest Max and the others would be placed in mortal danger. That left but one option. Within—Peter paused to calculate—fourteen blocks or less than eight minutes he would have to escape.

Peter's left wrist had been handcuffed to a metal loop on the rear door, but he could get free in seconds using his belt buckle if it weren't for the agent sitting next to him holding a Kurz pistol. Peter closed his eyes and considered the options. His feet were useless, as was his left arm. His right arm was available, but for what? He had nothing in his pockets and . . . wait. That wasn't exactly true. He still had some salt from the church in his shirt pocket—perfect for seasoning the stew he was in. Or maybe . . .

Peter began scratching his upper chest with his right hand. "I have an itch," he said before the agent next to him could ask what he was doing.

"Probably fleas," the agent said as Peter scratched more vigorously, providing enough cover to reach into his shirt pocket and snatch some of the salt, which he concealed between his thumb and fingertips. Then he brought up the map of Berlin in his mind. They only had to go another nine blocks, which, given the nearly empty streets of early-morning Berlin, should take under six minutes. Time was getting tight. Peter checked the map again. In two blocks they should make a left turn. That's what he needed. He waited, but the two blocks came and went without a turn. Had he misread the map? Impossible.

"Hey, you missed the turn!" the agent in the back shouted. "Where is your head?"

"So what?" the agent driving shot back. "I'll turn at the next block and then get us back on the right street."

True to his word, when they reached the intersecting street the driver turned the car sharply to the left, and Peter saw the rising sun directly in front of him. They were headed east, and he was ready.

Peter jerked his body forward, as if in response to the turn, and in the same motion flicked the salt from his fingertips quickly three times, each time reciting under his breath, "White folks go an' don't come back—go yuh way an' let me alone."

It was a desperation move. When the irrational is the only thing left to grab on to, you do. Delta had told Peter that saying the hoodoo incantation three times while throwing salt at the rising sun would keep the police away. Did Peter believe it could work? Of course not. Technically the police were already here. And, like them, he was also "white folk," although the term had to do with more than just color. Besides, Peter was never a stickler for the rules.

The driver had zigzagged back to the right street and as they cruised along Peter's mental odometer counted down: five blocks and less than three minutes. So much for grabbing on to the irrational. Next stop. 8 Prinz-Albrecht-Strasse.

Or it would have been, if the car didn't halt abruptly to avoid crashing into the side of another vehicle blocking the road. When horn honking didn't work, the Gestapo agent next to the driver—the same one who had briefly interrogated Peter—leapt out and stormed toward the other car. He rapped angrily on the window, identified himself as Gestapo, then fumed while he waited for the two men sitting in the front to emerge.

"How dare you block this road," he raged as the car doors opened. "You better have a good explanation and you better be prepared to give it at Gestapo headquarters."

"I think not," replied one of the two, a striking, impeccably attired man who looked like he had just stepped out of a Leyendecker *Vanity Fair* ad. "We are not going to Gestapo headquarters and neither is the person you have apprehended. He is going with us."

The man took a slim leather wallet from his right breast pocket and handed it to the Gestapo agent, who opened it, then flipped it shut with an air of obvious contempt. "Abwehr." He tossed the wallet back. "That man is a Jew runner. The Abwehr has no jurisdiction in this."

"Who are you to say what the Abwehr's jurisdiction is? As far as Jew running, I could care less. We have had him under surveillance for some time, an operation that you have now ruined. As a result, we must take him earlier than we had planned."

"You are telling me that he is involved somehow in military intelligence?"

"I am telling you nothing except to hand the man over immediately and be on your way."

"That won't happen."

"Do I need to remind you that Himmler himself issued an order forbidding the Gestapo to interfere with military matters? This is a military matter and you are interfering. Should you choose to press it, then we *will* indeed go to Gestapo headquarters and sort it out, but I would consider the consequences very carefully. I am a senior military officer entrusted with top-secret matters while you and your friends are mere functionaries. I will win the day at your expense. Is that what you want?"

Suddenly the Gestapo agent was uncharacteristically quiet.

"Well?" the Abwehr officer pressed him.

The Gestapo agent turned to the car and barked, "Bring him here!"

"A wise decision." The Abwehr officer reached into his breast pocket again, this time taking out a pad and pencil. "Let me see your identification."

The agent drew out his own wallet and handed it over. "I need the names of the others as well," the officer said, and the agent told him.

In the meantime, Peter, released from his handcuffs, had been brought over.

"Put him in the car," the officer said to his companion, then focused again on the agent. "You know who I am, so you are free to report this when you get to your headquarters. But if you do, I promise I will find out and it will be the end of three careers in the Gestapo, a very unpleasant end. Are we clear about this?"

The agent muttered something.

"I said are we clear about this!"

"Yes, we are clear."

"Good, now let us all return to our cars and go about our lives as if these last five minutes had never happened."

The Abwehr car sped off first, with Peter in the backseat, unfettered and uninformed since he hadn't been able to hear any of the conversation. "Am I allowed to ask who you are?"

The resultant silence left Peter to supply his own, disturbing answer.

More white folk!

The exterior of Abwehr headquarters conveyed a much different message from that of the Gestapo headquarters. The four-story sandstone building at 72-76 Tirpitzufer, a tree-lined street of once-elegant homes, backed on the Landwehr Canal, and was adjacent to the headquarters of the OKW—the German Supreme Military Command—to which it reported.

"Put this on and button it."

As the car pulled to a stop, a trench coat came flying over the front seat. Peter caught it and did as told.

"When we get out, you carry this."

This time a leather briefcase came over the seat, handed, not tossed.

"And try to look like you know what you're doing."

While the actor in Peter had no problem with improvisation, usually there was a setup of some kind. Here he had no idea what he was supposed to be doing.

"Come on, let's go."

The man in the passenger seat got out and Peter followed.

"Walk next to me and make small talk—family, weather, I don't care. But nothing military."

The two proceeded up the steps and into the building, chatting as if they were longtime friends. At the same time, Peter did his customary sensory sweep of the strange environment. All the input converged in a single descriptive word: "chaos." This was a town house—no, a few town houses—hastily joined and consequently disjointed. A staircase here, a dining room there, over that way maid quarters, diagonal to that a kitchen and everywhere corridors running to even more disorder. People, some in uniform, were darting in and out, only to disappear in a wink. It was a dictionary definition of "warren," with "pandemonium" as a suitable synonym.

"This way." Peter's still-unnamed companion led him to a rickety elevator, which shook and rattled as it took them to the fourth floor, where the pace was much less frenetic.

"We've arrived," Peter's escort said after a short walk down a deserted hallway, and swung open the door to an office. "Please, go in. I will only be a minute."

"Please?" It was the first civil word Peter had heard since leaving the church and it threw him momentarily. As he entered, Peter glanced at the nameplate on the door: *Major Karl Albrecht, Helfer dem Abgeordneten, Abwehr, Abteilung Z.* Peter had known he was in Abwehr hands. Now he knew who those hands belonged to. One more thing remained. Peter called up Abwehr from memory and found Abteilung Z. the Central Division, which ran the entire organization. And Albrecht, in turn, was the aide to the Abwehr's second in command. Donovan had briefed Peter on the Abwehr's big cheese, Admiral Wilhelm Canaris, speaking of him with muted admiration. He said that while Canaris was the head, day-to-day operations were handled by his second in command, who was—Peter glanced at his mental notes—Oster. Colonel Hans Oster. So Albrecht must be Oster's right-hand man, which would put him pretty high in the pecking order.

Albrecht's office looked like the study it probably had been when it was part of a town house. It was modestly yet nicely furnished with an oak desk and matching visitor chairs, a small sofa, a wooden map table and a bookcase, which held literary works by Goethe, Lessing and Herder shelved next to military classics by Moltke, Clausewitz and Schlichting. There was an interior door, which Peter assumed led to another office. Behind the desk was a bank of three windows from which the Tiergarten, Friedrich the First's magnificent urban park, was visible. The office exuded a certain tranquility that belied its function.

"I've brought us both some coffee." Albrecht came into the office carrying a tray with a carafe and cups, which he set on the desk. "I hope you will forgive my earlier behavior, but it was necessary."

Again, civility along with an apology. Even goodies. Peter tried to sort it out.

"Let me introduce myself. I am Karl Albrecht, a major in the Abwehr."

"And I'm confused. Why are both the Gestapo and the Abwehr so interested in a man whose only transgression was to seek shelter in a church?"

"Come now, Herr Kepler, give yourself more credit than that."

Herr Kepler. This was a bad sign. "Herr Kepler?"

"Yes, Peter Kepler."

No, this was a *very* bad sign. "Major, I fear you're mistaken. My name is—"

Albrecht held up his hand. "Please, no need to waste time with a name we both know is false. Have a seat and help yourself to some coffee."

Peter figured he might as well. It was obvious he wasn't about to be released.

"Good. I'll join you." Albrecht poured some coffee and sat down behind the desk. "You see, Herr Kepler, we have—"

There was a knock and then the door of an adjacent office opened. Albrecht shot up as soon as he saw the new arrival, who hadn't waited for an invitation to enter.

"So formal, Karl," the man said, and waved Albrecht back into his chair. "Herr Kepler is almost family."

From what Peter had already gathered, this soldier-trim man with a knowing face had to be Hans Oster. That was confirmed with a handshake as he sat down next to Peter.

"So how did our friends in the Gestapo take your little welcoming surprise?" Oster asked Albrecht.

"Furious at having to turn over a Jew runner. He was a big catch for them."

"They have no idea how big." Oster turned to Peter. "Can you imagine how furious they would be if they knew they really handed over the weapon that will kill Hitler?"

OK, forget bad—this was catastrophic. "How can I make you understand that I am not who you think I am? Besides, such talk about the *Führer* is treason. I will not be part of it."

"It's really a good performance, Herr Kepler," Oster said. "I particularly like disavowing any talk against Hitler, as if you were afraid we might be baiting you or that there was listening equipment in the room. A very nice touch."

"Is there no way I can convince you?" Peter asked.

"Actually, I think it's we who must convince you," Oster said. "Karl?"

Albrecht rose and went into Oster's office, returning with a man in civilian garb. "He's a tough one," Albrecht said. He closed the door and remained standing, obscuring Peter's view.

"Don't I know," the man replied.

The voice. Peter couldn't see the face, but the voice! "Father Fritz?"

"I hear you had a very successful night." Father Fritz stepped forward and took a spot on the sofa. "But not as good a morning. Let me see if I can make it better by clearing up your confusion."

"Why are you—"

"Peter, please." Father Fritz held up his hand. "Listen first, then I—we—will try to answer any questions. The members of Kobo were watching you, just in case something went wrong. Ingrid was the lookout at the church. As soon as she saw the Gestapo, she called me from the home of a nearby friend, a member of the resistance. I, in turn, called Colonel Oster, who dispatched Major Albrecht and his companion. Both were at the ready just in case."

So it wasn't the hoodoo incantation but, as Peter suspected, there was a nonmagical explanation for the intervention that saved him from the Gestapo. It had all been planned. And while the logistics were obviously fine, the logic troubled Peter. "Colonel Oster, Major Albrecht and Major

Albrecht's companion are officers in the Abwehr, the Reich's military spy organization," he said to Father Fritz. "Did you happen to forget that?"

"What I didn't forget is that their primary allegiance isn't to the Abwehr, but to The Black Orchestra."

"The Black Orchestra? What the hell is the Black Orchestra?"

"It's a term the Gestapo uses for those military officers committed to overthrowing Hitler," Oster said. "The Gestapo doesn't know who they are, only that they exist. Many of the Orchestra members are here in the Abwehr."

"Right under the nose of Canaris?" Peter asked.

"Arm-in-arm with Canaris. He and some others in the Black Orchestra have also been working with another group, which includes diplomats, theologians and political figures past and present, setting people in place to assume the running of government and the military once Hitler is dead."

"So the whole world knows about my mission?" Peter's angry question was aimed more at Father Fritz than Oster, although it was the colonel who answered.

"We were preparing to act against Hitler on our own. Many of these people have been committed to this for a long time. I, for example, have been trying to rid Germany of this blight since 1938. That's when Father Fritz and I met. We bonded over our common interest and have worked together since then. I've kept his secret and he's kept mine. And, no, the whole world doesn't know about you and your mission. Within the Abwehr, only Admiral Canaris, Major Albrecht and I know, just as we are the only ones who know about Father Fritz's resistance work."

"And the man who was with Major Albrecht?" Peter said.

"He only knows that you couldn't fall into Gestapo hands, not why. He's a member of the Black Orchestra, but he has no idea about Zodiac."

"Until this morning, everything seemed to be going fine." Father Fritz reentered the conversation. "It didn't look like the Abwehr would have to get actively involved."

"Actively involved?" Peter said.

"Behind the scenes, Major Albrecht has been keeping an eye out for any orders or directives that could compromise your mission," Oster said.

"If you're upset, blame me, not them," Father Fritz said. "I'm used to it."

How many times had Peter said he needed to know everything that involved the mission, no matter how minor it might seem? And this wasn't exactly minor. This was the leadership of the god damn Abwehr! He could blow up, justifiably, but to what end? He wasn't going to abandon the mission, and by now they knew that. Instead he would take a different tack and see if that might prove more effective. "Colonel Oster, Major Albrecht, Father Fritz—I want to thank you all for making sure this mission wasn't ended prematurely."

Oster and Albrecht looked relieved. Father Fritz, however, looked surprised. Good, Peter thought. I've thrown him off. He now has to wonder if he knows me as well as he believes he does.

"Herr Kepler—"

"I think we can dispense with formalities," Peter said to Albrecht.

"See, Karl, I told you he was almost family," Oster said.

"Peter, then. If you have—"

This time Albrecht was interrupted by the ringing of his telephone. He picked up the receiver. "Yes? . . . Well, where is Werner? . . . Damn. . . . Yes, of course put him through. . . . Admiral, how is the meeting going? . . . Yes, I understand, but certainly it's nothing that can't be handled. . . . Yes, Werner gave me a report on them about a half hour ago."

Oster began to chuckle quietly as Albrecht rustled some papers on his desk. "Ah, here it is. I have it right in front of me." Albrecht wasn't looking at anything. Father Fritz joined in, enjoying whatever joke was eluding Peter. "Ate heartily and eliminated in the same fashion. . . . Of course. . . . Yes. . . . We will see you later then."

With the conversation completed both Oster and Father Fritz laughed out loud while Albrecht shook his head, then proclaimed, "If Werner is not at his post one more time I will fight the Legions of Hell to make sure he is demoted!"

Albrecht's remark only made Oster and Father Fritz laugh harder. Since neither was in any shape to address Peter's bewilderment, the task fell to Albrecht. "Admiral Canaris' two dachshunds. He values them more than people. When he travels he requires a separate room for them. This morning he got called to an early meeting at the Reich Chancellery. Normally one of his staff, Werner, watches the dogs and gives the admiral a report when he calls. And he always calls. But today, Werner was among the missing. So . . ."

"Don't you like dogs?" Peter asked.

"I love dogs. Colonel Oster loves dogs. All the secretaries love dogs. Every person serving in the Abwehr who wishes to continue to serve or who hopes to get ahead loves dogs."

Oster had finally composed himself enough to speak. "So we make fun, but the admiral has his reasons. I once asked him about his attachment to the dogs, and he told me he believes in the inherent goodness of animals. He said that his dachshunds are discreet and will never betray him, something he couldn't say for human beings."

Peter hadn't met Canaris, but he already liked him, just as he instinctively liked Oster and Albrecht. The morning—after the awful Gestapo incident—had actually gone better than Peter had thought. It had given him a few more reasons to believe there might be some hope for Germany if he and the others succeeded.

And the odds of that happening had just tilted a little bit more in their favor.

33

Berlin: October 15, 1942
Your Stars Today: Take advantage of the opportunity to firm up those ideas that are swirling around right now. Concentrate on real projects, since the conditions are perfect for turning plans into realities.

Peter knocked on the rectory door and braced himself for another cold greeting from Father Fritz's overly protective housekeeper. Hildie may have accepted Peter's regular visits to the rectory, but she never seemed to approve of him. Not that Peter cared, as long as she didn't interfere with what he had to do. Today that meant using Father Fritz's library to research a special gift for Himmler, one that could help ensure the mission's success.

Peter glanced at his watch: 2:20 P.M. He knocked louder. Nothing. Normally Peter would had accepted the obvious and come back later, but he was on a tight schedule. When his third series of knocks went unanswered, Peter resorted to a pocketknife, which, in his deft hands, turned the lock as well as a key. He pushed the door open and entered the foyer. "Hello!" he shouted, but there was no reply. There was, however, the smell of cigar smoke and, tacked to a wood panel with hooks for hanging keys, a note from Father Fritz to Hildie saying he was on a sick call. No telling how long that would take, and Peter couldn't afford to wait. Besides, he had already broken in. So he made his way down the corridor and entered the study.

Again Peter was hit by lingering cigar smoke, which grew more pronounced as he approached the high wooden bookcases lining the wall behind the desk. Obviously Father Fritz had been using the study before he left. Peter glanced at the fresh ashes in an oval glass tray on the desktop, gray and white, the sign of a good cigar. Cheap cigars burned black. Sir Arthur, who loved smoking, had taught Peter how to find clues in tobacco and its residue. Consequently, he could tell that, despite its being a good cigar, Father Fritz wasn't enjoying it. If he was, the ashes in the tray would have been at least an inch long and cone shaped. Instead they were short and flat; some were even broken and scattered from being tapped off instead of gently pressed against the side of the tray. No, this was a nervous, distracted smoke, not a relaxed one. But whatever may have been bothering Father Fritz wasn't Peter's problem. He needed books on ancient Germanic magic; locating them promised to be a time-consuming task. Father Fritz counseled parishioners in his study, so he had covered the titles on the spines of books on the occult. Without him as a guide, Peter would have to go through each of them in hopes of finding what he was after. Not quite a needle in a haystack, but close enough.

Resigned to the inevitable, he removed a book, looked at the title page and then put it back. He flipped open another book, causing a ribbon, which was marking a spot, to fall out and flutter to the floor. When he bent down to retrieve it, Peter noticed a more pungent tobacco smell. Getting on his knees, he inhaled deeply, forcing air across the patch of cells in the nasal cavity that transmitted scents to the brain for analysis. In milliseconds, the results came back: wet tobacco leaf and tars. The odor was most intense on the bottom shelf, which was filled with theological tomes, their ponderous-sounding names clearly visible. Peter put his face close to the books and sniffed. The scent led to a thin black volume wedged between two volumes on Canon Law. Peter pulled it out and saw it was more of an elongated binder, which he probably otherwise would have overlooked. Peter pressed his nose against a small, slightly damp spot on the front cover. There was the source of the smell. Cigar wrapper tobacco moistened by saliva and left by fingertips. Father Fritz must have been reading this when he was called away. Did something in it trigger his anxiety?

Peter put the book on the desk and looked at the contents—pasted-in newspaper accounts of the deaths and funerals of several prominent Nazi Party members. Why would Father Fritz be gathering these articles? Peter saw no mention of him presiding at any of the ceremonies honoring the lives and accomplishments of the deceased, so it wasn't vanity. Nor could Peter see a common thread linking those in the book. What was he missing?

"Are you looking for something?"

Damn! Peter had been so engrossed in the scrapbook that he didn't hear Father Fritz enter the room.

"Actually, I'm looking *at* something." Holding an end in each hand, Peter lifted the open book. "Something very interesting."

"You have no idea what you're looking at." Father Fritz pressed his lips together so tightly they almost disappeared completely, which only drew more attention to the anger in his eyes. He stormed over to Peter and grabbed the book.

"Curious hobby, collecting obituaries of dead Nazis, then listing them along with a few powerful people who are still alive: Ernst Kaltenbrunner, Alb—"

"I know who's on the list." Father Fritz slammed the book shut.

But Peter wasn't about to stop. "Here's the interesting part: each name has a date next to it. For the dead, it's the day they died. But what about the three who are still alive? Are those the dates when they're going to die, because if so, it means—"

"I'd have to be involved in their impending deaths." Father Fritz's heavy sigh seemed to vent any remaining anger. "I'm not a murderer, if that's what you're asking." He tossed the book back on the desk and sat down in one of the easy chairs. "Not anymore."

Not anymore? Peter sat down across from Father Fritz.

"And so, finally, it's confession time for the priest. In many ways, it will be a relief." Father Fritz held up his right hand. "How many fingers do you see?"

"Five."

"That's how many people know what I'm about to tell you. No one else. Not Max, not Otto, not even Hitler."

"Yet you're prepared to tell me?" Peter braced for a trick.

"I was going to tell you anyway, because it's important to the mission that you know. It might as well be now. The information could enhance your credibility with Himmler."

Despite any lingering reservations he might have about Father Fritz, Peter's gut said to trust him on this.

"The men whose names you saw on that list are or were members of a secret SS order. When inducted, each took a blood oath to destroy Russia and establish an SS kingdom on its soil."

"And how many members does this secret order have?"

"Now?" Father Fritz again held up his hand with fingers spread apart.

"Five?"

"The same five. There were twelve members originally, ruthless men who had worked tirelessly during the late 1920s and early 1930s to mold what would become the SS so they could use it for their own ends. The order never expanded beyond those twelve. There was no need. The ancient seers of Germany prophesized that at least one of them would be left to found the kingdom when the time came."

Should he laugh? While not the most ridiculous yarn Peter ever heard, it still deserved a laugh. But then so did this entire mission when Donovan first explained it. Peter restrained himself. "And just when did the ancients reveal this prophecy?"

"In 1933."

Peter could no longer hold back. "Forgive me. I'm no archaeologist, but I always thought 'ancient' referred to things a little older than nine years."

"The ancients we're talking about lived thousands of years ago. But in 1933 they entrusted their prophecy to one of their self-proclaimed descendants, a clairvoyant who established contact with them."

Normally, Peter would have reached his breaking point by now. After all, how many so-called contacts with the departed had he exposed when working with Houdini? And, later, how often had Peter faked contact with the dead to con a gullible mark? No, by right Peter should have been rolling on the rug, doubled over with laughter. Instead, he stiffened in the chair, his facial muscles taut. This ridiculous yarn wasn't funny anymore. It was serious. Deadly serious. Father Fritz was testing at the same time he was telling, and Peter knew the answer.

"Wiligut."

"Wiligut." Father Fritz rose and turned away from Peter, as if ashamed of uttering the name, took a few steps in no particular direction, then sat down again. "The man responsible for most of the occult nonsense that Himmler and the SS hold as sacred."

"And a certified lunatic whose own wife had him committed."

"Who better?"

Good point. "So the Order was Wiligut's idea?"

"No, it was Himmler's. Since childhood, Himmler's been obsessed with conquering Russia. This war was his chance to turn fantasy into reality."

"Stalin may have other ideas."

"It doesn't matter. Germany's victory is inevitable."

"According to Wiligut."

Father Fritz lifted his right forefinger and Peter immediately corrected himself. "Sorry. I forgot. According to the ancients as conveyed through Wiligut."

"I know it sounds crazy."

"Obviously not to an elite handful of powerful men."

"Understand, each had his reasons for joining. Some, like Werner Ebling, shared Himmler's dream. Others, like Heydrich and Kaltenbrunner, simply pretended to. But they all had one reason in common: legitimacy. You see, there was a second part to the prophecy. The ancients said that Hitler would rise to command a great Reich and then be succeeded by a member of the Order."

"So after Hitler, the German people would just anoint this person as their leader?" Peter asked.

"Unlike an undistinguished corporal who failed as a painter?" Father Fritz placed the question in its proper perspective. "When that time comes, the Ahnenerbe will unleash a barrage of scientific rubbish to validate Wiligut's channeling of the prophecy. That will secure the backing of the SS, since Hitler would be followed by one of their own. Nothing else matters. As always, the military, citing loyalty and duty, will blindly obey while the people, fearing for their lives, will cheer and follow. That explains Germany today and, unless something's done, tomorrow as well."

Irrational as it sounded, everything Father Fritz said made chilling sense. But something was missing. "You said twelve members, but there are only ten names on the list. Who are the others?"

"The two men who founded the order."

"Himmler, obviously, and Wiligut."

"Wiligut added the Order's pomp and trappings, much as he did for the SS, but he was never a member. The Order dates back to the 1920s, well before he ever entered the picture."

"So Himmler and . . . ?"

Instead of speaking, Father Fritz plucked a plain circular gold-colored cuff link from the left sleeve of his clerical shirt and rolled up the cuff until most of his forearm was exposed. He slid his right hand down until it cradled his wrist; then he turned his arm slightly toward Peter. Hesitating twice, as if fighting against some terrible inner turmoil, Father Fritz finally removed his hand, revealing a small tattoo just above his wrist.

"You?"

Father Fritz simply sat. Peter had wanted more and now he had it. What he didn't have was a good explanation for being surprised, since he had sensed what might be coming. Was it because he didn't want it to come? If so, that raised another set of questions. Yes, Peter had lowered his guard by letting Max into his life, but he had no choice. Having resisted love for so long, he had forgotten its power. But Father Fritz? To Peter, all clergy were con artists and priests were the worst, scamming people for their so-called souls and their money. Why should it bother him to discover that a priest, about whom he always had doubts, helped create an entity that, from what little Peter had already learned, might be the first among evils? Peter wanted—no, needed—to find that out. "You were that involved in the Nazi Party and were that high up in its structure?"

"Priests are Germans, too. I fought in the war and I was disgusted by the terms the victors imposed on us, the economic suffering they caused. So, yes, priests became Nazis and so did Protestant ministers. I regret it now and I've lived my life trying to make amends. But in the early years I, too, saw Hitler and the Party as Germany's salvation."

"You still keep your ties."

"The better to do what I must do. I could openly oppose Hitler and be sent to a concentration camp. That wouldn't frighten me. But being a martyr when you could instead save lives is a selfish choice."

"Yet you—"

"Enough! I've told you more than I intended, beyond what was necessary." Father Fritz was now in full priest mode. "Now, what do you see?"

Father Fritz held his arm closer to Peter's face, enabling him to study the tattoo. It appeared to be some kind of rune—one of the twenty-four characters that made up the old Germanic alphabet. But Peter knew those runes and their variants, and this didn't match any of them. Instead, some of the characters had been combined. "It's a bindrune, formed from two . . ." Peter gently ran his right forefinger over the symbol. "Yes, two runes. One is definitely Algiz."

Taking a fountain pen from his breast pocket, Father Fritz screwed off the top, hunched over and on the white edge of a newspaper lying on the table between his chair and Peter's drew a large *Y* with the top of its base protruding slightly above the point where the two diagonal lines met. "Algiz. The rune of protection."

"And the other is Thurisaz," Peter said.

This time Father Fritz drew a vertical line with a rotated *V* pointing outward from its right side. "Thurisaz, the gateway rune, leading to new opportunities."

"Through violence and destruction," Peter added. "Appropriate."

"Now, if we superimpose them." Father Fritz drew another symbol. "We get . . ." He handed Peter the newspaper with his right hand and held his up his left wrist again so that both the drawing and the tattoo were visible. "This—"

"Only there's a significant difference," Peter said. "The symbol on your wrist is reversed. It's a wendrune."

"And why's that significant?"

Not that it mattered, but, for some reason, Father Fritz hadn't finished testing him. "Reversing a rune supposedly gives it magical powers. But for those who believe, a bindrune is already magical. Making it a wendrune dangerously increases its powers, sometimes to a level that its wearer can't control."

Father Fritz nodded his approval and again held up his wrist. "Now tell me what images you see in this particular wendrune."

"Maybe it's my forced Catholic upbringing, but it looks a little like someone being crucified."

"Not just someone. Baldur-Chrestos."

Baldur-Chrestos. Obviously the name was supposed to mean something to Peter. But as hard as he tried, he came up dry. Sometimes, on those rare occasions when he was rattled, Peter had trouble retrieving items from his memory. This wasn't one of those occasions, however, which meant he had never heard of Baldur-Chrestos. The old encyclopedia he memorized at the orphanage didn't even mention him. "And who is Baldur-Chrestos?"

"Who is Baldur-Chrestos?" The sound of the fountain pen smashing on the tabletop made it unnecessary for Father Fritz to raise his voice, but he did anyway. "Didn't I tell you what you needed to study?" Lifting his right hand in the air, he swept it from left to right, taking in a row of bookcases on the wall. "Specific books that you have to know?"

"I've been a little busy," Peter shot back.

"And you'll be a lot dead if you don't do what I tell you."

Suddenly Peter was six again, hearing but not listening to the words of the parish priest who came to say daily mass for the nuns at the orphanage: *"And you'll go to hell if you don't do what I tell you. There, in hell, with all the other bad boys who started out just like you. In hell—forever!"* Except, even at six, Peter knew that priest was full of crap. This priest wasn't. "Noted and accepted. But for the time being, can I get the short version?"

Father Fritz pinched the pen by the bottom of its black barrel and lifted it from the pool of ink that had squirted onto the table. He gently dabbed the nib before putting the cap back on.

"This isn't the first pen I've ruined that way," he said, which Peter understood to be an apology for losing his temper. "According to Wiligut, some twelve thousand years ago Germans practiced Irminism, a religion with a savior named Krist. Then in 960 B.C. the adherents of Wotanism, a rival religion crucified Baldur-Chrestos, Irminism's greatest prophet. But Baldur-Chrestos was resurrected and escaped to the east. Meanwhile, the two religions continued to fight each other and the war engulfed all Germany. Ultimately the Wotanists won, and ruled Germany until Charlemagne defeated them in the eighth century and forced their conversion to Christianity."

"Some of this sounds familiar."

"If you believe Wiligut, that's because the Christians stole and corrupted the Bible, which had originally been written in Germany by Irmanists. Anyway, Wiligut created the wendrune for our group. I forgot: he's the one other person besides the five who knows about it. We never had a formal name or a formal installation, but in 1933 we became the Order of the Wendrune during a ceremony Wiligut presided over. Each member was formally inducted in a different month—Himmler in January, me in February and so on. It symbolized the Order's connection with time and eternity. That's when we received the tattoos."

"So is Wiligut or Hitler the risen Baldur-Chrestos?"

Father Fritz shrugged his shoulders. "Maybe neither. Wiligut never said. For Himmler, Baldur-Chrestos represents the transcendent leadership that will arise from the order. Wiligut, however, became a major embarrassment for Himmler in 1939 when the closely guarded secret of his earlier confinement in a mental institution leaked out. He retired from the SS, citing ill health. But Himmler, who never abandoned Wiligut's delusions, still provided for him: a nice dwelling in Goslar, a housekeeper and enough money for his basic needs, which, these days, are mostly alcohol."

"Leaving Himmler without a guide to the occult."

"There were the astrologers and the psychics he gathered around him, although they weren't Wiligut. Then you appeared and were able to do something none of them could. You've managed to tap deep into Himmler's overwhelming romantic nostalgia for a Germany that never was. That's why this may prove valuable."

Father Fritz rose and got the scrapbook from the desk and put it on the table as he sat. He opened it to the list at the back. "Of the seven dead members, two were killed in battle and one—Heydrich—was assassinated. The other four, including Werner Ebling, supposedly died from natural or accidental causes."

"Supposedly?"

"I find it odd that each died on the month and day of his wendrune order induction."

So there *was* a pattern connecting the deaths. Peter couldn't see it because he lacked the necessary background information. Now he was fascinated. "And the living members?"

"Besides Himmler and myself . . ." Father Fritz put his right forefinger on the list and pointed to the names as he spoke. "Albert Sang, commander of Hitler's personal security, Kurt Veidt, in charge of all occupied eastern territories and Ernst Kaltenbrunner, head of the Reich Main Security Service. If I'm right, Sang will be the next person killed."

Peter looked at the date corresponding to Sang's name. "On November 2, his induction date."

"Now let me suggest how knowledge of Sang's impending death might be used to our advantage," Father Fritz said. "Weave it into the astrological charts you prepare for Himmler, but in such a way that you don't specifically identify Sang. A precaution, in case Himmler suspects that somehow you've learned about the Order."

What Father Fritz was suggesting held promise. It just needed some refining. Peter thought for a moment. "I could tell Himmler that someone close to him is in danger."

"He's not close to Sang. They've grown apart."

"What about someone close to Hitler?"

"That could work. Sang is close to Hitler, both personally and, because of his responsibilities, physically."

Peter clasped his right hand over his left fist and drew them to his chin. "The best thing would be for Himmler to single out the possible people and set the stage."

"That's certainly cryptic."

"Finding the album was an accident. I came here looking for help on ancient Germanic religion and mystical practices and you've given me a lot to go on. The mission's reached a critical point. We're twelve weeks away from our target date, so it's time to get the matches. In nine days we light the fuse by pulling off a mind-boggling deception that exploits Himmler's passion for the mythic past."

"And what exactly will this deception do to further the mission?"

"Link Himmler's sacred destiny—and Germany's—to Hitler's death."

34

Horn-Bad Meinberg: October 24, 1942
Your Stars Today: This is a good time for outdoor activities, taking the initiative, risky ventures, speculations, enterprise and quick judgments. Confident thinking leads to positive results.

To most people the Externsteine—seven tall, narrow limestone columns shooting up from the southern hills of the Teutoberg Forest to form a four-hundred-meter-long horn-shaped wall—were simply a magnificent act of nature.

Wiligut's disciples weren't most people.

They believed that here, twelve hundred years before Christ's birth, followers of the god Irman, driven into exile by rival Wotan worshipers, rebuilt their temple. The temple was the center of ancient Germany's true religion until, in 410 C.E., the Saxons, a tribe of Wotanists, seized and profaned it with their gods. Then, in 782 C.E., Charlemagne conquered the Saxons, destroyed the temple and turned the Externsteine into a Christian holy place.

"Tragic. So very tragic." Unaccustomed to physical exercise but determined to put on a show of vigor, Himmler, hands on hips, huffed between the words, unable to hide his heavy breathing from Peter and Max. After making their way up a staircase carved into one of the rocks, Himmler had bolted ahead, crossing a stone bridge to the Externsteine's highest and narrowest rock and entering a semi-enclosed chamber. Eschewing SS garb, Himmler was dressed for hiking but otherwise unprepared, and it showed. His companions, who had caught up with him, pretended not to notice.

"What happened here was unforgivable," Himmler continued as they walked through the chamber to an outside area dominated by a stone altar at the far end. "The Saxons may have corrupted the old religion, but at least it was still Germanic. Charlemagne all but wiped it out."

"And you, dear Heinrich, will be the one to restore it." Max placed a consoling hand on Himmler's forearm, pressing just enough so he could feel her touch through the cotton of his shirt.

"I believe it a sacred charge." Himmler put his hand over Max's just as she started to pull it away. "The spirit of this place resonates in my soul."

"I felt the same way when filming here for the SS documentary," Max said as she finally managed to free her hand.

"And you brought your equipment today as well." Himmler pointed to a medium-sized case on the ground.

"You know I rarely go anywhere without my camera, Heinrich. Besides, I wanted to have footage of you up here among the ruins. It's important that future generations of Germans appreciate how you returned the Externsteine to its true purpose and glory."

"So much to be done. The Ahnenerbe archaeologists excavate and uncover more artifacts, but the real work must wait until we win the war."

"Which is why we're here today," Max said.

"Yes, this dream you said Peter had. I still don't quite understand what the Externsteine has to do with it. You were vague."

"Vague because I didn't know any of the particulars. I still don't. Yet you met us here."

"I can never refuse you, Max. Besides, Peter has repeatedly demonstrated his extraordinary gifts. I trust this will not be an exception."

That was Peter's cue, and the performer in him was anxious to take center stage. "It could be, *Reichsführer*. Or nothing may happen. I'm simply acting on a dream."

"But not an ordinary dream," Max said.

"Ordinary dreams come from our own minds and experiences," Peter said. "Another mind with other experiences planted this dream in my mind, and I felt as if I had been transported into a different reality." Peter stopped, so that he could gauge Himmler's enthusiasm by silently counting the seconds until he reacted.

"Go on."

Four seconds. He was drawing Himmler in without a fight. "In this dream I couldn't make out any distinct images. Instead, I was enveloped by multi-hued mists swirling in all directions and filled with voices, thousands of voices, yet they all spoke as one. And although I didn't know the language, I understood all they commanded me to do."

"These voices." Himmler's eyes, which had been growing wider as he listened, now seemed to fill the round lenses in his wire-framed glasses. "Whose were they?"

"They were the voices of the flame kindlers who founded our race so long ago."

"Wiligut's ancestors," Himmler blurted out.

"I'm sorry, *Reichsführer?*"

"What you just said made me think of Wiligut. He had this amazing ability to communicate with his ancestors who lived twelve thousand years ago."

"Of course! The Ueiskunings—the Ice King descendants of the Gods." Thanks to Father Fritz, Peter was well prepped on lunatic history and could rattle off bits and pieces with authority. "I hadn't made that association, but you're right. They must be the same."

"Then you can speak to the Ancient Ones as well," Himmler said.

"No, *Reichsführer.* Wiligut can speak to them. I can only listen. Further, Wiligut can open the portals of the past at will, while I need the Ancient Ones to open them for me."

"And does this happen often?"

"Only once before, again in a dream, when I was told to immediately prepare Heydrich's horoscope in a very special way—using his current location rather than his birthplace. I was further told to send the horoscope to you as soon as it was completed."

"So this relocation technique was revealed to you in a dream." Himmler turned to Max. "I never knew that part."

"Neither did I," Max said.

Once more Max came through exactly as Peter had hoped. He was creating some of this on the fly and relying on her to play along. "That was deliberate. When I sent the horoscope, I didn't understand how truly attuned you were to the old ways, *Reichsführer.* I feared you might think me a lunatic and blame Max for interceding on my behalf."

"So, at great risk, you prepared and sent the horoscope knowing the Reich had banned the practice of astrology." Himmler seemed impressed.

"I prepared the horoscope purely out of curiosity. When I saw the tragedy it portended, I was amazed, but not convinced. Then, as a test, I chose days that had already passed, and prepared charts for other people using both the conventional method and this new one that had been revealed to me. In each instance, the new method was far more accurate. As a loyal German, my duty was to send you it, *Reichsführer,* no matter what the consequences. Our Reich is more important than any individual." A good con man has balls of brass and a great one has balls of steel. Peter's balls were titanium.

"Perhaps there was more to that dream, Heinrich," Max said.

"How so?" Himmler asked.

Peter wondered the same thing. He had just concocted the story about the first dream; Max was improvising.

"Through trying to save poor Heydrich's life, the Ancient Ones used the dream to bring you and Peter together, so that, through him, they might communicate with you."

Brilliant! Peter saw Max wasn't simply improvising; she was manipulating Himmler by stoking his ego. On a set or off, she was a master director.

"Using these?" Himmler unfastened a bag secured to his lederhosen and drew out a handful of short ash-tree branches. "I gathered them as you asked, Max."

"After grumbling about it on the phone."

"Gathered nonetheless. All from trees at the base of the Externsteine. It took nearly a half hour. Had any of my men seen, they would have thought me mad."

If a man believes the earth is hollow and that he had been a German prince nine hundred years ago, he's sane. But if he innocently picks up some sticks, he's mad. Peter had stopped trying to understand the Nazi mentality beyond what was necessary to con Himmler, kill Hitler and leave loony land.

Taking Max with him.

"So, Peter, you will tell me what to do with them?" Himmler asked.

Shove them up your ass and let your Ahnenerbe archaeologists use them to excavate there for the artifact that's your brain. Peter resisted saying that and went in a much safer direction. "This is what the Ancient Ones instructed me to do." He drew a pocketknife from his trousers, took one of the branches from Himmler's hand and began stripping off the bark. "We need to prepare twenty-four sticks in this manner. They should be at least a quarter inch in diameter, which will allow for carving."

"What sort of carving?" Himmler scattered the branches in his hand, and those remaining in the pouch, on the ground, then crouched down and began sorting through them.

"Rune symbols." Peter joined Himmler in his search for the right-sized branches. "Wiligut's rune symbols, given to him by his ancestors."

"Can I help?" Max asked.

"Not yet, but soon," Peter said. "Without you, all of this is meaningless."

"I'm ready to do whatever the Ancient Ones directed." Her reply was preplanned, to encourage Himmler to show equal patience while awaiting the will of the Ancient Ones, rather than barraging Peter with questions. And it worked. Following Peter's lead, Himmler took out his own pocketknife and silently proceeded to remove bark from the sticks.

When twenty-four branches were ready, Peter removed one from the pile and with a few deft strokes of his knife carved a crude circle with a cross inside. "Tel, the first of Wiligut's runes." He held up the branch for Himmler and Max to see, then set it down.

"What am I to carve?" Himmler said.

"This." Peter reached over and took Himmler's left hand. "Each of the staves must have your blood on them. You're to make a small cut here that will quickly heal." Peter placed his forefinger an inch below Himmler's middle finger and traced a straight line that ended an inch above his wrist. "By doing this, you're opening your life line to the Ancient Ones, allowing them to determine your destiny. When I complete a rune, I'll give you the stave. Wrap your hand around it, then place it on the ground to let the blood soak into the etched depression and stain it."

"You want me to slice my hand?" Himmler flinched as he spoke.

"Very slightly." The psychology professor in Peter was fascinated by how Himmler could torture and kill millions of people in the most horrible ways imaginable yet weaken at the thought of drawing a bit of his own blood.

"Wait a moment until I get Mickey Mouse out of his hole," Max said, using the name Himmler had given her movie camera because the two film reels on top reminded him of Mickey Mouse's ears.

"I'm not sure all this should be filmed," Himmler said.

Probably because Himmler didn't want a record of him fainting over what was essentially a glorified paper cut was Peter's guess.

"I'll be selective." Max had already set up her tripod and was removing the camera from its case. "Later we can decide what, if anything, to use. But if we don't film, we may regret the missed opportunity." Max secured the camera to the tripod as she spoke. "You know how valuable all the photographs and movies of the *Führer* have been, especially mine. They may prove equally beneficial to you, dear Heinrich, at the appropriate time."

"*Reichsführer,* your hand?" Peter said, turning Himmler's attention away from the camera. "I've readied more than half the staves."

"Yes, the hand." Resigned to his task and seeing that Max was watching, although not yet filming him, Himmler put the point of his knife blade on the spot Peter indicated and, closing his eyes, pressed the blade down and drew it two inches across his flesh. Immediately a reddish streak appeared; soon blood began to well and trickle along the edges, slowly at first, then more profusely. Himmler picked up a stave and, after clutching it for a moment, laid it on the ground.

"Perfect," Peter said. "All of them, just like that."

Meanwhile Max clamped a metal bar with two movie lights to the tripod and connected them and the camera to a battery.

"Will Mickey work in the dark?" Himmler asked despite his qualms over filming.

"Look at it, Heinrich." Max swept her arms open, embracing the sky. "The full moon and its glorious glow. I probably don't even need the lights, though I'll use them just to be sure."

"You mentioned Charlemagne's destruction of this temple, *Reichsführer*," Peter said. "But the last followers of the old ways suffered other indignities. Those who didn't convert Charlemagne either slaughtered or enslaved, consigning them to the lead mines, which had been unworked for centuries. Often monks oversaw the mines, making them masters of the Saxons. Tonight we will break those past bonds of servitude and reassert the primacy of the Teutonic ways over those of the usurpers."

Both Himmler and Max were visibly intrigued by Peter's tale, much as he had been when, as a boy, he sat around a hobo jungle campfire and listened to the old-timers spin yarns. Soon he, too, became adept at holding people in his thrall with nothing more than words woven into stories, most of which were made up. But what he was now relating was true, on the off chance that Himmler might check.

"And how will you accomplish this bond breaking?" Himmler, saucer eyed again, asked.

"With this." Peter reached into a backpack on the ground next to him and took out a small, lead-framed stained-glass panel that showed a red-robed warrior on a white horse. The warrior was holding his sword high, ready to smite a yellow-bearded man in a white cloak cowering before him. Peter handed the panel to Himmler. "Charlemagne is on the horse and the figure he's about to kill is the last Saxon priest in Germany. This piece was part of a large church window commemorating Charlemagne's victories over the pagans that brought about the triumph of Christianity."

"And the rest of the window?" Himmler asked.

"Demolished. This is the only intact portion." Peter again dug into the backpack and took out first a small iron pot with a handle and then a bunch of thin metal pieces in various sizes and shapes. "These pieces of lead were used to separate the pieces of window glass." He dropped them into the pot. "And now, *Reichsführer*, you must destroy the remnant you're holding and deposit the lead into the pot. There, at the altar." He handed Himmler a small pick hammer that was secured to his belt. "Chip away any remnants still adhering to the lead. When you're done, toss the metal pieces into the pot."

Without further questioning, Himmler did as directed. "Have we now completed all the preparations?" he asked when finished.

"Almost." Peter made another foray into the backpack and fished out two iron bowls, one small and circular, the other larger and oblong.

"Did you pack an entire kitchen in there, hearth and all?" Himmler joked.

"The hearth wouldn't fit," Peter said after some false laughter to humor Himmler. "But we'll remedy that. Max, you brought the extra tripod?"

Max took the tripod from her case, opened it and gave it to Peter, who set it down in front of the stone altar. "And now—" He hung the bowl with lead on the panning handle protruding from the tripod. Then he scooped up a clump of branches that weren't needed for the rune staves and piled them beneath the bowl. The rest of the branches he used to line the bottom of the larger bowl.

"So we are finished?" Himmler said.

Peter thrust his right forefinger in the air, signaling to wait, and Himmler sighed at another delay. After a long moment, Peter said, "We need just two more ingredients, *Reichsführer,* and then everything will be in place." He took the hammer and went to a spot on the right side of the altar where a piece of the rock jutted over the edge of the pillar. Steadying himself, he leaned over and tapped the rock with the head of the hammer. "It's right here." Peter turned the hammer to the pick side and began outlining a rectangle in the rock about a foot long and eight inches wide.

"What are you doing?" an alarmed Himmler demanded.

"What the voices told me to do. Would you have me disobey them?"

That shut Himmler up. Peter chipped away without further interruption, reaching a point where he could toss the hammer aside and wedge his fingertips beneath the stone section, then rock it back and forth like a loose tooth until it came free.

"Here's the first ingredient." As he walked to the altar, Peter held up the piece of rock for Himmler and Max to see. "And it goes here." Peter placed the rock in the oblong pot. "A good fit."

"And the second?" Himmler asked.

Seeming not to hear, Peter removed his hiking bottle from his belt and poured water into the small empty pot. "How is your cut?"

Himmler looked at his hand. "It's started to close over."

"Here, let me see." Peter took Himmler's hand and, after a quick examination, squeezed it hard enough to break the thin scabbing and restart the bleeding. Immediately he turned the hand and held it over the pot so that some blood dropped into the water.

Himmler, startled by Peter's action, jerked his hand away. "What are you doing?"

"We only needed a little." Peter stirred the blood and water together with a branch and then placed the pot at the altar's edge. "And now, *Reichs-führer*, we are ready."

"This is the part I want to film." Max's anticipation had spilled over to giddiness.

"Sorry, but I'm going to need your help," Peter said.

Max looked crestfallen. "Then I'll set the focus and the camera will run automatically. It's not my preference, but it'll work." Max made her needed adjustments and then flicked on the camera lights.

"Ready?" Peter asked.

"I think so." Max pressed the switch and the camera started to hum. She took one last look through the viewfinder. "It seems fine. So, what must I do?"

"Take off your clothes."

"What did you tell her to do?" said a startled Himmler.

There was enough moonlight for Peter to see that Himmler's face was flushed, probably more from titillation than prudishness. "Again, *Reichs-führer*, I'm only the messenger conveying what the Ancient Ones tell me must be done."

"It's all right, Heinrich." Max's tone was soft and soothing. "I wasn't expecting this, but I'm prepared to do whatever is necessary."

"I don't want you to suffer any embarrassment," Himmler said.

"There's no embarrassment. The Aryan body is a thing of beauty." As Max spoke, she shed her shawl, slipped off the shoulder straps of her dirndl and began unbuttoning her blouse. "How many times have I photographed naked women and men—athletes—the pride of Germany?" Max removed her blouse and tossed it on the ground, then unhooked her bra and set it free with a shake of her shoulders. "And you, yourself, lifted the laws that prohibited nude sunbathing and swimming, Heinrich." After taking off her dirndl, Max placed her thumbs in the elastic band of her lace panties, slowly pulled them down to her knees and let them drop to her ankles so she could step out of them. "No, I'm not ashamed of my body. Let's continue. What comes next, Peter?"

While his eyes were on Max, Peter's ears were tuned to Himmler, who was breathing heavily again, and not from exertion. Besides repulsing Peter, the sound kicked his brain into high gear. Maybe he couldn't kill Himmler, but he could play with his mind. "Stand by the altar and spread out your shawl before it," Peter told Max. "And you, *Reichsführer*—gather the rune staves and toss them onto the shawl."

Kneeling, the nipples of her supple breasts, firm from the night air, hovering an inch above the ground, Max spread her shawl out while Himmler watched transfixed.

"*Reichsführer?*" Peter said.

His trance broken, Himmler scooped up the staves and threw them on the shawl, never taking his eyes off Max.

"Please step back, *Reichsführer,*" Peter said, and Himmler reluctantly complied. "Max, close your eyes, empty your mind of any conscious thoughts and simply listen. Then, when the moment feels right, draw a stick that you feel directed to, stand and place it in the large pot. You are to do this three times."

Himmler asked, "What is the significance of—"

"Shhh." Peter placed a finger to his lips. "There must be total silence."

Eyes shut tight, Max remained motionless for a few seconds. Then she opened her eyes and slowly passed her right hand back and forth over the staves until, like a hawk, her fingers dove and snatched her target. "This," she whispered. Rising, then turning, she released her catch, watched it plummet into the pot and returned to the staves on the shawl to repeat the process.

When the final stave had been cast, Peter went to the altar, placed his hands above the pot and began reciting an incantation in a strange language. Himmler was too focused on Max's naked body to notice that, as he blessed the pot, Peter dropped in two wads of cotton from small bottles in his pocket. One wad was saturated with ammonia, the other with diluted hydrochloric acid.

With the pot primed Peter dismissed Max, who snatched her shawl for covering and returned to the camera. Himmler followed her with his ogling eyes, which were reduced to slits by the brightness of the photo lights. It was the distraction Peter needed. Again he reached into his pocket, and pulled out three pieces of wax, each of which held a short, thin pin with a large bead of rubber cement at the tip. With Himmler still looking away, Peter stuck the wax pieces in a small crevice in the back of the altar stand and then pushed the wads of cotton until they were almost touching one another. Within seconds white smoke began to billow from the pot.

"Look!" Max shouted, and Himmler swung his neck toward the altar.

"What is that?" he exclaimed. "What is causing the smoke?"

"The wooden rune staves interacting with the chipped-off stone," Peter said, blending fact with fiction. It was definitely an interaction, but it was between the gases from the evaporating ammonium and hydrogen chloride. The very fine particles of ammonium chloride it produced looked like smoke.

"Next." Peter picked up the remaining rune staves, threw them into the oblong pot and removed a branch, which yet hadn't started to burn, from the fire beneath the lead. He plunged the tip of the branch into the flames until it caught, then, holding it with both hands, lit the rune staves in the large pot. Immediately a ball of fire shot from the pot, traveling ten feet into the air before vanishing. Wanting to surprise Max, Peter hadn't mentioned this little extra, which left both her and Himmler awestruck. Amazing what effect a dash of finely ground lycopodium—club moss—could have when slipped into a pot and touched with a burning branch.

"Unbelievable!" Max said. "That's why I knew we had to film this, Heinrich."

Himmler tried to look at Max, who was now controlling the camera manually, but this time the lights proved too much and he turned his head away. While keeping Himmler from seeing the camera wasn't necessary, it provided Peter with an additional safeguard for the untested illusion he was about to attempt.

"Only the ceremony, Max," Himmler said, an indication that the filming still disturbed him.

"I understand. Move over to your right, Heinrich, so you're completely out of the shot."

Max's seemingly offhanded but deliberate direction positioned Himmler perfectly for the effect. With the sight lines set up, Peter could proceed.

"The pot of blood has been prepared, the lead has been melted, the staves have been cast upon the sacred stone and blessed in the words I was given and the holy fire kindled." Peter craned his neck toward the sky. "All has been done as told." Then, to better set up the Catholic-raised Himmler, Peter threw in a line from the mass: "May our subsequent actions be acceptable to you." Now came the first of several tricky parts: "So that my hand may do what must be done, I purify it with blood, the blood of one who has been chosen by the Ancient Ones." With that Peter thrust his right hand into the pot of blood mixed with water. "This blood has cleansed my hand, enabling it to triumph over the servitude endured by the Saxons, the last of our kind, in the mines of lead." Peter withdrew his hand and held it aloft, allowing the liquid to stream down his arm for effect, before plunging it into the pot of molten lead.

Himmler gasped, then grimaced, but Peter, who pulled his hand from the pot and shook off any adhering lead, was unharmed—and chuckling silently. Agriculture degree aside, Himmler must have been asleep during some of the chemistry classes or he might have learned about the Leidenfrost effect, named for the eighteenth-century German scientist who studied it.

The heat from the lead evaporated the coating of bloody water on Peter's hand, and the resulting layer of steam protected him from burns. But the temperature of the lead had to be kept within a very tight range, which was why Peter, unbeknownst to Himmler, kept "adjusting" the fire by kicking it with his foot. However, the trick relied heavily on "feel," with little room for miscalculation, making the devastating, logic-defying display so dangerous that it was seldom performed, and then only by those with steady nerves and great self-confidence. And Peter never lacked for either.

"By breaking the bonds of disgrace, we are able to set history back on its true course with he who the Ancient Ones say has been chosen." Peter slipped his right hand behind the altar and pressed his forefinger against one of the wax pieces until it adhered. Standing behind Himmler, at her camera, Max gave an emphatic nod, signaling that she was ready.

Peter spoke again. "This was the first rune chosen." As he solemnly uttered the words, he mentally began counting off exactly twenty seconds, precisely pacing his words and actions. He slowly waved his hand in the air to eat up another small block of time; then, with seven seconds left, he stabbed his forefinger into the flames, which ignited the ball of rubber cement. When three seconds remained, he jerked his finger, its tip seemingly ablaze, from the pot and rapidly drew a shape with fire in the night sky—a rough Y with a line protruding from the point where the two diagonal lines met. "Algiz. The rune of the Irminsul. The rune that opens the realm of heaven. The rune of the man who becomes a god."

Himmler was aghast; Peter was delighted. He had to admit that the illusion, which he had designed and Otto and Ammon built, was amazing: so simple in concept, yet so effective. The camera was really a projector controlled by Max, its beam camouflaged by the movie lights. And the smoke that Peter stirred up acted as a screen. Everything was timed perfectly: twenty seconds after Max started the projector, an image of a rune would appear where Peter's flaming finger was, linger for four seconds—long enough to be implanted in Himmler's mind—then disappear. By saying the rune's name, Peter reinforced the image. So damn simple! Now for the next rune. Peter didn't want to give Himmler too much time to think. Again Peter stuck his hand in the blood and water, the lead, and then, with another wax piece in place and once Max had nodded, into the fire.

"This was the second rune chosen." The shape Peter drew in the air with two quick strokes resembled the letter V with its point facing to the right side instead of down. "Thurisaz, the gateway rune, whose power only the truly committed can harness. Thurisaz destroys the weak and anoints the strong. It leads to new opportunities through the conquest of enemies, but only for the decisive."

While Himmler remained enthralled by the fire-drawing illusion, he was also being drawn in by Peter's carefully constructed message. That meant the moment had come for Peter to deliver the sucker punch or, as they said in con circles, "sting the mark."

Peter's hand went from the bloody water to the lead, only this time he felt it. Just slightly, but enough to realize he could no longer control the fire. The temperature in the pot was moving beyond the safety range. Any further attempt would result in a severe scalding or worse. Fortunately, there was no blistering, so Peter was able to attach the wax easily enough. When it was secure, he looked at Max and waited for her signal.

But Max wasn't looking at him. Instead she was furiously adjusting the controls on the fake camera, shaking, not nodding, her head.

"The last and the most important rune." Whatever the problem was, Peter had to stall, giving Max time to correct it. "The rune the Ancient Ones said would determine the fate of our great nation.

"Come on, Max," Peter exhorted under his breath, concerned that the longer the delay, the greater the chances that the mood he had created would shatter. But Max was still laboring on the device and growing more frustrated as she did. So it was back to dragging things out. "Entrusted to the right person, this rune will be stamped on Germany and from there the world. But that person must be willing to accept the charge, even if it should be at great personal risk."

Himmler was beginning to sway in place—not a good sign. His interest was flagging. Worse, Max had stopped playing with the controls and was waiting for Peter's cue, her thumb downturned. "Hey, rube!" The carnie cry for help ricocheted off the walls of Peter's brain. He only used it once, when he was seventeen and scammed some guy in Kansas trying to impress a girl by tossing balls into a box and winning a Kewpie doll. Only the game was rigged. The sucker couldn't beat it no matter how much cash he put up— and he put up a lot. Later he came back with a bunch of his friends looking for blood. But one loud "Hey, rube" brought everyone in the carnival running to Peter's defense, from the burly, "take no shit" roustabouts who set up everything to the three-hundred-pound bearded lady, and after two quick broken jaws the local boys got the message and fled.

Except in the Externsteine there were no roustabouts for Peter to call, nor were there bearded ladies. Just an agitated Max, an anxious Himmler and, if Peter was lucky, another two minutes in which to act. After that, the mystical bubble would burst, reality would set in and he would lose Himmler.

Think, damn it, think, while Himmler still believed the bullshit he was being handed. Believe—bullshit—believe—Beloit—Be—Bennett—Beloit, Bennett—Beloit, Bennett! Beloit, Wisconsin, Sister Chastity Bennett. June 1927. Sister Chastity, God's anointed, queen of the revival and healing tent shows, the beautiful bunko who taught Peter the ins and outs of fleecing religious dupes—and so much more.

Sister Chastity. During her revival meetings, she made the lame walk. But first her associates would set the stage by providing an array of spiritual entertainments: music, singing and testimonies—lots of testimonies—all of them from planted stooges. By the time Sister Chastity appeared, the crowd was primed to believe, ready to witness the miraculous. If she described a halo over her head, the suckers saw it. Not thought they saw it, actually saw it. Such was their state of suggestibility.

Just like Himmler's.

And Peter knew what to do. The odds said it wouldn't succeed, but the odds never stopped Peter, especially when he had a chance to stack them more in his favor. What was a worrisome snag moments ago had become an exhilarating challenge. And he was ready. "This, then, is the rune of destiny!" Peter proclaimed, his arms spread out, his palms face up toward the heavens. "Let nothing distract from this, the most solemn of moments. The woman shall step forward and stand beside the man." That sounded pretty damn good, Peter thought—the woman next to the man. Primordial, like he was summoning the first couple or some such crap. It was more officious than the language used in Chastity's tent, but there the listeners were simply gullible, not insane.

"As the Ancient Ones command." Script or not, the actress in Max took over, as Peter had hoped. She abandoned the camera, then the shawl, and moved to Himmler's right. With no lights to contend with, Himmler rotated his neck and gaped, making up for lost opportunities.

"What I draw from the pot will signify all that will come and will designate he who will make it so." Peter lowered his eyes toward the pot. "Signify and designate, oh rune of the ancients; signify and designate." Down went Peter's forefinger, into the pot, into the flame, then suddenly up and out, ablaze.

"There, Heinrich, there!" Max, without any subtle urging from Peter, tried to do her part. "You saw it! You saw it!"

"Yes, I saw it!" Himmler was more excited than Max and he wasn't acting. "I saw it! The *Sig* rune! There, in the sky! The *Sig* rune."

"Yes, the Sig rune!" Max, who knew what rune was supposed to be projected, exclaimed. Peter could tell that Max was astonished. Later she would

want him to tell her how, using nothing but his flaming fingertip, he got
Himmler to see not just a rune but the right one. And Peter would explain
about a verbal force, using certain words like "signify" and "designate" and
placing a little extra emphasis on "sig" to plant the image of the rune in
Himmler's mind. The trick was to do it immediately before the fire writing
so the two were connected. But that would be later. Now it was time to
hook Himmler completely.

"May I return to the camera?" Max whispered, in keeping with the solemn tone Peter had set.

Peter motioned her back with his hand, welcoming the chance to get her
away from Himmler. "Sig. The rune that encapsulates the values of the SS
and conveys its true purpose. Sig. The rune that no man can command,
although over the centuries a certain select few have been allowed to bond
with it. You alone in this century, *Reichsführer,* are among them." It was a
nice touch, reinforcing that Himmler, not Hitler, had been called to greatness. Unsure of whether to speak, Himmler bowed his head. For him it was
an act of humility; to Peter it showed Himmler's surrender. He had the
bastard.

"We are near the end of the ceremony." Peter lifted the pot of blood and
water and poured its contents into the rune bowl, which he then placed on
the ground. The fire doused, Peter reached into the bowl, removed the piece
of stone that he had chipped off and placed it on the altar. "Come forward,
both of you, and observe."

With Max and Himmler flanking him Peter rubbed his right palm over
the stone, removing the char and ash and revealing an image that had been
seared into it.

More than his face, Himmler's hands said it all—they were glued to the
sides of the altar to keep him from toppling over. He opened his mouth,
but nothing came out.

"Two of the chosen runes." His finger hovering above the stone, Peter
pointed as he spoke. "Algiz and Thurisaz combined into a bind rune." Peter
glanced at Himmler, who was so shaken that his eyes remained fixed on
the symbol rather than Max's body. "And here is the third rune, Sig." Peter's
finger circled what looked like a *Z* on the left side of the symbol. "Only, like
the Thurisaz, it's reversed. That makes this bindrune exceptional."

"Why is that?" Max asked.

"Because it's a wendrune." Himmler's voice had returned, but that was all he volunteered, leaving Peter to pick up the slack.

"In the right hands, wendrunes can have incredible power, including the ability to turn situations around, to make the impossible possible."

"Then could—"

Peter cut Max off by raising his hand. "The time for questions will come. Now go dress. The ceremony is over."

When Max left, Himmler snatched a twig from the ground and tossed it into the pot of lead. It dissolved immediately.

"Do you doubt?" Peter began stomping out the fire under the pot.

"No, not at all." Himmler's answer had an apprehensive undertone, as if he was afraid of offending the Ancient Ones, who might then choose another to guide Germany to its destiny.

But for Peter, Himmler's smell more clearly indicated his fear—and his fervor. It had been building through the whole ceremony, and what was faint at first Peter, with his hyper-developed senses, now found overpowering. Himmler's apocrine glands were reacting to his emotional state, secreting sweat containing cellular matter that bacteria were breaking down. Himmler's armpits were bad enough, but the odor it produced in Himmler's groin area was brutal and even in the crisp evening air Peter felt like a prisoner in an outhouse. Only the reappearance of a fully clothed, fresh-smelling Max carrying a film reel kept him from keeling over.

"What do you have?" Himmler asked.

"Nothing anymore." Max tossed the reel into the lead. "I should have trusted your instincts, Heinrich. What we witnessed tonight must remain private."

Perfect. Peter watched the last tiny bubbles of dissolving celluloid. That took care of the film used to project the runes, leaving one last piece of evidence to dispose of.

"What comes next, given the profound import of all that's happened here?" Max asked, turning to Peter.

"I can't say for sure, but I believe it has something to do with the wendrune. *Reichsführer*, does the wendrune hold any particular meaning for you?"

Himmler gripped his left wrist as if to hide the tattoo, which was already covered by his shirtsleeve, but said nothing.

"*Reichsführer*, the wendrune didn't simply appear. The Ancient Ones had a purpose, one that wasn't communicated to me. I believe it was intended as a message for you. Do you know what that message might be?"

"Russia."

Short but sufficient. "Russia? In what respect?"

Had Himmler hoped to resume his silence, Max wasn't going to let him. "Peter, you said wendrunes could turn things around. Even wars?"

"If matters are going badly, yes, even wars. Again, it depends on who uses them."

"Then perhaps this wendrune has something to do with the war in Russia," Max said. "I've heard talk—some rumor, some seemingly informed—that things are not going well there." She looked at Himmler. "Heinrich?"

Now it was Peter's turn to prod when Himmler didn't respond. "*Reichsführer*, please, if I'm out of line, I apologize, but this is too important. Herr Goebbels paints a positive picture for the people; is that the true situation in Russia?"

This was the test. Peter's con-man instincts said Himmler had been completely sucked in by the sham ceremony. But Peter's con-man experience said any hustle could suddenly go sour. There was no way Himmler would discuss what was really happening in Russia with him or Max, unless he had something to gain from it, and even then it was dicey.

"Herr Kepler . . ."

Herr Kepler and not Peter. That wasn't encouraging.

"You are indeed out of line, very much so, and so am I, because I am going to tell you what the real situation is in Russia. On the surface, we are winning. Paulus and his Sixth Army have ninety percent of Stalingrad under their control. But the remaining ten percent is proving impossible to take. The Russians holed up in the city are like wild animals and our soldiers haven't been able to pry them out of their lairs. Paulus' lines are stretched thin, supply delivery grows more difficult and the Luftwaffe can't provide the support needed. The longer the offensive drags on, the worse the situation becomes. Paulus grows more mired while his options narrow."

"And winter will soon be there," Max said, helpfully reminding Himmler of the brutal Russian winter.

Himmler grimaced as if Max's words were salt, which she sprinkled on a still-festering wound. It had been a year since the Ahnenerbe's Meteorology Section had forecast a mild Russian winter using a half-baked theory that ice was the fundamental substance of the universe. Hitler had accepted the forecast and the Germany military was equipped accordingly. And so when the forecast proved wrong, German soldiers had to fight in sub-zero temperatures wearing flimsy summer uniforms, backed up by malfunctioning tanks that hadn't been properly winterized. The monumental debacle contributed greatly to prolonging the war in Russia and cast serious doubt on Himmler's so-called scientific projects.

"I am very aware of the seasons, thank you."

"And I'm sure the generals are also aware," Peter said, shifting the blame. "Although from what you're saying, Reichsführer, they don't seem to be handling things very well."

"The generals handle nothing!" Himmler said in disgust. "The *Führer*, and only the *Führer*, handles every aspect of the war in Russia. All decisions are his alone and he is confident that they will lead to Stalingrad falling in a matter of days."

Himmler's remarks were a surprise to Peter. "It would appear as if he has a different view of the situation than you described, and while decisive, the *Führer's* actions also appear to be inconsistent with those the Ancient Ones have called for. However, there is obviously much I don't know."

Instead of defending Hitler, Himmler said nothing. Did the silence mean Himmler was finally admitting to himself that Hitler was responsible for the failures in Russia and that, without a change in strategy, the Eastern Front would be lost, along with his dream of establishing an SS empire on Soviet soil? Peter, turning away from Himmler, busied himself with his post-ceremony cleanup while he waited.

Finally Himmler spoke. "So what must I do?"

Peter turned back to Himmler. The die was cast. Caesar had crossed the Rubicon, not to be the assassinated but the assassin and Peter had to ensure that the knife was at the ready.

"The Ancient Ones didn't specify beyond your willingly accepting responsibility for Germany's future greatness, *Reichsführer*. Are you indeed ready? Are you prepared to do what is necessary, even if it might place you in grave danger? If so, then I can offer advice if you so desire."

"I so desire."

Peter nodded, then asked Max, "May I use your shawl again?"

"Of course." Max took it from her neck and handed it to him.

Peter wrapped the stone with the wendrune in the shawl, placed it on the ground and then smashed it repeatedly with the hammer until nothing but small fragments of rock remained.

"Reichsführer." Peter rose, holding the scarf between his hands like a basket, and directed Himmler to take three of the shards. "As for the rest." Peter tossed the other pieces over the edge of the column, shaking the shawl to make sure all had been disposed of. "What occurred here tonight was not intended for others to see," Peter said. What he didn't say was *another gimmick gone.*

"What am I to do with these?" Himmler held out his palm with the three small pieces of rock.

"Nothing yet." Peter placed them in the shawl along with a kindling branch that hadn't been too charred by the fire, and folded it. "But within seven days, you will use them to great advantage."

"More mystic doings?" Himmler asked, although Peter took his question as coming from an interested believer rather than a skeptic. Still, Peter had to be careful: Himmler might be mad, but he wasn't stupid.

"Scientific, actually. But, please, you must wait."

"Then I imagine we're finished for now," Himmler said. "Shall we?"

"You and Max go on," Peter said. "I have to let the lead cool so I can clean up here."

"Nonsense. Leave it. I'll send someone to take care of it. We're all going back together." Himmler glanced at his watch. "Nearly ten P.M. You and Max will stay at Wewelsburg tonight. In the morning you can fly back to Berlin with me."

"That's sweet of you, Heinrich." Max squeezed his cheek. "Let me pack up my equipment."

"Leave that as well. My men will fetch it before we take off tomorrow."

"It'll only take a moment," Max said.

"I insist, Max. Leave it."

Always expect the unexpected, although Peter wouldn't have thought of this. Even if he could step in, which he couldn't, Himmler wasn't going to budge.

"A compromise. I'll just take my camera."

"No need. They'll bring it all back."

"I don't go anywhere without my camera. You know that, Heinrich. If it stays, I stay."

"She has a real stubborn streak," Himmler said to Peter. "She's also more attached to her cameras than most mothers are to their children." He turned to Max. "A compromise, then. Go get your camera."

Max quickly removed the fake camera from its tripod and, instead of its heavier case, placed it in a canvas bag she had brought along. "I'm going to shut down the photo lights," she said, and Peter and Himmler took flashlights from their pockets.

"I'm more familiar with the area," Himmler said when Max returned. "I'll go ahead across the bridge and shine my light on it so you both can safely cross."

"You're a dear, Heinrich." One more pat on the cheek from Max sent Himmler on his way. Once his back was to them, Max kissed Peter. "You were magnificent."

"You were pretty good yourself."

"Considering you held a few things back. Whatever happened to our no-secrets agreement?"

"Come on—minor stuff. A flash of light."

"I'm talking about what's going to happen within a week."

"I didn't hold that back. I have no idea what's going to happen. I made it up on the spot. That's the bad news."

"What's the good news?"

"I may not know what I'm going to do, but I do know how I'm going to do it."

When Himmler returned to Wewelsburg with Peter and Max, a communiqué from Berlin marked *Urgent* was waiting. Though short, it gave Himmler a message that went far beyond its content.

"What's the matter, Heinrich?" Max asked.

"Montgomery has attacked at El Alamein. Rommel was caught totally unprepared. It appears he may be headed for a massive defeat."

35

Berlin: October 25, 1942
Your Stars Today: Be prepared: turbulent conditions will bring
about strategy sessions on critical matters of far-reaching
concern.

The Berlin papers that greeted Peter and Max when they returned with
Himmler the next day said nothing about Rommel. Instead, they were buzz-
ing with Goebbels-issued stories on the impending victory at Stalingrad, a
sure sign that the German army was in a desperate situation, with the end
near. But how near was key to Peter revealing something dramatic and
definitive to Himmler within the week, as he had promised on the Extern-
esteine. That meant getting access to the top-secret information that only
the most highly placed intelligence officials would be privy to, officials like
Karl Albrecht.

If Albrecht didn't have the information, he could probably get it. Then
there was Father Fritz, who undoubtedly had other sources. If only Peter
could resolve his lingering doubts about the priest. There was no rational
reason to distrust Father Fritz. He had always protected Peter. And Father
Fritz did come clean about being a member of the wendrune order. Still,
something about him just didn't seem right. Reservations aside, Peter arranged for the necessary meeting.

It was a dinnertime gathering for three in the rectory study—Father
Fritz, Albrecht and Peter—but the only thing on the menu was Russia. Father
Fritz and Albrecht already knew the Externsteine plan had succeeded, so
Peter offered only a brief summary.

"And what do you intend to tell Himmler?" Albrecht asked when Peter
finished, echoing Max's question.

"That depends on what you can tell me," Peter said.

"What I can tell you." Albrecht, dressed casually and ensconced in an
easy chair, sliced the end from one of the cigars Father Fritz had passed
around and threw the silver cutter on the table. "What I can tell you."
Albrecht lit a match, ran it along the length of the cigar to warm the
wrapper, then held the flame under the tip. He took a puff and slowly

released the smoke from his mouth. "I can tell you everything Himmler said about the Eastern Front is correct. In fact, it's actually worse than he described. He doesn't see all the dispatches and the intelligence reports."

"And does Hitler?" Peter asked.

"Hitler sees what he wants to see. When the news is bad—as it has constantly been of late—he closes his eyes to it and blames the field or staff generals. Lately he's taken to simply dismissing them."

"Like Halder, head of the Eastern Front Command," Father Fritz said through a mist of bluish smoke from his own cigar

"Former head." Albrecht corrected him. "Halder's a brilliant general, although as a person he's an elitist prig. His nose is always up in the air, but it was never up Hitler's ass and that was his downfall. From the start, Hitler was adamant about fighting a two-front war within Russia. He created two armies. One, Army A, was to capture the oil and wheat fields in the Caucasus while the other, Army B, was to take Stalingrad. Halder never liked the plan, and rightly so. Neither army had been able to accomplish its objective and the losses had been staggering. Finally, about a month ago, Halder couldn't stay silent any longer and openly disagreed with Hitler's Russian strategy. So Hitler tossed him out and replaced him with Kurt Zeitzler."

"Zeitzler is nowhere near Halder's caliber," Father Fritz said. "He's more prone to hold his fire around Hitler."

"Not true," Albrecht said. "Halder held his fire around Hitler many times." Both Albrecht and Father Fritz broke out laughing.

"Obviously I'm missing something," Peter said.

"You are," Albrecht replied. "Some years ago, Halder was so opposed to Hitler and his plans for Germany that he took to carrying around a pistol in his pocket, determined to finish him off. But each time he had a chance, he backed down."

"A typical German officer, bound more to duty and oath than to a greater morality," Father Fritz added.

"Absolutely," Albrecht agreed. "Halder continued to flirt with joining the resistance against Hitler, even recently, but each time his toe hit the water, he found it too cold."

"So now there's another toady at Hitler's side," Peter said.

"Yes and no," Albrecht said. "Even Zeitzler couldn't remain blind to the obvious. I understand he's hinted during meetings that Paulus should be allowed to pull his army back before it's too late."

"I didn't know that," Father Fritz said. "That must have put the *Führer* in an especially jolly mood."

"On one occasion when Zeitzler mentioned withdrawal, I hear Hitler went into a rage, shouting, 'I won't leave the Volga! I won't go back from the Volga!' over and over, insisting that holding Stalingrad will have a devastating psychological effect on the Russians and will cause their defeat."

"Can Stalingrad be held?" Peter asked Albrecht.

"It can and will be, but not by us, not the way Hitler's going about things. Our front line is fragmented. If Paulus was allowed to withdraw, there's a chance he could restore it. But that won't happen."

All of this was valuable background, but Peter had yet to hear anything that he could use with Himmler. "Karl, can you tell me more of what your intelligence sources are saying?"

"There's some buildup of Soviet troops in the Stalingrad area, near our Third Romanian Army, although not enough to mount a major offensive. They're probably getting ready to try to sever the train lines there and cut off supplies. No, the Russians have been hitting us more in the central and northern regions and haven't deployed their strategic reserves near Moscow to Stalingrad. We also intercepted a detailed Stavka directive on defensive measures to be put into place for winter. Looks as if they're relying on the weather to do what their military can't."

"And this is the information you've been sending to Hitler?" Peter asked.

"We send it, but he also gets the same information from Gehlen."

"Reinhard Gehlen," Father Fritz said, anticipating Peter's question. "He heads Foreign Armies East, the General Staff's Russian intelligence-gathering unit."

"And the information Gehlen gathers usually comes from our sources. His own sources simply confirm what ours report, only several days later," Albrecht said, contempt in his voice.

"You place a great deal of faith in your Russian inside operations," Peter said.

"Complete faith. And with good reason. It's overseen by someone that is completely reliable. He's been checked, double-checked and triple-checked."

But not Peter-checked. "I assume he has a name."

Albrecht took a sip of brandy. "His code name is Komerad Kostya and—"

"You named him Komerad Kostya?" Peter asked.

"It was a collaborative effort. He chose Kostya. Oster tacked on 'Komerad.' He likes alliteration. Why?"

But Peter wasn't about to be sidetracked. "Do you happen to know if Komerad Kostya likes the theater?"

Father Fritz leaned forward in his chair. "That's a strange question, Peter, even for you."

"Perhaps. Do either of you know the book *An Actor Prepares,* in which the great Russian director Stanislavsky explains his theories?"

"I don't," Father Fritz said. "Karl?" Albrecht shook his head.

"The book is a collection of notes taken by Kostya, a young student, during his first year of acting class."

"Interesting, but Kostya isn't an uncommon Russian name," Albrecht said. "Isn't it short for Konstantine?"

"Which was Stanislavsky's own first name," Peter said. "However, put it together with the name 'Skrobat'—"

"You mean Komerad Kostya never mentioned Skrobat? No, of course he wouldn't."

"Peter, what's this all about?" Father Fritz asked.

"Gentlemen, pour some more brandy and relax. I'm about to tell you some circus tales. And when I finish those, I'm going to tell you why you can't trust Komerad Kostya. And finally I'm going to tell you what the Russians actually intend to do at Stalingrad."

Wewelsburg: October 31, 1942
Your Stars Today: The rise of alternative perspectives leads
to radical ideas for change and an urge to rule and achieve
fanatical objectives can generate power struggles.

Clad in his customary uniform, Reichsführer-SS Heinrich Himmler entered the Wewelsburg woods unaware that on this particular morning he was dressed for battle.

Peter, wearing more casual clothes, was already at the assigned meeting spot. They exchanged pleasantries, made a few comments about the beauty of the dawn sky that was just beginning to give way to day and then got down to the business at hand.

"So, at last I'm to learn how to fulfill the destiny of the Ancient Ones. I have been waiting for this moment."

That was good. Himmler still bought in to all the mystical malarkey Peter had staged for his benefit.

"I was surprised, however, at the location," Himmler continued. "I would have thought we'd be returning to the Externsteine."

Peter was ready for that. "As you have said, some places such as the Externsteine possess a geo-mystical energy that man could connect with. However, different purposes require different places with different energies. What we are about to do requires the energy from here. Your historic destiny, like that of these woods, is linked to Russia." He stopped to give Himmler an opportunity to pick up on his hint.

"*Schlacht am Birkenbaum,*" Himmler said immediately, much to Peter's satisfaction.

"Exactly, *Reichsführer.* The Battle of the Birch Tree, the ultimate confrontation between the armies of the West and the hordes of the East. Most think it a mere legend."

"But things thought of as legend will be shown as fact," Himmler added. "How many times did Wiligut say that? He was convinced that the Battle of the Birch Tree would occur right here. It was why he insisted I purchase Wewelsburg Castle and make it the center of the SS. We will be ready when the time comes."

Usually Otto provided Peter with the best setup lines, but Himmler had him beat. "The time *has* come."

Himmler looked around. "I don't see any armies or any barbarian invaders."

"Nor will you. I've thought hard on this, *Reichsführer,* and I believe the confrontation won't physically occur here. Instead, it's occurring as we speak, on the Eastern Front. However, the decisions made here will determine the outcome. And those will be decisions you make. That was what the Ancient Ones were telling us. Of course, you understand I could be mistaken."

Himmler considered Peter's words before speaking. "No, I don't think so. It's all so clear once you see the entire picture instead of small parts of it."

Peter felt his juices flowing. Himmler had taken the bait. "I had the same reaction. It was all so clear, and so overwhelming."

"As to these decisions I'm supposed to make. I would assume they revolve around Stalingrad."

"You and the *Führer* have both said that whoever controlled Stalingrad would control the East."

"Which is likely to be Stalin." Himmler's face tightened when he mentioned the Soviet leader's name.

"Now, yes, but not necessarily later. If Paulus withdraws, then waits until he's better equipped and our other armies in the East move in to support—"

"I've told you, the *Führer* won't hear of pulling back and there's nothing I can do." Himmler's burst of frustration was followed quickly by calm. "I'm not one of his top military advisers."

This was the first time Himmler admitted being excluded from high level military planning. Peter jumped on the opening. "And yet you were right about what would happen in North Africa."

"With your assistance."

"All leaders have assistance. The test of leadership is acting, not receiving counsel. Would you act on Stalingrad if you could?"

Himmler hesitated. "You know how concerned I am about Paulus and his army. However, our information indicates that a Russian offensive won't be launched any time soon. So there's still a chance Paulus can withstand it when it does come."

"Conventional information." Peter lifted a small pouch that was beside him on the ground and pulled out something to show Himmler. "Do you recognize this?"

"It looks like the three bits of stone from the Externsteine, taped and attached by strings of different lengths to the branch that also came from there."

"It's a triple pendulum, which can give us some direction."

"I'm familiar with pendulums," Himmler said, lifting his right hand and then swinging his palm downward dismissively. "We've tried using them to locate enemy ships, with very mixed results."

"Like relocation in the astrology charts, perhaps a different method would produce a more useful outcome." Peter knew Himmler wasn't going to argue that point. Again Peter reached into the pouch, took out an oversized piece of paper and unfolded it. "An enlarged map of Stalingrad." Peter knelt on the ground and spread out the map. "Would you join me, please, *Reichsführer.*"

Once Himmler settled into position, Peter held up the triple pendulum and pressed one end against his palm. "Please do the same with the other end," he said to Himmler, "and then press lightly, as will I, so the branch is stable yet still flexible." Peter waited until he was sure Himmler was holding the pendulum properly. "Now, both of us must think only of the word 'Stalingrad,' and nothing else, as we slowly move the pendulum bar back and forth over the map. The pendulums, however, must be kept still. Move only the bar and try to avoid any jiggling. Again, our minds must focus only on the word 'Stalingrad.' Are you ready?"

Himmler nodded and Peter took the lead, starting to move his hand. Himmler tried to follow but dropped his end of the branch.

"Keeping the proper tension takes a little doing," Peter said. "Let's try it again."

This time Himmler almost lost his end but, with a little more pressure, kept it from falling.

"Good," Peter said. "That's the way. Now, focus on nothing but Stalingrad."

As the two moved the bar across the map, the pendulum in the middle began to rotate in a clockwise direction, gradually building up speed. Then the pendulum at the end nearest to Himmler started to rotate in the opposite direction. Soon they were both spinning rapidly.

"Now pull your hand back from the end of the bar," Peter said as he did the same. The bar and all the pendulums fell onto the map. Peter took a pencil from his pocket and circled where the pendulum that didn't rotate landed. "*Reichsführer*, would you remove the tape holding the string to the stone pieces?"

Himmler first unmasked the two pieces that had been spinning. When he got to the third, he saw that it was the only piece with something etched on it: the wendrune. "What is this?" he exclaimed, proclaiming his amazement.

"This" was the ideomotor effect, the ability of thoughts to control the swing of pendulums, which had been known and studied for centuries. However, Peter's ability to make two specific pendulums on a common bar rotate in opposite directions while keeping a third stationary never failed to fool even those well acquainted with the effect.

"Wait. Let's see where it landed," Peter said and the two peered at the circle. "Here."

"That's not the heart of Stalingrad," Himmler said. "If I remember correctly, that's where Paulus' left flank is."

You remember perfectly, Peter thought. That's why he made sure to maneuver the bar to drop where it did. That's where the Soviet attack would come—there and on Paulus' other flank. *Maskirovka*. The Germans were expecting an attack at Stalingrad, but not for months, since the Russians had to regroup. That's what the Germans had been led to expect. But they were wrong. What they'd seen was Skrobat falling from the trapeze. What they hadn't seen yet was how he grabbed the rope at the end, leaving them dazzled. And, in the case of the German army, dead. "That is where the Russians will attack, and soon. Probably before the end of the month."

"Impossible," Himmler said, but Peter could see that wasn't what he really believed.

"Perhaps. But I'm convinced that this information shouldn't be disregarded."

"We shall see." Himmler rose. "If it proves correct, we will discuss what steps to take. But if it doesn't prove correct—"

"I did say I could be mistaken, *Reichsführer*," Peter quickly interjected.

What Peter didn't say was that if he was wrong, the mission, and quite possibly all those associated with it, would be finished.

36

Berlin: November 2, 1942
Your Stars Today: Change is in the wind and it could prove
a turning point for important matters that are pending.

"He's dead."

That was the news Peter received when he arrived at the rectory, summoned by Father Fritz for an early-morning cup of coffee. Peter didn't have to ask. He knew who was dead: Albert Sang. Today was the day that Father Fritz had singled out. Peter looked at his watch: just a few minutes after 7:00 A.M. "That didn't take long. The day's just starting. What happened?"

"According to Albrecht, he fell down the stairs and broke his neck."

"An accident?"

"Of sorts. Seems he had been drinking." Father Fritz took a sip of coffee and held it in his mouth as he reflected, then swallowed. "Sang and alcohol had been friends for years, although usually on good terms. He could be surly, but that had more to do with his personality. He was surly sober. Still, people change." Father Fritz drifted off again for a brief spell. "How well I know that."

"What more do we know?" Peter asked.

"I told Albrecht certain things about the wendrune order, without going into great detail, and asked that he keep watch on Sang's home. Last night Sang had a visitor—Kurt Veidt. Veidt arrived about ten thirty P.M. and stayed until around midnight. A few minutes later some of the lights in the house went out, and that was it until six this morning when Sang's aide brought the early briefing reports and discovered the body on the marble floor of the foyer. The stairs are fairly steep. Supposedly, Sang was badly bruised. His right arm was also broken along with his neck."

"They couldn't have finished the autopsy already. What makes them think he had been drinking?"

The phone rang, but Father Fritz left it for Hildie to answer.

"The smell of liquor on his clothes. He must have spilled some."

"I assume you'll be able to find out what the final report says."

"Through Albrecht, yes."

"Then keep me informed."

The phone rang again. "Excuse me—Hildie must be indisposed." Father Fritz got up, went to his desk and picked up the receiver. "Hello. . . . He's right here. Do you need to speak with him? . . . No, I'll tell him. . . . Right. Good-bye." Father Fritz put the receiver back in its cradle. "Looks like you might be keeping me informed. That was Max. Himmler called you and when there was no answer he called her. He wants you to come to his office this afternoon at two P.M. Given your prediction about harm coming to someone close to Hitler, and your prior deceptions, I think Himmler suspects something."

"What do you think he suspects?"

"That you're the genuine article."

"You've heard about Sang, of course." Himmler didn't waste any time with cordialities once Peter had been shown into his office. "Just as you predicted, one of the three possible deaths. I am saddened beyond words over the loss of such a pillar of the Reich."

"Yet you did warn him, *Reichsführer*."

"I warned all of them," Himmler replied, although Peter wasn't so sure.

"In that case, there is nothing more you could do. The stars merely direct us. We can change outcomes, but only if we listen to what they tell us."

"It was so foolish, so needless," Himmler said. "A lack of discipline, of self-control, and this is the result." He opened a folder he had carried with him from his desk marked *Höchste Geheimhaltung*—Highest Secrecy—in bold Gothic letters. "An excessive amount of alcohol in the blood . . . severe cranial and cerebral trauma . . . asphyxiation caused by a fracturing of the fourth cervical vertebra . . . consistent with the impact of the head on hard marble." Himmler removed some pictures from the folder and handed them to Peter. "Here—see for yourself."

The autopsy pictures were a visual rehash of what Himmler had read. Peter handed them back.

"Not pretty." Himmler stuck them back in the folder, leaving Peter to ponder how the *Reichsführer* might characterize pictures of the victims tortured and slaughtered by his command. "But it will not be how he is remembered. He will be remembered as a hero of the Reich, viciously murdered by an enemy of the Reich. We will, of course, apprehend this fiend."

"But there is no murderer, *Reichsführer*."

"There will be, when the time is right."

"And the autopsy report?"

"This?" Himmler held up the folder, then tore it into pieces and tossed it on the table in front of the sofa. "No, the real report is being prepared, with all the graphic details of this monstrous crime. There will be a state funeral. Goebbels stages them whenever he can. Good for morale."

"What can I do to help in this matter, *Reichsführer*?"

"Nothing. You already provided tremendous help. Unfortunately, it was for nothing, since your cautions weren't heeded."

"Then can I assist you in some other way?"

"At this moment, no. I simply wanted to tell you how impressed I am with your knowledge and skills. But soon I may need to call on you—and them—again."

"I and they are always at your disposal."

"I know." Himmler put his hand on Peter's shoulder, then withdrew it. "You have been a valuable ally. And you've been a friend. Sometimes I feel guilty. I draw on you and give nothing back."

"I believe myself a patriot. Anything I can do for our *Führer* and the Reich I do so willingly, without any thought of return."

Himmler smiled. "Just remember, if there's something I can do, you will tell me."

"I promise I will tell you," Peter said, adding silently *and very soon*.

37

On Monday, November 9, Peter received a telephone command from Himmler couched as an invitation to visit Hegewald, his Eastern Front headquarters near the Ukrainian town of Zhitomir.

"Max filmed here earlier, but said you still need to write the narration," Himmler, who was already at Hegewald, said. "It would be good if you spent a few days and saw the model resettlement colony for ethnic Germans I've established. Once we are victorious, similar colonies will spread throughout the east, producing farm goods that will sustain them and the Reich."

Peter didn't like Himmler's reference to Germany being victorious. Was it a slip or a sign that he had backslid and was again blindly accepting Hitler's flawed view of the situation in Russia? Whatever it was, Peter had to keep Himmler on course, and being together at Hegewald could help.

Buying time to confer with Father Fritz and the others, Peter told Himmler he was in the middle of an important segment for the documentary and asked if it was possible for him to have the rest of the week and leave on Saturday.

It was, and Himmler arranged for Peter to travel the seven hundred miles aboard a military train from Berlin. Peter wasted no time and assembled the group the next day. All agreed that Peter's trip could be beneficial. Max, the only one who had been to Hegewald, offered her impressions, while Karl Albrecht summarized the most current intelligence reports on the Eastern Front and Father Fritz provided some background on Himmler's resettlement plan. Then they said their good-byes.

Two nights before Peter was scheduled to leave, Father Fritz called, asking that he come to the rectory immediately for an urgent meeting with Albrecht. "I don't know anything more," Father Fritz said when Peter pressed him. "Albrecht was rushed. Our conversation lasted less than a minute."

Albrecht arrived at the rectory a half hour after Peter. "I'm sorry I'm late. It's been chaos." Albrecht didn't bother with being asked but headed straight for the side table, poured a glass of brandy and took a sip. "That's better," he said, and sat down.

"For heaven's sake, Karl, what's this all about?" Father Fritz asked.

"It's about a lengthy meeting that Oster and I had with Canaris today. He came back from Spain this afternoon with some disturbing news. Word is that Roosevelt has convinced Churchill to accept only an unconditional German surrender."

"What!" Father Fritz exclaimed. "Unconditional surrender?"

"They're setting up another Allied conference to announce it."

"So even if Himmler replaces Hitler, there's no chance of a separate peace with the Allies."

"Himmler or anyone else," Albrecht said. "It's a potentially devastating strategic shift. Stalin's been applying pressure for a second front in Europe, but Roosevelt and Churchill have been stalling. Unconditional surrender could be a placatory gesture to ensure him the United States and Britain won't join forces with Germany against Russia.

"Hold on a second," Peter said. "Back up. Where's Canaris getting this so-called word from?"

"From sources even you would concede are in a position to know," Albrecht said.

"Try me."

"Menzies and Donovan."

Albrecht's disclosure wasn't just convincing; it was stunning. "Are you saying that the head of Germany's military espionage service spoke to his British and American counterparts?"

"Last night, over dinner at an understandably secret location in Spain," Albrecht said. "The three of them go back a long time. They have a lot of respect for one another. They also have the same goal—trying to forge a peace."

Peter looked at Father Fritz. "Did you know about this?"

"Only that they had gotten together before and that they were trying to arrange another meeting. Karl, does the admiral know when this next conference will take place?"

"Not until January, but that's only a guess based on what he was told."

"Did Donovan and Menzies talk about Zodiac?" Peter asked.

"They didn't have to. Everyone knew that if the mission isn't completed before the announcement, it's over."

"But they didn't call it off," Peter said.

"That's the last thing they'd want to do," Albrecht said. "If Hitler's assassinated before the announcement, then a negotiated peace may still be possible."

"But we would have to change the date," Father Fritz said. "January 6 won't work. The conference could be underway by then."

"There's no way of knowing, so it's the wisest course," Albrecht said. "Peter?"

"What do you expect me to say? It is what it is."

"We still have a problem." Albrecht got up, poured another brandy and sat back down. "Hitler's heading for the Wolfschanze, his East Prussian Field Headquarters, later this month and intends to stay there at least for the rest of the year. He feels he can run the campaign more effectively by being closer to the front."

"Closer to the front?" Father Fritz roared. "The front's in Stalingrad, a thousand miles from the Wolfschanze."

"Nevertheless, he's going to be holed up there, although he's kept the graduation and commissioning ceremonies at the SS officer training school in Bad Tölz on the calendar."

The Allies weren't the only ones shifting strategy, Peter thought. "Wasn't it essential that the assassination take place in Berlin so Himmler could head off an immediate leadership challenge?" This time Peter did the calculations. "Bad Tölz is at least four hundred miles from the capital."

"Berlin would have certainly have made things easier," Albrecht said. "Even so, we always intended to have people in place to ensure control. For example, General Friedrich Olbricht, who runs the General Army Office headquarters in Berlin, can communicate with and mobilize reserve units all over Germany using an independent system that can't be monitored or blocked."

"He's part of the Black Orchestra?" Peter asked.

"You'd be surprised," Albrecht said. "No, Bad Tölz will be inconvenient, that's all. The more important consideration is that during the ceremonies Bad Tölz will be swarming with SS members loyal to Himmler. In that respect, it's perfect."

"Are you forgetting something?" Peter asked.

Albrecht smiled at him. "The date? I haven't forgotten. I just wasn't rushing to tell you. December 22, fifteen days sooner. Will that make a big difference?"

"What would you do if I said yes? Fortunately, I haven't gotten Himmler to the point of settling on a date. Don't worry. I'll make it work." Peter rose and smiled. "In the circus, being shot through a hoop from a cannon is always dangerous and exciting, more so if you set the hoop on fire. So if you'll excuse me, I have to find my asbestos underwear."

Hegewald: November 17, 1942
Your Stars Today: Your penchant for seeking the truth is strong today and you know how to go about getting beneath the surface for the information you seek. But be careful that your zeal doesn't put you in a precarious situation.

Peter was delayed getting to Hegewald by troop transport trains, which had track priority. Himmler was still awake and they chatted for twenty minutes or so. Then he advised Peter to get some rest. "Tomorrow we'll tour the villages that are part of the colony. Afterwards we'll dine here with some of the administrative staff who will explain the colony's agricultural and economic workings in greater detail. I want to make sure you have all that you need for this part of the documentary."

As a result, Peter's first full day at Hegewald was fatiguing and his evening boring. Worse, it was unproductive, since he had no chance to speak privately with Himmler. Still, Peter held out hope.

The next morning Peter rose early. Himmler, however, rose earlier.

"The *Reichsführer* apologizes, but he was called back to Berlin on urgent business," one of Himmler's adjutants told Peter. "He departed before daylight. But feel free to remain here as long as you like."

Without Himmler, Peter had no reason to stay. However, before leaving, he wanted to collect root samples from some local medicinal plants. So, after a quick breakfast of sausages and coffee, he headed for a wooded area on the outskirts of the headquarters. While Peter couldn't locate all the species he sought, there were enough to make at least this part of his Ukraine trip a success. He was gathering the last specimens when he heard a rustling and then a voice calling out, "Herr Kepler!"

Peter turned to his right, where he saw a man in uniform. The lack of a shoulder patch insignia said he was a *Mann,* the SS equivalent of a private. "Where did you come from?" Peter asked.

"I was over there." The soldier thrust his open right hand toward a clump of trees. "I've been looking for you. They're concerned at headquarters that you might have gotten lost."

That seemed innocent enough, but Peter was bothered by something he noticed. "I have a fairly good sense of direction. The headquarters are over there." Peter extended his right forefinger toward a clearing.

"It's a good thing I showed up. That's south and headquarters is east." The soldier again pointed at the trees with his open hand. "See, where I showed you before."

There it was again, and it convinced Peter that he better tread cautiously. "Really? Well, now that I know the way back I can stay a while longer and you can return and assure your superiors that everything's fine."

"If I had my way, Herr Kepler, but I don't. I was told to fetch you."

Peter's uneasiness was building. "I thought you were simply sent to make sure I hadn't gotten lost."

"Please, Herr Kepler." The soldier walked toward him. "I'm only following orders."

Time was running out. Peter had to test him now. "And where did those orders come from—Hegewald or Skrobat?"

It was involuntary and fleeting—a second if that long—and would have escaped notice if Peter weren't looking for it. The mention of Skrobat, which would have flown right past an ordinary German soldier, caught this one by surprise, causing his eyebrows to involuntarily rise slightly, then fall immediately back down.

"Skrobat? Who is Skrobat?"

Who, not what. Peter had very deliberately phrased his question. How did the soldier know Skrobat was a person and not a place like Hegewald? "Would you have a better idea if I asked in Russian?"

"Russian? I have no idea what you're talking about. I was sent to find you and bring you back to the *Reichsführer's* compound. Please, Herr Kepler, it would be best if we returned."

The guy was good. Peter gave him that. He wasn't budging. Yet. Now the question became why would a Russian disguised as a lowly SS soldier be lurking around in these woods?

"Are you coming?"

And you're not helping me out. What could Skrobat be up to? A skilled Russian operative, with perfect command of German, who would be able to get through Eastern resistance lines, disguise himself as an inconspicuous SS soldier assigned to Himmler's Ukraine headquarters? There's one obvious answer, of course: kill Himmler. That's how Skrobat would think and that's what Skrobat has planned. "You realize what Skrobat will do to you when he learns Himmler left before you could act."

"What do you know about Skrobat?" the soldier barked.

Well, so much for pretense. Peter had his proof, although it might end up being small comfort. "What does anyone know about Skrobat?"

"The only thing one needs to know—fear." He emphasized the point by drawing his gun.

Peter had tried for stalling but would have to rely on bluffing. "If you intend to kill me, be prepared for a lot of explaining, provided he gives you a chance."

"He who? Himmler? As you correctly figured out, I'm inconspicuous. I don't exist for Himmler."

"Himmler? I care nothing for Himmler. I'm talking about Skrobat, the man we both answer to."

"You answer to Skrobat? Don't make me laugh."

"I want to make you think. You're here to kill Himmler. Good for you. The sooner he's gone, the better. But I doubt Skrobat's orders included killing the man he personally sent on another important assignment. It has nothing to do with getting rid of Himmler, so don't worry—you won't have to share that honor. But you will have to answer for getting rid of me. So, again, I suggest you weigh your actions very carefully."

"Let's go." The soldier moved close enough to point the barrel of the gun just inches from Peter's forehead.

So much for bluffing. "Where to?"

"Turn around, drop that bag you're holding—"

"They're nothing but root samples."

"Drop them and walk!"

Damn. Peter was afraid of that. He's one of Skrobat's *biryuks*. What was it Medov said? *Biryuks* won't stop until they've completed their tasks. There was no chance the soldier would have believed Peter was on a mission for Skrobat. *Biryuks* are trained to trust no one. Killing Himmler was all that mattered to this *biryuk*, so Peter had to be removed.

Peter continued to talk as they walked, but it was a one-sided conversation. Then, after a few minutes, he noticed that the footsteps behind him were softer and had a different cadence. Then he heard "Stop," followed by "you can turn around," but the voice was different. And, when Peter turned around, he saw the person was different as well.

"Who the hell are you?" Peter asked as he took stock of the new arrival, also wearing an SS uniform, but with shoulder patches identifying him as a *Hauptsturmführer*, or captain.

"Someone who answers directly to Major Albrecht. That should be sufficient for you to figure out why I've been keeping watch on you."

"How can I be sure you're telling the truth?"

"Zodiac."

Peter narrowed his eyes. "And what's that supposed to mean?"

"I don't know. Major Albrecht just said to mention it if I needed to."

"What happened to the other one?"

"He had an unfortunate encounter with a garrote about twenty meters back."

"Do you have any idea who he was?"

"A man who was about to kill you. I have his wallet if you want his name."

"Don't bother. It's false. He was Russian, not German," Peter said.

"How do you know that?"

"Where did you say you left him?"

"Back about twenty meters."

"Show me."

"We don't have time. Major Albrecht said I was to get you back to Berlin immediately if there was any trouble. The train's waiting."

"Just show me." Peter turned his head in one direction, then another.

"There!" He thrust his right forefinger straight out. "Back there."

"That's how I knew. He didn't point with his forefinger the way Germans do. He pointed with his open hand, the way Russians do. He was sent here to kill Himmler, and I represented a potential obstacle. Let Albrecht know. I assume you'll be returning to Berlin with me."

"No. I wish I were. I haven't been home to see my wife and children in months. But I can't leave here. Someone else will be watching over you on the train. It's better that you don't know who that is, but you'll be safe. He'll also bring the wallet to the major."

"One last thing before we go." Peter walked over to a patch of dead plants and broke up the soil by kicking it repeatedly with the heel of his shoe. Then he crouched down, dug into the soil with his hands and pulled out some of the plants with their roots attached. "Here's a gift for saving my life." He broke off the roots, shook the dirt from them and handed them to the captain. "Slice these into thin strips and dry them indoors until they turn from white to light brown, then chop them. Take maybe five grams and add a cup of boiling water, then let it steep for three hours before you drink it."

"And after I drink this concoction will I thank you for this gift?"

"No, but your wife will."

38

Berlin: November 19, 1942
Your Stars Today: The Sun in Scorpio bodes well for your
power to persuade, even coerce, others. This, coupled with
your ability to detect motives, can prove advantageous, although you may have to resort to manipulation to achieve
your goals.

On November 19, it snowed in Stalingrad, the first heavy winter storm. But
that was nothing compared to the torrent of Russian troops, more than a
million, that pounded the German army, a surprise attack on Paulus' flanks.

In Berlin, it was cool but dry, although in Himmler's office at Gestapo
headquarters, where Peter was becoming a regular visitor, it was steaming.

"Like you said, the flanks," Himmler ranted. "The flanks. The Russians
are going to encircle Paulus. Everyone knows that now but Hitler. He still
stands firm. Decisive action is needed."

Peter liked what he was hearing. "Action that you could provide, *Reichsführer.*"

"I *would* provide it. But the ability to do so comes at a terrible cost. We
must remember what Hitler has done for Germany."

"If I may I speak freely, *Reichsführer,*" Peter said, and Himmler nodded
his head. "If we continue on our present course, I fear we will only remember
what the *Führer* has done *to* Germany. And for one who has been honored,
dishonor is worse than death."

While not immediate, Himmler's response was the one Peter was hoping
for. "The Bhagavad Gita. Prince Arjuna's charioteer urging him to enter
battle. I'm very much taken with the Gita. I often turn to it for advice on
matters of great consequence."

So Father Fritz was right about Himmler and the Gita, Now Peter knew
what to say next. "Then it's no wonder that you were so familiar with this
portion in which Arjuna despairs at the prospect of killing kinsmen who
are part of the opposing army. His reluctance is much like yours. However,
the charioteer reminds Arjuna of his duty. He tells him he must harden
himself and transcend his concerns. Not to do so is to sin."

"Yes, but Arjuna knows he is really being guided by Sri Krishna, the Supreme Being, who has assumed the form of a charioteer. I have no such direct guidance. Mine comes through others."

And it had been going so well. Himmler was obviously having doubts—or looking for excuses. But more than once Peter had to convince someone to do what needed to be done. "And what would give you such certainty?"

"A clear sign that I must perform this extreme deed that will change the course of the world. A sign that's not delivered through others. Krishna spoke to Arjuna directly. Open the portal to the Ancient Ones and ask them to communicate their will directly to me."

Damn! So close! "The Ancient Ones have their own ways, *Reichsführer*."

"And I have mine. But I swear this to you and them: if I receive an unambiguous sign, I will act without further hesitation."

"I will do what I can, *Reichsführer*," Peter said, knowing that he had no choice but to satisfy Himmler's request.

"Understand, if this doesn't occur, it will merely mean the time isn't right for me to ascend." Himmler placed his arm around Peter's shoulders. "But it will come. And when it does, I'll you put there by my side, in appreciation of everything you've done."

If Himmler only knew everything Peter had done. *You were born to be hanged,* Donovan had told him. Peter wondered if Donovan knew that in the Third Reich there were three punishments for everything he had done: one was to be shot; another was to be guillotined; the third, as Donovan would have appreciated, was to be hanged with piano wire from a meat hook.

Father Fritz called him to the meeting and, as always, offered his rectory study. He and Peter were joined by Karl Albrecht, Max and Otto.

Peter went first and summed up his conversation with Himmler: "He wants personal confirmation of his destiny before he acts. If he gets it, he promised no more delays. If he doesn't, then it's over."

"That really puts us in a bind," Albrecht said. "I thought the Externsteine deception and the Stalingrad prediction would be enough."

"You forget how Himmler can vacillate," Father Fritz said. "However, once he makes up his mind, he won't be swayed."

"Why are you worrying?" Otto said. "Peter will come up with something, like always. Right, Peter?"

"I'm the one you should be talking to about miracles," Father Fritz said.

"But he's not," Peter said. "He's talking magic. And if a mystical message is what it takes to steel Himmler, he'll get one. The Bad Tölz ceremonies are still four weeks away. That gives us the next two weeks to—" It was the way Father Fritz looked at Albrecht that made Peter stop. "What?"

"We don't have four weeks," Father Fritz said, and Max and Otto appeared as taken aback as Peter. "Please. Before you say anything, let Karl explain."

"Nothing was being kept from you," Albrecht said. "We only confirmed this yesterday, and immediately put together this meeting. The problem has to do with the soldier Peter came across in the Ukrainian woods."

"The Russian sent to kill Himmler?" Peter said.

"Not to kill Himmler," Albrecht said. "To kill you."

Max gasped. "Kill Peter? What are you talking about?"

"This was tucked into a hidden compartment of the Russian's wallet." Albrecht took out his own wallet and removed a piece of paper, which he gave to Peter—a portion of a photograph taken in a classroom, copied and enlarged. Magnification had blurred the picture, but not enough to obscure its subject: Professor David Walker. "We have to assume the mission's been compromised, that the Russians know about the Hitler assassination and that they believe Peter's the assassin."

"But wouldn't the Russians want Hitler dead?" Otto said.

"They did, or at least Stalin did," Albrecht replied. "We know that he had ordered assassination plans drawn up."

Otto persisted, "Then why the change?"

"Probably because he sees the same thing we do," Father Fritz said. "Hitler's military blunders are costing Germany the war in the East. Hitler's the best weapon Stalin has, so why should he take it out of service?"

"There's something else," Albrecht said. "Some powerful people in government like Foreign Minister von Ribbentrop are trying to persuade Hitler to make peace with Stalin. Let the Russians take the East and Germany can take Europe. They argue that we can settle the score with Russia later."

"Himmler knows about this?" Peter, who had been taking in all this without showing any sign of concern, asked.

"If I do, he does," Albrecht said.

"That's good," Peter said. "It should make him more determined to act if he gets the assurance he wants."

"He won't be the only one who will be more determined," Albrecht said. "Having failed to kill you in the Ukraine, the Russians will redouble their resolve when they try to kill you here in Germany. You may not be concerned, but I have to be. And short of keeping you under house arrest, I can't protect you. We have to move the assassination date up."

Like it or not, Peter knew Albrecht was right. "How much time do I have?"

"The Russians don't know when you'll strike, so they'll act as quickly as possible."

"Karl, how much time?" Peter repeated his question.

"Nineteen days."

Max's jaw dropped. "You can't be serious!"

"Even that long makes me nervous," Albrecht said. "Keeping Peter alive has become a lot more complicated."

"Nineteen days?" Otto said. "Why so specific? Why not eighteen or twenty?"

"Think about it, Otto," Father Fritz answered. "What's the date?"

Otto counted the days on his fingers. "December 8. December 8 . . . Decem—ah, Heinz Ritter. Now I understand the significance."

"But Peter may not." Father Fritz turned to Peter. "Heinz Ritter was a very persuasive recruiter during the early days of the Nazi Party. Too persuasive for the German communists. On December 8, 1929, while Ritter was organizing a major rally in Münster, they broke into his office and killed him. In less than a week, Goebbels had made Ritter into a Party martyr and used his death to gain support for the Nazi cause. Now Goebbels wants to boost national morale by again using Ritter's death. He's convinced Hitler to leave the Wolfschanze on December 8 and fly to Dortmund, where he will make a late-morning speech and place a wreath on Ritter's statue. Dortmund is less than an hour away from Paderborn by air."

"Help me understand this." Max shot up and began circling the room as she talked. "Himmler's still not ready to kill Hitler, and even if he was there are no plans for Hitler to visit Wewelsburg. Yet within nineteen days we have to turn both of those around." She stopped in front of Father Fritz and Albrecht. "Is that essentially the situation?"

"I think we can get him to Wewelsburg," Father Fritz said as Max returned to her chair. "If you told Goebbels that you need some footage of Hitler at the castle with Himmler."

Max waited a few seconds. "It might work. Goebbels really wants the film finished. But that would be the easy part."

Albrecht picked up the discussion. "What do you think, Peter? It's certainly not the first impossible task you've taken on. Given a few days do you—?"

"We don't have a few days," Peter said. "Start reckoning time in hours and minutes."

"Then we call it off?" Otto asked.

"Like hell!" Peter said. "I'm not walking away from the biggest scam in history." Then after a glance at Max, he dropped the bravado. "But more importantly, I'm not walking away from a cause, and from people that I've come to believe in." He turned to Father Fritz. "It may not be God, but it's still belief."

"Given the circumstances, say three Hail Marys and I'll absolve you." Father Fritz provided the meeting's first laugh.

"I probably should, not to be absolved but to make this work," Peter said. "Last July, when I was detained at Wewelsburg, I was shown Himmler's private quarters, which he named for Henry the Fowler. All the trappings were medieval."

"And all of them were authentic, taken from various museums," Max said. "I filmed his quarters for the documentary."

"There was also something in a leather sheath on his desk, a dagger perhaps. It was about that size. Obviously I couldn't examine it."

"The replica of the lance," Max said.

Father Fritz chimed in. "The Holy Lance, which, legend says, the Roman soldier Longinus used to pierce Christ's side during the crucifixion. Himmler was always fascinated by the lance and its supposed powers."

"The lance was the model for the reconstruction of Wewelsburg," Max added. "It's clear from the plans. The castle itself is the lance's tip and the north tower its point."

Peter made a fist with his right hand and slammed it into the palm of his left. "Perfect."

"Does that mean you have an idea?" Max asked.

"More of a gamble. I can't guarantee it'll work. Even if it does, it may not produce the desired results."

"We're in no position to be choosy," Albrecht said. "How long do you need to set up?"

"I could try it tomorrow, but to better convince Himmler that I've been in contact with the Ancient Ones I'll wait a day or two."

"See, I told you he wouldn't let us down," Otto said. "What are you going to do, Peter?"

"Me? Nothing. Himmler's going to do this all by himself."

Himmler left Berlin for a series of prearranged inspections of SS units in occupied territories. So Peter wasn't able to see him until the morning of November 24 and spell out the instructions received from the Ancient Ones.

"The Ancient Ones have directed I do these things?" Himmler was clearly incredulous upon hearing them.

"I was surprised at them myself, *Reichsführer*. However, I think with the mind of a man, and am therefore incapable of comprehending the ways of the Ancient Ones."

"And I am to carry them out privately this evening at Wewelsburg? I have an engagement this evening, here in Berlin. Why must I go to Wewelsburg?"

"If the Ancient Ones have willed that the rebirth of Germany under your leadership occur at Wewelsburg, then it must be part of everything associated with that rebirth. Everything."

"And if I do go there this evening and carry out the instructions, what will happen?"

"If everything is done exactly as directed, then tonight you will dream you are on a path in a wooded area. You are to follow the path until you come to a bridge spanning a stream. Cross over and, on the other side, there will be a man. You may ask this man one very specific question, but only one. The answer he gives will be what the Ancient Ones require of you."

"And you will also be there, at Wewelsburg?"

"No, *Reichsführer*. I will be in Berlin. I don't want my presence to influence matters in any way. You requested that the Ancient Ones directly speak to you of your destiny. They will, but only in response to one question and only tonight."

"What question should I ask?"

"I can't tell you that, *Reichsführer*. I can play no further part in this. The sign you want will be the answer to a question that has meaning for you. Depending on that answer, you must then either act decisively to claim your destiny, and all that implies, or draw back and relinquish it forever. The choice you make will determine your future and Germany's."

Himmler appeared to be mulling over Peter's words. "This engagement has been on my calendar for a long time," he finally said. "I'm to receive an award, so it isn't something one easily backs out of." Himmler made a soft sound that was close to but not exactly *hmm*, then added, "I will think on this."

"Of course, *Reichsführer*." Peter showed himself out of the office. Never before had he put all his chips into the poker pot, called the hand and left not knowing whether he was flush or broke.

Dead broke.

At 7:15 on the evening of November 24, Reichsführer-SS Heinrich Himmler boarded his private plane and left Berlin. At 8:00 P.M. he landed at the Paderborn airport, and at 8:20 P.M. his chauffeured military Mercedes arrived at the entrance of Wewelsburg Castle. At 8:30 P.M. he ate a light supper and read a few reports. At 9:14 P.M., still dressed in his uniform, he went alone into the woods by the castle, a flashlight in one hand, an empty drinking glass in the other. At 9:21 P.M. he placed a handful of dirt in the glass, and at 9:24 P.M. he found a small stick lying on the ground, which he put in his pocket. At 9:36 P.M. he returned to the castle and retired to his second-floor quarters. At 9:42 P.M. he bathed and put on a dressing robe. At 9:53 P.M. he took the glass, got on his knees and sprinkled the dirt on the carpet beneath his bed. At 9:54 P.M. he filled the glass halfway with water, placed it under the bed as well and laid the stick from the woods across its rim. At 9:56 P.M. he unsheathed the replica of the Holy Lance, which was on his desk, and put it under the bed next to the glass. At 9:59 P.M. he extinguished the lights, removed his robe and, naked, climbed into the bed. At 10:11 P.M. Reichsführer-SS Heinrich Himmler was sound asleep.

It was early afternoon the following day when Himmler returned to his Berlin headquarters. As he had requested before leaving Wewelsburg, Peter was waiting for him. Their conversation was brief and to the point.

"It was as the Ancient Ones told you it would be," Himmler said. "Almost exactly. The man was there, on the other side of the bridge, dressed in knight's armor and holding the lance. I asked my question, which I had crafted very precisely, and he answered, then handed me the lance."

That was a recounting, but Peter was waiting for a decision.

"When I awakened, I thought about my dream and recalled something from the Gita: about with the sword of self-knowledge severing the ignorant doubt in your heart."

Peter retrieved the Gita from his memory and quickly found the quote, part of Krishna's fourth teaching, reread it in context and concluded that Himmler probably didn't really understand what it meant.

"For the wise, those who have true vision, knowledge and action are one," Peter replied with his own paraphrased quote from the Gita, trying to move Himmler along, and asked, "Then have you reached a decision, *Reichsführer*?"

This time Himmler reached for a small leather-bound volume that lay open on his desk, held it up and read, "'Perform that duty that you are obliged to, for action is better than inaction.'" He placed the book down.

"For the good of Germany, I will perform my duty and act. The Ancient Ones will set the date, since nothing has been scheduled. But when the *Führer* next visits Wewelsburg, he will die and Germany will be reborn."

Max was the first to hear that Peter's stratagem had succeeded. He told her before they enjoyed a quiet dinner in the Berlin house that served as both her home and postproduction studio. However, he held back on telling her why it had succeeded until they had finished.

"You always do this to me, Peter," Max said. "You always torture me, making me wait for you to explain how something's done. Maybe now I don't want to know."

"That's fine with me. So how was your day?"

"Damn you, Peter!" Max threw her napkin across the table at him. "You know I want to know! How could you possibly implant a dream in Himmler's mind? Did you hypnotize him in some way?"

"I didn't hypnotize him, although there was some suggestion involved."

"Then what magic trick did you resort to?"

"No magic. It's all psychology and presentation. I told Himmler what he would dream provided he did certain things that weren't part of his regular routine—collecting the dirt, finding the stick, placing items under his bed. Then, while he was sleeping, his brain tried to structure these unfamiliar activities so it could process them. To do this, it sought a connection that would put these pieces of information in some kind of order. Here it was easy. There was a ready-made visual connection—the bridge over the stream, which I had already planted in Himmler's mind. His brain identified that and used it to sequence all the unfamiliar information. His dream was the result of this processing. The fact that he believed he would have the dream if he satisfied the instructions also helped. Sometimes the brain mixes up information and misinformation, making it difficult to know what's true and what's false or what happened and what didn't happen."

"I'm still amazed," Max said. "And also concerned. How long do you think Himmler will be committed to act?"

"You heard Father Fritz the other day talk about Himmler not swaying once he's made up his mind," Peter replied. "But I agree with you about him possibly reconsidering. That's why a tight timetable works to our advantage."

"We're down to thirteen days."

"Are you superstitious?" Peter asked.

"As I said, concerned. We don't have much margin for error."

"Then let's not have any error. The next move is yours."

"I'll make it a point to see Goebbels tomorrow," Max said.

"Are you ready?" Peter said, and the look on Max's face made him add, "Stupid question. Maybe you should simply cook him a meal like this." Peter tapped his dinner plate. "He wouldn't be able to refuse you anything."

"That's funny, because I'm actually preparing an old German specialty for him. You may know it: *Honig im Mund. Galle im Herzen.*"

Peter did indeed know that old German specialty, a saying actually. Max was going to serve Goebbels "a tongue of honey and a heart of gall."

39

Berlin: November 25, 1942
Your Stars Today: With the Sun in Sagittarius, your natural magnetism is particularly strong. Thanks to that, your propensity to be forthright and direct, even in difficult dealings, will be particularly well received today and you could enjoy tremendous success.

Goebbels had been pestering Max about progress on the SS documentary, so she invited him to view some edited segments. He accepted and sat next to her in the small screening room, watching thirty-five minutes of film. When it was over, Goebbels made no attempt to downplay his satisfaction.

"I'm only sorry that we have to waste your genius on Himmler, Elie. But there are times when art must accommodate politics. You understand that, of course, which is why I needed you for this project."

"And now you need me to finish it more quickly than you anticipated. Morale's sagging."

"I didn't say that, nor will I ever!" Goebbels snapped. Then he smiled at Max. "Not publicly. I could always talk honestly to you, Elie. It's true. The war has fatigued everyone. Victory may take longer than planned, which will mean privation will grow. The rationing of food and clothing will become more severe, assigned jobs more demanding. However, our people must never forget why they are sacrificing. Our soldiers must never doubt the righteousness of our cause. The SS documentary will be part of a new initiative to ensure that, despite the sacrifices, faith in the *Führer* and his vision for Germany never wavers. I want it to be ready to show by the tenth anniversary of the Reich next month."

Max feigned shock. "Joseph, do you realize how little time this leaves me?"

"Elie—"

"If I had known about this constraint when I started, or even a month or two ago—"

"Enough, Elie!" It was another outburst, followed by calm. "Things happen. When you started the documentary, I couldn't have cared less when

you finished or even whether you finished. Just the fact that you were working on it suited my purpose. But now I have a new purpose and I need you
to adapt to it."

"You leave me no choice." Max was deliberately brusque and she made
certain that the look on her face reinforced her tone of voice.

"I'm sorry, Elie. I really am. How much do you have left to do?"

"Filming is the biggest problem. I have three short segments, two of
which I could leave out if I had to."

"And the third?"

"The third is the *Führer* with Himmler at Wewelsburg. We were on the
verge of scheduling it twice, but, as you said, things happen."

"So leave it out as well."

"Himmler won't hear of it. He had a short list of segments that must be
included and this was at the top."

"It won't happen. The *Führer* will be rooted into Wolfschanze through
the end of the year and probably into January."

"Be honest with me, Joseph, because I'll find out anyway. He has no
events in Germany scheduled for December?"

"Two. A late-afternoon commissioning ceremony at the Bad Tölz SS
Training Academy on December 22, which was set long ago, and a quick
morning speech honoring Heinz Ritter in Dortmund on December 8, which
I forced him into."

"Joseph, Dortmund is perfect. It's what, fifty miles or so from Paderborn,
practically next door. I could finish filming in early December and—"

"I'm sorry, Elie, but it's out of the question. It's enough I was able to pry
the *Führer* away for the Ritter speech. He's not going to dally, even as a
favor to you."

"This isn't a favor, Joseph. Give me this and then with a spate of sleepless
stretches in the editing room I guarantee you'll have your documentary for
the anniversary. Without it—well, I said Himmler's adamant. If you want
to battle with him over Wewelsburg—"

"Himmler and his damn mystical fantasies. We should have shot that
old demented drunk Wiligut who fed him that foolishness when we had
the chance."

"But you didn't. Besides, Himmler had those fantasies long before Wiligut. Wiligut saw that and built on it."

"Because Himmler's a gullible fool."

"Yes, but a dangerous gullible fool, Joseph, one who will forever be in
your debt if he's pleased with the documentary. Funny you haven't men-

tioned that. Wasn't that your real intention when you insisted that I handle the project?"

Goebbels conceded the point by not responding. Knowing she had pierced his armor, Max sought to widen the opening. "So? Wolf will be close by, Joseph," she said, deliberately using Hitler's nickname to remind Goebbels of her special relationship with him. "And we're not talking a lot of time." Max watched how Goebbels reacted to her words. He was definitely weighing them. "It's not like asking him to do this when he's much further away at Bad Tölz."

"Bad Tölz is part of the problem. The *Führer's* not pleased at being away from Wolfschanze again instead of carefully monitoring the situation on the Eastern Front and making immediate military decisions."

As Max had hoped, Goebbels seized on Bad Tölz, giving her the opportunity she needed. "I know. How nice it would be if events were better coordinated. Think of how we do it in film, Joseph. Instead of shooting in sequence, we lump together all the scenes involving particular actors or locations. It's much less costly that way and much more efficient."

"It certainly would make life easier." Goebbels paused a few seconds. "I wonder . . . Suppose the *Führer's* two days of events were combined into one. The date of Ritter's death can't be changed, but the ceremony at Bad Tölz—"

Yes! "You mean move the ceremonies?"

"Just the when, not the where. The *Führer* could speak at Dortmund in the morning and then attend the Bad Tölz ceremonies in the later afternoon."

"Can you change the Bad Tölz date?" Max asked.

"Not as easily as Himmler. He created and commands the SS officer-training schools. No one is going to argue with him."

Max couldn't have been more pleased. "So you're going to ask Himmler? Do you think he'll agree?"

"He'll be hard-pressed not to. We desperately need officers for North Africa and the Eastern Front. This will make some of them available two weeks earlier than planned. In war two weeks can make a difference. No, I don't anticipate a problem, especially if the day includes lunch at Wewelsburg."

"Lunch at Wewelsburg." Max leaned over and kissed him. "I knew you wouldn't disappoint me, Joseph. It's a brilliant plan."

"Yes, but I'm not certain who really came up with it, you or me. Not that it matters. We both get what we want."

As she nodded her head in agreement, Max thought, *And you, Joseph, will also get much more than you expected.*

Berlin: December 1, 1942
Your Stars Today: A major turning point in an ongoing situation could be at hand and new plans may emerge.

Peter arrived at Max's house with a smile on his face and a bottle of Champagne in his hand. "Already chilled." He gave Max the bottle and removed his topcoat.

"French." Max studied the bottle. "And a fine vintage."

"The best the black market has to offer, according to Otto." Peter took the Champagne and began twisting the cork as he walked to the living room. Max fetched two flutes and followed.

"Just in time." Peter jiggled the cork back and forth until it erupted, shooting into the air and hitting the ceiling, then plummeting to the floor, taking along a small glass vase. "A war wound." Peter picked up the vase and inspected it. "But fortunately not fatal." He put the vase on a coffee table and poured the Champagne. "A toast," he said, handing a flute to Max, then lifting his own. "Here's to women and successful shills. In other words, here's to you." Peter clinked his flute against Max's, took a sip of Champagne and sat down on the sofa.

Max sat down next to him and put her hand on his arm. "Himmler?"

"Wrapped up with a bow. He called me to his office this afternoon and told me that the Bad Tölz ceremonies are being changed to December 8, which will allow Hitler to lunch at Wewelsburg. He wants me to determine whether that date will be favorable for the assassination. Tomorrow Himmler will be reminded that December 8 is a New Moon, making it a perfect date for ending the old and beginning the new."

"Thank God!" Max exclaimed. "I was beginning to worry. There's only a week left. So Goebbels came through."

"*You* came through," Peter said, and watched Max's reaction, a mixture of satisfaction and excitement. "Your first foray as a grifter and you pulled it off brilliantly."

Max quickly corrected him. "Have you forgotten the Externsteine?"

"Ah, but I was there to keep everything in line. I wasn't there with Goebbels. You duped him all by yourself." Peter clinked Max's flute again. "We make a pretty good team." The moment the words left his mouth, Peter saw

Max's mood shift and he knew why. "So I see no reason to break it up once the mission is over."

"Not reason—reality."

"Here's the reality." Peter put his arm around Max and drew her closer to him. "When Himmler succeeds Hitler, people like Canaris and Albrecht and their friends among the Allies will take over the next phase of the mission. If they want our help, we'll help. Together."

"But Stalin wants you dead."

"Stalin only wants me dead because he wants Hitler alive. Soon that's going to be a moot point. And when it is, Stalin will have a lot more on his mind than killing me."

"Then you would stay here, in Germany?" Max said, and snuggled closer.

"Of course I'd stay. Everything I care about is here." Peter gently kissed her brow. "Right here."

"And if something went wrong? It could, you know."

"If something went wrong, there would be a lot of people trying to kill both of us. And we'd face that together." Peter placed his right finger under Max's chin and gently lifted her head, then looked into her eyes. "Together. Do you understand?"

"Yes."

"Good, then let's stop worrying about what-ifs and concentrate on better things we can do together."

Max's smile returned. "Don't you have a chart to prepare?"

"I already prepared one—for tonight." Peter moved his hand from Max's chin to the top button on her blouse. "And it's very, very favorable."

Berlin: December 7, 1942
Your Stars Today: This is a time of great flux and a significant shift in direction looms. Be ready to cope with change.

Although normally expansive, this night Father Fritz kept his journal entries short and routine. The only allusion to the next day's planned assassination was a quote from Matthew—"Take no thought for tomorrow; for tomorrow shall take thought for the things of itself."

Finished, Father Fritz rose and walked over to the fireplace, removed the loose brick and slid the journal back into its hiding place. Only something was blocking it. He stuck his hand into the opening and removed a wooden box, put there long ago and forgotten, which had fallen over. He returned to his desk, sat down and emptied the contents of the box onto his blotter. It was a small collection of assorted items—some faded pictures and folded papers, a few patches and a ring—all of which he tossed back into the box, closing it.

Father Fritz stood up, about to put the box back, then fell back into his chair. He reopened the box, turned it over, pulled the ring from the scattering contents and stared at it. Suddenly he grabbed the phone and placed a call to Karl Albrecht's private number. Following a few minutes of animated discussion, Father Fritz hung up the receiver and put everything but the ring back into the box. Once the box and journal were safely ensconced in the fireplace, he poured a snifter of brandy, settled into his reading chair and waited.

It was a two-snifter wait, enough time for Father Fritz to read a new, privately published monograph by the philosopher Martin Heidegger—or most of it before he threw it down in disgust. How could such a brilliant mind embrace the Nazi ideology so completely and apologize for it so consistently? Father Fritz wondered. The question fascinated him, perhaps because he lived it himself at one time and still couldn't completely comprehend why. Or perhaps because he could. A knock at the rectory door interrupted his pondering.

"I have what you asked for," was Karl Albrecht's version of "hello" when Father Fritz let him in. "But not without exerting a lot of influence."

"I appreciate what you had to go through." Father Fritz took the small packet from Albrecht, leaving him to tend to his overcoat and his own brandy.

"Then how about an explanation? Why you were so insistent I get Albert Sang's SS Death's Head ring?"

"If I'm right, you'll have your explanation."

Father Fritz tore open the packet and examined the ring while Albrecht, between sips of his brandy, kept talking. "Well, you were certainly right about the ring still being at the SS Personnel Bureau here in Berlin. I thought they sent them up regularly to Wewelsburg. I had no idea the Bureau was holding all of them until the shrine to hold them is built. Let me tell you, though—getting an official to open the office at ten P.M. . . . well, that's a story in itself. Let's just say it's a good thing I'm not SS. If my ring ever showed up there while that fellow was on duty, he would melt it down immediately. He kept muttering about not knowing what to say if he was ever asked about Sang's ring."

"He won't have to worry." Father Fritz finally looked up and flipped the ring to Albrecht, who was looking over his shoulder. "It's not Sang's."

Albrecht glanced at the ring. "What are you talking about? I saw the paperwork. And look here." Albrecht held the ring so Father Fritz could see inside. "Sang's name, Himmler's signature and the issuance number are all properly engraved."

"I saw them. Still, it's not Sang's ring."

"How do you know?"

Father Fritz picked up the ring that had been in the fireplace box and handed it to Albrecht. "Compare this ring with the one you think is Sang's."

Albrecht looked at each ring carefully, his eyes darting from one to the other. "The runes. The ring I brought you has four."

"A Sig rune in a triangle on either side of the Death's Head for the SS," Father Fritz said from memory. "A swastika on the right in a quadrangle for loyalty to the *Führer,* a Hagall rune in a hexagon on the left for faith in the victory of the Nazi philosophy and a double rune on the back, designed by Wiligut to symbolize God."

"Exactly. But the ring you just gave me has an additional rune on the back."

"A wendrune. Only twelve men have a ring with that extra rune, the twelve members of the Order I told you about months ago. Besides their powerful symbolic significance, those rings can help to legitimize their owners in the eyes of the SS. The ring I showed you is mine. Sang had one as well. He knew that upon his death the ring would be removed and stored. He would never part with it, so he acquired a regular Death's Head ring—the one you're holding."

"If what you're saying is true, then Sang is still alive and he's the wendrune murderer."

"He may be much more than that, and if so we have to stop him quickly."

"It sounds like you know where he is."

"I know where he'll be—Wewelsburg."

40

Your Stars Today: Tread cautiously. Beware of exaggerated hopes and expectations during this time of resignations, unravelings, and uncertainties.

It was a cold and rainy morning, but Himmler was beaming.

Not only had Hitler, notorious for last-minute cancellations, arrived, but he also was early enough to hobnob with some prominent supporters and members of the Ahnenerbe and their wives at a preluncheon reception. Himmler led Hitler around and introduced him while the *Führer*, in turn, praised his host for his dedication and loyalty.

"*Reichsführer*, if I might?"

Himmler didn't know the young officer who approached him, but he knew the uniform. The officer was a member of Hitler's protection detail, which gave him the authority to intrude on Himmler's special moment.

"Yes, what is it?" Himmler asked, after excusing himself.

"There's a security problem that needs your attention."

"Security problem? What security problem?"

"It might be better if we talked about this in your study."

Himmler, who knew better than to argue when it came to the *Führer's* security, nodded his head in agreement and started down the hall.

"Heinrich, I'm glad you could make it."

The words hit Himmler the moment he stepped through the study door and left him wobbly. "Sang," he said in a voice weak with disbelief.

"Well, aren't you going to say something customary, like 'I thought you were dead'?"

But all Himmler could say was, "Sang."

"Sorry to arrive unannounced. It was necessary, however."

"I demand an explanation!" Himmler had almost recovered his composure.

"You demand? Remember that in just a few minutes." Sang motioned for the officer who had fetched Himmler to leave, then opened the door to the small side room of the study. "I'm afraid I had to detain two of your guests," Sang said as Peter and Max emerged.

"What is going on, Sang?" Himmler was again rattled. "I want to know immediately."

"What is going on, *Reichsführer*, is something that sickens me. A vast conspiracy directed against the *Führer* and the Reich, which I staged my own death to uncover."

"All of this, and I knew nothing about it?" Himmler was furious.

"The *Führer* knew about it and that's all that matters. To everyone else, I was dead. Even my own men, my own trusted officers, thought so, until this morning, when I resumed my command."

"You couldn't have done this without help." Himmler said. "Word would have gotten out that you were alive."

Sang merely smiled. "There are ways of ensuring that certain deep secrets remain hidden." He turned to Peter. "Isn't that right, Dr. Walker?"

"Who?" Himmler asked.

"Oh, I forgot, Heinrich. Allow me to do the honors. Meet Dr. David Walker, a professor of psychology at Princeton University, a breeding ground for OSS spies." Sang took a picture from his pocket and gave it to Himmler. "Dr. Walker is a man who wears many hats, including, for the past few months, that of an Allied operative sent to kill the *Führer*. He planned on carrying out his mission today here at Wewelsburg."

Himmler looked at the picture, then at Peter, then at the picture again. Meanwhile, the young officer had returned to the study and nodded to Sang.

"You needn't say I'm right, but you can see that I am," Sang continued. "Then there's the Grand Elise, the *Führer*'s favorite director, only lately she's been directing his assassination. She used her friendship with you to position Dr. Walker so he could strike at the right time."

"Max, this can't be true." Himmler shook his head. "Tell me Sang has gone completely insane."

"Why would she tell you the truth now, Heinrich? However, I believe my aide has located someone else who might." Sang opened the door to the study. "Please escort him in," he said, and two of his men entered, bringing Father Fritz with them. "You can let him go." The men released Father Fritz and left. "Another friend of ours, from the old days, Heinrich. And, I'm ashamed to say, another traitor to the Reich."

"Now I know where your help came from." Father Fritz made a muffled laughing sound. "So Sang, you sold your soul to Stalin. I should have realized that Veidt wasn't up to that sort of thing."

"Stalin?" Himmler was totally thrown. "Sang is aligned with the Russians?"

"He's their master agent in Germany," Father Fritz said. "Ask him."

"No, first I will ask you. Are you a part of any so-called conspiracy against the *Führer*?"

"I won't deny it," Father Fritz said.

"And you, Sang? Is what he said about the Russians true?"

"Whether he admits it or not, Sang isn't who he seems," Father Fritz said.

"And are you, Fritz?" Sang said. "Everyone here knows you're a conspirator, but do Fräulein Elise and Dr. Walker know what else you are? Do they know about Christmas Eve 1933." Sang moved closer to Max and Peter. "You see, Father Fritz is a genius at scheming. This conspiracy was very clever, but his masterpiece was a plan that allowed the Nazi Party to increase its grip on the German people and further inflame hatred toward the Jews. Since he's too modest to discuss it—"

"That's enough, Sang!" Father Fritz issued an order. "I'll do it."

"Please, go ahead," Sang said. "Heinrich and I never tire of the story, do we *Reichsführer*?"

"Understand that this has haunted me since it happened." Father Fritz spoke slowly. "Sang is right. As a member of the wendrune order, I had devised a plan with an ugly purpose, achieved by an even uglier means. I told you about Heinz Ritter, Peter—"

"David," Sang interjected.

Father Fritz ignored him. "What I didn't tell you is that on Christmas Eve 1933 Ritter's wife and two young children were murdered."

"'Murdered' is a kind word," Max said. "They were butchered in the most ghastly fashion."

"They were supposed to be beaten, not killed," Father Fritz said. "A horrible incident that would be blamed on Jewish members of the German Communist Party, linking it to Ritter's own death at its members' hands. Sang, Heydrich and Ebling were to handle the task." Father Fritz stared at Sang, then turned back to Max and Peter. "Sang was godfather to Liesl, Ritter's six-year-old daughter. Ever since her father was killed, Sang would visit on Christmas Eve, bringing presents for her and her eight-year-old brother. The door was always left open for him. The plan—my plan—called for Sang to enter, with his face hidden, and administer the beatings while Heydrich kept watch outside. Only Sang and Heydrich altered the plan without telling anyone. To create greater drama and incite more powerful anti-Semitic and anti-communist passions, they decided to kill the children and their mother in a gruesome way that mocked Christian, and especially Catholic, beliefs. After mass, I went by the house to check on things, and that's when I found out what they had done. The horror of it was my road to Damascus. My blindness was lifted and I could see the monster I had become. But, as it has so many sinners, God's unqualified love sustained me, and I resolved to save Jews and any others I could rescue from a horrible fate I had helped bring about. Continuing to act as though I was Hitler's Priest allowed me to do this more effectively. The conspiracy—ridding Germany of the vermin I helped spawn—was my final act of contrition."

"Bravo, Fritz!" Sang clapped his hands. "Such a heartrending and self-serving account. But the truth is, you set something in motion that not even your God could stop. It's a shame that you'll never receive the credit you deserve for the success of our glorious Reich. The greater shame is that I didn't also kill you that night, Fritz. You were always the most dangerous member of the wendrune order and, because of my moment of weakness, you became one of Germany's most dangerous enemies. Your execution will be *my* final act of contrition for not preventing that."

Father Fritz was too concerned with how his confession affected Max to pay Sang any heed. "I wanted to tell you, but I couldn't bring myself to. Now I ask you to forgive me. Though the request is simple, the granting is difficult, maybe even impossible. But I must ask."

"If you had told me . . ." Max was crying softly. "You didn't have to bear this alone." She put her arms around Father Fritz and embraced him as a child would a parent. "Of course I forgive you. But you have to forgive yourself."

Father Fritz raised his head so he could see Peter over Max's shoulder. "You were always suspicious of me, and with good reason. Properly used, your ability to read a person's soul can prove a blessing."

Peter responded, but to Sang, not Father Fritz. "Let's see what can I read in that void left when your soul departed. You crave only power, the kind of power that Stalin can bestow by making you the leader of a defeated Germany." Peter looked at Himmler. "Hitler's successor will wear the wendrune ring, just as Wiligut foretold."

"It's a little premature to speak about Hitler's successor, since the *Führer* is still quite alive, no thanks to any of you," Sang shot back. "I wonder how he'll react upon learning that his loyal Heinrich has been harboring an assassin and providing him with SS protection."

"So you haven't told Hitler yet," Peter said.

"Stalin wanted the assassination to occur," Sang said. "Then, at the last minute, he changed his mind. With Russia now having the upper hand in

Stalingrad, he's convinced Hitler's authority and effectiveness will wane. The greater threat could come from those most likely to succeed Hitler were he assassinated. You should feel honored, Heinrich. Stalin believes you the most dangerous because of the backing of the SS. Of course that means you must be eliminated, and once I disclose your role in the conspiracy that will be taken care of. However, because of our past I'm willing to offer you an officer's death by suicide, rather than torture and a humiliating public execution. It's your choice. I can just as easily disclose your treasonous acts to Hitler at the reception. Oh, and don't try to alert your SS guards. There's someone currently in the castle with a sealed envelope containing ironclad proof of your involvement, someone who has immediate access to Hitler. So which will it be?"

"With an officer's death, do I also have an officer's privilege of writing a note?" Himmler appeared to have made his choice.

"Do so quickly." Sang pointed to the small inner office. "You don't have a lot of time." Himmler left and, after calling back his aide and instructing him to watch Max, Peter and Father Fritz joined him.

"The aide—I recognize him," Father Fritz whispered to Peter and Max, then, in a normal voice, said, "Hans Eisner, right? We talked once in Berlin after mass. I remember you telling me about the dreams you were having, filled with the voices of people you shot while part of the *Einsatzgruppen*. How are you doing?"

"Actually, Father, I'm no longer plagued by them. Each night I confess to God, and say an act of contrition. I've come to accept what you told me, that what I did was what I had to do. I think because of this, the voices are silent." A beatific smile lit up Eisner's face, but only for a moment. Then solemnity returned. "I don't understand how you got involved in this plot, Father. Why would Hitler's Priest want to kill him?"

There was no hesitancy, nor any longer a reason to dodge the question. "Why? To stop my own terrible nightmares and to save my soul. We all have our paths, and yours, my son, is a dangerous one. Watch out for Sang. Never trust him. His loyalty is to Stalin—not Hitler—and he'll use anything and anyone to do his master's work. You may not believe what I'm saying, but at the very least, be careful."

As he spoke, Father Fritz watched Eisner's face to see if his words had any impact but he couldn't tell. He considered saying more until a burst of loud shouting from Himmler's inner office ruled that out.

"Go to hell, then, you stupid bastard!" The voice was clearly Sang's.

"That honor will be yours. The *Führer* will never take your word over mine. Yours is the neck he'll watch dangling from a piano wire noose at Panazee!"

The door flew open and Sang, propelled by rage, stormed through, heading for Eisner and yelling over his shoulder, "I offered you an officer's death, but you want to gamble? Fine! Gamble!" Sang made a fist with one hand and slammed it into the palm of his other. "That stupid *Arschloch* thinks the *Führer* will simply disregard his traitorous acts, as if they were nothing more than an accidental belch in public. 'I plotted to kill you, my *Führer*, so please excuse me.' Unbelievable!"

Sang's venting seemed to calm him. "For the good of the Reich, I had hoped not to make a spectacle of this," he said to no one in particular. "But what is, is." More controlled, he walked over and once more opened the door leading to the hallway. "In here, now!" he barked, then stepped back as the two men who had brought in Father Fritz entered clutching rifles. They drew to a sudden halt before Sang and thrust their right arms forward.

Sang returned their salute by pointing to the study's inner chamber. "In there is Reichsführer-SS Heinrich Himmler, the deadliest threat to our glorious Reich. More deadly than the Russians, than the Allies, than any of our military enemies. He has betrayed our *Führer* and our people and is to be treated accordingly. As members of the *Führer's* elite protection guard, you answer to me, not to him. No matter what he says, you are to keep him confined to that room. Should he try to escape, you are to use your guns, not to wound, but to kill. I trust my orders are completely clear."

Again the two soldiers gave a stiff-armed salute.

"Good." Sang turned his attention to the others. "Come, let's join the festivities. I'm sure the *Führer* will want to know what his favorite film director and his priest have been up to lately." Then, moving closer to Peter until their foreheads almost touched, Sang added, "And he certainly will want to meet the man who has contributed so much to Himmler's special project."

Over the months, Father Fritz had learned how to catch glimpses of the interior Peter, the one whose mind was now working at unfathomable speed on ways to stop Sang, even while the exterior Peter remained calm. Sang, on the other hand, as always, wore his emotions like a weapon, a broadsword that could slice others into submission. Looking at Sang, Father Fritz saw what he himself had nearly become: a raging beast restrained only by a collar of weak clerical cloth, which could conveniently be broken at will. It had happened to others—ministers, priests, bishops, even cardinals.

In the public's mind, he was still Hitler's Priest, even though his Nazi involvement ended long ago, when he chose not to make the cross a sidearm. Then it had been a difficult decision, which could have gone the other way. Now, in Sang, Father Fritz saw the path he had been tempted to take. He saw, and he was deeply ashamed.

"Then we're off." Sang grabbed Peter by the arm and strode into the hallway. "Fritz, you and the woman will follow me. Eisner, you will walk behind us, in case any of them should try to break away."

"Yes, sir." Eisner turned to Max and Father Fritz. "Come along."

Max walked past Eisner without a glance, but Father Fritz paused and peered into his eyes. "There's still time to do what's right. Obey God's orders, not Sang's. Try to save Max and your own soul."

"I told you, Father—I no longer hear the voices." Eisner lowered his head, away from Father Fritz's gaze.

"Where's the priest?"

Responding immediately to Sang's bellow, Eisner grabbed the lapels of Father Fritz's black jacket and propelled him forward with great force. "You heard him. Move!" Off-balance, Father Fritz teetered, but the same hands that pushed him quickly reached out and caught him before he fell. "Just do what he says." Eisner steadied the priest. "Don't make me be the one who kills you."

"Killing me will be your own decision, but I'll make it easier." Father Fritz shook free of Eisner. "I'm going."

"Good," Eisner said. "Quickly, then. And Father, pray for me at the hour of death."

Max was a step away from entering the reception area when she felt someone grasp her shoulders, restraining her. Then she heard a voice whisper, "Flee. Now, while you still can."

Turning, then craning her neck, Max saw the face of Hans Eisner.

"Now," Eisner said, as forcefully as he could without shouting, then shoved her away from the reception. After two or three seconds of hesitation, Max took off. Satisfied that she was gone, Eisner went into the room.

Sang was already there, still clutching Peter's arm and making his way toward Hitler, who had just finished exchanging a few words with a small group of adulatory women. "My *Führer*," Sang said when he drew close enough to be heard.

"Sang. I am surprised to see you. Have you brought news?"

"My *Führer*." Sang was now standing face-to-face with Hitler. "I have—"

Sang was interrupted by two quick pistol shots, one that hit him in the neck, the other in the side. He staggered to his right, leaving Hitler exposed.

"Finally Germany's nightmares end!" Hans Eisner fired another shot from the small Mauser he had kept concealed in his trousers and the bullet pierced Hitler's right arm. Eisner got off another round, but the security detail had already shielded Hitler with their bodies. They rushed him from the castle, slicing through the crowd of terrified people also trying to flee, their panic intensified by the sound of SS guards riddling Eisner's body with bullets.

As soon as Hitler's car sped away, some remaining members of the security detail took up positions at the front door so as to prevent anyone from leaving. Others went inside and clustered around Eisner's body. Father Fritz approached and glared at the detail guards, who recognized Hitler's Priest and let him through. Kneeling next to the bloody corpse, Father Fritz draped a stole over his neck and began giving Eisner absolution.

Off to the side, Sang tried to gasp for assistance, but the words wouldn't come. Instead, he was left to lurch in pain, straining to give some direction to his random movements. He headed toward the dining hall, which was adjacent to the reception room, a forgotten man to all but Peter.

While he gladly would have let Father Fritz handle Sang, Peter didn't want to risk him somehow escaping. Not knowing whether Sang was armed, Peter searched for a weapon and found a carving knife from the reception. It would do.

Peter scanned the room, which was still teeming with panicked people, and spotted a figure who could be Sang trying to open the dining-room door. By the time Peter was able to weave a path through the confusion, the figure was gone and the dining-room door closed. Keeping a firm grip on the knife, Peter slowly cracked the door open enough to look in. It was indeed Sang, and his wounds were taking more of a toll. As Peter watched, Sang placed his palms on the large wooden dining table for balance and worked his way around, trying to find a way out, other than the reception area.

Peter could tell that Sang was nearing the end of his endurance. The loss of blood, coupled with the internal injuries Eisner had inflicted, was proving too severe. But there was no guarantee that there was enough damage to kill Sang and, with all that he knew, unless he was dead he was dangerous. Peter would have to provide his own guarantee and he had no compunctions about doing so.

He opened the door even wider but still waited. Weakened wasps could still sting. Sang made one last attempt to steady himself using the table but was unsuccessful. Instead, he collapsed onto the cushioned seat of the chair reserved for Hitler at the table's head. Seeing his opportunity, Peter, his arm cocked and the knife ready, stepped into the dining room.

The terrifying whoosh and brutal force of a cyclonic wind; the blinding brilliance and horrible heat of ten thousand stage lights flicked on at once; the simultaneous sensation of being bitten by bees and battered by bricks: never had Peter experienced anything like the bomb blast.

One moment he was steps away from killing Sang; the next Peter was airborne, a man-missile, propelled away from his target by a concussive shock that burst from the spot where the luncheon table had been. The violent explosion compressed time, in the same instant lifting Peter, then slamming him against the far reception hall wall some thirty yards away. Spared death by first hitting a cushion of piled body parts from guests caught a split second earlier by the more rapidly moving front of furiously expanding gases, Peter ricocheted from the wall to the floor, where he rolled over fragments of uprooted, broken tile before coming to a rest on his right side.

There he lay, dazed, coughing out foul air and particulates from his lungs and slowly becoming aware of a persistent pealing of bells. While Peter could still hear the sounds of suffering, along with assorted shouts, they were muffled and impossible to distinguish. He had been through this once before, although on a much lesser scale, when he stood too close to a carnival cannon that shot a scantily clad woman into a net. One of the clowns, a former doctor who had lost his license to booze, said the loud noise had temporarily messed up the microscopic ear canal hairs that transmitted sound-producing impulses to the brain. Within an hour Peter's hearing had returned to normal; he was hoping that would happen again. Or the intensity of the explosion may have permanently damaged his eardrums, perhaps even his auditory nerve. Either way, for the moment Peter was functionally deaf.

There was more. The brilliant flash of light from the detonation had filled his eyes with bright, free-floating patches and spots, and these effectively blocked any outside images. Even if this hadn't happened, it would have been difficult enough for him to see clearly. Smoke and billowing ash had transformed the once-bright room into greens and grays, decorated with deformed shadowy shapes created from what used to be people and furniture.

As with his hearing, Peter had no way of telling whether his vision damage was permanent or temporary. If his retinas were burned, he might never regain full sight; if they were just oversaturated, he would soon see normally, although not necessarily soon enough to do him much good. Sight or no sight, Peter had to get up and find Max. He rolled over from his side to his back, and as he did so his left shoulder struck something. An agonizing jolt shot through his neck and head, fusing his teeth together in a clench of agony.

What the hell just happened? Looking for an answer, Peter cast his left hand onto the floor, angled around a bit and fished up a hard, sharp object partially covered in a wet, pulpy wrapping. By feel, Peter knew he was holding a bone—or part of one—and, from the size, most likely from a leg, a portion of tibia still partially covered by muscle made into mush by the explosion. Rolling over it would hurt, but the pain wouldn't be excruciating. OK, Peter, make an instant diagnosis. Think. What's plausible? Maybe I raised my shoulder instinctively to protect my head when I was thrown into the wall by the blast, and the impact probably broke or badly bruised it. That's why it hurt like hell when it hit the leg bone. Fortunately, the injury wasn't the kind that should prevent him from standing. However, the throbbing in the front of his right thigh might be a different story.

Seeking the cause, Peter raised his upper body slightly and extended his right arm. This time he didn't need to speculate. A long shaft of wood had shot through the skin and soft tissue of his thigh and lodged in the underlying muscle. While bad, the warm blood around the entry point could be worse, depending on its color. Moderate red indicated broken capillaries; deeper red, a damaged vein; and bright red, a severed femoral artery, which, without immediate medical treatment, would be deadly. Since Peter couldn't rely on his vision, he resorted to a less certain method.

With his right hand cupped around the shaft and over the wound, he took a deep breath, then forcibly exhaled, ensuring a strong heartbeat, which would send blood coursing through his body and, if the femoral artery was severed, powerfully spurting onto his palm. He waited but felt nothing. Just to make sure, he repeated the process, with the same result. The wound might be serious, but it wasn't fatal. Relieved, Peter grasped the piece of wood with both hands and carefully snapped it close to where it had penetrated the skin, tossing the exposed segment aside and leaving the other part embedded to stanch the bleeding.

Satisfied that he had done all he could, Peter brushed his hands over his body, this time applying more pressure and noting any abnormal sensations. Most of his skin seemed fine, although on his right side, which had been exposed to the full blast when he cracked open the oak dining-room door, there were some damp, uncomfortable patches where the protective epidermal layer had been seared. It wouldn't take long for the burns to blister and the pain to increase, possibly enough to incapacitate him. Outside, there were natural remedies like tinder polypore, a fungus easily found at the base of a birch tree that Peter could have applied to the burns. But here among the rubble and remains there was nothing, except his willingness to take a leap of logic by talking the fire from his body.

Taught the technique by one of Delta's healer friends, Peter had used it on a hobo badly scalded by an unsteady pot of nail stew. And it worked. Peter, then eleven, didn't believe magic had anything to do with the healing, especially since Trotter had taught him how the hypnotized mind could influence the body in startling ways. But right now, none of that mattered. He only wanted it to work again.

And to see if it would, he needed saliva, not easy to come by in a mouth parched from the heat of the still-active fires scattered throughout the room. Resorting to an old actor's trick for mouth moistening under hot stage lights, Peter gently bit the tip of his tongue repeatedly, which stimulated the production of saliva. When he had enough, he wet his hands with it and softly patted them on the most painful burns, while repeating a prayer three times: "Angels God did send, one bearing fire, the other salt. Out fire, I command thee, out and go into salt as is ordained."

Much to his amazement, when he finished the heat seemed to recede. Was it really magic or did he block out the burns through sheer will? Those were questions he would ponder later, provided there was a later. Peter's immediate task was to survey the surroundings and size up the situation, even though his hearing was still shot and his sight remained limited. That left logic.

Logic said most of Hitler's security force had fled with him after the shooting, and some of the few members remaining behind to investigate were likely injured or killed by the explosion. Considering the chaos and devastation, any SS guards who escaped the blast probably hadn't effectively regrouped yet. Even if they had, entering the room was still too dangerous. So they would be directing operations from outside, although that would change after the castle's small fire brigade brought things somewhat under control. Given all those factors, Peter figured he had ten minutes to find Max without interference. Yet as he was arriving at his perfectly reasoned conclusions, a snippet from "A Scandal in Bohemia" popped into his head. It was as though Sir Arthur, through Holmes, was warning him against theorizing before having data, which could make him "twist facts to suit theories rather than theories to suit facts." It was sound advice, although Peter would have preferred knowing how Holmes would have gotten a feel for his surroundings without his eyes and ears to . . .

Feel for his . . . Feel for . . . Feel—

"Feel anything?"

And just as suddenly as he had been eleven, Peter was nine, in a field outside of Chicago, his fingers on a train rail. "Not yet."

Trotter squatted next to him. "No wonder. Look at your fingers. They're white. You're pressing them down so hard, you're numbing any sensation. Lightly. Just graze the rail." Trotter lifted Peter's hand and set it down properly. "Like that. Now, concentrate. Anything?"

"A little—sort of like the rail's moving."

"Good. It's a start. And by the time I finish, you'll not only be able to tell when a train's coming, but what kind and how many cars it's pulling. Hoboes respect someone who can read vibrations. You'll also discover it's a skill with value far beyond railroads."

Just as Trotter predicted, Peter did occasionally read vibrations, usually when pulling off a con but never when his life was on the line. Now, lying back flat to keep his body from moving, he stretched out his right arm and, with his open hand, swept pieces of the shattered floor tiles into a small pile. Then he brushed the tip of his index finger back and forth over the coarse cement-and-gravel floor base, scraping away enough skin to sharpen his sense of touch. It was an old safecracker's trick: file the fingertips and expose those nerve endings best able to detect high-frequency changes in vibrating lock tumblers. Lost in the process were other types of nerve endings, which responded better to lower-frequency vibrations but weren't needed to crack open a safe. Anyway, the lost layers of skin eventually grew back. But Peter wasn't dealing with a safe and he needed access to the full frequency range. So he scraped only the tip of his index finger, which he then rested, along with the unscathed tip of his middle finger, on the tile mound. Once he did, Peter was transformed. No longer a man, he had become a spider, attached to his web of smashed tile and waiting for it to shake with information. Supposedly, spiders can distinguish between prey and potential mates through web vibrations. Peter would settle for getting a rough idea of how many people were alive and where they were clustered.

Just as Peter anticipated, the tile pieces acted as an antenna, picking up motion waves and transmitting them to his fingers. He detected no strong vibrations, the kind that might come from a group of men stomping around in heavy combat boots. Any movement seemed random, which he attributed to either contortions of the maimed trying to right themselves or stumbling steps of those able to stand, who were seeking escape. Sitting up again, with his hands planted on the floor to act as body jacks, Peter was ready to learn which camp he would be in.

He managed to get to his feet, albeit unsteadily. Then, due to shock and blood loss, nausea assailed him. Once the queasiness passed, Peter tested his left shoulder, his taut lips anticipating the agony to come. The slow rotations hurt, but not as badly as he thought they might. The shoulder moved too well to be dislocated or broken, so most likely it was only severely bruised. Even if a piece of bone had chipped off, the shoulder was functional. Knowing that, Peter extended both arms to his sides and slowly turned around twice trying to get a fix on the fires and their intensity by sensing the rising heat. He used his fingers like thermometers to register gradations of temperature differences. One area was clearly hotter than the others, a perception supported by the heavier concentration of smoke. It had to be the dining room where the explosion occurred. Peter now had his bearings and knew how to reach the sole set of doors leading out of the reception room. That was where Max would have headed unless she was hurt or— Peter refused to consider the alternative and began moving in that direction. With each step he swung his raised foot forward before planting it on the floor. Repeatedly he kicked air, but once he struck a body he couldn't see and managed to avoid tripping over it.

As he cautiously proceeded, Peter called out Max's name, hoping for a response. Unlike his hearing and his vision, his sense of smell hadn't been compromised. So he inhaled slowly, hoping to catch a whiff of her distinctive perfume. Most of the other women at the reception had dabbed on Chanel, easily obtained from Nazi-occupied Paris. That Coco Chanel was a Nazi sympathizer living with a high-ranking German officer only made her fragrances that much more popular. For those same reasons, Max refused to touch Chanel, opting instead for her own dwindling prewar reserve of Zibeline, a seductive scent from the House of Weil meant to evoke the forests of Russia with its hints of coriander, bergamot and lemon resting on a heavier concentration of iris, gardenia, jasmine and rose, all held together by a base of ambergris, honey, amber, musk and civet. To Peter, Zibeline was the Tsarist St. Petersburg of tales Trotter would spin around a hobo campfire—tales of evenings iced like crystal aglow with the radiance of beautiful women in ball-bound sleighs, smothered in rich furs and gaily laughing as they sipped fine Champagne. Many a youthful night Peter had lived those wondrous tales in his mind and then, later, relived them in the flesh with Max each time she took down one of her cherished cut-glass bottles and dotted prewar Zibeline on various parts of her naked body, proclaiming herself, when finished, "properly dressed for the occasion." No, even without his heightened sense of smell Peter would have been able to detect the alluring fragrance, a blend of Zibeline and Max's own natural essence.

But instead of jasmine and ambergris, traces of urine and feces, released by the relaxed sphincter and bowel muscles of the dead, filled Peter's nostrils, along with a sharp metallic odor, like that produced when a coin was rubbed over skin, only much stronger. Having encountered the smell before, Peter knew it came from the iron in human blood combining with body sweat, its pungency reflecting the massive scope of injury and death.

In contrast, he also caught a faint whiff of burnt almonds, a common scent, which normally would be difficult to identify. But there was no mistaking this: hydrogen cyanide in the smoke, a deadly toxin with a surer kill rate than carbon monoxide, its better-known companion. The weakness of the odor meant there was a decent amount of fresh air nearby, but even dissipated the lethal gas would eventually take its toll.

Hydrogen cyanide rose, so Peter gambled that by crouching low to the ground he could avoid being poisoned. Once more he shouted out Max's name; then he constricted his throat, trapping whatever air was inside his lungs. Absent his noxious surroundings and with some quick prepping, Peter could have held his breath for five minutes or more, longer than Houdini, who had taught him how. Under these circumstances, though, he thought he'd be lucky to manage maybe three minutes. During that time he would stay put, monitoring the smoldering confusion swirling around him for any sight or sound of Max.

"Peter!"

Seconds after the barely audible voice, a figure emerged from orangey gray billows, taking on more specific shape until Peter saw it was Father Fritz. Apparently he had followed the calls for Max, which Peter had scattered around the reception hall like bread crumbs.

"Are you all right?" Father Fritz dropped to his knees, removed a water-soaked napkin that he had been holding across his mouth and pressed it over Peter's lips. The cool, filtered air momentarily soothed the searing in his lungs.

"Where's Max?" Peter forced his words through the napkin.

"Come on," Father Fritz put his free arm around Peter's shoulder and tried to lift him up. But Peter remained rooted. Pushing away the napkin, he shouted, "We've got to find Max!"

"No, we've got to take advantage of all this chaos and get out of here before there's a clampdown."

"Not without Max. We're not leaving without Max. *I'm* not leaving without Max." Peter shook off Father Fritz's grip.

"Listen to me, Peter—Max is already gone. Eisner warned her just before we entered the reception room."

"But how—"

"Once we're safely away. Please. Seconds count."

A phalanx of SS soldiers wearing gas masks was already staking out positions and Peter knew that soon the only way out for him and Father Fritz would be in their custody. Nodding, Peter lifted the right lapel of his suit jacket so that it partly shielded his face. "The toxins," he said and told Father Fritz to do the same.

"Don't worry. After World War One, I developed a great respect for poisonous vapors." Father Fritz rose, then gripped Peter's arm and helped him up. "Stay close. We're going to make it look like we're heading for the front door."

"'Make it look'? And where are we heading?"

"Valhalla."

41

———————

Peter had only been to Valhalla in Wewelsburg's north tower once. So he wasn't familiar with its nuances, such as the cleverly concealed passageway that led to a grove where Himmler conducted outdoor occult ceremonies.

"Come on, Peter, hold on to the back of my jacket as we go through," Father Fritz said. "It's not all that long, but it can be tricky."

As Peter walked, he began reacting to scents barely there, dissipated vestiges overpowered by earth and mold. Coriander, bergamot and perhaps lemon. Traces of iris, gardenia, jasmine and rose? Ambergris, honey and amber, musk and civet. "Did Max know about this passageway?"

"She never spoke of it."

Maybe not, but she was speaking of it now and the language she was using was Zibeline! Finally, Peter could accept that Max had escaped.

"I see some light ahead," Father Fritz said. "We're almost there."

"Almost" was another five hundred feet. When they emerged, they could see the heavy smoke encircling Wewelsburg.

"Now we cut through the woods to a little-used road. Albrecht's waiting for us." Father Fritz put his arm around Peter, who had been limping.

"My thigh looks like a coatrack," Peter said and accepted the assistance. "What do you think happened back there?"

"I think Himmler was true to form. He lacked the courage to shoot Hitler, so he planted explosives in his chair to do the job. Hitler sits and *bam.*"

"Like a big whoopee cushion," Peter said.

"Of course, Himmler would have found a reason to excuse himself before Hitler sat down," Father Fritz said.

"Yes, but the other guests would have been killed or maimed."

"Large-scale murder never bothered Himmler."

After what seemed like hours but must have been only minutes of walking, they sighted the car. Albrecht rushed over to greet them. "We were concerned. We thought we heard an explosion."

"You did," Father Fritz said.

"And Hitler?"

"Alive, but not for want of trying."

"So Himmler really did attempt it."

"Not just Himmler," Father Fritz said. "One of Hitler's security detail as well, a young man named Hans Eisner."

"Eisner?" Albrecht looked surprised.

"Do you know him?" Peter asked.

"We recently brought him into the Black Orchestra. He had wanted to join earlier, but we needed to check him out thoroughly to make certain Sang wasn't planting him. Ironically, it worked the other way: he kept us informed. But he didn't say anything about Sang being alive."

"He didn't know," Father Fritz said. "No one but Hitler, Sang's confederates, and some high-level Russian operatives knew."

"Then Eisner didn't betray us," Albrecht said. "I'm glad to hear that. Because of his unique security position, he volunteered to kill Hitler. However, with Zodiac in play, we said no. I wonder what prompted him to act anyway."

"It could have been any one of thousands of voices, or all of them," Father Fritz replied. "Peter, will you excuse us for a moment?"

Father Fritz took Albrecht aside and they talked briefly. When they returned, Albrecht put his hand on Peter's shoulder.

"Come. We'll get you medical attention and there's a plane waiting to take you to Switzerland."

"Then this is where I leave you," Father Fritz said.

"What are you talking about?" Peter said. "You're not safe here, not with what Himmler knows."

"And what will he do, tell Hitler, and expose himself? Eventually he'll start searching for me, but it'll be too late."

"He won't have to. Sang said another person at the reception had the proof of Himmler's involvement and of ours."

"This." From his inside jacket pocket Father Fritz pulled an oversized manila envelope that had been folded in half to fit. "Eisner gave it to me as we were leaving Himmler's study." Father Fritz took out his lighter, flicked the spark wheel and touched the flame to the envelope. "A little more fire's not going to make a difference."

"You didn't open it."

"I've got a good idea of what it contains."

"There could be copies."

"There could, but I doubt it." Father Fritz dropped the burning envelope and watched as it turned totally to ash. "Sang would want to make sure he controlled such valuable information. Besides, he was arrogant enough to believe that nothing could go wrong. Himmler's safe for now."

Peter turned to Albrecht. "Now can I have a minute?"

Albrecht nodded and went to the car.

"Look, I may have been a little quick to judge you."

"But you judged correctly," Father Fritz said.

"Still, I owe you a lot, way beyond thanks."

"Peter, come," Albrecht called out from the car.

"They're waiting," Father Fritz said.

"One last thing. Will I see Max again?"

"Peter, I'm a priest, not a prophet."

"I just have this feeling that you know the answer to my question. I don't know—maybe I'm just seeking some hope, so humor me. Will I see her again?"

"I can't answer that."

"You won't answer that." Peter grabbed Father Fritz's shoulders. "Please. Tell me something."

"If she's the love of your life the Gypsy spoke about—"

"What?" Peter dropped his hands and stared, astonished. "The Gypsy? How did you know about the Gypsy?"

"Max mentioned her."

"Max may have mentioned a gypsy she encountered. But she never knew about *my* dealings with a gypsy. How did you?"

"Peter, don't—"

"Never mind the Gypsy. I care about Max, not the Gypsy. You have to tell me—will I see her again?"

"Peter—"

"You know. Don't say you don't."

Father Fritz pressed his lips so tightly together that his lower cheek muscles began to bulge.

"Please! I'm begging you! For God's sake, tell me!"

Whether or not it was in response to Peter's heartfelt appeal, Father Fritz relented. "If Max is indeed the love of your life, you'll see her again, but only if you look for her."

"I won't stop searching until I find her."

"Searching isn't looking. If you search, you'll never find her."

Father Fritz wasn't making sense. The blast, the stress—traumatic neurosis. For a moment, Peter the psychologist took over.

But Albrecht shouted to Peter the spy, "We have to go right now!"

Now Father Fritz clasped Peter. "You have to leave. Quickly."

"Who are you?"

"A sinner."

"Goddamn you!" Anger, frustration and stress claimed Peter.

"He has, but because of you I can finally die."

"I don't understand any of this."

"Because you don't want to understand. But you already understand more than you know. The rest you can find out, should you choose. It's your decision."

"That's it, Peter!" Albrecht had left the car to retrieve him.

"Bless you, my son, whether you want to be or not," Father Fritz said. "And when you get back, don't forget to get paid."

"Paid?" Peter brushed Albrecht away. "I didn't do this for money."

"What about the hobo nickel?"

"How did you—"

"Enough!" This time Albrecht wouldn't be denied. He grabbed Peter by the arm and pulled him away. "I'd handcuff you, but I realize it wouldn't do any good."

Peter didn't resist. He couldn't. He was stunned, more by Father Fritz's words than by the explosion. He got into the back of the car without a struggle and, once he closed the door, they sped off. Peter looked out the rear window, but Father Fritz was gone.

Albrecht, who was sitting in the passenger's seat, turned his head toward the backseat. "Father Fritz will be all right. There's an abbey not too far away. The nuns there help him get Jews out of Germany. He'll be safe in their care. Here." Albrecht pulled a bundled handkerchief from his pocket. "This is what Father Fritz and I were speaking about privately. He asked me to give it to you."

Peter took the handkerchief, undid it, looked at what it held and then lapsed into silence.

"Well, what is it?" Albrecht asked.

Peter held the contents up so Albrecht could see: a strangely hued blue string, which held a rusted iron carpenter's nail twisted into a cross.

With a stack of books piled in one hand and a cup of coffee in the other, he made his way through the door to his office and over to the desk, where he let the books drop. Three or four more trips should do it, he thought, then took a sip from the cup and gazed at the window, admiring the view of the

Berkshire Mountains. They weren't the Bavarian Alps, but they were beautiful and tranquil, which he considered more than a fair exchange.

Although classes wouldn't start until September, there was a lot to do: research and scholarly papers to catch up on, syllabi to prepare, a slew of obligatory meetings. Still, he wasn't complaining. His getting a tenured professorship was one of John Goddard's conditions for taking over the chairmanship of the psychology department at Williams, a small, prestigious college in the northwest corner of Massachusetts. Williams didn't put up a fight.

He sat, swept away some of the scattered books and began to tackle a small stack of mail, starting with a package that actually had been hand delivered an hour earlier and left on his desk. There was no return address. He cut the twine with his pocketknife and tore away the heavy brown wrapping paper. Inside, between two pieces of heavy, protective cardboard was a doctoral diploma from Harvard and an unsigned note that read: *This time you earned it. Should anyone bother to check, they'll find a set of extremely impressive credentials. It's the least we could do. Hang it proudly knowing that you were born to be hanged.*

He put the note aside and took another look at the diploma. Beautifully lettered and inserted right after *Quoniam* whereas and before *studio diligentiore* —diligent study—was the name *Peter Kepler*.

He smiled, but it was a sad smile. How he wished Max were here to share this with him. Then he would have laughed—they both would have laughed, just as Donovan must have laughed when he sent the diploma to him. For a moment he was back in Nazi Germany, but only for a moment, and when he returned he took a pen from the desk—a newly acquired Montblanc, like the one Father Fritz always used—removed the cap and, with a single, deft stroke drew a line through *Peter Kepler*. Then, after waiting a few seconds for the ink to dry, he wrote two words in the space above the line.

Luke Six.